PENGUIN CLASSICS

SELECTED WRITINGS

SAMUEL JOHNSON

Samuel Johnson was born in Lichfield in 1709, the son of a book-seller, and was educated at Lichfield Grammar School and, for a short time, at Pembroke College, Oxford. He taught for a while, after which he worked for a Birmingham printer, for whom he translated Lobo's *A Voyage to Abyssinia*. In 1735 he married Elizabeth Jervis Porter and with her money opened a boarding academy. The school was a failure and in 1737 Johnson left for London. There, he became a regular contributor to the *Gentleman's Magazine* and struggled to earn a living from writing. His *London: A Poem In Imitation of the Third Satire of Juvenal* was published anonymously in 1738 and attracted some attention. *The Vanity of Human Wishes: The Tenth Satire of Juvenal Imitated* appeared under his own name in 1749. From 1750 to 1752 he issued the *Rambler*, a periodical written almost entirely by himself, and consolidated his position as a notable moral essayist with some twenty-five essays in the *Adventurer*. The *Idler* essays, lighter in tone, appeared weekly between 1758 and 1760. When his *Dictionary of the English Language* was published in 1755, Johnson took on the proportions of a literary monarch in the London of his day. In need of money to visit his sick mother, he wrote *Rasselas* (1759) reportedly in the evenings of one week, finishing a couple of days after his mother's death. In 1763 Boswell became his faithful follower and it is mainly to his *Life* that we owe our intimate knowledge of Johnson. Founded in 1764, 'The Club' (of literary men) was the perfect forum for the exercise of Johnson's great conversational art. His edition of Shakespeare's plays appeared in 1765. From August to November 1773 he and Boswell toured Scotland and in 1775 his *Journey to the Western Islands of Scotland* appeared. His last major work was *Lives of the Poets*. He died in December 1784.

•

Patrick Cruttwell is Emeritus Professor of English at Carleton University, Ottawa. He is the author of *The English Sonnet* (1966) and *The Shakespearian Moment and its Place in Poetry in the 17th Century* (1970).

SAMUEL JOHNSON

Selected Writings

EDITED WITH
AN INTRODUCTION AND NOTES
BY PATRICK CRUTTWELL

PENGUIN BOOKS

Penguin Books Ltd, Harmondsworth, Middlesex, England
Viking Penguin Inc., 40 West 23rd Street, New York, New York 10010, U.S.A.
Penguin Books Australia Ltd, Ringwood, Victoria, Australia
Penguin Books Canada Limited, 2801 John Street, Markham, Ontario, Canada L3R 1B4
Penguin Books (N.Z.) Ltd, 182–190 Wairau Road, Auckland 10, New Zealand

—

Published in the Penguin English Library 1968
Reprinted 1982, 1983, 1984
Reprinted in Penguin Classics 1986

—

—

Printed and bound in Great Britain by
Cox & Wyman Ltd, Reading
Set in Monotype Bembo

CONTENTS

Contents

Part III: 1762–84

'GREAT CHAM OF LITERATURE'

PREFACE

THIS selection has been made in accordance with two principles: to supply a conspectus of Johnson's mind and literary personality throughout his career, and to include as much of his less familiar work as could be accommodated without excessive sacrifice of the better-known masterpieces.

His literary career seems to divide quite naturally into three stages. Up to 1749, he is the desperately poor, bitter, Grub Street journalist. The great works of this stage are *London* and *The Life of Savage*. From 1749 to 1762, he wins and consolidates his position as moralist and lexicographer; the monuments of this stage are *The Vanity of Human Wishes*, the three series of essays (*Rambler*, *Adventurer*, and *Idler*), the *Dictionary*, and *Rasselas*. The second stage is concluded by his reception of a pension. This radically altered both his way of life and his way of writing; it made him into the figure we know from Boswell, the 'Great Cham of Literature' (in Smollett's phrase), and the greatest recorded talker in the language. The works of this stage – more relaxed, sprawling, colloquial – are the edition of Shakespeare, the *Journey to the Western Islands*, and *The Lives of the Poets*. Through all three stages, but very sparsely in the first and in much the greatest mass in the third, is a stream of letters, prayers and journals, which ought to be regarded as no less part of his work than those writings which he printed.

I have tried consistently to stress Johnson's less familiar work by giving more space than most selections to the letters, essays, prayers and journals, and to the *Journey to the Western Islands*. Only one major work is omitted: *Rasselas*. This omission is regrettable, but there is some compensation for the exclusion of *Rasselas* in that the major themes of the novel have already been explored in *The Vanity of Human Wishes*.

The texts are taken from a variety of editions, but in all of them the spelling, capitalization and italicization are modernized. The language and printing conventions of the eighteenth century were not so remote from our own as to make an essential difference; to modernize an Elizabethan or medieval text is to make a radical change, but to write 'critic' and 'public' for *critick* and *publick*, and to remove the capital initials from abstract nouns and the italics from proper names, is merely to get rid of irritating quaintnesses. Johnson is *not* a quaint, old-world writer; he is a writer of raw power and disturbing immediacy.

INTRODUCTION

SAMUEL JOHNSON was born in 1709, the son of a poor and unsuccessful bookseller in Lichfield, Staffordshire. He was thus a provincial, a Midlander: of which fact, in spite of his well-known passion for London, he was never forgetful. He made regular pilgrimages back to his home-country – what he calls in a letter his 'annual ramble into the middle counties'. He inserted a tribute to his birthplace in one of the entries in his *Dictionary*. And his voice, all through his life, retained strong traces of the Midland accent; Garrick used to imitate his pronunciation of punch – 'Who's for *poonsh*?' (Boswell, 23 March 1776).

Lichfield, which is a cathedral city, was at that time the very High Church and High Tory capital of a county which had similar affiliations; when Boswell and Johnson (28 April 1778) affected to believe in the virtual impossibility of there existing such a creature as a 'Staffordshire Whig', they were not entirely jesting. No doubt this played a part in forming some of Johnson's subsequent opinions, but it is important to note that this could not have been through the direct way of gratitude and respect, for Johnson had no reason at all to feel grateful to Church or State in Lichfield; to this exceptionally, and from the start, obviously, gifted boy they gave no help whatsoever. It is odd that his earliest local friends and helpers seem to have included a remarkably high proportion of 'Staffordshire Whigs' and a remarkably low proportion of Staffordshire Tories; notable among the former were Gilbert Walmsley, superbly remembered some fifty years later in the *Lives of the Poets* (p. 467 below), and the Aston family, of whom the beautiful 'Molly' was later described by Johnson (according to Mrs Piozzi) as 'a beauty and a scholar, and a wit and whig; and she talked all in praise of liberty . . . She was the loveliest creature I ever saw!' (*Anecdotes of Johnson*, London 1925, p. 103). It is characteristic of Johnson's honesty that in both instances he admitted they were Whigs.

The same process seems to have continued when he went to Oxford in 1728. His learning, already immense, and the power of his mind, were immediately shown by the Latin verse-translation which he made of Pope's *Messiah*. This (in Boswell's words) he performed 'with uncommon rapidity, and in so masterly a manner, that he obtained great applause from it, which ever after kept him high in the estimation of his College, and, indeed, of all the University'. Its fame went even further; for Pope himself (then at the zenith of his glory) 'expressed himself concerning it in terms of strong approbation'. All this, however, did Johnson no good; for his poverty was such that after little more than a year he was forced to withdraw. Johnson's record at Oxford is in truth a thorough disgrace to the University; nor is it any good to argue that this was the unenlightened un-Welfared eighteenth century, for Addison had received a scholarship at Magdalen for exactly the same kind of feat – a copy of Latin verses – which failed to secure anything for Johnson, and later in the century the career of the great Hellenist, Porson, was to show that the age was not entirely lacking in ladders for talent: Porson, born into a poor cottage-weaver's family in Norfolk, was helped by the local parson and squirearchy first to Eton and then to Cambridge.

Johnson's *real* experience of his university was terrible; it is summed up in his own words to Boswell:

Ah, Sir, I was mad and violent. It was bitterness which they mistook for frolic. I was miserably poor, and I thought to fight my way by my literature and my wit, so I disregarded all power and all authority. (Boswell, 1729)

Yet in later years he became a totally uncritical admirer and defender of Oxford, quite unable to admit, perhaps even to see, those deficiencies and pettinesses which he himself had experienced and which Gibbon was to expose in his autobiography. This is one of the basic characteristics of Johnson's mind. It never reacts *in the expected way*. It takes, on the contrary, a farouche delight in going the *other* way. Given what everyone else would consider sound cause for becoming an embittered rebel, he becomes a starry-eyed defender. Exactly the same can be seen in his reaction to his Lichfield schooling. His teacher, Hunter, was obviously – from Johnson's own accounts – a brute whose stupidity and cruelty were exceptional even for eighteenth-century schoolmasters; yet Johnson emerged as the most intransigent defender of teaching by fear. 'A child is afraid of being whipped, and gets his task, and there's an end on't' is the summing-up of his educational theory, and it is perhaps the least attractive or impressive part of his mind. There may be some truth in Bernard Shaw's suggestion, in the preface to *Misalliance*, that Johnson's 'great mind' had been 'lamed' for life by Hunter's treatment. I feel sure, at anyrate, that this sort of reaction – this process of declining the natural, rational consequence and insisting on its opposite – can hardly be indulged in without paying a price; and the price Johnson paid was that tenseness, that tendency to sudden and disproportionate violence, which was always lurking behind his behaviour and his writings.

His real literary career began – after some unsuccessful and miserable efforts at teaching – when he went to London in 1737, at the age of twenty-eight. He at once became a regular contributor to the just-started *Gentleman's Magazine* – 'enlisted', in Boswell's words, 'by Mr Cave as a regular coadjutor in his magazine, by which he probably obtained a tolerable livelihood'. Edward Cave was the magazine's first proprietor and editor; eighteen years later, Johnson was to remember his first patron by naming him in the *Dictionary* entry for *magazine*. Johnson thus became, what in a sense he was always to remain, a miscellaneous journalist. How miscellaneous, we may estimate from Boswell's remark: 'I indeed doubt if he could have remembered every one of [his early writings] as they were so numerous, so varied, and scattered in such a multiplicity of unconnected publications; nay, several of them published under the names of other persons, to whom he liberally contributed from the abundance of his mind' (Boswell, 1738).

He became not only a miscellaneous, but also, quintessentially, a metropolitan journalist; for then began that passionate love-hate relationship with London which was to dominate the rest of his life. There was a bigger infusion of hate in it than the sentimentalized picture of Johnson as eminently 'clubbable', the mighty talker in drawing-rooms, is willing to allow for; no one was more sensitive than he to the miseries of urban poverty, squalor and vice, and he shared the age's widespread uneasiness about the fast-growing urbanization and commercialization of English society. What he found in London was exactly what Henry James found: the constant stimulus, imaginative and intellectual, provided by (in James's words, which might well be Johnson's) 'the biggest aggregation of human life – the most complete compendium of the world' (*Notebooks*, Oxford 1947, p. 28). It is therefore appropriate that his first two major works should derive directly from his early experience of the metropolis and of the journalist's life there. These are the poem *London* (1738) and the *Life of Richard Savage* (1744).

London is an 'Imitation' of Juvenal's third satire. The 'Imitation' was a favourite eighteenth-century form (it has been revived in our own time, by Ezra Pound and Robert Lowell among others); it grew out of a seventeenth-century controversy between free and literal translators, and is really an extension of the principle of free translation. The object of the 'imitator' is to make a poem which follows an ancient original closely enough to convey effects of echo, parody, etc., to a reader who knows the original, but which is also a new poem, a genuine remaking of the old form for contemporary use. Readers who know the original derive a special pleasure from the contrasts or comparisons; those who do not, read the imitation simply as a contemporary poem. A certain tact is required of the imitator (which, in my view, Pound's and Lowell's imitations do not always show); he must neither go so much against the grain of his original as to irritate those who know and love it, nor depart from it so little as to forfeit any claim to creation.

The first requisite is clearly to pick an original with which the imitator is in sympathy. Pope had done this in his *Imitations of Horace*, and Johnson did the same when he picked Juvenal. For Johnson and Juvenal have much in common. Both are poets of the metropolis; Juvenal's Rome, huge centre of an expanding empire, must have had some real resemblances to eighteenth-century London. Both know literary poverty, the life of the hack in his garret. Both are insular; Juvenal's contempt for the Greeks is paralleled by Johnson's for the French. Both write a poetry devoid of lyrical fancifulness, firmly based on the real life they knew. Both are rhetorical writers; their work has the quality of formal, studied delivery. Both, above all, are moralists (or claim to be, perhaps one should say in the case of Juvenal): they are writers who distil general reflections, philosophical conclusions, out of their contemplation of the lives of men.

Johnson follows closely the structure of Juvenal's poem. The poet is bidding farewell to a friend who is leaving the metropolis in disgust and disillusion; the bulk of the poem consists of the latter's denunciation of the city he is leaving. The friend is merely a rhetorical device, a mouthpiece for the poet's own utterance. It is usually said of *London* that the poem is flawed by a degree of insincerity, in that Johnson himself was devoted to the city and cannot have really 'meant' the poem's denunciation of it: but there are points to be made against this commonplace. For, firstly, as I have suggested, Johnson was never an uncritical or sentimental adorer of London, and the experience he had had of it so far was overwhelmingly one of poverty, frustration and resentment. There can be no doubt of the personal feeling behind the finest passage in the poem, that on the miseries and humiliations of poverty (line 158, etc.), which drives on with splendid power to its climax in the capitalized line 'SLOW RISES WORTH, BY POVERTY DEPRESS'D.'

Secondly, *London* reflects a great deal of the young Johnson's fierce anger against Walpole's apparently irremovable regime and the corrupting effects which he thought it was having on the moral fibre of England. This belief was widely held by the 'wits'; it was given passionate, almost hysterical, expression in Pope's *Epilogue to the Satires*, published in the same year of 1738:

> Hear her [Vice's] black trumpet thro' the land proclaim,
> That NOT TO BE CORRUPTED IS THE SHAME.

And in *London* one finds the same conviction in such lines as 'with slavish tenets taint our poison'd youth' (55) or '. . . where all are slaves to gold, Where looks are merchandise, and smiles are sold' (178). In later life, Johnson repudiated this youthful fierceness against Walpole's government, but it was real and deep at the time.

Moreover, although *London* is a completely sincere poem, it is not, throughout, a *solemn* one. There is much deliberate exaggeration and farcical wit. 'Here falling houses thunder on your head, And here a female atheist talks you dead' (17-18): the female atheist is not in Juvenal. Such wit disarms one's objections by anticipating them; the exaggeration is admitted.

London, in critical esteem, has been somewhat overshadowed by *The Vanity of Human Wishes.* The latter is certainly the greater poem; but *London* has its own merits, and they are great. Take it as part of that art and writing of the eighteenth century which found its material in the vast and swift-growing city, object alike of revulsion and delight; see it in the company of Swift's *City Shower,* Gay's *Trivia* and *Beggar's Opera,* and Hogarth's *Gin Lane* and *Rake's Progress.* In this context, it holds its own: one of the monuments to the beginnings of Megalopolis and the changing of England from a rural to an urban and industrial community – not so alien as one might think from Blake's *London:*

> I wander thro each charter'd street
> Near where the charter'd Thames does flow,
> And mark in ev'ry face I meet
> Marks of weakness, marks of woe ...

The *Life of Savage* was included, thirty-five years after its first publication, among *The Lives of the Poets* – where it looks thoroughly out of place – but it is not best thought of either as biography or as criticism. It is really an elegy, almost a poem, which is concerned with a man maniacally bent on self-destruction and with the kind of existence he lived – the desperate, savage, hand to mouth life of Grub Street at its worst in what was probably its worst period. If one looked for analogues in later literature, one might find them in such works as Gissing's *New Grub Street,* Malcolm Lowry's letters, or Malcolm Brinnin's *Dylan Thomas in America.* Johnson's *Life* accepts unquestioningly two premises of which Johnson himself may have been, in private, a trifle doubtful: the complete truth of Savage's own tale that he was the illegitimate, disowned and hideously persecuted son of the Countess of Macclesfield, and the validity of his claim to be a distinguished poet. Johnson states these premises in his second paragraph –

a man whose writings entitle him to an eminent rank in the classes of learning, and whose misfortunes claim a degree of compassion not always due to the unhappy, as they were often the consequences of the crimes of others rather than his own . . .

– and they give to the narrative of Savage's follies, crimes and compulsively repetitive self-induced disasters a tragic dignity they would never possess if one were allowed to remember that he was probably no more than a crazy poetaster. With what one suspects to be artistic tact, Johnson gives no hint of the other side in the story of Savage's parentage – and quotes very little of his poetry.

The best possible introduction to the *Life of Savage* is provided by these sentences from Boswell:

. . . Richard Savage, a man of whom it is difficult to speak impartially, without wondering that he was for some time the intimate companion of Johnson; for his character was marked by profligacy, insolence, and ingratitude . . . It is melancholy to reflect that Johnson and Savage were sometimes in such extreme indigence that they could not pay for a lodging; so that they have wandered together whole nights in the streets. . .[Johnson] told Sir Joshua Reynolds that one night in particular, when Savage and he walked round St James's Square for want of a lodging, they were not at all depressed by their situation; but in high spirits and brimful of patriotism, traversed the square for several hours, inveighed against the minister, and 'resolved they would *stand by their country*'.

I am afraid, however, that by associating with Savage, who was habituated to the dissipation and licentiousness of the town, Johnson, though his good principles remained steady, did not entirely preserve that conduct for which, in days of greater simplicity, he was remarked . . . but was imperceptibly led into some indulgence which occasioned much distress to his virtuous mind.

We learn here from Boswell what we would never learn from the *Life* itself – the close intimacy between Savage and Johnson and the fact that Johnson had shared in the kind of life he lived. In the biography Johnson hardly appears at all, nor are there any of the numerous details, scabrous or crapulous, which he could certainly have provided if he had cared to. But it is, as it were, the unseen *pressure* of this intimacy, this common experience, which makes the *Life of Savage* so moving. Again and again, as one can see when one knows the truth, the moments of concrete fact are such as only a sharer could have known:

There [in the fields or the streets] he used to walk and form his speeches, and afterwards step into a shop, beg for a few moments the use of the pen and ink, and write down what he had composed upon paper which he had picked up by accident . . .
. . . walked about the streets till he was weary, and lay down in the summer upon a bulk, or in the winter, with his associates in poverty, among the ashes of a glass-house.

The work is organized, very largely, round such cameos of fact; between them, through a marching sequence of solid and stately paragraphs, Johnson builds up his tragic yet sardonic picture of a self-destroying man. And as the picture emerges, one sees that Boswell had no right to express amazement that Savage and Johnson had been friends, for in fact the character of Savage was very close to that of the bitter and wounded 'young Sam Johnson' whom Boswell never knew; and at many points Johnson is telling us so. When he writes that it was 'in no time of Mr Savage's life any part of his character to be the first of the company that desired to separate', he must have known that that was just as true of Samuel Johnson. When he relates an instance of Savage's crazy, heroic, pathetic pride – how, though 'his clothes were worn out', he nevertheless refused to accept some new ones left by an unknown benefactor – he could hardly have failed to remember how he, at Oxford, had thrown away 'with indignation' a pair of new shoes which had been charitably put at his door. When he comments that for Savage the worst effect of poverty was the humiliation it brought – 'not the want of lodging or of food, but the neglect and contempt which it drew upon him' – he knew that, as he had written in *London*, the case was his also:

> Of all the ills that harass the distress'd,
> Sure the most bitter is a scornful jest.

Thus, what the *Life of Savage* gives us, indirectly, is that part of Johnson's experience which Boswell did not know. But the effect of it remained with him all his life; it gave him his completely charitable, but also completely unsentimental, knowledge of the 'poor naked wretches', and their 'looped and windowed raggedness', who lived in his London. Johnson had none of the 'progressive's' optimism about poverty – he did not think it would ever be mitigated – but also he had none of the reforming zealot's well-meaning cruelty. Moreover, the experience behind the *Life of Savage* settled another thing for Johnson. It sealed him for ever of the tribe of those who earn their bread with their pens. The eighteenth century was the first age in which to do this became generally possible. The modern structure of the literary world, with its publishers and their establishments, its periodicals and their editors, all resting on the basis of the great anonymous public which pays for what it reads, was beginning to emerge. The whole structure, in turn, rested on a steady growth in population, urbanization, and literacy. Of this way of organizing literature, Johnson entirely approved, in spite of his bitter knowledge of its hardships (is this another example of the 'opposite-reacting' bent of his mind?). He always defended the big commercial publishers (a new race then) against charges of extortion or philistinism. The commercializing of literature he thought a definite gain, as he argued with Dr Watson at St Andrews:

. . Now learning itself is a trade. A man goes to a bookseller, and gets what he can. We have done with patronage . . . With patronage, what flattery! what falsehood! While a man is in equilibrio, he throws truth among the multitude, and lets them take it as they please . . . *Watson.* But is not the case now, that, instead of flattering one person, we flatter the age? *Johnson.* No, Sir. The world always lets a man tell what he thinks, his own way. (*Journal of a Tour to the Hebrides*, 19 August)

We today, after 200 years of 'throwing truth among the multitude', may well feel there is more to Dr Watson's objection than Johnson allowed; but Johnson's confidence rested, ultimately, on his faith in the 'common reader'. He invented the phrase; his age, almost, invented the thing – the anonymous, multitudinous arbiter of taste; but the common reader of the eighteenth century was a great deal more genuinely independent, more uncorrupted, than his descendant in the twentieth.

The Vanity of Human Wishes was published in 1749. Like *London*, it is an Imitation of one of Juvenal's satires, the tenth. It seems, on the whole, to follow its original less closely than *London*: a difference which is signalled by the fact that whereas the complete Latin text was given at the bottom of the page in the first edition of *London*, only line-references were given for this poem.

The basic organization of the poem is that which had been perfected by Pope in his *Moral Essays*. A moral proposition is first stated as a generalization, and then enforced by a series of character-sketches of people or careers, real or imaginary. Thus, the general proposition of Pope's second *Moral Essay* is stated in its second line – 'Most women have no characters at all' – and this is illustrated by a number of feminine portraits, including at least one, 'Atossa', based on a real woman, the Duchess of Marlborough. The method was entirely suited to the Augustan genius, with its bent for pragmatism, for testing a generalization by applying it to real people in real and contemporary society; it is in fact the equivalent in verse of Addison's enterprise in the *Spectator* – 'to enliven Morality with Wit, and to temper Wit with Morality'. Neither 'morality' nor 'wit' meant quite what it means today; both were less specialized, less restrictive, in application. 'Wit' meant something like Matthew Arnold's 'free play of the mind'. 'Morality' had the force of the French *mœurs*: a concept which united questions of right and wrong with questions of social behaviour.

The Vanity of Human Wishes is squarely in this tradition; it is one of its greatest achievements. Eliot's comment defines its quality as well as possible:

It is the certainty, the ease with which he hits the bull's-eye every time, that makes Johnson a poet.

But whence does Johnson derive that certainty and ease? From the complete fusion of *morality* and *wit*: he is never merely 'clever', as Pope is sometimes, and rarely merely sententious, as Addison and Crabbe are often. This total fusion results in the *compression* which is the great strength of the character-sketches. Take the one of Charles XII of Sweden – the greatest passage in the poem, which Eliot was right to single out for special praise with the comment: 'If these lines are not poetry, I do not know what poetry is.' In that passage, the effect is not merely of *one* military conqueror's entire career being compressed into thirty lines of verse, but of the whole of military glory being so compressed. It is a masterpiece of varying tempos. It begins with a rush of crowded, excited lines describing Charles's powers and successes:

> A frame of adamant, a soul of fire,
> No dangers fright him, and no labours tire ...

These are slowed down to a stately march –

> The march begins in military state
> And nations on his eye suspended wait

– slowed down to a dead halt at the climactic line recalling his disaster –

> Hide, blushing Glory, hide Pultowa's day ...

Then the rhythm changes again to a broken, limping anticlimax –

> The vanquish'd hero leaves his broken bands,
> And shows his miseries in distant lands

– expiring, at the very end, in the mocking remark that all the mighty Charles is now good for is to supply material for a passage in a poem by Samuel Johnson:

> He left the name, at which the world grew pale,
> To point a moral, or adorn a tale.

To my mind, this is not only poetry, but great poetry. I have found for myself – if personal experience is of any value in criticism –

that this poem has 'stayed with me' through more than thirty years of knowing it, in a way that very, very little of the poetry of romanticism has managed to do. Walter Scott seems to have found the same: he said to Ballantyne (as reported in chapter 20 of Lockhart's *Life*) that

Neither his own, nor any modern popular style of composition, was that from which he derived most pleasure. I asked him what it was. He answered – Johnson's; and that he had more pleasure in reading *London* and *The Vanity of Human Wishes*, than any other poetical composition he could mention.

And another perhaps surprising witness is Byron. 'Read Johnson's *Vanity of Human Wishes*', he noted in his journal for 9 January 1821:

all the examples and mode of giving them sublime, as well as the latter part, with the exception of an occasional couplet ... But 'tis a grand poem – and *so true*!

Byron drew from the poem reinforcement for his own pessimism: everything changes, so he felt it proved,

except man himself, who has always been, and always will be, an unlucky rascal. The infinite variety of lives conduct but to death, and the infinity of wishes lead but to disappointment.

Byron's rather facile disillusionment is a long way below Johnson's Stoic-Christian blending: but there is no need to doubt his admiration.

Johnson wrote, or was considerably involved in, three series of periodical essays. The first, *The Rambler*, was begun in 1750 and continued, at the rate of two issues a week, for almost exactly two years. *The Adventurer* (1753) was really the enterprise of one of Johnson's dearest friends, an unsuccessful doctor named Bathurst; but Johnson wrote many essays for it, under the pseudonym 'T'. The third series, *The Idler*, was begun in 1758 and continued, at the rate of one issue per week, for two years. Altogether, between the three series, he wrote over 300 periodical essays. In his own time, these essays formed the most read and most admired part of his work – especially the bound volumes of *Ramblers* and *Idlers*. They are now, probably, the least read and least admired.

Introduction

For this fate – which is undeserved – Boswell may provide, unwittingly, part of the reason. He announces the beginning of Johnson's career as essayist with great pomp and solemnity:

In 1750 he came forth in the character for which he was eminently qualified, a majestic teacher of moral and religious wisdom ... With what devout and conscientious sentiments this paper was undertaken is evidenced by the following prayer, which he composed and offered up on the occasion: Almighty God, the giver of all good things, without whose help all labour is ineffectual, and without whose grace all wisdom is folly: grant, I beseech thee, that in this undertaking thy Holy Spirit may not be with-held from me, but that I may promote thy glory, and the salvation of myself and others: grant this, O Lord, for the sake of thy son, Jesus Christ. Amen.

It is quite true that the general tone of Johnson's essays is much graver, much more that of a preacher, than the tone of Addison or Lamb; but Johnson regarded the basic duty of *all* his writing to be 'making the world better', and he would have offered up a prayer for the beginning of any such undertaking. Where Boswell gives a false – and perhaps a damaging – impression is in suggesting that *The Rambler* was peculiarly 'moralizing'. Johnson's essays have in truth a wide range of subject-matter; they include literary criticism (such as *Rambler* 4, on the novel); social and political comment (e.g., *Idler* 81, on European imperialism in North America); and satirical portrayals of social types, like the Dick Minim *Idlers*.

The impression of uniformity is due to the style rather than the matter. *The Rambler*, in fact, became the main vehicle for the 'Johnsonian prose' which, already in his lifetime, was 'censured by some shallow critics, as involved and turgid, and abounding with antiquated and hard words' (Boswell). That prose style has been magisterially analysed by W. K. Wimsatt:* essentially, it is a use of language designed to give to the raw, chaotic, disparate material of human life a quality of generalization, order and cohesion which will render it bearable, controllable, usable. Many of Johnson's best essays owe their power to the large element of self-analysis within

* See Select Bibliography, p. 37.

them: Johnson is *there*, in the essay, as he was in the *Life of Savage*, but here also his presence is unacknowledged. *Rambler* 155, for example, and *Idler* 31, are both devoted to that sin of which Johnson felt himself more guilty than of any other, the sin of Sloth. An essayist in the Lamb tradition might have started off in this style: 'I am myself – dare I admit it, dear Reader? – the *laziest* of mortals. Breakfast in Bed is *delicious* unto me, and a feather mattress is Heaven!' But one would never know, without external information, that there was any personal reference at all in Johnson's essays. The private human pain is made a part of universal experience and the driving-power for a moral lesson.

Johnson's essays were not particularly successful in their periodical form, but when they appeared as bound volumes they became widely read and deeply influential. They took over from the *Spectator* the role of lay-moralist, and filled that role into the early nineteenth century; they express the essential morality of Scott and Jane Austen. They have less sparkle than the *Spectator*, but much of the difference reflects a difference between the epochs which produced the two series. The mid-eighteenth century *is* a heavier, less witty, less spark-ling age than the age of Swift, Pope and Gay; one can feel in the air from the 1750s onwards a certain sobriety, and more than a tinge of Romantic introspection and melancholia.

If the essays, and especially *The Rambler*, provided the first step whereby Johnson advanced from the embittered hack of his early years to the much-admired scholar and moralist of the middle part of his life, it was the *Dictionary* which provided the second. These two monuments – now, probably, the least-known part of his work – were then the most important. They moved him into a position which scarcely any other English writer has occupied: for though we have had no lack of great moralists, or of great scholars, we have not had many who were both. Add to these his stature as poet and critic, and it will not seem excessive to claim that as *man of letters* no one in the English language can stand beside him.

Recent research on the *Dictionary* – considered as a work in the field of lexicography – has exploded some of the easy assumptions which used to present it as a towering mountain arising out of nothing. Johnson was by no means the first of English lexicographers, and he was far from independent of his predecessors. The conclusions of Professors Sledd and Kolb represent the general verdict of contemporary linguists and lexicographers:

Johnson's *Dictionary*, a booksellers' project, was what its age demanded – a standard and standardizing dictionary which included a history of the language, a grammar, and an extensive list of words selected with some care, explained by divided and classified definitions, and illustrated with quotations from authorities. Like Johnson's ideas about the nature of language in general and the history and structure of English in particular, his techniques in lexicography do not seem new when they are viewed against the background of earlier work . . . Not all parts of his work are of the same high quality. His grammar and history of the language and his etymologies are mediocre . . . His influence on the development of the language is dubious at best, and too much has been made of the Latinity of his word-list and definitions. The magnitude of his achievement remains, more clearly seen when he is not judged in unnatural isolation (James Sledd and Gwin Kolb: *Dr Johnson's Dictionary*, Chicago 1955).

To which may be added a comment from the viewpoint of literary criticism – Johnson's *Dictionary*, like his Shakespeare, possesses virtues which seem more literary than scholarly, more humane than scientific, and which perhaps could not have been found in it at all but for the fact that literary and linguistic scholarship in the eighteenth century was not particularly scholarly and most certainly not at all scientific. The *Dictionary* is full of the sense of an individual personality, the unique, unmistakable personality of its maker. From the moving pride and sorrow of the Preface to many of the actual entries, one is never in the impersonal world of 'exact scholarship'; one is as much in the world of Samuel Johnson's mind as in *The Vanity of Human Wishes* or in his private prayers. Even the quotations he chooses as examples – not only do these give a revealing picture of his literary tastes, but they were chosen, as Boswell tells us, in accordance with a private system of censorship. 'It should not pass unobserved, that he has quoted no author whose writings had a tendency to hurt sound religion and morality.'

The third and last stage of Johnson's career – from 1762 to his death in 1784 – is far better known to us than the preceding years. This is due to James Boswell, who met him in 1763. But the meeting with Boswell was not the great thing for Johnson that it was for Boswell himself, or for posterity. For Johnson, the decisive event had happened in the previous year – the granting of a Government pension of £300 a year for the rest of his life.

State patronage of writers is usually such a sorry, anguish-ridden business, that any instance of its succeeding is worth recording. In this case, both sides behaved with admirable dignity and generosity. Lord Bute, the Prime Minister, said to Johnson (who had expressed some scruples): 'It is not given you for any thing you are to do, but for what you have done' – and repeated the words twice, to 'set his mind perfectly at ease'. Johnson, on his side, wrote Bute a letter which is one of the finest examples of his 'public' epistolary style:

To the Right Honourable the Earl of Bute
My Lord,
When the bills were yesterday delivered to me by Mr Wedderburne, I was informed by him of the future favours which his Majesty has, by your Lordship's recommendation, been induced to intend for me.

Bounty always receives part of its value from the manner in which it is bestowed; your Lordship's kindness includes every circumstance that can gratify delicacy, or enforce obligation. You have conferred your favours on a man who has neither alliance nor interest, who has not merited them by services, nor courted them by officiousness; you have spared him the shame of solicitation, and the anxiety of suspense.

What has been thus elegantly given will, I hope, not be reproachfully enjoyed; I shall endeavour to give your Lordship the only recompense which generosity desires, – the gratification of finding that your benefits are not improperly bestowed. I am, my Lord,

Your Lordship's most obliged,
Most obedient, and most humble servant,
20 July 1762   Sam. Johnson

Johnson's scruples were due mostly to his past opposition to the Government and Court and to his very strong Jacobite sympathies. As late as 1783, he was saying to Boswell: 'This Hanoverian family is *isolée* here. They have no friends.' Nor did his enemies let him forget his dictionary definitions of *pension* and *pensioner* (see p. 248). Johnson was obviously right to disregard the innuendoes of malice and envy; if ever a man had deserved well of the State, it was he; if ever public money was well spent, it was the money which made possible the way of life which, in turn, made possible the work of Boswell. And it would be nonsense to suggest that Johnson was in any way a 'lost leader', a figure like Southey as seen by Byron – youthful Radical turning his coat into middle-aged conformer. Johnson's was a subtler case; no pat formula will do for him.

But there is a case for suggesting that the pension, and the life it made possible, did 'tame' something in Johnson. Bernard Shaw, in the preface to *Misalliance*, complains of Johnson's 'trifling with literary fools in taverns, when he should have been shaking England with the thunder of his spirit'. Is Shaw entirely wrong? I do feel that a certain *wholeness* was lost to Johnson, that he became something of a split man – and that this happened because a mind and soul which remained, to the end, sultry, volcanic, always 'in opposition', had now to live in uneasy combination with a man living comfortably, a social prize whom it was a triumph to secure for one's salon, the gruff heart-of-gold roarer whom people delighted, half-trembling, to prod and tease. The split becomes visible if one compares the two accounts of the Hebridean journey. Boswell's is a fascinating, amusing, lively piece of gossip; Johnson's is a serious, sombre, almost tragic investigation of a society in its death-agonies. And in many areas of his mind there seems an increasing degree of self-conflict and confusion; one has often the impression of an immensely powerful but tortured mind which finds it desperately difficult to settle itself in anything. He mocks at those who denounce 'luxury', but is himself always deploring the spread of commerce and its values. He becomes, outwardly, a more and more bigoted High Churchman, bellowing hysterically against Methodists, Quakers, Presbyterians, non-conformists of all sorts; but his private prayers and journals show a man tortured to the end by doubts and scruples. His political opinions show a similar hardening; the quite inaccurate picture of Johnson as an absurdly reactionary 'Tory' is largely derived from the utter-ances of his last fifteen years or so. In almost all respects, there is a basic alienation from the society of which, on the surface, he was an admired and comfortable member. The free-thinking of Hume and Gibbon; the pre-romantic poetry of Gray, Collins, etc., and the critical stance which went with it; the political radicalism of Wilkes and the American colonists: with all these he was utterly out of sympathy. It is a strange paradox: the young Johnson – poor, embittered, rebellious – was nevertheless more in tune with the intellectual life around him than the pensioned and conforming Johnson of his later years.

And a sign of it is a hardening of the sensibility and a narrowing of the imagination. Of this his utterances on the public executions at Tyburn and the processions of death from Newgate give a striking example. When the processions were abolished in 1783, this was his comment:

He said to Sir William Scott, 'The age is running mad after innovation; and all the business of the world is to be done in a new way; men are to be hanged in a new way; Tyburn itself is not free from the fury of in-novation.' It having been argued that this was an improvement. – 'No Sir, (said he, eagerly,) it is *not* an improvement; they object, that the old method drew together a number of spectators. Sir, executions are in-tended to draw spectators. If they do not draw spectators, they don't answer their purpose. The old method was most satisfactory to all parties; the public was gratified by a procession; the criminal was sup-ported by it. Why is all this to be swept away?' (30 March 1783.)

But if one turns to No. 114 of the *Rambler*, one finds this:

The learned, the judicious, the pious Boerhaave relates, that he never saw a criminal dragged to execution without asking himself, 'Who knows whether this man is not less culpable than me?' On the days when the prisons of this city are emptied into the grave, let every spectator of the dreadful procession put the same question to his own heart. Few among those who crowd in thousands to the legal massacre, and look with carelessness, perhaps with triumph, on the utmost exacerbations of human misery, would then be able to return without horror and misery.

It is hard to believe that it was the same man who spoke the former passage and wrote the latter: there are thirty-three years between them.

The major works of Johnson's last period are three: the edition of Shakespeare (1765), the *Journey to the Western Islands of Scotland* (1775), and *The Lives of the Poets* (1779–81). It is not a large output for more than twenty years – and his prayers and journals are fuller than ever before of self-reproaches for indolence – but there are far more letters than before (presumably because people now kept letters from the great man); and these, together with the unbalanced structure of Boswell's biography, which devotes about four-fifths of its length to the last twenty years, contribute to the misleading impression that Johnson's last decade or two was more productive than all the years before.

An edition of Shakespeare had been in Johnson's mind for many years before it appeared. He had published 'Proposals' for it in 1745, and renewed them, more elaborately, in 1756. The latter, as Boswell remarks, are very impressive: they show 'that he perfectly well knew what a variety of research such an undertaking required'. He also made use of the old-fashioned method of publishing 'by subscription': that is, he asked for advance contributions, to be repaid with a copy of the book. But it took him another nine years to produce it – the eventual goad being supplied by the satire of Charles Churchill:

> He for subscribers baits his hook,
> And takes your cash; but where's the book?

In producing an edition of Shakespeare, Johnson was taking his part in one of the eighteenth century's major literary tasks – the establishing of Shakespeare as an 'edited' classic. He is in the succession which began with Rowe in 1709, when the completely unedited Folios of the seventeenth century were becoming inadequate. It is clear that Boswell is a trifle embarrassed about Johnson's Shakespeare; he greets it with far less enthusiasm than he does the *Rambler* or *Dictionary*, and is particularly uneasy about its value as scholarship:

His researches were not so ample, and his investigations so acute, as they might have been; which we now certainly know from the labours of other able and ingenious critics who have followed him.

The last words are a compliment to the great Shakespearean scholar Edmond Malone, who had helped Boswell greatly over writing the *Life* and had no doubt informed him of Johnson's deficiencies in Shakespearean scholarship. Boswell, accordingly, puts the weight of his praise on to the Preface. The *Preface to Shakespeare* is much more than simply a preface. It is a critical manifesto, a public statement, and its style is appropriately dignified. What this manifesto says is, first of all, that Shakespeare is now a classic. He can no longer be harmed by captious denigration; he is no longer in need of patriotic defence. But the fact that he is a classic does not mean that we must therefore revere him absolutely and uncritically. It means the opposite: that we may now examine his work – including its defects and limitations – calmly and reasonably, secure that it cannot be overthrown.

Why, then, is he a classic? Because he is 'the poet of nature' – because his work reaches that core of human behaviour which is not changed by all the changes of time and place. This for Johnson, as for all classical criticism, is the vital thing. Without this, nothing will do; with it, no faults, however great or many, and no flouting of the 'Rules', can prove fatal. But Shakespeare does have faults, and faults big enough to destroy anyone else. They are *not* the ones that conventional criticism has accused him of: in two memorable and magnificent passages Johnson demolishes the cases against Shakespeare's 'mixing comic and tragic scenes' and against his disregard of the 'Unities'. No: Shakespeare's real faults, says Johnson, are these: his neglect of moral instruction; his carelessness in structure and frequent indifference to probability and consistency; and his tendency to pointless elaboration of language – to bombast, declamation, far-fetched conceits and contemptible word-play.

Johnson's account of Shakespeare's faults, like all his criticism, is trenchant and forthright – so much so that his preface was widely regarded by contemporaries as an attempt at 'debunking' Shakespeare. This, of course, is ridiculous; his love and reverence are everywhere apparent. But he loved and revered on his own terms and no others: *independence* is the central quality of his mind. The faults he believes to be Shakespeare's are those he has found for himself; he has not borrowed them from any reach-me-down theory. And is he – if we assume, as he did, that Shakespeare is unassailably great – is he entirely wrong in the faults he finds? I suspect, myself, that his Shakespeare – always fallible, sometimes a cynical audience-pleaser, often careless, often bewitched to his harm by his own immense power over words – is nearer the truth than the always right and bottomlessly subtle monstrosity which our Bardolatry has invented.

Whether we agree or not, it is certain that Johnson in this Preface has accomplished what he set out to do. He has not only settled Shakespeare firmly on the pedestal of a classic; he has also given, as he sees it, the valid reasons why he *is* a classic and the valid reasons why, in spite of that, he is not perfect. He has demolished, on the one hand, the wrong arguments against him (the neo-classicist formulae), and has protested, on the other hand, against the beginnings of a senseless adulation. I doubt if Shakespeare himself would have asked for any other kind of tribute.

But the real value of the edition is found in the critical notes and in the summaries which Johnson supplies for each play. These establish him as one of the greatest (*the* greatest, in my view) of Shakespearean critics. His Shakespearean criticism is distinguished by three main qualities.

First, he has a passionate admiration for Shakespeare, and responds to his work as intensely as any reader ever has. One can hardly doubt that, if one reads his reason for quasi-approving Nahum Tate's 'happy ending' for *King Lear* (see p. 296) or his comment on the scene of Desdemona's death:

I am glad that I have ended my revisal of this dreadful scene. It is not to be endured.

But his admiration does not lead him to what Shaw was to call 'Bardolatry'. He never forgets that Shakespeare, however towering a genius, was still a hardworking professional writer, dependent on public support – no less than Samuel Johnson was. His notes are peppered with remarks like '. . . it produces merriment, which our author found more useful than probability' . . . 'our author well knew what would please the audience for which he wrote', and so on. He can say such things without any implication of derogation; he has nothing of the post-romantic assumption, that the popular and commercial *must* be the inferior.

Second, Johnson is extremely conservative (which, in fact, was then revolutionary) in his treatment of the text. All editorial interference he regards with profound scepticism. In this he anticipates contemporary scholarship, and is well in advance of that of his own day, which regarded the Folio text as more or less worthless, fair game for editorial ingenuity or critical superiority. 'The explanation is very good, but the text does not require to be amended . . . There is no need of change . . . No emendation is necessary . . . I am not much a friend to conjectural emendation' – such is Johnson's invariable tenor. Part of this was derived from his respect, as a lexicographer, for the language – his awareness that Elizabethan English had its rights. 'All the modern editions', he notes, substitute 'in private' for Claudius's 'in hugger-mugger to inter him' (*Hamlet*, IV.v); Johnson restores 'hugger-mugger,' with the comment:

That the words now replaced are better, I do not undertake to prove; it is sufficient that they are Shakespeare's. If phraseology is to be changed as words grow uncouth by disuse, or gross by vulgarity, the history of every language will be lost; we shall no longer have the words of any author; and, as these alterations will be often unskilfully made, we shall in time have very little of his meaning.

The third quality is Johnson's invariable practice of relating the plays to real life, and testing them by their fidelity to real life. Again and again, this is the criterion by which he judges. Would a real man, in such a situation, feel, speak, act like this? 'This is one of our author's observations upon life . . . These are observations worthy of a man who has surveyed human nature with the closest attention . . . Richard speaks here the language of nature.' The general principle he had laid down in the Preface:

Shakespeare has no heroes; his scenes are occupied only by men, who act and speak as the reader thinks that he should himself have spoken or acted on the same occasion; even where the agency is supernatural, the dialogue is level with life.

Against Johnson's criticism of Shakespeare it has been argued that it suffers from a deficient appreciation of the Shakespearean poetry. This is argued by Dr Leavis:

His limitation in the face of Shakespearean tragedy goes with a limitation in the face of Shakespearean poetry. He cannot appreciate the Shakespearean handling of language . . . He doesn't respond fully to Shakespeare's poetry. He cannot, because his training opposes.

('Johnson and Augustanism' in *The Common Pursuit*, London, 1952)

It is certainly true that Johnson did not entirely approve of many qualities of Shakespeare's writing. He disliked his addiction to word-play, his mixed and far-fetched metaphors, and his 'conceits'. But however much he disapproved in theory, there is no doubt that he understood, in practice. He always resisted any attempts to make Shakespeare 'correct'. Warburton, for example, wanted to change 'a leaven'd and prepared choice' into 'level'd'; Johnson answers: 'No emendation is necessary. *Leaven'd* is one of Shakespeare's harsh metaphors.' Warburton, again, is upset by the mixed metaphor in 'falling into the *flaws* of her own youth, Hath blister'd her report', and wants to put 'flames' for 'flaws' – on which Johnson caustically remarks: 'Who does not see that upon such principles there is no end of correction?' He recognized that the basis of Shakespeare's poetic diction is the colloquial language.

Such is the English idiom, which our author commonly prefers to grammatical nicety . . . The language of Shakespeare is very licentious [i.e., indifferent to rules], and his words have often meanings remote from the proper and original use.

I suspect that he enjoyed Shakespeare's poetry a good deal more thoroughly than some of his critical principles allowed him to admit.

He did not enjoy it from the critical standpoint of the twentieth century – why should he? or rather, how could he? – and from that standpoint he missed a good deal and got a good deal more a little wrong: but perhaps we miss just as much which he did not miss. He certainly appreciated, more than we do, the gnomic, moralizing element in Shakespeare; he appreciated also the Shakespearean use of the plain style. This one can see from his noble praise of Macbeth's 'I dare do all that may become a man . . .' (p. 297.) What he did not entirely approve of was the baroque, 'metaphysical' manner: but that is only one of Shakespeare's almost innumerable 'styles'. No one can achieve a complete and even appreciation of all that there is in Shakespeare. We all make our own selections; and Johnson's was no narrower than ours.

Boswell tells us that Johnson had been interested in the Scottish Highlands – had even thought of visiting them – long before he actually went there in 1773. There were two main motives. First came his deep emotional attachment to the Jacobite cause. Boswell, commenting on the fact that he apparently wrote little or nothing during the years 1745 and '46, suggests that some may imagine this was caused by a 'sympathetic anxiety [which] impeded the exertion of his intellectual powers'. This seems dubious; but there is no doubt of the sympathy. It included also a strong tinge of guilt; for Johnson knew very well that the English Jacobites, however heartily they drank to the Stuarts, had scarcely risked a penny or a limb when the crunch came: while the Highland Jacobites had staked, and lost, their entire way of life. A deep respect and admiration, almost an elegiac tenderness, suffuse the *Journey to the Western Islands* whenever the '45 or its aftermath is mentioned.

But in addition to the Jacobite interest, there was the prospect of seeing a genuinely 'savage' society – a wild, primitive, *different* way of living. However caustically Johnson mocked at the cult of the Noble Savage, he shared his age's absorption in the exotic and the barbarous, whether found among American Indians, Chinese sages, or Celtic warriors. His mind was deeply interested too in the age's great debate about 'luxury' – i.e., commercialism, the replacement of rank by wealth as the standard of society. In the Highlands, he thought and hoped, he would find a society living still according to the ancient forms – feudal, traditional, pre-commercial – the kind of society which, in theory, he revered and longed for, though in practice he would always have fled from it (as he fled from Lichfield) to the 'full tide of human existence' at Charing Cross.

Yet when he did come to the Highlands, what he found was the ancient society in its death-throes. It was dying partly through defeat by external forces, partly through its own desire: its people were 'now losing their distinction and hastening to mingle with the general community'. They were emigrating to America; they were drifting to the cities; they were joining the British Army as mercenaries. They were becoming like everyone else. Was this to be welcomed – or deplored? Johnson could not decide: the *Journey to the Western Islands* is the record of his indecision.

The Lives of the Poets, like the *Dictionary*, began as a co-operative commercial venture by a group of London publishers. They had decided to produce

an elegant and uniform edition of 'The English Poets' ... with a concise account of the life of each author, by Dr Samuel Johnson ... The Doctor very politely undertook it, and seemed exceedingly pleased with the prospect. As to the terms, it was left entirely to the Doctor to name his own; he mentioned 200 guineas; it was immediately agreed to ... (Letter from Edward Dilly, one of the publishers, quoted in Boswell, September 1777)

The proposal was made first in 1777. The original intention was that Johnson should write no more than a very brief 'notice' for each poet; but as he got his teeth into it,

the subject swelled in such a manner, that instead of prefaces to each poet, of no more than a few pages ... he produced an ample, rich, and most entertaining view of them in every respect. (Boswell, September 1777)

He worked away at it for over three years, in the manner inimitably described by himself – 'in my usual way, dilatorily and hastily, unwilling to work, and working with vigour and haste'. Boswell opines that of all Johnson's works *The Lives of the Poets* is the one which 'will perhaps be read most generally, and with most pleasure'; and this is so, he suggests, because the subject was exactly suited to Johnson's deepest interests. Biography had always been his favourite branch of literature; criticism, and especially the criticism of English poetry, was one of his chosen fields. *The Lives of the Poets* combined the two. The actual choice of poets was not his, but the publishers': he himself merely added a few, including (for the sake of his piety rather than his poetry) the hymn-writer Isaac Watts. The selection is heavily loaded in favour of the eighteenth century, and it is obvious that a collection of 'The English Poets' in which the earliest are Milton and Cowley is absurd. But as a repository of information, gossip, wit and criticism, *The Lives of the Poets* is unsurpassable. Boswell's epithets are perfect: 'ample, rich, and most entertaining.'

The general reception of the *Lives* was far from universally favourable. Johnson expected they would be attacked, as he said to Boswell (26 March 1779), and attacked they were – for their lack of respect towards Milton, Lyttelton and Gray in particular. The fact is that the taste which they represent was already, by 1780, old-fashioned: in this again Johnson had become alienated from his age. He was upholding the Augustan standards; the age was groping its way, half-consciously, to romanticism. Hence the defiant note in his praise of Pope – 'if Pope be not a poet, where is poetry to be found?' – and hence, to some degree, his depreciation of Milton, whose shorter poems were a major source of eighteenth-century romanticism, and his scathing contempt for the odes of Gray. In all the lives, his method is the same. He gives first his subject's biography, and then a critical survey of his work. He does not try to interweave the one with the other, or to indicate the bearings of 'Life' on 'Work': a critically primitive technique, perhaps, but it does make for clarity and ease. The whole work, indeed, has an air of ease; its prose is relaxed and colloquial, the paragraphs and sentences simple and short. It reflects the Indian summer of Johnson's life, the few years of fame, comfort and tranquillity, before the physical collapse and emotional misery of the last year or two. Amid the rest, the *Life of Savage*, inserted unchanged as it had been written thirty-five years before, stands out enormously different, 'young Sam Johnson' enclosed, but far from killed, within the venerable sage he had become.

Johnson is not an easy writer to sum up. His personality – which *is* his work – was complicated and changeable; to different people, and at different times, he presented a bewildering variety of facets. For my own part, I would suggest as the basis of it all his thoroughly proletarian and provincial origin, and the poverty and frustration which that entailed in his early years. No writer I know of has seen this as clearly, or expressed it as memorably, as Carlyle. He may exaggerate, to the point of caricature; he may, one suspects, be thinking as much of Thomas Carlyle as of Samuel Johnson; but he does understand:

At College . . . a rugged wildman of the desert, awakened to the feeling of himself; proud as the proudest, poor as the poorest; stoically shut up, silently enduring the incurable . . . A flood of black indignation mantling beneath. A truculent, raw-boned figure! . . . An English plebeian, and moving rag-and-dust mountain, coarse, proud, irascible, imperious.

This was the beginning. But Johnson could not (as many modern writers can and do) *exploit* it. He believed in a hierarchical society. He believed in the classical and Anglican values: in sobriety, restraint and resignation. He longed desperately to embody them in himself and uphold them in his work. He never imagined for a moment that there was anything praiseworthy or of positive value in a life of poverty and bohemianism or in living for the senses and the moment rather than for the soul and eternity. He would have treated as wicked raving Blake's saying: 'The road of excess leads to the palace of wisdom', and if you had suggested that he himself was a proof of its truth, he would have roared with tormented rage. But it *was* the truth of him. He was an enormously 'excessive' character, always 'in extremes', as he said of himself to Mrs Thrale. He forced those 'excesses' into a sternly classical mode of expression; he tailored the 'extremes', as best he could, into the semblance of a devout High Churchman and respectable Conservative. His admirers were taken in; they accepted and venerated this noble facade, and explained away the occasional outbursts, the moments of agony or almost hysterical joviality, as due merely to his 'temperament', his 'constitutional melancholia'. But this is too easy. The true analysis of Johnson will show a man in whom there was a built-in principle of *contradiction*. Show him anything, and his spontaneous reaction is to stand for its opposite. His first biographer, Sir John Hawkins, tells a revealing anecdote which shows that even Johnson's churchmanship was tinged with this quality. He tells us that Johnson's loudly proclaimed reverence for the Church did not prevent him from being remarkably rude and combative whenever he encountered individual clerics he disapproved of. And Hawkins suggests why:

He had been bred in an university, and must there have had in prospect those advantages, those stations in life, or perhaps those dignities, which an academic education leads to. Missing these by his adverse fortunes, he looked on every dignity under a bishop . . . as occupying a station to which himself had a better title. (Abridged edition of Hawkins' *Life*, London, 1962: p. 106)

He was a man always 'in opposition' – and he was so, largely, because he was a 'disappointed man'. Hawkins tells us something else which seems to me both true and revealing – that Johnson had not at all *wanted* to be a writer, not, at least, the kind of writer – professional, miscellaneous, secular – that he did become:

As the narrowness of his father's circumstances had shut him out of those professions for which an university education is a necessary qualification, and his project of an academy had failed . . . the profession of an author was the only one in his power to adopt. (ibid., p. 68)

Like Swift, Johnson had longed to be more 'respectable', more unquestionably a member of that fixed hierarchy which he venerated, though the principle of contradiction within him was always impelling him to criticize and satirize in detail what he revered in gross. The lady who, having listened with horror to one of his outbursts of bitter misanthropy, murmured ('in a low voice'): 'This is worse than Swift!', was perfectly right. He was much more akin to Swift than he realized or would have liked to acknowledge. And that was why he hated Swift.

36

SELECT BIBLIOGRAPHY

On Johnson's life, the primary authority is of course Boswell, and the definitive edition is L. F. Powell's revision of Birkbeck Hill's edition (Oxford, 1934 etc.). *Johnsonian Miscellanies*, edited by Birkbeck Hill (Oxford, 1897, and reprinted, 1966), gives a great deal of biographical information not in Boswell. The best edition of Johnson's letters is that edited by R. W. Chapman (Oxford, 1952); there is a good selection from this in the World's Classics. A very useful collection is *The Critical Opinions of Samuel Johnson*, edited by J. E. Brown (Princeton, 1926). There is at present no definitive modern edition of Johnson's complete works, though the Yale edition, currently coming out, will probably become this.

Of critical comment on his work that of Boswell himself is much better than is commonly realized; his little introductions to the works as they appear are often full of relevant information and intelligent comment. The next notable commentator, apart from stray remarks by Scott and Byron, is Carlyle, whose 'review' of Croker's edition of Boswell (it is some sixty pages long and is usually included in his *Critical and Miscellaneous Essays*) is full of eccentric but valid insight. Leslie Stephen's *English Men of Letters* volume (London, 1878) is worth reading, so is Sir Walter Raleigh's *Six Essays on Johnson* (Oxford, 1910). More recent criticism which I have found valuable includes the following:

T. S. Eliot: 'Eighteenth Century Poetry' in *Pelican Guide to English Literature, Dryden to Johnson* (London, 1957).

F. R. Leavis: 'Johnson and Augustanism' in *The Common Pursuit* (London, 1952).

W. K. Wimsatt, Jr.: *The Prose Style of Samuel Johnson* (New Haven, 1941).

J. W. Krutch: *Samuel Johnson* (New York, 1944; London, 1948).

B. H. Bronson: *Johnson Agonistes* (Berkeley, 1944; Cambridge, 1946).

W. J. Bate: *The Achievement of Samuel Johnson* (New York, 1955).

Samuel Johnson

J. L. Clifford: *Young Sam Johnson* (New York, 1955).
J. Sledd and G. Kolb: *Dr Johnson's Dictionary* (Chicago, 1955).
D. J. Greene: *The Politics of Samuel Johnson* (New Haven, 1960).
Robert Voitle: *Samuel Johnson the Moralist* (Harvard, 1961).

Part I: 1709–49

GRUB STREET JOURNALIST

TRANSLATION OF HORACE: ODES
BOOK II. 14 ·

ALAS, dear friend, the fleeting years
In everlasting circles run,
In vain you spend your vows and prayers,
They roll, and ever will roll on.

Should hecatombs each rising morn   5
On cruel Pluto's altar die,
Should costly loads of incense burn,
Their fumes ascending to the sky;

You could not gain a moment's breath,
Or move the haughty King below,   10
Nor would inexorable Death
Defer an hour the fatal blow.

In vain we shun the din of war,
And terrors of the stormy main,
In vain with anxious breasts we fear   15
Unwholesome Sirius'[1] sultry reign;

We all must view the Stygian flood
That silent cuts the dreary plains,
And cruel Danaus'[2] bloody brood
Condemn'd to everduring pains.   20

Your shady groves, your pleasing wife,
And fruitful fields, my dearest friend,
You'll leave together with your life;
Alone the cypress shall attend.

After your death, the lavish heir   25
Will quickly drive away his woe,
The wine you kept with so much care
Along the marble floor shall flow.

LONDON

A POEM

IN IMITATION OF THE THIRD SATIRE OF JUVENAL

Quis ineptae
Tam patiens urbis, tam ferreus ut teneat se?

JUV.

THO' grief and fondness in my breast rebel,
When injur'd THALES bids the town farewell,
Yet still my calmer thoughts his choice commend,
I praise the hermit, but regret the friend,
5   Resolved at length, from vice and LONDON far,
To breathe in distant fields a purer air,
And, fix'd on Cambria's solitary shore,
Give to St David one true Briton more.
    For who would leave, unbrib'd, Hibernia's land,
10 Or change the rocks of Scotland for the Strand?
There none are swept by sudden fate away,
But all whom hunger spares, with age decay:
Here malice, rapine, accident, conspire,
And now a rabble rages, now a fire;
15 Their ambush here relentless ruffians lay,
And here the fell attorney prowls for prey;
Here falling houses thunder on your head,
And here a female atheist talks you dead.
    While THALES waits the wherry that contains
20 Of dissipated wealth the small remains,
On Thames's banks, in silent thought we stood,
Where Greenwich smiles upon the silver flood:
Struck with the seat that gave Eliza birth,[1]
We kneel, and kiss the consecrated earth;
25 In pleasing dreams the blissful age renew,
And call Britannia's glories back to view;
Behold her cross triumphant on the main,
The guard of commerce, and the dread of Spain,
Ere masquerades debauch'd, excise[2] oppress'd,

Or English honour grew a standing jest.   30
   A transient calm the happy scenes bestow,
And for a moment lull the sense of woe.
At length awaking, with contemptuous frown,
Indignant THALES eyes the neighb'ring town.
   Since worth, he cries, in these degen'rate days,   35
Wants ev'n the cheap reward of empty praise;
In those curs'd walls, devote to vice and gain,
Since unrewarded science toils in vain;
Since hope but soothes to double my distress,
And ev'ry moment leaves my little less;   40
While yet my steady steps no staff sustains,
And life still vig'rous revels in my veins;
Grant me, kind heaven. to find some happier place,
Where honesty and sense are no disgrace;
Some pleasing bank where verdant osiers play,   45
Some peaceful vale with nature's paintings gay;
Where once the harass'd Briton found repose,
And safe in poverty defy'd his foes;
Some secret cell, ye pow'rs, indulgent give.
Let — live here, for — has learn'd to live.   50
Here let those reign, whom pensions can incite
To vote a patriot black, a courtier white;
Explain their country's dear-bought rights away,
And plead for pirates in the face of day;
With slavish tenets taint our poison'd youth,   55
And lend a lie the confidence of truth.
   Let such raise palaces, and manors buy,
Collect a tax, or farm a lottery,
With warbling eunuchs[3] fill a licens'd stage,[4]
And lull to servitude a thoughtless age.   60
   Heroes, proceed! what bounds your pride shall hold?
What check restrain your thirst of pow'r and gold?
Behold rebellious virtue quite o'erthrown,
Behold our fame, our wealth, our lives your own.
   To such, a groaning nation's spoils are giv'n,   65
When public crimes inflame the wrath of heav'n:
But what, my friend, what hope remains for me,

    Who start at theft, and blush at perjury?
    Who scarce forbear, tho' BRITAIN'S Court he sing,
70   To pluck a titled Poet's borrow'd wing;
    A Statesman's logic unconvinc'd can hear,
    And dare to slumber o'er the Gazetteer;[5]
    Despise a fool in half his pension dress'd,
    And strive in vain to laugh at H — Y's[6] jest.
75   Others with softer smiles, and subtler art,
    Can sap the principles, or taint the heart;
    With more address a lover's note convey,
    Or bribe a virgin's innocence away.
    Well may they rise, while I, whose rustic tongue
80   Ne'er knew to puzzle right, or varnish wrong,
    Spurn'd as a beggar, dreaded as a spy,
    Live unregarded, unlamented die.
     For what but social guilt the friend endears?
    Who shares Orgilio's crimes, his fortune shares.
85   But thou, should tempting villainy present
    All Marlb'rough hoarded, or all Villiers spent,
    Turn from the glitt'ring bribe thy scornful eye,
    Nor sell for gold, what gold could never buy,
    The peaceful slumber, self-approving day,
90   Unsullied fame, and conscience ever gay.
      The cheated nation's happy fav'rites, see!
    Mark whom the great caress, who frown on me!
    LONDON! the needy villain's gen'ral home,
    The common shore of Paris and of Rome;
95   With eager thirst, by folly or by fate,
    Sucks in the dregs of each corrupted state.
    Forgive my transports on a theme like this,
    I cannot bear a French metropolis.
      Illustrious EDWARD![7] from the realms of day,
100   The land of heroes and of saints survey;
    Nor hope the British lineaments to trace,
    The rustic grandeur, or the surly grace,
    But lost in thoughtless ease, and empty show,
    Behold the warrior dwindled to a beau;
105   Sense, freedom, piety, refin'd away,

Of France the mimic,[8] and of Spain the prey.
    All that at home no more can beg or steal,
Or like a gibbet better than a wheel;
Hiss'd from the stage, or hooted from the court,
Their air, their dress, their politics import;   110
Obsequious, artful, voluble and gay,
On Britain's fond credulity they prey.
No gainful trade their industry can 'scape,
They sing, they dance, clean shoes, or cure a clap;
All sciences a fasting Monsieur knows,   115
And bid him go to hell, to hell he goes.
    Ah! what avails it, that, from slav'ry far,
I drew the breath of life in English air;
Was early taught a Briton's right to prize,
And lisp the tale of HENRY's victories;   120
If the gull'd conqueror receives the chain,
And flattery subdues when arms are vain?
    Studious to please, and ready to submit,
The supple Gaul was born a parasite:
Still to his int'rest true, where'er he goes,   125
Wit, brav'ry, worth, his lavish tongue bestows;
In ev'ry face a thousand graces shine,
From ev'ry tongue flows harmony divine.
These arts in vain our rugged natives try,
Strain out with falt'ring diffidence a lie,   130
And get a kick for awkward flattery.
    Besides, with justice, this discerning age
Admires their wond'rous talents for the stage:
Well may they venture on the mimic's art,
Who play from morn to night a borrow'd part;   135
Practis'd their master's notions to embrace,
Repeat his maxims, and reflect his face;
With ev'ry wild absurdity comply,
And view each object with another's eye;
To shake with laughter ere the jest they hear,   140
To pour at will the counterfeited tear,
And as their patron hints the cold or heat,
To shake in dog-days, in December sweat.

How, when competitors like these contend,
145 Can surly virtue hope to fix a friend?
Slaves that with serious impudence beguile,
And lie without a blush, without a smile;
Exalt each trifle, ev'ry vice adore,
Your taste in snuff, your judgement in a whore;
150 Can Balbo's eloquence applaud, and swear
He gropes[9] his breeches with a monarch's air.

For arts like these preferr'd, admir'd, caress'd,
They first invade your table, then your breast;
Explore your secrets with insidious art,
155 Watch the weak hour, and ransack all the heart;
Then soon your ill-plac'd confidence repay,
Commence your lords, and govern or betray.

By numbers here from shame or censure free,
All crimes are safe, but hated poverty.[10]
160 This, only this, the rigid law pursues,
This, only this, provokes the snarling muse.
The sober trader at a tatter'd cloak,
Wakes from his dream, and labours for a joke;
With brisker air the silken courtiers gaze,
165 And turn the varied taunt a thousand ways.
Of all the griefs that harass the distress'd,
Sure the most bitter is a scornful jest;
Fate never wounds more deep the gen'rous heart,
Than when a blockhead's insult points the dart.

170 Has heaven reserv'd, in pity to the poor,
No pathless waste, or undiscover'd shore;
No secret island in the boundless main?
No peaceful desert yet unclaim'd by Spain?[11]
Quick let us rise, the happy seats explore,
175 And bear oppression's insolence no more.
This mournful truth is ev'ry where confess'd,
SLOW RISES WORTH, BY POVERTY DEPRESS'D:
But here more slow, where all are slaves to gold,
Where looks are merchandise, and smiles are sold;
180 Where won by bribes, by flatteries implor'd,
The groom retails the favours of his lord.

But hark! th' affrighted crowd's tumultuous cries
Roll thro' the streets, and thunder to the skies;
Rais'd from some pleasing dream of wealth and pow'r,
Some pompous palace, or some blissful bow'r,   185
Aghast you start, and scarce with aching sight
Sustain th' approaching fire's tremendous light;
Swift from pursuing horrors take your way,
And leave your little ALL to flames a prey;
Then thro' the world a wretched vagrant roam,   190
For where can starving merit find a home?
In vain your mournful narrative disclose,
While all neglect, and most insult your woes.

Should heaven's just bolts Orgilio's wealth confound,[12]
And spread his flaming palace on the ground,   195
Swift o'er the land the dismal rumour flies,
And public mournings pacify the skies;
The laureat tribe in servile verse relate,
How virtue wars with persecuting fate;
With well-feign'd gratitude the pension'd band   200
Refund the plunder of the beggar'd land.
See! while he builds, the gaudy vassals come,
And crowd with sudden wealth the rising dome;
The price of boroughs and of souls restore,
And raise his treasures higher than before.   205
Now bless'd with all the baubles of the great,
The polish'd marble, and the shining plate,
Orgilio sees the golden pile aspire,
And hopes from angry heav'n another fire.

Could'st thou resign the park and play content,   210
For the fair banks of Severn or of Trent;
There might'st thou find some elegant retreat,
Some hireling senator's deserted seat;
And stretch thy prospects o'er the smiling land,
For less than rent the dungeons of the Strand;   215
There prune thy walks, support thy drooping flow'rs,
Direct thy rivulets, and twine thy bow'rs;
And, while thy grounds a cheap repast afford,
Despise the dainties of a venal lord:

220   There ev'ry bush with nature's music rings,
       There ev'ry breeze bears health upon its wings;
       On all thy hours security shall smile,
       And bless thine evening walk and morning toil.
       Prepare for death, if here at night you roam,
225   And sign your will before you sup from home.
       Some fiery fop, with new commission vain,
       Who sleeps on brambles till he kills his man;
       Some frolic drunkard, reeling from a feast,
       Provokes a broil, and stabs you for a jest.
230   Yet ev'n these heroes, mischievously gay,
       Lords of the street, and terrors of the way;
       Flush'd as they are with folly, youth and wine,
       Their prudent insults to the poor confine;
       Afar they mark the flambeau's bright approach,
235   And shun the shining train, and golden coach.
       In vain, these dangers past, your doors you close,
       And hope the balmy blessings of repose:
       Cruel with guilt, and daring with despair,
       The midnight murd'rer bursts the faithless bar;
240   Invades the sacred hour of silent rest,
       And leaves, unseen, a dagger in your breast.
       Scarce can our fields, such crowds at Tyburn[13] die,
       With hemp the gallows and the fleet supply.
       Propose your schemes, ye Senatorian band,
245   Whose Ways and Means[14] support the sinking land;
       Lest ropes be wanting in the tempting spring,
       To rig another convoy for the k — g.[15]
       A single jail, in ALFRED's golden reign,
       Could half the nation's criminals contain;
250   Fair Justice then, without constraint ador'd,
       Held high the steady scale, but deep'd the sword;[16]
       No spies were paid, no special juries known,
       Blest age! but ah! how diff'rent from our own!
       Much could I add, – but see the boat at hand,
255   The tide retiring, calls me from the land:
       Farewell! – When youth, and health, and fortune spent,
       Thou fly'st for refuge to the wilds of Kent;[17]

And tir'd like me with follies and with crimes,
In angry numbers warn'st succeeding times;
Then shall thy friend, nor thou refuse his aid,   260
Still foe to vice, forsake his Cambrian shade;
In virtue's cause once more exert his rage,
Thy satire point, and animate thy page.

AN ACCOUNT OF THE LIFE OF
MR RICHARD SAVAGE, SON OF THE
EARL RIVERS

IT has been observed in all ages, that the advantages of nature or of fortune have contributed very little to the promotion of happiness; and that those whom the splendour of their rank, or the extent of their capacity, have placed upon the summits of human life, have not often given any just occasion to envy in those who look up to them from a lower station: whether it be that apparent superiority incites great designs, and great designs are naturally liable to fatal miscarriages; or that the general lot of mankind is misery, and the misfortunes of those whose eminence drew upon them an universal attention, have been more carefully recorded, because they were more generally observed, and have in reality been only more conspicuous than those of others, not more frequent, or more severe.

That affluence and power, advantages extrinsic and adventitious, and therefore easily separable from those by whom they are possessed, should very often flatter the mind with expectations of felicity which they cannot give, raises no astonishment; but it seems rational to hope, that intellectual greatness should produce better effects: that minds qualified for great attainments should first endeavour their own benefit; and that they who are most able to teach others the way to happiness, should with most certainty follow it themselves.

But this expectation, however plausible, has been very frequently disappointed. The heroes of literary as well as civil history have been very often no less remarkable for what they have suffered than for what they have achieved; and volumes have been written only to enumerate the miseries of the learned, and relate their unhappy lives and untimely deaths.

To these mournful narratives, I am about to add the Life of Richard Savage, a man whose writings entitle him to an eminent rank in the classes of learning, and whose misfortunes claim a degree of compassion, not always due to the unhappy, as they were often the consequences of the crimes of others, rather than his own.

In the year 1697, Anne Countess of Macclesfield, having lived for some time upon very uneasy terms with her husband, thought a public confession of adultery the most obvious and expeditious method of obtaining her liberty; and therefore declared, that the child, with which she was then great, was begotten by the Earl Rivers. This, as may be imagined, made her husband no less desirous of a separation than herself, and he prosecuted his design in the most effectual manner; for he applied not to the ecclesiastical courts for a divorce, but to the parliament for an act, by which his marriage might be dissolved, the nuptial contract totally annulled, and the children of his wife illegitimated. This act, after the usual deliberation, he obtained, though without the approbation of some, who considered marriage as an affair only cognizable by ecclesiastical judges; and on March 3rd was separated from his wife, whose fortune, which was very great, was repaid her, and who having, as well as her husband, the liberty of making another choice, was in a short time married to Colonel Brett.

While the Earl of Macclesfield was prosecuting this affair, his wife was, on the 10th of January 1697-8, delivered of a son, and the Earl Rivers, by appearing to consider him as his own, left none any reason to doubt of the sincerity of her declaration; for he was his godfather, and gave him his own name, which was by his direction inserted in the register of St Andrew's parish in Holborn, but unfortunately left him to the care of his mother, whom, as she was now set free from her husband, he probably imagined likely to treat with great tenderness the child that had contributed to so pleasing an event. It is not indeed easy to discover what motives could be found to over-balance that natural affection of a parent, or what interest could be promoted by neglect or cruelty. The dread of shame or of poverty, by which some wretches have been incited to abandon or to murder their children, cannot be supposed to have affected a woman who had proclaimed her crimes and solicited reproach, and on whom the clemency of the legislature had undeservedly bestowed a fortune, which would have been very little diminished by the expenses which the care of her child could have brought upon her. It was therefore not likely that she would be wicked without temptation, that she would look upon her son from his birth with a kind of resentment and abhorrence; and, instead of supporting, assisting, and defending him, delight to see him struggling with misery, or that she would take every opportunity of aggravating his misfortunes, and obstructing his resources, and with an implacable and restless cruelty continue her persecution from the first hour of his life to the last.

But whatever were her motives, no sooner was her son born, than she discovered a resolution of disowning[1] him; and in a very short time removed him from her sight, by committing him to the care of a poor woman, whom she directed to educate him as her own, and enjoined never to inform him of his true parents.

Such was the beginning of the life of Richard Savage. Born with a legal claim to honour and to affluence, he was in two months illegitimated by the parliament, and disowned by his mother, doomed to poverty and obscurity, and launched upon the ocean of life, only that he might be swallowed by its quicksands, or dashed upon its rocks.

His mother could not indeed infect others with the same cruelty. As it was impossible to avoid the inquiries which the curiosity or tenderness of her relations made after her child, she was obliged to give some account of the measures that she had taken; and her mother, the Lady Mason, whether in approbation of her design, or to prevent more criminal contrivances, engaged to transact with the nurse, to pay her for her care, and to superintend the education of the child.

In this charitable office she was assisted by his godmother Mrs Lloyd, who, while she lived, always looked upon him with that tenderness, which the barbarity of his mother made peculiarly necessary; but her death, which happened in his tenth year, was another of the misfortunes of his childhood; for though she kindly endeavoured to alleviate his loss by a legacy of three hundred pounds; yet, as he had none to prosecute his claim, to shelter him from oppression, or call in law to the assistance of justice, her will was eluded by the executors, and no part of the money was ever paid.

He was, however, not yet wholly abandoned. The Lady Mason still continued her care, and directed him to be placed at a small grammar-school near St Alban's, where he was called by the name of his nurse, without the least intimation that he had a claim to any other.

Here he was initiated in literature, and passed through several of the classes, with what rapidity or what applause cannot now be known. As he always spoke with respect of his master, it is probable that the mean rank, in which he then appeared, did not hinder his genius from being distinguished, or his industry from being rewarded; and if in so low a state he obtained distinction and rewards, it is not likely that they were gained but by genius and industry.

It is very reasonable to conjecture, that his application was equal to his abilities, because his improvement was more than proportioned to the opportunities which he enjoyed; nor can it be doubted, that if his earliest productions had been preserved like those of happier students, we might in some have found vigorous sallies of that sprightly humour which distinguishes *The Author to be let*,[2] and in others strong touches of that ardent imagination which painted the solemn scenes of *The Wanderer*.[3]

While he was thus cultivating his genius, his father the Earl Rivers was seized with a distemper, which in a short time put an end to his life. He had frequently inquired after his son, and had always been amused with fallacious and evasive answers;[4] but, being now in his own opinion on his death-bed, he thought it his duty to provide for him among his other natural children, and therefore demanded a positive account of him, with an importunity not to be diverted or denied. His mother, who could no longer refuse an answer, determined at least to give such as should cut him off for ever from that happiness which competence affords, and therefore declared that he was dead; which is perhaps the first instance of a lie invented by a mother to deprive her son of a provision which was designed him by another, and which she could not expect herself, though he should lose it.

This was therefore an act of wickedness which could not be

defeated, because it could not be suspected; the Earl did not imagine there could exist in a human form a mother that would ruin her son without enriching herself, and therefore bestowed upon some other person six thousand pounds, which he had in his will bequeathed to Savage.

The same cruelty which incited his mother to intercept this provision which had been intended him, prompted her in a short time to another project, a project worthy of such a disposition. She endeavoured to rid herself from the danger of being at any time made known to him, by sending him secretly to the American plantations.

By whose kindness this scheme was counteracted, or by whose interposition she was induced to lay aside her design, I know not; it is not improbable that the Lady Mason might persuade or compel her to desist, or perhaps she could not easily find accomplices wicked enough to concur in so cruel an action; for it may be conceived, that those who had by a long gradation of guilt hardened their hearts against the sense of common wickedness, would yet be shocked at the design of a mother to expose her son to slavery and want, to expose him without interest, and without provocation; and Savage might on this occasion find protectors and advocates among those who had long traded in crimes, and whom compassion had never touched before.

Being hindered, by whatever means, from banishing him into another country, she formed soon after a scheme for burying him in poverty and obscurity in his own; and, that his station of life, if not the place of his residence, might keep him for ever at a distance from her, she ordered him to be placed with a shoemaker in Holborn, that, after the usual time of trial, he might become his apprentice.

It is generally reported, that this project was for some time successful, and that Savage was employed at the awl longer than he was willing to confess; nor was it perhaps any great advantage to him, that an unexpected discovery determined him to quit his occupation.

About this time his nurse, who had always treated him as her own son, died; and it was natural for him to take care of those effects, which by her death were, as he imagined, become his own; he therefore went to her house, opened her boxes, and examined her papers, among which he found some letters written to her by the Lady Mason, which informed him of his birth, and the reasons for which it was concealed.

He was no longer satisfied with the employment which had been allotted him, but thought he had a right to share the affluence of his mother; and therefore without scruple applied to her as her son, and made use of every art to awaken her tenderness, and attract her regard. But neither his letters, nor the interposition of those friends which his merit or his distress procured him, made any impression upon her mind. She still resolved to neglect, though she could no longer disown him.

It was to no purpose that he frequently solicited her to admit him to see her; she avoided him with the most vigilant precaution, and ordered him to be excluded from her house, by whomsoever he might be introduced, and what reason soever he might give for entering it.

Savage was at the same time so touched with the discovery of his real mother, that it was his frequent practice to walk in the dark evenings for several hours before her door, in hopes of seeing her as she might come by accident to the window, or cross her apartment with a candle in her hand.

But all his assiduity and tenderness were without effect, for he could neither soften her heart, nor open her hand, and was reduced to the utmost miseries of want, while he was endeavouring to awaken the affection of a mother. He was therefore obliged to seek some other means of support; and, having no profession, became by necessity an author.

At this time the attention of all the literary world was engrossed by the Bangorian controversy,[5] which filled the press with pamphlets, and the coffee-houses with disputants. Of this subject, as most popular, he made choice for his first attempt, and, without any other knowledge of the question than he had casually collected from conversation, published a poem against the Bishop.

What was the success or merit of this performance, I know not; it was probably lost among the innumerable pamphlets to which that dispute gave occasion. Mr Savage was himself in a little time ashamed of it, and endeavoured to suppress it, by destroying all the copies that he could collect.

He then attempted a more gainful kind of writing, and in his eighteenth year offered to the stage a comedy borrowed from a Spanish plot, which was refused by the players, and was therefore given by him to Mr Bullock, who, having more interest, made some slight alterations, and brought it upon the stage, under the title of *Woman's a Riddle*, but allowed the unhappy author no part of the profit.

Not discouraged, however, at his repulse, he wrote two years afterwards *Love in a Veil*, another comedy, borrowed likewise from the Spanish, but with little better success than before; for though it was received and acted, yet it appeared so late in the year, that the author obtained no other advantage from it, than the acquaintance of Sir Richard Steele, and Mr Wilks, by whom he was pitied, caressed,[6] and relieved.

Sir Richard Steele, having declared in his favour with all the ardour of benevolence which constituted his character, promoted his interest with the utmost zeal, related his misfortunes, applauded his merit, took all the opportunities to recommending him, and asserted, that the inhumanity of his mother had given him a right to find every good man his father.

Nor was Mr Savage admitted to his acquaintance only, but to his confidence, of which he sometimes related an instance too extraordinary to be omitted, as it affords a very just idea of his patron's character.

He was once desired by Sir Richard, with an air of the utmost importance, to come very early to his house the next morning. Mr Savage came as he had promised, found the chariot at the door, and Sir Richard waiting for him, and ready to go out. What was intended, and whither they were to go, Savage could not conjecture, and was not willing to inquire; but immediately seated himself with Sir Richard; the coachman was ordered to drive, and they hurried with the utmost expedition to Hyde-Park Corner, where they stopped at a petty tavern, and retired to a private room. Sir Richard then informed him, that he intended to publish a pamphlet, and that he had desired him to come thither that he might write for him. They soon sat down to the work. Sir Richard dictated, and Savage wrote, till the dinner that had been ordered was put upon the table. Savage was surprised at the meanness of the entertainment, and after some hesitation ventured to ask for wine, which Sir Richard, not without reluctance, ordered to be brought. They then finished their dinner, and proceeded in their pamphlet, which they concluded in the afternoon.

Mr Savage then imagined his task over, and expected that Sir Richard would call for the reckoning, and return home; but his expectations deceived him, for Sir Richard told him, that he was without money, and that the pamphlet must be sold before the dinner could be paid for; and Savage was therefore obliged to go and offer their new production to sale for two guineas, which with some difficulty he obtained. Sir Richard then returned home, having retired that day only to avoid his creditors, and composed the pamphlet only to discharge his reckoning.

Mr Savage related another fact equally uncommon, which, though it has no relation to his life, ought to be preserved. Sir Richard Steele having one day invited to his house a great number of persons of the first quality, they were surprised at the number of liveries which surrounded the table; and after dinner, when wine and mirth had set them free from the observation of a rigid ceremony, one of them inquired of Sir Richard, how such an expensive train of domestics could be consistent with his fortune. Sir Richard very frankly confessed, that they were fellows of whom he would very willingly be rid. And being then asked, why he did not discharge them, declared that they were bailiffs who had introduced themselves with an execution,[7] and whom, since he could not send them away, he had thought it convenient to embellish with liveries, that they might do him credit while they stayed.

His friends were diverted with the expedient, and, by paying the debt, discharged their attendance, having obliged Sir Richard to promise that they should never again find him graced with a retinue of the same kind.

Under such a tutor, Mr Savage was not likely to learn prudence or frugality; and perhaps many of the misfortunes, which the want of those virtues brought upon him in the following parts of his life, might be justly imputed to so unimproving an example.

Nor did the kindness of Sir Richard end in common favours. He proposed to have established him in some settled scheme of life, and to have contracted a kind of alliance with him, by marrying him to a natural daughter, on whom he intended to bestow a thousand pounds. But though he was always lavish of future bounties, he conducted his affairs in such a manner, that he was very seldom able to keep his promises, or execute his own intentions; and, as he was never able to raise the sum which he had offered, the marriage was delayed. In the mean time he was officiously informed, that Mr Savage had ridiculed him; by which he was so much exasperated, that he withdrew the allowance which he had paid him, and never afterwards admitted him to his house.

It is not-indeed unlikely that Savage might, by his imprudence, expose himself to the malice of a tale-bearer; for his patron had many follies, which, as his discernment easily discovered, his imagination might sometimes incite him to mention too ludicrously. A little knowledge of the world is sufficient to discover that such weakness is very common, and that there are few who do not sometimes, in the wantonness of thoughtless mirth, or the heat of transient resentment, speak of their friends and benefactors with levity and contempt, though in their cooler moments they want neither sense of their kindness, nor reverence for their virtue. The fault therefore of Mr Savage was rather negligence than ingratitude; but Sir Richard must likewise be acquitted of severity, for who is there that can patiently bear contempt from one whom he has relieved and supported, whose establishment he has laboured, and whose interest he has promoted?

He was now again abandoned to fortune, without any other friend than Mr Wilks; a man who, whatever were his abilities or skill as an actor, deserves at least to be remembered for his virtues, which are not often to be found in the world, and perhaps less often in his profession than in others.[8] To be humane, generous, and candid, is a very high degree of merit in any case; but those qualities deserve still greater praise, when they are found in that condition which makes almost every other man, for whatever reason, contemptuous, insolent, petulant, selfish, and brutal.

As Mr Wilks was one of those to whom calamity seldom complained without relief, he naturally took an unfortunate wit into his protection, and not only assisted him in any casual distresses, but continued an equal and steady kindness to the time of his death.

By his interposition Mr Savage once obtained from his mother fifty pounds, and a promise of one hundred and fifty more; but it was the fate of this unhappy man, that few promises of any advantage to him were performed. His mother was infected among others with the general madness of the South Sea traffic; and, having been disappointed in her expectations, refused to pay what perhaps nothing but the prospect of sudden affluence prompted her to promise.

Being thus obliged to depend upon the friendship of Mr Wilks, he was consequently an assiduous frequenter of the theatres; and in a short time the amusements of the stage took such possession of his mind, that he never was absent from a play in several years.

This constant attendance naturally procured him the acquaintance of the players, and, among others, of Mrs Oldfield,[9] who was so much pleased with his conversation, and touched with his misfortunes, that she allowed him a settled pension of fifty pounds a year, which was during her life regularly paid.

That this act of generosity may receive its due praise, and that the good actions of Mrs Oldfield may not be sullied by her general character, it is proper to mention what Mr Savage often declared in the strongest terms, that he never saw her alone, or in any other place than behind the scenes.

At her death he endeavoured to show his gratitude in the most decent manner, by wearing mourning as for a mother; but did not celebrate her in elegies, because he knew that too great profusion of praise would only have revived those faults which his natural equity did not allow him to think less, because they were committed by one who favoured him; but of which, though his virtue would not endeavour to palliate them, his gratitude would not suffer him to prolong the memory, or diffuse the censure.

In his *Wanderer*, he has indeed taken an opportunity of mentioning her, but celebrates her not for her virtue, but her beauty, an excellence which none ever denied her: this is the only encomium with which he has rewarded her liberality, and perhaps he has even in this been too lavish of his praise. He seems to have thought, that never to mention his benefactress would have the appearance of ingratitude, though to have dedicated any particular performance to her memory would have only betrayed an officious partiality, that, without exalting her character, would have depressed his own.

He had sometimes, by the kindness of Mr Wilks, the advantage of a benefit, on which occasions he often received uncommon marks of regard and compassion; and was once told by the Duke of Dorset, that it was just to consider him as an injured nobleman, and that in his opinion the nobility ought to think themselves obliged, without solicitation, to take every opportunity of supporting him by their countenance and patronage. But he had generally the mortification to hear that the whole interest of his mother was employed to frustrate his applications, and that she never left any expedient untried, by which he might be cut off from the possibility of supporting life. The same disposition she endeavoured to diffuse among all those over whom nature or fortune gave her any influence, and indeed succeeded too well in her design; but could not always propagate her effrontery with her cruelty, for some of those, whom she incited against him, were ashamed of their own conduct, and boasted of that relief which they never gave him.

In this censure I do not indiscriminately involve all his relations; for he has mentioned with gratitude the humanity of one lady, whose name I am now unable to recollect, and to whom therefore I cannot pay the praises which she deserves for having acted well in opposition to influence, precept, and example.

The punishment which our laws inflict upon those parents who murder their infants is well known, nor has its justice ever been contested; but if they deserve death who destroy a child in its birth, what pains can be severe enough for her who forbears to destroy him only to inflict sharper miseries upon him; who prolongs his life only to make him miserable; and who exposes him, without care and without pity, to the malice of oppression, the caprices of chance, and the temptations of poverty; who rejoices to see him overwhelmed with calamities; and, when his own industry, or the charity of others, has enabled him to rise for a short time above his miseries, plunges him again into his former distress?

The kindness of his friends not affording him any constant supply, and the prospect of improving his fortune by enlarging his acquaintance necessarily leading him to places of expense, he found it necessary to endeavour once more at dramatic poetry, for which he was now better qualified by a more extensive knowledge, and longer observation. But having been unsuccessful in comedy, though rather for want of opportunities than genius, he resolved now to try whether he should not be more fortunate in exhibiting a tragedy.

The story which he chose for the subject was that of Sir Thomas Overbury,[10] a story well adapted to the stage, though perhaps not far enough removed from the present age, to admit properly the fictions necessary to complete the plan: for the mind, which naturally loves truth, is always most offended with the violation of those truths of which we are most certain; and we of course conceive those facts most certain, which approach nearest to our own time.

Out of this story he formed a tragedy, which, if the circumstances in which he wrote it be considered, will afford at once an uncommon proof of strength of genius, and evenness of mind, of a serenity not to be ruffled, and an imagination not to be suppressed.

During a considerable part of the time in which he was employed upon this performance, he was without lodging, and often without meat; nor had he any other conveniences for study than the fields or the street allowed him; there he used to walk and form his speeches, and afterwards step into a shop, beg for a few moments the use of the pen and ink, and write down what he had composed, upon paper which he had picked up by accident.

If the performance of a writer thus distressed is not perfect, its faults ought surely to be imputed to a cause very different from want of genius, and much rather excite pity than provoke censure.

But when under these discouragements the tragedy was finished, there yet remained the labour of introducing it on the stage, an undertaking, which, to an ingenuous mind, was in a very high degree vexatious and disgusting; for, having little interest or reputation, he was obliged to submit himself wholly to the players, and admit, with whatever reluctance, the emendations of Mr Cibber, which he always considered as the disgrace of his performance.

He had indeed in Mr Hill[11] another critic of a very different class, from whose friendship he received great assistance on many occasions, and whom he never mentioned but with the utmost tenderness and regard. He had been for some time distinguished by him with very particular kindness, and on this occasion it was natural to apply to him as an author of an established character. He therefore sent this tragedy to him, with a short copy of verses, in which he desired his correction. Mr Hill, whose humanity and politeness are generally known, readily complied with his request; but as he is remarkable for singularity of sentiment, and bold experiments in language, Mr Savage did not think his play much improved by his innovation, and had even at that time the courage to reject several passages which he could not approve; and what is still more laudable, Mr Hill had the generosity not to resent the neglect of his alterations, but wrote the prologue and epilogue, in which he touches on the circumstances of the author with great tenderness.

After all these obstructions and compliances, he was only able to bring his play upon the stage in the summer, when the chief actors had retired, and the rest were in possession of the house for their own advantage. Among these, Mr Savage was admitted to play the part of Sir Thomas Overbury, by which he gained no great reputation, the theatre being a province for which nature seemed not to have designed him; for neither his voice, look, nor gesture, were such as were expected on the stage; and he was so much ashamed of having been reduced to appear as a player, that he always blotted out his name from the list, when a copy of his tragedy was to be shown to his friends.

In the publication of his performance he was more successful, for the rays of genius that glimmered in it, that glimmered through all the mists which poverty and Cibber had been able to spread over it, procured him the notice and esteem of many persons eminent for their rank, their virtue, and their wit.

Of this play, acted, printed, and dedicated, the accumulated profits arose to an hundred pounds, which he thought at that time a very large sum, having been never master of so much before.

In the Dedication, for which he received ten guineas, there is nothing remarkable. The Preface contains a very liberal encomium on the blooming excellences of Mr Theophilus Cibber, which Mr Savage could not in the latter part of his life see his friends about to read without snatching the play out of their hands. The generosity of Mr Hill did not end on this occasion; for afterwards, when Mr Savage's necessities returned, he encouraged a subscription to a Miscellany of Poems in a very extraordinary manner, by publishing his story in the *Plain Dealer*, with some affecting lines, which he asserts to have been written by Mr Savage upon the treatment received by him from his mother, but of which he was himself the author, as Mr Savage afterwards declared. These lines, and the paper in which they were inserted, had a very powerful effect upon all but his mother, whom, by making her cruelty more public, they only hardened in her aversion.

Mr Hill not only promoted the subscription to the Miscellany, but furnished likewise the greatest part of the Poems of which it is composed, and particularly *The Happy Man*, which he published as a specimen.

The subscriptions of those whom these papers should influence to patronize merit in distress, without any other solicitation, were directed to be left at Button's coffee-house[12]; and Mr Savage going thither a few days afterwards, without expectation of any effect from his proposal, found to his surprise seventy guineas, which had been sent him in consequence of the compassion excited by Mr Hill's pathetic representation.

To this Miscellany he wrote a Preface, in which he gives an account of his mother's cruelty in a very uncommon strain of humour, and with a gaiety of imagination, which the success of his subscription probably produced.

The Dedication is addressed to the Lady Mary Wortley Montague, whom he flatters without reserve and, to confess the truth, with very little art. The same observation may be extended to all his Dedications: his compliments are constrained and violent, heaped together without the grace of order, or the decency of introduction: he seems to have written his panegyrics for the perusal only of his patrons, and to have imagined that he had no other task than to pamper them with praises however gross, and that flattery would make its way to the heart, without the assistance of elegance or invention.

Soon afterwards, the death of the king furnished a general subject for a poetical contest, in which Mr Savage engaged, and is allowed to have carried the prize of honour from his competitors; but I know not whether he gained by his performance any other advantage than the increase of his reputation; though it must certainly have been with farther views that he prevailed upon himself to attempt a species of writing, of which all the topics had been long before exhausted, and which was made at once difficult by the multitudes that had failed in it, and those that had succeeded.

He was now advancing in reputation, and though frequently involved in very distressful perplexities, appeared however to be gaining upon mankind, when both his fame and his life were endangered by an event, of which it is not yet determined, whether it ought to be mentioned as a crime or a calamity.

On the 20th of November 1727, Mr Savage came from Richmond, where he then lodged, that he might pursue his studies with less interruption, with an intent to discharge another lodging[13] which he had in Westminster; and accidentally meeting two gentlemen his acquaintances, whose names were Merchant and Gregory, he went in with them to a neighbouring coffee-house, and sat drinking till it was late, it being in no time of Mr Savage's life any part of his character to be the first of the company that desired to separate. He would willingly have gone to bed in the same house; but there was not room for the whole company, and therefore they agreed to ramble about the streets, and divert themselves with such amusements as should offer themselves till morning.

In this walk they happened unluckily to discover a light in Robinson's coffee-house, near Charing-cross, and therefore went in. Merchant, with some rudeness, demanded a room, and was told that there was a good fire in the next parlour, which the company were about to leave, being then paying their reckoning. Merchant, not satisfied with this answer, rushed into the room, and was followed by his companions. He then petulantly placed himself between the company and the fire, and soon after kicked down the table. This produced a quarrel, swords were drawn on both sides, and one Mr James Sinclair was killed. Savage, having wounded likewise a maid that held him, forced his way with Merchant out of the house; but being intimidated and confused, without resolution either to fly or stay, they were taken in a back-court by one of the company and some soldiers whom he had called to his assistance.

Being secured and guarded that night, they were in the morning carried before three justices, who committed them to the Gatehouse, from whence, upon the death of Mr Sinclair, which happened the same day, they were removed in the night to Newgate, where they were however treated with some distinction, exempted from the ignominy of chains, and confined, not among the common criminals, but in the Press-yard.

When the day of trial came, the court was crowded in a very unusual manner, and the public appeared to interest itself as in a cause of general concern. The witnesses against Mr Savage and his friends were, the woman who kept the house, which was a house of ill fame, and her maid, the men who were in the room with Mr Sinclair, and a woman of the town, who had been drinking with them, and with whom one of them had been seen in bed. They swore in general, that Merchant gave the provocation, which Savage and Gregory drew their swords to justify; that Savage drew first, and that he stabbed Sinclair when he was not in a posture of defence, or while Gregory commanded his sword; that after he had given the thrust he turned pale, and would have retired, but the maid clung round him, and one of the company endeavoured to detain him, from whom he broke, by cutting the maid on the head, but was afterwards taken in a court.

There was some difference in their depositions; one did not see Savage give the wound, another saw it given when Sinclair held his point towards the ground; and the woman of the town asserted, that she did not see Sinclair's sword at all: this difference however was very far from amounting to inconsistency; but it was sufficient to show, that the hurry of the dispute was such, that it was not easy to discover truth with relation to particular circumstances, and that therefore some deductions were to be made from the credibility of the testimonies.

Sinclair had declared several times before his death, that he received his wound from Savage, nor did Savage at his trial deny the fact, but endeavoured partly to extenuate it, by urging the suddenness of the whole action, and the impossibility of any ill design or premeditated malice, and partly to justify it by the necessity of self-defence, and the hazard of his own life, if he had lost that opportunity of giving the thrust: he observed, that neither reason nor law obliged a man to wait for the blow which was threatened, and which, if he should suffer it, he might never be able to return; that it was always allowable to prevent an assault, and to preserve life by taking away that of the adversary, by whom it was endangered.

With regard to the violence with which he endeavoured to escape, he declared, that it was not his design to fly from justice, or decline a trial, but to avoid the expenses and severities of a prison; and that he intended to have appeared at the bar without compulsion.

This defence, which took up more than an hour, was heard by the multitude that thronged the court with the most attentive and respectful silence: those who thought he ought not to be acquitted, owned that applause could not be refused him; and those who before pitied his misfortunes, now reverenced his abilities.

The witnesses which appeared against him were proved to be persons of characters which did not entitle them to much credit; a common strumpet, a woman by whom strumpets were entertained, and a man by whom they were supported; and the character of Savage was by several persons of distinction asserted to be that of a modest inoffensive man, not inclined to broils, or to insolence, and who had, to that time, been only known for his misfortunes and his wit.

Had his audience been his judges, he had undoubtedly been acquitted; but Mr Page,[14] who was then upon the bench, treated him with his usual insolence and severity, and when he had summed up the evidence, endeavoured to exasperate the jury, as Mr Savage used to relate it, with this eloquent harangue:

'Gentlemen of the jury, you are to consider that Mr Savage is a very great man, a much greater man than you or I, gentlemen of the jury; that he wears very fine clothes, much finer clothes than you or I, gentlemen of the jury; that he has abundance of money in his pocket, much more money than you or I, gentlemen of the jury; but, gentlemen of the jury, is it not a very hard case, gentlemen of the jury, that Mr Savage should therefore kill you or me, gentlemen of the jury?'

Mr Savage, hearing his defence thus misrepresented, and the men who were to decide his fate incited against him by invidious comparisons, resolutely asserted, that his cause was not candidly[15] explained, and began to recapitulate what he had before said with regard to his condition, and the necessity of endeavouring to escape the expenses of imprisonment; but the judge having ordered him to be silent, and repeated his orders without effect, commanded that he should be taken from the bar by force.

The jury then heard the opinion of the judge, that good characters were of no weight against positive evidence, though they might turn the scale where it was doubtful; and that though, when two men attack each other, the death of either is only manslaughter; but where one is the aggressor, as in the case before them, and, in pursuance of his first attack, kills the other, the law supposes the action, however sudden, to be malicious. They then deliberated upon their verdict, and determined that Mr Savage and Mr Gregory were guilty of murder, and Mr Merchant, who had no sword, only of manslaughter.

Thus ended this memorable trial, which lasted eight hours. Mr Savage and Mr Gregory were conducted back to prison, where they were more closely confined, and loaded with irons of fifty pounds weight: four days afterwards they were sent back to the court to receive sentence; on which occasion Mr Savage made, as far as it could be retained in memory, the following speech.

'It is now, my Lord, too late to offer any thing by way of defence or vindication; nor can we expect from your Lordships, in this court, but the sentence which the law requires you, as judges, to pronounce against men of our calamitous condition. – But we are also persuaded, that as mere men, and out of this seat of rigorous justice, you are susceptive of the tender passions, and too humane, not to commiserate the unhappy situation of those, whom the law some-times perhaps – exacts – from you to pronounce upon. No doubt you distinguish between offences, which arise out of premeditation, and a disposition habituated to vice or immorality, and transgressions, which are the unhappy and unforeseen effects of casual absence of reason, and sudden impulse of passion: we therefore hope you will contribute all you can to an extension of that mercy, which the gentlemen of the jury have been pleased to show Mr Merchant, who (allowing facts as sworn against us by the evidence) has led us into this our calamity. I hope this will not be construed, as if we meant to reflect upon that gentleman, or remove any thing from us upon him, or that we repine the more at our fate, because he has no participation of it: No, my Lord! For my part, I declare nothing could more soften my grief, than to be without any companion in so great a misfortune.'

Mr Savage had now no hopes of life, but from the mercy of the crown, which was very earnestly solicited by his friends, and which, with whatever difficulty the story may obtain belief, was obstructed only by his mother.

To prejudice the Queen against him, she made use of an incident, which was omitted in the order of time, that it might be mentioned together with the purpose which it was made to serve. Mr Savage, when he had discovered his birth, had an incessant desire to speak to his mother, who always avoided him in public, and refused him admission into her house. One evening walking, as it was his custom, in the street that she inhabited, he saw the door of her house by accident open; he entered it, and, finding no person in the passage to hinder him, went up stairs to salute her. She discovered him before he could enter her chamber, alarmed the family with the most distressful outcries, and when she had by her screams gathered them about her, ordered them to drive out of the house that villain, who had forced himself in upon her, and endeavoured to murder her. Savage, who had attempted with the most submissive tenderness to soften her rage, hearing her utter so detestable an accusation, thought it prudent to retire; and, I believe, never attempted afterwards to speak to her.

But, shocked as he was with her falsehood and her cruelty, he imagined that she intended no other use of her lie, than to set herself free from his embraces and solicitations, and was very far from suspecting that she would treasure it in her memory, as an instrument of future wickedness, or that she would endeavour for this fictitious assault to deprive him of his life.

But when the Queen was solicited for his pardon, and informed of the severe treatment which he had suffered from his judge, she answered, that, however unjustifiable might be the manner of his trial, or whatever extenuation the action for which he was condemned might admit, she could not think that man a proper object of the King's mercy, who had been capable of entering his mother's house in the night, with an intent to murder her.

By whom this atrocious calumny had been transmitted to the Queen; whether she that invented had the front[16] to relate it; whether she found any one weak enough to credit it, or corrupt enough to concur with her in her hateful design, I know not: but methods had been taken to persuade the Queen so strongly of the truth of it, that she for a long time refused to hear any one of those who petitioned for his life.

Thus had Savage perished by the evidence of a bawd, a strumpet, and his mother, had not justice and compassion procured him an advocate of rank too great to be rejected unheard, and of virtue too eminent to be heard without being believed. His merit and his calamities happened to reach the ear of the Countess of Hertford, who engaged in his support with all the tenderness that is excited by pity, and all the zeal which is kindled by generosity; and, demanding an audience of the Queen, laid before her the whole series of his mother's cruelty, exposed the improbability of an accusation by which he was charged with an intent to commit a murder that could produce no advantage, and soon convinced her how little his former conduct could deserve to be mentioned as a reason for extraordinary severity.

The interposition of this lady was so successful, that he was soon after admitted to bail, and, on the 9th of March 1728, pleaded the King's pardon.

It is natural to inquire upon what motives his mother could prosecute him in a manner so outrageous and implacable; for what reason she could employ all the arts of malice, and all the snares of calumny, to take away the life of her own son, of a son who never injured her, who was never supported by her expense, nor obstructed any prospect of pleasure or advantage; why she should endeavour to destroy him by a lie – a lie which could not gain credit, but must vanish of itself at the first moment of examination, and of which only this can be said to make it probable, that it may be observed from her conduct, that the most execrable crimes are sometimes committed without apparent temptation.

This mother is still alive, and may perhaps even yet, though her malice was so often defeated, enjoy the pleasure of reflecting, that the life, which she often endeavoured to destroy, was at least shortened by her maternal offices; that though she could not transport her son to the plantations, bury him in the shop of a mechanic, or hasten the hand of the public executioner, she has yet had the satisfaction of embittering all his hours, and forcing him into exigences that hurried on his death.

It is by no means necessary to aggravate the enormity of this woman's conduct, by placing it in opposition to that of the Countess of Hertford; no one can fail to observe how much more amiable it is to relieve, than to oppress, and to rescue innocence from destruction, than to destroy without an injury.

Mr Savage, during his imprisonment, his trial, and the time in which he lay under sentence of death, behaved with great firmness and equality of mind, and confirmed by his fortitude the esteem of those who before admired him for his abilities. The peculiar circumstances of his life were made more generally known by a short account, which was then published, and of which several thousands were in a few weeks dispersed over the nation: and the compassion of mankind operated so powerfully in his favour, that he was enabled, by frequent presents, not only to support himself, but to assist Mr Gregory in prison; and, when he was pardoned and released, he found the number of his friends not lessened.

The nature of the act for which he had been tried was in itself doubtful; of the evidences which appeared against him, the character of the man was not unexceptionable, that of the woman notoriously infamous: she, whose testimony chiefly influenced the jury to condemn him, afterwards retracted her assertions. He always himself denied that he was drunk, as had been generally reported. Mr Gregory, who is now Collector of Antigua, is said to declare him far less criminal than he was imagined, even by some who favoured him: and Page himself afterwards confessed, that he had treated him with uncommon rigour. When all these particulars are rated together, perhaps the memory of Savage may not be much sullied by his trial.

Some time after he obtained his liberty, he met in the street the woman who had sworn with so much malignity against him. She informed him, that she was in distress, and, with a degree of confidence not easily attainable, desired him to relieve her. He, instead of insulting her misery, and taking pleasure in the calamities of one who had brought his life into danger, reproved her gently for her perjury; and changing the only guinea that he had, divided it equally between her and himself.

This is an action which in some ages would have made a saint, and perhaps in others a hero, and which, without any hyperbolical encomiums, must be allowed to be an instance of uncommon generosity, an act of complicated virtue; by which he at once relieved the poor, corrected the vicious, and forgave an enemy; by which he at once remitted the strongest provocations, and exercised the most ardent charity.

Compassion was indeed the distinguishing quality of Savage; he never appeared inclined to take advantage of weakness, to attack the defenceless, or to press upon the falling: whoever was distressed was certain at least of his good wishes; and when he could give no assistance to extricate them from misfortunes, he endeavoured to soothe them by sympathy and tenderness.

But when his heart was not softened by the sight of misery, he was sometimes obstinate in his resentment, and did not quickly lose remembrance of an injury. He always continued to speak with anger of the insolence and partiality of Page, and a short time before his death revenged it by a satire.

It is natural to inquire in what terms Mr Savage spoke of this fatal action, when the danger was over, and he was under no necessity of using any art to set his conduct in the fairest light. He was not willing to dwell upon it; and, if he transiently mentioned it, appeared neither to consider himself as a murderer, nor as a man wholly free from the guilt of blood. How much and how long he regretted it, appeared in a poem which he published many years afterwards. On occasion of a copy of verses, in which the failings of good men were recounted, and in which the author had endeavoured to illustrate his position, that, 'the best may sometimes deviate from virtue, by an instance of murder committed by Savage in the heat of wine, Savage remarked, that it was no very just representation of a good man, to suppose him liable to drunkenness, and disposed in his riots to cut throats.

He was now indeed at liberty, but was, as before, without any other support than accidental favours and uncertain patronage afforded him; sources by which he was sometimes very liberally supplied, and which at other times were suddenly stopped; so that he spent his life between want and plenty; or, what was yet worse, between beggary and extravagance; for as whatever he received was the gift of chance, which might as well favour him at one time as another, he was tempted to squander what he had, because he always hoped to be immediately supplied.

Another cause of his profusion was the absurd kindness of his friends, who at once rewarded and enjoyed his abilities, by treating him at taverns, and habituating him to pleasures which he could not afford to enjoy, and which he was not able to deny himself, though he purchased the luxury of a single night by the anguish of cold and hunger for a week.

The experience of these inconveniences determined him to endeavour after some settled income, which, having long found submission and entreaties fruitless, he attempted to extort from his mother by rougher methods. He had now, as he acknowledged, lost that tenderness for her, which the whole series of her cruelty had not been able wholly to repress, till he found, by the efforts which she made for his destruction, that she was not content with refusing to assist him, and being neutral in his struggles with poverty, but was as ready to snatch every opportunity of adding to his misfortunes, and that she was to be considered an enemy implacably malicious, whom nothing but his blood could satisfy. He therefore threatened to harass her with lampoons, and to publish a copious narrative of her conduct, unless she consented to purchase an exemption from infamy, by allowing him a pension.

This expedient proved successful. Whether shame still survived, though virtue was extinct, or whether her relations had more delicacy than herself, and imagined that some of the darts which satire might point at her would glance upon them; Lord Tyrconnel, whatever were his motives, upon his promise to lay aside his design of exposing the cruelty of his mother, received him into his family, treated him as his equal, and engaged to allow him a pension of two hundred pounds a year.

This was the golden part of Mr Savage's life; and for some time he had no reason to complain of fortune; his appearance was splendid, his expenses large, and his acquaintance extensive. He was courted by all who endeavoured to be thought men of genius, and caressed by all who valued themselves upon a refined taste. To admire Mr Savage, was a proof of discernment; and to be acquainted with him, was a title to poetical reputation. His presence was sufficient to make any place of public entertainment popular; and his approbation and example constituted the fashion. So powerful is genius, when it is invested with the glitter of affluence! Men willingly pay to fortune that regard which they owe to merit, and are pleased when they have an opportunity at once of gratifying their vanity, and practising their duty.

This interval of prosperity furnished him with opportunities of enlarging his knowledge of human nature, by contemplating life from its highest gradations to its lowest; and, had he afterwards applied to dramatic poetry, he would perhaps not have had many superiors; for as he never suffered any scene to pass before his eyes without notice, he had treasured in his mind all the different combinations of passions, and the innumerable mixtures of vice and virtue, which distinguish one character from another; and, as his conception was strong, his impressions were clear, he easily received impressions from objects, and very forcibly transmitted them to others.

Of his exact observations on human life he has left a proof, which would do honour to the greatest names, in a small pamphlet, called, *The Author to be let*, where he introduces Iscariot Hackney, a prostitute scribbler, giving an account of his birth, his education, his disposition and morals, habits of life, and maxims of conduct. In the introduction are related many secret histories of the petty writers of that time, but sometimes mixed with ungenerous reflections on their birth, their circumstances, or those of their relations; nor can it be denied, that some passages are such as Iscariot Hackney might himself have produced.

He was accused likewise of living in an appearance of friendship with some whom he satirized, and of making use of the confidence which he gained by a seeming kindness to discover failings and expose them: it must be confessed, that Mr Savage's esteem was no very certain possession, and that he would lampoon at one time those whom he had praised at another.

It may be alleged, that the same man may change his principles, and that he, who was once deservedly commended, may be afterwards satirized with equal justice, or that the poet was dazzled with the appearance of virtue, and found the man whom he had celebrated, when he had an opportunity of examining him more narrowly, unworthy of the panegyric which he had too hastily bestowed; and that, as a false satire ought to be recanted, for the sake of him whose reputation may be injured, false praise ought likewise to be obviated, lest the distinction between vice and virtue should be lost, lest a bad man should be trusted upon the credit of his encomiast, or lest others should endeavour to obtain the like praises by the same means.

But though these excuses may be often plausible, and sometimes just, they are very seldom satisfactory to mankind; and the writer, who is not constant to his subject, quickly sinks into contempt, his satire loses its force, and his panegyric its value, and he is only considered at one time as a flatterer, and as a calumniator at another.

To avoid these imputations, it is only necessary to follow the rules of virtue, and to preserve an unvaried regard to truth. For though it is undoubtedly possible, that a man, however cautious, may be sometimes deceived by an artful appearance of virtue, or by false evidences of guilt, such errors will not be frequent; and it will be allowed, that the name of an author would never have been made contemptible, had no man ever said what he did not think, or misled others but when he was himself deceived.

The Author to be let was first published in a single pamphlet, and afterwards inserted in a collection of pieces relating to the *Dunciad*, which were addressed by Mr Savage to the Earl of Middlesex, in a dedication which he was prevailed upon to sign, though he did not write it, and in which there are some positions, that the true author[17] would perhaps not have published under his own name, and on which Mr Savage afterwards reflected with no great satisfaction; the enumeration of the bad effects of the uncontrolled freedom of the press, and the assertion that the 'liberties taken by the writers of Journals with their superiors were exorbitant and unjustifiable,' very ill became men, who have themselves not always shown the exactest regard to the laws of subordination in their writings, and who have often satirized those that at least thought themselves their superiors, as they were eminent for their hereditary rank, and employed in the highest offices of the kingdom. But this is only an instance of that partiality which almost every man indulges with regard to himself; the liberty of the press is a blessing when we are inclined to write against others, and a calamity when we find ourselves overborne by the multitude of our assailants; as the power of the crown is always thought too great by those who suffer by its influence, and too little by those in whose favour it is exerted; and a standing army is generally accounted necessary by those who command, and dangerous and oppressive by those who support it.

Mr Savage was likewise very far from believing, that the letters annexed to each species of bad poets in the *Bathos*, were, as he was directed to assert, 'set down at random'; for when he was charged by one of his friends with putting his name to such an improbability, he had no other answer to make, than that 'he did not think of it'; and his friend had too much tenderness to reply, that next to the crime of writing contrary to what he thought was that of writing without thinking.

After having remarked what is false in this dedication, it is proper that I observe the impartiality which I recommend, by declaring what Savage asserted, that the account of the circumstances which attended the publication of the *Dunciad*, however strange and improbable, was exactly true.

The publication of this piece at this time raised Mr Savage a great number of enemies among those that were attacked by Mr Pope, with whom he was considered as a kind of confederate, and whom he was suspected of supplying with private intelligence and secret incidents: so that the ignominy of an informer was added to the terror of a satirist.

That he was not altogether free from literary hypocrisy, and that he sometimes spoke one thing, and wrote another, cannot be denied; because he himself confessed, that, when he lived with great familiarity with Dennis, he wrote an epigram against him.

Mr Savage however set all the malice of all the pigmy writers at defiance, and thought the friendship of Mr Pope cheaply purchased by being exposed to their censure and their hatred; nor had he any reason to repent of the preference, for he found Mr Pope a steady and un-alienable friend almost to the end of his life.

About this time, notwithstanding his avowed neutrality with re-gard to party, he published a panegyric on Sir Robert Walpole, for which he was rewarded by him with twenty guineas, a sum not very large, if either the excellence of the performance, or the affluence of the patron be considered; but greater than he afterwards obtained from a person of yet higher rank, and more desirous in appearance of being distinguished as a patron of literature.

As he was very far from approving the conduct of Sir Robert Walpole, and in conversation mentioned him sometimes with acri-mony, and generally with contempt; as he was one of those who were always zealous in their assertions of the justice of the late opposition, jealous of the rights of the people, and alarmed by the long-continued triumph of the court; it was natural to ask him what could induce him to employ his poetry in praise of that man who was, in his op-inion, an enemy to liberty, and an oppressor of his country? He alleg-ed, that he was then dependent upon the Lord Tyrconnel, who was an implicit follower of the ministry; and that being enjoined by him, not without menaces, to write in praise of his leader, he had not res-olution sufficient to sacrifice the pleasure of affluence to that of in-tegrity.

On this, and on many other occasions, he was ready to lament the misery of living at the tables of other men, which was his fate from the beginning to the end of his life; for I know not whether he ever had, for three months together, a settled habitation, in which he could claim a right of residence.

To this unhappy state it is just to impute much of the inconstancy of his conduct; for though a readiness to comply with the inclination of others was no part of his natural character, yet he was sometimes ob-liged to relax his obstinacy, and submit his own judgement, and even his virtue, to the government of those by whom he was supported: so that, if his miseries were sometimes the consequences of his faults, he ought not yet to be wholly excluded from compassion, because his faults were very often the effects of his misfortunes.

In this gay period of his life, while he was surrounded by affluence and pleasure, he published *The Wanderer*, a moral poem, of which the design is comprised in these lines:

> I fly all public care, all venal strife,
> To try the still compar'd with active life;
> To prove, by these the sons of men may owe
> The fruits of bliss to bursting clouds of woe;
> That ev'n calamity, by thought refin'd,
> Inspirits and adorns the thinking mind.

And more distinctly in the following passage:

> By woe, the soul to daring action swells;
> By woe, in plaintless patience it excels;
> From patience, prudent clear experience springs,
> And traces knowledge thro' the course of things!
> Thence hope is form'd, thence fortitude, success,
> Renown: – whate'er men covet and caress.

This performance was always considered by himself as his masterpiece; and Mr Pope, when he asked his opinion of it, told him, that he read it once over, and was not displeased with it, that it gave him more pleasure at the second perusal, and delighted him still more at the third.

It has been generally objected to *The Wanderer*, that the disposition of the parts is irregular; that the design is obscure, and the plan perplexed; that the images, however beautiful, succeed each other without order; and that the whole performance is not so much a regular fabric, as a heap of shining materials thrown together by accident, which strikes rather with the solemn magnificence of a stupendous ruin, than the elegant grandeur of a finished pile.

This criticism is universal, and therefore it is reasonable to believe it at least in a great degree just; but Mr Savage was always of a contrary opinion, and thought his drift could only be missed by negligence or stupidity, and that the whole plan was regular, and the parts distinct.

It was never denied to abound with strong representations of nature, and just observations upon life; and it may easily be observed, that most of his pictures have an evident tendency to illustrate his first great position, 'that good is the consequence of evil'. The sun that burns up the mountains, fructifies the vales; the deluge that rushes down the broken rocks with dreadful impetuosity, is separated into purling brooks; and the rage of the hurricane purifies the air.

Even in this poem he has not been able to forbear one touch upon the cruelty of his mother, which, though remarkably delicate and tender, is a proof how deep an impression it had upon his mind.

This must be at least acknowledged, which ought to be thought equivalent to many other excellences, that this poem can promote no other purposes than those of virtue, and that it is written with a very strong sense of the efficacy of religion.

But my province is rather to give the history of Mr Savage's performances, than to display their beauties, or to obviate the criticisms which they have occasioned; and therefore I shall not dwell upon the particular passages which deserve applause: I shall neither show the excellence of his descriptions, nor expatiate on the terrific portrait of suicide, nor point out the artful touches, by which he had distinguished the intellectual features of the rebels, who suffered death in his last canto. It is, however, proper to observe, that Mr Savage always declared the characters wholly fictitious, and without the least allusion to any real persons or actions.

From a poem so diligently laboured, and so successfully finished, it might be reasonably expected that he should have gained considerable advantage; nor can it, without some degree of indignation and concern, be told, that he sold the copy for ten guineas,[18] of which he afterwards returned two, that the two last sheets of the work might be reprinted, of which he had in his absence intrusted the correction to a friend, who was too indolent to perform it with accuracy.

A superstitious regard to the correction of his sheets[19] was one of Mr Savage's peculiarities: he often altered, revised, recurred to his first reading or punctuation, and again adopted the alteration; he was dubious and irresolute without end, as on a question of the last importance, and at last was seldom satisfied: the intrusion or omission of a comma was sufficient to discompose him, and he would lament an error of a single letter as a heavy calamity. In one of his letters relating to an impression of some verses, he remarks, that he had, with regard to the correction of the proof, 'a spell upon him'; and indeed the anxiety with which he dwelt upon the minutest and most trifling niceties, deserved no other name than that of fascination.

That he sold so valuable a performance for so small a price, was not to be imputed either to necessity, by which the learned and ingenious are often obliged to submit to very hard conditions; or to avarice, by which the booksellers are frequently incited to oppress that genius by which they are supported; but to that intemperate desire of pleasure, and habitual slavery to his passions, which involved him in many perplexities. He happened at that time to be engaged in the pursuit of some trifling gratification, and, being without money for the present occasion, sold his poem to the first bidder, and perhaps for the first price that was proposed, and would probably have been content with less, if less had been offered him.

This poem was addressed to the Lord Tyrconnel, not only in the first lines, but in a formal dedication filled with the highest strains of panegyric, and the warmest professions of gratitude, but by no means remarkable for delicacy of connexion or elegance of style.

These praises in a short time he found himself inclined to retract, being discarded by the man on whom he had bestowed them, and whom he then immediately discovered not to have deserved them. Of this quarrel, which every day made more bitter, Lord Tyrconnel and Mr Savage assigned very different reasons, which might perhaps all in reality concur, though they were not all convenient to be alleged by either party. Lord Tyrconnel affirmed, that it was the constant practice of Mr Savage to enter a tavern with any company that proposed it, drink the most expensive wines with great profusion, and when the reckoning was demanded, to be without money. If, as it often happened, his company were willing to defray his part, the affair ended, without any ill consequences; but, if they were refractory, and expected that the wine should be paid for by him that drank it, his method of composition was, to take them with him to his own apartment, assume the government of the house, and order the butler in an imperious manner to set the best wine in the cellar before his company, who often drank till they forgot the respect due to the house in which they were entertained, indulged themselves in the utmost extravagance of merriment, practised the most licentious frolics, and committed all the outrages of drunkenness.

Nor was this the only charge which Lord Tyrconnel brought against him. Having given him a collection of valuable books, stamped with his own arms, he had the mortification to see them in a short time exposed to sale upon the stalls, it being usual with Mr Savage, when he wanted a small sum, to take his books to the pawnbroker.

Whoever was acquainted with Mr Savage easily credited both these accusations: for, having been obliged, from his first entrance into the world, to subsist upon expedients, affluence was not able to exalt him above them; and so much was he delighted with wine and conversation, and so long had he been accustomed to live by chance, that he would at any time go to the tavern without scruple, and trust for the reckoning to the liberality of his company, and frequently of company to whom he was very little known. This conduct indeed very seldom drew upon him those inconveniences that might be feared by any other person; for his conversation was so entertaining, and his address so pleasing, that few thought the pleasure which they received from him dearly purchased, by paying for his wine. It was his peculiar happiness, that he scarcely ever found a stranger, whom he did not leave a friend; but it must likewise be added, that he had not often a friend long, without obliging him to become a stranger.

Mr Savage, on the other hand, declared, that Lord Tyrconnel quarrelled with him, because he would subtract from his own luxury and extravagance what he had promised to allow him, and that his resentment was only a plea for the violation of his promise. He asserted that he had done nothing that ought to exclude him from that subsistence which he thought not so much a favour, as a debt, since it was offered him upon conditions, which he had never broken; and that his only fault was, that he could not be supported with nothing.

He acknowledged, that Lord Tyrconnel often exhorted him to regulate his method of life, and not to spend all his nights in taverns, and that he appeared desirous, that he would pass those hours with him, which he so freely bestowed upon others. This demand Mr Savage considered as a censure of his conduct, which he could never patiently bear; and which, in the latter and cooler part of his life, was so offensive to him, that he declared it as his resolution, 'to spurn that friend who should presume to dictate to him'; and it is not likely, that in his earlier years he received admonitions with more calmness.

He was likewise inclined to resent such expectations, as tending to infringe his liberty, of which he was very jealous, when it was necessary to the gratification of his passions; and declared, that the request was still more unreasonable, as the company to which he was to have been confined was insupportably disagreeable. This assertion affords another instance of that inconsistency of his writings with his conversation, which was so often to be observed. He forgot how lavishly he had, in his Dedication to *The Wanderer*, extolled the delicacy and penetration, the humanity and generosity, the candour and politeness of the man, whom, when he no longer loved him, he declared to be a wretch without understanding, without good-nature, and without justice; of whose name he thought himself obliged to leave no trace in any future edition of his writings; and accordingly blotted it out of that copy of *The Wanderer* which was in his hands.

During his continuance with the Lord Tyrconnel, he wrote *The Triumph of Health and Mirth,* on the recovery of Lady Tyrconnel from a languishing illness. This performance is remarkable, not only for the gaiety of the ideas, and the melody of the numbers, but for the agreeable fiction upon which it is formed. Mirth, overwhelmed with sorrow for the sickness of her favourite, takes a flight in quest of her sister Health, whom she finds reclined upon the brow of a lofty mountain, amidst the fragrance of perpetual spring, with the breezes of the morning sporting about her. Being solicited by her sister Mirth, she readily promises her assistance, flies away in a cloud, and impregnates the waters of Bath with new virtues, by which the sickness of Belinda is relieved.

As the reputation of his abilities, the particular circumstances of his birth and life, the splendour of his appearance, and the distinction which was for some time paid him by Lord Tyrconnel, entitled him to familiarity with persons of higher rank than those to whose conversation he had been before admitted, he did not fail to gratify that curiosity, which induced him to take a nearer view of those whom their birth, their employments, or their fortunes, necessarily place at a distance from the greatest part of mankind, and to examine whether their merit was magnified or diminished by the medium through which it was contemplated; whether the splendour with which they dazzled their admirers was inherent in themselves, or only reflected on them by the objects that surrounded them; and whether great men were selected for high stations, or high stations made great men.

For this purpose he took all opportunities of conversing familiarly with those who were most conspicuous at that time for their power or their influence; he watched their looser moments, and examined their domestic behaviour, with that acuteness which nature had given him, and which the uncommon variety of his life had contributed to increase, and that inquisitiveness which must always be produced in a vigorous mind, by an absolute freedom from all pressing or domestic engagements. His discernment was quick, and therefore he soon found in every person, and in every affair, something that deserved attention; he was supported by others, without any care for himself, and was therefore at leisure to pursue his observations.

More cirumstances to constitute a critic on human life could not easily concur; nor indeed could any man, who assumed from accidental advantages more praise than he could justly claim from his real merit, admit an acquaintance more dangerous than that of Savage; of whom likewise it must be confessed, that abilities really exalted above the common level, or virtue refined from passion, or proof against corruption, could not easily find an abler judge, or a warmer advocate.

What was the result of Mr Savage's inquiry, though he was not much accustomed to conceal his discoveries, it may not be entirely safe to relate, because the persons whose characters he criticized are powerful; and power and resentment are seldom strangers; nor would it perhaps be wholly just, because what he asserted in conversation might, though true in general, be heightened by some momentary ardour of imagination, and, as it can be delivered only from memory, may be imperfectly represented; so that the picture at first aggravated, and then unskilfully copied, may be justly suspected to retain no great resemblance of the original.

It may however be observed, that he did not appear to have formed very elevated ideas of those to whom the administration of affairs, or the conduct of parties, has been intrusted; who have been considered as the advocates of the crown, or the guardians of the people; and who have obtained the most implicit confidence, and the loudest applauses. Of one particular person,[20] who has been at one time so popular as to be generally esteemed, and at another so formidable as to be universally detested, he observed, that his acquisitions had been small, or that his capacity was narrow, and that the whole range of his mind was from obscenity to politics, and from politics to obscenity.

But the opportunity of indulging his speculations on great characters was now at an end. He was banished from the table of Lord Tyrconnel, and turned again adrift upon the world, without prospect of finding quickly any other harbour. As prudence was not one of the virtues by which he was distinguished, he had made no provision against a misfortune like this. And though it is not to be imagined but that the separation must for some time have been preceded by coldness, peevishness, or neglect, though it was undoubtedly the consequence of accumulated provocations on both sides; yet every one that knew Savage will readily believe, that to him it was sudden as a stroke of thunder; that, though he might have transiently suspected it, he had never suffered any thought so unpleasing to sink into his mind, but that he had driven it away by amusements, or dreams of future felicity and affluence, and had never taken any measures by which he might prevent a precipitation from plenty to indigence.

This quarrel and separation, and the difficulties to which Mr Savage was exposed by them, were soon known both to his friends and enemies; nor was it long before he perceived, from the behaviour of both, how much is added to the lustre of genius by the ornaments of wealth.

His condition did not appear to excite much compassion; for he had not always been careful to use the advantages he enjoyed with that moderation which ought to have been with more than usual caution preserved by him, who knew, if he had reflected, that he was only a dependant on the bounty of another, whom he could expect to support him no longer than he endeavoured to preserve his favour by complying with his inclinations, and whom he nevertheless set at defiance, and was continually irritating by negligence or encroachments.

Examples need not be sought at any great distance to prove, that superiority of fortune has a natural tendency to kindle pride, and that pride seldom fails to exert itself in contempt and insult; and if this is often the effect of hereditary wealth, and of honours enjoyed only by the merit of others, it is some extenuation of any indecent triumphs to which this unhappy man may have been betrayed, that his prosperity was heightened by the force of novelty, and made more intoxicating by a sense of the misery in which he had so long languished, and perhaps of the insults which he had formerly borne, and which he might now think himself entitled to revenge. It is too common for those who have unjustly suffered pain, to inflict it likewise in their turn with the same injustice, and to imagine that they have a right to treat others as they have themselves been treated.

That Mr Savage was too much elevated by any good fortune, is generally known; and some passages of his Introduction to *The Author to be let* sufficiently show, that he did not wholly refrain from such satire as he afterwards thought very unjust, when he was exposed to it himself; for when he was afterwards ridiculed[21] in the character of a distressed poet, he very easily discovered, that distress was not a proper subject for merriment, or topic of invective. He was then able to discern, that, if misery be the effect of virtue, it ought to be reverenced; if of ill-fortune, to be pitied; and if of vice, not to be insulted, because it is perhaps itself a punishment adequate to the crime by which it was produced. And the humanity of that man can deserve no panegyric, who is capable of reproaching a criminal in the hands of the executioner.

But these reflections, though they readily occurred to him in the first and last parts of his life, were, I am afraid, for a long time forgotten; at least they were, like many other maxims, treasured up in his mind, rather for show than use, and operated very little upon his conduct, however elegantly he might sometimes explain, or however forcibly he might inculcate, them.

His degradation therefore from the condition which he had enjoyed with such wanton thoughtlessness, was considered by many as an occasion of triumph. Those who had before paid their court to him without success, soon returned the contempt which they had suffered; and they who had received favours from him, for of such favours as he could bestow he was very liberal, did not always remember them. So much more certain are the effects of resentment than of gratitude: it is not only to many more pleasing to recollect those faults which place others below them, than those virtues by which they are themselves comparatively depressed; but it is likewise more easy to neglect, than to recompense; and though there are few who will practise a laborious virtue, there will never be wanting multitudes that will indulge an easy vice.

Savage, however, was very little disturbed at the marks of contempt which his ill-fortune brought upon him, from those whom he never esteemed, and with whom he never considered himself as levelled by any calamities: and though it was not without some uneasiness that he saw some, whose friendship he valued, change their behaviour; he yet observed their coldness without much emotion, considered them as the slaves of fortune and the worshippers of prosperity, and was more inclined to despise them, than to lament himself.

It does not appear that, after this return of his wants, he found mankind equally favourable to him, as at his first appearance in the world. His story, though in reality not less melancholy, was less affecting, because it was no longer new; it therefore procured him no new friends; and those that formerly relieved him, thought they might now consign him to others. He was now likewise considered by many rather as criminal, than as unhappy; for the friends of Lord Tyrconnel, and of his mother, were sufficiently industrious to publish his weaknesses, which were indeed very numerous; and nothing was forgotten, that might make him either hateful or ridiculous.

It cannot but be imagined, that such representations of his faults must make great numbers less sensible of his distress; many, who had only an opportunity to hear one part, made no scruple to propagate the account which they received; many assisted their circulation from malice or revenge; and perhaps many pretended to credit them, that they might with a better grace withdraw their regard, or withhold their assistance.

Savage, however, was not one of those, who suffered himself to be injured without resistance, nor was less diligent in exposing the faults of Lord Tyrconnel, over whom he obtained at least this advantage, that he drove him first to the practice of outrage and violence; for he was so much provoked by the wit and virulence of Savage, that he came with a number of attendants, that did no honour to his courage, to beat him at a coffee-house. But it happened that he had left the place a few minutes, and his lordship had, without danger, the pleasure of boasting how he would have treated him. Mr Savage went next day to repay his visit at his own house; but was prevailed on, by his domestics, to retire without insisting upon seeing him.

Lord Tyrconnel was accused by Mr Savage of some actions, which scarcely any provocations will be thought sufficient to justify; such as seizing what he had in his lodgings, and other instances of wanton cruelty, by which he increased the distress of Savage, without any advantage to himself.

These mutual accusations were retorted on both sides, for many years, with the utmost degree of virulence and rage; and time seemed rather to augment than diminish their resentment. That the anger of Mr Savage should be kept alive, is not strange, because he felt every day the consequences of the quarrel; but it might reasonably have been hoped, that Lord Tyrconnel might have relented, and at length have forgot those provocations, which, however they might have once inflamed him, had not in reality much hurt him.

The spirit of Mr Savage indeed never suffered him to solicit a reconciliation; he returned reproach for reproach, and insult for insult; his superiority of wit supplied the disadvantages of his fortune, and enabled him to form a party, and prejudice great numbers in his favour.

But though this might be some gratification of his vanity, it afforded very little relief to his necessities; and he was very frequently reduced to uncommon hardships, of which, however, he never made any mean or importunate complaints, being formed rather to bear misery with fortitude, than enjoy prosperity with moderation.

He now thought himself again at liberty to expose the cruelty of his mother, and therefore, I believe about this time, published *The Bastard*, a poem remarkable for the vivacious sallies of thought in[22] the beginning, where he makes a pompous enumeration of the imaginary advantages of base birth; and the pathetic sentiments at the end, where he recounts the real calamities which he suffered by the crime of his parents.

The vigour and spirit of the verses, the peculiar circumstances of the author, the novelty of the subject and the notoriety of the story to which the allusions are made, procured this performance a very favourable reception; great numbers were immediately dispersed, and editions were multiplied with unusual rapidity.

One circumstance attended the publication, which Savage used to relate with great satisfaction. His mother, to whom the poem was with 'due reverence' inscribed, happened then to be at Bath, where she could not conveniently retire from censure, or conceal herself from observation; and no sooner did the reputation of the poem begin to spread, than she heard it repeated in all places of concourse, nor could she enter the assembly-rooms, or cross the walks, without being saluted with some lines from *The Bastard*.

This was perhaps the first time that ever she discovered a sense of shame, and on this occasion the power of wit was very conspicuous; the wretch who had, without scruple, proclaimed herself an adulteress, and who had first endeavoured to starve her son, then to transport him, and afterwards to hang him, was not able to bear the representation of her own conduct; but fled from reproach, though she felt no pain from guilt, and left Bath with the utmost haste, to shelter herself among the crowds of London.

Thus Savage had the satisfaction of finding, that, though he could not reform his mother, he could punish her, and that he did not always suffer alone.

The pleasure which he received from this increase of his poetical reputation, was sufficient for some time to overbalance the miseries of want, which this performance did not much alleviate; for it was sold for a very trivial sum to a bookseller, who, though the success was so uncommon that five impressions were sold, of which many were undoubtedly very numerous, had not generosity sufficient to admit the unhappy writer to any part of the profit.

The sale of this poem was always mentioned by Savage with the utmost elevation of heart, and referred to by him as an incontestable proof of a general acknowledgement of his abilities. It was indeed the only production of which he could justly boast a general reception.

But though he did not lose the opportunity which success gave him, of setting a high rate on his abilities, but paid due deference to the suffrages of mankind when they were given in his favour, he did not suffer his esteem of himself to depend upon others, nor found any thing sacred in the voice of the people when they were inclined to censure him; he then readily showed the folly of expecting that the public should judge right, observed how slowly poetical merit had often forced its way into the world; he contented himself with the applause of men of judgement, and was somewhat disposed to exclude all those from the character of men of judgement who did not applaud him.

But he was at other times more favourable to mankind[23] than to think them blind to the beauties of his works, and imputed the slowness of their sale to other causes; either they were published at a time when the town was empty, or when the attention of the public was engrossed by some struggle in the parliament, or some other object of general concern; or they were by the neglect of the publisher not diligently dispersed, or by his avarice not advertised with sufficient frequency. Address, or industry, or liberality, was always wanting; and the blame was laid rather on any person than the author.

By arts like these, arts which every man practises in some degree, and to which too much of the little tranquillity of life is to be ascribed, Savage was always able to live at peace with himself. Had he indeed only made use of these expedients to alleviate the loss or want of fortune or reputation, or any other advantages, which it is not in man's power to bestow upon himself, they might have been justly mentioned as instances of a philosophical mind, and very properly proposed to the imitation of multitudes, who, for want of diverting their imaginations with the same dexterity, languish under afflictions which might be easily removed.

It were doubtless to be wished, that truth and reason were universally prevalent; that every thing were esteemed according to its real value; and that men would secure themselves from being disappointed in their endeavours after happiness, by placing it only in virtue, which is always to be obtained; but if adventitious and foreign pleasures must be pursued, it would be perhaps of some benefit, since that pursuit must frequently be fruitless, if the practice of Savage could be taught, that folly might be an antidote to folly, and one fallacy be obviated by another.

But the danger of this pleasing intoxication must not be concealed; nor indeed can anyone, after having observed the life of Savage, need to be cautioned against it. By imputing none of his miseries to himself, he continued to act upon the same principles, and to follow the same path; was never made wiser by his sufferings, nor preserved by one misfortune from falling into another. He proceeded throughout his life to tread the same steps on the same circle; always applauding his past conduct, or at least forgetting it, to amuse himself with phantoms of happiness, which were dancing before him; and willingly turned his eyes from the light of reason, when it would have discovered the illusion, and shown him, what he never wished to see, his real state.

He is even accused after having lulled his imagination with those ideal opiates, of having tried the same experiment upon his conscience; and, having accustomed himself to impute all deviations from the right to foreign causes, it is certain that he was upon every occasion too easily reconciled to himself, and that he appeared very little to regret those practices which had impaired his reputation. The reigning error of his life was, that he mistook the love for the practice of virtue, and was indeed not so much a good man, as the friend of goodness.[24]

This at least must be allowed him, that he always preserved a strong sense of the dignity, the beauty, and the necessity of virtue, and that he never contributed deliberately to spread corruption amongst mankind. His actions, which were generally precipitate, were often blameable; but his writings, being the productions of study, uniformly tended to the exaltation of the mind, and the propagation of morality and piety.

These writings may improve mankind, when his failings shall be forgotten; and therefore he must be considered, upon the whole, as a benefactor to the world; nor can his personal example do any hurt, since, whoever hears of his faults, will hear of the miseries which they brought upon him, and which would deserve less pity, had not his condition been such as made his faults pardonable. He may be considered as a child exposed to all the temptations of indigence, at an age when resolution was not yet strengthened by conviction, nor virtue confirmed by habit; a circumstance which in his *Bastard* he laments in a very affecting manner:

> – No Mother's care
> Shielded my infant innocence with prayer:
> No Father's guardian-hand my youth maintain'd,
> Call'd forth my virtues, or from vice restrain'd.

The Bastard, however it might provoke or mortify his mother, could not be expected to melt her to compassion, so that he was still under the same want of the necessities of life; and he therefore exerted all the interest which his wit, or his birth, or his misfortunes, could procure, to obtain, upon the death of Eusden,[25] the place of Poet Laureate, and prosecuted his application with so much diligence, that the King publicly declared it his intention to bestow it upon him; but such was the fate of Savage, that even the King, when he intended his advantage, was disappointed in his schemes; for the Lord Chamberlain, who has the disposal of the laurel, as one of the appendages of his office, either did not know the King's design, or did not approve it, or thought the nomination of the Laureate an encroachment upon his rights, and therefore bestowed the laurel upon Colley Cibber.

Mr Savage, thus disappointed, took a resolution of applying to the Queen, that, having once given him life, she would enable him to support it, and therefore published a short poem on her birth-day, to which he gave the odd title of *Volunteer Laureat*. The event of this essay he has himself related in the following letter, which he prefixed to the poem, when he afterwards reprinted it in *The Gentleman's Magazine*, from whence I have copied it entire, as this was one of the few attempts in which Mr Savage succeeded.

MR URBAN,

In your Magazine for February you published the last *Volunteer Laureat*, written on a very melancholy occasion, the death of the royal patroness of arts and literature in general, and of the author of that poem in particular; I now send you the first that Mr Savage wrote under that title. – This gentleman, notwithstanding a very considerable interest, being, on the death of Mr Eusden, disappointed of the Laureat's place, wrote the before-mentioned poem; which was no sooner published, but the late Queen sent to a bookseller for it: the author had not at that time a friend either to get him introduced, or his poem presented at court; yet such was the unspeakable goodness of that Princess, that notwithstanding this act of ceremony was wanting, in a few days after publication, Mr Savage received a bank-bill of fifty pounds and a gracious message from her Majesty, by the Lord North and Guilford, to this effect: 'That her Majesty was highly pleased with the verses; that she took particularly kind his lines there relating to the King; that he had permission to write annually on the same subject; and that he should yearly receive the like present, till something better (which was her Majesty's intention) could be done for him.' After this, he was permitted to present one of his annual poems to her Majesty, had the honour of kissing her hand, and met with the most gracious reception.

Yours, &c.

Such was the performance, and such its reception; a reception which, though by no means unkind, was yet not in the highest degree generous: to chain down the genius of a writer to an annual panegyric, showed in the Queen too much desire of hearing her own praises, and a greater regard to herself than to him on whom her bounty was conferred. It was a kind of avaricious generosity, by which flattery was rather purchased, than genius rewarded.

Mrs Oldfield had formerly given him the same allowance with much more heroic intention; she had no other view than to enable him to prosecute his studies, and to set himself above the want of assistance, and was contented with doing good without stipulating for encomiums.

Mr Savage, however, was not at liberty to make exceptions, but was ravished with the favours which he had received, and probably yet more with those which he was promised; he considered himself now as a favourite of the Queen, and did not doubt but a few annual poems would establish him in some profitable employment.

He therefore assumed the title of *Volunteer Laureat*, not without some reprehensions from Cibber, who informed him, that the title of *Laureate* was a mark of honour conferred by the King, from whom all honour is derived, and which therefore no man has a right to bestow upon himself; and added, that he might with equal propriety, style himself a Volunteer Lord, or Volunteer Baronet. It cannot be denied that the remark was just; but Savage did not think any title, which was conferred upon Mr Cibber, so honourable as that the usurpation of it could be imputed to him as an instance of very exorbitant vanity, and therefore continued to write under the same title, and received every year the same reward.

He did not appear to consider these encomiums as tests of his abilities, or as any thing more than annual hints to the Queen of her promise, or acts of ceremony, by the performance of which he was entitled to his pension, and therefore did not labour them with great diligence, or print more than fifty each year, except that for some of the last years he regularly inserted them in *The Gentleman's Magazine*, by which they were dispersed over the kingdom.

Of some of them he had himself so low an opinion that he intended to omit them in the collection of poems, for which he printed proposals, and solicited subscriptions; nor can it seem strange, that, being confined to the same subject, he should be at some times indolent, and at others unsuccessful; that he should sometimes delay a disagreeable task, till it was too late to perform it well; or that he should sometimes repeat the same sentiment on the same occasion, or at others be misled by an attempt after novelty to forced conceptions and far-fetched images.

He wrote indeed with a double intention, which supplied him with some variety; for his business was to praise the Queen for the favours which he had received, and to complain to her of the delay of those which she had promised: in some of his pieces, therefore, gratitude is predominant, and in some discontent; in some he represents himself as happy in her patronage, and in others as disconsolate to find himself neglected.

Her promise, like other promises made to this unfortunate man, was never performed, though he took sufficient care that it should not be forgotten. The publication of his *Volunteer Laureat* procured him no other reward than a regular remittance of fifty pounds.

He was not so depressed by his disappointments as to neglect any opportunity that was offered of advancing his interests. When the Princess Anne was married, he wrote a poem upon her departure, only, as he declared, because it was expected from him, and he was not willing to bar his own prospects by any appearance of neglect.

He never mentioned any advantage gained by this poem, or any regard that was paid to it; and therefore it is likely that it was considered at court as an act of duty to which he was obliged by his dependence, and which it was therefore not necessary to reward by any new favour: or perhaps the Queen really intended his advancement, and therefore thought it superfluous to lavish presents upon a man whom she intended to establish for life.

About this time not only his hopes were in danger of being frustrated, but this pension likewise of being obstructed, by an accidental calumny. The writer of *The Daily Courant*, a paper then published under the direction of the ministry, charged him with a crime, which, though very great in itself, would have been remarkably invidious in him, and might very justly have incensed the Queen against him. He was accused by name of influencing elections against the court, by appearing at the head of a Tory mob; nor did the accuser fail to aggravate his crime, by representing it as the effect of the most atrocious ingratitude, and a kind of rebellion against the Queen, who had first preserved him from an infamous death, and afterwards distinguished him by her favour, and supported him by her charity. The charge, as it was open and confident, was likewise by good fortune very particular. The place of the transaction was mentioned, and the whole series of the rioter's conduct related. The exactness made Mr Savage's vindication easy; for he never had in his life seen the place which was declared to be the scene of his wickedness, nor ever had been present in any town when its representatives were chosen. This answer he therefore made haste to publish, with all the circumstances necessary to make it credible; and very reasonably demanded, that the accusation should be retracted in the same paper, that he might no longer suffer the imputation of sedition and ingratitude. This demand was likewise pressed by him in a private letter to the author of the paper, who, either trusting to the protection of those whose defence he had undertaken, or having entertained some personal malice against Mr Savage, or fearing, lest, by retracting so confident an assertion, he should impair the credit of his paper, refused to give him that satisfaction.

Mr Savage therefore thought it necessary, to his own vindication, to prosecute him in the King's Bench; but as he did not find any ill effects from the accusation, having sufficiently cleared his innocence, he thought any farther procedure would have the appearance of revenge; and therefore willingly dropped it.

He saw soon afterwards a process commenced in the same court against himself, on an information in which he was accused of writing and publishing an obscene pamphlet.

It was always Mr Savage's desire to be distinguished; and, when any controversy became popular, he never wanted some reason for engaging in it with great ardour, and appearing at the head of the party which he had chosen. As he was never celebrated for his prudence, he had no sooner taken his side, and informed himself of the chief topics of the dispute, than he took all opportunities of asserting and propagating his principles, without much regard to his own interest, or any other visible design than that of drawing upon himself the attention of mankind.

The dispute between the Bishop of London and the Chancellor[26] is well known to have been for some time the chief topic of political conversation; and therefore Mr Savage, in pursuance of his character, endeavoured to become conspicuous among the controvertists with which every coffee-house was filled on that occasion. He was an indefatigable opposer of all the claims of ecclesiastical power, though he did not know on what they were founded; and was therefore no friend to the Bishop of London. But he had another reason for appearing as a warm advocate for Dr Rundle; for he was the friend of Mr Foster and Mr Thomson, who were the friends of Mr Savage.

Thus remote was his interest in the question, which however, as he imagined, concerned him so nearly, that it was not sufficient to harangue and dispute, but necessary likewise to write upon it.

He therefore engaged with great ardour in a new poem, called by him, *The Progress of a Divine*,[27] in which he conducts a profligate priest by all the gradations of wickedness from a poor curacy in the country, to the highest preferments of the church, and describes with that humour which was natural to him, and that knowledge which was extended to all the diversities of human life, his behaviour in every station; and insinuates, that this priest, thus accomplished, found at last a patron in the Bishop of London.

When he was asked by one of his friends, on what pretence he could charge the bishop with such an action, he had no more to say, than that he had only invented the accusation, and that he thought it reasonable to believe, that he, who obstructed the rise of a good man without reason, would for bad reasons promote the exaltation of a villain.

The clergy were universally provoked by this satire; and Savage, who, as was his constant practice, had set his name to his performance, was censured in *The Weekly Miscellany* with severity, which he did not seem inclined to forget.

But a return of invective was not thought a sufficient punishment. The Court of King's Bench was therefore moved against him, and he was obliged to return an answer to a charge of obscenity. It was urged, in his defence, that obscenity was criminal when it was intended to promote the practice of vice; but that Mr Savage had only introduced obscene ideas, with the view of exposing them to detestation, and of amending the age, by showing the deformity of wickedness. This plea was admitted; and Sir Philip Yorke, who then presided in that court, dismissed the information with encomiums upon the purity and excellence of Mr Savage's writings.

The prosecution, however, answered in some measure the purpose of those by whom it was set on foot; for Mr Savage was so far intimidated by it, that, when the edition of his poem was sold, he did not venture to reprint it; so that it was in a short time forgotten, or forgotten by all but those whom it offended.

It is said, that some endeavours were used to incense the Queen against him: but he found advocates to obviate at least part of their effect; for though he was never advanced, he still continued to receive his pension.

This poem drew more infamy upon him than any incident of his life; and, as his conduct cannot be vindicated, it is proper to secure his memory from reproach, by informing those whom he made his enemies, that he never intended to repeat the provocation; and that, though, whenever he thought he had any reason to complain of the clergy, he used to threaten them with a new edition of *The Progress of a Divine*, it was his calm and settled resolution to suppress it for ever.

He once intended to have made a better reparation for the folly or injustice with which he might be charged, by writing another poem, called *The Progress of a Free-thinker*, whom he intended to lead through all the stages of vice and folly, to convert him from virtue to wickedness, and from religion to infidelity, by all the modish sophistry used for that purpose; and at last to dismiss him by his own hand into the other world.

That he did not execute this design is a real loss to mankind, for he was too well acquainted with all the scenes of debauchery to have failed in his representations of them, and too zealous for virtue not to have represented them in such a manner as should expose them either to ridicule or detestation.

But this plan was, like others, formed and laid aside, till the vigour of his imagination was spent, and the effervescence of invention had subsided; but soon gave way to some other design, which pleased by its novelty for a while, and then was neglected like the former.

He was still in his usual exigences, having no certain support but the pension allowed him by the Queen, which, though it might have kept an exact economist from want, was very far from being sufficient for Mr Savage, who had never been accustomed to dismiss any of his appetites without the gratification which they solicited, and whom nothing but want of money withheld from partaking of every pleasure that fell within his view.

His conduct with regard to his pension was very particular.[28] No sooner had he changed the bill, than he vanished from the sight of all his acquaintances, and lay for some time out of the reach of all the inquiries that friendship or curiosity could make after him; at length he appeared again penniless as before, but never informed even those whom he seemed to regard most, where he had been, nor was his retreat ever discovered.

This was his constant practice during the whole time that he received the pension from the Queen: he regularly disappeared and returned. He indeed affirmed that he retired to study, and that the money supported him in solitude for many months; but his friends declared, that the short time in which it was spent sufficiently confuted his own account of his conduct.

His politeness and his wit still raised him friends, who were desirous of setting him at length free from that indigence by which he had been hitherto oppressed; and therefore solicited Sir Robert Walpole in his favour with so much earnestness, that they obtained a promise of the next place that should become vacant, not exceeding two hundred pounds a year. This promise was made with an uncommon declaration, 'that it was not the promise of a minister to a petitioner, but of a friend to his friend'.

Mr Savage now concluded himself set at ease for ever, and, as he observes in a poem written on that incident of his life, trusted and was trusted; but soon found that his confidence was ill-grounded, and this friendly promise was not inviolable. He spent a long time in solicitations, and at last despaired and desisted.

He did not indeed deny that he had given the minister some reason to believe that he should not strengthen his own interest by advancing him, for he had taken care to distinguish himself in coffee-houses as an advocate for the ministry of the last years of Queen Anne[29] and was always ready to justify the conduct, and exalt the character of Lord Bolingbroke, whom he mentions with great regard in an epistle upon authors, which he wrote about that time, but was too wise to publish, and of which only some fragments have appeared, inserted by him in the *Magazine* after his retirement.

To despair was not, however, the character of Savage; when one patronage failed, he had recourse to another. The prince was now extremely popular,[30] and had very liberally rewarded the merit of some writers whom Mr Savage did not think superior to himself, and therefore he resolved to address a poem to him.

For this purpose he made choice of a subject, which could regard only persons of the highest rank and greatest affluence, and which was therefore proper for a poem intended to procure the patronage of a prince; and having retired for some time to Richmond, that he might prosecute his design in full tranquillity, without the temptations of pleasure, or the solicitations of creditors, by which his meditations were in equal danger of being disconcerted, he produced a poem *On Public Spirit, with regard to Public Works.*

The plan of this poem is very extensive, and comprises a multitude of topics, each of which might furnish matter sufficient for a long performance, and of which some have already employed more eminent writers; but as he was perhaps not fully acquainted with the whole extent of his own design, and was writing to obtain a supply of wants too pressing to admit of long or accurate inquiries, he passes negligently over many public works, which, even in his own opinion, deserved to be more elaborately treated.

But though he may sometimes disappoint his reader by transient touches upon these subjects, which have often been considered, and therefore naturally raise expectations, he must be allowed amply to compensate his omissions, by expatiating, in the conclusion of his work, upon a kind of beneficence not yet celebrated by any eminent poet, though it now appears more susceptible of embellishments, more adapted to exalt the ideas, and affect the passions, than many of those which have hitherto been thought most worthy of the ornaments of verse. The settlement of colonies in uninhabited countries, the establishment of those in security, whose misfortunes have made their own country no longer pleasing or safe, the acquisition of property without injury to any, the appropriation of the waste and luxuriant bounties of nature, and the enjoyment of those gifts which heaven has scattered upon regions uncultivated and unoccupied, cannot be considered without giving rise to a great number of pleasing ideas, and bewildering the imagination in delightful prospects; and, therefore, whatever speculations they may produce in those who have confined themselves to political studies, naturally fixed the attention, and excited the applause, of a poet. The politician, when he considers men driven into other countries for shelter, and obliged to retire to forests and deserts, and pass their lives and fix their posterity in the remotest corners of the world, to avoid those hardships which they suffer or fear in their native place, may very properly inquire, why the legislature does not provide a remedy for these miseries, rather than encourage an escape from them. He may conclude, that the flight of every honest man is a loss to the community; that those who are unhappy without guilt ought to be relieved; and the life, which is over-burdened by accidental calamities, set at ease by the care of the public; and that those, who have by misconduct forfeited their claim to favour, ought rather to be made useful to the society which they have injured, than be driven from it. But the poet is employed in a more pleasing undertaking than that of proposing laws, which, however just or expedient, will never be made, or endeavouring to reduce to rational schemes of government societies which were formed by chance, and are conducted by the private passions of those who preside in them. He guides the unhappy fugitive from want and persecution, to plenty, quiet, and security, and seats him in scenes of peaceful solitude, and undisturbed repose.

Savage has not forgotten, amidst the pleasing sentiments which this prospect of retirement suggested to him, to censure those crimes which have been generally committed by the discoverers of new regions, and to expose the enormous wickedness of making war upon barbarous nations[31] because they cannot resist, and of invading countries because they are fruitful; of extending navigation only to propagate vice, and of visiting distant lands only to lay them waste. He has asserted the natural equality of mankind, and endeavoured to suppress that pride which inclines men to imagine that right is the consequence of power.

His description of the various miseries which force men to seek for refuge in distant countries, affords another instance of his proficiency in the important and extensive study of human life; and the tenderness with which he recounts them, another proof of his humanity and benevolence.

It is observable, that the close of this poem discovers a change which experience had made in Mr Savage's opinions. In a poem written by him in his youth, and published in his *Miscellanies*, he declares his contempt of the contracted views and narrow prospects of the middle state of life, and declares his resolution either to tower like the cedar, or be trampled like the shrub; but in this poem, though addressed to a prince, he mentions this state of life as comprising those who ought most to attract reward, those who merit most the confidence of power, and the familiarity of greatness; and, accidentally mentioning this passage to one of his friends, declared, that in his opinion all the virtue of mankind was comprehended in that state.

In describing villas and gardens, he did not omit to condemn that absurd custom which prevails among the English, of permitting servants to receive money from strangers for the entertainment that they receive, and therefore inserted in his poem these lines:

> But what the flowering pride of gardens rare,
> However royal, or however fair,
> If gates, which to access should still give way,
> Ope but, like Peter's paradise, for pay?
> If perquisited varlets frequent stand,
> And each new walk must a new tax demand?
> What foreign eye but with contempt surveys?
> What Muse shall from oblivion snatch their praise?

But before the publication of his performance he recollected, that the Queen allowed her garden and cave at Richmond to be shown for money, and that she so openly countenanced the practice, that she had bestowed the privilege of showing them as a place of profit on a man, whose merit she valued herself upon rewarding, though she gave him only the liberty of disgracing his country.

He therefore thought, with more prudence than was often exerted by him, that the publication of these lines might be officiously represented as an insult upon the Queen, to whom he owed his life and his subsistence; and that the propriety of his observation would be no security against the censures which the unseasonableness of it might draw upon him; he therefore suppressed the passage in the first edition, but after the Queen's death thought the same caution no longer necessary, and restored it to the proper place.

The poem was therefore published without any political faults, and inscribed to the Prince; but Mr Savage, having no friend upon whom he could prevail to present it to him, had no other method of attracting his observation than the publication of frequent advertisements, and therefore received no reward from his patron, however generous on other occasions.

This disappointment he never mentioned without indignation, being by some means or other confident that the Prince was not ignorant of his address to him; and insinuated, that, if any advances in popularity could have been made by distinguishing him, he had not written without notice, or without reward.

He was once inclined to have presented his poem in person, and sent to the printer for a copy with that design; but either his opinion changed, or his resolution deserted him, and he continued to resent neglect without attempting to force himself into regard.

Nor was the public much more favourable than his patron, for only seventy-two were sold, though the performance was much commended by some whose judgement in that kind of writing is generally allowed. But Savage easily reconciled himself to mankind without imputing any defect to his work, by observing that his poem was unluckily published two days after the prorogation of the parliament, and by consequence at a time when all those who could be expected to regard it were in the hurry of preparing for their departure, or engaged in taking leave of others upon their dismission from public affairs.

It must be however allowed, in justification of the public, that this performance is not the most excellent of Mr Savage's works; and that, though it cannot be denied to contain many striking sentiments, majestic lines, and just observations, it is in general not sufficiently polished in the language, or enlivened in the imagery, or digested in the plan.

Thus his poem contributed nothing to the alleviation of his poverty, which was such as very few could have supported with equal patience; but to which it must likewise be confessed, that few would have been exposed who received punctually fifty pounds a year; a salary which, though by no means equal to the demands of vanity and luxury, is yet found sufficient to support families above want, and was undoubtedly more than the necessities of life require.

But no sooner had he received his pension, than he withdrew to his darling privacy, from which he returned in a short time to his former distress, and for some part of the year generally lived by chance, eating only when he was invited to the tables of his acquaintances, from which the meanness of his dress often excluded him, when the politeness and variety of his conversation would have been thought a sufficient recompense for his entertainment.

He lodged as much by accident as he dined, and passed the night sometimes in mean houses, which are set open at night to any casual wanderers, sometimes in cellars, among the riot and filth of the meanest and most profligate of the rabble; and sometimes, when he had not money to support even the expenses of these receptacles, walked about the streets till he was weary, and lay down in the summer upon a bulk,[32] or in the winter, with his associates in poverty, among the ashes of a glass-house.

In this manner were passed those days and those nights which nature had enabled him to have employed in elevated speculations, useful studies, or pleasing conversation. On a bulk, in a cellar, or in a glass-house among thieves and beggars, was to be found the author of *The Wanderer*, the man of exalted sentiments, extensive views, and curious observations; the man whose remarks on life might have assisted the statesman, whose ideas of virtue might have enlightened the moralist, whose eloquence might have influenced senates, and whose delicacy might have polished courts.

It cannot but be imagined that such necessities might sometimes force him upon disreputable practices: and it is probable that these lines in *The Wanderer* were occasioned by his reflections on his own conduct:

> Though misery leads to happiness, and truth,
> Unequal to the load, this languid youth,
> (O, let none censure, if, untried by grief,
> If, amidst woe, untempted by relief,)
> He stoop'd reluctant to low arts of shame,
> Which then, ev'n then, he scorn'd, and blush'd to name.

Whoever was acquainted with him was certain to be solicited for small sums, which the frequency of the request made in time considerable, and he was therefore quickly shunned by those who were become familiar enough to be trusted with his necessities; but his rambling manner of life, and constant appearance at houses of public resort, always procured him a new succession of friends, whose kindness had not been exhausted by repeated requests; so that he was seldom absolutely without resources, but had in his utmost exigences this comfort, that he always imagined himself sure of speedy relief.

It was observed, that he always asked favours of this kind without the least submission or apparent consciousness of dependence, and that he did not seem to look upon a compliance with his request as an obligation that deserved any extraordinary acknowledgements; but a refusal was resented by him as an affront, or complained of as an injury; nor did he readily reconcile himself to those who either denied to lend, or gave him afterwards any intimation that they expected to be repaid.

He was sometimes so far compassionated by those who knew both his merit and distresses, that they received him into their families, but they soon discovered him to be a very incommodious inmate; for, being always accustomed to an irregular manner of life he could not confine himself to any stated hours, or pay any regard to the rules of a family, but would prolong his conversation till midnight, without considering that business might require his friend's application in the morning; and, when he had persuaded himself to retire to bed, was not, without equal difficulty, called up to dinner; it was therefore impossible to pay him any distinction without the entire subversion of all economy, a kind of establishment which, wherever he went, he always appeared ambitious to overthrow.

It must therefore be acknowledged, in justification of mankind, that it was not always by the negligence or coldness of his friends that Savage was distressed, but because it was in reality very difficult to preserve him long in a state of ease. To supply him with money was a hopeless attempt; for no sooner did he see himself master of a sum sufficient to set him free from care for a day, than he became profuse and luxurious. When once he had entered a tavern, or engaged in a scheme of pleasure, he never retired till want of money obliged him to some new expedient. If he was entertained in a family, nothing was any longer to be regarded there but amusements and jollity; wherever Savage entered, he immediately expected that order and business should fly before him, that all should thenceforward be left to hazard, and that no dull principle of domestic management should be opposed to his inclination, or intrude upon his gaiety.

His distresses, however afflictive, never dejected him; in his lowest state he wanted not spirit to assert the natural dignity of wit, and was always ready to repress that insolence which the superiority of fortune incited, and to trample on that reputation which rose upon any other basis than that of merit: he never admitted any gross familiarities, or su mitted to be treated otherwise than as an equal. Once, when he was without lodging, meat, or clothes, one of his friends, a man not indeed remarkable for moderation in his prosperity, left a message, that he desired to see him about nine in the morning. Savage knew that his intention was to assist him; but was very much disgusted that he should presume to prescribe the hour of his attendance, and, I believe, refused to visit him, and rejected his kindness.

The same invincible temper, whether firmness or obstinacy, appeared in his conduct to the Lord Tyrconnel, from whom he very frequently demanded, that the allowance which was once paid him should be restored; but with whom he never appeared to entertain for a moment the thought of soliciting a reconciliation, and whom he treated at once with all the haughtiness of superiority, and all the bitterness of resentment. He wrote to him, not in a style of supplication or respect,[33] but of reproach, menace, and contempt; and appeared determined, if he ever regained his allowance, to hold it only by the right of conquest.

As many more can discover, that a man is richer than that he is wiser than themselves, superiority of understanding is not so readily acknowledged as that of fortune; nor is that haughtiness, which the consciousness of great abilities incites, borne with the same submission as the tyranny of affluence; and therefore Savage, by asserting his claim to deference and regard, and by treating those with contempt whom better fortune animated to rebel against him, did not fail to raise a great number of enemies in the different classes of mankind. Those who thought themselves raised above him by the advantages of riches, hated him because they found no protection from the petulance of his wit.[34] Those who were esteemed for their writings feared him as a critic, and maligned him as a rival, and almost all the smaller wits were his professed enemies.

Among these Mr Miller so far indulged his resentment as to introduce him in a farce, and direct him to be personated on the stage, in a dress like that which he then wore; a mean insult, which only insinuated that Savage had but one coat, and which was therefore despised by him rather than resented; for though he wrote a lampoon against Miller, he never printed it: and as no other person ought to prosecute that revenge from which the person who was injured desisted, I shall not preserve what Mr Savage suppressed: of which the publication would indeed have been a punishment too severe for so impotent an assault.

The great hardships of poverty were to Savage not the want of lodging or of food, but the neglect and contempt which it drew upon him. He complained, that as his affairs grew desperate, he found his reputation for capacity visibly decline; that his opinion in questions of criticism was no longer regarded, when his coat was out of fashion; and that those who, in the interval of his prosperity, were always encouraging him to great undertakings by encomiums on his genius and assurances of success, now received any mention of his designs with coldness, thought that the subjects on which he proposed to write were very difficult, and were ready to inform him, that the event of a poem was uncertain, that an author ought to employ much time in the consideration of his plan, and not presume to sit down to write in confidence of a few cursory ideas, and a superficial knowledge; difficulties were started on all sides, and he was no longer qualified for any performance but *The Volunteer Laureat*.

Yet even this kind of contempt never depressed him; for he always preserved a steady confidence in his own capacity, and believed nothing above his reach which he should at any time earnestly endeavour to attain. He formed schemes of the same kind with regard to knowledge and to fortune, and flattered himself with advances to be made in science, as with riches, to be enjoyed in some distant period of his life. For the acquisition of knowledge he was indeed far better qualified than for that of riches; for he was naturally inquisitive and desirous of the conversation of those from whom any information was to be obtained, but by no means solicitous to improve those opportunities that were sometimes offered of raising his fortune; and he was remarkably retentive of his ideas, which, when once he was in possession of them, rarely forsook him; a quality which could never be communicated to his money.

While he was thus wearing out his life in expectation that the Queen would some time recollect her promise, he had recourse to the usual practice of writers, and published proposals for printing his works by subscription, to which he was encouraged by the success of many who had not a better right to the favour of the public; but, whatever was the reason, he did not find the world equally inclined to favour him; and he observed with some discontent, that, though he offered his works at half a guinea, he was able to procure but a small number in comparison with those who subscribed twice as much to Duck.[35]

Nor was it without indignation that he saw his proposals neglected by the Queen, who patronized Mr Duck's with uncommon ardour, and incited a competition among those who attended the court, who should most promote his interest, and who should first offer a subscription. This was a distinction to which Mr Savage made no scruple of asserting that his birth, his misfortunes, and his genius, gave a fairer title, than could be pleaded by him on whom it was conferred.

Savage's applications were, however, not universally unsuccessful; for some of the nobility countenanced his design, encouraged his proposals, and subscribed with great liberality. He related of the Duke of Chandos particularly, that, upon receiving his proposals, he sent him ten guineas.

But the money which his subscriptions afforded him was not less volatile than that which he received from his other schemes; whenever a subscription was paid him, he went to a tavern; and, as money so collected is necessarily received in small sums, he never was able to send his poems to the press, but for many years continued his solicitation, and squandered whatever he obtained.

This project of printing his works was frequently revived; and, as his proposals grew obsolete, new ones were printed with fresher dates. To form schemes for the publication was one of his favourite amusements; nor was he ever more at ease than when, with any friend who readily fell in with his schemes, he was adjusting the print, forming the advertisements, and regulating the dispersion of his new edition, which he really intended some time to publish, and which, as long as experience had shown him the impossibility of printing the volume together, he at last determined to divide into weekly or monthly numbers, that the profits of the first might supply the expenses of the next.

Thus, he spent his time in mean expedients and tormenting suspense, living for the greatest part in fear of prosecutions from his creditors, and consequently skulking in obscure parts of the town, of which he was no stranger to the remotest corners. But wherever he came, his address secured him friends, whom his necessities soon alienated; so that he had perhaps a more numerous acquaintance than any man ever before attained, there being scarcely any person eminent on any account to whom he was not known, or whose character he was not in some degree able to delineate.

To the acquisition of this extensive acquaintance every circumstance of his life contributed. He excelled in the arts of conversation, and therefore willingly practised them. He had seldom any home, or even a lodging in which he could be private; and therefore was driven into public-houses for the common conveniences of life and supports of nature. He was always ready to comply with every invitation, having no employment to withhold him, and often no money to provide for himself; and by dining with one company, he never failed of obtaining an introduction into another.

Thus dissipated was his life, and thus casual his subsistence; yet did not the distraction of his views hinder him from reflection, nor the uncertainty of his condition depress his gaiety. When he had wandered about without any fortunate adventure by which he was led into a tavern, he sometimes retired into the fields, and was able to employ his mind in study, or amuse it with pleasing imaginations; and seldom appeared to be melancholy, but when some sudden misfortune had just fallen upon him, and even then in a few moments he would disentangle himself from his perplexity, adopt the subject of conversation, and apply his mind wholly to the objects that others presented to it.

Samuel Johnson

This life, unhappy as it may be already imagined, was yet embittered, in 1738, with new calamities. The death of the Queen deprived him of all the prospects of preferment with which he so long entertained his imagination; and, as Sir Robert Walpole had before given him reason to believe that he never intended the performance of his promise, he was now abandoned again to fortune.

He was however, at that time, supported by a friend; and as it was not his custom to look out for distant calamities, or to feel any other pain than that which forced itself upon his senses, he was not much afflicted at his loss, and perhaps comforted himself that his pension would be now continued without the annual tribute of a panegyric.

Another expectation contributed likewise to support him: he had taken a resolution to write a second tragedy upon the story of Sir Thomas Overbury, in which he preserved a few lines of the former play, but made a total alteration of the plan, added new incidents, and introduced new characters; so that it was a new tragedy, not a revival of the former.

Many of his friends blamed him for not making choice of another subject; but, in vindication of himself, he asserted, that it was not easy to find a better; and that he thought it his interest to extinguish the memory of the first tragedy, which he could only do by writing one less defective upon the same story; by which he should entirely defeat the artifice of the booksellers, who, after the death of any author of reputation, are always industrious to swell his works, by uniting his worst productions with his best.

In the execution of this scheme, however, he proceeded but slowly, and probably only employed himself upon it when he could find no other amusement; but he pleased himself with counting the profits, and perhaps imagined, that the theatrical reputation which he was about to acquire, would be equivalent to all that he had lost by the death of his patroness.

He did not, in confidence of his approaching riches, neglect the measures proper to secure the continuance of his pension, though some of his favourers thought him culpable for omitting to write on her death; but on her birthday next year, he gave a proof of the solidity of his judgement, and the power of his genius. He knew that the track of elegy had been so long beaten, that it was impossible to travel in it without treading in the footsteps of those who had gone before him; and that therefore it was necessary, that he might distinguish himself from the herd of encomiasts, to find out some new walk of funeral panegyric.

This difficult task he performed in such a manner, that his poem may be justly ranked among the best pieces that the death of princes has produced. By transferring the mention of her death to her birthday, he has formed a happy combination of topics, which any other man would have thought it very difficult to connect in one view, but which he has united in such a manner, that the relation between them appears natural; and it may be justly said, that what no other man would have thought on, it now appears scarcely possible for any man to miss.

The beauty of this peculiar combination of images is so masterly, that it is sufficient to set this poem above censure; and therefore it is not necessary to mention many other delicate touches which may be found in it, and which would deservedly be admired in any other performance.

To these proofs of his genius may be added, from the same poem, an instance of his prudence, an excellence for which he was not so often distinguished; he does not forget to remind the King, in the most delicate and artful manner, of continuing his pension.

With regard to the success of his address, he was for some time in suspense, but was in no great degree solicitous about it; and continued his labour upon his new tragedy with great tranquillity, till the friend who had for a considerable time supported him, removing his family to another place, took occasion to dismiss him. It then became necessary to inquire more diligently what was determined in his affair, having reason to suspect that no great favour was intended him, because he had not received his pension at the usual time.

It is said, that he did not take those methods of retrieving his interest, which were most likely to succeed; and some of those who were employed in the Exchequer, cautioned him against too much violence in his proceedings; but Mr Savage, who seldom regulated his conduct by the advice of others, gave way to his passion, and demanded of Sir Robert Walpole, at his levee, the reason of the distinction that was made between him and the other pensioners of the Queen, with a degree of roughness which perhaps determined him to withdraw what had been only delayed.

Whatever was the crime of which he was accused or suspected, and whatever influence was employed against him, he received soon after an account that took from him all hopes of regaining his pension; and he had now no prospect of subsistence but from his play, and he knew no way of living for the time required to finish it.

So peculiar were the misfortunes of this man, deprived of an estate and title by a particular law, exposed and abandoned by a mother, defrauded by a mother of a fortune which his father had allotted him, he entered the world without a friend; and though his abilities forced themselves into esteem and reputation, he was never able to obtain any real advantage, and whatever prospects arose were always intercepted as he began to approach them. The King's intentions in his favour were frustrated; his dedication to the Prince, whose generosity on every other occasion was eminent, procured him no reward; Sir Robert Walpole, who valued himself upon keeping his promise to others, broke it to him without regret; and the bounty of the Queen was, after her death, withdrawn from him, and from him only.

Such were his misfortunes, which yet he bore, not only with decency, but with cheerfulness; nor was his gaiety clouded even by his last disappointments, though he was in a short time reduced to the lowest degree of distress, and often wanted both lodging and food. At this time he gave another instance of the insurmountable obstinacy of his spirit: his clothes were worn out; and he received notice, that at a coffee-house some clothes and linen were left for him: the person who sent them did not, I believe, inform him to whom he was to be obliged, that he might spare the perplexity of acknowledging the benefit; but though the offer was so far generous, it was made with some neglect of ceremonies, which Mr Savage so much resented, that he refused the present, and declined to enter the house till the clothes that had been designed for him were taken away.

His distress was now publicly known, and his friends, therefore, thought it proper to concert some measures for his relief; and one of them wrote a letter to him,[36] in which he expressed his concern 'for the miserable withdrawing of his pension'; and gave him hopes, that in a short time he should find himself supplied with a competence, 'without any dependence on those little creatures which we are pleased to call the Great.'

The scheme proposed for this happy and independent subsistence, was, that he should retire into Wales, and receive an allowance of fifty pounds a year, to be raised by a subscription, on which he was to live privately in a cheap place, without aspiring any more to affluence, or having any farther care of reputation.

This offer Mr Savage gladly accepted, though with intentions very different from those of his friends; for they proposed that he should continue an exile from London for ever, and spend all the remaining part of his life at Swansea; but he designed only to take the opportunity, which their scheme offered him, of retreating for a short time, that he might prepare his play for the stage, and his other works for the press, and then to return to London to exhibit his tragedy, and live upon the profits of his own labour.

With regard to his works, he proposed very great improvements, which would have required much time, or great application; and when he had finished them, he designed to do justice to his subscribers by publishing them according to his proposals.

As he was ready to entertain himself with future pleasures, he had planned out a scheme of life for the country, of which he had no knowledge but from pastorals and songs. He imagined that he should be transported to scenes of flowery felicity,[37] like those which one poet has reflected to another; and had projected a perpetual round of innocent pleasures, of which he suspected no interruption from pride, or ignorance, or brutality.

With these expectations he was so enchanted, that when he was once gently reproached by a friend for submitting to live upon a subscription, and advised rather by a resolute exertion of his abilities to support himself, he could not bear to debar himself from the happiness which was to be found in the calm of a cottage, or lose the opportunity of listening, without intermission, to the melody of the nightingale, which he believed was to be heard from every bramble, and which he did not fail to mention as a very important part of the happiness of a country life.

While this scheme was ripening, his friends directed him to take a lodging in the liberties of the Fleet,[38] that he might be secure from his creditors, and sent him every Monday a guinea, which he commonly spent before the next morning, and trusted, after his usual manner, the remaining part of the week to the bounty of fortune.

He now began very sensibly to feel the miseries of dependence. Those by whom he was to be supported, began to prescribe to him with an air of authority, which he knew not how decently to resent, nor patiently to bear; and he soon discovered, from the conduct of most of his subscribers, that he was yet in the hands of 'little creatures'.

Of the insolence that he was obliged to suffer, he gave many instances, of which none appeared to raise his indignation to a greater height, than the method which was taken of furnishing him with clothes. Instead of consulting him, and allowing him to send a tailor his orders for what they thought proper to allow him, they proposed to send for a tailor to take his measure, and then to consult how they should equip him.

This treatment was not very delicate, nor was it such as Savage's humanity would have suggested to him on a like occasion; but it had scarcely deserved mention, had it not, by affecting him in an uncommon degree, shown the peculiarity of his character. Upon hearing the design that was formed, he came to the lodging of a friend with the most violent agonies of rage; and, being asked what it could be that gave him such disturbance, he replied with the utmost vehemence of indignation, 'That they had sent for a tailor to measure him.'

How the affair ended was never inquired, for fear of renewing his uneasiness. It is probable, that, upon recollection, he submitted with a good grace to what he could not avoid and that he discovered no resentment where he had no power.

He was, however, not humbled to implicit and universal compliance; for when the gentleman, who had first informed him of the design to support him by a subscription, attempted to procure a reconciliation with the Lord Tyrconnel, he could by no means be prevailed upon to comply with the measures that were proposed.

A letter was written for him[39] to Sir William Lemon, to prevail upon him to interpose his good offices with Lord Tyrconnel, in which he solicited Sir William's assistance 'for a man who really needed it as much as any man could well do'; and informed him, that he was retiring 'for ever to a place where he should no more trouble his relations, friends, or enemies'; he confessed, that his passion had betrayed him to some conduct with regard to Lord Tyrconnel, for which he could not but heartily ask his pardon; and as he imagined Lord Tyrconnel's passion might be yet so high, that he would not 'receive a letter from him', begged that Sir William would endeavour to soften him; and expressed his hopes that he would comply with his request, and that 'so small a relation would not harden his heart against him'.

That any man should presume to dictate a letter to him, was not very agreeable to Mr Savage; and therefore he was, before he had opened it, not much inclined to approve it. But when he read it, he found it contained sentiments entirely opposite to his own, and, as he asserted, to the truth; and therefore, instead of copying it, wrote his friend a letter full of masculine resentment and warm expostulations. He very justly observed, that the style was too supplicatory, and the representation too abject, and that he ought at least to have made him complain with 'the dignity of a gentleman in distress'. He declared that he would not write the paragraph in which he was to ask Lord Tyrconnel's pardon; for, 'he despised his pardon, and therefore could not heartily, and would not hypocritically, ask it'. He remarked, that his friend made a very unreasonable distinction between himself and him; for, says he, when you mention men of high rank 'in your own character', they are 'those little creatures whom we are pleased to call the Great'; but when you address them 'in mine', no servility is sufficiently humble. He then with great propriety explained the ill-consequences which might be expected from such a letter, which his relations would print in their own defence, and which would for ever be produced as a full answer to all that he should allege against them; for he always intended to publish a minute account of the treatment which he had received. It is to be remembered, to the honour of the gentleman by whom this letter was drawn up, that he yielded to Mr Savage's reasons, and agreed that it ought to be suppressed.

After many alterations and delays, a subscription was at length raised, which did not amount to fifty pounds a year, though twenty were paid by one gentleman; such was the generosity of mankind, that what had been done by a player without solicitation, could not now be effected by application and interest; and Savage had a great number to court and to obey for a pension less than that which Mrs Oldfield paid him without exacting any servilities.

Mr Savage however was satisfied, and willing to retire, and was convinced that the allowance, though scanty, would be more than sufficient for him, being now determined to commence a rigid economist, and to live according to the exactest rules of frugality; for nothing was in his opinion more contemptible than a man, who, when he knew his income, exceeded it; and yet he confessed, that instances of such folly were too common, and lamented that some men were not to be trusted with their own money.

Full of these salutary resolutions, he left London in July 1739, having taken leave with great tenderness of his friends, and parted from the author of this narrative[40] with tears in his eyes. He was furnished with fifteen guineas, and informed, that they would be sufficient not only for the expense of his journey, but for his support in Wales for some time; and that there remained but little more of the first collection. He promised a strict adherence to his maxims of parsimony, and went away in the stage-coach; nor did his friends expect to hear from him, till he informed them of his arrival at Swansea.

But when they least expected, arrived a letter dated the fourteenth day after his departure, in which he sent them word, that he was yet upon the road, and without money; and that he therefore could not proceed without a remittance. They then sent him the money that was in their hands, with which he was enabled to reach Bristol, from whence he was to go to Swansea by water.

At Bristol he found an embargo laid upon the shipping,[41] so that he could not immediately obtain a passage; and being therefore obliged to stay there some time, he with his usual felicity, ingratiated himself with many of the principal inhabitants, was invited to their houses, distinguished at their public feasts, and treated with a regard that gratified his vanity, and therefore easily engaged his affection.

He began very early after his retirement to complain of the conduct of his friends in London, and irritated many of them so much by his letters, that they withdrew, however honourably, their contributions; and it is believed, that little more was paid him than the twenty pounds a year, which were allowed him by the gentleman who proposed the subscription.

After some stay at Bristol he retired to Swansea, the place originally proposed for his residence, where he lived about a year, very much dissatisfied with the diminution of his salary; but contracted, as in other places, acquaintance with those who were most distinguished in that country, among whom he has celebrated Mr Powel and Mrs Jones, by some verses which he inserted in *The Gentleman's Magazine*.

Here he completed his tragedy, of which two acts were wanting when he left London, and was desirous of coming to town to bring it upon the stage. This design was very warmly opposed, and he was advised by his chief benefactor to put it into the hands of Mr Thomson and Mr Mallet, that it might be fitted for the stage, and to allow his friends to receive the profits, out of which an annual pension should be paid him.

This proposal he rejected with the utmost contempt. He was by no means convinced that the judgement of those, to whom he was required to submit, was superior to his own. He was now determined, as he expressed it, to be 'no longer kept in leading-strings', and had no elevated idea of 'his bounty, who proposed to pension him out of the profits of his own labours'.

He attempted in Wales to promote a subscription for his works, and had once hopes of success; but in a short time afterwards formed a resolution of leaving that part of the country, to which he thought it not reasonable to be confined for the gratification of those who, having promised him a liberal income, had no sooner banished him to a remote corner, than they reduced his allowance to a salary scarcely equal to the necessities of life.

His resentment of this treatment, which, in his own opinion at least, he had not deserved, was such, that he broke off all correspondence with most of his contributors, and appeared to consider them as persecutors and oppressors; and in the latter part of his life declared, that their conduct toward him, since his departure from London, 'had been perfidiousness improving on perfidiousness, and inhumanity on inhumanity'.

It is not to be supposed, that the necessities of Mr Savage did not sometimes incite him to satirical exaggerations of the behaviour of those by whom he thought himself reduced to them. But it must be granted, that the diminution of his allowance was a great hardship, and that those who withdrew their subscription from a man, who, upon the faith of their promise, had gone into a kind of banishment, and abandoned all those by whom he had been before relieved in his distresses, will find it no easy task to vindicate their conduct.

It may be alleged, and perhaps justly, that he was petulant and contemptuous; that he more frequently reproached his subscribers for not giving him more, than thanked them for what he received; but it is to be remembered, that his conduct, and this is the worst charge that can be drawn up against him, did them no real injury; and that it therefore ought rather to have been pitied than resented; at least, the resentment it might provoke ought to have been generous and manly; epithets which his conduct will hardly deserve that starves the man whom he has persuaded to put himself into his power.

It might have been reasonably demanded by Savage, that they

should, before they had taken away what they promised, have replaced him in his former state, that they should have taken no advantages from the situation to which the appearance of their kindness had reduced him, and that he should have been recalled to London before he was abandoned. He might justly represent, that he ought to have been considered as a lion in the toils, and demand to be released before the dogs should be loosed upon him.

He endeavoured, indeed, to release himself, and, with an intent to return to London, went to Bristol, where a repetition of the kindness which he had formerly found invited him to stay. He was not only caressed and treated, but had a collection made for him of about thirty pounds, with which it had been happy if he had immediately departed for London; but his negligence did not suffer him to consider, that such proofs of kindness were not often to be expected, and that this ardour of benevolence was in a great degree the effect of novelty, and might, probably, be every day less; and therefore he took no care to improve the happy time, but was encouraged by one favour to hope for another, till at length generosity was exhausted, and officiousness wearied.

Another part of his misconduct was the practice of prolonging his visits to unseasonable hours, and disconcerting all the families into which he was admitted. This was an error in a place of commerce which all the charms of his conversation could not compensate; for what trader would purchase such airy satisfaction by the loss of solid gain, which must be the consequence of midnight merriment, as those hours which were gained at night were generally lost in the morning?

Thus Mr Savage, after the curiosity of the inhabitants was gratified, found the number of his friends daily decreasing, perhaps without suspecting for what reason their conduct was altered; for he still continued to harass, with his nocturnal intrusions, those that yet countenanced him, and admitted him to their houses.

But he did not spend all the time of his residence at Bristol in visits or at taverns, for he sometimes returned to his studies, and began several considerable designs. When he felt an inclination to write, he always retired from the knowledge of his friends, and lay hid in an obscure part of the suburbs, till he found himself again desirous of company, to which it is likely that intervals of absence made him more welcome.

He was always full of his design of returning to London, to bring his tragedy upon the stage; but, having neglected to depart with the money that was raised for him, he could not afterwards procure a sum sufficient to defray the expenses of his journey; nor perhaps would a fresh supply have had any other effect, than, by putting immediate pleasures in his power, to have driven the thoughts of his journey out of his mind.

While he was thus spending the day in contriving a scheme for the morrow, distress stole upon him by imperceptible degrees. His conduct had already wearied some of those who were at first enamoured of his conversation; but he might, perhaps, still have devolved to others, whom he might have entertained with equal success, had not the decay of his clothes made it no longer consistent with their vanity to admit him to their tables, or to associate with him in public places. He now began to find every man from home at whose house he called; and was therefore no longer able to procure the necessaries of life, but wandered about the town, slighted and neglected, in quest of a dinner, which he did not always obtain.

To complete his misery, he was pursued by the officers for small debts which he had contracted; and was therefore obliged to withdraw from the small number of friends from whom he had still reason to hope for favours. His custom was to lie in bed the greatest part of the day, and to go out in the dark with the utmost privacy, and after having paid his visit return again before morning to his lodging, which was in the garret of an obscure inn.

Being thus excluded on one hand, and confined on the other, he suffered the utmost extremities of poverty, and often fasted so long that he was seized with faintness, and had lost his appetite, not being able to bear the smell of meat, till the action of his stomach was restored by a cordial.

In this distress, he received a remittance of five pounds from London, with which he provided himself a decent coat, and determined to go to London, but unhappily spent his money at a favourite tavern. Thus was he again confined to Bristol, where he was every day hunted by bailiffs. In this exigence he once more found a friend, who sheltered him in his house, though at the usual inconveniences with which his company was attended; for he could neither be persuaded to go to bed in the night, nor to rise in the day.

It is observable, that in these various scenes of misery, he was always disengaged and cheerful: he at some times pursued his studies, and at others continued or enlarged his epistolary correspondence; nor was he ever so far dejected as to endeavour to procure an increase of his allowance by any other methods than accusations and reproaches.

He had now no longer any hopes of assistance from his friends at Bristol, who as merchants, and by consequence sufficiently studious of profit, cannot be supposed to have looked with much compassion upon negligence and extravagance, or to think any excellence equivalent to a fault of such consequence as neglect of economy. It is natural to imagine, that many of those, who would have relieved his real wants, were discouraged from the exertion of their benevolence by observation of the use which was made of their favours, and conviction that relief would only be momentary, and that the same necesssity would quickly return.

At last he quitted the house of his friend, and returned to his lodging at the inn, still intending to set out in a few days for London; but on the 10th of January, 1742–3, having been at supper with two of his friends, he was at his return to his lodgings arrested for a debt of about eight pounds, which he owed at a coffee-house, and conducted to the house of a sheriff's officer. The account which he gives of this misfortune, in a letter to one of the gentlemen with whom he had supped, is too remarkable to be omitted.

It was not a little unfortunate for me, that I spent yesterday's evening with you; because the hour hindered me from entering on my new lodging; however, I have now got one, but such an one as I believe nobody would choose.

I was arrested at the suit of Mrs Read, just as I was going up stairs to bed, at Mr Bowyer's; but taken in so private a manner, that I believe nobody at the White Lion is apprised of it. Though I let the officers know the strength (or rather weakness) of my pocket, yet they treated me with the utmost civility; and even when they conducted me to confinement, it was in such a manner, that I verily believe I could have escaped, which I would rather be ruined than have done, notwithstanding the whole amount of my finances was but threepence half-penny.

In the first place I must insist, that you will industriously conceal this from Mrs S — s, because I would not have her good-nature suffer that pain, which, I know, she would be apt to feel on this occasion.

Next, I conjure you, dear Sir, by all the ties of friendship, by no means to have one uneasy thought on my account; but to have the same pleasantry of countenance, and unruffled serenity of mind, which (God be praised!) I have in this, and have had in a much severer calamity. Furthermore, I charge you, if you value my friendship as truly I do yours, not to utter, or even harbour, the least resentment against Mrs Read. I believe she has ruined me, but I freely forgive her; and (though I will never more have any intimacy with her) I would, at a due distance, rather do her an act of good, than ill will. Lastly (pardon the expression), I absolutely command you not to offer me any pecuniary assistance, nor to attempt getting me any from any one of your friends. At another time, or on any other occasion, you may, dear friend, be well assured, I would rather write to you in the submissive style of a request, than that of a peremptory command.

However, that my truly valuable friend may not think I am too proud to ask a favour, let me entreat you to let me have your boy to attend me for this day, not only for the sake of saving me the expense of porters, but for the delivery of some letters to people whose names I would not have known to strangers.

The civil treatment I have thus far met from those whose prisoner I am, makes me thankful to the Almighty, that, though he has thought fit to visit me (on my birth-night) with affliction, yet (such is his great goodness!) my affliction is not without alleviating circumstances. I murmur not; but am all resignation to the divine will. As to the world, I hope that I shall be endued by Heaven with that presence of mind, that serene dignity in misfortune, that constitutes the character of a true nobleman; a dignity far beyond that of coronets; a nobility arising from the just principles of philosophy, refined and exalted by those of christianity.

He continued five days at the officer's, in hopes that he should be able to procure bail, and avoid the necessity of going to prison. The state in which he passed his time, and the treatment which he received, are very justly expressed by him in a letter which he wrote to a friend: 'The whole day,' says he, 'has been employed in various people's filling my head with their foolish chimerical systems, which had obliged me coolly (as far as nature will admit) to digest, and accommodate myself to, every different person's way of thinking; hurried from one wild system to another, till it has quite made a chaos of my imagination, and nothing done – promised – disappointed – ordered to send, every hour, from one part of the town to the other.'

When his friends, who had hitherto caressed and applauded, found that to give bail and pay the debt was the same, they all refused to preserve him from a prison at the expense of eight pounds; and therefore, after having been for some time at the officer's house, 'at an immense expense,' as he observes in his letter, he was at length removed to Newgate.

This expense he was enabled to support by the generosity of Mr Nash at Bath,[42] who, upon receiving from him an account of his condition, immediately sent him five guineas, and promised to promote his subscription at Bath with all his interest.

By his removal to Newgate, he obtained at least a freedom from suspense, and rest from the disturbing vicissitudes of hope and disappointment; he now found that his friends were only companions, who were willing to share his gaiety, but not to partake of his misfortunes; and therefore he no longer expected any assistance from them.

It must, however, be observed of one gentleman, that he offered to release him by paying the debt; but that Mr Savage would not consent, I suppose because he thought he had before been too burthensome to him.

He was offered by some of his friends, that a collection should be made for his enlargement; but he 'treated the proposal,' and declared, 'he should again treat it, with disdain. As to writing any mendicant letters, he had too high a spirit, and determined only to write to some ministers of state, to try to regain his pension.'

He continued to complain of those that had sent him into the country, and objected to them, that he had 'lost the profits of his play, which had been finished three years'; and in another letter declares his resolution to publish a pamphlet, that the world might know how 'he had been used'.

This pamphlet was never written; for he in a very short time recovered his usual tranquillity, and cheerfully applied himself to more inoffensive studies. He indeed steadily declared, that he was promised a yearly allowance of fifty pounds, and never received half the sum; but he seemed to resign himself to that as well as to other misfortunes, and lose the remembrance of it in his amusements and employments.

The cheerfulness with which he bore his confinement, appears from the following letter, which he wrote, January the 30th, to one of his friends in London:

'I now write to you from my confinement in Newgate, where I have been ever since Monday last was se'nnight,[43] and where I enjoy myself with much more tranquillity than I have known for upwards of a twelvemonth past; having a room entirely to myself, and pursuing the amusement of my poetical studies, uninterrupted, and agreeable to my mind. I thank the Almighty, I am now all collected in myself; and, though my person is in confinement, my mind can expatiate on ample and useful subjects with all the freedom imaginable. I am now more conversant with the Nine than ever; and if instead of a Newgate-bird, I may be allowed to be a bird of the Muses, I assure you Sir, I sing very freely in my cage; sometimes indeed in the plaintive notes of the nightingale; but, at others, in the cheerful strains of the lark.'

In another letter he observes, that he ranges from one subject to another, without confining himself to any particular task, and that he was employed one week upon one attempt, and the next upon another.

Surely the fortitude of this man deserves, at least, to be mentioned with applause; and, whatever faults may be imputed to him, the virtue of suffering well cannot be denied him. The two powers which, in the opinion of Epictetus, constituted a wise man, are those of bearing and forbearing, which cannot indeed be affirmed to have been equally possessed by Savage; and indeed the want of one obliged him very frequently to practise the other.

He was treated by Mr Dagg, the keeper of the prison, with great humanity; was supported by him at his own table without any certainty of recompense; had a room to himself, to which he could at any time retire from all disturbance; was allowed to stand at the door of the prison, and sometimes taken out into the fields; so that he suffered fewer hardships in prison than he had been accustomed to undergo in the greatest part of his life.

The keeper did not confine his benevolence to a gentle execution of his office, but made some overtures to the creditor for his release, though without effect; and continued, during the whole time of his imprisonment, to treat him with the utmost tenderness and civility.

Virtue is undoubtedly most laudable in that state which makes it most difficult; and therefore the humanity of a gaoler certainly deserves this public attestation; and the man, whose heart has not been hardened by such an employment, may be justly proposed as a pattern of benevolence. If an inscription was once engraved 'to the honest toll-gatherer,' less honours ought not to be paid 'to the tender gaoler.'

Mr Savage very frequently received visits, and sometimes presents from his acquaintances: but they did not amount to a subsistence, for the greater part of which he was indebted to the generosity of this keeper; but these favours, however they might endear to him the particular persons from whom he received them, were very far from impressing upon his mind any advantageous ideas of the people of Bristol, and therefore he thought he could not more properly employ himself in prison, than in writing a poem called *London and Bristol delineated*.

When he had brought this poem to its present state, which, without considering the chasm, is not perfect, he wrote to London an account of his design, and informed his friend, that he was determined to print it with his name; but enjoined him not to communicate his intention to his Bristol acquaintance. The gentleman, surprised at his resolution, endeavoured to dissuade him from publishing it, at least from prefixing his name; and declared, that he could not reconcile the injunction of secrecy with his resolution to own it at its first appearance. To this Mr Savage returned an answer agreeable to his character in the following terms:

I received yours this morning; and not without a little surprise at the contents. To answer a question with a question, you ask me concerning London and Bristol, Why will I add delineated? Why did Mr Woolaston add the same word to his *Religion of Nature?* I suppose that it was his will and pleasure to add it in his case; and it is mine to do so in my own. You are pleased to tell me, that you understand not why secrecy is enjoined, and yet I intend to set my name to it. My answer is – I have my private reasons, which I am not obliged to explain to any one. You doubt my friend Mr S – would not approve of it – And what is it to me whether he does or not? Do you imagine that Mr S – is to dictate to me! If any man who calls himself my friend should assume such an air, I would spurn at his friendship with contempt. You say, I seem to think so by not letting him know it – And suppose I do, what then? Perhaps I can give reasons for that disapprobation, very foreign from what you would imagine. You go on in saying, Suppose I should not put my name to it – My answer is, that I will not suppose any such thing, being determined to the contrary: neither, Sir, would I have you suppose, that I applied to you for want of another press: nor would I have you imagine, that I owe Mr S – obligations which I do not.

Such was his imprudence, and such his obstinate adherence to his own resolutions, however absurd. A prisoner! supported by charity! and, whatever insults he might have received during the latter part of his stay at Bristol, once caressed, esteemed, and presented with a liberal collection, he could forget on a sudden his danger and his obligations, to gratify the petulance of his wit, or the eagerness of his resentment, and publish a satire, by which he might reasonably expect that he should alienate those who then supported him, and provoke those whom he could neither resist nor escape.

This resolution, from the execution of which it is probable that only his death could have hindered him, is sufficient to show, how much he disregarded all considerations that opposed his present passions, and how readily he hazarded all future advantages for any immediate gratifications. Whatever was his predominant inclination, neither hope nor fear hindered him from complying with it; nor had opposition any other effect than to heighten his ardour, and irritate his vehemence.

This performance was however laid aside, while he was employed in soliciting assistance from several great persons; and one interruption succeeding another, hindered him from supplying the chasm, and perhaps from retouching the other parts, which he can hardly be imagined to have finished in his own opinion; for it is very unequal, and some of the lines are rather inserted to rhyme to others, than to support or improve the sense; but the first and last parts are worked up with great spirit and elegance.

His time was spent in the prison for the most part in study, or in receiving visits; but sometimes he descended to lower amusements, and diverted himself in the kitchen with the conversation of the criminals; for it was not pleasing to him to be much without company; and though he was very capable of a judicious choice, he was often contented with the first that offered; for this he was sometimes reproved by his friends, who found him surrounded with felons; but the reproof was on that, as on other occasions, thrown away; he continued to gratify himself, and to set very little value on the opinion of others.

But here, as in every other scene of his life, he made use of such opportunities as occurred of benefiting those who were more miserable than himself, and was always ready to perform any office of humanity to his fellow-prisoners.

He had now ceased from corresponding with any of his subscribers except one,[44] who yet continued to remit him the twenty pounds a year which he had promised him, and by whom it was expected that he would have been in a very short time enlarged, because he had directed the keeper to inquire after the state of his debts.

However, he took care to enter his name according to the forms of the court, that the creditor might be obliged to make him some allowance, if he was continued a prisoner, and when on that occasion he appeared in the hall was treated with very unusual respect.

But the resentment of the city was afterwards raised by some accounts that had been spread of the satire, and he was informed that some of the merchants intended to pay the allowance which the law required, and to detain him a prisoner at their own expense. This he treated as an empty menace; and perhaps might have hastened the publication, only to show how much he was superior to their insults, had not all his schemes been suddenly destroyed.

When he had been six months in prison, he received from one of his friends,[45] in whose kindness he had the greatest confidence, and on whose assistance he chiefly depended, a letter, that contained a charge of very atrocious ingratitude, drawn up in such terms as sudden resentment dictated. Henley, in one of his advertisements, had mentioned *Pope's treatment of Savage.* This was supposed by Pope to be the consequence of a complaint made by Savage to Henley, and was therefore mentioned by him with much resentment. Mr Savage returned a very solemn protestation of his innocence, but however appeared much disturbed at the accusation. Some days afterwards he was seized with a pain in his back and side, which, as it was not violent, was not suspected to be dangerous; but growing daily more languid and dejected, on the 25th of July he confined himself to his room, and a fever seized his spirits. The symptoms grew every day more formidable, but his condition did not enable him to procure any assistance. The last time that the keeper saw him was on July the 31st, 1743; when Savage, seeing him at his bed-side, said, with an uncommon earnestness, 'I have something to say to you, Sir'; but, after a pause, moved his hand in a melancholy manner; and, finding himself unable to recollect what he was going to communicate, said, ''Tis gone!' The keeper soon after left him; and the next morning he died. He was buried in the churchyard of St Peter, at the expense of the keeper.

Such were the life and death of Richard Savage, a man equally distinguished by his virtues and vices; and at once remarkable for his weaknesses and abilities.

He was of a middle stature, of a thin habit of body, a long visage, coarse features, and melancholy aspect; of a grave and manly deportment, a solemn dignity of mien; but which, upon a nearer acquaintance, softened into an engaging easiness of manners. His walk was slow, and his voice tremulous and mournful. He was easily excited to smiles, but very seldom provoked to laughter.

His mind was in an uncommon degree vigorous and active.[46] His judgement was accurate, his apprehension quick, and his memory so tenacious, that he was frequently observed to know what he had learned from others in a short time, better than those by whom he was informed; and could frequently recollect incidents, with all their combination of circumstances, which few would have regarded at the present time, but which the quickness of his apprehension impressed upon him. He had the peculiar felicity, that his attention never deserted him; he was present to every object, and regardful of the most trifling occurrences. He had the art of escaping from his own reflections, and accommodating himself to every new scene.

To this quality is to be imputed the extent of his knowledge, compared with the small time which he spent in visible endeavours to acquire it. He mingled in cursory conversation with the same steadiness of attention as others apply to a lecture; and, amidst the appearance of thoughtless gaiety, lost no new idea that was started, nor any hint that could be improved. He had therefore made in coffee-houses the same proficiency as others in their closets: and it is remarkable, that the writings of a man of little education and little reading have an air of learning scarcely to be found in any other performances, but which perhaps as often obscures as embellishes them.

His judgement was eminently exact both with regard to writings and to men. The knowledge of life was indeed his chief attainment; and it is not without some satisfaction, that I can produce the suffrage of Savage in favour of human nature, of which he never appeared to entertain such odious ideas as some, who perhaps had neither his judgement nor experience, have published, either in ostentation of their sagacity, vindication of their crimes, or gratification of their malice.

His method of life particularly qualified him for conversation, of which he knew how to practise all the graces. He was never vehement or loud, but at once modest and easy, open and respectful; his language was vivacious or elegant, and equally happy upon grave and humorous subjects. He was generally censured for not knowing when to retire; but that was not the defect of his judgement, but of his fortune; when he left his company, he was frequently to spend the remaining part of the night in the street, or at least was abandoned to gloomy reflections, which it is not strange that he delayed as long as he could; and sometimes forgot that he gave others pain to avoid it himself.

It cannot be said, that he made use of his abilities for the direction of his own conduct: an irregular and dissipated manner of life had made him the slave of every passion that happened to be excited by the presence of its object, and that slavery to his passions reciprocally produced a life irregular and dissipated. He was not master of his own motions, nor could promise any thing for the next day.

With regard to his economy, nothing can be added to the relation of his life. He appeared to think himself born to be supported by others, and dispensed from all necessity of providing for himself; he therefore never prosecuted any scheme of advantage, nor endeavoured even to secure the profits which his writings might have afforded him. His temper was, in consequence of the dominion of his passions, uncertain and capricious: he was easily engaged and easily disgusted; but he is accused of retaining his hatred more tenaciously than his benevolence.

He was compassionate both by nature and principle, and always ready to perform offices of humanity; but when he was provoked (and very small offences were sufficient to provoke him), he would prosecute his revenge with the utmost acrimony till his passion had subsided.

His friendship was therefore of little value: for though he was zealous in the support or vindication of those whom he loved, yet it was always dangerous to trust him, because he considered himself as discharged by the first quarrel from all ties of honour or gratitude; and would betray those secrets which, in the warmth of confidence, had been imparted to him. This practice drew upon him an universal accusation of ingratitude: nor can it be denied that he was very ready to set himself free from the load of an obligation; for he could not bear to conceive himself in a state of dependence, his pride being equally powerful with his other passions, and appearing in the form of insolence at one time, and of vanity at another. Vanity, the most innocent species of pride, was most frequently predominant. He could not easily leave off, when he had once begun to mention himself or his works; nor ever read his verses without stealing his eyes from the page, to discover, in the faces of his audience, how they were affected with any favourite passage.

A kinder name than that of vanity ought to be given to the delicacy with which he was always careful to separate his own merit from every other man's, and to reject that praise to which he had no claim. He did not forget, in mentioning his performances, to mark every line, that had been suggested or amended; and was so accurate, as to relate that he owed three words in *The Wanderer* to the advice of his friends.

His veracity was questioned, but with little reason; his accounts, though not indeed always the same, were generally consistent. When he loved any man, he suppressed all his faults; and, when he had been offended by him, concealed all his virtues: but his characters were generally true, so far as he proceeded; though it cannot be denied, that his partiality might have sometimes the effect of falsehood.

In cases indifferent, he was zealous for virtue, truth, and justice: he knew very well the necessity of goodness to the present and future happiness of mankind; nor is there perhaps any writer, who has less endeavoured to please by flattering the appetites, or perverting the judgement.

As an author, therefore, and he now ceases to influence mankind in any other character, if one piece which he had resolved to suppress be excepted, he has very little to fear from the strictest moral or religious censure. And though he may not be altogether secure against the objections of the critic, it must however be acknowledged, that his works are the productions of a genius truly poetical; and, what many writers who have been more lavishly applauded cannot boast, that they have an original air, which has no resemblance of any foregoing work, that the versification and sentiments have a cast peculiar to themselves, which no man can imitate with success, because what was nature in Savage, would in another be affectation. It must be confessed, that his descriptions are striking, his images animated, his fictions justly imagined, and his allegories artfully pursued; that his diction is elevated, though sometimes forced, and his numbers sonorous and majestic, though frequently sluggish and encumbered. Of his style, the general fault is harshness, and its general excellence is dignity; of his sentiments, the prevailing beauty is sublimity, and uniformity the prevailing defect.

For his life, or for his writings, none, who candidly consider his fortune, will think an apology either necessary or difficult. If he was not always sufficiently instructed in his subject, his knowledge was at least greater than could have been attained by others in the same state. If his works were sometimes unfinished, accuracy cannot reasonably be exacted from a man oppressed with want, which he has no hope of relieving but by a speedy publication. The insolence and resentment of which he is accused were not easily to be avoided by a great mind, irritated by perpetual hardships, and constrained hourly to return the spurns of contempt, and repress the insolence of prosperity; and vanity may surely readily be pardoned in him, to whom life afforded no other comforts than barren praises, and the consciousness of deserving them.

Those are no proper judges of his conduct, who have slumbered away their time on the down of plenty; nor will any wise man presume to say, 'Had I been in Savage's condition, I should have lived or written better than Savage.'

This relation will not be wholly without its use, if those, who languish under any part of his sufferings, shall be enabled to fortify their patience, by reflecting that they feel only those afflictions from which the abilities of Savage did not exempt him; or those, who, in confidence of superior capacities or attainments, disregard the common maxims of life, shall be reminded, that nothing will supply the want of prudence; and that negligence and irregularity, long continued, will make knowledge useless, wit ridiculous, and genius contemptible.

LETTERS*

To Edward Cave

Greenwich, next door to the Golden Heart,
Church-street, 12 July 1737

Sir

Having observed in your papers very uncommon offers of encouragement to men of letters, I have chosen, being a stranger in London, to communicate to you the following design, which, I hope, if you join in it, will be of advantage to both of us.

The *History of the Council of Trent* having been lately translated into French, and published with large notes by Dr Le Courayer, the reputation of that book is so much revived in England, that, it is presumed, a new translation of it from the Italian, together with Le Courayer's notes from the French, could not fail of a favourable reception.

If it be answered, that the History is already in English, it must be remembered, that there was the same objection against Le Courayer's undertaking, with this disadvantage, that the French had a version by one of their best translators, whereas you cannot read three pages of the English History without discovering that the style is capable of great improvements; but whether those improvements are to be expected from the attempt, you must judge from the specimen, which, if you approve the proposal, I shall submit to your examination.

Suppose the merit of the versions equal, we may hope that the addition of the notes will turn the balance in our favour, considering the reputation of the annotator.

Be pleased to favour me with a speedy answer, if you are not willing to engage in this scheme; and appoint me a day to wait upon you, if you are.

I am, Sir, your humble servant,
SAM: JOHNSON

Castle-street, Wednesday Morning.
[*No date.* 1738]

Sir

When I took the liberty of writing to you a few days ago, I did not expect a repetition of the same pleasure so soon; for a pleasure I shall always think it, to converse in any manner with an ingenious and candid man; but having the enclosed poem in my hands to dispose of for the benefit of the author, (of whose abilities I shall say nothing, since I send you his performance,) I believed I could not procure more advantageous terms from any person than from you, who have so much distinguished yourself by your generous encouragement of poetry; and whose judgment of that art nothing but your commendation of my trifle can give me any occasion to call in question. I do not doubt but you will look over this poem with another eye, and reward it in a different manner, from a mercenary bookseller, who counts the lines he is to purchase, and considers nothing but the bulk. I cannot help taking notice, that, besides what the author may hope for on account of his abilities, he has likewise another claim to your regard, as he lies at present under very disadvantageous circumstances of fortune. I beg, therefore, that you will favour me with a letter tomorrow, that I may know what you can afford to allow him, that he may either part with it to you, or find out, (which I do not expect,) some other way more to his satisfaction.

I have only to add, that as I am sensible I have transcribed it very coarsely, which, after having altered it, I was obliged to do, I will, if you please to transmit the sheets from the press, correct it for you; and will take the trouble of altering any stroke of satire which you may dislike.

By exerting on this occasion your usual generosity, you will not only encourage learning, and relieve distress, but (though it be in comparison of the other motives of very small account) oblige in a very sensible manner,

Sir, your very humble servant,
SAM: JOHNSON

MORALIST AND
LEXICOGRAPHER

THE
VANITY
OF
HUMAN WISHES
THE TENTH SATIRE OF JUVENAL IMITATED

LET observation with extensive view,
Survey mankind, from China to Peru;[1]
Remark each anxious toil, each eager strife,
And watch the busy scenes of crowded life;
Then say how hope and fear, desire and hate,   5
O'erspread with snares the clouded maze of fate,
Where wav'ring man, betray'd by vent'rous pride,
To tread the dreary paths without a guide,
As treach'rous phantoms in the mist delude,
Shuns fancied ills, or chases airy good;   10
How rarely reason guides the stubborn choice,
Rules the bold hand, or prompts the suppliant voice;
How nations sink, by darling schemes oppress'd,
When vengeance listens to the fool's request.
Fate wings with ev'ry wish th' afflictive[2] dart,   15
Each gift of nature, and each grace of art,
With fatal heat impetuous courage glows,
With fatal sweetness elocution flows,
Impeachment stops the speaker's pow'rful breath,
And restless fire precipitates on death.[3]   20
But scarce observ'd, the knowing and the bold
Fall in the gen'ral massacre of gold;
Wide-wasting pest! that rages unconfin'd,
And crowds with crimes the records of mankind;
For gold his sword the hireling ruffian draws,   25
For gold the hireling judge distorts the laws;
Wealth heap'd on wealth, nor truth nor safety buys,
The dangers gather as the treasures rise.[4]
Let hist'ry tell where rival kings command,
And dubious title shakes the madded land,   30
When statutes glean the refuse of the sword,

How much more safe the vassal than the lord;
Low skulks the hind beneath the rage of pow'r,
And leaves the wealthy traitor[5] in the Tow'r,
35   Untouch'd his cottage, and his slumbers sound,
Tho' confiscation's vultures hover round.[6]
    The needy traveller, serene and gay,
Walks the wild heath, and sings his toil away.
Does envy seize thee? crush th' upbraiding joy,
40   Increase his riches and his peace destroy;
Now fears in dire vicissitude invade,
The rustling brake alarms, and quiv'ring shade,
Nor light nor darkness bring his pain relief,
One shows the plunder, and one hides the thief.
45   Yet still one gen'ral cry the skies assails,
And gain and grandeur load the tainted gales;
Few know the toiling statesman's fear or care,
Th' insidious rival and the gaping heir.
    Once more, Democritus, arise on earth,
50   With cheerful wisdom and instructive mirth,
See motley life in modern trappings dress'd,
And feed with varied fools th' eternal jest:
Thou who couldst laugh where want enchain'd caprice,
Toil crush'd conceit, and man was of a piece;
55   Where wealth unlov'd without a mourner died,
And scarce a sycophant was fed by pride;
Where ne'er was known the form of mock debate,
Or seen a new-made mayor's unwieldy state;
Where change of fav'rites made no change of laws,
60   And senates heard before they judg'd a cause;
How wouldst thou shake at Britain's modish tribe,
Dart the quick taunt, and edge the piercing gibe?
Attentive truth and nature to descry,
And pierce each scene with philosophic eye,
65   To thee were solemn toys or empty show,
The robes of pleasure and the veils of woe:
All aid the farce, and all thy mirth maintain,
Whose joys are causeless, or whose griefs are vain.
    Such was the scorn that fill'd the sage's mind,

Renew'd at ev'ry glance on humankind;   70
How just that scorn ere yet thy voice declare,
Search every state, and canvass ev'ry pray'r.
 Unnumber'd suppliants crowd Preferment's gate,[7]
Athirst for wealth, and burning to be great;
Delusive Fortune hears th' incessant call,   75
They mount, they shine, evaporate, and fall.
On ev'ry stage the foes of peace attend,
Hate dogs their flight, and insult mocks their end.
Love ends with hope, the sinking statesman's door
Pours in the morning worshipper no more;   80
For growing names the weekly scribbler lies,
To growing wealth the dedicator flies,
From every room descends the painted face,
That hung the bright Palladium[8] of the place,
And smok'd in kitchens, or in auctions sold,   85
To better features yields the frame of gold;
For now no more we trace in ev'ry line
Heroic worth, benevolence divine:
The form distorted justifies the fall,
And detestation rids th' indignant wall.   90
 But will not Britain hear the last appeal,
Sign her foes' doom, or guard her fav'rites' zeal?
Through Freedom's sons no more remonstrance rings,
Degrading nobles and controlling kings;
Our supple tribes repress their patriot throats,   95
And ask no questions but the price of votes;
With weekly libels and septennial ale,
Their wish is full to riot and to rail.
 In full-blown dignity, see Wolsey[9] stand,
Law in his voice, and fortune in his hand: 100
To him the church, the realm, their pow'rs consign,
Thro' him the rays of regal bounty shine,
Turn'd by his nod the stream of honour flows,
His smile alone security bestows:
Still to new heights his restless wishes tow'r,   105
Claim leads to claim, and pow'r advances pow'r;
Till conquest unresisted ceas'd to please,

And rights submitted, left him none to seize.
At length his sov'reign frowns – the train of state
110   Mark the keen glance, and watch the sign to hate.
Where-e'er he turns he meets a stranger's eye,
His suppliants scorn him, and his followers fly;
At once is lost the pride of aweful state,
The golden canopy, the glitt'ring plate,
115   The regal palace, the luxurious board,
The liv'ried army, and the menial lord.
With age, with cares, with maladies oppress'd,
He seeks the refuge of monastic rest.
Grief aids disease, remember'd folly stings,
120   And his last sighs reproach the faith of kings.
     Speak thou, whose thoughts at humble peace repine,
Shall Wolsey's wealth, with Wolsey's end be thine?
Or liv'st thou now, with safer pride content,
The wisest justice[10] on the banks of Trent?
125   For why did Wolsey near the steeps of fate,
On weak foundations raise th' enormous weight?
Why but to sink beneath misfortune's blow,
With louder ruin to the gulfs below?
What gave great Villiers[11] to th' assassin's knife,
130   And fixed disease on Harley's[12] closing life?
What murder'd Wentworth,[13] and what exil'd Hyde,
By kings protected, and to kings allied?
What but their wish indulg'd in courts to shine,
And pow'r too great to keep, or to resign?
135   When first the college rolls receive his name,[14]
The young enthusiast quits his ease for fame;
Through all his veins the fever of renown
Burns from the strong contagion of the gown;
O'er Bodley's dome his future labours spread,
140   And Bacon's mansion trembles o'er his head.[15]
Are these thy views? proceed, illustrious youth,
And virtue guard thee to the throne of Truth!
Yet should thy soul indulge the gen'rous heat,
Till captive Science yields her last retreat;
145   Should Reason guide thee with her brightest ray,

And pour on misty Doubt resistless day;
Should no false Kindness lure to loose delight,
Nor Praise relax, nor Difficulty fright;
Should tempting Novelty thy cell refrain,
And Sloth effuse her opiate fumes in vain;   150
Should Beauty blunt on fops her fatal dart,
Nor claim the triumph of a letter'd heart;
Should no Disease thy torpid veins invade,
Nor Melancholy's phantoms haunt thy shade;
Yet hope not life from grief or danger free,   155
Nor think the doom of man revers'd for thee:
Deign on the passing world to turn thine eyes,
And pause awhile from letters, to be wise;
There mark what ills the scholar's life assail,
Toil, envy, want, the patron, and the jail.[16]   160
See nations slowly wise, and meanly just,
To buried merit raise the tardy bust.[17]
If dreams yet flatter, once again attend,
Hear Lydiat's[18] life, and Galileo's end.

Nor deem, when learning her last prize bestows,   165
The glitt'ring eminence exempt from foes;
See when the vulgar 'scape, despis'd or aw'd,
Rebellion's vengeful talons seize on Laud.
From meaner minds, tho' smaller fines content,
The plunder'd palace or sequester'd rent;   170
Mark'd out by dangerous parts he meets the shock,
And fatal Learning leads him to the block:[19]
Around his tomb let Art and Genius weep,
But hear his death, ye blockheads, hear and sleep.

The festal blazes, the triumphal show,   175
The ravish'd standard, and the captive foe,
The senate's thanks, the gazette's pompous tale,
With force resistless o'er the brave prevail.
Such bribes the rapid Greek[20] o'er Asia whirl'd,
For such the steady Romans shook the world;   180
For such in distant lands the Britons shine,
And stain with blood the Danube or the Rhine;
This pow'r has praise, that virtue scarce can warm,

143

Till fame supplies the universal charm.
185   Yet Reason frowns on War's unequal game,
Where wasted nations raise a single name,
And mortgag'd states their grandsires' wreaths regret,
From age to age in everlasting debt;
Wreaths which at last the dear-bought right convey
190   To rust on medals, or on stones decay.
    On what foundation stands the warrior's pride,
How just his hopes let Swedish Charles[21] decide;
A frame of adamant, a soul of fire,
No dangers fright him, and no labours tire;
195   O'er love, o'er fear, extends his wide domain,
Unconquer'd lord of pleasure and of pain;
No joys to him pacific sceptres yield,
War sounds the trump, he rushes to the field;
Behold surrounding kings their pow'r combine,
200   And one capitulate, and one resign;
Peace courts his hand, but spreads her charms in vain;
'Think nothing gain'd, he cries, till nought remain,
'On Moscow's walls till Gothic standards fly,
'And all be mine beneath the polar sky.'
205   The march begins in military state,
And nations on his eye suspended wait;
Stern Famine guards the solitary coast,
And Winter barricades the realms of Frost;
He comes, not want and cold his course delay; –
210   Hide, blushing Glory, hide Pultowa's day:[22]
The vanquish'd hero leaves his broken bands,
And shows his miseries in distant lands;
Condemn'd a needy supplicant to wait,
While ladies interpose, and slaves debate.
215   But did not Chance at length her error mend?
Did no subverted empire mark his end?
Did rival monarchs give the fatal wound?
Or hostile millions press him to the ground?
His fall was destin'd to a barren strand,
220   A petty fortress, and a dubious hand;
He left the name, at which the world grew pale,

To point a moral, or adorn a tale.[23]
   All times their scenes of pompous woes afford,
From Persia's tyrant to Bavaria's lord.
In gay hostility, and barb'rous pride,   225
With half mankind embattled at his side,
Great Xerxes comes to seize the certain prey,
And starves exhausted regions in his way;
Attendant Flatt'ry counts his myriads o'er,
Till counted myriads soothe his pride no more;   230
Fresh praise is tried till madness fires his mind,
The waves he lashes, and enchains the wind;
New pow'rs are claim'd, new pow'rs are still bestow'd,
Till rude resistance lops the spreading god;
The daring Greeks deride the martial show,   235
And heap their valleys with the gaudy foe;
Th' insulted sea with humbler thoughts he gains,
A single skiff to speed his flight remains;
Th' encumber'd oar scarce leaves the dreaded coast
Through purple billows and a floating host.[24]   240
   The bold Bavarian,[25] in a luckless hour,
Tries the dread summits of Caesarean pow'r,
With unexpected legions bursts away,
And sees defenceless realms receive his sway;
Short sway! fair Austria[26] spreads her mournful charms,   245
The queen, the beauty, sets the world in arms;
From hill to hill the beacons' rousing blaze
Spreads wide the hope of plunder and of praise:
The fierce Croatian, and the wild Hussar,
And all the sons of ravage crowd the war;   250
The baffled prince in honour's flatt'ring bloom
Of hasty greatness finds the fatal doom,
His foes' derision, and his subjects' blame,
And steals to death from anguish and from shame.
   Enlarge my life with multitude of days,   255
In health, in sickness, thus the suppliant prays;
Hides from himself his state, and shuns to know,
That life protracted is protracted woe.
Time hovers o'er, impatient to destroy,

260 And shuts up all the passages of joy:
  In vain their gifts the bounteous seasons pour,
  The fruit autumnal, and the vernal flow'r,
  With listless eyes the dotard views the store,
  He views, and wonders that they please no more;
265 Now pall the tasteless meats, and joyless wines,
  And Luxury[27] with sighs her slave resigns.
  Approach, ye minstrels, try the soothing strain,
  Diffuse the tuneful lenitives of pain:
  No sounds, alas, would touch th' impervious ear,
270 Though dancing mountains witness'd Orpheus near;
  Nor lute nor lyre his feeble pow'rs attend,
  Nor sweeter music of a virtuous friend,
  But everlasting dictates crowd his tongue,
  Perversely grave, or positively[28] wrong.
275 The still returning tale, and ling'ring jest,
  Perplex the fawning niece and pamper'd guest,
  While growing hopes scarce awe the gath'ring sneer,
  And scarce a legacy can bribe to hear;
  The watchful guests still hint the last offence,
280 The daughter's petulance, the son's expense,
  Improve his heady rage with treach'rous skill,
  And mould his passions till they make his will.[29]

  Unnumber'd maladies his joints invade,
  Lay siege to life and press the dire blockade;
285 But unextinguish'd Avarice still remains,
  And dreaded losses aggravate his pains;
  He turns, with anxious heart and crippled hands,
  His bonds of debt, and mortgages of lands;
  Or views his coffers with suspicious eyes,
290 Unlocks his gold, and counts it till he dies.

  But grant, the virtues of a temp'rate prime
  Bless with an age exempt from scorn or crime;
  An age that melts with unperceiv'd decay,
  And glides in modest Innocence away;
295 Whose peaceful day Benevolence endears,
  Whose night congratulating Conscience cheers;
  The gen'ral fav'rite as the gen'ral friend:

The Vanity of Human Wishes

Such age there is, and who shall wish its end?
  Yet ev'n on this her load Misfortune flings,
To press the weary minutes' flagging wings: 300
New sorrow rises as the day returns,
A sister sickens, òr a daughter mourns.
Now kindred Merit fills the sable bier,
Now lacerated Friendship claims a tear.
Year chases year, decay pursues decay, 305
Still drops some joy from with'ring life away;
New forms arise, and diff'rent views engage,
Superfluous lags the vet'ran on the stage,
Till pitying Nature signs the last release,
And bids afflicted worth retire to peace. 310
  But few there are whom hours like these await,
Who set unclouded in the gulfs of fate.
From Lydia's monarch[30] should the search descend,
By Solon caution'd to regard his end,
In life's last scene what prodigies surprise, 315
Fears of the brave, and follies of the wise?
From Marlb'rough's eyes the streams of dotage flow,
And Swift expires a driv'ler and a show.
  The teeming mother, anxious for her race,
Begs for each birth the fortune of a face: 320
Yet Vane[31] could tell what ills from beauty spring;
And Sedley[32] curs'd the form that pleas'd a king.
Ye nymphs of rosy lips and radiant eyes,[33]
Whom Pleasure keeps too busy to be wise,
Whom Joys with soft varieties invite, 325
By day the frolic, and the dance by night,
Who frown with vanity, who smile with art,
And ask the latest fashion of the heart,
What care, what rules your heedless charms shall save,
Each nymph your rival, and each youth your slave? 330
Against your fame with fondness hate combines,
The rival batters, and the lover mines.
With distant voice neglected Virtue calls,
Less heard and less, the faint remonstrance falls;
Tir'd with contempt, she quits the slipp'ry reign, 335

147

And Pride and Prudence take her seat in vain.
In crowd at once, where none the pass defend,
The harmless Freedom, and the private Friend.
The guardians yield, by force superior ply'd;
340   By Int'rest, Prudence; and by Flatt'ry, Pride.
Now beauty falls betray'd, despis'd, distress'd,
And hissing Infamy proclaims the rest.
    Where then shall Hope and Fear their objects find?[34]
Must dull Suspense corrupt the stagnant mind?
345   Must helpless man, in ignorance sedate,
Roll darkling down the torrent of his fate?[35]
Must no dislike alarm, no wishes rise,
No cries attempt the mercies of the skies?
Inquirer, cease, petitions yet remain,
350   Which heav'n may hear, nor deem religion vain.
Still raise for good the supplicating voice,
But leave to heav'n the measure and the choice,
Safe in his pow'r, whose eyes discern afar
The secret ambush of a specious pray'r.[36]
355   Implore his aid, in his decisions rest,
Secure whate'er he gives, he gives the best.
Yet when the sense of sacred presence fires,
And strong devotion to the skies aspires,
Pour forth thy fervours for a healthful mind,
360   Obedient passions, and a will resign'd;
For love, which scarce collective man can fill;
For patience sov'reign o'er transmuted ill;
For faith, that panting for a happier seat,
Counts death kind Nature's signal of retreat:
365   These goods for man the laws of heav'n ordain,
These goods he grants, who grants the pow'r to gain;
With these celestial wisdom calms the mind,
And makes the happiness she does not find.

THE RAMBLER*

NO. 4, SATURDAY, 31 MARCH 1750

Simul et jucunda et idonea dicere vitæ.
HORACE, *Ars Poetica*, 334.
And join both profit and delight in one.
CREECH

The works of fiction, with which the present generation seems more particularly delighted, are such as exhibit life in its true state, diversified only by accidents that daily happen in the world, and influenced by passions and qualities which are really to be found in conversing with mankind.

This kind of writing may be termed not improperly the comedy of romance, and is to be conducted nearly by the rules of comic poetry. Its province is to bring about natural events by easy means, and to keep up curiosity without the help of wonder: it is therefore precluded from the machines and expedients of the heroic romance, and can neither employ giants to snatch away a lady from the nuptial rites, nor knights to bring her back from captivity; it can neither bewilder its personages in deserts, nor lodge them in imaginary castles.

I remember a remark made by Scaliger upon Pontanus, that all his writings are filled with the same images; and that if you take from him his lilies and his roses, his satyrs and his dryads, he will have nothing left that can be called poetry. In like manner almost all the fictions of the last age will vanish, if you deprive them of a hermit and a wood, a battle and a shipwreck.

Why this wild strain of imagination found reception so long in polite and learned ages, it is not easy to conceive; but we cannot wonder that while readers could be procured, the authors were willing to continue it; for when a man had by practice gained some fluency of language, he had no further care than to retire to his closet, let loose his invention, and heat his mind with incredibilities; a book was thus

* See Editor's Notes.

produced without fear of criticism, without the toil of study, without knowledge of nature, or acquaintance with life.

The task of our present writers is very different; it requires, together with that learning which is to be gained from books, that experience which can never be attained by solitary diligence, but must arise from general converse and accurate observation of the living world. Their performances have, as Horace expresses it, *plus oneris quantum veniæ minus,* little indulgence, and therefore more difficulty. They are engaged in portraits of which every one knows the original, and can detect any deviation from exactness of resemblance. Other writings are safe, except from the malice of learning, but these are in danger from every common reader; as the slipper ill executed was censured by a shoemaker who happened to stop in his way at the Venus of Apelles.

But the fear of not being approved as just copiers of human manners, is not the most important concern that an author of this sort ought to have before him. These books are written chiefly to the young, the ignorant, and the idle, to whom they serve as lectures of conduct, and introductions into life. They are the entertainment of minds unfurnished with ideas, and therefore easily susceptible of impressions; not fixed by principles, and therefore easily following the current of fancy; not informed by experience, and consequently open to every false suggestion and partial account.

That the highest degree of reverence should be paid to youth, and that nothing indecent should be suffered to approach their eyes or ears, are precepts extorted by sense and virtue from an ancient writer, by no means eminent for chastity of thought. The same kind, though not the same degree, of caution, is required in every thing which is laid before them, to secure them from unjust prejudices, perverse opinions, and incongruous combinations of images.

In the romances formerly written, every transaction and sentiment was so remote from all that passes among men, that the reader was in very little danger of making any applications to himself; the virtues and crimes were equally beyond his sphere of activity; and he amused himself with heroes and with traitors, deliverers and persecutors, as with beings of another species, whose actions were regulated upon motives of their own, and who had neither faults nor excellencies in common with himself.

But when an adventurer is levelled with the rest of the world, and acts in such scenes of the universal drama, as may be the lot of any other man; young spectators fix their eyes upon him with closer attention, and hope, by observing his behaviour and success, to regulate their own practices, when they shall be engaged in the like part.

For this reason these familiar histories may perhaps be made of greater use than the solemnities of professed morality, and convey the knowledge of vice and virtue with more efficacy than axioms and definitions. But if the power of example is so great as to take possession of the memory by a kind of violence, and produce effects almost without the intervention of the will, care ought to be taken, that, when the choice is unrestrained, the best examples only should be exhibited; and that which is likely to operate so strongly, should not be mischievous or uncertain in its effects.

The chief advantage which these fictions have over real life is, that their authors are at liberty, though not to invent, yet to select objects, and to cull from the mass of mankind, those individuals upon which the attention ought most to be employed; as a diamond, though it cannot be made, may be polished by art, and placed in such a situation, as to display that lustre which before was buried among common stones.

It is justly considered as the greatest excellency of art, to imitate nature; but it is necessary to distinguish those parts of nature, which are most proper for imitation: greater care is still required in representing life, which is so often discoloured by passion, or deformed by wickedness. If the world be promiscuously described, I cannot see of what use it can be to read the account; or why it may not be as safe to turn the eye immediately upon mankind as upon a mirror which shows all that presents itself without discrimination.

It is therefore not a sufficient vindication of a character, that it is drawn as it appears; for many characters ought never to be drawn: nor of a narrative, that the train of events is agreeable to observation and experience; for that observation which is called knowledge of the world, will be found much more frequently to make men cunning than good. The purpose of these writings is surely not only to show mankind, but to provide that they may be seen hereafter with less hazard; to teach the means of avoiding the snares which are laid by Treachery for Innocence, without infusing any wish for that superiority with which the betrayer flatters his vanity; to give the power of counteracting fraud, without the temptation to practise it; to initiate youth by mock encounters in the art of necessary defence, and to increase prudence without impairing virtue.

Many writers, for the sake of following nature, so mingle good and bad qualities in their principal personages, that they are both equally conspicuous; and as we accompany them through their adventures with delight, and are led by degrees to interest ourselves in their favour, we lose the abhorrence of their faults, because they do not hinder our pleasure, or, perhaps, regard them with some kindness, for being united with so much merit.

There have been men indeed splendidly wicked, whose endowments threw a brightness on their crimes, and whom scarce any villainy made perfectly detestable, because they never could be wholly divested of their excellencies; but such have been in all ages the great corrupters of the world, and their resemblance ought no more to be preserved, than the art of murdering without pain.

Some have advanced, without due attention to the consequences of this notion, that certain virtues have their correspondent faults, and therefore that to exhibit either apart is to deviate from probability. Thus men are observed by Swift to be 'grateful in the same degree as they are resentful'. This principle, with others of the same kind, supposes man to act from a brute impulse, and pursue a certain degree of inclination, without any choice of the object; for, otherwise, though it should be allowed that gratitude and resentment arise from the same constitution of the passions, it follows not that they will be equally indulged when reason is consulted; yet, unless that consequence be admitted, this sagacious maxim becomes an empty sound, without any relation to practice or to life.

Nor is it evident, that even the first motions to these effects are always in the same proportion. For pride, which produces quickness of resentment, will obstruct gratitude, by unwillingness to admit that inferiority which obligation implies; and it is very unlikely that he who cannot think he receives a favour, will acknowledge or repay it.

It is of the utmost importance to mankind, that positions of this tendency should be laid open and confuted; for while men consider good and evil as springing from the same root, they will spare the one for the sake of the other, and in judging, if not of others at least of themselves, will be apt to estimate their virtues by their vices. To this fatal error all those will contribute, who confound the colours of right and wrong, and, instead of helping to settle their boundaries, mix them with so much art, that no common mind is able to disunite them.

In narratives where historical veracity has no place, I cannot discover why there should not be exhibited the most perfect idea of virtue; of virtue not angelical, nor above probability, for what we cannot credit, we shall never imitate, but the highest and purest that humanity can reach, which, exercised in such trials as the various revolutions of things shall bring upon it, may, by conquering some calamities, and enduring others, teach us what we may hope, and what we can perform. Vice, for vice is necessary to be shown, should always disgust; nor should the graces of gaiety, or the dignity of courage, be so united with it, as to reconcile it to the mind. Wherever it appears, it should raise hatred by the malignity of its practices, and contempt by the meanness of its stratagems: for while it is supported by either parts or spirit, it will be seldom heartily abhorred. The Roman tyrant was content to be hated, if he was but feared; and there are thousands of the readers of romances willing to be thought wicked, if they may be allowed to be wits. It is therefore to be steadily inculcated, that virtue is the highest proof of understanding, and the only solid basis of greatness; and that vice is the natural consequence of narrow thoughts; that it begins in mistake, and ends in ignominy.

No. 18, Saturday, 19 May 1750

Illic matre carentibus
Privignis mulier temperat innocens,
Nec dotata regit virum
Conjux, nec nitido fidit adultero:
  Dos est magna parentium
Virtus, et metuens alterius viri
Certo fædere castitas.

HORACE Liber iii Ode xxiv, 17

Not there the guiltless step-dame knows
The baleful draught for orphans to compose;
  No wife high portion'd rules her spouse,
Or trusts her essenc'd lover's faithless vows:
  The lovers there for dow'ry claim
The father's virtue, and the spotless fame,
  Which dares not break the nuptial tie.

FRANCIS

There is no observation more frequently made by such as employ themselves in surveying the conduct of mankind, than that marriage, though the dictate of nature, and the institution of Providence, is yet very often the cause of misery, and that those who enter into that state can seldom forbear to express their repentance, and their envy of those whom either chance or caution had withheld from it.

This general unhappiness has given occasion to many sage maxims among the serious, and smart remarks among the gay; the moralist and the writer of epigrams have equally shown their abilities upon it; some have lamented, and some have ridiculed it; but as the faculty of writing has been chiefly a masculine endowment, the reproach of making the world miserable has been always thrown upon the women, and the grave and the merry have equally thought themselves at liberty to conclude either with declamatory complaints, or satirical censures, of female folly or fickleness, ambition or cruelty, extravagance or lust.

Led by such a number of examples, and incited by my share in the common interest, I sometimes venture to consider this universal grievance, having endeavoured to divest my heart of all partiality, and place myself as a kind of neutral being between the sexes, whose clamours being equally vented on both sides with all the vehemence of distress, all the apparent confidence of justice, and all the indignation of injured virtue, seem entitled to equal regard. The men have, indeed, by their superiority of writing, been able to collect the evidence of many ages, and raise prejudices in their favour by the venerable testimonies of philosophers, historians, and poets; but the pleas of the ladies appeal to passions of more forcible operation than the reverence of antiquity. If they have not so great names on their side, they have stronger arguments: it is to little purpose that Socrates, or Euripides, are produced against the sighs of softness, and the tears of beauty. The most frigid and inexorable judge would at least stand suspended between equal powers, as Lucan was perplexed in the determination of the cause, where the deities were on one side, and Cato on the other.

But I, who have long studied the severest and most abstracted philosophy, have now, in the cool maturity of life, arrived at such command over my passions, that I can hear the vociferations of either sex without catching any of the fire from those that utter them. For I have found, by long experience, that a man will sometimes rage at his wife, when in reality his mistress has offended him; and a lady complain of the cruelty of her husband, when she has no other enemy than bad cards. I do not suffer myself to be any longer imposed upon by oaths on one side, or fits on the other; nor when the husband hastens to the tavern, and the lady retires to her closet, am I always confident that they are driven by their miseries; since I have sometimes reason to believe, that they purpose not so much to soothe their sorrows, as to animate their fury. But how little credit soever may be given to particular accusations, the general accumulation of the charge shows, with too much evidence, that married persons are not very often advanced in felicity; and, therefore, it may be proper to examine at what avenues so many evils have made their way into the world. With this purpose, I have reviewed the lives of my friends, who have been least successful in connubial contracts, and attentively considered by what motives they were incited to marry, and by what principles they regulated their choice.

One of the first of my acquaintances that resolved to quit the unsettled thoughtless condition of a bachelor, was Prudentius, a man of slow parts, but not without knowledge or judgement in things which he had leisure to consider gradually before he determined them. Whenever we met at a tavern, it was his province to settle the scheme of our entertainment, contract with the cook, and inform us when we had called for wine to the sum originally proposed. This grave considerer found, by deep meditation, that a man was no loser by marrying early, even though he contented himself with a less fortune; for estimating the exact worth of annuities, he found that considering the constant diminution of the value of life, with the probable fall of the interest of money, it was not worse to have ten thousand pounds at the age of two and twenty years, than a much larger fortune at thirty; for many opportunities, says he, occur of improving money, which if a man misses, he may not afterwards recover.

Full of these reflections, he threw his eyes about him, not in search of beauty or elegance, dignity or understanding, but of a woman with ten thousand pounds. Such a woman, in a wealthy part of the kingdom, it was not very difficult to find; and by artful management with her father, whose ambition was to make his daughter a gentlewoman, my friend got her, as he boasted to us in confidence two days after his marriage, for a settlement of seventy-three pounds a year less than her fortune might have claimed, and less than he would himself have given, if the fools had been but wise enough to delay the bargain.

Thus, at once delighted with the superiority of his parts and the augmentation of his fortune, he carried Furia to his own house, in which he never afterwards enjoyed one hour of happiness. For Furia was a wretch of mean intellects, violent passions, a strong voice, and low education, without any sense of happiness but that which consisted in eating and counting money. Furia was a scold. They agreed in the desire of wealth, but with this difference, that Prudentius was for growing rich by gain, Furia by parsimony. Prudentius would venture his money with chances very much in his favour; but Furia very wisely observing, that what they had was, while they had it, *their own*, thought all traffic too great a hazard, and was for putting it out at low interest, upon good security. Prudentius ventured, however, to insure a ship at a very unreasonable price, but happening to lose his money, was so tormented with the clamours of his wife, that he never durst try a second experiment. He has now grovelled seven and forty years under Furia's direction, who never once mentioned him, since his bad luck, by any other name than that of *the insurer*.

The next that married from our society was Florentius. He happened to see Zephyretta in a chariot at a horserace, danced with her at night, was confirmed in his first ardour, waited on her next morning, and declared himself her lover. Florentius had not knowledge enough of the world, to distinguish between the flutter of coquetry, and the sprightliness of wit, or between the smile of allurement, and that of cheerfulness. He was soon awaked from his rapture, by conviction that his pleasure was but the pleasure of a day. Zephyretta had in four and twenty hours spent her stock of repartee, gone round the circle of her airs, and had nothing remaining for him but childish insipidity, or for herself, but the practice of the same artifices upon new men.

Melissus was a man of parts, capable of enjoying and of improving life. He had passed through the various scenes of gaiety with that indifference and possession of himself, natural to men who have something higher and nobler in their prospect. Retiring to spend the summer in a village little frequented, he happened to lodge in the same house with Ianthe, and was unavoidably drawn to some acquaintance, which her wit and politeness soon invited him to improve. Having no opportunity of any other company, they were always together; and as they owed their pleasures to each other, they began to forget that any pleasure was enjoyed before their meeting. Melissus, from being delighted with her company, quickly began to be uneasy in her absence, and being sufficiently convinced of the force of her understanding, and finding, as he imagined, such a conformity of temper as declared them formed for each other, addressed her as a lover, after no very long courtship obtained her for his wife, and brought her next winter to town in triumph.

Now began their infelicity. Melissus had only seen her in one scene, where there was no variety of objects, to produce the proper excitements to contrary desires. They had both loved solitude and reflection where there was nothing but solitude and reflection to be loved; but when they came into public life, Ianthe discovered those passions which accident rather than hypocrisy had hitherto concealed. She was, indeed, not without the power of thinking, but was wholly without the exertion of that power when either gaiety or splendour played on her imagination. She was expensive in her diversions, vehement in her passions, insatiate of pleasure, however dangerous to her reputation, and eager of applause, by whomsoever it might be given. This was the wife which Melissus the philosopher found in his retirement, and from whom he expected an associate in his studies, and an assistant to his virtues.

Prosapius, upon the death of his younger brother, that the family might not be extinct, married his housekeeper, and has ever since been complaining to his friends that mean notions are instilled into his children, that he is ashamed to sit at his own table, and that his house is uneasy to him for want of suitable companions.

Avaro, master of a very large estate, took a woman of bad reputation, recommended to him by a rich uncle, who made that marriage the condition on which he should be his heir. Avaro now wonders to perceive his own fortune, his wife's and his uncle's, insufficient to give him that happiness which is to be found only with a woman of virtue.

I intend to treat in more papers on this important article of life, and shall, therefore, make no reflection upon these histories, except that all whom I have mentioned failed to obtain happiness, for want of considering that marriage is the strictest tie of perpetual friendship; that there can be no friendship without confidence, and no confidence without integrity; and that he must expect to be wretched, who pays to beauty, riches, or politeness, that regard which only virtue and piety can claim.

No. 21, Tuesday, 29 May 1750

Terra saluteres herbas, eademque nocentes,
Nutrit; et urticæ proxima sæpe rosa est.

OVID, *Remedia Amoris*, 45.

Our bane and physic the same earth bestows,
And near the noisome nettle blooms the rose.

Every man is prompted by the love of himself to imagine, that he possesses some qualities, superior, either in kind or in degree, to those which he sees allotted to the rest of the world; and, whatever apparent disadvantages he may suffer in the comparison with others, he has some invisible distinctions, some latent reserve of excellence, which he throws into the balance, and by which he generally fancies that it is turned in his favour.

The studious and speculative part of mankind always seem to consider their fraternity as placed in a state of opposition to those who are engaged in the tumult of public business; and have pleased themselves, from age to age, with celebrating the felicity of their own condition, and with recounting the perplexity of politics, the dangers of greatness, the anxieties of ambition, and the miseries of riches.

Among the numerous topics of declamation, that their industry has discovered on this subject, there is none which they press with greater efforts, or on which they have more copiously laid out their reason and their imagination, than the instability of high stations, and the uncertainty with which the profits and honours are possessed, that must be acquired with so much hazard, vigilance, and labour.

This they appear to consider as an irrefrágable argument against the choice of the statesman and the warrior; and swell with confidence of victory, thus furnished by the muses with the arms which never can be blunted, and which no art or strength of their adversaries can elude or resist.

It was well known by experience to the nations which employed elephants in war, that though by the terror of their bulk, and the violence of their impression, they often threw the enemy into disorder, yet there was always danger in the use of them, very nearly equivalent to the advantage; for if their first charge could be supported, they were easily driven back upon their confederates; they then broke through the troops behind them, and made no less havoc in the precipitation of their retreat, than in the fury of their onset.

I know not whether those who have so vehemently urged the inconveniencies and dangers of an active life, have not made use of arguments that may be retorted with equal force upon themselves; and whether the happiness of a candidate for literary fame be not subject to the same uncertainty with that of him who governs provinces, commands armies, presides in the senate, or dictates in the cabinet.

That eminence of learning is not to be gained without labour, at least equal to that which any other kind of greatness can require, will be allowed by those who wish to elevate the character of a scholar; since they cannot but know, that every human acquisition is valuable in proportion to the difficulty employed in its attainment. And that those who have gained the esteem and veneration of the world, by their knowledge or their genius, are by no means exempt from the solicitude which any other kind of dignity produces, may be conjectured from the innumerable artifices which they make use of to degrade a superior, to repress a rival, or obstruct a follower; artifices so gross and mean, as to prove evidently how much a man may excel in learning, without being either more wise or more virtuous than those whose ignorance he pities or despises.

Nothing therefore remains, by which the student can gratify his desire of appearing to have built his happiness on a more firm basis than his antagonist, except the certainty with which his honours are enjoyed. The garlands gained by the heroes of literature must be gathered from summits equally difficult to climb with those that bear the civic or triumphal wreaths, they must be worn with equal envy, and guarded with equal care from those hands that are always employed in efforts to tear them away; the only remaining hope is, that their verdure is more lasting, and that they are less likely to fade by time, or less obnoxious to the blasts of accident.

Even this hope will receive very little encouragement from the examination of the history of learning, or observation of the fate of scholars in the present age. If we look back into past times, we find innumerable names of authors once in high reputation, read perhaps by the beautiful, quoted by the witty, and commented upon by the grave; but of whom we now know only that they once existed. If we consider the distribution of literary fame in our own time, we shall find it a possession of very uncertain tenure; sometimes bestowed by a sudden caprice of the public, and again transferred to a new favourite, for no other reason than that he is new; sometimes refused to long labour and eminent desert, and sometimes granted to very slight pretensions; lost sometimes by security and negligence, and sometimes by too diligent endeavours to retain it.

A successful author is equally in danger of the diminution of his fame, whether he continues or ceases to write. The regard of the public is not to be kept but by tribute, and the remembrance of past service will quickly languish, unless successive performances frequently revive it. Yet in every new attempt there is new hazard, and there are few who do not at some unlucky time, injure their own characters by attempting to enlarge them.

There are many possible causes of that inequality which we may so frequently observe in the performances of the same man, from the influence of which no ability or industry is sufficiently secured, and which have so often sullied the splendour of genius, that the wit, as well as the conqueror, may be properly cautioned not to indulge his pride with too early triumphs, but to defer to the end of life his estimate of happiness.

> ... *Ultima semper*
> *Expectanda dies homini, dicique beatus*
> *Ante obitum nemo supremaque funera debet.*
>
> OVID, *Metamorphoses* iii, 135
>
> But no frail man, however great or high,
> Can be concluded blest before he die.
>
> ADDISON

Among the motives that urge an author to undertakings by which his reputation is impaired, one of the most frequent must be mentioned with tenderness, because it is not to be counted among his follies, but his miseries. It very often happens that the works of learning or of wit are performed at the direction of those by whom they are to be rewarded; the writer has not always the choice of his subject, but is compelled to accept any task which is thrown before him without much consideration of his own convenience, and without time to prepare himself by previous studies.

Miscarriages of this kind are likewise frequently the consequence of that acquaintance with the great, which is generally considered as one of the chief privileges of literature and genius. A man who has once learned to think himself exalted by familiarity with those whom nothing but their birth, or their fortunes, or such stations as are seldom gained by moral excellence, set above him, will not be long without submitting his understanding to their conduct; he will suffer them to prescribe the course of his studies, and employ him for their own purposes either of diversion or interest. His desire of pleasing those whose favour he has weakly made necessary to himself, will not suffer him always to consider how little he is qualified for the work imposed. Either his vanity will tempt him to conceal his deficiencies, or that cowardice, which always encroaches fast upon such as spend their lives in the company of persons higher than themselves, will not leave him resolution to assert the liberty of choice.

But, though we suppose that a man by his fortune can avoid the necessity of dependence, and by his spirit can repel the usurpations of patronage, yet he may easily, by writing long, happen to write ill. There is a general succession of events in which contraries are produced by periodical vicissitudes; labour and care are rewarded with success, success produces confidence, confidence relaxes industry, and negligence ruins that reputation which accuracy had raised.

He that happens not to be lulled by praise into supineness, may be animated by it to undertakings above his strength, or incited to fancy himself alike qualified for every kind of composition, and able to comply with the public taste through all its variations. By some opinion like this, many men have been engaged, at an advanced age, in attempts which they had not time to complete, and after a few weak efforts, sunk into the grave with vexation to see the rising generation gain ground upon them. From these failures the highest genius is not exempt; that judgement which appears so penetrating, when it is employed upon the works of others, very often fails where interest or passion can exert their power. We are blinded in examining our own labours by innumerable prejudices. Our juvenile composi- tions please us, because they bring to our minds the remembrance of youth; our later performances we are ready to esteem, because we are unwilling to think, that we have made no improvement; what flows easily from the pen charms us, because we read with pleasure that which flatters our opinion of our own powers; what was com- posed with great struggles of the mind we do not easily reject, be- cause we cannot bear that so much labour should be fruitless. But the reader has none of these prepossessions, and wonders that the author is so unlike himself, without considering that the same soil will, with different culture, afford different products.

No. 50, Saturday, 8 September 1750

Credebant hoc grande nefas, et morte piandum,
Si juvenis vetulo non assurrexerat, atque
Barbato cuicunque puer, licet ipse videret
Plura domi fraga, et majores glandis acervos.

JUVENAL, Satires xiii, 54

And had not men the hoary head rever'd,
And boys paid rev'rence when a man appear'd,
Both must have died, though richer skins they wore,
And saw more heaps of acorns in their store.

CREECH

I have always thought it the business of those who turn their specula- tions upon the living world, to commend the virtues, as well as to expose the faults of their contemporaries, and to confute a false as well as to support a just accusation; not only because it is peculiarly the business of a monitor to keep his own reputation untainted, lest those who can once charge him with partiality, should indulge themselves afterwards in disbelieving him at pleasure; but because he may find real crimes sufficient to give full employment to caution or repentance, without distracting the mind by needless scruples and vain solicitudes.

There are certain fixed and stated reproaches that one part of mankind has in all ages thrown upon another, which are regularly transmitted through continued successions, and which he that has once suffered them is certain to use with the same undistinguishing vehemence, when he has changed his station, and gained the prescriptive right of inflicting on others what he had formerly endured himself.

To these hereditary imputations, of which no man sees the justice, till it becomes his interest to see it, very little regard is to be shown; since it does not appear that they are produced by ratiocination or inquiry, but received implicitly, or caught by a kind of instantaneous contagion, and supported rather by willingness to credit, than ability to prove, them.

It has been always the practice of those who are desirous to believe themselves made venerable by length of time, to censure the new comers into life, for want of respect to grey hairs and sage experience, for heady confidence in their own understandings, for hasty conclusions upon partial views, for disregard of counsels, which their fathers and grandsires are ready to afford them, and a rebellious impatience of that subordination to which youth is condemned by nature, as necessary to its security from evils into which it would be otherwise precipitated, by the rashness of passion, and the blindness of ignorance.

Every old man complains of the growing depravity of the world, of the petulance and insolence of the rising generation. He recounts the decency and regularity of former times, and celebrates the discipline and sobriety of the age in which his youth was passed; a happy age, which is now no more to be expected, since confusion has broken in upon the world, and thrown down all the boundaries of civility and reverence.

It is not sufficiently considered how much he assumes who dares to claim the privilege of complaining; for as every man has, in his own opinion, a full share of the miseries of life, he is inclined to consider all clamorous uneasiness, as a proof of impatience rather than of affliction, and to ask, what merit has this man to show, by which he has acquired a right to repine at the distributions of nature? Or, why does he imagine that exemptions should be granted him from the general condition of man?[1] We find ourselves excited rather to captiousness than pity, and instead of being in haste to soothe his complaints by sympathy and tenderness, we inquire, whether the pain be proportionate to the lamentation; and whether, supposing the affliction real, it is not the effect of vice and folly, rather than calamity.

The querulousness and indignation which is observed so often to disfigure the last scene of life, naturally leads us to inquiries like these. For surely it will be thought at the first view of things, that if age be thus condemned and ridiculed, insulted and neglected, the crime must at least be equal on either part. They who have had opportunities of establishing their authority over minds ductile and unresisting, they who have been the protectors of helplessness, and the instructors of ignorance, and who yet retain in their own hands the power of wealth, and the dignity of command, must defeat their influence by their own misconduct, and make use of all these advantages with very little skill, if they cannot secure to themselves an appearance of respect, and ward off open mockery, and declared contempt.

The general story of mankind will evince, that lawful and settled authority is very seldom resisted when it is well employed. Gross corruption, or evident imbecility, is necessary to the suppression of that reverence with which the majority of mankind look upon their governors, and on those whom they see surrounded by splendour, and fortified by power. For though men are drawn by their passions into forgetfulness of invisible rewards and punishments, yet they are easily kept obedient to those who have temporal dominion in their hands, till their veneration is dissipated by such wickedness and folly as can neither be defended nor concealed.

It may, therefore, very reasonably be suspected that the old draw upon themselves the greatest part of those insults which they so much lament, and that age is rarely despised but when it is contemptible. If men imagine that excess of debauchery can be made reverend by time, that knowledge is the consequence of long life, however idly or thoughtlessly employed, that priority of birth will supply the want of steadiness or honesty, can it raise much wonder that their hopes are disappointed, and that they see their posterity rather willing to trust their own eyes in their progress into life, than enlist themselves under guides who have lost their way?

There are, indeed, many truths which time necessarily and certainly teaches, and which might, by those who have learned them from experience, be communicated to their successors at a cheaper rate: but dictates, though liberally enough bestowed, are generally without effect, the teacher gains few proselytes by instruction which his own behaviour contradicts; and young men miss the benefit of counsel, because they are not very ready to believe that those who fell below them in practice, can much excel them in theory. Thus the progress of knowledge is retarded, the world is kept long in the same state, and every new race is to gain the prudence of their predecessors by committing and redressing the same miscarriages.

To secure to the old that influence which they are willing to claim, and which might so much contribute to the improvement of the arts of life, it is absolutely necessary that they give themselves up to the duties of declining years; and contentedly resign to youth its levity, its pleasures, its frolics, and its fopperies. It is a hopeless endeavour to unite the contrarieties of spring and winter; it is unjust to claim the privileges of age, and retain the playthings of childhood. The young always form magnificent ideas of the wisdom and gravity of men, whom they consider as placed at a distance from them in the ranks of existence, and naturally look on those whom they find trifling with long beards, with contempt and indignation, like that which women feel at the effeminacy of men. If dotards will contend with boys in those performances in which boys must always excel them; if they will dress crippled limbs in embroidery, endeavour at gaiety with faltering voices, and darken assemblies of pleasure with the ghastliness of disease, they may well expect those who find their diversions obstructed will hoot them away; and that if they descend to competition with youth, they must bear the insolence of successful rivals.

> *Lusisti satis, edisti satis atque bibisti:*
> *Tempus abire tibi est.*
>
> You've had your share of mirth, of meat and drink;
> 'Tis time to quit the scene – 'tis time to think.
>
> ELPHINSTON

Another vice of age, by which the rising generation may be alienated from it, is severity and censoriousness, that gives no allowance to the failings of early life, that expects artfulness from childhood, and constancy from youth, that is peremptory in every command, and inexorable to every failure. There are many who live merely to hinder happiness,[2] and whose descendants can only tell of long life, that it produces suspicion, malignity, peevishness, and persecution; and yet even these tyrants can talk of the ingratitude of the age, curse their heirs for impatience, and wonder that young men cannot take pleasure in their father's company.

He that would pass the latter part of life with honour and decency, must, when he is young, consider that he shall one day be old; and remember, when he is old, that he has once been young. In youth, he must lay up knowledge for his support, when his powers of acting shall forsake him; and in age forbear to animadvert with rigour on faults which experience only can correct.

Samuel Johnson

No. 60, Saturday, 13 October 1750

Quid sit pulchrum, quid turpe, quid utile, quid non,
Plenius ac melius Chrysippo et Crantore dicit.

HORACE, *Liber* i, Epistle ii, 3

Whose works the beautiful and base contain,
Of vice and virtue more instructive rules,
Than all the sober sages of the schools.

FRANCIS

All joy or sorrow for the happiness or calamities of others is produced by an act of the imagination, that realizes the event however fictitious, or approximates it however remote, by placing us, for a time, in the condition of him whose fortune we contemplate; so that we feel, while the deception lasts, whatever motions would be excited by the same good or evil happening to ourselves.

Our passions are therefore more strongly moved, in proportion as we can more readily adopt the pains or pleasure proposed to our minds, by recognizing them as once our own, or considering them as naturally incident to our state of life. It is not easy for the most artful writer to give us an interest in happiness or misery, which we think ourselves never likely to feel, and with which we have never yet been made acquainted. Histories of the downfall of kingdoms, and revolutions of empires, are read with great tranquillity; the imperial tragedy pleases common auditors only by its pomp of ornament, and grandeur of ideas; and the man whose faculties have been engrossed by business, and whose heart never fluttered but at the rise or fall of the stocks, wonders how the attention can be seized, or the affection agitated, by a tale of love.

Those parallel circumstances and kindred images, to which we readily conform our minds, are, above all other writings, to be found in narratives of the lives of particular persons; and therefore no species of writing seems more worthy of cultivation than biography, since none can be more delightful or more useful, none can more certainly enchain the heart by irresistible interest, or more widely diffuse instruction to every diversity of condition.

The general and rapid narratives of history, which involve a thousand fortunes in the business of a day, and complicate innumerable incidents in one great transaction, afford few lessons applicable to private life, which derives its comforts and its wretchedness from the right or wrong management of things, which nothing but their frequency makes considerable, *Parva si non fiant quotidie*,[1] says Pliny, and which can have no place in those relations which never descend below the consultation of senates, the motions of armies, and the schemes of conspirators.

I have often thought that there has rarely passed a life of which a judicious and faithful narrative would not be useful. For, not only every man has, in the mighty mass of the world, great numbers in the same condition with himself, to whom his mistakes and miscarriages, escapes and expedients, would be of immediate and apparent use; but there is such an uniformity in the state of man, considered apart from adventitious and separable decorations and disguises, that there is scarce any possibility of good or ill, but is common to human kind. A great part of the time of those who are placed at the greatest distance by fortune, or by temper, must unavoidably pass in the same manner; and though, when the claims of nature are satisfied, caprice, and vanity, and accident, begin to produce discriminations and peculiarities, yet the eye is not very heedful or quick, which cannot discover the same causes still terminating their influence in the same effects, though sometimes accelerated, sometimes retarded, or perplexed by multiplied combinations. We are all prompted by the same motives, all deceived by the same fallacies, all animated by hope, obstructed by danger, entangled by desire, and seduced by pleasure.

It is frequently objected to relations of particular lives, that they are not distinguished by any striking or wonderful vicissitudes. The scholar who passed his life among his books, the merchant who conducted only his own affairs, the priest, whose sphere of action was not extended beyond that of his duty, are considered as no proper objects of public regard, however they might have excelled in their several stations, whatever might have been their learning, integrity, and piety. But this notion arises from false measures of excellence and dignity, and must be eradicated by considering, that in the esteem of uncorrupted reason, what is of most use is of most value.

It is, indeed, not improper to take honest advantages of prejudice, and to gain attention by a celebrated name; but the business of a biographer is often to pass slightly over those performances and incidents, which produce vulgar greatness, to lead the thoughts into domestic privacies, and display the minute details of daily life, where exterior appendages are cast aside, and men excel each other only by prudence and by virtue. The account of Thuanus is, with great propriety, said by its author to have been written, that it might lay open to posterity the private and familiar character of that man, *cujus ingenium et candorem ex ipsius scriptis sunt olim semper miraturi*, whose candour and genius will to the end of time be by his writings preserved in admiration.

There are many invisible circumstances which, whether we read as inquirers after natural and moral knowledge, whether we intend to enlarge our science, or increase our virtue, are more important than public occurrences. Thus Sallust, the great master of nature, has not forgot, in his account of Catiline, to remark that 'his walk was now quick, and again slow,' as an indication of a mind revolving something with violent commotion. Thus the story of Melancthon affords a striking lecture on the value of time, by informing us, that when he made an appointment, he expected not only the hour, but the minute to be fixed, that the day might not run out in the idleness of suspense: and all the plans and enterprises of De Witt are now of less importance to the world, than that part of his personal character, which represents him as 'careful of his health, and negligent of his life'.

But biography has often been allotted to writers who seem very little acquainted with the nature of their task, or very negligent about the performance.

They rarely afford any other account than might be collected from public papers, but imagine themselves writing a life when they exhibit a chronological series of actions or preferments; and so little regard the manners or behaviour of their heroes, that more knowledge may be gained of a man's real character, by a short conversation with one of his servants, than from a formal and studied narrative, begun with his pedigree, and ended with his funeral.

If now and then they condescend to inform the world of particular facts, they are not always so happy as to select the most important. I know not well what advantage posterity can receive from the only circumstance by which Tickell has distinguished Addison from the rest of mankind, 'the irregularity of his pulse': nor can I think myself overpaid for the time spent in reading the life of Malherbe by being enabled to relate after the learned biographer, that Malherbe had two predominant opinions; one, that the looseness of a single woman might destroy all her boast of ancient descent; the other, that the French beggars made use very improperly and barbarously of the phrase 'noble Gentleman', because either word included the sense to both.

There are, indeed, some natural reasons why these narratives are often written by such as were not likely to give much instruction or delight, and why most accounts of particular persons are barren and useless. If a life be delayed till interest and envy are at an end, we may hope for impartiality, but must expect little intelligence; for the incidents which give excellence to biography are of a volatile and evanescent kind, such as soon escape the memory, and are rarely transmitted by tradition. We know how few can portray a living acquaintance, except by his most prominent and observable particularities, and the grosser features of his mind; and it may be easily imagined how much of this little knowledge may be lost in imparting it, and how soon a succession of copies will lose all resemblance of the original.

If the biographer writes from personal knowledge, and makes haste to gratify the public curiosity, there is danger lest his interest, his fear, his gratitude, or his tenderness, overpower his fidelity, and tempt him to conceal, if not to invent. There are many who think it an act of piety to hide the faults or failings of their friends, even when they can no longer suffer by their detection; we therefore see whole ranks of characters adorned with uniform panegyric, and not to be known from one another, but by extrinsic and casual circumstances.

'Let me remember,' says Hale, 'when I find myself inclined to pity a criminal, that there is likewise a pity due to the country.' If we owe regard to the memory of the dead, there is yet more respect to be paid to knowledge, to virtue, and to truth.

NO. 144, SATURDAY, 3 AUGUST 1751

... *Daphnidis arcum*
Fregisti et calamos: quæ tu, perverse Menalca,
Et quum vidisti puero donata, dolebas;
Et si non aliqua nocuisses, mortuus esses.

VIRGIL, *Eclogues* iii, 12

The bow of Daphnis and the shafts you broke;
When the fair boy receiv'd the gift of right;
And but for mischief, you had dy'd for spite.

DRYDEN

It is impossible to mingle in conversation without observing the difficulty with which a new name makes its way into the world. The first appearance of excellence unites multitudes against it; unexpected opposition rises up on every side; the celebrated and the obscure join in the confederacy; subtlety furnishes arms to impudence, and invention leads on credulity.

The strength and unanimity of this alliance is not easily conceived. It might be expected that no man should suffer his heart to be inflamed with malice, but by injuries; that none should busy himself in contesting the pretensions of another, but when some right of his own was involved in the question; that at least hostilities, commenced without cause, should quickly cease; that the armies of malignity should soon disperse, when no common interest could be found to hold them together; and that the attack upon a rising character should be left to those who had something to hope or fear from the event.

The hazards of those that aspire to eminence, would be much diminished if they had none but acknowledged rivals to encounter. Their enemies would then be few, and, what is yet of greater importance, would be known. But what caution is sufficient to ward off the blows of invisible assailants, or what force can stand against uninterrupted attacks, and a continual succession of enemies? Yet such is the state of the world, that no sooner can any man emerge from the crowd, and fix the eyes of the public upon him, than he stands as a mark to the arrows of lurking calumny, and receives in the tumult of hostility, from distant and from nameless hands, wounds not always easy to be cured.

It is probable that the onset against the candidates for renown, is originally incited by those who imagine themselves in danger of suffering by their success; but, when war is once declared, volunteers flock to the standard, multitudes follow the camp only for want of employment, and flying squadrons are dispersed to every part, so pleased with an opportunity of mischief, that they toil without prospect of praise, and pillage without hope of profit.

When any man has endeavoured to deserve distinction, he will be surprised to hear himself censured where he could not expect to have been named; he will find the utmost acrimony of malice among those whom he never could have offended.

As there are to be found in the service of envy men of every diversity of temper and degree of understanding, calumny is diffused by all arts and methods of propagation. Nothing is too gross or too refined, too cruel or too trifling, to be practised; very little regard is had to the rules of honourable hostility, but every weapon is accounted lawful, and those that cannot make a thrust at life are content to keep themselves in play with petty malevolence, to tease with feeble blows and impotent disturbance.

But as the industry of observation has divided the most miscellaneous and confused assemblages into proper classes, and ranged the insects of the summer, that torment us with their drones or stings, by their several tribes; the persecutors of merit, notwithstanding their numbers, may be likewise commodiously distinguished into Roarers, Whisperers, and Moderators.

The Roarer is an enemy rather terrible than dangerous. He has no other qualification for a champion of controversy than a hardened front and strong voice. Having seldom so much desire to confute as to silence, he depends rather upon vociferation than argument, and has very little care to adjust one part of his accusation to another, to preserve decency in his language, or probability in his narratives. He has always a store of reproachful epithets and contemptuous appellations, ready to be produced as occasion may require, which by constant use he pours out with resistless volubility. If the wealth of a trader is mentioned, he without hesitation devotes him to bankruptcy; if the beauty and elegance of a lady be commended, he wonders how the town can fall in love with rustic deformity; if a new performance of genius happens to be celebrated, he pronounces the writer a hopeless idiot, without knowledge of books or life, and without the understanding by which it must be acquired. His exaggerations are generally without effect upon those whom he compels to hear them; and though it will sometimes happen that the timorous are awed by his violence, and the credulous mistake his confidence for knowledge, yet the opinions which he endeavours to suppress soon recover their former strength, as the trees that bend to the tempest erect themselves again when its force is past.

The Whisperer is more dangerous. He easily gains attention by a soft address, and excites curiosity by an air of importance. As secrets are not to be made cheap by promiscuous publication, he calls a select audience about him, and gratifies their vanity with an appearance of trust by communicating his intelligence in a low voice. Of the trader he can tell that, though he seems to manage an extensive commerce, and talks in high terms of the funds, yet his wealth is not equal to his reputation; he has lately suffered much by an expensive project, and had a greater share than is acknowledged in the rich ship that perished by the storm. Of the beauty he has little to say, but that they who see her in a morning do not discover all those graces which are admired in the Park. Of the writer he affirms with great certainty, that though the excellence of the work be incontestable, he can claim but a small part of the reputation; that he owed most of the images and sentiments to a secret friend; and that the accuracy and equality of the style was produced by the successive correction of the chief critics of the age.

As every one is pleased with imagining that he knows something not yet commonly divulged, secret history easily gains credit; but it is for the most part believed only while it circulates in whispers; and when once it is openly told, is openly confuted.

The most pernicious enemy is the man of Moderation. Without interest in the question, or any motive but honest curiosity, this impartial and zealous inquirer after truth is ready to hear either side, and always disposed to kind interpretations and favourable opinions. He hath heard the trader's affairs reported with great variation, and, after a diligent comparison of the evidence, concludes it probable that the splendid superstructure of business being originally built upon a narrow basis, has lately been found to totter; but between dilatory payment and bankruptcy there is a great distance; many merchants have supported themselves by expedients for a time, without any final injury to their creditors; and what is lost by one adventure may be recovered by another. He believes that a young lady pleased with admiration, and desirous to make perfect what is already excellent, may heighten her charms by artificial improvements, but surely most of her beauties must be genuine, and who can say that he is wholly what he endeavours to appear? The author he knows to be a man of diligence, who perhaps does not sparkle with the fire of Homer, but has the judgement to discover his own deficiencies, and to supply them by the help of others; and, in his opinion, modesty is a quality so amiable and rare, that it ought to find a patron wherever it appears, and may justly be preferred by the public suffrage to petulant wit and ostentatious literature.

He who thus discovers failings with unwillingness, and extenuates the faults which cannot be denied, puts an end at once to doubt or vindication; his hearers repose upon his candour and veracity, and admit the charge without allowing the excuse.

Such are the arts by which the envious, the idle, the peevish, and the thoughtless, obstruct that worth which they cannot equal, and, by artifices thus easy, sordid, and detestable, is industry defeated, beauty blasted, and genius depressed.

Samuel Johnson

... *Steriles transmisimus annos,*
Hæc ævi mihi prima dies, hæc limina vitæ.
STATIUS, i, 362

... Our barren years are past;
Be this of life the first, of sloth the last.
ELPHINSTON

No weakness of the human mind has more frequently incurred animadversion, than the negligence with which men overlook their own faults, however flagrant, and the easiness with which they pardon them, however frequently repeated.

It seems generally believed, that as the eye cannot see itself, the mind has no faculties by which it can contemplate its own state, and that therefore we have not means of becoming acquainted with our real characters; an opinion which, like innumerable other postulates, an inquirer finds himself inclined to admit upon very little evidence, because it affords a ready solution of many difficulties. It will explain why the greatest abilities frequently fail to promote the happiness of those who possess them; why those who can distinguish with the utmost nicety the boundaries of vice and virtue, suffer them to be confounded in their own conduct; why the active and vigilant resign their affairs implicitly to the management of others; and why the cautious and fearful make hourly approaches towards ruin, without one sigh of solicitude or struggle for escape.

When a position teems thus with commodious consequences, who can without regret confess it to be false? Yet it is certain that declaimers have indulged a disposition to describe the dominion of the passions as extended beyond the limits that nature assigned. Self-love is often rather arrogant than blind; it does not hide our faults from ourselves, but persuades us that they escape the notice of others, and disposes us to resent censures lest we should confess them to be just. We are secretly conscious of defects and vices, which we hope to conceal from the public eye, and please ourselves with innumerable impostures, by which, in reality, nobody is deceived.

In proof of the dimness of our internal sight, or the general inability of man to determine rightly concerning his own character, it is common to urge the success of the most absurd and incredible flattery, and the resentment always raised by advice, however soft, benevolent, and reasonable. But flattery, if its operation be nearly examined,[1] will be found to owe its acceptance, not to our ignorance, but knowledge of our failures, and to delight us rather as it consoles our wants than displays our possessions. He that shall solicit the favour of his patron by praising him for qualities which he can find in himself, will be defeated by the more daring panegyrist who enriches him with adscititious[2] excellence. Just praise is only a debt, but flattery is a present. The acknowledgement of those virtues on which conscience congratulates us, is a tribute that we can at any time exact with confidence; but the celebration of those which we only feign, or desire without any vigorous endeavours to attain them, is received as a confession of sovereignty over regions never conquered, as a favourable decision of disputable claims, and is more welcome as it is more gratuitous.

Advice is offensive, not because it lays us open to unexpected regret, or convicts us of any fault which had escaped our notice, but because it shows us that we are known to others as well as to ourselves; and the officious monitor is persecuted with hatred, not because his accusation is false, but because he assumes that superiority which we are not willing to grant him, and has dared to detect what we desired to conceal.

For this reason advice is commonly ineffectual. If those who follow the call of their desires, without inquiry whither they are going, had deviated ignorantly from the paths of wisdom, and were rushing upon dangers unforeseen, they would readily listen to information that recalls them from their errors, and catch the first alarm by which destruction or infamy is denounced. Few that wander in the wrong way mistake it for the right, they only find it more smooth and flowery, and indulge their own choice rather than approve it: therefore few are persuaded to quit it by admonition or reproof, since it impresses no new conviction, nor confers any powers of action or resistance. He that is gravely informed how soon profusion will annihilate his fortune, hears with little advantage what he knew before, and catches at the next occasion of expense, because advice has no force to suppress his vanity. He that is told how certainly intemperance will hurry him to the grave, runs with his usual speed to a new course of luxury, because his reason is not invigorated, nor his appetite weakened.

The mischief of flattery is, not that it persuades any man that he is what he is not, but that it suppresses the influence of honest ambition, by raising an opinion that honour may be gained without the toil of merit; and the benefit of advice arises commonly not from any new light imparted to the mind, but from the discovery which it affords of the public suffrages. He that could withstand conscience is frighted at infamy, and shame prevails when reason is defeated.

As we all know our own faults, and know them commonly with many aggravations which human perspicacity cannot discover, there is, perhaps, no man, however hardened by impudence or dissipated by levity, sheltered by hypocrisy or blasted by disgrace, who does not intend some time to review his conduct, and to regulate the remainder of his life by the laws of virtue. New temptations indeed attack him, new invitations are offered by pleasure and interest, and the hour of reformation is always delayed; every delay gives vice another opportunity of fortifying itself by habit; and the change of manners, though sincerely intended and rationally planned, is referred to the time when some craving passion shall be fully gratified, or some powerful allurement cease its importunity.

Thus procrastination is accumulated on procrastination, and one impediment succeeds another, till age shatters our resolution, or death intercepts the project of amendment. Such is often the end of salutary purposes, after they have long delighted the imagination, and appeased that disquiet which every mind feels from known misconduct, when the attention is not diverted by business or by pleasure.

Nothing surely can be more unworthy of a reasonable nature, than to continue in a state so opposite to real happiness, as that all the peace of solitude, and felicity of meditation, must arise from resolutions of forsaking it. Yet the world will often afford examples of men, who pass months and years in a continual war with their own convictions, and are daily dragged by habit, or betrayed by passion, into practices which they closed and opened their eyes with purposes to avoid; purposes which, though settled on conviction, the first impulse of momentary desire totally overthrows.

The influence of custom is indeed such, that to conquer it will require the utmost efforts of fortitude and virtue; nor can I think any man more worthy of veneration and renown, than those who have burst the shackles of habitual vice. This victory, however, has different degrees of glory as of difficulty; it is more heroic as the objects of guilty gratification are more familiar, and the recurrence of solicitation more frequent. He that, from experience of the folly of ambition, resigns his offices, may set himself free at once from temptation to squander his life in courts, because he cannot regain his former station. He who is enslaved by an amorous passion, may quit his tyrant in disgust, and absence will, without the help of reason, overcome by degrees the desire of returning. But those appetites to which every place affords their proper object, and which require no preparatory measures or gradual advances, are more tenaciously adhesive; the wish is so near the enjoyment, that compliance often precedes consideration, and, before the powers of reason can be summoned, the time for employing them is past.

Indolence is therefore one of the vices from which those whom it once infects are seldom reformed. Every other species of luxury operates upon some appetite that is quickly satiated, and requires some concurrence of art or accident which every place will not supply; but the desire of ease acts equally at all hours, and the longer it is indulged is the more increased. To do nothing is in every man's power; we can never want an opportunity of omitting duties. The lapse to indolence is soft and imperceptible, because it is only a mere cessation of activity; but the return to diligence is difficult, because it implies a change from rest to motion, from privation to reality:

Samuel Johnson

... Facilis descensus Averni:
Noctes atque dies patet atri janua ditis;
Sed revocare gradum, superasque evadere ad auras,
Hoc opus, hic labor est. ...

VIRGIL, *Æneid*, *Liber* vi, 126

The gates of hell are open night and day;
Smooth the descent, and easy is the way;
But to return, and view the cheerful skies,
In this the task and mighty labour lies.

DRYDEN

Of this vice, as of all others, every man who indulges it is conscious: we all know our own state, if we could be induced to consider it, and it might perhaps be useful to the conquest of all these ensnarers of the mind, if, at certain stated days, life was reviewed. Many things necessary are omitted, because we vainly imagine that they may be always performed; and what cannot be done without pain will for ever be delayed, if the time of doing it be left unsettled. No corruption is great but by long negligence, which can scarcely prevail in a mind regularly and frequently awakened by periodical remorse. He that thus breaks his life into parts, will find in himself a desire to distinguish every stage of his existence by some improvement, and delight himself with the approach of the day of recollection, as of the time which is to begin a new series of virtue and felicity.

No. 185, Tuesday, 24 December 1751

At vindicta bonum vita jucundius ipsa,
Nempe hoc indocti. . . .
Chrysippus non dicet idem, nec mite Thaletis
Ingenium, dulcique senex vicinus Hymetto,
Qui partem adceptæ sæva inter vincla Cicutæ
Adcusatori nollet dare. . . .
. . . Quippe minuti
Semper et infirmi est animi exiguique voluptas
Ultio.

JUVENAL, Satires xiii, 180

But O! revenge is sweet.
Thus think the crowd; who, eager to engage,
Take quickly fire, and kindle into rage.
Not so mild Thales nor Chrysippus thought,
Nor that good man, who drank the poisonous draught
With mind serene; and could not wish to see
H's vile accuser drink as deep as he:
Exalted Socrates! divinely brave!
Injur'd he fell, and dying he forgave!
Too noble for revenge; which still we find
The weakest frailty of a feeble mind.

DRYDEN

No vicious dispositions of the mind more obstinately resist both the counsels of philosophy and the injunctions of religion, than those which are complicated with an opinion of dignity; and which we cannot dismiss without leaving in the hands of opposition some advantage iniquitously obtained, or suffering from our own prejudices some imputation of pusillanimity.

For this reason scarcely any law of our Redeemer is more openly transgressed, or more industriously evaded, than that by which he commands his followers to forgive injuries, and prohibits, under the sanction of eternal misery, the gratification of the desire which every man feels to return pain upon him that inflicts it. Many who could have conquered their anger, are unable to combat pride, and pursue offences to extremity of vengeance, lest they should be insulted by the triumph of an enemy.

But certainly no precept could better become him, at whose birth *peace* was proclaimed *to the earth*. For, what would so soon destroy all the order of society, and deform life with violence and ravage, as a permission to every one to judge his own cause, and to apportion his own recompense for imagined injuries?

It is difficult for a man of the strictest justice not to favour himself too much, in the calmest moments of solitary meditation. Every one wishes for the distinctions for which thousands are wishing at the same time, in their own opinion, with better claims. He that, when his reason operates in its full force, can thus, by the mere prevalence of self-love, prefer himself to his fellow-beings, is very unlikely to judge equitably when his passions are agitated by a sense of wrong, and his attention wholly engrossed by pain, interest, or danger. Whoever arrogates to himself the right of vengeance, shows how little he is qualified to decide his own claims, since he certainly demands what he would think unfit to be granted to another.

Nothing is more apparent than that, however injured, or however provoked, some must at last be contented to forgive. For it can never be hoped, that he who first commits an injury, will contentedly acquiesce in the penalty required: the same haughtiness of contempt, or vehemence of desire, that prompt the act of injustice, will more strongly incite its justification; and resentment can never so exactly balance the punishment with the fault, but there will remain an overplus of vengeance which even he who condemns his first action will think himself entitled to retaliate. What then can ensue but a continual exacerbation of hatred, an unextinguishable feud, an incessant reciprocation of mischief, a mutual vigilance to entrap, and eagerness to destroy?

Since then the imaginary right of vengeance must be at last remitted, because it is impossible to live in perpetual hostility, and equally impossible that of two enemies, either should first think himself obliged by justice to submission, it is surely eligible to forgive early. Every passion is more easily subdued before it has been long accustomed to possession of the heart; every idea is obliterated with less difficulty, as it has been more slightly impressed, and less frequently renewed. He who has often brooded over his wrongs, pleased himself with schemes of malignity, and glutted his pride with the fancied supplications of humbled enmity, will not easily open his bosom to amity and reconciliation, or indulge the gentle sentiments of benevolence and peace.

It is easiest to forgive, while there is yet little to be forgiven. A single injury may be soon dismissed from the memory; but a long succession of ill offices by degrees associates itself with every idea; a long contest involves so many circumstances, that every place and action will recall it to the mind, and fresh remembrance of vexation must still enkindle rage, and irritate revenge.

A wise man will make haste to forgive, because he knows the true value of time, and will not suffer it to pass away in unnecessary pain. He that willingly suffers the corrosions of inveterate hatred, and gives up his days and nights to the gloom of malice, and perturbations of stratagem, cannot surely be said to consult his ease. Resentment is an union of sorrow with malignity, a combination of a passion which all endeavour to avoid, with a passion which all concur to detest. The man who retires to meditate mischief, and to exasperate his own rage; whose thoughts are employed only on means of distress and contrivances of ruin; whose mind never pauses from the remembrance of his own sufferings, but to indulge some hope of enjoying the calamities of another, may justly be numbered among the most miserable of human beings, among those who are guilty without reward, who have neither the gladness of prosperity, nor the calm of innocence.

Whoever considers the weakness both of himself and others, will not long want persuasives to forgiveness. We know not to what degree of malignity any injury is to be imputed; or how much its guilt, if we were to inspect the mind of him that committed it, would be extenuated by mistake, precipitance, or negligence; we cannot be certain how much more we feel than was intended to be inflicted, or how much we increase the mischief to ourselves by voluntary aggravations. We may charge to design the effects of accident; we may think the blow violent only because we have made ourselves delicate and tender; we are on every side in danger of error and of guilt; which we are certain to avoid only by speedy forgiveness.

From this pacific and harmless temper, thus propitious to others and ourselves, to domestic tranquillity and to social happiness, no man is withheld but by pride, by the fear of being insulted by his adversary, or despised by the world.

It may be laid down as an unfailing and universal axiom, that 'all pride is abject and mean'. It is always an ignorant, lazy, or cowardly acquiescence in a false appearance of excellence, and proceeds not from consciousness of our attainments, but insensibility of our wants.

Nothing can be great which is not right. Nothing which reason condemns can be suitable to the dignity of the human mind. To be driven by external motives from the path which our own heart approves, to give way to anything but conviction, to suffer the opinion of others to rule our choice, or overpower our resolves, is to submit tamely to the lowest and most ignominious slavery, and to resign the right of directing our own lives.

The utmost excellence at which humanity can arrive, is a constant and determinate pursuit of virtue, without regard to present dangers or advantage; a continual reference of every action to the divine will; an habitual appeal to everlasting justice; and an unvaried elevation of the intellectual eye to the reward which perseverance only can obtain. But that pride which many, who presume to boast of generous sentiments, allow to regulate their measures, has nothing nobler in view than the approbation of men, of beings whose superiority we are under no obligation to acknowledge, and who, when we have courted them with the utmost assiduity, can confer no valuable or permanent reward; of beings who ignorantly judge of what they do not understand, or partially determine what they never have examined; and whose sentence is therefore of no weight till it has received the ratification of our own conscience.

He that can descend to bribe suffrages like these, at the price of his innocence: he that can suffer the delight of such acclamations to withhold his attention from the commands of the universal Sovereign, has little reason to congratulate himself upon the greatness of his mind; whenever he awakes to seriousness and reflection, he must become despicable in his own eyes, and shrink with shame from the remembrance of his cowardice and folly.

Of him that hopes to be forgiven, it is indispensably required that he forgive. It is therefore superfluous to urge any other motive. On this great duty eternity is suspended, and to him that refuses to practise it, the Throne of mercy is inaccessible and the Saviour of the world has been born in vain.

THE ADVENTURER*

No. 67, Tuesday, 26 June 1753

Inventas – vitam excoluere per artes.
VIRGIL, Æneid, vi, 663
They polish life by useful arts.

THAT familiarity produces neglect, has been long observed. The effect of all external objects, however great or splendid, ceases with their novelty: the courtier stands without emotion in the royal presence; the rustic tramples under his foot the beauties of the spring, with little attention to their colour or their fragrance; and the inhabitant of the coast darts his eye upon the immense diffusion of waters, without awe, wonder or terror.

Those who have passed much of their lives in this great city, look upon its opulence and its multitudes, its extent and variety, with cold indifference; but an inhabitant of the remoter parts of the kingdom is immediately distinguished by a kind of dissipated curiosity, a busy endeavour to divide his attention amongst a thousand objects, and a wild confusion of astonishment and alarm.

The attention of a new-comer is generally first struck by the multiplicity of cries that stun him in the streets, and the variety of merchandise and manufactures which the shopkeepers expose on every hand; and he is apt, by unwary bursts of admiration, to excite the merriment and contempt of those, who mistake the use of their eyes for effects of their understanding, and confound accidental knowledge with just reasoning.

But, surely, these are subjects on which any man may without reproach employ his meditations: the innumerable occupations, among which the thousands that swarm in the streets of London are distributed, may furnish employment to minds of every cast, and capacities of every degree. He that contemplates the extent of this wonderful city, finds it difficult to conceive, by what method plenty is maintained in our markets, and how the inhabitants are regularly supplied

* See Editor's Notes.

with the necessaries of life; but when he examines the shops and ware-houses, sees the immense stores of every kind of merchandise piled up for sale, and runs over all the manufactures of art and products of nature, which are everywhere attracting his eye and soliciting his purse, he will be inclined to conclude, that such quantities cannot easily be exhausted, and that part of mankind must soon stand still for want of employment, till the wares already provided shall be worn out and destroyed.

As Socrates was passing through the fair at Athens, and casting his eyes over the shops and customers, 'how many things are here', says he, 'that I do not want!' The same sentiment is every moment rising in the mind of him that walks the streets of London, however inferior in philosophy to Socrates: he beholds a thousand shops crowded with goods, of which he can scarcely tell the use, and which, therefore, he is apt to consider as of no value: and, indeed, many of the arts by which families are supported, and wealth is heaped to-gether, are of that minute and superfluous kind, which nothing but experience could evince possible to be prosecuted with advantage, and which, as the world might easily want, it could scarcely be expected to encourage.

But so it is, that custom, curiosity, or wantonness, supplies every art with patrons, and finds purchasers for every manufacture; the world is so adjusted, that not only bread, but riches may be obtained without great abilities, or arduous performances: the most unskilful hand and unenlightened mind have sufficient incitements to industry; for he that is resolutely busy, can scarcely be in want. There is, indeed, no employment, however despicable, from which a man may not promise himself more than competence, when he sees thousands and myriads raised to dignity, by no other merit than that of contributing to supply their neighbours with the means of sucking smoke through a tube of clay; and others raising contributions upon those, whose elegance disdains the grossness of smoky luxury, by grinding the same materials into a powder, that may at once gratify and impair the smell.

Not only by these popular and modish trifles, but by a thousand unheeded and evanescent kinds of business, are the multitudes of this city preserved from idleness, and consequently from want. In the endless variety of tastes and circumstances that diversify mankind, nothing is so superfluous, but that some one desires it; or so common, but that some one is compelled to buy it. As nothing is useless but because it is in improper hands, what is thrown away by one is gathered up by another; and the refuse of part of mankind furnishes a subordinate class with the materials necessary to their support.

When I look round upon those who are thus variously exerting their qualifications, I cannot but admire the secret concatenation of society, that links together the great and the mean, the illustrious and the obscure; and consider with benevolent satisfaction, that no man, unless his body or mind be totally disabled, has need to suffer the mortification of seeing himself useless or burdensome to the community: he that will diligently labour, in whatever occupation, will deserve the sustenance which he obtains, and the protection which he enjoys; and may lie down every night with the pleasing consciousness, of having contributed something to the happiness of life.

Contempt and admiration are equally incident to narrow minds: he whose comprehension can take in the whole subordination of mankind, and whose perspicacity can pierce to the real state of things through the thin veils of fortune or of fashion, will discover meanness in the highest stations, and dignity in the meanest; and find that no man can become venerable but by virtue, or contemptible but by wickedness.

In the midst of this universal hurry, no man ought to be so little influenced by example, or so void of honest emulation, as to stand a lazy spectator of incessant labour; or please himself with the mean happiness of a drone, while the active swarms are buzzing about him: no man is without some quality, by the due application of which he might deserve well of the world; and whoever he be that has but little in his power, should be in haste to do that little, lest he be confounded with him that can do nothing.

By this general concurrence of endeavours, arts of every kind have been so long cultivated, that all the wants of man may be immediately supplied; idleness can scarcely form a wish which she may not gratify by the toil of others, or curiosity dream of a toy which the shops are not ready to afford her.

Happiness is enjoyed only in proportion as it is known; and such is the state or folly of man, that it is known only by experience of its contrary: we who have long lived amidst the conveniences of a town immensely populous, have scarce an idea of a place where desire cannot be gratified by money. In order to have a just sense of this artificial plenty, it is necessary to have passed some time in a distant colony, or those parts of our island which are thinly inhabited: he that has once known how many trades every man in such situations is compelled to exercise, with how much labour the products of nature must be accommodated to human use, how long the loss or defect of any common utensil must be endured, or by what awkward expedients it must be supplied, how far men may wander with money in their hands before any can sell them what they wish to buy, will know how to rate at its proper value the plenty and ease of a great city.

But that the happiness of man may still remain imperfect, as wants in this place are easily supplied, new wants likewise are easily created: every man, in surveying the shops of London, sees numberless instruments and conveniences, of which, while he did not know them, he never felt the need; and yet, when use has made them familiar, wonders how life could be supported without them. Thus it comes to pass, that our desires always increase with our possessions; the knowledge that something remains yet unenjoyed, impairs our enjoyment of the good before us.

They who have been accustomed to the refinements of science, and multiplications of contrivance, soon lose their confidence in the unassisted powers of nature, forget the paucity of our real necessities, and overlook the easy methods by which they may be supplied. It were a speculation worthy of a philosophical mind, to examine how much is taken away from our native abilities, as well as added to them by artificial expedients. We are so accustomed to give and receive assistance, that each of us singly can do little for himself; and there is scarce any one amongst us, however contracted may be his form of life, who does not enjoy the labour of a thousand artists.

But a survey of the various nations that inhabit the earth will inform us, that life may be supported with less assistance, and that the dexterity, which practice enforced by necessity produces, is able to effect much by very scanty means. The nations of Mexico and Peru erected cities and temples without the use of iron; and at this day the rude Indian supplies himself with all the necessaries of life: sent like the rest of mankind naked into the world, as soon as his parents have nursed him up to strength, he is to provide by his own labour for his own support. His first care is to find a sharp flint among the rocks; with this he undertakes to fell the trees of the forest; he shapes his bow, heads his arrows, builds his cottage, and hollows his canoe, and from that time lives in a state of plenty and prosperity; he is sheltered from the storms, he is fortified against beasts of prey, he is enabled to pursue the fish of the sea, and the deer of the mountains; and as he does not know, does not envy the happiness of polished nations, where gold can supply the want of fortitude and skill, and he whose laborious ancestors have made him rich, may lie stretched upon a couch, and see all the treasures of all the elements poured down before him.

This picture of a savage life, if it shows how much individuals may perform, shows likewise how much society is to be desired. Though the perseverance and address of the Indian excite our admiration, they nevertheless cannot procure him the conveniences which are enjoyed by the vagrant beggar of a civilized country: he hunts like a wild beast to satisfy his hunger; and when he lies down to rest after a successful chase, cannot pronounce himself secure against the danger of perishing in a few days; he is, perhaps, content with his condition, because he knows not that a better is attainable by man; as he that is born blind does not long for the perception of light, because he cannot conceive the advantages which light would afford him: but hunger, wounds and weariness are real evils, though he believes them equally incident to all his fellow creatures; and when a tempest compels him to lie starving in his hut, he cannot justly be concluded equally happy with those whom art has exempted from the power of chance, and who make the foregoing year provide for the following.

To receive and to communicate assistance, constitutes the happiness of human life: man may indeed preserve his existence in solitude, but can enjoy it only in society: the greatest understanding of an individual doomed to procure food and clothing for himself, will barely supply him with expedients to keep off death from day to day; but as one of a large community performing only his share of the common business, he gains leisure for intellectual pleasures, and enjoys the happiness of reason and reflection.

No. 99, Tuesday, 16 October 1753

... Magnis tamen excidit ausis.
OVID, Metamorphoses, ii, 328
But in the glorious enterprize he dy'd.
ADDISON

It has always been the practice of mankind, to judge of actions by the event. The same attempts, conducted in the same manner, but terminated by different success, produce different judgements: they who attain their wishes, never want celebrators of their wisdom and their virtue; and they that miscarry, are quickly discovered to have been defective not only in mental but in moral qualities. The world will never be long without some good reason to hate the unhappy; their real faults are immediately detected, and if those are not sufficient to sink them into infamy, an additional weight of calumny will be superadded: he that fails in his endeavours after wealth or power, will not long retain either honesty or courage.

This species of injustice has so long prevailed in universal practice, that it seems likewise to have infected speculation: so few minds are able to separate the ideas of greatness and prosperity, that even Sir William Temple has determined, that 'he who can deserve the name of a hero, must not only be virtuous but fortunate'.

By this unreasonable distribution of praise and blame, none have suffered oftener than projectors, whose rapidity of imagination and vastness of design, raise such envy in their fellow mortals, that every eye watches for their fall, and every heart exults at their distress: yet even a projector may gain favour by success; and the tongue that was prepared to hiss, then endeavours to excel others in loudness of applause.

When Coriolanus, in Shakespeare, deserted to Aufidius, the Volscian servants at first insulted him, even while he stood under the protection of the household gods; but when they saw that the project took effect, and the stranger was seated at the head of the table, one of them very judiciously observes, 'that he always thought there was more in him than he could think'.

Machiavel has justly animadverted on the different notice taken by all succeeding times, of the two great projectors Catiline and Caesar. Both formed the same project, and intended to raise themselves to power, by subverting the commonwealth: they pursued their design, perhaps, with equal abilities, and with equal virtue; but Catiline perished in the field, and Caesar returned from Pharsalia with unlimited authority: and from that time, every monarch of the earth has thought himself honoured by a comparison with Caesar; and Catiline has been never mentioned, but that his name might be applied to traitors and incendiaries.

In an age more remote, Xerxes projected the conquest of Greece, and brought down the power of Asia against it: but after the world had been filled with expectation and terror, his army was beaten, his fleet was destroyed and Xerxes has been never mentioned without contempt.

A few years afterwards, Greece likewise had her turn of giving birth to a projector; who invading Asia with a small army, went forward in search of adventures, and by his escape from one danger gained only more rashness to rush into another: he stormed city after city, over-ran kingdom after kingdom, fought battles only for barren victory, and invaded nations only that he might make his way through them to new invasions: but having been fortunate in the execution of his projects, he died with the name of Alexander the Great.

These are, indeed, events of ancient time; but human nature is always the same, and every age will afford us instances of public censures influenced by events. The great business of the middle centuries was the holy war; which undoubtedly was a noble project, and was for a long time prosecuted with a spirit equal to that with which it had been contrived: but the ardour of the European heroes only hurried them to destruction; for a long time they could not gain the territories for which they fought, and, when at last gained, they could not keep them: their expeditions, therefore, have been the scoff of idleness and ignorance, their understanding and their virtue have been equally vilified, their conduct has been ridiculed, and their cause has been defamed.

When Columbus had engaged King Ferdinand in the discovery of the other hemisphere, the sailors with whom he embarked in the expedition had so little confidence in their commander, that after having been long at sea looking for coasts which they expected never to find, they raised a general mutiny, and demanded to return. He found means to sooth them into a permission to continue the same course three days longer, and on the evening of the third day descried land. Had the impatience of his crew denied him a few hours of the time requested, what had been his fate but to have come back with the infamy of a vain projector, who had betrayed the king's credulity to useless expenses, and risked his life in seeking countries that had no existence: how would those that had rejected his proposals, have triumphed in their acuteness? and when would his name have been mentioned, but with the makers of potable gold and malleable glass?

The last royal projectors with whom the world has been troubled, were Charles of Sweden and the Czar of Muscovy. Charles, if any judgement may be formed of his designs by his measures and his inquiries, had purposed first to dethrone the Czar, then to lead his army through pathless deserts into China, thence to make his way by the sword through the whole circuit of Asia, and by the conquest of Turkey to unite Sweden with his new dominions: but this mighty project was crushed at Pultowa, and Charles has since been considered as a madman by those powers, who sent their ambassadors to solicit his friendship, and their generals 'to learn under him the art of war'.

The Czar found employment sufficient in his own dominions, and amused himself in digging canals, and building cities; murdering his subjects with insufferable fatigues, and transplanting nations from one corner of his dominions to another, without regretting the thousands that perished on the way: but he attained his end, he made his people formidable, and is numbered by fame among the Demi-gods.

I am far from intending to vindicate the sanguinary projects of heroes and conquerors, and would wish rather to diminish the reputation of their success, than the infamy of their miscarriages: for I cannot conceive, why he that has burnt cities, and wasted nations, and filled the world with horror and desolation, should be more kindly regarded by mankind, than he that died in the rudiments of wickedness; why he that accomplished mischief should be glorious, and he that only endeavoured it should be criminal: I would wish Caesar and Catiline, Xerxes and Alexander, Charles and Peter, huddled together in obscurity or detestation.

But there is another species of projectors, to whom I would willingly conciliate mankind; whose ends are generally laudable, and whose labours are innocent; who are searching out new powers of nature, or contriving new works of art; but who are yet persecuted with incessant obloquy, and whom the universal contempt with which they are treated, often debars from that success which their industry would obtain, if it were permitted to act without opposition.

They who find themselves inclined to censure new undertakings, only because they are new, should consider, that the folly of projection is very seldom the folly of a fool; it is commonly the ebullition of a capacious mind, crowded with variety of knowledge, and heated with intenseness of thought; it proceeds often from the consciousness of uncommon powers, from the confidence of those, who having already done much, are easily persuaded that they can do more: when Rowley had completed the orrery, he attempted the perpetual motion; when Boyle had exhausted the secrets of vulgar chemistry, he turned his thoughts to the work of transmutation.

A projector generally unites those qualities which have the fairest claim to veneration, extent of knowledge and greatness of design: it was said of Catiline, *immoderata, incredibilia, nimis alta semper cupiebat.* Projectors of all kinds agree in their intellects, though they differ in their morals; they all fail by attempting things beyond their power, by despising vulgar attainments, and aspiring to performances to which, perhaps, nature has not proportioned the force of man: when they fail, therefore, they fail not by idleness or timidity, but by rash adventure and fruitless diligence.

That the attempts of such men will often miscarry, we may reasonably expect; yet from such men, and such only, are we to hope for the cultivation of those parts of nature which lie yet waste, and the invention of those arts which are yet wanting to the felicity of life. If they are, therefore, universally discouraged, art and discovery can make no advances. Whatever is attempted without previous certainty of success, may be considered as a project, and amongst narrow minds may, therefore, expose its author to censure and contempt; and if the liberty of laughing be once indulged, every man will laugh at what he does not understand, every project will be considered as madness, and every great or new design will be censured as a project. Men, unaccustomed to reason and researches, think every enterprise impracticable, which is extended beyond common effects, or comprises many intermediate operations. Many that presume to laugh at projectors, would consider a flight through the air in a winged chariot, and the movement of a mighty engine by the steam of water, as equally the dreams of mechanic lunacy; and would hear, with equal negligence, of the union of the Thames and Severn by a canal, and the scheme of Albuquerque the viceroy of the Indies, who in the rage of hostility had contrived to make Egypt a barren desert, by turning the Nile into the Red Sea.

Those who have attempted much, have seldom failed to perform more than those who never deviate from the common roads of action: many valuable preparations of chemistry, are supposed to have risen from unsuccessful inquiries after the grand elixir: it is, therefore, just to encourage those, who endeavour to enlarge the power of art, since they often succeed beyond expectation; and when they fail, may sometimes benefit the world even by their miscarriages.

No. 107, Tuesday, 13 November 1753

... *Sub judice lis est.*

HORACE, Art of Poetry, l. 78

And of their vain disputings find no end

FRANCIS

It has been sometimes asked by those, who find the appearance of wisdom more easily attained by questions than solutions, how it comes to pass, that the world is divided by such difference of opinion; and why men, equally reasonable, and equally lovers of truth, do not always think in the same manner.

With regard to simple propositions, where the terms are understood, and the whole subject is comprehended at once, there is such an uniformity of sentiment among all human beings, that, for many ages, a very numerous set of notions were supposed to be innate, or necessarily coexistent with the faculty of reason; it being imagined, that universal agreement could proceed only from the invariable dictates of the universal parent.

In questions diffuse and compounded, this similarity of determination is no longer to be expected. At our first sally into the intellectual world, we all march together along one strait and open road; but as we proceed further, and wider prospects open to our view, every eye fixes upon a different scene; we divide into various paths, and, as we move forward, are still at a greater distance from each other. As a question becomes more complicated and involved, and extends to a greater number of relations, disagreement of opinion will always be multiplied, not because we are irrational, but because we are finite beings, furnished with different kinds of knowledge, exerting different degrees of attention, one discovering consequences which escape another, none taking in the whole concatenation of causes and effects, and most comprehending but a very small part; each comparing what he observes with a different criterion, and each referring it to a different purpose.

Where, then, is the wonder, that they, who see only a small part, should judge erroneously of the whole? or that they, who see different and dissimilar parts, should judge differently from each other?

Whatever has various respects, must have various appearances of good and evil, beauty or deformity: thus, the gardener tears up as a weed, the plant which the physician gathers as a medicine; and 'a general,' says Sir Kenelm Digby, 'will look with pleasure over a plain, as a fit place on which the fate of empires might be decided in battle; which the farmer will despise as bleak and barren, neither fruitful of pasturage, nor fit for tillage.'

Two men examining the same question, proceed commonly like the physician and gardener in selecting herbs, or the farmer and hero looking on the plain; they bring minds impressed with different notions, and direct their inquiries to different ends; they form, therefore, contrary conclusions, and each wonders at the other's absurdity.

We have less reason to be surprised or offended when we find others differ from us in opinion, because we very often differ from ourselves: how often we alter our minds, we do not always remark; because the change is sometimes made imperceptibly and gradually, and the last conviction effaces all memory of the former; yet every man, accustomed from time to time to take a survey of his own notions, will by a slight retrospection be able to discover, that his mind has suffered many revolutions, that the same things have in the several parts of his life been condemned and approved, pursued and shunned; and that on many occasions, even when his practice has been steady, his mind has been wavering, and he has persisted in a scheme of action, rather because he feared the censure of inconstancy, than because he was always pleased with his own choice.

Of the different faces shown by the same objects as they are viewed on opposite sides, and of the different inclinations which they must constantly raise in him that contemplates them, a more striking example cannot easily be found than two Greek epigrammatists will afford us in their accounts of human life, which I shall lay before the reader in English prose.

Posidippus, a comic poet, utters this complaint; 'Through which of the paths of life is it eligible to pass? In public assemblies are debates and troublesome affairs; domestic privacies are haunted with anxieties; in the country is labour; on the sea is terror; in a foreign land, he that has money must live in fear, he that wants it must pine in distress; are you married? you are troubled with suspicions; are you single? you languish in solitude; children occasion toil, and a childless life is a state of destitution; the time of youth is a time of folly, and grey hairs are loaded with infirmity. This choice only, therefore, can be made, either never to receive being, or immediately to lose it.'

Such and so gloomy is the prospect, which Posidippus has laid before us. But we are not to acquiesce too hastily in his determination against the value of existence, for Metrodorus, a philosopher of Athens, has shown, that life has pleasures as well as pains; and having exhibited the present state of man in brighter colours, draws, with equal appearance of reason, a contrary conclusion:

'You may pass well through any of the paths of life. In public assemblies are honours, and transactions of wisdom; in domestic privacy is stillness and quiet; in the country are the beauties of nature; on the sea is the hope of gain; in a foreign land, he that is rich is honoured, he that is poor may keep his poverty secret; are you married? you have a cheerful house; are you single? you are unencumbered; children are objects of affection; to be without children is to be without care; the time of youth is the time of vigour; and grey hairs are made venerable by piety. It will, therefore, never be a wise man's choice, either not to obtain existence, or to lose it; for every state of life has its felicity.'

In these epigrams are included most of the questions, which have engaged the speculations of the inquirers after happiness; and though they will not much assist our determinations, they may, perhaps, equally promote our quiet, by showing that no absolute determination ever can be formed.

Whether a public station, or private life be desirable, has always been debated. We see here both the allurements and discouragements of civil employments; on one side there is trouble, on the other honour; the management of affairs is vexatious and difficult, but it is the only duty in which wisdom can be conspicuously displayed: it must then still be left to every man to choose either ease or glory; nor can any general precept be given, since no man can be happy by the prescription of another.

Thus what is said of children by Posidippus, 'that they are occasions of fatigue,' and by Metrodorus, 'that they are objects of affection,' is equally certain; but whether they will give most pain or pleasure, must depend on their future conduct and dispositions, on many causes over which the parent can have little influence: there is, therefore, room for all the caprices of imagination, and desire must be proportioned to the hope or fear that shall happen to predominate.

Such is the uncertainty, in which we are always likely to remain with regard to questions, wherein we have most interest, and which every day affords us fresh opportunity to examine: we may examine, indeed, but we never can decide, because our faculties are unequal to the subject: we see a little, and form an opinion; we see more, and change it.

This inconstancy and unsteadiness, to which we must so often find ourselves liable, ought certainly to teach us moderation and forbearance towards those, who cannot accommodate themselves to our sentiments: if they are deceived, we have no right to attribute their mistake to obstinacy or negligence, because we likewise have been mistaken: we may, perhaps, again change our own opinion; and what excuse shall we be able to find for aversion and malignity conceived against him, whom we shall then find to have committed no fault, and who offended us only by refusing to follow us into error?

It may likewise contribute to soften that resentment, which pride naturally raises against opposition, if we consider, that he, who differs from us, does not always contradict us; he has one view of an object, and we have another; each describes what he sees with equal fidelity, and each regulates his steps by his own eyes: one man, with Posidippus, looks on celibacy as a state of gloomy solitude, without a partner in joy or a comforter in sorrow; the other considers it, with Metrodorus, as a state free from incumbrances, in which a man is at liberty to choose his own gratifications, to remove from place to place in quest of pleasure, and to think of nothing but merriment and diversion; full of these notions, one hastens to choose a wife, and the other laughs at his rashness, or pities his ignorance; yet it is possible that each is right, but that each is right only for himself.

Life is not the object of science: we see a little, very little; and what is beyond we only can conjecture. If we inquire of those who have gone before us, we receive small satisfaction; some have travelled life without observation, and some willingly mislead us. The only thought, therefore, on which we can repose with comfort, is that which presents to us the care of Providence, whose eye takes in the whole of things, and under whose direction all involuntary errors will terminate in happiness.

No. 137, Tuesday, 26 February 1754

Τί δ' ἔρεξα;

PYTHAGORAS, Aurea Carmina, 42
What have I been doing?

As man is a being very sparingly furnished with the power of prescience, he can provide for the future only by considering the past; and as futurity is all in which he has any real interest, he ought very diligently to use the only means by which he can be enabled to enjoy it, and frequently to revolve the experiments which he has hitherto made upon life, that he may gain wisdom from his mistakes and caution from his miscarriages.

Though I do not so exactly conform to the precepts of Pythagoras, as to practise every night this solemn recollection, yet I am not so lost in dissipation as wholly to omit it; nor can I forbear sometimes to inquire of myself, in what employments my life has passed away. Much of my time has sunk into nothing, and left no trace by which it can be distinguished, and of this I now only know, that it was once in my power and might once have been improved.

Of other parts of life memory can give some account: at some hours I have been gay, and at others serious; I have sometimes mingled in conversation, and sometimes meditated in solitude; one day has been spent in consulting the ancient sages, and another in writing *Adventurers*.

At the conclusion of any undertaking, it is usual to compute the loss and profit. As I shall soon cease to write *Adventurers*, I could not forbear lately to consider what has been the consequence of my labours; and whether I am to reckon the hours laid out in these compositions, as applied to a good and laudable purpose, or suffered to fume away in useless evaporations.

That I have intended well, I have the attestation of my own heart; but good intentions may be frustrated, when they are executed without suitable skill, or directed to an end unattainable in itself.

Some there are, who leave writers very little room for self congratulation; some who affirm, that books have no influence upon the public, that no age was ever made better by its authors, and that to call upon mankind to correct their manners, is, like Xerxes, to scourge the wind or shackle the torrent.

This opinion they pretend to support by unfailing experience. The world is full of fraud and corruption, rapine and malignity; interest is the ruling motive of mankind, and every one is endeavouring to increase his own stores of happiness by perpetual accumulation, without reflecting upon the numbers whom his superfluity condemns to want: in this state of things a book of morality is published, in which charity and benevolence are strongly enforced; and it is proved beyond opposition, that men are happy in proportion as they are virtuous, and rich as they are liberal. The book is applauded, and the author is preferred; he imagines his applause deserved, and receives less pleasure from the acquisition of reward, than the consciousness of merit. Let us look again upon mankind: interest is still the ruling motive, and the world is yet full of fraud and corruption, malevolence and rapine.

The difficulty of confuting this assertion, arises merely from its generality and comprehension: to overthrow it by a detail of distinct facts, requires a wider survey of the world than human eyes can take; the progress of reformation is gradual and silent, as the extension of evening shadows; we know that they were short at noon, and are long at sun-set, but our senses were not able to discern their increase; we know of every civil nation that it was once savage, and how was it reclaimed but by precept and admonition?

Mankind are universally corrupt, but corrupt in different degrees; as they are universally ignorant, yet with greater or less irradiations of knowledge. How has knowledge or virtue been increased and preserved in one place beyond another, but by diligent inculcation and rational enforcement?

Books of morality are daily written, yet its influence is still little in the world; so the ground is annually ploughed, and yet multitudes are in want of bread. But, surely, neither the labours of the moralist nor of the husbandman are vain: let them for a while neglect their tasks, and their usefulness will be known; the wickedness that is now frequent would become universal, the bread that is now scarce would wholly fail.

The power, indeed, of every individual is small, and the consequence of his endeavours imperceptible in a general prospect of the world. Providence has given no man ability to do much, that something might be left for every man to do. The business of life is carried on by a general cooperation; in which the part of any single man can be no more distinguished, than the effect of a particular drop when the meadows are floated by a summer shower: yet every drop increases the inundation, and every hand adds to the happiness or misery of mankind.

That a writer, however zealous or eloquent, seldom works a visible effect upon cities or nations, will readily be granted. The book which is read most, is read by few, compared with those that read it not; and of those few, the greater part peruse it with dispositions that very little favour their own improvement.

It is difficult to enumerate the several motives, which procure to books the honour of perusal: spite, vanity, and curiosity, hope and fear, love and hatred, every passion which incites to any other action, serves at one time or other to stimulate a reader.

Some are fond to take a celebrated volume into their hands, because they hope to distinguish their penetration, by finding faults which have escaped the public; others eagerly buy it in the first bloom of reputation, that they may join the chorus of praise, and not lag, as Falstaff terms it, in 'the rearward of the fashion'.

Some read for style, and some for argument: one has little care about the sentiment, he observes only how it is expressed; another regards not the conclusion, but is diligent to mark how it is inferred: they read for other purposes, than the attainment of practical knowledge; and are no more likely to grow wise by an examination of a treatise of moral prudence, than an architect to inflame his devotion by considering attentively the proportions of a temple.

Some read that they may embellish their conversation, or shine in dispute; some that they may not be detected in ignorance, or want the reputation of literary accomplishments: but the most general and prevalent reason of study, is the impossibility of finding another amusement equally cheap or constant, equally independent on the hour or the weather. He that wants money to follow the chase of pleasure through her yearly circuit, and is left at home when the gay world rolls to Bath or Tunbridge; he whose gout compels him to hear from his chamber, the rattle of chariots transporting happier beings to plays and assemblies, will be forced to seek in books a refuge from himself.

The author is not wholly useless, who provides innocent amusements for minds like these. There are in the present state of things so many more instigations to evil, than incitements to good, that he who keeps men in a neutral state, may be justly considered as a benefactor to life.

But, perhaps, it seldom happens, that study terminates in mere pastime. Books have always a secret influence on the understanding; we cannot at pleasure obliterate ideas; he that reads books of science, though without any fixed desire of improvement, will grow more knowing; he that entertains himself with moral or religious treatises, will imperceptibly advance in goodness; the ideas which are often offered to the mind, will at last find a lucky moment when it is disposed to receive them.

It is, therefore, urged without reason, as a discouragement to writers, that there are already books sufficient in the world; that all the topics of persuasion have been discussed, and every important question clearly stated and justly decided; and that, therefore, there is no room to hope, that pigmies should conquer where heroes have been defeated, or that petty copiers of the present time should advance the great work of reformation, which their predecessors were forced to leave unfinished.

Whatever be the present extent of human knowledge, it is not only finite, and therefore in its own nature capable of increase; but so narrow, that almost every understanding may by a diligent application of its powers hope to enlarge it. It is, however, not necessary, that a man should forbear to write, till he has discovered some truth unknown before; he may be sufficiently useful, by only diversifying the surface of knowledge, and luring the mind by a new appearance to a second view of those beauties which it had passed over inattentively before. Every writer may find intellects correspondent to his own, to whom his expressions are familiar, and his thoughts congenial; and, perhaps, truth is often more successfully propagated by men of moderate abilities, who, adopting the opinions of others, have no care but to explain them clearly, than by subtle speculatists and curious searchers, who exact from their readers powers equal to their own, and if their fabrics of science be strong take no care to render them accessible.

For my part, I do not regret the hours which I have laid out on these little compositions. That the world has grown apparently better, since the publication of the *Adventurer*, I have not observed; but am willing to think, that many have been affected by single sentiments, of which it is their business to renew the impression; that many have caught hints of truth, which it is now their duty to pursue; and that those who have received no improvement, have wanted not opportunity but intention to improve.

THE IDLER*

Surge tandem Carnifex

The rainy weather which has continued the last month, is said to have given great disturbance to the inspectors of barometers. The oraculous glasses have deceived their votaries; shower has succeeded shower, though they predicted sunshine and dry skies; and by fatal confidence in these fallacious promises, many coats have lost their gloss, and many curls been moistened to flaccidity.

This is one of the distresses to which mortals subject themselves by the pride of speculation. I had no part in this learned disappointment, who am content to credit my senses, and to believe that rain will fall when the air blackens, and that the weather will be dry when the sun is bright. My caution indeed does not always preserve me from a shower. To be wet may happen to the genuine Idler, but to be wet in opposition to theory, can befall only the Idler that pretends to be busy. Of those that spin out life in trifles, and die without a memorial, many flatter themselves with high opinions of their own importance, and imagine that they are every day adding some improvement to human life. To be idle and to be poor have always been reproaches, and therefore every man endeavours with his utmost care, to hide his poverty from others, and his idleness from himself.

Among those whom I never could persuade to rank themselves with Idlers, and who speak with indignation of my morning sleeps and nocturnal rambles; one passes the day in catching spiders that he may count their eyes with a microscope: another erects his head, and exhibits the dust of a marigold separated from the flower with dexterity worthy of Leeuwenhoeck himself. Some turn the wheel of electricity, some suspend rings to a loadstone, and find that what they did yesterday they can do again today. Some register the changes of the wind, and die fully convinced that the wind is changeable.

There are men yet more profound, who have heard that two col-

* See Editor's Notes.

ourless liquors may produce a colour by union, and that two cold bodies will grow hot if they are mingled: they mingle them, and produce the effect expected, say it is strange, and mingle them again.

The Idlers that sport only with inanimate nature may claim some indulgence; if they are useless they are still innocent: but there are others, whom I know not how to mention without more emotion than my love of quiet willingly admits. Among the inferior professors of medical knowledge, is a race of wretches, whose lives are only varied by varieties of cruelty; whose favourite amusement is to nail dogs to tables and open them alive; to try how long life may be continued in various degrees of mutilation, or with the excision or laceration of the vital parts; to examine whether burning irons are felt more acutely by the bone or tendon; and whether the more lasting agonies are produced by poison forced into the mouth or injected into the veins.

It is not without reluctance that I offend the sensibility of the tender mind with images like these. If such cruelties were not practised it were to be desired that they should not be conceived, but since they are published every day with ostentation, let me be allowed once to mention them, since I mention them with abhorrence.

Mead has invidiously remarked of Woodward that he gathered shells and stones, and would pass for a philosopher. With pretensions much less reasonable, the anatomical novice tears out the living bowels of an animal, and styles himself physician, prepares himself by familiar cruelty for that profession which he is to exercise upon the tender and the helpless, upon feeble bodies and broken minds, and by which he has opportunities to extend his arts of torture, and continue those experiments upon infancy and age, which he has hitherto tried upon cats and dogs.

What is alleged in defence of these hateful practices, everyone knows; but the truth is, that by knives, fire, and poison, knowledge is not always sought, and is very seldom attained. The experiments that have been tried, are tried again; he that burned an animal with irons yesterday; will be willing to amuse himself with burning another tomorrow. I know not, that by living dissections any discovery has been made by which a single malady is more easily cured. And if the knowledge of physiology has been somewhat increased, he surely buys knowledge dear, who learns the use of the lacteals at the expense of his humanity. It is time that universal resentment should arise against these horrid operations, which tend to harden the heart, extinguish those sensations which give man confidence in man, and make the physician more dreadful than the gout or stone.

No. 18, Saturday, 12 August 1758

To The Idler

Sir,

It commonly happens to him who endeavours to obtain distinction by ridicule, or censure, that he teaches others to practise his own arts against himself, and that, after a short enjoyment of the applause paid to his sagacity, or of the mirth excited by his wit, he is doomed to suffer the same severities of scrutiny, to hear inquiry detecting his faults, and exaggeration sporting with his failings.

The natural discontent of inferiority will seldom fail to operate in some degree of malice against him, who professes to superintend the conduct of others, especially if he seats himself uncalled in the chair of judicature, and exercises authority by his own commission.

You cannot, therefore, wonder that your observations on human folly, if they produce laughter at one time, awaken criticism at another; and that among the numbers whom you have taught to scoff at the retirement of Drugget, there is one that offers his apology.

The mistake of your old friend is by no means peculiar. The public pleasures of far the greater part of mankind are counterfeit. Very few carry their philosophy to places of diversion, or are very careful to analyse their enjoyments. The general condition of life is so full of misery, that we are glad to catch delight without inquiring whence it comes, or by what power it is bestowed.

The mind is seldom quickened to very vigorous operations but by pain, or the dread of pain. We do not disturb ourselves with the detection of fallacies which do us no harm, nor willingly decline a pleasing effect to investigate its cause. He that is happy, by whatever means, desires nothing but the continuance of happiness, and is no more solicitous to distribute his sensations into their proper species, than the common gazer on the beauties of the spring to separate light into its original rays.

Pleasure is therefore seldom such as it appears to others, nor often such as we represent it to ourselves. Of the ladies that sparkle at a musical performance, a very small number has any quick sensibility of harmonious sounds. But every one that goes has her pleasure. She has the pleasure of wearing fine clothes, and of showing them, of outshining those whom she suspects to envy her; she has the pleasure of appearing among other ladies in a place whither the race of meaner mortals seldom intrudes, and of reflecting that, in the conversations of the next morning, her name will be mentioned among those that sat in the first row; she has the pleasure of returning courtesies, or refusing to return them, of receiving compliments with civility, or rejecting them with disdain. She has the pleasure of meeting some of her acquaintance, of guessing why the rest are absent, and of telling them that she saw the opera, on pretence of inquiring why they would miss it. She has the pleasure of being supposed to be pleased with a refined amusement, and of hoping to be numbered among the votresses of harmony. She has the pleasure of escaping for two hours the superiority of a sister, or the control of a husband; and from all these pleasures she concludes that heavenly music is the balm of life.

All assemblies of gaiety are brought together by motives of the same kind. The theatre is not filled with those, that know or regard the skill of the actor, nor the ballroom, by those who dance, or attend to the dancers. To all places of general resort, where the standard of pleasure is erected, we run with equal eagerness, or appearance of eagerness, for very different reasons. One goes that he may say he has been there, another because he never misses. This man goes to try what he can find, and that to discover what others find. Whatever diversion is costly will be frequented by those who desire to be thought rich; and whatever has, by any accident, become fashionable, easily continues its reputation, because every one is ashamed of not partaking it.

To every place of entertainment we go with expectation, and desire of being pleased; we meet others who are brought by the same motives; no one will be the first to own the disappointment; one face reflects the smile of another, till each believes the rest delighted, and endeavours to catch and transmit the circulating rapture. In time, all are deceived by the cheat to which all contribute. The fiction of happiness is propagated by every tongue, and confirmed by every look, till at last all profess the joy which they do not feel, content to yield to the general delusion; and when the voluntary dream is at an end, lament that bliss is of so short a duration.

If Drugget pretended to pleasures, of which he had no perception, or boasted of one amusement where he was indulging another, what did he which is not done by all those who read his story? of whom some pretend delight in conversation, only because they dare not be alone; some praise the quiet of solitude, because they are envious of sense and impatient of folly; and some gratify their pride, by writing characters which expose the vanity of life.

I am, Sir,

Your humble servant.

No. 22, Saturday, 9 September 1758

Many naturalists are of opinion, that the animals which we commonly consider as mute, have the power of imparting their thoughts to one another. That they can express general sensations is very certain; every being that can utter sounds, has a different voice for pleasure and for pain. The hound informs his fellows when he scents his game; the hen calls her chickens to their food by her cluck, and drives them from danger by her scream.

Birds have the greatest variety of notes; they have indeed a variety, which seems almost sufficient to make a speech adequate to the purposes of a life, which is regulated by instinct, and can admit little change or improvement. To the cries of birds, curiosity or superstition has been always attentive, many have studied the language of the feathered tribes, and some have boasted that they understood it.

The most skilful or most confident interpreters of the silvan dialogues have been commonly found among the philosophers of the East, in a country where the calmness of the air, and the mildness of the seasons, allow the student to pass a great part of the year in groves and bowers. But what may be done in one place by peculiar opportunities, may be performed in another by peculiar diligence. A shepherd of Bohemia has, by long abode in the forests, enabled himself to understand the voice of birds, at least he relates with great confidence a story of which the credibility may be considered by the learned.

'As I was sitting, (said he) within a hollow rock, and watching my sheep that fed in the valley, I heard two vultures interchangeably crying on the summit of the cliff. Both voices were earnest and deliberate. My curiosity prevailed over my care of the flock; I climbed slowly and silently from crag to crag, concealed among the shrubs, till I found a cavity where I might sit and listen without suffering, or giving disturbance.

'I soon perceived, that my labour would be well repaid; for an old vulture was sitting on a naked prominence, with her young about her, whom she was instructing in the arts of a vulture's life, and preparing, by the last lecture, for their final dismission to the mountains and the skies.

'"My children," said the old vulture, "you will the less want my instructions because you have had my practice before your eyes; you have seen me snatch from the farm the household fowl, you have seen me seize the leveret in the bush, and the kid in the pasture, you know how to fix your talons, and how to balance your flight when you are laden with your prey. But you remember the taste of more delicious food; I have often regaled you with the flesh of man." "Tell us," said the young vultures, "where man may be found, and how he may be known; his flesh is surely the natural food of a vulture. Why have you never brought a man in your talons to the nest?"

"He is too bulky," said the mother; "when we find a man, we can only tear away his flesh and leave his bones upon the ground." "Since man is so big," said the young ones, "how do you kill him? You are afraid of the wolf and of the bear, by what power are vultures superior to man, is man more defenceless than a sheep?" "We have not the strength of man," returned the mother, "and I am sometimes in doubt whether we have the subtlety; and the vultures would seldom feast upon his flesh, had not nature, that devoted him to our uses, infused into him a strange ferocity, which I have never observed in any other being that feeds upon the earth. Two herds of men will often meet and shake the earth with noise, and fill the air with fire. When you hear noise and see fire which flashes along the ground, hasten to the place with your swiftest wing, for men are surely destroying one another; you will then find the ground smoking with blood and covered with carcasses, of which many are dismembered and mangled for the convenience of the vulture." "But when men have killed their prey," said the pupil, "why do they not eat it? When the wolf has killed a sheep he suffers not the vulture to touch it till he has satisfied himself. Is not man another kind of wolf?" "Man", said the mother, "is the only beast who kills that which he does not devour, and this quality makes him so much a benefactor to our species." "If men kill our prey and lay it in our way," said the young one, "what need shall we have of labouring for ourselves?" "Because man will, sometimes," replied the mother, "remain for a long time quiet in his den. The old vultures will tell you when you are to watch his motions. When you see men in great numbers moving close together, like a flight of storks, you may conclude that they are hunting, and that you will soon revel in human blood." "But still," said the young one, "I would gladly know the reason of this mutual slaughter. I could never kill what I could not eat." "My child," said the mother, "this is a question which I cannot answer, tho' I am reckoned the most subtle bird of the mountain. When I was young I used frequently to visit the ayry of an old vulture who dwelt upon the Carpathian rocks; he had made many observations; he knew the places that afforded prey round his habitation, as far in every direction as the strongest wing can fly between the rising and setting of the summer sun; he had fed year after year on the entrails of men. His opinion was, that men had only the appearance of animal life, being really vegetables with a power of motion; and that as the boughs of an oak are dashed together by the storm, that swine may fatten upon the falling acorns, so men are by some unaccountable power driven one against another, till they lose their motion, that vultures may be fed. Others think they have observed something of contrivance and policy among these mischievous beings, and those that hover more closely round them, pretend that there is, in every herd, one that gives directions to the rest, and seems to be more eminently delighted with a wide carnage. What it is that entitles him to such pre-eminence we know not; he is seldom the biggest or the swiftest, but he shows by his eagerness and diligence that he is, more than any of the others, a friend to vultures." '

No. 30, Saturday, 11 November 1758

The desires of man increase with his acquisitions; every step which he advances brings something within his view, which he did not see before, and which, as soon as he sees it, he begins to want. Where necessity ends curiosity begins, and no sooner are we supplied with every thing that nature can demand, than we sit down to contrive artificial appetites.

By this restlessness of mind, every populous and wealthy city is filled with innumerable employments, for which the greater part of mankind is without a name; with artificers whose labour is exerted in producing such petty conveniences, that many shops are furnished with instruments, of which the use can hardly be found without inquiry, but which he that once knows them, quickly learns to number among necessary things.

Such is the diligence, with which, in countries completely civilized, one part of mankind labours for another, that wants are supplied faster than they can be formed, and the idle and luxurious find life stagnate, for want of some desire to keep it in motion. This species of distress furnishes a new set of occupations, and multitudes are busied, from day to day, in finding the rich and the fortunate something to do.

It is very common to reproach those artists as useless, who produce only such superfluities as neither accommodate the body nor improve the mind; and of which no other effect can be imagined, than that they are the occasions of spending money, and consuming time.

But this censure will be mitigated, when it is seriously considered, that money and time are the heaviest burdens of life, and that the unhappiest of all mortals are those who have more of either than they know how to use. To set himself free from these incumbrances, one hurries to Newmarket; another travels over Europe; one pulls down his house and calls architects about him; another buys a seat in the country, and follows his hounds over hedges and through rivers; one makes collections of shells, and another searches the world for tulips and carnations.

He is surely a public benefactor who finds employment for those to whom it is thus difficult to find it for themselves. It is true that this is seldom done merely from generosity or compassion, almost every man seeks his own advantage in helping others, and therefore it is too common for mercenary officiousness, to consider rather what is grateful than what is right.

We all know that it is more profitable to be loved than esteemed, and ministers of pleasure will always be found, who study to make themselves necessary, and to supplant those who are practising the same arts.

One of the amusements of idleness is reading without the fatigue of close attention, and the world therefore swarms with writers whose wish is not to be studied but to be read.

No species of literary men has lately been so much multiplied as the writers of news. Not many years ago the nation was content with one *Gazette*; but now we have not only in the metropolis papers for every morning and every evening, but almost every large town has its weekly historian, who regularly circulates his periodical intelligence, and fills the villages of his district with conjectures on the events of war, and with debates on the true interest of Europe.

To write news in its perfection requires such a combination of qualities, that a man completely fitted for the task is not always to be found. In Sir Henry Wotton's jocular definition, 'An ambassador' is said to be 'a man of virtue sent abroad to tell lies for the advantage of his country'; a news-writer is 'a man without virtue, who writes lies at home for his own profit.' To these compositions is required neither genius nor knowledge, neither industry nor sprightliness, but contempt of shame and indifference to truth are absolutely necessary. He who by a long familiarity with infamy has obtained these qualities, may confidently tell today what he intends to contradict tomorrow; he may affirm fearlessly what he knows that he shall be obliged to recant, and may write letters from Amsterdam or Dresden to himself.

In a time of war the nation is always of one mind, eager to hear something good of themselves and ill of the enemy. At this time the task of news-writers is easy, they have nothing to do but to tell that a battle is expected, and afterwards that a battle has been fought, in which we and our friends, whether conquering or conquered, did all, and our enemies did nothing.

Scarce any thing awakens attention like a tale of cruelty. The writer of news never fails in the intermission of action to tell how the enemies murdered children and ravished virgins; and if the scene of action be somewhat distant, scalps half the inhabitants of a province.

Among the calamities of war may be justly numbered the diminution of the love of truth, by the falsehoods which interest dictates and credulity encourages. A peace will equally leave the warrior and relator of wars destitute of employment; and I know not whether more is to be dreaded from streets filled with soldiers accustomed to plunder, or from garrets filled with scribblers accustomed to lie.

Many moralists have remarked that pride has of all human vices the widest dominion, appears in the greatest multiplicity of forms, and lies hid under the greatest variety of disguises; of disguises, which, like the moon's 'veil of brightness,' are both its 'lustre and its shade,' and betray it to others, tho' they hide it from ourselves.

It is not my intention to degrade pride from this pre-eminence of mischief, yet I know not whether idleness may not maintain a very doubtful and obstinate competition.

There are some that profess idleness in its full dignity who call themselves the 'Idle', as Busiris in the play 'calls himself the Proud'; who boast that they do nothing, and thank their stars that they have nothing to do; who sleep every night till they can sleep no longer, and rise only that exercise may enable them to sleep again; who prolong the reign of darkness by double curtains, and never see the sun but to 'tell him how they hate his beams', whose whole labour is to vary the postures of indulgence, and whose day differs from their night but as a couch or chair differs from a bed.

These are the true and open votaries of idleness, for whom she weaves the garlands of poppies, and into whose cup she pours the waters of oblivion; who exist in a state of unruffled stupidity, forgetting and forgotten; who have long ceased to live, and at whose death the survivors can only say, that they have ceased to breathe.

But idleness predominates in many lives where it is not suspected, for being a vice which terminates in itself, it may be enjoyed without injury to others, and is therefore not watched like fraud, which endangers property, or like pride which naturally seeks its gratifications in another's inferiority. Idleness is a silent and peaceful quality, that neither raises envy by ostentation, nor hatred by opposition; and therefore no body is busy to censure or detect it.

As pride sometimes is hid under humility, idleness is often covered by turbulence and hurry. He that neglects his known duty and real employment, naturally endeavours to crowd his mind with something that may bar out the remembrance of his own folly, and does anything but what he ought to do with eager diligence, that he may keep himself in his own favour.

Some are always in a state of preparation, occupied in previous measures, forming plans, accumulating materials, and providing for the main affair. These are certainly under the secret power of idleness. Nothing is to be expected from the workman whose tools are for ever to be sought. I was once told by a great master, that no man ever excelled in painting, who was eminently curious about pencils and colours.

There are others to whom idleness dictates another expedient, by which life may be passed unprofitably away without the tediousness of many vacant hours. The art is, to fill the day with petty business, to have always something in hand which may raise curiosity, but not solicitude, and keep the mind in a state of action, but not of labour.

This art has for many years been practised by my old friend Sober, with wonderful success. Sober is a man of strong desires and quick imagination, so exactly balanced by the love of ease, that they can seldom stimulate him to any difficult undertaking; they have, however, so much power, that they will not suffer him to lie quite at rest, and though they do not make him sufficiently useful to others, they make him at least weary of himself.

Mr Sober's chief pleasure is conversation; there is no end of his talk or his attention; to speak or to hear is equally pleasing; for he still fancies that he is teaching or learning something, and is free for the time from his own reproaches.

But there is one time at night when he must go home, that his friends may sleep; and another time in the morning, when all the world agrees to shut out interruption. These are the moments of which poor Sober trembles at the thought. But the misery of these tiresome intervals, he has many means of alleviating. He has persuaded himself that the manual arts are undeservedly overlooked; he has observed in many trades the effects of close thought, and just ratiocination. From speculation he proceeded to practice, and supplied himself with the tools of a carpenter, with which he mended his coal-box very successfully, and which he still continues to employ, as he finds occasion.

He has attempted at other times the crafts of the shoemaker, tin-man, plumber, and potter; in all these arts he has failed, and resolves to qualify himself for them by better information. But his daily amusement is chemistry. He has a small furnace, which he employs in distillation, and which has long been the solace of his life. He draws oils and waters, and essences and spirits, which he knows to be of no use; sits and counts the drops as they come from his retort, and forgets that, while a drop is falling, a moment flies away.

Poor Sober! I have often teased him with reproof, and he has often promised reformation; for no man is so much open to conviction as the idler, but there is none on whom it operates so little. What will be the effect of this paper I know not; perhaps he will read it and laugh, and light the fire in his furnace; but my hope is that he will quit his trifles, and betake himself to rational and useful diligence.

No. 32, Saturday, 25 November 1758

Among the innumerable mortifications that waylay human arrogance on every side may well be reckoned our ignorance of the most common objects and effects, a defect of which we become more sensible by every attempt to supply it. Vulgar and inactive minds confound familiarity with knowledge, and conceive themselves informed of the whole nature of things when they are shown their form or told their use; but the speculatist, who is not content with superficial views, harasses himself with fruitless curiosity, and still as he inquires more perceives only that he knows less.

Sleep is a state in which a great part of every life is passed. No animal has been yet discovered, whose existence is not varied with intervals of insensibility; and some late philosophers have extended the empire of sleep over the vegetable world.

Yet of this change so frequent, so great, so general, and so necessary, no searcher has yet found either the efficient or final cause; or can tell by what power the mind and body are thus chained down in irresistible stupefaction; or what benefits the animal receives from this alternate suspension of its active powers.

Whatever may be the multiplicity or contrariety of opinions upon this subject, nature has taken sufficient care that theory shall have little influence on practice. The most diligent inquirer is not able long to keep his eyes open; the most eager disputant will begin about midnight to desert his argument, and once in four and twenty hours, the gay and the gloomy, the witty and the dull, the clamorous and the silent, the busy and the idle, are all overpowered by the gentle tyrant, and all lie down in the equality of sleep

Philosophy has often attempted to repress insolence by asserting that all conditions are levelled by death; a position which, however it may deject the happy, will seldom afford much comfort to the wretched. It is far more pleasing to consider that sleep is equally a leveller with death; that the time is never at a great distance, when the balm of rest shall be effused alike upon every head, when the diversities of life shall stop their operation, and the high and the low shall lie down together.

It is somewhere recorded of Alexander, that in the pride of conquests, and intoxication of flattery, he declared that he only perceived himself to be a man by the necessity of sleep. Whether he considered sleep as necessary to his mind or body it was indeed a sufficient evidence of human infirmity; the body which required such frequency of renovation gave but faint promises of immortality; and the mind which, from time to time, sunk gladly into insensibility, had made no very near approaches to the felicity of the supreme and self-sufficient nature.

I know not what can tend more to repress all the passions that disturb the peace of the world, than the consideration that there is no height of happiness or honour, from which man does not eagerly descend to a state of unconscious repose; that the best condition of life is such, that we contentedly quit its good to be disentangled from its evils; that in a few hours splendour fades before the eye, and praise itself deadens in the ear; the senses withdraw from their objects, and reason favours the retreat.

What then are the hopes and prospects of covetousness, ambition and rapacity? Let him that desires most have all his desires gratified, he never shall attain a state, which he can, for a day and a night, contemplate with satisfaction, or from which, if he had the power of perpetual vigilance, he would not long for periodical separations.

All envy would be extinguished if it were universally known that there are none to be envied, and surely none can be much envied who are not pleased with themselves. There is reason to suspect that the distinctions of mankind have more show than value, when it is found that all agree to be weary alike of pleasures and of cares, that the powerful and the weak, the celebrated and obscure, join in one common wish, and implore from nature's hand the nectar of oblivion.

Such is our desire of abstraction from ourselves, that very few are satisfied with the quantity of stupefaction which the needs of the body force upon the mind. Alexander himself added intemperance to sleep, and solaced with the fumes of wine the sovereignty of the world. And almost every man has some art, by which he steals his thoughts away from his present state.

It is not much of life that is spent in close attention to any important duty. Many hours of every day are suffered to fly away without any traces left upon the intellects. We suffer phantoms to rise up before us, and amuse ourselves with the dance of airy images, which after a time we dismiss for ever, and know not how we have been busied.

Many have no happier moments than those that they pass in solitude, abandoned to their own imagination, which sometimes puts sceptres in their hands or mitres on their heads, shifts the scene of pleasure with endless variety, bids all the forms of beauty sparkle before them, and gluts them with every change of visionary luxury.

It is easy in these semi-slumbers to collect all the possibilities of happiness, to alter the course of the sun, to bring back the past, and anticipate the future, to unite all the beauties of all seasons, and all the blessings of all climates, to receive and bestow felicity, and forget that misery is the lot of man. All this is a voluntary dream, a temporary recession from the realities of life to airy fictions; and habitual subjection of reason to fancy.

Others are afraid to be alone, and amuse themselves by a perpetual succession of companions, but the difference is not great, in solitude we have our dreams to ourselves, and in company we agree to dream in concert. The end sought in both is forgetfulness of ourselves.

No. 38, Saturday, 6 January 1759

Since the publication of the letter, concerning the condition of those who are confined in gaols by their creditors, an inquiry is said to have been made, by which it appears that more than twenty thousand are at this time prisoners for debt.

We often look with indifference on the successive parts of that, which, if the whole were seen together, would shake us with emotion. A debtor is dragged to prison, pitied for a moment, and then forgotten; another follows him, and is lost alike in the caverns of oblivion; but when the whole mass of calamity rises up at once, when twenty thousand reasonable beings are heard all groaning in unnecessary misery, not by the infirmity of nature, but the mistake or negligence of policy, who can forbear to pity and lament, to wonder and abhor.

There is here no need of declamatory vehemence; we live in an age of commerce and computation; let us therefore coolly inquire what is the sum of evil which the imprisonment of debtors brings upon our country.

It seems to be the opinion of the later computists, that the inhabitants of England do not exceed six millions, of which twenty thousand is the three-hundredth part. What shall we say of the humanity or the wisdom of a nation, that voluntarily sacrifices one in every three hundred to lingering destruction!

The misfortunes of an individual do not extend their influence to many; yet, if we consider the effects of consanguinity and friendship, and the general reciprocation of wants and benefits, which make one man dear or necessary to another, it may reasonably be supposed, that every man languishing in prison gives trouble of some kind to two others who love or need him. By this multiplication of misery we see distress extended to the hundredth part of the whole society.

If we estimate at a shilling a day what is lost by the inaction and consumed in the support of each man thus chained down to involuntary idleness, the public loss will rise in one year to three hundred thousand pounds; in ten years to more than a sixth part of our circulating coin.

I am afraid that those who are best acquainted with the state of our prisons, will confess that my conjecture is too near the truth, when I suppose that the corrosion of resentment, the heaviness of sorrow, the corruption of confined air, the want of exercise, and sometimes of food, the contagion of diseases from which there is no retreat, and the severity of tyrants against whom there can be no resistance, and all the complicated horrors of a prison, put an end every year to the life of one in four of those that are shut up from the common comforts of human life.

Thus perish yearly five thousand men, overborne with sorrow, consumed by famine, or putrefied by filth; many of them in the most vigorous and useful part of life; for the thoughtless and imprudent are commonly young, and the active and busy are seldom old.

According to the rule generally received, which supposes that one in thirty dies yearly, the race of man may be said to be renewed at the end of thirty years. Who would have believed till now, that of every English generation an hundred and fifty thousand perish in our gaols! That in every century, a nation eminent for science, studious of commerce, ambitious of empire, should willingly lose, in noisome dungeons, five hundred thousand of its inhabitants: a number greater than has ever been destroyed in the same time by the pestilence and sword!

A very late occurrence may show us the value of the number which we thus condemn to be useless; in the re-establishment of the trained bands, thirty thousand are considered as a force sufficient against all exigencies: while, therefore, we detain twenty thousand in prison, we shut up in darkness and uselessness two thirds of an army which our-selves judge equal to the defence of our country.

The monastic institutions have been often blamed, as tending to retard the increase of mankind. And perhaps retirement ought rarely to be permitted, except to those whose employment is consistent with abstraction, and who, tho' solitary, will not be idle; to those whom infirmity makes useless to the commonwealth, or to those who have paid their due proportion to society, and who, having lived for others, may be honourably dismissed to live for themselves. But whatever be the evil or the folly of these retreats, those have no right to censure them whose prisons contain greater numbers than the monasteries of other countries. It is, surely, less foolish and less criminal to permit inaction than compel it; to comply with doubtful opinions of happiness, than condemn to certain and apparent misery; to indulge the extravagancies of erroneous piety, than to multiply and enforce temptations to wickedness.

The misery of gaols is not half their evil; they are filled with every corruption which poverty and wickedness can generate between them; with all the shameless and profligate enormities that can be produced by the impudence of ignominy, the rage of want, and the malignity of despair. In a prison the awe of the public eye is lost, and the power of the law is spent; there are few fears, there are no blushes. The lewd inflame the lewd, the audacious harden the audacious. Every one fortifies himself as he can against his own sensibility, en-deavours to practise on others the arts which are practised on himself; and gains the kindness of his associates by similitude of manners.

Thus some sink amidst their misery, and others survive only to propagate villainy. It may be hoped that our lawgivers will at length take away from us this power of starving and depraving one another: but, if there be any reason why this inveterate evil should not be re-moved in our age, which true policy has enlightened beyond any former time, let those, whose writings form the opinions and the practices of their contemporaries, endeavour to transfer the reproach of such imprisonment from the debtor to the creditor, till universal infamy shall pursue the wretch, whose wantonness of power, or revenge of disappointment, condemns another to torture and to ruin; till he shall be hunted through the world as an enemy to man, and find in riches no shelter from contempt.

Surely, he whose debtor has perished in prison, though he may acquit himself of deliberate murder, must at least have his mind clouded with discontent, when he considers how much another has suffered from him; when he thinks on the wife bewailing her husband, or the children begging the bread which their father would have earned. If there are any made so obdurate by avarice or cruelty, as to revolve these consequences without dread or pity, I must leave them to be awakened by some other power, for I write only to human beings.

No. 60, Saturday, 9 June 1759

Criticism is a study by which men grow important and formidable at very small expense. The power of invention has been conferred by nature upon few, and the labour of learning those sciences which may, by mere labour, be obtained, is too great to be willingly endured; but every man can exert such judgement as he has upon the works of others; and he whom nature has made weak, and idleness keeps ignorant, may yet support his vanity by the name of a critic.

I hope it will give comfort to great numbers who are passing thro' the world in obscurity, when I inform them how easily distinction may be obtained. All the other powers of literature are coy and haughty, they must be long courted, and at last are not always gained; but criticism is a goddess easy of access and forward of advance, who will meet the slow and encourage the timorous; the want of meaning she supplies with words, and the want of spirit she recompenses with malignity.

This profession has one recommendation peculiar to itself, that it gives vent to malignity without real mischief. No genius was ever blasted by the breath of critics. The poison which, if confined, would have burst the heart, fumes away in empty hisses, and malice is set at ease with very little danger to merit. The critic is the only man whose triumph is without another's pain, and whose greatness does not rise upon another's ruin.

To a study at once so easy and so reputable, so malicious and so harmless, it cannot be necessary to invite my readers by a long or laboured exhortation; it is sufficient, since all would be critics if they could, to show by one eminent example that all can be critics if they will.

Dick Minim, after the common course of puerile studies, in which he was no great proficient, was put apprentice to a brewer, with whom he had lived two years, when his uncle died in the city, and left him a large fortune in the stocks. Dick had for six months before used the company of the lower players, of whom he had learned to scorn a trade, and being now at liberty to follow his genius, he resolved to be a man of wit and humour. That he might be properly initiated in his new character, he frequented the coffee-houses near the theatres, where he listened very diligently day after day, to those who talked of language and sentiments, and unities and catastrophes, till by slow degrees he began to think that he understood something of the stage, and hoped in time to talk himself.

But he did not trust so much to natural sagacity, as wholly to neglect the help of books. When the theatres were shut, he retired to Richmond with a few select writers, whose opinions he impressed upon his memory by unwearied diligence; and when he returned with other wits to the town, was able to tell, in very proper phrases, that the chief business of art is to copy nature; that a perfect writer is not to be expected, because genius decays as judgement increases; that the great art is the art of blotting, and that according to the rule of Horace every piece should be kept nine years.

Of the great authors he now began to display the characters, laying down as an universal position that all had beauties and defects. His opinion was, that Shakespeare, committing himself wholly to the impulse of nature, wanted that correctness which learning would have given him; and that Jonson, trusting to learning, did not sufficiently cast his eye on nature. He blamed the stanza of Spenser, and could not bear the hexameters of Sidney. Denham and Waller he held the first reformers of English numbers, and thought that if Waller could have obtained the strength of Denham, or Denham the sweetness of Waller, there had been nothing wanting to complete a poet. He often expressed his commiseration of Dryden's poverty, and his indignation at the age which suffered him to write for bread; he repeated with rapture the first lines of *All for Love*, but wondered at the corruption of taste which could bear any thing so unnatural as rhyming tragedies. In Otway he found uncommon powers of moving the passions, but was disgusted by his general negligence, and blamed him for making a conspirator his hero; and never concluded his disquisition, without remarking how happily the sound of the clock is made to alarm the audience. Southern would have been his favourite, but that he mixes comic with tragic scenes, intercepts the natural course of the passions, and fills the mind with a wild confusion of mirth and melancholy. The versification of Rowe he thought too melodious for the stage, and too little varied in different passions. He made it the great fault of Congreve, that all his persons were wits, and that he always wrote with more art than nature. He considered *Cato* rather as a poem than a play, and allowed Addison to be the complete master of allegory and grave humour, but paid no great deference to him as a critic. He thought the chief merit of Prior was in his easy tales and lighter poems, tho' he allowed that his *Solomon* had many noble sentiments elegantly expressed. In Swift he discovered an inimitable vein of irony, and an easiness which all would hope and few would attain. Pope he was inclined to degrade from a poet to a versifier, and thought his numbers rather luscious than sweet. He often lamented the neglect of *Phaedra and Hippolitus*, and wished to see the stage under better regulations.

These assertions passed commonly uncontradicted; and if now and then an opponent started up, he was quickly repressed by the suffrages of the company, and Minim went away from every dispute with elation of heart and increase of confidence.

He now grew conscious of his abilities, and began to talk of the present state of dramatic poetry; wondered what was become of the comic genius which supplied our ancestors with wit and pleasantry, and why no writer could be found that durst now venture beyond a farce. He saw no reason for thinking that the vein of humour was exhausted, since we live in a country where liberty suffers every character to spread itself to its utmost bulk, and which therefore produces more originals than all the rest of the world together. Of tragedy he concluded business to be the soul, and yet often hinted that love predominates too much upon the modern stage.

He was now an acknowledged critic, and had his own seat in the coffee-house, and headed a party in the pit. Minim has more vanity than ill-nature, and seldom desires to do much mischief; he will perhaps murmur a little in the ear of him that sits next him, but endeavours to influence the audience to favour, by clapping when an actor exclaims 'ye Gods,' or laments the misery of his country.

By degrees he was admitted to rehearsals, and many of his friends are of opinion, that our present poets are indebted to him for their happiest thoughts; by his contrivance the bell was rung twice in *Barbarossa*, and by his persuasion the author of *Cleone* concluded his play without a couplet; for what can be more absurd, said Minim, than that part of a play should be rhymed, and part written in blank verse? and by what acquisition of faculties is the speaker who never could find rhymes before, enabled to rhyme at the conclusion of an act!

He is the great investigator of hidden beauties, and is particularly delighted when he finds 'the sound an echo to the sense'. He has read all our poets with particular attention to this delicacy of versification, and wonders at the supineness with which their works have been hitherto perused, so that no man has found the sound of a drum in this distich,

> When pulpit, drum ecclesiastic,
> Was beat with fist instead of a stick;

and the wonderful lines upon honour and a bubble have hitherto passed without notice.

> Honour is like the glassy bubble,
> Which costs philosophers such trouble,
> Where one part crack'd, the whole does fly,
> And wits are crack'd to find out why.

In these verses, says Minim, we have two striking accommodations of the sound to the sense. It is impossible to utter the two lines emphatically without an act like that which they describe; 'bubble' and 'trouble' causing a momentary inflation of the cheeks by the retention of the breath, which is afterwards forcibly emitted, as in the practice of 'blowing bubbles'. But the greatest excellence is in the third line, which is 'crack'd' in the middle to express a crack, and then shivers into monosyllables. Yet has this diamond lain neglected with common stones, and among the innumerable admirers of *Hudibras* the observation of this superlative passage has been reserved for the sagacity of Minim.

No. 73, Saturday, 8 September 1759

That every man would be rich if a wish could obtain riches, is a position, which, I believe, few will contest, at least in a nation like ours, in which commerce has kindled an universal emulation of wealth, and in which money receives all the honours which are the proper right of knowledge and of virtue.

Yet tho' we are all labouring for gold as for the chief good, and, by the natural effort of unwearied diligence, have found many expeditious methods of obtaining it, we have not been able to improve the art of using it, or to make it produce more happiness than it afforded in former times, when every declaimer expatiated on its mischiefs, and every philosopher taught his followers to despise it.

Many of the dangers imputed of old to exorbitant wealth, are now at an end. The rich are neither waylaid by robbers, nor watched by informers; there is nothing to be dreaded from proscriptions, or seizures. The necessity of concealing treasure has long ceased; no man now needs counterfeit mediocrity,[1] and condemn his plate and jewels to caverns and darkness, or feast his mind with the consciousness of clouded splendour, of finery which is useless till it is shown, and which he dares not show.

In our time the poor are strongly tempted to assume the appearance of wealth, but the wealthy very rarely desire to be thought poor; for we are all at full liberty to display riches by every mode of ostentation. We fill our houses with useless ornaments, only to show that we can buy them; we cover our coaches with gold, and employ artists in the discovery of new fashions of expense; and yet it cannot be found that riches produce happiness.

Of riches, as of every thing else, the hope is more than the enjoyment; while we consider them as the means to be used, at some future time, for the attainment of felicity, we press on our pursuit ardently and vigorously, and that ardour secures us from weariness of ourselves; but no sooner do we sit down to enjoy our acquisitions, than we find them insufficient to fill up the vacuities of life.

One cause which is not always observed of the insufficiency of riches, is, that they very seldom make their owner rich. To be rich, is to have more than is desired, and more than is wanted; to have something which may be spent without reluctance and scattered without care, with which the sudden demands of desire may be gratified, the casual freaks of fancy indulged, or the unexpected opportunities of benevolence improved.

Avarice is always poor,[2] but poor by her own fault. There is another poverty to which the rich are exposed with less guilt by the officiousness of others. Every man, eminent for exuberance of fortune, is surrounded from morning to evening, and from evening to midnight, by flatterers, whose art of adulation consists in exciting artificial wants, and in forming new schemes of profusion.

Tom Tranquil, when he came to age, found himself in possession of a fortune, of which the twentieth part might perhaps have made him rich. His temper is easy, and his affections soft; he receives every man with kindness, and hears him with credulity. His friends took care to settle him by giving him a wife, whom, having no particular inclination, he rather accepted than chose, because he was told that she was proper for him.

He was now to live with dignity proportionate to his fortune. What his fortune requires or admits Tom does not know, for he has little skill in computation, and none of his friends think it their interest to improve it. If he was suffered to live by his own choice he would leave everything as he finds it, and pass thro' the world distinguished only by inoffensive gentleness. But the ministers of luxury have marked him out as one at whose expense they may exercise their arts. A companion, who has just learned the names of the Italian masters, runs from sale to sale, and buys pictures, for which Mr Tranquil pays, without inquiring where they shall be hung. Another fills his garden with statues which Tranquil wishes away, but dares not remove. One of his friends is learning architecture by building him a house, which he passed by, and inquired to whom it belonged; another has been for three years digging canals and raising mounts, cutting trees down in one place, and planting them in another, on which Tranquil looks with serene indifference, without asking what will be the cost. Another projector tells him that a water-work, like that of Versailles, will complete the beauties of his seat, and lays his draughts before him; Tranquil turns his eyes upon them, and the artist begins his explanations; Tranquil raises no objections, but orders him to begin the work that he may escape from talk which he does not understand.

Thus a thousand hands are busy at his expense, without adding to his pleasures. He pays and receives visits, and has loitered in public or in solitude, talking in summer of the town, and in winter of the country, without knowing that his fortune is impaired, till his steward told him this morning, that he could pay the workmen no longer but by mortgaging a manor.

No. 81, Saturday, 3 November 1759

As the English army was passing towards Quebec along a soft savanna between a mountain and a lake, one of the petty chiefs of the inland regions stood upon a rock surrounded by his clan, and from behind the shelter of the bushes contemplated the art and regularity of European war. It was evening, the tents were pitched, he observed the security with which the troops rested in the night, and the order with which the march was renewed in the morning. He continued to pursue them with his eye till they could be seen no longer, and then stood for some time silent and pensive.

Then turning to his followers, 'My children,' said he, 'I have often heard from men hoary with long life, that there was a time when our ancestors were absolute lords of the woods, the meadows, and the lakes, wherever the eye can reach or the foot can pass. They fished and hunted, feasted and danced, and when they were weary lay down under the first thicket, without danger and without fear. They changed their habitations as the seasons required, convenience prompted, or curiosity allured them, and sometimes gathered the fruits of the mountain, and sometimes sported in canoes along the coast.

'Many years and ages are supposed to have been thus passed in plenty and security; when at last, a new race of men entered our country from the great ocean. They inclosed themselves in habitations of stone, which our ancestors could neither enter by violence, nor destroy by fire. They issued from those fastnesses, sometimes covered like the armadillo with shells, from which the lance rebounded on the striker, and sometimes carried by mighty beasts which had never been seen in our vales or forests, of such strength and swiftness, that flight and opposition were vain alike. Those invaders ranged over the continent, slaughtering in their rage those that resisted, and those that submitted, in their mirth. Of those that remained, some were buried in caverns, and condemned to dig metals for their masters; some were employed in tilling the ground, of which foreign tyrants devour the produce; and when the sword and the mines have destroyed the natives, they supply their place by human beings of another colour, brought from some distant country to perish here under toil and torture.

'Some there are who boast their humanity, and content themselves to seize our chases and fisheries, who drive us from every tract of ground where fertility and pleasantness invite them to settle, and make no war upon us except when we intrude upon our own lands.

'Others pretend to have purchased a right of residence and tyranny; but surely the insolence of such bargains is more offensive than the avowed and open dominion of force. What reward can induce the possessor of a country to admit a stranger more powerful than himself? Fraud or terror must operate in such contracts; either they promised protection which they never have afforded, or instruction which they never imparted. We hoped to be secured by their favour from some other evil, or to learn the arts of Europe, by which we might be able to secure ourselves. Their power they have never exerted in our defence, and their arts they have studiously concealed from us. Their treaties are only to deceive, and their traffic only to defraud us. They have a written law among them, of which they boast as derived from him who made the earth and sea, and by which they profess to believe that man will be made happy when life shall forsake him. Why is not this law communicated to us? It is concealed because it is violated. For how can they preach it to an Indian nation, when I am told that one of its first precepts forbids them to do to others what they would not that others should do to them?

'But the time perhaps is now approaching when the pride of usurpation shall be crushed, and the cruelties of invasion shall be revenged. The sons of rapacity have now drawn their swords upon each other, and referred their claims to the decision of war; let us look unconcerned upon the slaughter, and remember that the death of every European delivers the country from a tyrant and a robber; for what is the claim of either nation, but the claim of the vulture to the leveret, of the tiger to the fawn? Let them then continue to dispute their title to regions which they cannot people, to purchase by danger and blood the empty dignity of dominion over mountains which they will never climb, and rivers which they will never pass. Let us endeavour, in the mean time, to learn their discipline, and to forge their weapons; and when they shall be weakened with mutual slaughter, let us rush down upon them, force their remains to take shelter in their ships, and reign once more in our native country.'

Samuel Johnson

'Ανέχου καὶ ἀπέχου

How evil came into the world; for what reason it is that life is over-spread with such boundless varieties of misery; why the only thinking being of this globe is doomed to think merely to be wretched, and to pass his time from youth to age in fearing or in suffering calamities, is a question which philosophers have long asked, and which philosophy could never answer.

Religion informs us that misery and sin were produced together. The depravation of human will was followed by a disorder of the harmony of nature; and by that providence which often places antidotes in the neighbourhood of poisons, vice was checked by misery, lest it should swell to universal and unlimited dominion.

A state of innocence and happiness is so remote from all that we have ever seen, that though we can easily conceive it possible, and may therefore hope to attain it, yet our speculations upon it must be general and confused. We can discover that where there is universal innocence there will probably be universal happiness; for why should afflictions be permitted to infest beings who are not in danger of corruption from blessings, and where there is no use of terror nor cause of punishment? But in a world like ours, where our senses assault us, and our hearts betray us, we should pass on from crime to crime, heedless and remorseless, if misery did not stand in our way, and our own pains admonish us of our folly.

Almost all the moral good which is left among us, is the apparent effect of physical evil.

Goodness is divided by divines into soberness, righteousness, and godliness. Let it be examined how each of these duties would be practised if there were no physical evil to enforce it.

Sobriety, or temperance, is nothing but the forbearance of pleasure; and if pleasure was not followed by pain, who would forbear it? We see every hour those in whom the desire of present indulgence overpowers all sense of past and all foresight of future misery. In a remission of the gout the drunkard returns to his wine, and the glutton to his feast; and if neither disease nor poverty were felt or dreaded, every one would sink down in idle sensuality, without any care of others, or of himself. To eat and drink, and lie down to sleep, would be the whole business of mankind.

Righteousness, or the system of social duty, may be subdivided into justice and charity. Of justice one of the heathen sages has shown, with great acuteness, that it was impressed upon mankind only by the inconveniences which injustice had produced. 'In the first ages,' says he, 'men acted without any rule but the impulse of desire, they practised injustice upon others, and suffered it from others in their turn; but in time it was discovered, that the pain of suffering wrong was greater than the pleasure of doing it, and mankind, by a general compact, submitted to the restraint of laws, and resigned the pleasure to escape the pain.'

Of charity it is superfluous to observe, that it could have no place if there were no want; for of a virtue which could not be practised, the omission could not be culpable. Evil is not only the occasional but the efficient cause of charity; we are incited to the relief of misery by the consciousness that we have the same nature with the sufferer, that we are in danger of the same distresses, and may sometime implore the same assistance.

Godliness, or piety, is elevation of the mind towards the supreme being, and extension of the thoughts to another life. The other life is future, and the supreme being is invisible. None would have recourse to an invisible power, but that all other subjects had eluded their hopes. None would fix their attention upon the future, but that they are discontented with the present. If the senses were feasted with perpetual pleasure, they would always keep the mind in subjection. Reason has no authority over us, but by its power to warn us against evil.

In childhood, while our minds are yet unoccupied, religion is impressed upon them, and the first years of almost all who have been well educated are passed in a regular discharge of the duties of piety. But as we advance forward into the crowds of life, innumerable delights solicit our inclinations, and innumerable cares distract our attention; the time of youth is passed in noisy frolics; manhood is led on from hope to hope, and from project to project; the dissoluteness of pleasure, the inebriation of success, the ardour of expectation, and the vehemence of competition, chain down the mind alike to the present scene, nor is it remembered how soon this mist of trifles must be scattered, and the bubbles that float upon the rivulet of life be lost for ever in the gulf of eternity. To this consideration scarce any man is awakened but by some pressing and resistless evil. The death of those from whom he derived his pleasures, or to whom he destined his possessions, some disease which shows him the vanity of all external acquisitions, or the gloom of age, which intercepts his prospects of long enjoyment, forces him to fix his hopes upon another state, and when he has contended with the tempests of life till his strength fails him, he flies at last to the shelter of religion.

That misery does not make all virtuous, experience too certainly informs us; but it is no less certain that of what virtue there is, misery produces far the greater part. Physical evil may be therefore endured with patience, since it is the cause of moral good; and patience itself is one virtue by which we are prepared for that state in which evil shall be no more.

FROM THE PREFACE TO THE DICTIONARY

THUS have I laboured to settle the orthography, display the analogy, regulate the structures, and ascertain the signification of English words, to perform all the parts of a faithful lexicographer: but I have not always executed my own scheme, or satisfied my own expectations. The work, whatever proofs of diligence and attention it may exhibit, is yet capable of many improvements: the orthography which I recommend is still controvertible, the etymology which I adopt is uncertain, and perhaps frequently erroneous; the explanations are sometimes too much contracted, and sometimes too much diffused, the significations are distinguished rather with subtlety than skill, and the attention is harassed with unnecessary minuteness.

The examples are too often injudiciously truncated, and perhaps sometimes, I hope very rarely, alleged in a mistaken sense; for in making this collection I trusted more to memory,[1] than, in a state of disquiet and embarrassment, memory can contain, and purposed to supply at the review what was left incomplete in the first transcription.

Many terms appropriated to particular occupations, though necessary and significant, are undoubtedly omitted, and of the words most studiously considered and exemplified, many senses have escaped observation.

Yet these failures, however frequent, may admit extenuation and apology. To have attempted much is always laudable, even when the enterprise is above the strength that undertakes it. To rest below his own aim is incident to every one whose fancy is active, and whose views are comprehensive; nor is any man satisfied with himself because he has done much, but because he can conceive little. When first I engaged in this work, I resolved to leave neither words nor things unexamined, and pleased myself with a prospect of the hours which I should revel away in feasts of literature, the obscure recesses of northern learning,[2] which I should enter and ransack, the treasures with which I expected every search into those neglected mines to reward my labour, and the triumph with which I should display my acquisitions to mankind. When I had thus inquired into the original of words, I resolved to show likewise my attention to things; to pierce deep into every science, to inquire the nature of every substance of which I inserted the name, to limit every idea by a definition strictly logical, and exhibit every production of art or nature in an accurate description, that my book might be in place of all other dictionaries whether appellative or technical.[3] But these were the dreams of a poet doomed at last to wake a lexicographer. I soon found that it is too late to look for instruments, when the work calls for execution, and that whatever abilities I had brought to my task, with those I must finally perform it. To deliberate whenever I doubted, to inquire whenever I was ignorant, would have protracted the undertaking without end, and, perhaps, without much improvement; for I did not find by my first experiments, that what I had not of my own was easily to be obtained: I saw that one inquiry only gave occasion to another, that book referred to book, that to search was not always to find, and to find was not always to be informed; and that thus to pursue perfection, was, like the first inhabitants of Arcadia, to chase the sun, which, when they had reached the hill where he seemed to rest, was still beheld at the same distance from them.

I then contracted my design, determining to confide in myself, and no longer to solicit auxiliaries, which produced more incumbrance than assistance: by this I obtained at least one advantage, that I set limits to my work, which would in time be finished, though not completed.

Despondency has never so far prevailed as to depress me to negligence; some faults will at last appear to be the effects of anxious diligence and persevering activity. The nice and subtle ramifications of meaning were not easily avoided by a mind intent upon accuracy, and convinced of the necessity of disentangling combinations, and separating similitudes. Many of the distinctions which to common readers appear useless and idle, will be found real and important by men versed in the school philosophy, without which no dictionary ever shall be accurately compiled, or skilfully examined.

Some senses however there are, which, though not the same, are yet so nearly allied, that they are often confounded. Most men think indistinctly, and therefore cannot speak with exactness; and consequently some examples might be indifferently put to either signification: this uncertainty is not to be imputed to me, who do not form, but register the language; who do not teach men how they should think, but relate how they have hitherto expressed their thoughts.

The imperfect sense of some examples I lamented, but could not remedy, and hope they will be compensated by innumerable passages selected with propriety, and preserved with exactness; some shining with sparks of imagination, and some replete with treasures of wisdom.

The orthography and etymology, though imperfect, are not imperfect for want of care, but because care will not always be successful, and recollection or information come too late for use.

That many terms of art and manufacture are omitted, must be frankly acknowledged; but for this defect I may boldly allege that it was unavoidable: I could not visit caverns to learn the miner's language, nor take a voyage to perfect my skill in the dialect of navigation, nor visit the warehouses of merchants, and shops of artificers, to gain the names of wares, tools and operations, of which no mention is found in books; what favourable accident or easy inquiry brought within my reach, has not been neglected; but it had been a hopeless labour to glean up words, by courting living information, and contesting with the sullenness of one, and the roughness of another.

To furnish the academicians della Crusca[4] with words of this kind, a series of comedies called *la Fiera*, or *the Fair*, was professedly written by Buonaroti; but I had no such assistant, and therefore was content to want what they must have wanted likewise, had they not luckily been so supplied.

Nor are all words which are not found in the vocabulary, to be lamented as omissions. Of the laborious and mercantile part of the people, the diction is in a great measure casual and mutable; many of their terms are formed for some temporary or local convenience, and though current at certain times and places, are in others utterly unknown. This fugitive cant,[5] which is always in a state of increase or decay, cannot be regarded as any part of the durable materials of a language, and therefore must be suffered to perish with other things unworthy of preservation.

Care will sometimes betray to the appearance of negligence. He that is catching opportunities which seldom occur, will suffer those to pass by unregarded, which he expects hourly to return; he that is searching for rare and remote things, will neglect those that are obvious and familiar: thus many of the most common and cursory words[6] have been inserted with little illustration, because in gathering the authorities, I forbore to copy those which I thought likely to occur, whenever they were wanted. It is remarkable that, in reviewing my collection, I found the word *sea* unexemplified.

Thus it happens, that in things difficult there is danger from ignorance, and in things easy from confidence; the mind, afraid of greatness, and disdainful of littleness, hastily withdraws herself from painful searches, and passes with scornful rapidity over tasks not adequate to her powers, sometimes too secure for caution, and again too anxious for vigorous effort; sometimes idle in a plain path, and sometimes distracted in labyrinths, and dissipated by different intentions.

A large work is difficult because it is large, even though all its parts might singly be performed with facility; where there are many things to be done, each must be allowed its share of time and labour, in the proportion only which it bears to the whole; nor can it be expected, that the stones which form the dome of a temple, should be squared and polished like the diamond of a ring.

Of the event of this work, for which, having laboured it with so much application, I cannot but have some degree of parental fondness, it is natural to form conjectures. Those who have been persuaded to think well of my design, require that it should fix our language, and put a stop to those alterations which time and chance have hitherto been suffered to make in it without opposition. With this consequence I will confess that I flattered myself for a while; but now begin to fear that I have indulged expectation which neither reason nor experience can justify. When we see men grow old and die at a certain time one after another, from century to century, we laugh at the elixir that promises to prolong life to a thousand years; and with equal justice may the lexicographer be derided, who being able to produce no example of a nation that has preserved their words and phrases from mutability, shall imagine that his dictionary can embalm his language, and secure it from corruption and decay, that it is in his power to change sublunary nature, or clear the world at once from folly, vanity, and affectation.

With this hope, however, academies have been instituted, to guard the avenues of their languages, to retain fugitives, and repulse intruders; but their vigilance and activity have hitherto been vain; sounds are too volatile and subtle for legal restraints; to enchain syllables, and to lash the wind, are equally the undertakings of pride, unwilling to measure its desires by its strength. The French language has visibly changed[7] under the inspection of the academy; the style of Amelot's translation of father Paul is observed by Le Courayer to be *un peu passé*; and no Italian will maintain, that the diction of any modern writer is not perceptibly different from that of Boccace, Machiavel, or Caro.

Total and sudden transformations of a language seldom happen; conquests and migrations are now very rare; but there are other causes of change, which, though slow in their operation, and invisible in their progress, are perhaps as much superior to human resistance, as the revolutions of the sky, or intumescence of the tide. Commerce, however necessary,[8] however lucrative, as it depraves the manners, corrupts the language; they that have frequent intercourse with strangers, to whom they endeavour to accommodate themselves, must in time learn a mingled dialect, like the jargon which serves the traffickers on the Mediterranean and Indian coasts. This will not always be confined to the exchange, the warehouse, or the port, but will be communicated by degrees to other ranks of the people, and be at last incorporated with the current speech.

There are likewise internal causes equally forcible. The language most likely to continue long without alteration, would be that of a nation raised a little, and but a little, above barbarity, secluded from strangers, and totally employed in procuring the conveniences of life; either without books, or, like some of the Mahometan countries, with very few: men thus busied and unlearned, having only such words as common use requires, would perhaps long continue to express the same notions by the same signs. But no such constancy can be expected in a people polished by arts, and classed by subordination, where one part of the community is sustained and accommodated by the labour of the other. Those who have much leisure to think, will always be enlarging the stock of ideas, and every increase of knowledge, whether real or fancied, will produce new words, or combinations of words. When the mind is unchained from necessity, it will range after convenience; when it is left at large in the fields of speculation, it will shift opinions; as any custom is disused, the words that expressed it must perish with it; as any opinion grows popular, it will innovate speech in the same proportion as it alters practice.

As by the cultivation of various sciences, a language is amplified, it will be more furnished with words deflected from their original sense;[9] the geometrician will talk of a courtier's zenith, or the eccentric virtue of a wild hero, and the physician of sanguine expectations and phlegmatic delays. Copiousness of speech will give opportunities to capricious choice, by which some words will be preferred, and others degraded; vicissitudes of fashion will enforce the use of new, or extend the signification of known terms. The tropes of poetry will make hourly encroachments, and the metaphorical will become the current sense: pronunciation will be varied by levity or ignorance, and the pen must at length comply with the tongue; illiterate writers will at one time or other, by public infatuation, rise into renown, who, not knowing the original import of words, will use them with colloquial licentiousness, confound distinction, and forget propriety. As politeness increases, some expressions will be considered as too gross and vulgar for the delicate, others as too formal and ceremonious for the gay and airy; new phrases are therefore adopted, which must, for the same reasons, be in time dismissed. Swift, in his petty treatise on the English language, allows that new words must sometimes be introduced, but proposes that none should be suffered to become obsolete. But what makes a word obsolete, more than general agreement to forbear it? and how shall it be continued, when it conveys an offensive idea, or recalled again into the mouths of mankind, when it has once by disuse become unfamiliar, and by unfamiliarity unpleasing?

There is another cause of alteration more prevalent than any other, which yet in the present state of the world cannot be obviated. A mixture of two languages will produce a third distinct from both, and they will always be mixed, where the chief part of education, and the most conspicuous accomplishment, is skill in ancient or in foreign tongues. He that has long cultivated another language, will find its words and combinations crowd upon his memory; and haste and negligence, refinement and affectation, will obtrude borrowed terms and exotic expressions.

The great pest of speech is frequency of translation. No book was ever turned from one language into another, without imparting something of its native idiom; this is the most mischievous and comprehensive innovation; single words may enter by thousands, and the fabric of the tongue continue the same, but new phraseology changes much at once; it alters not the single stones of the building, but the order of the columns. If an academy should be established for the cultivation of our style, which I, who can never wish to see dependence multiplied, hope the spirit of English liberty will hinder or destroy, let them, instead of compiling grammars and dictionaries, endeavour, with all their influence, to stop the licence of translators, whose idleness and ignorance, if it be suffered to proceed, will reduce us to babble a dialect of France.[10]

If the changes that we fear be thus irresistible, what remains but to acquiesce with silence, as in the other insurmountable distresses of humanity? it remains that we retard what we cannot repel, that we palliate what we cannot cure. Life may be lengthened by care, though death cannot be ultimately defeated: tongues, like governments, have a natural tendency to degeneration; we have long preserved our constitution, let us make some struggles for our language.

In hope of giving longevity to that which its own nature forbids to be immortal, I have devoted this book, the labour of years, to the honour of my country, that we may no longer yield the palm of philology to the nations of the continent. The chief glory of every people arises from its authors: whether I shall add anything by my own writings to the reputation of English literature, must be left to time: much of my life has been lost under the pressures of disease; much has been trifled away; and much has always been spent in provision for the day that was passing over me; but I shall not think my employment useless or ignoble, if by my assistance foreign nations, and distant ages, gain access to the propagators of knowledge, and understand the teachers of truth; if my labours afford light to the repositories of science, and add celebrity to Bacon, to Hooker, to Milton and to Boyle.

When I am animated by this wish, I look with pleasure on my book, however defective, and deliver it to the world with the spirit of a man that has endeavoured well. That it will immediately become popular I have not promised to myself: a few wild blunders, and risible absurdities, from which no work of such multiplicity was ever free, may for a time furnish folly with laughter, and harden ignorance in contempt; but useful diligence will at last prevail, and there never can be wanting some who distinguish desert; who will consider that no dictionary of a living tongue ever can be perfect, since while it is hastening to publication, some words are budding, and some falling away; that a whole life cannot be spent upon syntax and etymology, and that even a whole life would not be sufficient; that he, whose design includes whatever language can express, must often speak of what he does not understand; that a writer will sometimes be hurried by eagerness to the end, and sometimes faint with weariness under a task, which Scaliger compares to the labours of the anvil and the mine; that what is obvious is not always known, and what is known is not always present; that sudden fits of inadvertency will surprise vigilance, slight avocations will seduce attention, and casual eclipses of the mind will darken learning; and that the writer shall often in vain trace his memory at the moment of need, for that which yesterday he knew with intuitive readiness, and which will come uncalled into his thoughts tomorrow.

In this work, when it shall be found that much is omitted, let it not be forgotten that much likewise is performed; and though no book was ever spared out of tenderness to the author, and the world is little solicitous to know whence proceeded the faults of that which it condemns; yet it may gratify curiosity to inform it, that the *English Dictionary* was written with little assistance of the learned, and without any patronage of the great;[11] not in the soft obscurities of retirement, or under the shelter of academic bowers, but amidst inconvenience and distraction, in sickness and in sorrow: and it may repress the triumph of malignant criticism to observe, that if our language is not here fully displayed, I have only failed in an attempt which no human powers have hitherto completed. If the lexicons of ancient tongues, now immutably fixed, and comprised in a few volumes, be yet, after the toil of successive ages, inadequate and delusive; if the aggregated knowledge, and cooperating diligence of the Italian academicians, did not secure them from the censure of Beni, if the embodied critics of France, when fifty years had been spent upon their work, were obliged to change its economy, and give their second edition another form, I may surely be contented without the praise of perfection, which, if I could obtain, in this gloom of solitude,[12] what would it avail me? I have protracted my work till most of those whom I wished to please, have sunk into the grave, and success and miscarriage are empty sounds: I therefore dismiss it with frigid tranquillity, having little to fear or hope from censure or from praise.

SELECTIONS FROM THE ENGLISH DICTIONARY

This selection from the Dictionary aims at choosing examples of six types of entry. First, some of those in which Johnson gives his opinions on matters of linguistic usage:—

Immaterial. (1) Incorporated; distinct from matter; void of matter.

(2) Unimportant; without weight; impertinent; without relation. This sense has crept into the conversation and writings of barbarians, but ought to be utterly rejected.

Nowadays. (This word, though common and used by the best writers, is perhaps barbarous.) In the present age.

Paramour. (1) A lover or wooer.

(2) A mistress. It is obsolete in both senses, though not inelegant or unmusical.

To partialize. To make partial. A word, perhaps, peculiar to Shakespeare, and not unworthy of general use.

> Such neighbour-nearness to our sacred blood
> Should nothing privilege him, nor *partialize*
> Th' unstooping firmness of my upright soul. Shakespeare.

Precarious. Dependent; uncertain, because depending on the will of another; held by courtesy; changeable or alienable at the pleasure of another. No word is more unskilfully used than this with its derivatives. It is used for *uncertain* in all its senses; but it only means uncertain, as dependent on others: thus there are authors who mention the *precariousness* of an *account*, of the *weather*, of a *die*.

Precariousness. Uncertainty; dependence on others. The following passage from a book, otherwise elegantly written, affords an example of the impropriety mentioned at the word *precarious*.

> Most consumptive people die of the discharge they spit up, which, with the *precariousness* of the symptoms of an oppressed diaphragm from a mere lodgment of extravasated matter, render the operation but little adviseable. Sharp's *Surgery*.

Rapport. Relation; reference; proportion. A word introduced by the innovator, Temple, but not copied by others.

Reputeless. Disreputable; disgraceful. A word not inelegant, but out of use.

> Opinion, that did help me to the crown,
> Had left me in reputeless banishment,
> A fellow of no mark nor livelihood. Shakespeare *Henry IV.*

Trait. A stroke; a touch. Scarce English.

Traverse. (2) Something that thwarts, crosses, or obstructs; cross accident; thwarting obstacle. This is a sense rather French than English.

Vastidity. Wideness; immensity. A barbarous word.

> Perpetual durance,
> Through all the world's *vastidity.* Shakespeare.

Vaulty. Arched; concave. A bad word.

> I will kiss thy detestable bones,
> And put my eye-balls in thy *vaulty* brows,
> And ring these fingers with thy housbold worms. Shakespeare.

Second, entries which show Johnson's conjectures (or honest admissions of failure) on etymologies:—

Booby. (A word of no certain etymology. Henshaw thinks it a corruption of *bull-beef* ridiculously; Skinner imagines it to be derived from *bobo*, foolish, Span. Junius finds *bowbard* to be an old Scottish word for a *coward*, a *contemptible fellow*; from which he naturally deduces *booby*; but the original of *bowbard* is not known.) A dull, heavy, stupid fellow; a lubber.*

Penguin. (1) A bird. This bird was found with this name, as is supposed, by the first discoverers of America; and *penguin* signifying in Welsh a white head, and the head of this fowl being white, it has

---

* The accepted etymology is Skinner's: Spanish *bobo*, from Latin *balbus*, a stammerer (Ed.)

been imagined, that America was peopled from Wales; whence *Hudibras:*

> British Indians nam'd from *penguins.*

Grew gives another account of the name, deriving it from *pinguis,* Lat. *fat;* but is, I believe, mistaken.*

Sleeveless. (2) Wanting reasonableness; wanting propriety; wanting solidity. (This sense, of which the word has been long possessed, I know not well how it obtained; Skinner thinks it properly *liveless* or *lifeless;* to this I cannot heartily agree, though I know not what better to suggest. Can it come from *sleeve,* a knot, or *skein,* and so signify *unconnected, hanging ill together*? or from *sleeve,* a cover; and therefore means *plainly absurd*; foolish without palliation?)†

Tatterdemalion. (*Tatter* and *I know not what.*) A ragged fellow.‡

Third, entries of scientific interest:—

Asthma. A frequent, difficult, and short respiration, joined with a hissing sound and a cough, especially in the night-time, and when the body is in a prone posture; because then the contents of the lower belly bear so against the diaphragm, as to lessen the capacity of the breast, whereby the lungs have less room to move. Quincy.

Bat. An animal having the body of a mouse and the wings of a bird; not with feathers, but with a sort of skin which is extended. It lays no eggs, but brings forth its young alive, and suckles them. It never grows tame, feeds upon flies, insects, and fatty substances, such as candles, oil, and cheese; and appears only in the summer evenings, when the weather is fine. Calmet.

Electricity. A property in some bodies, whereby, when rubbed so as to grow warm, they draw little bits of paper, or such like substances, to them. Quincy.

Such was the account given a few years ago of electricity; but

* The derivation from Welsh *pen,* head, and *gwyn,* white, is usually accepted. (Ed.)

† The O.E.D. knows no better than Johnson the origin of this sense (now obsolete) of *sleeveless.* (Ed.)

§ Again, the O.E.D. does no better, but covers its ignorance with some impressive polysyllables. '*Tatter,* or more prob. *tattered,* with a factitious element suggesting an ethnic or descriptive derivative.' (Ed.)

the industry of the present age, first excited by the experiments of Gray, has discovered in electricity a multitude of philosophical wonders. Bodies electrified by a sphere of glass, turned nimbly round, not only emit flame, but may be fitted with such a quantity of the electrical vapour, as, if discharged at once upon a human body, would endanger life. The force of this vapour has hitherto appeared instantaneous, persons at both ends of a long chain seeming to be struck at once. The philosophers are now endeavouring to intercept the strokes of lightning.

Ostrich. Ostrich is ranged among birds. It is very large, its wings very short, and the neck about four or five spans. The feathers of its wings are in great esteem, and are used as an ornament for hats, beds, canopies: they are stained of several colours, and made into pretty tufts. They are hunted by way of course, for they never fly; but use their wings to assist them in running more swiftly. The *ostrich* swallows bits of iron or brass, in the same manner as other birds will swallow small stones or gravel, to assist in digesting or comminuting their food. It lays its eggs upon the ground, hides them under the sand, and the sun hatches them. Calmet.

Plethora. The state in which the vessels are fuller of humours than is agreeable to a natural state of health; arises either from a diminution of some natural evacuations, or from debauch and feeding higher or more in quantity than the ordinary powers of the viscera can digest: evacuations and exercise are its remedies.

Fourth, entries relating to literature and literary criticism:—

Comedy. A dramatic representation of the lighter faults of mankind.

Epic. Narrative; comprising narrations, not acted, but rehearsed. It is usually supposed to be heroic, or to contain one great action achieved by a hero.

Novel. A small tale, generally of love.

Pastoral. A poem in which any action or passion is represented by its effects upon a country life; or according to the common practice in which speakers take upon them the character of shepherds; an idyll; a bucolic.

Romance. A military fable of the middle ages; a tale of wild adventures in war and love.

Romantic: (1) Resembling the tales of romances; wild.

(2) Improbable; false.

(3) Fanciful; full of wild scenery.

Sonnet. A short poem consisting of fourteen lines, of which the rhymes are adjusted by a particular rule. It is not very suitable to the English language, and has not been used by any man of eminence since Milton.

Sonnetteer. A small poet, in contempt.

Fifth, entries revealing some of Johnson's social or political opinions:—

Dedication. A servile address to a patron.

Dedicator. One who inscribes his work to a patron with compliment and servility.*

Enthusiasm. (1) A vain belief of private revelation; a vain confidence of divine favour or communication.

Patriot. One whose ruling passion is the love of his country. It is sometimes used for a factious disturber of the government.†

Patron. One who countenances, supports or protects. Commonly a wretch who supports with insolence, and is paid with flattery.‡

Pension. An allowance made to any one without an equivalent. In England it is generally understood to mean pay given to a state hireling for treason to his country.§

Plaid. A striped or variegated cloth; an outer loose weed worn much by the highlanders in Scotland: there is a particular kind worn too by the women; but both these modes seem now nearly extirpated

* Cf. the line in *The Vanity of Human Wishes:* 'To growing names the dedicator flies.' (Ed.)

† The second sentence of this definition was added in the fourth edition. It is largely (but not entirely) in this sense that Johnson was using the word in one of his most famous sayings: 'Patriotism is the last refuge of a scoundrel.' (Ed.)

‡ Cf. the definitions of *dedication* and *dedicator*, and of course the letter to Lord Chesterfield. (Ed.)

§ This definition reflects the younger, anti-establishment Johnson. When he himself became a pensioner, his enemies did not let him forget it. (Ed.)

among them; the one by act of parliament, and the other by adopting the English dresses of the sex.*

Stockjobber. A low wretch who gets money by buying and selling shares in the funds.†

Tory. One who adheres to the ancient constitution of the state, and the apostolical hierarchy of the church of England, opposed to a whig.

Whig. The name of a faction.

Sixth, a few entries in which personal references are slyly inserted:—

Grubstreet. Originally the name of a street in Moorfields, in London, much inhabited by writers of small histories, dictionaries, and temporary poems; whence any mean production is called grub-street.

*Χαῖρ' 'Ιθάκη. μετ' ἄεθλα, μετ' ἄλγεα πικρὰ
ἀσπασίως τεὸν οὖδας ἱκάνομαι.‡*

Lexicographer. A writer of dictionaries; a harmless drudge, that busies himself in tracing the original, and detailing the signification of words.

Lich. A dead carcase; whence *lichwake*, the time or act of watching by the dead; *lichgate*, the gate through which the dead are carried to the grave; *Lichfield*, the field of the dead, a city in Staffordshire, so

* This shows Johnson's sympathetic interest in Highland society already active eighteen years before he made the journey to the Hebrides. 'Act of parliament' refers to the measure passed after the Forty-five making the wearing of the kilt illegal. (Ed.)

† The modern equivalent is 'stockbroker'. The hostility of this definition reflects Johnson's abiding suspicion of the growing commercialism of English society. (Ed.)

‡ The Greek lines are from the Anthology, and mean: 'Hail, Ithaca! after labours, after bitter sorrows, safely I reach your shore . . .' It is not quite clear what Johnson intended by this. A recognition that he too was, or had been, a 'grubstreeter'? or a hope that perhaps the publication of the *Dictionary* would deliver him from the hand-to-mouth drudgery of Grubstreet? If the latter, his hope was not fulfilled. (Ed.)

named from martyred christians. *Salve magna parens. Lichwake* is
still retained in Scotland in the same sense.*

Oats. A grain, which in England is generally given to horses, but in
Scotland supports the people.†

Pastern. The knee of an horse.‡

* The Latin words after *Lichfield* mean 'Hail, great parent!', and are Johnson's way of telling his readers that he was born and brought up in Lichfield
and is proud of it. (Ed.)

† It seems doubtful if this was intended as a crack at the Scots (it was in fact a
perfectly accurate statement); but when, later, Johnson became celebrated for
his 'anti-Scottish prejudices', this was often quoted as a specimen. (Ed.)

‡ Johnson's best-known mistake – it is really a part of the horse's foot –
which owes its fame largely to his cheerful explanation of it to a feminine
inquirer: 'Ignorance, madam, pure ignorance.' (Ed.)

To Thomas Warton

Dear Sir

I am extremely sensible of the favour done me, both by Mr Wise and yourself. The book[1] cannot, I think, be printed in less than six weeks, nor probably so soon; and I will keep back the title-page, for such an insertion as you seem to promise me. Be pleased to let me know what money I should send you, for bearing the expense of the affair, and I will take care that you may have it ready in your hand.

I had lately the favour of a letter from your brother, with some account of poor Collins,[2] for whom I am much concerned. I have a notion, that by very great temperance, or more properly abstinence, he might yet recover.

There is an old English and Latin book of poems by Barclay, called *The Ship of Fools*; at the end of which are a number of *Eglogues* (so he writes it, from *Ægloga*) which are probably the first in our language. If you cannot find the book I will get Mr Dodsley to send it you.

I shall be extremely glad to hear from you soon again, to know if the affair proceeds. I have mentioned it to none of my friends for fear of being laughed at for my disappointment.

You know poor Mr Dodsley has lost his wife; I believe he is much affected. I hope he will not suffer so much as I yet suffer for the loss of mine.[3]

Οἴμοι. τί δ᾽ οἴμοι; θνῆτα γὰρ πεπόνθαμεν.

I have ever since seemed to myself broken off from mankind; a kind of solitary wanderer in the wild of life, without any certain direction, or fixed point of view: a gloomy gazer on a world to which I have little relation. Yet I would endeavour, by the help of you and your brother, to supply the want of closer union, by friendship: and hope to have long the pleasure of being,

dear Sir, most affectionately yours,

[London,] 21 December 1754　　　　Sam: Johnson

* See Editor's Notes.

To the Right Honourable the Earl
of Chesterfield

7 February 1755

My Lord

I have been lately informed, by the proprietor of *The World*, that two papers, in which my Dictionary is recommended to the public, were written by your Lordship. To be so distinguished, is an honour, which, being very little accustomed to favours from the great, I know not well how to receive, or in what terms to acknowledge.

When, upon some slight encouragement, I first visited your Lordship, I was overpowered, like the rest of mankind, by the enchantment of your address; and could not forbear to wish that I might boast myself *Le vainqueur du vainqueur de la terre*; – that I might obtain that regard for which I saw the world contending; but I found my attendance so little encouraged, that neither pride nor modesty would suffer me to continue it. When I had once addressed your Lordship in public, I had exhausted all the art of pleasing which a retired and uncourtly scholar can possess. I had done all that I could; and no man is well pleased to have his all neglected, be it ever so little.

Seven years, my Lord, have now past, since I waited in your outward rooms, or was repulsed from your door; during which time I have been pushing on my work through difficulties, of which it is useless to complain, and have brought it, at last, to the verge of publication, without one act of assistance, one word of encouragement, or one smile of favour. Such treatment I did not expect, for I never had a Patron before.

The shepherd in Virgil grew at last acquainted with Love, and found him a native of the rocks.[1]

Is not a Patron, my Lord, one who looks with unconcern on a man struggling for life in the water, and, when he has reached ground, encumbers him with help? The notice which you have been pleased to take of my labours, had it been early, had been kind; but it has been delayed till I am indifferent, and cannot enjoy it; till I am solitary,[2] and cannot impart it; till I am known, and do not want it.

I hope it is no very cynical[3] asperity not to confess obligations where no benefit has been received, or to be unwilling that the Public should consider me as owing that to a Patron, which Providence has enabled me to do for myself.

Having carried on my work thus far with so little obligation to any favourer of learning, I shall not be disappointed though I should conclude it, if less be possible, with less; for I have been long wakened from that dream of hope, in which I once boasted myself with so much exultation, my Lord,

your Lordship's most humble,
most obedient servant,
SAM: JOHNSON

TO SAMUEL RICHARDSON

Sir

I am obliged to entreat your assistance. I am now under an arrest for five pounds eighteen shillings. Mr Strahan, from whom I should have received the necessary help in this case, is not at home; and I am afraid of not finding Mr Millar. If you will be so good as to send me this sum, I will very gratefully repay you, and add it to all former obligations.

I am, Sir,
Your most obedient
and most humble servant,
SAM: JOHNSON

Gough Square, 16 March [1756]

TO JOSEPH WARTON

15 April 1756

Dear Sir

Though when you and your brother were in town you did not think my humble habitation worth a visit, yet I will not so far give way to sullenness as not to tell you that I have lately seen an octavo book[1] which I suspect to be yours, though I have not yet read above ten pages. That way of publishing, without acquainting your friends, is a wicked trick. However, I will not so far depend upon a mere conjecture as to charge you with a fraud which I cannot prove you to have committed.

I should be glad to hear that you are pleased with your new situation. You have now a kind of royalty, and are to be answerable for your conduct to posterity. I suppose you care not now to answer a letter except there be a lucky concurrence of a post-day with a holiday. These restraints are troublesome for a time, but custom makes them easy, with the help of some honour, and a great deal of profit, and I doubt not but your abilities will obtain both.

For my part, I have not lately done much. I have been ill in the winter, and my eye has been inflamed; but I please myself with the hopes of doing many things, with which I have long pleased and deceived myself.

What becomes of poor dear Collins?[2] I wrote him a letter which he never answered. I suppose writing is very troublesome to him. That man is no common loss. The moralists all talk of the uncertainty of fortune, and the transitoriness of beauty; but it is yet more dreadful to consider that the powers of the mind are equally liable to change; that understanding may make its appearance and depart, that it may blaze and expire.

Let me not be long without a letter, and I will forgive you the omission of the visit; and if you can tell me that you are now more happy than before, you will give great pleasure to,

Dear Sir,

Your most affectionate
and most humble servant,

SAM: JOHNSON

To Bennet Langton, Esq., at Langton,
near Spilsby, Lincolnshire

Dear Sir

I should be sorry to think that what engrosses the attention of my friend, should have no part of mine. Your mind is now full of the fate of Dury; but his fate is past, and nothing remains but to try what reflection will suggest to mitigate the terrors of a violent death, which is more formidable at the first glance, than on a nearer and more steady view. A violent death is never very painful; the only danger is lest it should be unprovided. But if a man can be supposed to make no provision for death in war, what can be the state that would have awakened him to the care of futurity? When would that man have prepared himself to die, who went to seek death without preparation? What then can be the reason why we lament more him that dies of a wound, than him that dies of a fever? A man that languishes with disease, ends his life with more pain, but with less virtue; he leaves no example to his friends, nor bequeaths any honour to his descendants. The only reason why we lament a soldier's death, is, that we think he might have lived longer; yet this cause of grief is common to many other kinds of death which are not so passionately bewailed. The truth is, that every death is violent which is the effect of accident; every death, which is not gradually brought on by the miseries of age, or when life is extinguished for any other reason than that it is burnt out. He that dies before sixty, of a cold or consumption, dies, in reality, by a violent death; yet his death is borne with patience only because the cause of his untimely end is silent and invisible. Let us endeavour to see things as they are, and then inquire whether we ought to complain. Whether to see life as it is, will give us much consolation, I know not; but the consolation which is drawn from truth, if any there be, is solid and durable; that which may be derived from error must be, like its original, fallacious and fugitive.

I am, dear, dear Sir,

your most humble servant,

21 September 1758   Sam: Johnson

PRAYERS
1752 AND 1759*

PRAYERS COMPOSED BY ME ON THE DEATH OF MY WIFE, AND
REPOSITED AMONG HER MEMORIALS,
8 MAY 1752. *Deus exaudi. – Heu!*

24 APRIL 1752. Almighty and most merciful Father, who lovest
those whom thou punishest, and turnest away thy anger from the
penitent, look down with pity upon my sorrows, and grant that the
affliction which it has pleased thee to bring upon me, may awaken
my conscience, enforce my resolutions of a better life, and impress
upon me such conviction of thy power and goodness, that I may place
in thee my only felicity, and endeavour to please thee in all my
thoughts, words, and actions. Grant, O Lord, that I may not languish
in fruitless and unavailing sorrow, but that I may consider from whose
hand all good and evil is received, and may remember that I am
punished for my sins, and hope for comfort only by repentance.
Grant, O merciful God, that by the assistance of thy Holy Spirit I may
repent, and be comforted, obtain that peace which the world cannot
give, pass the residue of my life in humble resignation and cheerful
obedience; and when it shall please thee to call me from this mortal
state, resign myself into thy hands with faith and confidence, and
finally obtain mercy and everlasting happiness, for the sake of Jesus
Christ our Lord. Amen.

26 APRIL 1752, BEING AFTER 12 AT NIGHT OF THE 25TH. O Lord,
Governor of Heaven and Earth, in whose hands are embodied and
departed spirits, if thou hast ordained the souls of the dead to minister
to the living, and appointed my departed wife to have care of me,
grant that I may enjoy the good effects of her attention and ministra-
tion, whether exercised by appearance, impulses, dreams, or in any
other manner agreeable to thy government; forgive my presumption, enlighten my ignorance, and however meaner agents are employed, grant me the blessed influences of thy Holy Spirit, through
Jesus Christ our Lord. Amen.

* See Editor's Notes.

'GREAT CHAM OF LITERATURE'

Prayers

15 APRIL 1759. Almighty and most merciful Father, look down with pity upon my sins. I am a sinner, good Lord, but let not my sins burden me for ever. Give me thy Grace to break the chain of evil custom. Enable me to shake off idleness and sloth; to will and to do what thou hast commanded, grant me to be chaste in thoughts, words, and actions; to love and frequent thy worship, to study and understand thy word; to be diligent in my calling, that I may support myself and relieve others.

Forgive me, O Lord, whatever my Mother has suffered by my fault, whatever I have done amiss, and whatever duty I have neglected. Let me not sink into useless dejection; but so sanctify my affliction, O Lord, that I may be converted and healed; and that, by the help of thy Holy Spirit, I may obtain everlasting life through Jesus Christ our Lord.

And O Lord, so far as it may be lawful, I commend unto thy fatherly goodness my father, brother, wife and mother, beseeching thee to make them happy for Jesus Christ's sake. Amen.

SCRUPLES

O Lord, who wouldst that all men should be saved, and who knowest that without thy grace we can do nothing acceptable to thee, have mercy upon me. Enable me to break the chain of my sins, to reject sensuality in thought, and to overcome and suppress vain scruples; and to use such diligence in lawful employment as may enable me to support myself and do good to others. O Lord, forgive me the time lost in idleness; pardon the sins which I have committed, and grant that I may redeem the time misspent, and be reconciled to thee by true repentance, that I may live and die in peace, and be received to everlasting happiness. Take not from me, O Lord, thy holy spirit, but let me have support and comfort for Jesus Christ's sake. Amen.

Transcribed 26 June 1768. Of this prayer there is no date, nor can I conjecture when it was composed. [1759?]

FROM PREFACE TO SHAKESPEARE

That praises are without reason lavished on the dead, and that the honours due only to excellence are paid to antiquity, is a complaint likely to be always continued by those, who, being able to add nothing to truth, hope for eminence from the heresies of paradox; or those, who, being forced by disappointment upon consolatory expedients, are willing to hope from posterity what the present age refuses, and flatter themselves that the regard which is yet denied by envy, will be at last bestowed by time.

Antiquity, like every other quality that attracts the notice of mankind, has undoubtedly votaries that reverence it, not from reason, but from prejudice. Some seem to admire indiscriminately whatever has been long preserved, without considering that time has sometimes cooperated with chance; all perhaps are more willing to honour past than present excellence; and the mind contemplates genius through the shades of age, as the eye surveys the sun through artificial opacity. The great contention of criticism is to find the faults of the moderns, and the beauties of the ancients. While an author is yet living we estimate his powers by his worst performance, and when he is dead we rate them by his best.

To works, however, of which the excellence is not absolute and definite, but gradual and comparative; to works not raised upon principles demonstrative and scientific, but appealing wholly to observation and experience, no other test can be applied than length of duration and continuance of esteem. What mankind have long possessed they have often examined and compared, and if they persist to value the possession, it is because frequent comparisons have confirmed opinion in its favour. As among the works of nature no man can properly call a river deep or a mountain high, without the knowledge of many mountains and many rivers; so in the productions of genius, nothing can be styled excellent till it has been compared with other works of the same kind. Demonstration immediately displays its power, and has nothing to hope or fear from the flux of years; but works tentative and experimental must be estimated by their proportion to the general and collective ability of man, as it is discovered in a long succession of endeavours. Of the first building that was raised, it might be with certainty determined that it was round or square, but whether it was spacious or lofty must have been referred to time. The Pythagorean scale of numbers was at once discovered to be perfect; but the poems of Homer we yet know not to transcend the common limits of human intelligence, but by remarking, that nation after nation, and century after century, has been able to do little more than transpose his incidents, new name his characters, and paraphrase his sentiments.

The reverence due to writings that have long subsisted arises therefore not from any credulous confidence in the superior wisdom of past ages, or gloomy persuasion of the degeneracy of mankind, but is the consequence of acknowledged and indubitable positions, that what has been longest known has been most considered, and what is most considered is best understood.

The Poet, of whose works I have undertaken the revision, may now begin to assume the dignity of an ancient, and claim the privilege of established fame and prescriptive veneration.[1] He has long outlived his century, the term commonly fixed as the test of literary merit. Whatever advantages he might once derive from personal allusions, local customs, or temporary opinions, have for many years been lost; and every topic of merriment or motive of sorrow, which the modes of artificial life afforded him, now only obscure the scenes which they once illuminated. The effects of favour and competition are at an end; the tradition of his friendships and his enmities has perished; his works support no opinion with arguments, nor supply any faction with invectives; they can neither indulge vanity nor gratify malignity, but are read without any other reason than the desire of pleasure, and are therefore praised only as pleasure is obtained; yet, thus unassisted by interest or passion, they have passed through variations of taste and changes of manners, and, as they devolved from one generation to another, have received new honours at every transmission.

But because human judgement, though it be gradually gaining upon certainty, never becomes infallible; and approbation, though long continued, may yet be only the approbation of prejudice or fashion; it is proper to inquire, by what peculiarities of excellence Shakespeare has gained and kept the favour of his countrymen.

Nothing can please many, and please long, but just representations of general nature. Particular manners can be known to few, and therefore few only can judge how nearly they are copied. The irregular combinations of fanciful invention may delight a while, by that novelty of which the common satiety of life sends us all in quest; but the pleasures of sudden wonder are soon exhausted, and the mind can only repose on the stability of truth.

Shakespeare is above all writers, at least above all modern writers,[2] the poet of nature; the poet that holds up to his readers a faithful mirror of manners and of life. His characters are not modified by the customs of particular places, unpractised by the rest of the world; by the peculiarities of studies or professions, which can operate but upon small numbers; or by the accidents of transient fashions or temporary opinions: they are the genuine progeny of common humanity, such as the world will always supply, and observation will always find. His persons act and speak by the influence of those general passions and principles by which all minds are agitated, and the whole system of life is continued in motion. In the writings of other poets a character is too often an individual; in those of Shakespeare it is commonly a species.

It is from this wide extension of design that so much instruction is derived. It is this which fills the plays of Shakespeare with practical axioms and domestic wisdom. It was said of Euripides, that every verse was a precept; and it may be said of Shakespeare, that from his works may be collected a system of civil and economical prudence. Yet his real power is not shown in the splendour of particular passages, but by the progress of his fable,[3] and the tenor of his dialogue; and he that tries to recommend him by select quotations, will succeed like the pedant in *Hierocles*, who, when he offered his house to sale, carried a brick in his pocket as a specimen.

It will not easily be imagined how much Shakespeare excels in accommodating his sentiments to real life, but by comparing him with other authors. It was observed of the ancient schools of declamation, that the more diligently they were frequented, the more was the student disqualified for the world, because he found nothing there which he should ever meet in any other place. The same remark may be applied to every stage but that of Shakespeare. The theatre, when it is under any other direction, is peopled by such characters as were never seen conversing in a language which was never heard, upon topics which will never arise in the commerce of mankind. But the dialogue of this author is often so evidently determined by the incident which produces it, and is pursued with so much ease and simplicity, that it seems scarcely to claim the merit of fiction, but to have been gleaned by diligent selection out of common conversation, and common occurrences.

Upon every other stage the universal agent is love, by whose power all good and evil is distributed, and every action quickened or retarded. To bring a lover, a lady and a rival into the fable; to entangle them in contradictory obligations, perplex them with oppositions of interest, and harass them with violence of desires inconsistent with each other; to make them meet in rapture and part in agony; to fill their mouths with hyperbolical joy and outrageous sorrow; to distress them as nothing human ever was distressed; to deliver them as nothing human ever was delivered, is the business of a modern dramatist. For this probability is violated, life is misrepresented, and language is depraved. But love is only one of many passions, and as it has no great influence upon the sum of life, it has little operation in the dramas of a poet, who caught his ideas from the living world, and exhibited only what he saw before him. He knew, that any other passion, as it was regular or exorbitant, was a cause of happiness or calamity.

Characters thus ample and general were not easily discriminated and preserved, yet perhaps no poet ever kept his personages more distinct from each other. I will not say with Pope that every speech may be assigned to the proper speaker, because many speeches there are which have nothing characteristical; but perhaps, though some may be equally adapted to every person, it will be difficult to find any that can be properly transferred from the present possessor to another claimant. The choice is right, when there is reason for choice.

Other dramatists can only gain attention by hyperbolical or aggravated characters, by fabulous and unexampled excellence or depravity, as the writers of barbarous romances invigorated the reader by a giant and a dwarf; and he that should form his expectations of human affairs from the play, or from the tale, would be equally deceived. Shakespeare has no heroes; his scenes are occupied only by men, who act and speak as the reader thinks that he should himself have spoken or acted on the same occasion. Even where the agency is supernatural the dialogue is level with life. Other writers disguise the most natural passions and most frequent incidents; so that he who contemplates them in the book will not know them in the world: Shakespeare approximates the remote, and familiarizes the wonderful; the event which he represents will not happen, but if it were possible, its effects would probably be such as he has assigned; and it may be said, that he has not only shown human nature as it acts in real exigencies, but as it would be found in trials, to which it cannot be exposed.

This therefore is the praise of Shakespeare, that his drama is the mirror of life; that he who has mazed his imagination, in following the phantoms which other writers raise up before him, may here be cured of his delirious ecstasies, by reading human sentiment in human language; by scenes from which a hermit may estimate the transactions of the world, and a confessor predict the progress of the passions.

His adherence to general nature has exposed him to the censure of critics, who form their judgements upon narrower principles. Dennis and Rhymer think his Romans not sufficiently Roman;[4] and Voltaire censures his kings as not completely royal. Dennis is offended, that Menenius, a senator of Rome, should play the buffoon; and Voltaire perhaps thinks decency violated when the Danish usurper is represented as a drunkard. But Shakespeare always makes nature predominate over accident; and if he preserves the essential character, is not very careful of distinctions superinduced and adventitious. His story requires Romans or kings, but he thinks only on men. He knew that Rome, like every other city, had men of all dispositions; and wanting a buffoon, he went into the senate-house for that which the senate-house would certainly have afforded him. He was inclined to show a usurper and a murderer not only odious but despicable; he therefore added drunkenness to his other qualities, knowing that kings love wine like other men, and that wine exerts its natural power upon kings. These are the petty cavils of petty minds; a poet overlooks the casual distinction of country and condition, as a painter, satisfied with the figure, neglects the drapery.

The censure which he has incurred by mixing comic and tragic scenes, as it extends to all his works, deserves more consideration. Let the fact be first stated, and then examined.

Shakespeare's plays are not in the rigorous and critical sense either tragedies or comedies, but compositions of a distinct kind; exhibiting the real state of sublunary nature, which partakes of good and evil, joy and sorrow, mingled with endless variety of proportion and in-numerable modes of combination; and expressing the course of the world, in which the loss of one is the gain of another; in which, at the same time, the reveller is hasting to his wine, and the mourner burying his friend; in which the malignity of one is sometimes defeated by the frolic of another; and many mischiefs and many benefits are done and hindered without design.

Out of this chaos of mingled purposes and casualties the ancient poets, according to the laws which custom had prescribed, selected some the crimes of men, and some their absurdities; some the mo-mentous vicissitudes of life, and some the lighter occurrences; some the terrors of distress, and some the gaieties of prosperity. Thus rose the two modes of imitation, known by the names of *tragedy* and *comedy*, compositions intended to promote different ends by contrary means, and considered as so little allied, that I do not recollect among the Greeks or Romans a single writer who attempted both.

Shakespeare has united the powers of exciting laughter and sorrow not only in one mind but in one composition. Almost all his plays are divided between serious and ludicrous characters, and, in the successive evolutions of the design, sometimes produce seriousness and sorrow, and sometimes levity and laughter.

That this is a practice contrary to the rules of criticism will be readily allowed; but there is always an appeal open from criticism to nature. The end of writing is to instruct; the end of poetry is to instruct by pleasing. That the mingled drama may convey all the instruction of tragedy or comedy cannot be denied, because it includes both in its alternations of exhibition, and approaches nearer than either to the appearance of life, by showing how great machinations and slender designs may promote or obviate one another, and the high and the low co-operate in the general system by unavoidable concatenation.

It is objected, that by this change of scenes the passions are interrupted in their progression, and that the principal event, being not advanced by a due gradation of preparatory incidents, wants at last the power to move, which constitutes the perfection of dramatic poetry. This reasoning is so specious, that it is received as true even by those who in daily experience feel it to be false. The interchanges of mingled scenes seldom fail to produce the intended vicissitudes of passion. Fiction cannot move so much, but that the attention may be easily transferred; and though it must be allowed that pleasing melancholy be sometimes interrupted by unwelcome levity, yet let it be considered likewise, that melancholy is often not pleasing, and that the disturbance of one man may be the relief of another; that different auditors have different habitudes; and that, upon the whole, all pleasure consists in variety.

The players, who in their edition[5] divided our author's works into comedies, histories, and tragedies, seem not to have distinguished the three kinds, by any very exact or definite ideas.

An action which ended happily to the principal persons, however serious or distressful through its intermediate incidents, in their opinion constituted a comedy. This idea of a comedy continued long amongst us, and plays were written, which, by changing the catastrophe, were tragedies today and comedies tomorrow.

Tragedy was not in those times a poem of more general dignity or elevation than comedy; it required only a calamitous conclusion, with which the common criticism of that age was satisfied, whatever lighter pleasure it afforded in its progress.

History was a series of actions, with no other than chronological succession, independent on each other, and without any tendency to introduce or regulate the conclusion. It is not always very nicely distinguished from tragedy. There is not much nearer approach to unity of action in the tragedy of *Antony and Cleopatra*, than in the history of *Richard the Second*. But a history might be continued through many plays; as it had no plan, it had no limits.

Through all these denominations of the drama, Shakespeare's mode of composition is the same; an interchange of seriousness and merriment, by which the mind is softened at one time, and exhilarated at another. But whatever be his purpose, whether to gladden or depress, or to conduct the story, without vehemence or emotion, through tracts of easy and familiar dialogue, he never fails to attain his purpose; as he commands us, we laugh or mourn, or sit silent with quiet expectation, in tranquillity without indifference.

When Shakespeare's plan is understood, most of the criticisms of Rhymer and Voltaire vanish away. The play of *Hamlet* is opened, without impropriety, by two sentinels; Iago bellows at Brabantio's window, without injury to the scheme of the play, though in terms which a modern audience would not easily endure; the character of Polonius is seasonable and useful; and the grave-diggers themselves may be heard with applause.

Shakespeare engaged in the dramatic poetry with the world open before him; the rules of the ancients were yet known to few;[6] the public judgement was unformed; he had no example of such fame as might force him upon imitation, nor critics of such authority as might restrain his extravagance. He therefore indulged his natural disposition, and his disposition, as Rhymer has remarked, led him to comedy. In tragedy he often writes with great appearance of toil and study, what is written at last with little felicity; but in his comic scenes, he seems to produce without labour, what no labour can improve. In tragedy he is always struggling after some occasion to be comic, but in comedy he seems to repose, or to luxuriate, as in a mode of thinking congenial to his nature. In his tragic scenes there is always something wanting, but his comedy often surpasses expectation or desire. His comedy pleases by the thoughts and the language, and his tragedy for the greater part by incident and action. His tragedy seems to be skill, his comedy to be instinct.

The force of his comic scenes has suffered little diminution from the changes made by a century and a half, in manners or in words. As his personages act upon principles arising from genuine passion, very little modified by particular forms, their pleasures and vexations are communicable to all times and to all places; they are natural, and therefore durable; the adventitious peculiarities of personal habits, are only superficial dies, bright and pleasing for a little while, yet soon fading to a dim tinct, without any remains of former lustre; but the discriminations of true passion are the colours of nature; they pervade the whole mass, and can only perish with the body that exhibits them. The accidental compositions of heterogeneous modes are dissolved by the chance which combined them; but the uniform simplicity of primitive qualities neither admits increase, nor suffers decay. The sand heaped by one flood is scattered by another, but the rock always continues in its place. The stream of time, which is continually washing the dissoluble fabrics of other poets, passes without injury by the adamant of Shakespeare.

If there be, what I believe there is, in every nation, a style which never becomes obsolete, a certain mode of phraseology so consonant and congenial to the analogy and principles of its respective language as to remain settled and unaltered; this style is probably to be sought in the common intercourse of life, among those who speak only to be understood, without ambition of elegance. The polite are always catching modish innovations, and the learned depart from established forms of speech, in hope of finding or making better; those who wish for distinction forsake the vulgar, when the vulgar is right; but there is a conversation above grossness and below refinement, where propriety resides, and where this poet seems to have gathered his comic dialogue. He is therefore more agreeable to the ears of the present age than any other author equally remote, and among his other excellencies deserves to be studied as one of the original masters of our language.

These observations are to be considered not as unexceptionably constant, but as containing general and predominant truth. Shakespeare's familiar dialogue is affirmed to be smooth and clear, yet not wholly without ruggedness or difficulty; as a country may be eminently fruitful, though it has spots unfit for cultivation. His characters are praised as natural, though their sentiments are sometimes forced, and their actions improbable; as the earth upon the whole is spherical, though its surface is varied with protuberances and cavities.

Shakespeare with his excellencies has likewise faults, and faults sufficient to obscure and overwhelm any other merit. I shall show them in the proportion in which they appear to me, without envious malignity or superstitious veneration. No question can be more innocently discussed than a dead poet's pretensions to renown; and little regard is due to that bigotry which sets candour higher than truth.

His first defect is that to which may be imputed most of the evil in books or in men. He sacrifices virtue to convenience, and is so much more careful to please than to instruct, that he seems to write without any moral purpose. From his writings indeed a system of social duty may be selected, for he that thinks reasonably must think morally; but his precepts and axioms drop casually from him; he makes no just distribution of good or evil, nor is always careful to show in the virtuous a disapprobation of the wicked; he carries his persons indifferently through right and wrong, and at the close dismisses them without further care, and leaves their examples to operate by chance. This fault the barbarity of his age cannot extenuate; for it is always a writer's duty to make the world better, and justice is a virtue independent on time or place.

The plots are often so loosely formed, that a very slight consideration may improve them, and so carelessly pursued, that he seems not always fully to comprehend his own design. He omits opportunities of instructing or delighting which the train of his story seems to force upon him, and apparently rejects those exhibitions which would be more affecting, for the sake of those which are more easy.

It may be observed, that in many of his plays the latter part is evidently neglected. When he found himself near the end of his work, and in view of his reward, he shortened the labour to snatch the profit. He therefore remits his efforts where he should most vigorously exert them, and his catastrophe is improbably produced or imperfectly represented.

He had no regard to distinction of time or place, but gives to one age or nation, without scruple, the customs, institutions, and opinions of another, at the expense not only of likelihood, but of possibility. These faults Pope has endeavoured, with more zeal than judgement, to transfer to his imagined interpolators. We need not wonder to find Hector quoting Aristotle, when we see the loves of Theseus and Hippolyta combined with the Gothic mythology of fairies.[7] Shakespeare, indeed, was not the only violator of chronology, for in the same age Sidney, who wanted not the advantages of learning, has, in his *Arcadia*, confounded the pastoral with the feudal times, the days of innocence, quiet and security, with those of turbulence, violence, and adventure.

In his comic scenes he is seldom very successful, when he engages his characters in reciprocations of smartness and contests of sarcasm; their jests are commonly gross, and their pleasantry licentious; neither his gentlemen nor his ladies have much delicacy, nor are sufficiently distinguished from his clowns by any appearance of refined manners. Whether he represented the real conversation of his time is not easy to determine; the reign of Elizabeth is commonly supposed to have been a time of stateliness, formality and reserve; yet perhaps the relaxations of that severity were not very elegant. There must, however, have been always some modes of gaiety preferable to others, and a writer ought to choose the best.

In tragedy his performance seems constantly to be worse, as his labour is more. The effusions of passion which exigence forces out are for the most part striking and energetic; but whenever he solicits his invention, or strains his faculties, the offspring of his throes is tumour, meanness, tediousness, and obscurity.

In narration he affects a disproportionate pomp of diction, and a wearisome train of circumlocution, and tells the incident imperfectly in many words, which might have been more plainly delivered in few. Narration in dramatic poetry is naturally tedious, as it is unanimated and inactive, and obstructs the progress of the action; it should therefore always be rapid, and enlivened by frequent interruption. Shakespeare found it an encumbrance, and instead of lightening it by brevity, endeavoured to recommend it by dignity and splendour.

His declamations or set speeches are commonly cold and weak, for his power was the power of nature; when he endeavoured, like other tragic writers, to catch opportunities of amplification, and instead of inquiring what the occasion demanded, to show how much his stores of knowledge could supply, he seldom escapes without the pity or resentment of his reader.

It is incident to him to be now and then entangled with an unwieldy sentiment, which he cannot well express, and will not reject; he struggles with it a while, and if it continues stubborn, comprises it in words such as occur, and leaves it to be disentangled and evolved by those who have more leisure to bestow upon it.

Not that always where the language is intricate the thought is subtle, or the image always great where the line is bulky; the equality of words to things is very often neglected, and trivial sentiments and vulgar ideas disappoint the attention, to which they are recommended by sonorous epithets and swelling figures.

But the admirers of this great poet have never less reason to indulge their hopes of supreme excellence, than when he seems fully resolved to sink them in dejection, and mollify them with tender emotions by the fall of greatness, the danger of innocence, or the crosses of love. He is not long soft and pathetic without some idle conceit, or contemptible equivocation. He no sooner begins to move, than he counteracts himself; and terror and pity, as they are rising in the mind, are checked and blasted by sudden frigidity.

A quibble is to Shakespeare,[8] what luminous vapours are to the traveller; he follows it at all adventures, it is sure to lead him out of his way, and sure to engulf him in the mire. It has some malignant power over his mind, and its fascinations are irresistible. Whatever be the dignity or profundity of his disquisition, whether he be enlarging knowledge or exalting affection, whether he be amusing attention with incidents, or enchaining it in suspense, let but a quibble spring up before him, and he leaves his work unfinished. A quibble is the golden apple for which he will always turn aside from his career, or stoop from his elevation. A quibble, poor and barren as it is, gave him such delight, that he was content to purchase it, by the sacrifice of reason, propriety and truth. A quibble was to him the fatal Cleopatra for which he lost the world, and was content to lose it.

It will be thought strange, that, in enumerating the defects of this writer, I have not yet mentioned his neglect of the unities; his violation of those laws which have been instituted and established by the joint authority of poets and of critics.

For his other deviations from the art of writing, I resign him to critical justice, without making any other demand in his favour, than that which must be indulged to all human excellence; that his virtues be rated with his failings: but, from the censure which this irregularity may bring upon him, I shall, with due reverence to that learning which I must oppose, adventure to try how I can defend him.

His histories, being neither tragedies nor comedies, are not subject to any of their laws; nothing more is necessary to all the praise which they expect, than that the changes of action be so prepared as to be understood, that the incidents be various and affecting, and the characters consistent, natural and distinct. No other unity is intended, and therefore none is to be sought.

In his other works he has well enough preserved the unity of action. He has not, indeed, an intrigue regularly perplexed and regularly unravelled; he does not endeavour to hide his design only to discover it, for this is seldom the order of real events, and Shakespeare is the poet of nature: but his plan has commonly what Aristotle requires, a beginning, a middle, and an end; one event is concatenated with another, and the conclusion follows by easy consequence. There are perhaps some incidents that might be spared, as in other poets there is much talk that only fills up time upon the stage; but the general system makes gradual advances, and the end of the play is the end of expectation.

To the unities of time and place he has shown no regard, and perhaps a nearer view of the principles on which they stand will diminish their value, and withdraw from them the veneration which, from the time of Corneille, they have very generally received, by discovering that they have given more trouble to the poet, than pleasure to the auditor.

The necessity of observing the unities of time and place arises from the supposed necessity of making the drama credible. The critics hold it impossible, that an action of months or years can be possibly believed to pass in three hours; or that the spectator can suppose himself to sit in the theatre, while ambassadors go and return between distant kings, while armies are levied and towns besieged, while an exile wanders and returns, or till he whom they saw courting his mistress, shall lament the untimely fall of his son. The mind revolts from evident falsehood, and fiction loses its force when it departs from the resemblance of reality.

From the narrow limitation of time necessarily arises the contraction of place. The spectator, who knows that he saw the first act at Alexandria, cannot suppose that he sees the next at Rome, at a distance to which not the dragons of Medea could, in so short a time, have transported him; he knows with certainty that he has not changed his place; and he knows that place cannot change itself; that what was a house cannot become a plain; that what was Thebes can never be Persepolis.

Such is the triumphant language with which a critic exults over the misery of an irregular poet, and exults commonly without resistance or reply. It is time therefore to tell him, by the authority of Shakespeare, that he assumes, as an unquestionable principle, a position, which, while his breath is forming it into words, his understanding pronounces to be false. It is false, that any representation is mistaken for reality; that any dramatic fable in its materiality was ever credible, or, for a single moment, was ever credited.

The objection arising from the impossibility of passing the first hour at Alexandria, and the next at Rome, supposes, that when the play opens, the spectator really imagines himself at Alexandria, and believes that his walk to the theatre has been a voyage to Egypt, and that he lives in the days of Antony and Cleopatra. Surely he that imagines this may imagine more. He that can take the stage at one time for the palace of the Ptolemies, may take it in half an hour for the promontory of Actium. Delusion, if delusion be admitted, has no certain limitation; if the spectator can be once persuaded, that his old acquaintance are Alexander and Caesar, that a room illuminated with candles is the plain of Pharsalia, or the bank of Granicus, he is in a state of elevation above the reach of reason, or of truth, and from the heights of empyrean poetry, may despise the circumscriptions of terrestrial nature. There is no reason why a mind thus wandering in ecstasy[9] should count the clock, or why an hour should not be a century in that calenture[10] of the brains that can make the stage a field.

The truth is, that the spectators are always in their senses,[11] and know, from the first act to the last, that the stage is only a stage, and that the players are only players. They came to hear a certain number of lines recited with just gesture and elegant modulation. The lines relate to some action, and an action must be in some place; but the different actions that complete a story may be in places very remote from each other; and where is the absurdity of allowing that space to represent first Athens, and then Sicily, which was always known to be neither Sicily nor Athens, but a modern theatre?

By supposition, as place is introduced time may be extended; the time required by the fable elapses for the most part between the acts; for, of so much of the action as is represented, the real and poetical duration is the same. If, in the first act, preparations for war against Mithridates are represented to be made in Rome, the event of the war may without absurdity, be represented, in the castastrophe, as happening in Pontus; we know that there is neither war, nor preparation for war; we know that we are neither in Rome nor Pontus; that neither Mithridates nor Lucullus are before us. The drama exhibits successive imitations of successive actions, and why may not the second imitation represent an action that happened years after the first; if it be so connected with it, that nothing but time can be supposed to intervene. Time is, of all modes of existence, most obsequious to the imagination; a lapse of years is as easily conceived as a passage of hours. In contemplation we easily contract the time of real actions, and therefore willingly permit it to be contracted when we only see their imitation.

It will be asked, how the drama moves, if it is not credited. It is credited with all the credit due to a drama. It is credited, whenever it moves, as a just picture of a real original; as representing to the auditor what he would himself feel, if he were to do or suffer what is there feigned to be suffered or to be done. The reflection that strikes the heart is not, that the evils before us are real evils, but that they are evils to which we ourselves may be exposed. If there be any fallacy, it is not that we fancy the players, but that we fancy ourselves unhappy for a moment; but we rather lament the possibility than suppose the presence of misery, as a mother weeps over her babe, when she remembers that death may take it from her. The delight of tragedy proceeds from our consciousness of fiction; if we thought murders and treasons real, they would please no more.

Imitations produce pain or pleasure, not because they are mistaken for realities, but because they bring realities to mind. When the imagination is recreated by a painted landscape, the trees are not supposed capable to give us shade, or the fountains coolness; but we consider, how we should be pleased with such fountains playing beside us, and such woods waving over us. We are agitated in reading the history of *Henry the Fifth,* yet no man takes his book for the field of Agincourt. A dramatic exhibition is a book recited with concomitants that increase or diminish its effect. Familiar comedy is often more powerful in the theatre, than on the page; imperial tragedy is always less. The humour of Petruchio may be heightened by grimace;

but what voice or what gesture can hope to add dignity or force to the soliloquy of Cato ?

A play read, affects the mind like a play acted. It is therefore evident, that the action is not supposed to be real, and it follows that between the acts a longer or shorter time may be allowed to pass, and that no more account of space or duration is to be taken by the auditor of a drama, than by the reader of a narrative, before whom may pass in an hour the life of a hero, or the revolutions of an empire.

Whether Shakespeare knew the unities, and rejected them by design, or deviated from them by happy ignorance, it is, I think, impossible to decide, and useless to inquire. We may reasonably suppose, that, when he rose to notice, he did not want the counsels and admonitions of scholars and critics, and that he at last deliberately persisted in a practice, which he might have begun by chance. As nothing is essential to the fable, but unity of action, and as the unities of time and place arise evidently from false assumptions, and, by circumscribing the extent of the drama, lessen its variety, I cannot think it much to be lamented, that they were not known by him, or not observed: nor, if such another poet could arise, should I very vehemently reproach him, that his first act passed at Venice, and his next in Cyprus. Such violations of rules merely positive, become the comprehensive genius of Shakespeare, and such censures are suitable to the minute and slender criticism of Voltaire:

> *Non usque adeo permiscuit imis*
> *Longus summa dies, ut non, si voce Metelli*
> *Serventur leges, malint a Cæsare tolli.*[12]

Yet when I speak thus slightly of dramatic rules, I cannot but recollect how much wit and learning may be produced against me; before such authorities I am afraid to stand, not that I think the present question one of those that are to be decided by mere authority, but because it is to be suspected, that these precepts have not been so easily received but for better reasons than I have yet been able to find. The result of my inquiries, in which it would be ludicrous to boast of impartiality, is, that the unities of time and place are not essential to a just drama, that though they may sometimes conduce to pleasure, they are always to be sacrificed to the nobler beauties of variety and instruction; and that a play, written with nice observation of critical rules, is to be contemplated as an elaborate curiosity, as the product of superfluous and ostentatious art, by which is shown, rather what is possible, than what is necessary.

He that, without diminution of any other excellence, shall preserve all the unities unbroken, deserves the like applause with the architect, who shall display all the orders of architecture in a citadel, without any deduction from its strength; but the principal beauty of a citadel is to exclude the enemy; and the greatest graces of a play, are to copy nature and instruct life.

Perhaps, what I have here not dogmatically but deliberately written, may recall the principles of the drama to a new examination. I am almost frightened at my own temerity; and when I estimate the fame and the strength of those that maintain the contrary opinion, am ready to sink down in reverential silence; as Æneas withdrew from the defence of Troy, when he saw Neptune shaking the wall, and Juno heading the besiegers.

Those whom my arguments cannot persuade to give their approbation to the judgement of Shakespeare, will easily, if they consider the condition of his life, make some allowance for his ignorance.

Every man's performances, to be rightly estimated,[13] must be compared with the state of the age in which he lived, and with his own particular opportunities; and though to the reader a book be not worse or better for the circumstances of the author, yet as there is always a silent reference of human works to human abilities, and as the inquiry, how far man may extend his designs, or how high he may rate his native force, is of far greater dignity than in what rank we shall place any particular performance, curiosity is always busy to discover the instruments, as well as to survey the workmanship, to know how much is to be ascribed to original powers, and how much to casual and adventitious help. The palaces of Peru or Mexico were certainly mean and incommodious habitations, if compared to the houses of European monarchs; yet who could forbear to view them with astonishment, who remembered that they were built without the use of iron?

The English nation, in the time of Shakespeare, was yet struggling to emerge from barbarity. The philology of Italy[14] had been transplanted hither in the reign of Henry the Eighth; and the learned languages had been successfully cultivated by Lilly, Linacre and More; by Pole, Cheke, and Gardiner; and afterwards by Smith, Clerk, Haddon, and Ascham. Greek was now taught to boys in the principal schools; and those who united elegance with learning, read, with great diligence, the Italian and Spanish poets. But literature was yet confined to professed scholars, or to men and women of high rank. The public was gross and dark; and to be able to read and write, was an accomplishment still valued for its rarity.

Nations, like individuals, have their infancy. A people newly awakened to literary curiosity, being yet unacquainted with the true state of things, knows not how to judge of that which is proposed as its resemblance. Whatever is remote from common appearance is always welcome to vulgar, as to childish credulity; and of a country unenlightened by learning, the whole people is the vulgar. The study of those who then aspired to plebeian learning was laid out upon adventures, giants, dragons, and enchantments. *The Death of Arthur*[15] was the favourite volume.

The mind, which has feasted on the luxurious wonders of fiction, has no taste of the insipidity of truth. A play which imitated only the common occurrences of the world, would upon the admirers of *Palmerin* and *Guy of Warwick*, have made little impression; he that wrote for such an audience was under the necessity of looking round for strange events and fabulous transactions, and that incredibility, by which maturer knowledge is offended, was the chief recommendation of writings, to unskilful curiosity.

Our author's plots are generally borrowed from novels, and it is reasonable to suppose, that he chose the most popular, such as were read by many, and related by more; for his audience could not have followed him through the intricacies of the drama, had they not held the thread of the story in their hands.

The stories, which we now find only in remoter authors, were in his time accessible and familiar. The fable of *As you like it*, which is supposed to be copied from Chaucer's *Gamelyn*, was a little pamphlet of those times; and old Mr Cibber remembered the tale of *Hamlet* in plain English prose, which the critics have now to seek in *Saxo Grammaticus*.

His English histories he took from English chronicles and English ballads; and as the ancient writers were made known to his countrymen by versions, they supplied him with new subjects; he dilated some of Plutarch's lives into plays, when they had been translated by North.

His plots, whether historical or fabulous, are always crowded with incidents, by which the attention of a rude people was more easily caught than by sentiment or argumentation; and such is the power of the marvellous even over those who despise it, that every man finds his mind more strongly seized by the tragedies of Shakespeare than of any other writer; others please us by particular speeches, but he always makes us anxious for the event, and has perhaps excelled all but Homer in securing the first purpose of a writer, by exciting restless and unquenchable curiosity, and compelling him that reads his work to read it through.

The shows and bustle with which his plays abound, have the same original. As knowledge advances, pleasure passes from the eye to the ear, but returns, as it declines, from the ear to the eye. Those to whom our author's labours were exhibited had more skill in pomps or processions than in poetical language, and perhaps wanted some visible and discriminated events, as comments on the dialogue. He knew how he should most please; and whether his practice is more agreeable to nature, or whether his example has prejudiced the nation, we still find that on our stage something must be done as well as said, and inactive declamation is very coldly heard, however musical or elegant, passionate or sublime.

Voltaire expresses his wonder, that our author's extravagances are endured by a nation, which has seen the tragedy of *Cato*. Let him be answered, that Addison speaks the language of poets, and Shakespeare, of men. We find in *Cato* innumerable beauties which enamour us of its author, but we see nothing that acquaints us with human sentiments or human actions; we place it with the fairest and the noblest progeny which judgement propagates by conjunction with learning, but *Othello* is the vigorous and vivacious offspring of observation impregnated by genius. *Cato* affords a splendid exhibition of artificial and fictitious manners, and delivers just and noble sentiments, in diction easy, elevated and harmonious, but its hopes and fears communicate no vibration to the heart; the composition refers us only to the writer; we pronounce the name of *Cato*, but we think on Addison.

The work of a correct and regular writer is a garden accurately formed and diligently planted, varied with shades, and scented with flowers; the composition of Shakespeare is a forest, in which oaks extend their branches, and pines tower in the air, interspersed sometimes with weeds and brambles, and sometimes giving shelter to myrtles and to roses; filling the eye with awful pomp, and gratifying the mind with endless diversity. Other poets display cabinets of precious rarities, minutely finished, wrought into shape, and polished unto brightness. Shakespeare opens a mine which contains gold and diamonds in unexhaustible plenty, though clouded by incrustations, debased by impurities, and mingled with a mass of meaner minerals.

It has been much disputed, whether Shakespeare owed his excellence to his own native force, or whether he had the common helps of scholastic education, the precepts of critical science, and the examples of ancient authors.

There has always prevailed a tradition, that Shakespeare wanted learning, that he had no regular education, nor much skill in the dead languages. Jonson, his friend, affirms, that 'he had small Latin, and no Greek';[16] who, besides that he had no imaginable temptation to falsehood, wrote at a time when the character and acquisitions of Shakespeare were known to multitudes. His evidence ought therefore to decide the controversy, unless some testimony of equal force could be opposed.

Some have imagined, that they have discovered deep learning in many imitations of old writers; but the examples which I have known urged, were drawn from books translated in his time; or were such easy coincidences of thought, as will happen to all who consider the same subjects; or such remarks on life or axioms of morality as float in conversation, and are transmitted through the world in proverbial sentences.

I have found it remarked, that, in this important sentence, 'Go before, I'll follow', we read a translation of, *I prae, sequar*. I have been told, that when Caliban, after a pleasing dream, says, 'I cry'd to sleep again,'[17] the author imitates Anacreon, who had, like every other man, the same wish on the same occasion.

There are a few passages which may pass for imitations, but so few, that the exception only confirms the rule; he obtained them from accidental quotations, or by oral communication, and as he used what he had, would have used more if he had obtained it.

The *Comedy of Errors* is confessedly taken from the *Menæchmi* of Plautus; from the only play of Plautus which was then in English. What can be more probable, than that he who copied that, would have copied more; but that those which were not translated were inaccessible?

Whether he knew the modern languages is uncertain. That his plays have some French scenes proves but little; he might easily procure them to be written, and probably, even though he had known the language in the common degree, he could not have written it without assistance. In the story of *Romeo and Juliet* he is observed to have followed the English translation, where it deviates from the Italian; but this on the other part proves nothing against his knowledge of the original. He was to copy, not what he knew himself, but what was known to his audience.

It is most likely that he had learned Latin sufficiently to make him acquainted with construction, but that he never advanced to an easy perusal of the Roman authors. Concerning his skill in modern languages, I can find no sufficient ground of determination; but as no imitations of French or Italian authors have been discovered, though the Italian poetry was then high in esteem, I am inclined to believe, that he read little more than English, and chose for his fables only such tales as he found translated.

That much knowledge is scattered over his works is very justly observed by Pope, but it is often such knowledge as books did not supply. He that will understand Shakespeare, must not be content to study him in the closet, he must look for his meaning sometimes among the sports of the field, and sometimes among the manufactures of the shop.

There is however proof enough that he was a very diligent reader, nor was our language then so indigent of books, but that he might very liberally indulge his curiosity without excursion into foreign literature. Many of the Roman authors were translated, and some of the Greek; the reformation had filled the kingdom with theological learning; most of the topics of human disquisition had found English writers; and poetry had been cultivated, not only with diligence, but success. This was a stock of knowledge sufficient for a mind so capable of appropriating and improving it.

But the greater part of his excellence was the product of his own genius. He found the English stage in a state of the utmost rudeness; no essays either in tragedy or comedy had appeared, from which it could be discovered to what degree of delight either one or other might be carried. Neither character nor dialogue were yet understood. Shakespeare may be truly said to have introduced them both amongst us, and in some of his happier scenes to have carried them both to the utmost height.

By what gradations of improvement he proceeded, is not easily known; for the chronology of his works is yet unsettled. Rowe is of opinion, that

perhaps we are not to look for his beginning, like those of other writers, in his least perfect works; art had so little, and nature so large a share in what he did, that for ought I know, [says he] the performances of his youth, as they were the most vigorous, were the best.

But the power of nature is only the power of using to any certain purpose the materials which diligence procures, or opportunity supplies. Nature gives no man knowledge, and when images are collected by study and experience, can only assist in combining or applying them. Shakespeare, however favoured by nature, could impart only what he had learned; and as he must increase his ideas, like other mortals, by gradual acquisition, he, like them, grew wiser as he grew older, could display life better, as he knew it more, and instruct with more efficacy, as he was himself more amply instructed.

There is a vigilance of observation and accuracy of distinction which books and precepts cannot confer; from this almost all original and native excellence proceeds. Shakespeare must have looked upon mankind with perspicacity, in the highest degree curious and attentive. Other writers borrow their characters from preceding writers, and diversify them only by the accidental appendages of present manners; the dress is a little varied, but the body is the same. Our author had both matter and form to provide; for except the characters of Chaucer, to whom I think he is not much indebted, there were no writers in English, and perhaps not many in other modern languages, which showed life in its native colours.

The contest about the original benevolence or malignity of man had not yet commenced. Speculation had not yet attempted to analyse the mind, to trace the passions to their sources, to unfold the seminal principles of vice and virtue, or sound the depths of the heart for the motives of action. All those inquiries, which from that time that human nature became the fashionable study, have been made sometimes with nice discernment, but often with idle subtlety, were yet unattempted. The tales, with which the infancy of learning was satisfied, exhibited only the superficial appearances of action, related the events but omitted the causes, and were formed for such as delighted in wonders rather than in truth. Mankind was not then to be studied in the closet; he that would know the world, was under the necessity of gleaning his own remarks, by mingling as he could in its business and amusements.

Boyle congratulated himself upon his high birth, because it favoured his curiosity, by facilitating his access. Shakespeare had no such advantage; he came to London a needy adventurer, and lived for a time by very mean employments. Many works of genius and learning have been performed in states of life, that appear very little favourable to thought or to inquiry; so many, that he who considers them is inclined to think that he sees enterprise and perseverance predominating over all external agency, and bidding help and hindrance vanish before them. The genius of Shakespeare was not to be depressed by the weight of poverty, not limited by the narrow conversation to which men in want are inevitably condemned; the incumbrances of his fortune were shaken from his mind, 'as dewdrops from a lion's mane'.[18]

Though he had so many difficulties to encounter, and so little assistance to surmount them, he has been able to obtain an exact knowledge of many modes of life, and many casts of native dispositions; to vary them with great multiplicity; to mark them by nice distinctions; and to show them in full view by proper combinations. In this part of his performances he had none to imitate, but has himself been imitated by all succeeding writers; and it may be doubted, whether from all his successors more maxims of theoretical knowledge, or more rules of practical prudence, can be collected, than he alone has given to his country.

Nor was his attention confined to the actions of men; he was an exact surveyor of the inanimate world; his descriptions have always some peculiarities, gathered by contemplating things as they really exist. It may be observed, that the oldest poets of many nations preserve their reputation, and that the following generations of wit, after a short celebrity, sink into oblivion. The first, whoever they be, must take their sentiments and descriptions immediately from knowledge; the resemblance is therefore just, their descriptions are verified by every eye, and their sentiments acknowledged by every breast. Those whom their fame invites to the same studies, copy partly them, and partly nature, till the books of one age gain such authority, as to stand in the place of nature to another, and imitation, always deviating a little, becomes at last capricious and casual. Shakespeare, whether life or nature be his subject, shows plainly, that he has seen with his own eyes; he gives the image which he receives, not weakened or distorted by the intervention of any other mind; the ignorant feel his representations to be just, and the learned see that they are complete.

Perhaps it would not be easy to find any author, except Homer, who invented so much as Shakespeare, who so much advanced the studies which he cultivated, or effused so much novelty upon his age or country. The form, the characters, the language, and the shows of the English drama are his. He seems, says Dennis,

to have been the very original of our *English* tragical harmony, that is, the harmony of blank verse, diversified often by dissyllable and trissyllable terminations. For the diversity distinguishes it from heroic harmony, and by bringing it nearer to common use makes it more proper to gain attention, and more fit for action and dialogue. Such verse we make when we are writing prose; we make such verse in common conversation.

I know not whether this praise is rigorously just. The dissyllable termination, which the critic rightly appropriates to the drama, is to be found, though, I think, not in *Gorboduc* which is confessedly before our author; yet in *Hieronimo*, [19] of which the date is not certain, but which there is reason to believe at least as old as his earliest plays. This however is certain, that he is the first who taught either tragedy or comedy to please, there being no theatrical piece of any older writer, of which the name is known, except to antiquaries and collectors of books, which are sought because they are scarce, and would not have been scarce, had they been much esteemed.

To him we must ascribe the praise, unless Spenser may divide it with him, of having first discovered to how much smoothness and harmony the English language could be softened. He has speeches, perhaps sometimes scenes, which have all the delicacy of Rowe, without his effeminacy. He endeavours indeed commonly to strike by the force and vigour of his dialogue, but he never executes his purpose better, than when he tries to soothe by softness.

Yet it must be at last confessed that as we owe every thing to him, he owes something to us; that, if much of his praise is paid by perception and judgement, much is likewise given by custom and veneration. We fix our eyes upon his graces, and turn them from his deformities, and endure in him what we should in another loathe or despise. If we endured without praising, respect for the father of our drama might excuse us; but I have seen, in the book of some modern critic, a collection of anomalies, which show that he has corrupted language by every mode of depravation, but which his admirer has accumulated as a monument of honour.

He has scenes of undoubted and perpetual excellence, but perhaps not one play, which, if it were now exhibited as the work of a contemporary writer, would be heard to the conclusion. I am indeed far from thinking, that his works were wrought to his own ideas of perfection; when they were such as would satisfy the audience, they satisfied the writer. It is seldom that authors, though more studious of fame than Shakespeare, rise much above the standard of their own age; to add a little to what is best will always be sufficient for present praise, and those who find themselves exalted into fame, are willing to credit their encomiasts, and to spare the labour of contending with themselves.

It does not appear, that Shakespeare thought his works worthy of posterity, that he levied any ideal tribute upon future times, or had any further prospect, than of present popularity and present profit. When his plays had been acted, his hope was at an end; he solicited no addition of honour from the reader. He therefore made no scruple to repeat the same jests in many dialogues, or to entangle different plots by the same knot of perplexity, which may be at least forgiven him, by those who recollect, that of Congreve's four comedies, two are concluded by a marriage in a mask, by a deception, which perhaps never happened, and which, whether likely or not, he did not invent.

So careless was this great poet of future fame, that, though he retired to ease and plenty, while he was yet little 'declined into the vale of years'[20], before he could be disgusted with fatigue, or disabled by infirmity, he made no collection of his works, nor desired to rescue those that had been already published from the depravations that obscured them, or secure to the rest a better destiny, by giving them to the world in their genuine state.

Of the plays which bear the name of Shakespeare in the late editions, the greater part were not published till about seven years after his death, and the few which appeared in his life were apparently thrust into the world without the care of the author, and therefore probably without his knowledge.

NOTES ON SHAKESPEARE*

A MIDSUMMER NIGHT'S DREAM

I. ii. Enter Quince *the carpenter*, Snug *the joiner*, Bottom *the weaver*, Flute *the bellows-mender*, Snout *the tinker, and* Starveling *the tailor*.

In this scene Shakespeare takes advantage of his knowledge of the theatre to ridicule the prejudices and competitions of the players. Bottom, who is generally acknowledged the principal actor, declares his inclination to be for a tyrant, for a part of fury, tumult, and noise, such as every young man pants to perform when he first steps upon the stage. The same Bottom, who seems bred in a tiring room, has another histrionical passion. He is for engrossing every part and would exclude his inferiors from all possibility of distinction. He is therefore desirous to play Pyramus, Thisbe, and the Lion at the same time.

MEASURE FOR MEASURE

III. i. 17. *Duke.*

> Thy best of rest is sleep,
> And that thou oft provok'st; yet grossly fear'st
> Thy death, which is no more.

Here Dr Warburton might have found a sentiment worthy of his animadversion. I cannot without indignation find Shakespeare saying that *death is only sleep*, lengthening out his exhortation by a sentence which in the friar is impious, in the reasoner is foolish, and in the poet trite and vulgar.

III. i. 32. *Duke.*

> Thou hast nor youth nor age;
> But, as it were, an after-dinner's sleep,
> Dreaming on both.]

This is exquisitely imagined. When we are young, we busy ourselves in forming schemes for succeeding time and miss the gratifications that are before us; when we are old, we amuse the languor of age with

* See Editor's Notes.

the recollection of youthful pleasures or performances; so that our life, of which no part is filled with the business of the present time, resembles our dreams after dinner, when the events of the morning are mingled with the designs of the evening.

III. i. 137. *Isabella.* Is't not a kind of incest, to take life / From thine own sister's shame?]

In Isabella's declamation there is something harsh and something forced and far-fetched. But her indignation cannot be thought violent when we consider her not only as a virgin but as a nun.

V. i. 448. *Isabella.* Till he did look on me]

The duke has justly observed that Isabel is *importuned against all sense* to solicit for Angelo, yet here *against all sense* she solicits for him. Her argument is extraordinary.

> A due sincerity govern'd his deeds,
> Till he did look on me: since it is so,
> Let him not die.

That Angelo had committed all the crimes charged against him, as far as he could commit them, is evident. The only *intent* which *his* act did not overtake was the defilement of Isabel. Of this Angelo was only intentionally guilty.

Angelo's crimes were such as must sufficiently justify punishment, whether its end be to secure the innocent from wrong or to deter guilt by example; and I believe every reader feels some indignation when he finds him spared. From what extenuation of his crime can Isabel, who yet supposes her brother dead, form any plea in his favour. *Since he was good, 'till he looked on me, let him not die.* I am afraid our varlet poet intended to inculcate that women think ill of nothing that raises the credit of their beauty and are ready, however virtuous, to pardon any act which they think incited by their own charms.

As You Like It

General Observation. Of this play the fable is wild and pleasing. I know not how the ladies will approve the facility with which both

Rosalind and Celia give away their hearts. To Celia much may be forgiven for the heroism of her friendship. The character of Jaques is natural and well preserved. The comic dialogue is very sprightly, with less mixture of low buffoonery than in some other plays; and the graver part is elegant and harmonious. By hastening to the end of his work, Shakespeare suppressed the dialogue between the usurper and the hermit and lost an opportunity of exhibiting a moral lesson in which he might have found matter worthy of his highest powers.

LOVE'S LABOUR'S LOST

V. i. 2. *Sir Nathaniel.* Your reasons at dinner have been sharp and sententious.]

I know not well what degree of respect Shakespeare intends to obtain for this vicar, but he has here put into his mouth a finished representation of colloquial excellence. It is very difficult to add any thing to this character of the schoolmaster's table-talk, and perhaps all the precepts of Castiglione will scarcely be found to comprehend a rule for conversation so justly delineated, so widely dilated, and so nicely limited.

General Observation. In this play, which all the editors have concurred to censure and some have rejected as unworthy of our poet, it must be confessed that there are many passages mean, childish, and vulgar; and some which ought not to have been exhibited, as we are told they were, to a maiden queen. But there are scattered through the whole many sparks of genius; nor is there any play that has more evident marks of the hand of Shakespeare.

TWELFTH NIGHT

General Observation. This play is in the graver part elegant and easy, and in some of the lighter scenes exquisitely humorous. Aguecheek is drawn with great propriety, but his character is, in a great measure, that of natural fatuity and is therefore not the proper prey of a satirist. The soliloquy of Malvolio is truly comic; he is betrayed to ridicule merely by his pride. The marriage of Olivia and the succeeding perplexity, though well enough contrived to divert on the stage, wants credibility and fails to produce the proper instruction required in the drama, as it exhibits no just picture of life.

ALL'S WELL THAT ENDS WELL

V. iii.

Shakespeare is now hastening to the end of the play, finds his matter sufficient to fill up his remaining scenes, and therefore, as on other such occasions, contracts his dialogue and precipitates his action. Decency required that Bertram's double crime of cruelty and disobedience, joined likewise with some hypocrisy, should raise more resentment; and that though his mother might easily forgive him, his king should more pertinaciously vindicate his own authority and Helen's merit. Of all this Shakespeare could not be ignorant, but Shakespeare wanted to conclude his play.

HENRY IV, PARTS 1 AND 2

None of Shakespeare's plays are more read than the *First and Second Parts of Henry the Fourth*. Perhaps no author has ever in two plays afforded so much delight. The great events are interesting, for the fate of kingdoms depends upon them; the slighter occurrences are diverting and, except one or two, sufficiently probable; the incidents are multiplied with wonderful fertility of invention, and the characters diversified with the utmost nicety of discernment and the profoundest skill in the nature of man.

The prince, who is the hero both of the comic and tragic part, is a young man of great abilities and violent passions, whose sentiments are right, though his actions are wrong; whose virtues are obscured by negligence, and whose understanding is dissipated by levity. In his idle hours he is rather loose than wicked; and when the occasion forces out his latent qualities, he is great without effort and brave without tumult. The trifler is roused into a hero, and the hero again reposes in the trifler. This character is great, original, and just.

Percy is a rugged soldier, choleric, and quarrelsome, and has only the soldier's virtues, generosity and courage.

But Falstaff, unimitated, unimitable Falstaff, how shall I describe thee? Thou compound of sense and vice; of sense which may be admired but not esteemed, of vice which may be despised but hardly detested. Falstaff is a character loaded with faults, and with those faults which naturally produce contempt. He is a thief and a glutton, a coward and a boaster, always ready to cheat the weak and prey upon the poor; to terrify the timorous and insult the defenceless. At once obsequious and malignant, he satirizes in their absence those whom he lives by flattering. He is familiar with the prince only as an agent of vice, but of this familiarity he is so proud as not only to be supercilious and haughty with common men but to think his interest of importance to the Duke of Lancaster. Yet the man thus corrupt, thus despicable, makes himself necessary to the prince that despises him, by the most pleasing of all qualities, perpetual gaiety, by an unfailing power of exciting laughter, which is the more freely indulged as his wit is not of the splendid or ambitious kind but consists in easy escapes and sallies of levity, which make sport but raise no envy. It must be observed that he is stained with no enormous or sanguinary crimes, so that his licentiousness is not so offensive but that it may be borne for his mirth.

The moral to be drawn from this representation is that no man is more dangerous than he that, with a will to corrupt, hath the power to please; and that neither wit nor honesty ought to think themselves safe with such a companion when they see Henry seduced by Falstaff.

HENRY V

II. iii. 27. *Hostess*. Cold as any stone.]

Such is the end of Falstaff, from whom Shakespeare had promised us in his epilogue to *Henry IV* that we should receive more entertainment. It happened to Shakespeare, as to other writers, to have his imagination crowded with a tumultuary confusion of images which, while they were yet unsorted and unexamined, seemed sufficient to

furnish a long train of incidents and a new variety of merriment;
but which, when he was to produce them to view, shrunk suddenly
from him or could not be accommodated to his general design. That
he once designed to have brought Falstaff on the scene again, we know
from himself; but whether he could contrive no train of adventures
suitable to his character, or could match him with no companions
likely to quicken his humour, or could open no new vein of pleasantry, and was afraid to continue the same strain lest it should not find
the same reception, he has here for ever discarded him, perhaps for
the same reason for which Addison killed Sir Roger, that no other
hand might attempt to exhibit him.

Let meaner authors learn from this example that it is dangerous to
sell the bear which is not yet hunted; to promise to the public what
they have not written.

V. i. 92. *Pistol.*

> To England will I steal, and there I'll steal:
> And patches will I get unto these cudgell'd scars,
> And swear I got them in the Gallia wars.]

The comic scenes of *The History of Henry the Fourth* and *Fifth* are
now at an end, and all the comic personages are now dismissed. Falstaff and Mrs Quickly are dead; Nym and Bardolph are hanged;
Gadshill was lost immediately after the robbery; Poins and Peto have
vanished since, one knows not how; and Pistol is now beaten into
obscurity. I believe every reader regrets their departure.

King Lear

IV. vi. 12. *Edgar.* How fearful / And dizzy 'tis to cast one's eyes so low!]

This description has been much admired since the time of Addison,
who has remarked, with a poor attempt at pleasantry, that 'he who
can read it without being giddy has a very good head or a very bad
one'. The description is certainly not mean, but I am far from thinking
it wrought to the utmost excellence of poetry. He that looks from a

precipice finds himself assailed by one great and dreadful image of irresistible destruction. But this overwhelming idea is dissipated and enfeebled from the instant that the mind can restore itself to the observation of particulars and diffuse its attention to distinct objects. The enumeration of the choughs and crows, the samphire-man, and the fishers, counteracts the great effect of the prospect, as it peoples the desert of intermediate vacuity and stops the mind in the rapidity of its descent through emptiness and horror.

General Observation. The tragedy of *Lear* is deservedly celebrated among the dramas of Shakespeare. There is perhaps no play which keeps the attention so strongly fixed; which so much agitates our passions and interests our curiosity. The artful involutions of distinct interests, the striking opposition of contrary characters, the sudden changes of fortune, and the quick succession of events, fill the mind with a perpetual tumult of indignation, pity, and hope. There is no scene which does not contribute to the aggravation of the distress or conduct of the action, and scarce a line which does not conduce to the progress of the scene. So powerful is the current of the poet's imagination that the mind which once ventures within it is hurried irresistibly along.

On the seeming improbability of Lear's conduct i t may be observed that he is represented according to the histories at that time vulgarly received as true. And perhaps if we turn our thoughts upon the barbarity and ignorance of the age to which this story is referred, it will appear not so unlikely as while we estimate Lear's manners by our own. Such preference of one daughter to another, or resignation of dominion on such conditions, would be yet credible if told of a petty prince of Guinea or Madagascar. Shakespeare, indeed, by the mention of his earls and dukes, has given us the idea of times more civilized and of life regulated by softer manners; and the truth is that though he so nicely discriminates and so minutely describes the characters of men, he commonly neglects and confounds the characters of ages, by mingling customs ancient and modern, English and foreign.

My learned friend Mr Warton, who has in the *Adventurer* very minutely criticized this play, remarks that the instances of cruelty are too savage and shocking, and that the intervention of Edmund destroys the simplicity of the story. These objections may, I think, be answered by repeating that the cruelty of the daughters is an historical fact, to which the poet has added little, having only drawn it into a series by dialogue and action. But I am not able to apologize with equal plausibility for the extrusion of Gloucester's eyes, which seems an act too horrid to be endured in dramatic exhibition, and such as must always compel the mind to relieve its distress by incredulity. Yet let it be remembered that our author well knew what would please the audience for which he wrote.

The injury done by Edmund to the simplicity of the action is abundantly recompensed by the addition of variety, by the art with which he is made to cooperate with the chief design, and the opportunity which he gives the poet of combining perfidy with perfidy and connecting the wicked son with the wicked daughters, to impress this important moral, that villainy is never at a stop, that crimes lead to crimes and at last terminate in ruin.

But though this moral be incidentally enforced, Shakespeare has suffered the virtue of Cordelia to perish in a just cause, contrary to the natural ideas of justice, to the hope of the reader, and, what is yet more strange, to the faith of chronicles. Yet this conduct is justified by the Spectator, who blames Tate for giving Cordelia success and happiness in his alteration and declares that, in his opinion, *the tragedy has lost half its beauty*. Dennis has remarked, whether justly or not, that to secure the favourable reception of *Cato*, *the town was poisoned with much false and abominable criticism*, and that endeavours had been used to discredit and decry poetical justice. A play in which the wicked prosper and the virtuous miscarry may doubtless be good, because it is a just representation of the common events of human life; but since all reasonable beings naturally love justice, I cannot easily be persuaded that the observation of justice makes a play worse; or that, if other excellencies are equal, the audience will not always rise better pleased from the final triumph of persecuted virtue.

In the present case the public has decided. Cordelia, from the time of Tate, has always retired with victory and felicity. And, if my sensations could add anything to the general suffrage, I might relate , I was many years ago so shocked by Cordelia's death that I know not whether I ever endured to read again the last scenes of the play till I undertook to revise them as an editor.

MACBETH

I. vii. 28. *Enter* Lady Macbeth.

The arguments by which Lady Macbeth persuades her husband to commit the murder afford a proof of Shakespeare's knowledge of human nature. She urges the excellence and dignity of courage, a glittering idea which has dazzled mankind from age to age and animated sometimes the housebreaker and sometimes the conqueror; but this sophism Macbeth has forever destroyed, by distinguishing true from false fortitude, in a line and a half; of which it may almost be said that they ought to bestow immortality on the author, though all his other productions had been lost;

> I dare do all that may become a man,
> Who dares do more, is none.

This topic, which has been always employed with too much success, is used in this scene with peculiar propriety, to a soldier by a woman. Courage is the distinguishing virtue of a soldier, and the reproach of cowardice cannot be borne by any man from a woman, without great impatience.

She then urges the oaths by which he had bound himself to murder Duncan, another art of sophistry by which men have sometimes deluded their consciences and persuaded themselves that what would be criminal in others is virtuous in them; this argument Shakespeare, whose plan obliged him to make Macbeth yield, has not confuted, though he might easily have shown that a former obligation could not be vacated by a latter; that obligations laid on us by a higher power could not be overruled by obligations which we lay upon ourselves.

II. i. 49. *Macbeth.* Now o'er the one half-world / Nature seems dead.]

That is, *over our hemisphere all action and motion seem to have ceased.* This image, which is perhaps the most striking that poetry can produce, has been adopted by Dryden in his *Conquest of Mexico:*

> All things are hush'd as Nature's self lay dead,
> The mountains seem to nod their drowsy head;
> The little birds in dreams their songs repeat,
> And sleeping flow'rs beneath the night dews sweat.
> Even lust and envy sleep!

These l ines, though so well known, I have transcribed, that the contrast between them and this passage of Shakespeare may be more accurately observed.

Night is described by two great poets, but one describes a night of quiet, the other of perturbation. In the night of Dryden, all the disturbers of the world are laid asleep; in that of Shakespeare, nothing but sorcery, lust, and murder i s awake. He that reads Dryden finds himself lulled with serenity and disposed to solitude and contemplation. He that peruses Shakespeare looks round alarmed and starts to find himself alone. One is the night of a lover, the other, of a murderer.

II. ii. 57. *Lady Macbeth.* Gild the faces of the grooms withal; / For it must seem their guilt.]

Could Shakespeare possibly mean to play upon the similitude of *gild* and *guilt*?

II. iii. 118. *Macbeth.* Here lay Duncan, / His silver skin lac'd with his golden blood.]

Mr Pope has endeavoured to improve one of these lines by substituting *gory blood* for *golden blood;* but it may easily be admitted that he who could on such occasion talk of *lacing the silver skin* would *lace it* with *golden blood.* No amendment can be made to this line, of which every word is equally faulty, but by a general blot.

It is not improbable that Shakespeare put these forced and unnatural metaphors into the mouth of Macbeth as a mark of artifice and dissimulation, to show the difference between the studied language of hypocrisy and the natural outcries of sudden passion. This whole speech so considered is a remarkable instance of judgement, as it consists entirely of antithesis and metaphor.

General Observation. This play is deservedly celebrated for the propriety of its fictions, and solemnity, grandeur, and variety of its action; but it has no nice discriminations of character, the events are too great to admit the influence of particular dispositions, and the course of the action necessarily determines the conduct of the agents.

The danger of ambition is well described; and I know not whether it may not be said in defence of some parts which now seem improbable, that, in Shakespeare's time, it was necessary to warn credulity against vain and illusive predictions.

The passions are directed to their true end. Lady Macbeth is merely detested; and though the courage of Macbeth preserves some esteem, yet every reader rejoices at his fall.

CORIOLANUS

General Observation. The tragedy of *Coriolanus* is one of the most amusing of our author's performances. The old man's merriment in Menenius; the lofty lady's dignity in Volumnia; the bridal modesty in Virgilia; the patrician and military haughtiness in Coriolanus; the plebeian malignity and tribunitian insolence in Brutus and Sicinius, make a very pleasing and interesting variety; and the various revolutions of the hero's fortune fill the mind with anxious curiosity. There is, perhaps, too much bustle in the first act and too little in the last.

ANTONY AND CLEOPATRA

IV. ix. 15. *Enobarbus.*

> Throw my heart
> Against the flint and hardness of my fault,
> Which, being dried with grief, will break to powder,
> And finish all foul thoughts.]

The pathetic of Shakespeare too often ends in the ridiculous. It is

painful to find the gloomy dignity of this noble scene destroyed by
the intrusion of a conceit so farfetched and unaffecting.

V. ii. 7. *Cleopatra.*

>   It is great
>   To do that thing that ends all other deeds,
>   Which shackles accidents, and bolts up change,
>   Which sleeps, and never palates more the dung,
>   The beggar's nurse and Caesar's.]

The difficulty of this passage, if any difficulty there be, arises only
from this, that the act of suicide and the state which is the effect of
suicide are confounded. Voluntary death, says she, is an act *which
bolts up change;* it produces a state,

>   Which sleeps, and never palates more the dung,
>   The beggar's nurse, and Caesar's.

Which has no longer need of the gross and terrene sustenance, in the
use of which Caesar and the beggar are on a level.

The speech is abrupt, but perturbation in such a state is surely
natural.

General Observation. This play keeps curiosity always busy and the
passions always interested. The continual hurry of the action, the
variety of incidents, and the quick succession of one personage to
another, call the mind forward without intermission from the first
act to the last. But the power of delighting is derived principally from
the frequent changes of the scene; for, except the feminine arts, some
of which are too low, which distinguish Cleopatra, no character is
very strongly discriminated. Upton, who did not easily miss what he
desired to find, has discovered that the language of Antony is, with
great skill and learning, made pompous and superb, according to his
real practice. But I think his diction not distinguishable from that of
others; the most tumid speech in the play is that which Caesar makes
to Octavia.

The events, of which the principal are described according to
history, are produced without any art of connexion or care of
disposition.

CYMBELINE

General Observation. This play has many just sentiments, some natural dialogues, and some pleasing scenes, but they are obtained at the expense of much incongruity.

To remark the folly of the fiction, the absurdity of the conduct, the confusion of the names and manners of different times, and the impossibility of the events in any system of life, were to waste criticism upon unresisting imbecility, upon faults too evident for detection, and too gross for aggravation.

ROMEO AND JULIET

General Observation. This play is one of the most pleasing of our author's performances. The scenes are busy and various, the incidents numerous and important, the catastrophe irresistibly affecting, and the process of the action carried on with such probability, at least with such congruity to popular opinions, as tragedy requires.

Here is one of the few attempts of Shakespeare to exhibit the conversation of gentlemen, to represent the airy sprightliness of juvenile elegance. Mr Dryden mentions a tradition, which might easily reach his time, of a declaration made by Shakespeare, that *he was obliged to kill Mercutio in the third act, lest he should have been killed by him.* Yet he thinks him *no such formidable person but that he might have lived through the play and died in his bed,* without danger to a poet. Dryden well knew, had he been in quest of truth, that in a pointed sentence more regard is commonly had to the words than the thought, and that it is very seldom to be rigorously understood. Mercutio's wit, gaiety, and courage will always procure him friends that wish him a longer life; but his death is not precipitated, he has lived out the time allotted him in the construction of the play; nor do I doubt the ability of Shakespeare to have continued his existence, though some of his sallies were perhaps out of the reach of Dryden, whose genius was not very fertile of merriment nor ductile to humour, but acute, argumentative, comprehensive, and sublime.

The nurse is one of the characters in which the author delighted; he has with great subtlety of distinction, drawn her at once loquacious and secret, obsequious and insolent, trusty and dishonest.

His comic scenes are happily wrought, but his pathetic strains are always polluted with some unexpected depravations. His persons, however distressed, *have a conceit left them in their misery, a miserable conceit.*

HAMLET

II. ii. 86–167. *Polonius*. My liege, and madam, to expostulate —]

Polonius is a man bred in courts, exercised in business, stored with observations, confident of his knowledge, proud of his eloquence, and declining into dotage. His mode of oratory is truly represented as designed to ridicule the practice of those times, of prefaces that made no introduction, and of method that embarrassed rather than explained. This part of his character is accidental, the rest is natural. Such a man is positive and confident, because he knows that his mind was once strong and knows not that it is become weak. Such a man excels in general principles but fails in the particular application. He is knowing in retrospect and ignorant in foresight. While he depends upon his memory and can draw from his repositories of knowledge, he utters weighty sentences and gives useful counsel; but as the mind in its enfeebled state cannot be kept long busy and intent, the old man is subject to sudden dereliction of his faculties, he loses the order of his ideas and entangles himself in his own thoughts, till he recovers the leading principle and falls again into his former train. This idea of dotage encroaching upon wisdom will solve all the phenomena of the character of Polonius.

III. i. 59. *Hamlet*. Or to take arms against a sea of troubles]

Mr Pope proposed *siege*. I know not why there should be so much solicitude about this metaphor. Shakespeare breaks his metaphors often, and in this desultory speech there was less need of preserving them.

III. iii. 94. *Hamlet.* His soul may be as damn'd and black / As hell, whereto it goes.]

This speech, in which Hamlet, represented as a virtuous character, is not content with taking blood for blood, but contrives damnation for the man he would punish, is too horrible to be read or to be uttered.

General Observation. If the dramas of Shakespeare were to be characterized each by the particular excellence which distinguishes it from the rest, we must allow to the tragedy of *Hamlet* the praise of variety. The incidents are so numerous that the argument of the play would make a long tale. The scenes are interchangeably diversified with merriment and solemnity; with merriment that includes judicious and instructive observations, and solemnity not strained by poetical violence above the natural sentiments of man. New characters appear from time to time in continual succession, exhibiting various forms of life and particular modes of conversation. The pretended madness of Hamlet causes much mirth, the mournful distraction of Ophelia fills the heart with tenderness, and every personage produces the effect intended, from the apparition that in the first act chills the blood with horror to the fop in the last that exposes affectation to just contempt.

The conduct is perhaps not wholly secure against objections. The action is indeed for the most part in continual progression, but there are some scenes which neither forward nor retard it. Of the feigned madness of Hamlet there appears no adequate cause, for he does nothing which he might not have done with the reputation of sanity. He plays the madman most when he treats Ophelia with so much rudeness, which seems to be useless and wanton cruelty.

Hamlet is, through the whole play, rather an instrument than an agent. After he has, by the stratagem of the play, convicted the king, he makes no attempt to punish him, and his death is at last effected by an incident which Hamlet has no part in producing.

OTHELLO

General Observation. The beauties of this play impress themselves so strongly upon the attention of the reader that they can draw no aid from critical illustration. The fiery openness of Othello, magnanimous, artless, and credulous, boundless in his confidence, ardent in his affection, inflexible in his resolution, and obdurate in his revenge; the cool malignity of Iago, silent in his resentment, subtle in his designs, and studious at once of his interest and his vengeance; the soft simplicity of Desdemona, confident of merit and conscious of innocence, her artless perseverance in her suit, and her slowness to suspect that she can be suspected, are such proofs of Shakespeare's skill in human nature as, I suppose, it is vain to seek in any modern writer. The gradual progress which Iago makes in the Moor's conviction and the circumstances which he employs to enflame him are so artfully natural that, though it will perhaps not be said of him, as he says of himself, that he is *a man not easily jealous*, yet we cannot but pity him when at last we find him *perplexed in the extreme*.

There is always danger lest wickedness, conjoined with abilities, should steal upon esteem, though it misses of approbation; but the character of Iago is so conducted that he is from the first scene to the last hated and despised.

Even the inferior characters of this play would be very conspicuous in any other piece, not only for their justness but their strength. Cassio is brave, benevolent, and honest, ruined only by his want of stubbornness to resist an insidious invitation. Roderigo's suspicious credulity and impatient submission to the cheats which he sees practised upon him, and which by persuasion he suffers to be repeated, exhibit a strong picture of a weak mind betrayed by unlawful desires to a false friend; and the virtue of Emilia is such as we often find, worn loosely but not cast off, easy to commit small crimes but quickened and alarmed at atrocious villainies.

The scenes from the beginning to the end are busy, varied by happy interchanges, and regularly presenting the progression of the story;

and the narrative in the end, though it tells but what is known already, yet is necessary to produce the death of Othello.

Had the scene opened in Cyprus, and the preceding incidents been occasionally related, there had been little wanting to a drama of the most exact and scrupulous regularity.

FROM A JOURNEY TO THE WESTERN ISLANDS OF SCOTLAND

... W E were now to bid farewell to the luxury of travelling, and to enter a country upon which perhaps no wheel has ever rolled. We could indeed have used our post-chaise one day longer, along the military road to Fort Augustus, but we could have hired no horses beyond Inverness, and we were not so sparing of ourselves, as to lead them, merely that we might have one day longer the indulgence of a carriage.

At Inverness therefore we procured three horses for ourselves and a servant, and one more for our baggage, which was no very heavy load. We found in the course of our journey the convenience of having disencumbered ourselves, by laying aside whatever we could spare; for it is not to be imagined without experience, how in climbing crags, and treading bogs, and winding through narrow and obstructed passages, a little bulk will hinder, and a little weight will burden; or how often a man that has pleased himself at home with his own resolution, will, in the hour of darkness and fatigue, be content to leave behind him everything but himself.

Lough Ness

We took two Highlanders to run beside us, partly to show us the way, and partly to take back from the seaside the horses, of which they were the owners. One of them was a man of great liveliness and activity, of whom his companion said, that he would tire any horse in Inverness. Both of them were civil and ready-handed. Civility seems part of the national character of Highlanders. Every chieftain is a monarch, and politeness, the natural product of royal government, is diffused from the laird through the whole clan. But they are not commonly dexterous: their narrowness of life confines them to a few operations, and they are accustomed to endure little wants more than to remove them.

We mounted our steeds on the thirtieth of August, and directed our guides to conduct us to Fort Augustus. It is built at the head of Lough Ness, of which Inverness stands at the outlet. The way between them has been cut by the soldiers, and the greater part of it runs along a rock levelled with great labour and exactness, near the water-side.

Most of this day's journey was very pleasant. The day, though bright, was not hot; and the appearance of the country, if I had not seen the Peak, would have been wholly new. We went upon a surface so hard and level, that we had little care to hold the bridle, and were therefore at full leisure for contemplation. On the left were high and steep rocks shaded with birch, the hardy native of the North, and covered with fern or heath. On the right the limpid waters of Lough Ness were beating their bank, and waving their surface by a gentle agitation. Beyond them were rocks sometimes covered with verdure, and sometimes towering in horrid nakedness. Now and then we espied a little cornfield, which served to impress more strongly the general barrenness.

Lough Ness is about twenty-four miles long, and from one mile to two miles broad. It is remarkable that Boethius, in his description of Scotland, gives it twelve miles of breadth. When historians or geographers exhibit false accounts of places far distant, they may be forgiven, because they can tell but what they are told; and that their accounts exceed the truth may be justly supposed, because most men exaggerate to others, if not to themselves; but Boethius lived at no great distance; if he never saw the lake, he must have been very incurious, and if he had seen it, his veracity yielded to very slight temptations.

Lough Ness, though not twelve miles broad, is a very remarkable diffusion of water without islands. It fills a large hollow between two ridges of high rocks, being supplied partly by the torrents which fall into it on either side, and partly, as is supposed, by springs at the bottom. Its water is remarkably clear and pleasant, and is imagined by the natives to be medicinal. We were told, that it is in some places a hundred and forty fathoms deep, a profundity scarcely credible,[1] and which probably those that relate it have never sounded. Its fish are salmon, trout, and pike.

It was said at Fort Augustus, that Lough Ness is open in the hardest winters, though a lake not far from it is covered with ice. In discussing these exceptions from the course of nature, the first question is, whether the fact be justly stated. That which is strange is delightful, and a pleasing error is not willingly detected. Accuracy of narration is not very common, and there are few so rigidly philosophical, as not to represent as perpetual, what is only frequent, or as constant, what is really casual. If it be true that Lough Ness never freezes, it is either sheltered by its high banks from the cold blasts, and exposed only to those winds which have more power to agitate than congeal; or it is kept in perpetual motion by the rush of streams from the rocks that inclose it. Its profundity, though it should be such as is represented, can have little part in this exemption; for though deep wells are not frozen, because their water is secluded from the external air, yet where a wide surface is exposed to the full influence of a freezing atmosphere, I know not why the depth should keep it open. Natural philosophy is now one of the favourite studies of the Scottish nation, and Lough Ness well deserves to be diligently examined.

The road on which we travelled, and which was itself a source of entertainment, is made along the rock, in the direction of the lough, sometimes by breaking off protuberances, and sometimes by cutting the great mass of stone to a considerable depth. The fragments are piled in a loose wall on either side, with apertures left at very short spaces, to give a passage to the wintry currents. Part of it is bordered with low trees, from which our guides gathered nuts, and would have had the appearance of an English lane, except that an English lane is almost always dirty. It has been made with great labour, but has this advantage, that it cannot, without equal labour, be broken up.

Within our sight there were goats feeding or playing. The mountains have red deer, but they came not within view; and if what is said of their vigilance and subtlety be true, they have some claim to that palm of wisdom, which the eastern philosopher, whom Alexander interrogated, gave to those beasts which live furthest from men.

Near the way, by the water side, we espied a cottage. This was the first Highland hut that I had seen; and as our business was with life and manners, we were willing to visit it. To enter a habitation without leave, seems to be not considered here as rudeness or intrusion. The old laws of hospitality still give this licence to a stranger.

A hut is constructed with loose stones, ranged for the most part with some tendency to circularity. It must be placed where the wind cannot act upon it with violence, because it has no cement; and where the water will run easily away, because it has no floor but the naked ground. The wall, which is commonly about six feet high, declines from the perpendicular a little inward. Such rafters as can be procured are then raised for a roof, and covered with heath, which makes a strong and warm thatch, kept from flying off by ropes of twisted heath, of which the ends, reaching from the centre of the thatch to the top of the wall, are held firm by the weight of a large stone. No light is admitted but at the entrance, and through a hole in the thatch, which gives vent to the smoke. This hole is not directly over the fire, lest the rain should extinguish it; and the smoke therefore naturally fills the place before it escapes. Such is the general structure of the houses in which one of the nations of this opulent and powerful island has been hitherto content to live. Huts however are not more uniform than palaces; and this which we were inspecting was very far from one of the meanest, for it was divided into several apartments; and its inhabitants possessed such property as a pastoral poet might exalt into riches.

When we entered we found an old woman[2] boiling goats-flesh in a kettle. She spoke little English, but we had interpreters at hand, and she was willing enough to display her whole system of economy. She has five children, of which none are yet gone from her. The eldest, a boy of thirteen, and her husband, who is eighty years old, were at work in the wood. Her two next sons were gone to Inverness to buy *meal*, by which oatmeal is always meant. Meal she considered as expensive food, and told us, that in spring, when the goats gave milk, the children could live without it. She is mistress of sixty goats, and I saw many kids in an enclosure at the end of her house. She had also some poultry. By the lake we saw a potato-garden, and a small spot of ground on which stood four shucks, containing each twelve sheaves of barley. She has all this from the labour of their own hands, and for what is necessary to be bought, her kids and her chickens are sent to market.

With the true pastoral hospitality, she asked us to sit down and drink whisky. She is religious, and though the kirk is four miles off, probably eight English miles, she goes thither every Sunday. We gave her a shilling, and she begged snuff; for snuff is the luxury of a Highland cottage.

Soon afterwards we came to the *General's Hut*, so called because it was the temporary abode of Wade,[3] while he superintended the works upon the road. It is now a house of entertainment for passengers, and we found it not ill stocked with provisions . . .

Fort Augustus

In the morning we viewed the fort, which is much less than that of St George, and is said to be commanded by the neighbouring hills. It was not long ago taken by the Highlanders. But its situation seems well chosen for pleasure, if not for strength; it stands at the head of the lake, and, by a sloop of sixty tons, is supplied from Inverness with great convenience.

We were now to cross the Highlands towards the western coast, and to content ourselves with such accommodations, as a way so little frequented could afford. The journey was not formidable, for it was but of two days, very unequally divided, because the only house, where we could be entertained, was not further off than a third of the way. We soon came to a high hill, which we mounted by a military road, cut in traverses, so that as we went upon a higher stage, we saw the baggage following us below in a contrary direction. To make this way, the rock has been hewn to a level with labour that might have broken the perseverance of a Roman legion.

The country is totally denuded of its wood, but the stumps both of oaks and firs, which are still found, show that it has been once a forest of large timber. I do not remember that we saw any animals, but we were told that, in the mountains, there are stags, roebucks, goats and rabbits.

We did not perceive that this tract was possessed by human beings, except that once we saw a corn field, in which a lady was walking with some gentlemen. Their house was certainly at no great distance, but so situated that we could not descry it.

Passing on through the dreariness of solitude, we found a party of soldiers from the fort, working on the road, under the superintendence of a sergeant. We told them how kindly we had been treated at the garrison, and as we were enjoying the benefit of their labours, begged leave to show our gratitude by a small present.

Anoch

Early in the afternoon we came to Anoch, a village in Glenmollison of three huts, one of which is distinguished by a chimney. Here we were to dine and lodge, and were conducted through the first room, that had the chimney, into another lighted by a small glass window. The landlord attended us with great civility, and told us what he could give us to eat and drink. I found some books on a shelf, among which were a volume or more of Prideaux's Connexion.[4]

This I mentioned as something unexpected, and perceived that I did not please him. I praised the propriety of his language, and was answered that I need not wonder, for he had learned it by grammar.

By subsequent opportunities of observation, I found that my host's diction had nothing peculiar. Those Highlanders that can speak English, commonly speak it well, with few of the words, and little of the tone by which a Scotchman is distinguished. Their language seems to have been learned in the army or the navy, or by some communication with those who could give them good examples of accent and pronunciation. By their Lowland neighbours they would not willingly be taught; for they have long considered them as a mean and degenerate race. These prejudices are wearing fast away; but so much of them still remains, that when I asked a very learned minister in the islands, which they considered as their most savage clans: 'Those', said he, 'that live next the Lowlands'.

As we came hither early in the day, we had time sufficient to survey the place. The house was built like other huts of loose stones, but the part in which we dined and slept was lined with turf and wattled with twigs, which kept the earth from falling. Near it was a garden of turnips and a field of potatoes. It stands in a glen, or valley, pleasantly watered by a winding river. But this country, however it may delight the gazer or amuse the naturalist, is of no great advantage to its owners. Our landlord told us of a gentleman, who possesses lands, eighteen Scotch miles in length, and three in breadth; a space containing at least a hundred square English miles. He has raised his rents, to the danger of depopulating his farms, and he fells his timber, and by exerting every art of augmentation, has obtained an yearly revenue of four hundred pounds, which for a hundred square miles is three halfpence an acre.

Some time after dinner we were surprised by the entrance of a young woman, not inelegant either in mien or dress, who asked us whether we would have tea. We found that she was the daughter of our host, and desired her to make it. Her conversation, like her appearance, was gentle and pleasing. We knew that the girls of the Highlands are all gentlewomen, and treated her with great respect, which she received as customary and due, and was neither elated by it, nor confused, but repaid my civilities without embarrassment, and told me how much I honoured her country by coming to survey it.

She had been at Inverness to gain the common female qualifications, and had, like her father, the English pronunciation. I presented her with a book,[5] which I happened to have about me, and should not be pleased to think that she forgets me.

In the evening the soldiers, whom we had passed on the road, came to spend at our inn the little money that we had given them. They had the true military impatience of coin in their pockets, and had marched at least six miles to find the first place where liquor could be bought. Having never been before in a place so wild and unfrequented, I was glad of their arrival, because I knew that we had made them friends, and to gain still more of their good will, we went to them, where they were carousing in the barn, and added something to our former gift. All that we gave was not much, but it detained them in the barn, either merry or quarrelling, the whole night, and in the morning they went back to their work, with great indignation at the bad qualities of whisky.

We had gained so much the favour of our host, that, when we left his house in the morning, he walked by us a great way, and entertained us with conversation both on his own condition, and that of the country. His life seemed to be merely pastoral, except that he differed from some of the ancient nomads in having a settled dwelling. His wealth consists of one hundred sheep, as many goats, twelve milk-cows, and twenty-eight beeves ready for the drover.

From him we first heard of the general dissatisfaction, which is now driving the Highlanders into the other hemisphere; and when I asked whether they would stay at home, if they were well treated, he answered with indignation, that no man willingly left his native country. Of the farm, which he himself occupied, the rent had, in twenty-five years, been advanced from five to twenty pounds, which he found himself so little able to pay, that he would be glad to try his fortune in some other place. Yet he owned the reasonableness of raising the Highland rents in a certain degree, and declared himself willing to pay ten pounds for the ground which he had formerly had for five.

Our host having amused us for a time, resigned us to our guides. The journey of this day was long, not that the distance was great, but that the way was difficult. We were now in the bosom of the Highlands, with full leisure to contemplate the appearance and properties of mountainous regions, such as have been, in many countries, the last shelters of national distress, and are everywhere the scenes of adventures, stratagems, surprises and escapes.

Mountainous countries are not passed but with difficulty, not merely from the labour of climbing; for to climb is not always necessary: but because that which is not mountain is commonly bog, through which the way must be picked with caution. Where there are hills, there is much rain, and the torrents pouring down into the intermediate spaces, seldom find so ready an outlet, as not to stagnate, till they have broken the texture of the ground.

Of the hills, which our journey offered to the view on either side, we did not take the height, nor did we see any that astonished us with their loftiness. Towards the summit of one, there was a white spot, which I should have called a naked rock, but the guides, who had better eyes, and were acquainted with the phenomena of the country, declared it to be snow. It had already lasted to the end of August, and was likely to maintain its contest with the sun, till it should be reinforced by winter.

The height of mountains, philosophically considered, is properly computed from the surface of the next sea;[6] but as it affects the eye or imagination of the passenger, as it makes either a spectacle or an obstruction, it must be reckoned from the place where the rise begins to make a considerable angle with the plain. In extensive continents the land may, by gradual elevation, attain great height, without any other appearance than that of a plane gently inclined, and if a hill placed upon such raised ground be described, as having its altitude equal to the whole space above the sea, the representation will be fallacious.

These mountains may be properly enough measured from the inland base; for it is not much above the sea. As we advanced at evening towards the western coast, I did not observe the declivity to be greater than is necessary for the discharge of the inland waters.

We passed many rivers and rivulets, which commonly ran with a clear shallow stream over a hard pebbly bottom. These channels, which seem so much wider than the water that they convey would naturally require, are formed by the violence of wintry floods, produced by the accumulation of innumerable streams that fall in rainy weather from the hills, and bursting away with resistless impetuosity, make themselves a passage proportionate to their mass.

Such capricious and temporary waters cannot be expected to produce many fish. The rapidity of the wintry deluge sweeps them away, and the scantiness of the summer stream would hardly sustain them above the ground. This is the reason why in fording the northern rivers, no fishes are seen, as in England, wandering in the water.

Of the hills many may be called with Homer's Ida *abundant in springs*, but few can deserve the epithet which he bestows upon Pelion by *waving their leaves.* They exhibit very little variety; being almost wholly covered with dark heath, and even that seems to be checked in its growth. What is not heath is nakedness, a little diversified by now and then a stream rushing down the steep. An eye accustomed to flowery pastures and waving harvests is astonished and repelled by this wide extent of hopeless sterility. The appearance is that of matter incapable of form or usefulness, dismissed by nature from her care and disinherited of her favours, left in its original elemental state, or quickened only with one sullen power of useless vegetation.

It will very readily occur, that this uniformity of barrenness can afford very little amusement to the traveller; that it is easy to sit at home and conceive rocks and heath, and waterfalls; and that these journeys are useless labours, which neither impregnate the imagination, nor enlarge the understanding. It is true that of far the greater part of things, we must content ourselves with such knowledge as description may exhibit, or analogy supply; but it is true likewise, that these ideas are always incomplete, and that at least, till we have compared them with realities, we do not know them to be just. As we see more, we become possessed of more certainties, and consequently gain more principles of reasoning, and found a wider basis of analogy.

Regions mountainous and wild, thinly inhabited, and little cultivated, make a great part of the earth, and he that has never seen them, must live unacquainted with much of the face of nature, and with one of the great scenes of human existence.

As the day advanced towards noon, we entered a narrow valley not very flowery, but sufficiently verdant. Our guides told us, that the horses could not travel all day without rest or meat, and entreated us to stop here, because no grass would be found in any other place. The request was reasonable and the argument cogent. We therefore willingly dismounted and diverted ourselves as the place gave us opportunity.

I sat down on a bank,[7] such as a writer of Romance might have delighted to feign. I had indeed no trees to whisper over my head, but a clear rivulet streamed at my feet. The day was calm, the air soft, and all was rudeness, silence, and solitude. Before me, and on either side, were high hills, which by hindering the eye from ranging, forced the mind to find entertainment for itself. Whether I spent the hour well I know not; for here I first conceived the thought of this narration.

We were in this place at ease and by choice, and had no evils to suffer or to fear; yet the imaginations excited by the view of an unknown and untravelled wilderness are not such as arise in the artificial solitude of parks and gardens, a flattering notion of self-sufficiency, a placid indulgence of voluntary delusions, a secure expansion of the fancy, or a cool concentration of the mental powers. The phantoms which haunt a desert are want, and misery, and danger; the evils of dereliction rush upon the thoughts; man is made unwillingly acquainted with his own weakness, and meditation shows him only how little he can sustain, and how little he can perform. There were no traces of inhabitants, except perhaps a rude pile of clods called a summer hut, in which a herdsman had rested in the favourable seasons. Whoever had been in the place where I then sat, unprovided with provisions and ignorant of the country, might, at least before the roads were made, have wandered among the rocks, till he had perished with hardship, before he could have found either food or shelter. Yet what are these hillocks to the ridges of Taurus, or these spots of wildness to the deserts[8] of America?

It was not long before we were invited to mount, and continued our journey along the side of a loch, kept full by many streams, which with more or less rapidity and noise, crossed the road from the hills on the other hand. These currents, in their diminished state, after several dry months, afford, to one who has always lived in level countries, an unusual and delightful spectacle; but in the rainy season, such as every winter may be expected to bring, must precipitate an impetuous and tremendous flood. I suppose the way by which we went, is at that time impassable.

Glensheals

The loch at last ended in a river broad and shallow like the rest, but that it may be passed when it is deeper, there is a bridge over it. Beyond it is a valley called Glensheals, inhabited by the clan of Macrae. Here we found a village called Auknasheals, consisting of many huts, perhaps twenty, built all of *dry-stone*, that is, stones piled up without mortar.

We had, by the direction of the officers at Fort Augustus, taken bread for ourselves, and tobacco for those Highlanders who might show us any kindness. We were now at a place where we could obtain milk, but must have wanted bread if we had not brought it. The people of this valley did not appear to know any English, and our guides now became doubly necessary as interpreters. A woman, whose hut was distinguished by greater spaciousness and better architecture, brought out some pails of milk. The villagers gathered about us in considerable numbers, I believe without any evil intention, but with a very savage wildness[9] of aspect and manner. When our meal was over, Mr Boswell sliced the bread, and divided it amongst them, as he supposed them never to have tasted a wheaten loaf before. He then gave them little pieces of twisted tobacco, and among the children we distributed a small handful of halfpence, which they received with great eagerness. Yet I have been since told, that the people of that valley are not indigent; and when we mentioned them afterwards as needy and pitiable, a Highland lady let us know, that we might spare our commiseration; for the dame whose milk we drank had probably more than a dozen milk-cows. She seemed unwilling to take any price, but being pressed to make a demand, at last named a shilling. Honesty is not greater where elegance is less. One of the by-standers, as we were told afterwards, advised her to ask more, but she said a shilling was enough. We gave her half a crown, and I hope got some credit by our behaviour; for the company said, if our interpreters did not flatter us, that they had not seen such a day since the old laird of Macleod passed through their country.

The Macraes, as we heard afterwards in the Hebrides, were originally an indigent and subordinate clan, and having no farms nor stock, were in great numbers servants to the Maclellans, who, in the war of Charles the First, took arms at the call of the heroic Montrose, and were, in one of his battles, almost all destroyed. The women that were left at home, being thus deprived of their husbands, like the Scythian ladies of old, married their servants, and the Macraes became a considerable race.

The Highlands

As we continued our journey, we were at leisure to extend our speculations, and to investigate the reason of those peculiarities by which such rugged regions as these before us are generally distinguished.

Mountainous countries commonly contain the original, at least the oldest race of inhabitants, for they are not easily conquered, because they must be entered by narrow ways, exposed to every power of mischief from those that occupy the heights; and every new ridge is a new fortress, where the defendants have again the same advantages. If the assailants either force the strait, or storm the summit, they gain only so much ground; their enemies are fled to take possession of the next rock, and the pursuers stand at gaze, knowing neither where the ways of escape wind among the steeps, nor where the bog has firmness to sustain them: besides that, mountaineers have an agility in climbing and descending distinct from strength or courage, and attainable only by use.

If the war be not soon concluded, the invaders are dislodged by hunger; for in those anxious and toilsome marches, provisions cannot easily be carried, and are never to be found. The wealth of mountains is cattle, which, while the men stand in the passes, the women drive away. Such lands at last cannot repay the expense of conquest, and therefore perhaps have not been so often invaded by the mere ambition of dominion, as by resentment of robberies and insults, or the desire of enjoying in security the more fruitful provinces.

As mountains are long before they are conquered, they are likewise long before they are civilized. Men are softened by intercourse mutually profitable, and instructed by comparing their own notions with those of others. Thus Caesar found the maritime parts of Britain made less barbarous by their commerce with the Gauls. Into a barren and rough tract no stranger is brought either by the hope of gain or of pleasure. The inhabitants having neither commodities for sale, nor money for purchase, seldom visit more polished places, or if they do visit them, seldom return.

It sometimes happens that by conquest, intermixture, or gradual refinement, the cultivated parts of a country change their language. The mountaineers then become a distinct nation, cut off by dissimilitude of speech from conversation with their neighbours. Thus in Biscay, the original Cantabrian, and in Dalecarlia, the old Swedish still subsists. Thus Wales and the Highlands speak the tongue of the first inhabitants of Britain, while the other parts have received first the Saxon, and in some degree afterwards the French, and then formed a third language between them.

That the primitive manners are continued where the primitive language is spoken, no nation will desire me to suppose, for the manners of mountaineers are commonly savage, but they are rather produced by their situation than derived from their ancestors.

Such seems to be the disposition of man, that whatever makes a distinction produces rivalry. England, before other causes of enmity were found, was disturbed for some centuries by the contests of the northern and southern counties; so that at Oxford, the peace of study could for a long time be preserved only by choosing annually one of the Proctors from each side of the Trent. A tract intersected by many ridges of mountains, naturally divides its inhabitants into petty nations, which are made by a thousand causes enemies to each other. Each will exalt its own chiefs, each will boast the valour of its men, or the beauty of its women, and every claim of superiority irritates competition; injuries will sometimes be done, and be more injuriously defended; retaliation will sometimes be attempted, and the debt exacted with too much interest.

In the Highlands it was a law, that if a robber was sheltered from justice, any man of the same clan might be taken in his place. This was a kind of irregular justice, which, though necessary in savage times, could hardly fail to end in a feud, and a feud once kindled among an idle people with no variety of pursuits to divert their thoughts, burnt on for ages either sullenly glowing in secret mischief, or openly blazing into public violence. Of the effects of this violent judicature, there are not wanting memorials. The cave is now to be seen to which one of the Campbells, who had injured the Macdonalds, retired with a body of his own clan. The Macdonalds required the offender, and being refused, made a fire at the mouth of the cave, by which he and his adherents were suffocated together.

Mountaineers are warlike, because by their feuds and competitions they consider themselves as surrounded with enemies, and are always prepared to repel incursions, or to make them. Like the Greeks in their unpolished state, described by Thucydides, the Highlanders, till lately, went always armed, and carried their weapons to visits, and to church.

Mountaineers are thievish, because they are poor, and having neither manufactures nor commerce, can grow richer only by robbery. They regularly plunder their neighbours, for their neighbours are commonly their enemies; and having lost that reverence for property, by which the order of civil life is preserved, soon consider all as enemies, whom they do not reckon as friends, and think themselves licensed to invade whatever they are not obliged to protect.

By a strict administration of the laws, since the laws have been introduced into the Highlands, this disposition to thievery is very much repressed. Thirty years ago no herd had ever been conducted through the mountains, without paying tribute in the night, to some of the clans; but cattle are now driven, and passengers travel without danger, fear, or molestation.

Among a warlike people, the quality of highest esteem is personal courage, and with the ostentatious display of courage are closely connected promptitude of offence and quickness of resentment. The Highlanders, before they were disarmed, were so addicted to quarrels, that the boys used to follow any public procession or ceremony, however festive, or however solemn, in expectation of the battle, which was sure to happen before the company dispersed.

Mountainous regions are sometimes so remote from the seat of government, and so difficult of access, that they are very little under the influence of the sovereign, or within the reach of national justice. Law is nothing without power; and the sentence of a distant court could not be easily executed, nor perhaps very safely promulgated, among men ignorantly proud and habitually violent, unconnected with the general system, and accustomed to reverence only their own lords. It has therefore been necessary to erect many particular jurisdictions, and commit the punishment of crimes, and the decision of right to the proprietors of the country who could enforce their own decrees. It immediately appears that such judges will be often ignorant, and often partial; but in the immaturity of political establishments no better expedient could be found. As government advances towards perfection, provincial judicature is perhaps in every empire gradually abolished.

Those who had thus the dispensation of law, were by consequence themselves lawless. Their vassals had no shelter from outrages and oppressions; but were condemned to endure, without resistance, the caprices of wantonness, and the rage of cruelty.

In the Highlands, some great lords had an hereditary jurisdiction over counties; and some chieftains over their own lands; till the final conquest of the Highlands afforded an opportunity of crushing all the local courts, and of extending the general benefits of equal law to the low and the high, in the deepest recesses and obscurest corners.

While the chiefs had this resemblance of royalty, they had little inclination to appeal, on any question, to superior judicatures. A claim of lands between two powerful lairds, was decided like a contest for dominion between sovereign powers. They drew their forces into the field, and right attended on the strongest. This was, in ruder times, the common practice, which the kings of Scotland could seldom control.

Even so lately as in the last years of King William, a battle was fought at Mull Roy, on a plain a few miles to the south of Inverness, between the clans of Mackintosh and Macdonald of Keppoch. Col. Macdonald, the head of a small clan, refused to pay the dues demanded from him by Mackintosh, as his superior lord. They disdained the interposition of judges and laws, and calling each his followers to maintain the dignity of the clan, fought a formal battle, in which several considerable men fell on the side of Mackintosh, without a complete victory to either. This is said to have been the last open war made between the clans by their own authority.

The Highland lords made treaties, and formed alliances, of which some traces may still be found, and some consequences still remain as lasting evidences of petty regality. The terms of one of these confederacies were, that each should support the other in the right, or in the wrong, except against the king.

The inhabitants of mountains form distinct races, and are careful to preserve their genealogies. Men in a small district necessarily mingle blood by intermarriages, and combine at last into one family, with a common interest in the honour and disgrace of every individual. Then begins that union of affections, and cooperation of endeavours, that constitute a clan. They who consider themselves as ennobled by their family, will think highly of their progenitors, and they who through successive generations live always together in the same place, will preserve local stories and hereditary prejudice. Thus every Highlander can talk of his ancestors, and recount the outrages which they suffered from the wicked inhabitants of the next valley.

Such are the effects of habitation among mountains, and such were the qualities of the Highlanders, while their rocks secluded them from the rest of mankind, and kept them an unaltered and discriminated race. They are now losing their distinction, and hastening to mingle with the general community.

Glenelg

We left Auknasheals and the Macraes in the afternoon, and in the evening came to Ratiken, a high hill on which a road is cut, but so steep and narrow, that it is very difficult. There is now a design of making another way round the bottom. Upon one of the precipices, my horse, weary with the steepness of the rise, staggered a little, and I called in haste to the Highlander to hold him. This was the only moment of my journey, in which I thought myself endangered.

Having surmounted the hill at last, we were told that at Glenelg, on the sea-side, we should come to a house of lime and slate and glass. This image of magnificence raised our expectation. At last we came to our inn weary and peevish,[10] and began to inquire for meat and beds.

Of the provisions the negative catalogue was very copious. Here was no meat, no milk, no bread, no eggs, no wine. We did not express much satisfaction. Here however we were to stay. Whisky we might have, and I believe at last they caught a fowl and killed it. We had some bread, and with that we prepared ourselves to be contented, when we had a very eminent proof of Highland hospitality. Along some miles of the way, in the evening, a gentleman's servant had kept us company on foot with very little notice on our part. He left us near Glenelg, and we thought on him no more till he came to us again, in about two hours, with a present from his master of rum and sugar. The man had mentioned his company, and the gentleman, whose name, I think, is Gordon, well knowing the penury of the place, had this attention to two men, whose names perhaps he had not heard, by whom his kindness was not likely to be ever repaid, and who could be recommended to him only by their necessities.

We were now to examine our lodging. Out of one of the beds, on which we were to repose, started up, at our entrance, a man black as a Cyclops from the forge. Other circumstances of no elegant recital concurred to disgust us. We had been frighted by a lady at Edinburgh, with discouraging representations of Highland lodgings. Sleep, however, was necessary. Our Highlanders had at last found some hay, with which the inn could not supply them. I directed them to bring a bundle into the room, and slept upon it in my riding coat. Mr Boswell being more delicate, laid himself sheets with hay over and under him, and lay in linen like a gentleman.

Sky: Armidel

In the morning, September the second, we found ourselves on the edge of the sea. Having procured a boat, we dismissed our Highlanders, whom I would recommend to the service of any future travellers, and were ferried over to the Isle of Sky. We landed at Armidel, where we were met on the sands by Sir Alexander Macdonald, who was at that time there with his lady, preparing to leave the island and reside at Edinburgh.

Armidel is a neat house, built where the Macdonalds had once a seat, which was burnt in the commotions that followed the Revolution. The walled orchard, which belonged to the former house, still remains. It is well shaded by tall ash trees, of a species, as Mr Janes the fossilist informed me, uncommonly valuable. This plantation is very properly mentioned by Dr Campbell, in his new account of the state of Britain, and deserves attention; because it proves that the present nakedness of the Hebrides is not wholly the fault of Nature.

As we sat at Sir Alexander's table, we were entertained, according to the ancient usage of the North, with the melody of the bagpipe. Every thing in those countries has its history. As the bagpiper was playing, an elderly gentleman informed us, that in some remote time, the Macdonalds of Glengary having been injured, or offended by the inhabitants of Culloden, and resolving to have justice or vengeance, came to Culloden on a Sunday, where finding their enemies at worship, they shut them up in the church, which they set on fire; and this, said he, is the tune that the piper played while they were burning.

Narrations like this, however uncertain, deserve the notice of a traveller, because they are the only records of a nation that has no historians, and afford the most genuine representation of the life and character of the ancient Highlanders.

Under the denomination of Highlander are comprehended in Scotland all that now speak the Erse language, or retain the primitive manners, whether they live among the mountains or in the islands; and in that sense I use the name, when there is not some apparent reason for making a distinction.

In Sky I first observed the use of brogues, a kind of artless shoes, stitched with thongs so loosely, that though they defend the foot from stones, they do not exclude water. Brogues were formerly made of raw hides, with the hair inwards, and such are perhaps still used in rude and remote parts; but they are said not to last above two days. Where life is somewhat improved, they are now made of leather tanned with oak bark, as in other places, or with the bark of birch, or roots of tormentil, a substance recommended in defect of bark, about forty years ago, to the Irish tanners, by one to whom the parliament of that kingdom voted a reward. The leather of Sky is not completely penetrated by vegetable matter, and therefore cannot be very durable.

My inquiries about brogues, gave me an early specimen of Highland information. One day I was told, that to make brogues was a domestic art, which every man practised for himself, and that a pair of brogues was the work of an hour. I supposed that the husband made brogues as the wife made an apron, till next day it was told me, that a brogue-maker was a trade, and that a pair would cost half a crown. It will easily occur that these representations may both be true, and that, in some places, men may buy them, and in others, make them for themselves; but I had both the accounts in the same house within two days.

Many of my subsequent inquiries upon more interesting topics ended in the like uncertainty. He that travels in the Highlands may easily saturate his soul with intelligence, if he will acquiesce in the first account. The Highlander gives to every question an answer so prompt and peremptory, that scepticism itself is dared into silence, and the mind sinks before the bold reporter in unresisting credulity; but, if a second question be ventured, it breaks the enchantment; for it is immediately discovered, that what was told so confidently was told at hazard, and that such fearlessness of assertion was either the sport of negligence, or the refuge of ignorance.

If individuals are thus at variance with themselves, it can be no wonder that the accounts of different men are contradictory. The traditions of an ignorant and savage people have been for ages negligently heard, and unskilfully related. Distant events must have been mingled together, and the actions of one man given to another. These, however, are deficiencies in story, for which no man is now to be censured. It were enough, if what there is yet opportunity of examining were accurately inspected, and justly represented; but such is the laxity of Highland conversation, that the inquirer is kept in continual suspense, and by a kind of intellectual retrogradation, knows less as he hears more.

In the islands the plaid is rarely worn. The law by which the Highlanders have been obliged to change the form of their dress, has, in all the places that we have visited, been universally obeyed. I have seen only one gentleman completely clothed in the ancient habit, and by him it was worn only occasionally and wantonly. The common people do not think themselves under any legal necessity of having coats; for they say that the law against plaids was made by Lord Hardwicke, and was in force only for his life: but the same poverty that made it then difficult for them to change their clothing, hinders them now from changing it again.

The fillibeg, or lower garment, is still very common, and the bonnet almost universal; but their attire is such as produces, in a sufficient degree, the effect intended by the law, of abolishing the dissimilitude of appearance between the Highlanders and the other inhabitants of Britain; and, if dress be supposed to have much influence, facilitates their coalition with their fellow-subjects.

What we have long used we naturally like, and therefore the Highlanders were unwilling to lay aside their plaid, which yet to an unprejudiced spectator must appear an incommodious and cumbersome dress; for hanging loose upon the body, it must flutter in a quick motion, or require one of the hands to keep it close. The Romans always laid aside the gown when they had any thing to do. It was a dress so unsuitable to war, that the same word which signified a gown signified peace. The chief use of a plaid seems to be this, that they could commodiously wrap themselves in it, when they were obliged to sleep without a better cover.

In our passage from Scotland to Sky, we were wet for the first time with a shower. This was the beginning of the Highland winter, after which we were told that a succession of three dry days was not to be expected for many months. The winter of the Hebrides consists of little more than rain and wind. As they are surrounded by an ocean never frozen, the blasts that come to them over the water are too much softened to have the power of congelation. The salt lochs, or inlets of the sea, which shoot very far into the island, never have any ice upon them, and the pools of fresh water will never bear the walker. The snow that sometimes falls, is soon dissolved by the air, or the rain.

This is not the description of a cruel climate, yet the dark months are here a time of great distress; because the summer can do little more than feed itself, and winter comes with its cold and its scarcity upon families very slenderly provided.

Coriatachan in Sky

The third or fourth day after our arrival at Armidel, brought us an invitation to the isle of Raasay, which lies east of Sky. It is incredible how soon the account of any event is propagated in these narrow countries by the love of talk, which much leisure produces, and the relief given to the mind in the penury of insular conversation by a new topic. The arrival of strangers at a place so rarely visited, excites rumour, and quickens curiosity. I know not whether we touched at any corner, where Fame had not already prepared us a reception.

To gain a commodious passage to Raasay, it was necessary to pass over a large part of Sky. We were furnished therefore with horses and a guide. In the Islands there are no roads, nor any marks by which a stranger may find his way. The horseman has always at his side a native of the place, who, by pursuing game or tending cattle, or being often employed in messages or conduct, has learned where the ridge of the hill has breadth sufficient to allow a horse and his rider a passage, and where the moss or bog is hard enough to bear them. The bogs are avoided as toilsome at least, if not unsafe, and therefore the journey is made generally from precipice to precipice; from which if the eye ventures to look down, it sees below a gloomy cavity, whence the rush of water is sometimes heard.

But there seems to be in all this more alarm than danger. The Highlander walks carefully before, and the horse, accustomed to the ground, follows him with little deviation. Sometimes the hill is too steep for the horseman to keep his seat, and sometimes the moss is too tremulous to bear the double weight of horse and man. The rider then dismounts, and all shift as they can.

Journeys made in this manner are rather tedious than long. A very few miles require several hours. From Armidel we came at night to Coriatachan, a house very pleasantly situated between two brooks, with one of the highest hills of the island behind it. It is the residence of Mr Mackinnon, by whom we were treated with very liberal hospitality, among a more numerous and elegant company than it could have been supposed easy to collect.

The hill behind the house we did not climb. The weather was rough, and the height and steepness discouraged us. We were told that there is a cairn upon it. A cairn is a heap of stones thrown upon the grave of one eminent for dignity of birth, or splendour of achievements. It is said that by digging, an urn is always found under these cairns: they must therefore have been thus piled by a people whose custom was to burn the dead. To pile stones is, I believe, a northern custom, and to burn the body was the Roman practice; nor do I know when it was that these two acts of sepulture were united.

The weather was next day too violent for the continuation of our journey; but we had no reason to complain of the interruption. We saw in every place, what we chiefly desired to know, the manners of the people. We had company, and, if we had chosen retirement, we might have had books.

I never was in any house of the Islands, where I did not find books in more languages than one, if I stayed long enough to want them, except one from which the family was removed. Literature is not neglected by the higher rank of the Hebridians.

It need not, I suppose, be mentioned, that in countries so little frequented as the Islands, there are no houses where travellers are entertained for money. He that wanders about these wilds, either procures recommendations to those whose habitations lie near his way, or, when night and weariness come upon him, takes the chance of general hospitality. If he finds only a cottage, he can expect little more than shelter; for the cottagers have little more for themselves:

but if his good fortune brings him to the residence of a gentleman, he will be glad of a storm to prolong his stay. There is, however, one inn by the sea-side at Sconsor, in Sky, where the post-office is kept.

At the tables where a stranger is received, neither plenty nor delicacy is wanting. A tract of land so thinly inhabited, must have much wildfowl; and I scarcely remember to have seen a dinner without them. The moorgame[11] is everywhere to be had. That the sea abounds with fish, needs not be told, for it supplies a great part of Europe. The Isle of Sky has stags and roebucks, but no hares. They sell very numerous droves of oxen yearly to England, and therefore cannot be supposed to want beef at home. Sheep and goats are in great numbers, and they have the common domestic fowls.

But as here is nothing to be bought, every family must kill its own meat, and roast part of it somewhat sooner than Apicius[12] would prescribe. Every kind of flesh is undoubtedly excelled by the variety and emulation of English markets; but that which is not best may be yet very free from bad, and he that shall complain of his fare in the Hebrides, has improved his delicacy more than his manhood.

Their fowls are not like those plumped for sale by the poulterers of London, but they are as good as other places commonly afford, except that the geese, by feeding in the sea, have universally a fishy rankness.

These geese seem to be of a middle race, between the wild and domestic kinds. They are so tame as to own a home, and so wild as sometimes to fly quite away.

Their native bread is made of oats, or barley. Of oatmeal they spread very thin cakes, coarse and hard, to which unaccustomed palates are not easily reconciled, the barley cakes are thicker and softer; I began to eat them without unwillingness; the blackness of their colour raises some dislike, but the taste is not disagreeable. In most houses there is wheat flour, with which we were sure to be treated, if we stayed long enough to have it kneaded and baked. As neither yeast nor leaven are used among them, their bread of every kind is unfermented. They make only cakes, and never mould a loaf.

A man of the Hebrides, for of the women's diet I can give no account, as soon as he appears in the morning, swallows a glass of whisky; yet they are not a drunken race, at least I never was present at much intemperance; but no man is so abstemious as to refuse the morning dram, which they call a *skalk*.

The word whisky signifies water, and is applied by way of eminence to *strong water*, or distilled liquor. The spirit drunk in the North is drawn from barley. I never tasted it, except once for experiment at the inn in Inverary, when I thought it preferable to any English malt brandy. It was strong, but not pungent, and was free from the empyreumatic[13] taste or smell. What was the process I had no opportunity of inquiring, nor do I wish to improve the art of making poison pleasant.[14]

Not long after the dram, may be expected the breakfast, a meal in which the Scots, whether of the lowlands or mountains, must be confessed to excel us. The tea and coffee are accompanied not only with butter, but with honey, conserves, and marmalades. If an epicure could remove by a wish, in quest of sensual gratifications, wherever he had supped he would breakfast in Scotland.

In the islands however, they do what I found it not very easy to endure. They pollute the tea-table by plates piled with large slices of Cheshire cheese, which mingles its less grateful odours with the fragrance of the tea.

Where many questions are to be asked, some will be omitted. I forgot to inquire how they were supplied with so much exotic luxury. Perhaps the French may bring them wine for wool, and the Dutch give them tea and coffee at the fishing season, in exchange for fresh provision. Their trade is unconstrained; they pay no customs; for there is no officer to demand them, whatever therefore is made dear only by impost, is obtained here at an easy rate.

A dinner in the Western Islands differs very little from a dinner in England, except that in the place of tarts, there are always set different preparations of milk. This part of their diet will admit some improvement. Though they have milk, and eggs, and sugar, few of them know how to compound them in a custard. Their gardens afford them no great variety, but they have always some vegetables on the table. Potatoes at least are never wanting, which, though they have not known them long, are now one of the principal parts of their food. They are not of the mealy, but the viscous kind.

Their more elaborate cookery, or made dishes, an Englishman at the first taste is not likely to approve, but the culinary compositions of every country are often such as become grateful to other nations only by degrees; though I have read a French author, who, in the elation of his heart, says, that French cookery pleases all foreigners, but foreign cookery never satisfies a Frenchman.

Their suppers, are, like their dinners, various and plentiful. The table is always covered with elegant linen. Their plates for common use are often of that kind of manufacture which is called cream coloured, or queen's ware. They use silver on all occasions where it is common in England, nor did I ever find the spoon of horn, but in one house.

The knives are not often either very bright, or very sharp. They are indeed instruments of which the Highlanders have not been long acquainted with the general use. They were not regularly laid on the table, before the prohibition of arms, and the change of dress. Thirty years ago the Highlander wore his knife as a companion to his dirk or dagger, and when the company sat down to meat, the men who had knives, cut the flesh into small pieces for the women, who with their fingers conveyed it to their mouths.

There was perhaps never any change of national manners so quick, so great, and so general, as that which has operated in the Highlands, by the last conquest, and the subsequent laws. We came thither too late to see what we expected, a people of peculiar appearance, and a system of antiquated life. The clans retain little now of their original character, their ferocity of temper is softened, their military ardour is extinguished, their dignity of independence is depressed, their contempt of government subdued, and their reverence for their chiefs abated. Of what they had before the late conquest of their country, there remain only their language and their poverty. Their language is attacked on every side. Schools are erected, in which English only is taught, and there were lately some who thought it reasonable to refuse them a version of the holy scriptures,[15] that they might have no monument of their mother-tongue.

That their poverty is gradually abated, cannot be mentioned among the unpleasing consequences of subjection. They are now acquainted with money, and the possibility of gain will by degrees make them industrious. Such is the effect of the late regulations, that a longer journey than to the Highlands must be taken by him whose curiosity pants for savage virtues and barbarous grandeur.

Raasay

At the first intermission of the stormy weather we were informed, that the boat, which was to convey us to Raasay, attended us on the coast. We had from this time our intelligence facilitated, and our conversation enlarged by the company of Mr Macqueen, minister of a parish in Sky, whose knowledge and politeness give him a title equally to kindness and respect, and who, from this time, never forsook us till we were preparing to leave Sky, and the adjacent places.

The boat was under the direction of Mr Malcolm Macleod, a gentleman of Raasay. The water was calm, and the rowers were vigorous; so that our passage was quick and pleasant. When we came near the island, we saw the laird's house, a neat modern fabric, and found Mr Macleod, the proprietor of the island, with many gentlemen, expecting us on the beach . . .

The number of this little community has never been counted by its ruler, nor have I obtained any positive account, consistent with the result of political computation. Not many years ago, the late Laird led out one hundred men upon a military expedition. The sixth part of a people is supposed capable of bearing arms: Raasay had therefore six hundred inhabitants. But because it is not likely that every man able to serve in the field would follow the summons, or that the chief would leave his lands totally defenceless, or take away all the hands qualified for labour, let it be supposed, that half as many might be permitted to stay at home. The whole number will then be nine hundred, or nine to a square mile; a degree of populousness greater than those tracts of desolation can often show. They are content with their country, and faithful to their chiefs, and yet uninfected with the fever of migration.

Near the house, at Raasay, is a chapel unroofed and ruinous, which has long been used only as a place of burial. About the churches, in the Islands, are small squares inclosed with stone, which belong to particular families, as repositories for the dead. At Raasay, there is one, I think, for the proprietor, and one for some collateral house.

It is told by Martin[16] that at the death of the Lady of the Island, it has been here the custom to erect a cross. This we found not to be true. The stones that stand about the chapel at a small distance, some of which perhaps have crosses cut upon them, are believed to have been not funeral monuments, but the ancient boundaries of the sanctuary or consecrated ground.

Martin was a man not illiterate: he was an inhabitant of Sky, and therefore was within reach of intelligence, and with no great difficulty might have visited the places which he undertakes to describe; yet with all his opportunities, he has often suffered himself to be deceived. He lived in the last century, when the chiefs of the clans had lost little of their original influence. The mountains were yet unpenetrated, no inlet was opened to foreign novelties, and the feudal institutions operated upon life with their full force. He might therefore have displayed a series of subordination and a form of government, which, in more luminous and improved regions, have been long forgotten, and have delighted his readers with many uncouth customs that are now disused, and wild opinions that prevail no longer. But he probably had not knowledge of the world sufficient to qualify him for judging what would deserve or gain the attention of mankind. The mode of life which was familiar to himself, he did not suppose unknown to others, nor imagined that he could give pleasure by telling that of which it was, in his little country, impossible to be ignorant.

What he has neglected cannot now be performed. In nations, where there is hardly the use of letters, what is once out of sight is lost for ever. They think but little, and of their few thoughts, none are wasted on the past, in which they are neither interested by fear nor hope. Their only registers are stated observances and practical representations. For this reason an age of ignorance is an age of ceremony. Pageants, and processions, and commemorations, gradually shrink away, as better methods come into use of recording events, and preserving rights.

It is not only in Raasay that the chapel is unroofed and useless; through the few islands which we visited, we neither saw nor heard of any house of prayer, except in Sky, that was not in ruins. The malignant influence of Calvinism has blasted ceremony and decency together; and if the remembrance of papal superstition is obliterated, the monuments of papal piety are likewise effaced.

It has been, for many years, popular to talk of the lazy devotion of the Romish clergy; over the sleepy laziness of men that erected churches we may indulge our superiority with a new triumph, by comparing it with the fervid activity of those who suffer them to fall.

Of the destruction of churches, the decay of religion must in time be the consequence; for while the public acts of the ministry are now performed in houses, a very small number can be present; and as the greater part of the Islanders make no use of books, all must necessarily live in total ignorance who want the opportunity of vocal instruction.

From these remains of ancient sanctity, which are everywhere to be found, it has been conjectured, that, for the last two centuries, the inhabitants of the Islands have decreased in number. This argument, which supposes that the churches have been suffered to fall, only because they were no longer necessary, would have some force, if the houses of worship still remaining were sufficient for the people. But since they have now no churches at all, these venerable fragments do not prove the people of former times to have been more numerous, but to have been more devout. If the inhabitants were doubled with their present principles, it appears not that any provision for public worship would be made. Where the religion of a country enforces consecrated buildings, the number of those buildings may be supposed to afford some indication, however uncertain, of the populousness of the place; but where by a change of manners a nation is contented to live without them, their decay implies no diminution of inhabitants.

Some of these dilapidations are said to be found in islands now uninhabited; but I doubt whether we can thence infer that they were ever peopled. The religion of the middle age, is well known to have placed too much hope in lonely austerities. Voluntary solitude was the great art of propitiation, by which crimes were effaced, and conscience was appeased; it is therefore not unlikely, that oratories were often built in places where retirement was sure to have no disturbance.

Raasay has little that can detain a traveller, except the Laird and his family; but their power wants no auxiliaries. Such a seat of hospitality, amidst the winds and waters, fills the imagination with a delightful contrariety of images. Without is the rough ocean and the rocky land, the beating billows and the howling storm; within is plenty and elegance, beauty and gaiety, the song and the dance. In Raasay, if I could have found an Ulysses, I had fancied a Phœacia.[17]

Dunvegan

At Raasay, by good fortune, Macleod, so the chief of the clan is called, was paying a visit, and by him we were invited to his seat at Dunvegan. Raasay has a stout boat, built in Norway, in which, with six oars, he conveyed us back to Sky. We landed at Port Re, so called, because James the Fifth of Scotland, who had curiosity to visit the Islands, came into it. The port is made by an inlet of the sea, deep and narrow, where a ship lay waiting to dispeople Sky, by carrying the natives away to America.

In coasting Sky, we passed by the cavern in which it was the custom, as Martin relates, to catch birds in the night, by making a fire at the entrance. This practice is disused; for the birds, as is known often to happen, have changed their haunts.

Here we dined at a public house, I believe the only inn of the island, and having mounted our horses, travelled in the manner already described, till we came to Kingsborough, a place distinguished by that name, because the King lodged here when he landed at Port Re. We were entertained with the usual hospitality by Mr Macdonald and his lady, Flora Macdonald,[18] a name that will be mentioned in history, and if courage and fidelity be virtues, mentioned with honour. She is a woman of middle stature, soft features, gentle manners, and elegant presence.

In the morning we sent our horses round a promontory to meet us, and spared ourselves part of the day's fatigue, by crossing an arm of the sea. We had at last some difficulty in coming to Dunvegan; for our way led over an extensive moor, where every step was to be taken with caution, and we were often obliged to alight, because the ground could not be trusted. In travelling this watery flat, I perceived that it had a visible declivity, and might without much expense or difficulty be drained. But difficulty and expense are relative terms, which have different meanings in different places.

To Dunvegan we came, very willing to be at rest, and found our fatigue amply recompensed by our reception. Lady Macleod, who had lived many years in England, was newly come hither with her son and four daughters, who knew all the arts of southern elegance, and all the modes of English economy. Here therefore we settled, and did not spoil the present hour with thoughts of departure.

Dunvegan is a rocky prominence, that juts out into a bay, on the west side of Sky. The house, which is the principal seat of Macleod, is partly old and partly modern; it is built upon the rock, and looks upon the water. It forms two sides of a small square; on the third side is the skeleton of a castle of unknown antiquity, supposed to have been a Norwegian fortress, when the Danes were masters of the Islands. It is so nearly entire, that it might have easily been made habitable, were there not an ominous tradition in the family, that the owner shall not long outlive the reparation. The grandfather of the present Laird, in defiance of prediction, began the work, but desisted in a little time, and applied his money to worse uses.

As the inhabitants of the Hebrides lived, for many ages, in continual expectation of hostilities, the chief of every clan resided in a fortress.

This house was accessible only from the water, till the last possessor opened an entrance by stairs upon the land.

They had formerly reason to be afraid, not only of declared wars and authorized invaders, or of roving pirates, which, in the northern seas, must have been very common; but of inroads and insults from rival clans, who, in the plenitude of feudal independence, asked no leave of their Sovereign to make war on one another. Sky has been ravaged by a feud between the two mighty powers of Macdonald and Macleod. Macdonald having married a Macleod, upon some discontent dismissed her, perhaps because she had brought him no children. Before the reign of James the Fifth, a Highland Laird made a trial of his wife for a certain time, and if she did not please him, he was then at liberty to send her away. This however must always have offended, and Macleod resenting the injury, whatever were its circumstances, declared, that the wedding had been solemnized without a bonfire, but that the separation should be better illuminated; and raising a little army, set fire to the territories of Macdonald, who returned the visit, and prevailed.

Another story may show the disorderly state of insular neighbourhood. The inhabitants of the Isle of Egg, meeting a boat manned by Macleods, tied the crew hand and foot, and set them adrift. Macleod landed upon Egg and demanded the offenders; but the inhabitants refusing to surrender them, retreated to a cavern, into which they thought their enemies unlikely to follow them. Macleod choked them with smoke, and left them lying dead by families as they stood.

Here the violence of the weather confined us for some time, not at all to our discontent or inconvenience. We would indeed very willingly have visited the Islands, which might be seen from the house scattered in the sea, and I was particularly desirous to have viewed Isay; but the storms did not permit us to launch a boat, and we were condemned to listen in idleness to the wind, except when we were better engaged by listening to the ladies.

We had here more wind than waves, and suffered the severity of a tempest, without enjoying its magnificence. The sea being broken by the multitude of islands, does not roar with so much noise, nor beat the shore with such foamy violence, as I have remarked on the coast of Sussex. Though, while I was in the Hebrides, the wind was extremely turbulent, I never saw very high billows.

The country about Dunvegan is rough and barren. There are no trees, except in the orchard, which is a low sheltered spot surrounded with a wall.

When this house was intended to sustain a siege, a well was made in the court, by boring the rock downwards, till water was found, which though so near to the sea, I have not heard mentioned as brackish, though it has some hardness, or other qualities, which make it less fit for use; and the family is now better supplied from a stream, which runs by the rock, from two pleasing water-falls.

Here we saw some traces of former manners, and heard some standing traditions.[19] In the house is kept an ox's horn, hollowed so as to hold perhaps two quarts, which the heir of Macleod was expected to swallow at one draught, as a test of his manhood, before he was permitted to bear arms, or could claim a seat among the men. It is held that the return of the Laird to Dunvegan, after any considerable absence, produces a plentiful capture of herrings; and that, if any woman crosses the water to the opposite Island, the herrings will desert the coast. Boetius tells the same of some other place. This tradition is not uniform. Some hold that no woman may pass, and others that none may pass but a Macleod.

Among other guests, which the hospitality of Dunvegan brought to the table, a visit was paid by the Laird and Lady of a small island south of Sky, of which the proper name is Muack, which signifies swine. It is commonly called Muck, which the proprietor not liking, has endeavoured, without effect, to change to Monk. It is usual to call gentlemen in Scotland by the name of their possessions, as Raasay, Bernera, Loch Buy, a practice necessary in countries inhabited by clans, where all that live in the same territory have one name, and must be therefore discriminated by some addition. This gentleman, whose name, I think, is Maclean, should be regularly called Muck; but the appellation, which he thinks too coarse for his Island, he would like still less for himself, and he is therefore addressed by the title of, Isle of Muck.

This little island, however it be named, is of considerable value. It is two English miles long, and three quarters of a mile broad, and consequently contains only nine hundred and sixty English acres. It is chiefly arable. Half of this little dominion the Laird retains in his own hand, and on the other half, live one hundred and sixty persons, who pay their rent by exported corn. What rent they pay, we were not told, and could not decently inquire. The proportion of the people to the land is such, as the most fertile countries do not commonly maintain.

The Laird having all his people under his immediate view, seems to be very attentive to their happiness. The devastation of the small-pox, when it visits places where it comes seldom, is well known. He has disarmed it of its terror at Muack, by inoculating eighty of his people. The expense was two shillings and sixpence a head. Many trades they cannot have among them, but upon occasion, he fetches a smith from the Isle of Egg, and has a tailor from the main land, six times a year. This island well deserved to be seen, but the Laird's absence left us no opportunity.

Every inhabited island has its appendant and subordinate islets. Muck, however small, has yet others smaller about it, one of which has only ground sufficient to afford pasture for three wethers.

At Dunvegan I had tasted lotus,[20] and was in danger of forgetting that I was ever to depart, till Mr Boswell sagely reproached me with my sluggishness and softness. I had no very forcible defence to make; and we agreed to pursue our journey. Macleod accompanied us to Ulinish, where we were entertained by the sheriff of the island . . .

Talisker in Sky

From Ulinish, our next stage was to Talisker, the house of Colonel Macleod, an officer in the Dutch service, who, in this time of universal peace, has for several years been permitted to be absent from his regiment. Having been bred to physic, he is consequently a scholar, and his lady, by accompanying him in his different places of residence, is become skilful in several languages. Talisker is the place beyond all that I have seen, from which the gay and the jovial seem utterly excluded; and where the hermit might expect to grow old in meditation, without possibility of disturbance or interruption. It is situated very near the sea, but upon a coast where no vessel lands but when it is driven by a tempest on the rocks. Towards the land are lofty hills streaming with water-falls. The garden is sheltered by firs or pines, which grow there so prosperously, that some, which the present inhabitant planted, are very high and thick.

At this place we very happily met Mr Donald Maclean, a young gentleman, the eldest son of the Laird of Col, heir to a very great extent of land, and so desirous of improving his inheritance, that he spent a considerable time among the farmers of Hertfordshire, and Hampshire, to learn their practice. He worked with his own hands at the principal operations of agriculture, that he might not deceive himself by a false opinion of skill, which, if he should find it deficient at home, he had no means of completing. If the world has agreed to praise the travels and manual labours of the Czar of Muscovy,[21] let Col have his share of the like applause, in the proportion of his dominions to the empire of Russia.

This young gentleman was sporting in the mountains of Sky, and when he was weary with following his game, repaired for lodging to Talisker. At night he missed one of his dogs, and when he went to seek him in the morning, found two eagles feeding on his carcass.

Col, for he must be named by his possessions, hearing that our intention was to visit Iona, offered to conduct us to his chief, Sir Allan Maclean, who lived in the isle of Inch Kenneth, and would readily find us a convenient passage. From this time was formed an acquaintance, which being begun by kindness, was accidentally continued by constraint; we derived much pleasure from it, and I hope have given him no reason to repent it.

The weather was now almost one continued storm, and we were to snatch some happy intermission to be conveyed to Mull, the third island of the Hebrides, lying about a degree south of Sky, whence we might easily find our way to Inch Kenneth, where Sir Allan Maclean resided, and afterward to Iona.

For this purpose, the most commodious station that we could take was Armidel, which Sir Alexander Macdonald had now left to a gentleman, who lived there as his factor or steward.

In our way to Armidel was Coriatachan, where we had already been, and to which therefore we were very willing to return. We stayed however so long at Talisker, that a great part of our journey was performed in the gloom of the evening. In travelling even thus almost without light thro' naked solitude, when there is a guide whose conduct may be trusted, a mind not naturally too much disposed to fear, may preserve some degree of cheerfulness; but what must be the solicitude of him who should be wandering, among the crags and hollows, benighted, ignorant and alone?

The fictions of the Gothic romances were not so remote from credibility as they are now thought. In the full prevalence of the feudal institution, when violence desolated the world, and every baron lived in a fortress, forests and castles were regularly succeeded by each other, and the adventurer might very suddenly pass from the gloom of woods, or the ruggedness of moors, to seats of plenty, gaiety, and magnificence. Whatever is imagined in the wildest tale, if giants, dragons and enchantment be excepted, would be felt by him, who, wandering in the mountains without a guide, or upon the sea without a pilot, should be carried amidst his terror and uncertainty, to the hospitality and elegance of Raasay or Dunvegan.

To Coriatachan at last we came, and found ourselves welcomed as before. Here we stayed two days, and made such inquiries as curiosity suggested. The house was filled with company, among whom Mr Macpherson and his sister distinguished themselves by their politeness and accomplishments. By him we were invited to Ostig, a house not far from Armidel, where we might easily hear of a boat, when the weather would suffer us to leave the Island.

Ostig in Sky

At Ostig, of which Mr Macpherson is minister, we were entertained for some days, then removed to Armidel, where we finished our observations on the island of Sky.

As this Island lies in the fifty-seventh degree, the air cannot be supposed to have much warmth. The long continuance of the sun above the horizon, does indeed sometimes produce great heat in northern latitudes; but this can only happen in sheltered places, where the atmosphere is to a certain degree stagnant, and the same mass of air continues to receive for many hours the rays of the sun, and the vapours of the earth. Sky lies open on the west and north to a vast extent of ocean, and is cooled in the summer by perpetual ventilation, but by the same blasts is kept warm in winter. Their weather is not pleasing. Half the year is deluged with rain. From the autumnal to the vernal equinox, a dry day is hardly known, except when the showers are suspended by a tempest. Under such skies can be expected no great exuberance of vegetation. Their winter overtakes their summer, and their harvest lies upon the ground drenched with rain. The autumn struggles hard to produce some of our early fruits. I gathered gooseberries in September; but they were small, and the husk was thick.

Their winter is seldom such as puts a full stop to the growth of plants, or reduces the cattle to live wholly on the surplusage of the summer. In the year Seventy-one they had a severe season, remembered by the name of the Black Spring, from which the island has not yet recovered. The snow lay long upon the ground, a calamity hardly known before. Part of their cattle died for want, part were unseasonably sold to buy sustenance for the owners; and, what I have not read or heard of before, the kine that survived were so emaciated and dispirited, that they did not require the male at the usual time. Many of the roebucks perished.

The soil, as in other countries, has its diversities. In some parts there is only a thin layer of earth spread upon a rock, which bears nothing but short brown heath, and perhaps is not generally capable of any better product. There are many bogs or mosses of greater or less extent, where the soil cannot be supposed to want depth, though it is too wet for the plough. But we did not observe in these any aquatic plants. The valleys and the mountains are alike darkened with heath. Some grass, however, grows here and there, and some happier spots of earth are capable of tillage.

Their agriculture is laborious, and perhaps rather feeble than unskilful. Their chief manure is sea-weed, which, when they lay it to rot upon the field, gives them a better crop than those of the Highlands.[22] They heap sea shells upon the dunghill, which in time moulder into a fertilizing substance. When they find a vein of earth where they cannot use it, they dig it up, and add it to the mould of a more commodious place.

Their corn grounds often lie in such intricacies among the crags, that there is no room for the action of a team and plough. The soil is then turned up by manual labour, with an instrument called a crooked spade,[23] of a form and weight which to me appeared very incommodious, and would perhaps be soon improved in a country where workmen could be easily found and easily paid. It has a narrow blade of iron fixed to a long and heavy piece of wood, which must have, about a foot and a half above the iron, a knee or flexure with the angle downwards. When the farmer encounters a stone which is the great impediment of his operations, he drives the blade under it, and bringing the knee or angle to the ground, has in the long handle a very forcible lever.

According to the different mode of tillage, farms are distinguished into *long land* and *short land*. Long land is that which affords room for a plough, and short land is turned up by the spade.

The grain which they commit to the furrows thus tediously formed, is either oats or barley. They do not sow barley without very copious manure, and then they expect from it ten for one, an increase equal to that of better countries; but the culture is so operose that they content themselves commonly with oats; and who can relate without compassion, that after all their diligence they are to expect only a triple increase? It is in vain to hope for plenty, when a third part of the harvest must be reserved for seed.

When their grain is arrived at the state which they must consider as ripeness, they do not cut, but pull the barley: to the oats they apply the sickle. Wheel carriages they have none, but make a frame of timber, which is drawn by one horse with the two points behind pressing on the ground. On this they sometimes drag home their sheaves, but often convey them home in a kind of open panier, or frame of sticks upon the horse's back.

Of that which is obtained with so much difficulty, nothing surely ought to be wasted; yet their method of clearing their oats from the husk is by parching them in the straw. Thus with the genuine improvidence of savages, they destroy that fodder for want of which their cattle may perish. From this practice they have two petty conveniences. They dry the grain so that it is easily reduced to meal, and they escape the theft of the thresher. The taste contracted from the fire by the oats, as by every other scorched substance, use must long ago have made grateful. The oats that are not parched must be dried in a kiln.

The barns of Sky I never saw. That which Macleod of Raasay had erected near his house was so contrived, because the harvest is seldom brought home dry, as by perpetual perflation[24] to prevent the mow from heating.

Of the gardens I can judge only from their tables. I did not observe that the common greens were wanting, and suppose, that by choosing an advantageous exposition, they can raise all the more hardy esculent plants. Of vegetable fragrance or beauty they are not yet studious. Few vows are made to Flora in the Hebrides.

They gather a little hay, but the grass is mown late; and is so often almost dry and again very wet, before it is housed, that it becomes a collection of withered stalks without taste or fragrance; it must be eaten by cattle that have nothing else, but by most English farmers would be thrown away.

In the Islands I have not heard that any subterraneous treasures have been discovered, though where there are mountains, there are commonly minerals. One of the rocks in Col has a black vein, imagined to consist of the ore of lead; but it was never yet opened or essayed. In

Sky a black mass was accidentally picked up, and brought into the house of the owner of the land, who found himself strongly inclined to think it a coal, but unhappily it did not burn in the chimney. Common ores would be here of no great value; for what requires to be separated by fire, must if it were found, be carried away in its mineral state, here being no fuel for the smelting-house or forge. Perhaps by diligent search in this world of stone, some valuable species of marble might be discovered. But neither philosophical curiosity, nor commercial industry, have yet fixed their abode here, where the importunity of immediate want supplied but for the day, and craving on the morrow, has left little room for excursive knowledge or the pleasing fancies of distant profit.

They have lately found a manufacture considerably lucrative. Their rocks abound with kelp, a sea-plant, of which the ashes are melted into glass. They burn kelp in great quantities, and then send it away in ships, which come regularly to purchase them. This new source of riches has raised the rents of many maritime farms; but the tenants pay, like all other tenants, the additional rent with great unwillingness; because they consider the profits of the kelp as the mere product of personal labour, to which the landlord contributes nothing. However, as any man may be said to give, what he gives the power of gaining, he has certainly as much right to profit from the price of kelp as of any thing else found or raised upon his ground.

This new trade has excited a long and eager litigation between Macdonald and Macleod, for a ledge of rocks, which, till the value of kelp was known, neither of them desired the reputation of possessing.

The cattle of Sky are not so small as is commonly believed. Since they have sent their beeves in great numbers to southern marts, they have probably taken more care of their breed. At stated times the annual growth of cattle is driven to a fair, by a general drover, and with the money, which he returns to the farmer, the rents are paid.

The price regularly expected, is from two to three pounds a head: there was once one sold for five pounds. They go from the Islands very lean, and are not offered to the butcher, till they have been long fatted in English pastures.

Of their black cattle, some are without horns, called by the Scots *humble* cows, as we call a bee an *humble* bee, that wants a sting. Whether this difference be specific, or accidental, though we inquired with great diligence, we could not be informed. We are not very sure that the bull is ever without horns, though we have been told, that such bulls there are. What is produced by putting a horned and unhorned male and female together, no man has ever tried, that thought the result worthy of observation.

Their horses are, like their cows, of a moderate size. I had no difficulty to mount myself commodiously by the favour of the gentlemen. I heard of very little cows in Barra, and very little horses in Rum, where perhaps no care is taken to prevent that diminution of size, which must always happen, where the greater and the less copulate promiscuously, and the young animal is restrained from growth by penury of sustenance.

The goat is the general inhabitant of the earth, complying with every difference of climate, and of soil. The goats of the Hebrides are like others: nor did I hear any thing of their sheep, to be particularly remarked.

In the penury of these malignant[25] regions, nothing is left that can be converted to food. The goats and the sheep are milked like the cows. A single meal[26] of a goat is a quart, and of a sheep a pint. Such at least was the account, which I could extract from those of whom I am not sure that they ever had inquired.

The milk of goats is much thinner than that of cows, and that of sheep is much thicker. Sheep's milk is never eaten before it is boiled: as it is thick, it must be very liberal of curd, and the people of St Kilda form it into small cheeses.

The stags of the mountains are less than those of our parks, or forests, perhaps not bigger than our fallow deer. Their flesh has no rankness, nor is inferior in flavour to our common venison. The roebuck I neither saw nor tasted. These are not countries for a regular chase. The deer are not driven with horns and hounds. A sportsman, with his gun in his hand, watches the animal, and when he has wounded him, traces him by the blood.

They have a race of brinded greyhounds, larger and stronger than those with which we course hares, and those are the only dogs used by them for the chase.

Man is by the use of fire-arms made so much an overmatch for other animals, that in all countries, where they are in use, the wild part of the creation sensibly diminishes. There will probably not be long, either stags or roebucks in the Islands. All the beasts of chase would have been lost long ago in countries well inhabited, had they not been preserved by laws for the pleasure of the rich.

There are in Sky neither rats nor mice, but the weasel is so frequent, that he is heard in houses rattling behind chests or beds, as rats in England. They probably owe to his predominance that they have no other vermin; for since the great rat took possession of this part of the world, scarce a ship can touch at any port, but some of his race are left behind. They have within these few years begun to infest the isle of Col, where being left by some trading vessel, they have increased for want of weasels to oppose them.

The inhabitants of Sky, and of the other Islands, which I have seen, are commonly of the middle stature, with fewer among them very tall or very short, than are seen in England, or perhaps, as their numbers are small, the chances of any deviation from the common measure are necessarily few. The tallest men that I saw are among those of higher rank. In regions of barrenness and scarcity, the human race is hindered in its growth by the same causes as other animals.

The ladies have as much beauty here as in other places, but bloom and softness are not to be expected among the lower classes, whose faces are exposed to the rudeness of the climate, and whose features are sometimes contracted by want, and sometimes hardened by the blasts. Supreme beauty is seldom found in cottages or work-shops, even where no real hardships are suffered. To expand the human face to its full perfection, it seems necessary that the mind should cooperate by placidness of content, or consciousness of superiority.

Their strength is proportionate to their size, but they are accustomed to run upon rough ground, and therefore can with great agility skip over the bog, or clamber the mountain. For a campaign in the wastes of America, soldiers better qualified could not have been found. Having little work to do, they are not willing, nor perhaps able to endure a long continuance of manual labour, and are therefore considered as habitually idle.

Having never been supplied with these accommodations, which life extensively diversified with trades affords, they supply their wants by very insufficient shifts, and endure many inconveniences, which a little attention would easily relieve. I have seen a horse carrying home the harvest on a crate. Under his tail was a stick for a crupper, held at the two ends by twists of straw. Hemp will grow in their islands, and therefore ropes may be had. If they wanted hemp, they might make better cordage of rushes, or perhaps of nettles, than of straw.

Their method of life neither secures them perpetual health, nor exposes them to any particular diseases. There are physicians in the Islands, who, I believe, all practice chirurgery,[27] and all compound their own medicines.

It is generally supposed, that life is longer in places where there are few opportunities of luxury; but I found no instance here of extraordinary longevity. A cottager grows old over his oaten cakes, like a citizen at a turtle feast. He is indeed seldom incommoded by corpulence. Poverty preserves him from sinking under the burden of himself, but he escapes no other injury of time. Instances of long life are often related, which those who hear them are more willing to credit than examine. To be told that any man has attained a hundred years, gives hope and comfort to him who stands trembling on the brink of his own climacteric.[28]

Length of life is distributed impartially to very different modes of life in very different climates; and the mountains have no greater examples of age and health than the low lands, where I was introduced to two ladies of high quality; one of whom, in her ninety-fourth year, presided at her table with the full exercise of all her powers; and the other has attained her eighty-fourth, without any diminution of her vivacity, and with little reason to accuse time of depredations on her beauty.

In the Islands, as in most other places, the inhabitants are of different rank, and one does not encroach here upon another. Where there is no commerce nor manufacture, he that is born poor can scarcely become rich; and if none are able to buy estates, he that is born to land cannot annihilate his family by selling it. This was once the state of these countries. Perhaps there is no example, till within a century and half, of any family whose estate was alienated otherwise than by violence or forfeiture. Since money has been brought amongst them, they have found, like others, the art of spending more than they receive; and I saw with grief the chief of a very ancient clan, whose Island was condemned by law to be sold for the satisfaction of his creditors.

The name of highest dignity is Laird, of which there are in the extensive Isle of Sky only three, Macdonald, Macleod, and Mackinnon. The Laird is the original owner of the land, whose natural power must be very great, where no man lives but by agriculture; and where the produce of the land is not conveyed through the labyrinths of traffic, but passes directly from the hand that gathers it to the mouth that eats it. The Laird has all those in his power that live upon his farms. Kings can, for the most part, only exalt or degrade. The Laird at pleasure can feed or starve, can give bread, or withhold it. This inherent power was yet strengthened by the kindness of consanguinity, and the reverence of patriarchal authority. The Laird was the father of the Clan, and his tenants commonly bore his name. And to these principles of original command was added, for many ages, an exclusive right of legal jurisdiction.

This multifarious, and extensive obligation operated with force scarcely credible. Every duty, moral or political, was absorbed in affection and adherence to the Chief. Not many years have passed since the clans knew no law but the Laird's will. He told them to whom they should be friends or enemies, what King they should obey, and what religion they should profess.

When the Scots first rose in arms against the succession of the house of Hanover, Lovat, the Chief of the Frasers, was in exile for a rape. The Frasers were very numerous, and very zealous against the government. A pardon was sent to Lovat. He came to the English camp, and the clan immediately deserted to him.

Next in dignity to the Laird is the Tacksman; a large taker or lease-holder of land, of which he keeps part, as a domain, in his own hand, and lets part to under tenants. The Tacksman is necessarily a man capable of securing to the Laird the whole rent, and is commonly a collateral relation. These *tacks*, or subordinate possessions, were long considered as hereditary, and the occupant was distinguished by the name of the place at which he resided. He held a middle station, by which the highest and the lowest orders were connected. He paid rent and reverence to the Laird, and received them from the tenants. This tenure still subsists, with its original operation, but not with the primitive stability. Since the islanders, no longer content to live, have learned the desire of growing rich, an ancient dependent is in danger of giving way to a higher bidder, at the expense of domestic dignity and hereditary power. The stranger, whose money buys him prefer-ence, considers himself as paying for all that he has, and is indifferent about the Laird's honour or safety. The commodiousness of money is indeed great; but there are some advantages which money cannot buy, and which therefore no wise man will by the love of money be tempted to forgo.

I have found in the hither parts of Scotland, men not defective in judgement or general experience, who consider the Tacksman as a useless burden of the ground, as a drone who lives upon the product of an estate, without the right of property, or the merit of labour, and who impoverishes at once the landlord and the tenant. The land, say they, is let to the Tacksman at six-pence an acre, and by him to the tenant at ten-pence. Let the owner be the immediate landlord to all the tenants; if he sets the ground at eight-pence, he will increase his revenue by a fourth part, and the tenant's burthen will be diminished by a fifth.

Those who pursue this train of reasoning, seem not sufficiently to inquire whither it will lead them, nor to know that it will equally show the propriety of suppressing all wholesale trade, of shutting up the shops of every man who sells what he does not make, and of extruding all whose agency and profit intervene between the manu-facturer and the consumer. They may, by stretching their understandings a little wider, comprehend, that all those who by undertaking large quantities of manufacture, and affording employment to many labourers, make themselves considered as benefactors to the public, have only been robbing their workmen with one hand, and their customers with the other. If Crowley had sold only what he could make, and all his smiths had wrought their own iron with their own hammers, he would have lived on less, and they would have sold their work for more. The salaries of superintendents and clerks would have been partly saved, and partly shared, and nails been sometimes cheaper by a farthing in a hundred. But then if the smith could not have found an immediate purchaser, he must have deserted his anvil; if there had by accident at any time been more sellers than buyers, the workmen must have reduced their profit to nothing, by underselling one another; and as no great stock could have been in any hand, no sudden demand of large quantities could have been answered, and the builder must have stood still till the nailer could supply him.

According to these schemes, universal plenty is to begin and end in universal misery. Hope and emulation will be utterly extinguished; and as all must obey the call of immediate necessity, nothing that requires extensive views, or provides for distant consequences, will ever be performed.

To the southern inhabitants of Scotland, the state of the mountains and the islands is equally unknown with that of Borneo or Sumatra: of both they have only heard a little, and guess the rest. They are strangers to the language and the manners, to the advantages and wants of the people, whose life they would model, and whose evils they would remedy.

Nothing is less difficult than to procure one convenience by the forfeiture of another. A soldier may expedite his march by throwing away his arms. To banish the Tacksman is easy, to make a country plentiful by diminishing the people, is an expeditious mode of husbandry; but that abundance, which there is nobody to enjoy, contributes little to human happiness.

As the mind must govern the hands, so in every society the man of intelligence must direct the man of labour. If the Tacksmen be taken away, the Hebrides must in their present state be given up to grossness and ignorance; the tenant, for want of instruction, will be unskilful, and for want of admonition will be negligent. The Laird in these wide estates, which often consist of islands remote from one another, cannot extend his personal influence to all his tenants; and the steward having no dignity annexed to his character, can have little authority among men taught to pay reverence only to birth, and who regard the Tacksman as their hereditary superior; nor can the steward have equal zeal for the prosperity of an estate profitable only to the Laird, with the Tacksman, who has the Laird's income involved in his own.

The only gentlemen in the Islands are the Lairds, the Tacksmen, and the Ministers, who frequently improve their livings by becoming farmers. If the Tacksmen be banished, who will be left to impart knowledge, or impress civility? The Laird must always be at a distance from the greater part of his lands; and if he resides at all upon them, must drag his days in solitude, having no longer either a friend or a companion; he will therefore depart to some more comfortable residence, and leave the tenants to the wisdom and mercy of a factor.

Of tenants there are different orders, as they have greater or less stock. Land is sometimes leased to a small fellowship, who live in a cluster of huts, called a Tenants Town, and are bound jointly and separately for the payment of their rent. These, I believe, employ in the care of their cattle, and the labour of tillage, a kind of tenants yet lower; who having a hut, with grass for a certain number of cows and sheep, pay their rent by a stipulated quantity of labour.

The condition of domestic servants, or the price of occasional labour, I do not know with certainty. I was told that the maids have sheep, and are allowed to spin for their own clothing; perhaps they have no pecuniary wages, or none but in very wealthy families. The state of life, which has hitherto been purely pastoral, begins now to be a little variegated with commerce; but novelties enter by degrees, and till one mode has fully prevailed over the other, no settled notion can be formed.

Such is the system of insular subordination, which, having little variety, cannot afford much delight in the view, nor long detain the mind in contemplation. The inhabitants were for a long time perhaps not unhappy; but their content was a muddy mixture of pride and ignorance, an indifference for pleasures which they did not know, a blind veneration for their chiefs, and a strong conviction of their own importance.

Their pride has been crushed by the heavy hand of a vindictive conqueror, whose severities have been followed by laws, which, though they cannot be called cruel, have produced much discontent, because they operate upon the surface of life, and make every eye bear witness to subjection. To be compelled to a new dress has always been found painful.

Their Chiefs being now deprived of their jurisdiction, have already lost much of their influence; and as they gradually degenerate from patriarchal rulers to rapacious landlords, they will divest themselves of the little that remains.

That dignity which they derived from an opinion of their military importance, the law, which disarmed them, has abated. An old gentleman, delighting himself with the recollection of better days, related, that forty years ago, a Chieftain walked out attended by ten or twelve followers, with their arms rattling. That animating rabble has now ceased. The Chief has lost his formidable retinue; and the Highlander walks his heath unarmed and defenceless, with the peaceable submission of a French peasant or English cottager.

Their ignorance grows every day less, but their knowledge is yet of little other use than to show them their wants. They are now in the period of education, and feel the uneasiness of discipline, without yet perceiving the benefit of instruction.

The last law, by which the Highlanders are deprived of their arms, has operated with efficacy beyond expectation. Of former statutes made with the same design, the execution had been feeble, and the effect inconsiderable. Concealment was undoubtedly practised, and perhaps often with connivance. There was tenderness, or partiality, on one side, and obstinacy on the other. But the law, which followed the victory of Culloden, found the whole nation dejected and intimidated; informations were given without danger, and without fear, and the arms were collected with such rigour, that every house was despoiled of its defence.

To disarm part of the Highlands, could give no reasonable occasion of complaint. Every government must be allowed the power of taking away the weapon that is lifted against it. But the loyal clans murmured with some appearance of justice, that after having defended the King, they were forbidden for the future to defend themselves; and that the sword should be forfeited, which had been legally employed. Their case is undoubtedly hard, but in political regulations, good cannot be complete, it can only be predominant.

Whether by disarming a people thus broken into several tribes, and thus remote from the seat of power, more good than evil has been produced, may deserve inquiry. The supreme power in every community has the right of debarring every individual, and every subordinate society from self-defence, only because the supreme power is able to defend them; and therefore where the governor cannot act, he must trust the subject to act for himself. These Islands might be wasted with fire and sword before their sovereign would know their distress. A gang of robbers, such as has been lately found confederating themselves in the Highlands, might lay a wide region under contribution. The crew of a petty privateer might land on the largest and most wealthy of the Islands, and riot without control in cruelty and waste. It was observed by one of the Chiefs of Sky, that fifty armed men might, without resistance, ravage the country. Laws that place the subjects in such a state, contravene the first principles of the compact of authority: they exact obedience, and yield no protection.

It affords a generous and manly pleasure to conceive a little nation gathering its fruits and tending its herds with fearless confidence, though it lies open on every side to invasion, where, in contempt of walls and trenches, every man sleeps securely with his sword beside him; where all on the first approach of hostility come together at the call to battle, as at a summons to a festal show; and committing their cattle to the care of those whom age or nature has disabled, engage the enemy with that competition for hazard and for glory, which operates in men that fight under the eye of those, whose dislike or kindness they have always considered as the greatest evil or the greatest good.

This was, in the beginning of the present century, the state of the Highlands. Every man was a soldier, who partook of national confidence, and interested himself in national honour. To lose this spirit, is to lose what no small advantage will compensate.

It may likewise deserve to be inquired, whether a great nation ought to be totally commercial? whether amidst the uncertainty of human affairs, too much attention to one mode of happiness may not endanger others? whether the pride of riches must not sometimes have recourse to the protection of courage? and whether, if it be necessary to preserve in some part of the empire the military spirit, it can subsist more commodiously in any place, than in remote and unprofitable provinces, where it can commonly do little harm, and whence it may be called forth at any sudden exigence?

It must however be confessed, that a man, who places honour only in successful violence, is a very troublesome and pernicious animal in time of peace; and that the martial character cannot prevail in a whole people, but by the diminution of all other virtues. He that is accustomed to resolve all right into conquest, will have very little tenderness or equity. All the friendship in such a life can be only a confederacy of invasion, or alliance of defence. The strong must flourish by force, and the weak subsist by stratagem.

Till the Highlanders lost their ferocity, with their arms, they suffered from each other all that malignity could dictate, or precipitance could act. Every provocation was revenged with blood, and no man that ventured into a numerous company, by whatever occasion brought together, was sure of returning without a wound. If they are now exposed to foreign hostilities, they may talk of the danger, but can seldom feel it. If they are no longer martial, they are no longer quarrelsome. Misery is caused for the most part, not by a heavy crush of disaster, but by the corrosion of less visible evils, which canker enjoyment, and undermine security. The visit of an invader is necessarily rare, but domestic animosities allow no cessation.

The abolition of the local jurisdictions, which had for so many ages been exercised by the chiefs, has likewise its evil and its good. The feudal constitution naturally diffused itself into long ramifications of subordinate authority. To this general temper of the government was added the peculiar form of the country, broken by mountains into many subdivisions scarcely accessible but to the natives, and guarded by passes, or perplexed with intricacies, through which national justice could not find its way.

The power of deciding controversies, and of punishing offences, as some such power there must always be, was intrusted to the Lairds of the country, to those whom the people considered as their natural judges. It cannot be supposed that a rugged proprietor of the rocks, unprincipled and unenlightened, was a nice resolver of entangled claims, or very exact in proportioning punishment to offences. But the more he indulged his own will, the more he held his vassals in dependence. Prudence and innocence, without the favour of the Chief, conferred no security; and crimes involved no danger, when the judge was resolute to acquit.

When the chiefs were men of knowledge and virtue, the convenience of a domestic judicature was great. No long journeys were necessary, nor artificial delays could be practised; the character, the alliances, and interests of the litigants were known to the court, and all false pretences were easily detected. The sentence, when it was passed, could not be evaded; the power of the Laird superseded formalities, and justice could not be defeated by interest or stratagem.

I doubt not but that since the regular judges have made their circuits through the whole country, right has been every where more wisely, and more equally distributed; the complaint is, that litigation is grown troublesome, and that the magistrates are too few, and therefore often too remote for general convenience.

Many of the smaller Islands have no legal officer within them. I once asked, If a crime should be committed, by what authority the offender could be seized? and was told, that the Laird would exert his right; a right which he must now usurp, but which surely necessity must vindicate, and which is therefore yet exercised in lower degrees, by some of the proprietors, when legal processes cannot be obtained.

In all greater questions, however, there is now happily an end to all fear or hope from malice or from favour. The roads are secure in those places through which, forty years ago, no traveller could pass without a convoy. All trials of right by the sword are forgotten, and the mean are in as little danger from the powerful as in other places. No scheme of policy has, in any country, yet brought the rich and poor on equal terms into courts of judicature. Perhaps experience, improving on experience, may in time effect it.

Those who have long enjoyed dignity and power, ought not to lose it without some equivalent. There was paid to the Chiefs by the public, in exchange for their privileges, perhaps a sum greater than most of them had ever possessed, which excited a thirst for riches, of which it showed them the use. When the power of birth and station ceases, no hope remains but from the prevalence of money. Power and wealth supply the place of each other. Power confers the ability of gratifying our desire without the consent of others. Wealth enables us to obtain the consent of others to our gratification. Power, simply considered, whatever it confers on one, must take from another. Wealth enables its owner to give to others, by taking only from himself. Power pleases the violent and proud: wealth delights the placid and the timorous. Youth therefore flies at power, and age grovels after riches.

The Chiefs, divested of their prerogatives, necessarily turned their thoughts to the improvement of their revenues, and expect more rent, as they have less homage. The tenant, who is far from perceiving that his condition is made better in the same proportion, as that of his landlord is made worse, does not immediately see why his industry is to be taxed more heavily than before. He refuses to pay the demand, and is ejected; the ground is then let to a stranger, who perhaps brings a larger stock, but who, taking the land at its full price, treats with the Laird upon equal terms, and considers him not as a Chief, but as a trafficker in land. Thus the estate perhaps is improved, but the clan is broken.

It seems to be the general opinion, that the rents have been raised with too much eagerness. Some regard must be paid to prejudice.

Those who have hitherto paid but little, will not suddenly be persuaded to pay much, though they can afford it. As ground is gradually improved, and the value of money decreases, the rent may be raised without any diminution of the farmer's profits: yet it is necessary in these countries, where the ejection of a tenant is a greater evil, than in more populous places, to consider not merely what the land will produce, but with what ability the inhabitant can cultivate it. A certain stock can allow but a certain payment; for if the land be doubled, and the stock remains the same, the tenant becomes no richer. The proprietors of the Highlands might perhaps often increase their income, by subdividing the farms, and allotting to every occupier only so many acres as he can profitably employ, but that they want people.

There seems now, whatever be the cause, to be through a great part of the Highlands a general discontent. That adherence, which was lately professed by every man to the chief of his name, has now little prevalence; and he that cannot live as he desires at home, listens to the tale of fortunate islands, and happy regions, where every man may have land of his own, and eat the product of his labour without a superior.

Those who have obtained grants of American lands, have, as is well known, invited settlers from all quarters of the globe; and among other places, where oppression might produce a wish for new habitations, their emissaries would not fail to try their persuasions in the Isles of Scotland, where at the time when the clans were newly disunited from their Chiefs, and exasperated by unprecedented exactions, it is no wonder that they prevailed.

Whether the mischiefs of emigration were immediately perceived, may be justly questioned. They who went first, were probably such as could best be spared; but the accounts sent by the earliest adventurers, whether true or false, inclined many to follow them; and whole neighbourhoods formed parties for removal; so that departure from their native country is no longer exile. He that goes thus accompanied, carries with him all that makes life pleasant. He sits down in a better climate, surrounded by his kindred and his friends: they carry with them their language, their opinions, their popular songs and hereditary merriment: they change nothing but the place of their abode; and of that change they perceive the benefit.

This is the real effect of emigration, if those that go away together settle on the same spot, and preserve their ancient union. But some relate that these adventurous visitants of unknown regions, after a voyage passed in dreams of plenty and felicity, are dispersed at last upon a sylvan wilderness, where their first years must be spent in toil, to clear the ground which is afterwards to be tilled, and that the whole effect of their undertaking is only more fatigue and equal scarcity.

Both accounts may be suspected. Those who are gone will endeavour by every art to draw others after them; for as their numbers are greater, they will provide for themselves. When Nova Scotia was first peopled, I remember a letter, published under the character of a New Planter, who related how much the climate put him in mind of Italy. Such intelligence the Hebridians probably receive from their transmarine correspondents. But with equal temptations of interest, and perhaps with no greater niceness of veracity, the owners of the Islands spread stories of American hardships to keep their people content at home.

Some method to stop this epidemic desire of wandering, which spreads its contagion from valley to valley, deserves to be sought with great diligence. In more fruitful countries, the removal of one only makes room for the succession of another: but in the Hebrides, the loss of an inhabitant leaves a lasting vacuity; for nobody born in any other parts of the world will choose this country for his residence; and an island once depopulated will remain a desert, as long as the present facility of travel gives every one, who is discontented and unsettled, the choice of his abode.

Let it be inquired, whether the first intention of those who are fluttering on the wing, and collecting a flock that they may take their flight, be to attain good, or to avoid evil. If they are dissatisfied with that part of the globe, which their birth has allotted them, and resolve not to live without the pleasures of happier climates; if they long for bright suns, and calm skies, and flowery fields, and fragrant gardens, I know not by what eloquence they can be persuaded, or by what offers they can be hired to stay.

But if they are driven from their native country by positive evils, and disgusted by ill-treatment, real or imaginary, it were fit to remove their grievances, and quiet their resentment; since, if they have been hitherto undutiful subjects, they will not much mend their principles by American conversation.[29]

To allure them into the army, it was thought proper to indulge them in the continuance of their national dress. If this concession could have any effect, it might easily be made. That dissimilitude of appearance, which was supposed to keep them distinct from the rest of the nation, might disincline them from coalescing with the Pennsylvanians, or people of Connecticut. If the restitution of their arms will reconcile them to their country, let them have again those weapons which will not be more mischievous at home than in the Colonies. That they may not fly from the increase of rent, I know not whether the general good does not require that the landlords be, for a time, restrained in their demands, and kept quiet by pensions proportionate to their loss.

To hinder insurrection, by driving away the people, and to govern peaceably, by having no subjects, is an expedient that argues no great profundity of politics. To soften the obdurate, to convince the mistaken, to mollify the resentful, are worthy of a statesman; but it affords a legislator little self-applause to consider, that where there was formerly an insurrection, there is now a wilderness.

It has been a question often agitated without solution, why those northern regions are now so thinly peopled, which formerly overwhelmed with their armies the Roman empire. The question supposes what I believe is not true, that they had once more inhabitants than they could maintain, and overflowed only because they were full.

This is to estimate the manners of all countries and ages by our own. Migration, while the state of life was unsettled, and there was little communication of intelligence between distant places, was among the wilder nations of Europe, capricious and casual. An adventurous projector heard of a fertile coast unoccupied, and led out a colony; a chief of renown for bravery, called the young men together, and led them out to try what fortune would present. When Caesar was in Gaul, he found the Helvetians preparing to go they knew not whither, and put a stop to their motions. They settled again in their own country, where they were so far from wanting room, that they had accumulated three years provision for their march.

The religion of the North was military; if they could not find enemies, it was their duty to make them: they travelled in quest of danger, and willingly took the chance of Empire or Death. If their troops were numerous, the countries from which they were collected are of vast extent, and without much exuberance of people great armies may be raised where every man is a soldier. But their true numbers were never known. Those who were conquered by them are their historians, and shame may have excited them to say, that they were overwhelmed with multitudes. To count is a modern practice, the ancient method was to guess; and when numbers are guessed they are always magnified.

Thus England has for several years been filled with the achievements of seventy thousand Highlanders employed in America. I have heard from an English officer, not much inclined to favour them, that their behaviour deserved a very high degree of military praise; but their number has been much exaggerated. One of the ministers told me, that seventy thousand men could not have been found in all the Highlands, and that more than twelve thousand never took the field. Those that went to the American war, went to destruction. Of the old Highland regiment, consisting of twelve hundred, only seventy-six survived to see their country again.

The Gothic swarms have at least been multiplied with equal liberality. That they bore no great proportion to the inhabitants, in whose countries they settled, is plain from the paucity of northern words now found in the provincial languages. Their country was not deserted for want of room, because it was covered with forests of vast extent; and the first effect of plenitude of inhabitants is the destruction of wood. As the Europeans spread over America, the lands are gradually laid naked.

I would not be understood to say, that necessity had never any part in their expeditions. A nation, whose agriculture is scanty or unskilful, may be driven out by famine. A nation of hunters may have exhausted their game. I only affirm that the northern regions were not, when their irruptions subdued the Romans, overpeopled with regard to their real extent of territory, and power of fertility. In a country fully inhabited, however afterward laid waste, evident marks will remain of its former populousness. But of Scandinavia and Germany, nothing is known but that as we trace their state upwards into antiquity, their woods were greater, and their cultivated ground was less.

That causes very different from want of room may produce a general disposition to seek another country is apparent from the present conduct of the Highlanders, who are in some places ready to threaten a total secession. The numbers which have already gone, though like other numbers they may be magnified, are very great, and such as if they had gone together and agreed upon any certain settlement, might have founded an independent government in the depths of the western continent. Nor are they only the lowest and most indigent; many men of considerable wealth have taken with them their train of labourers and dependents; and if they continue the feudal scheme of polity, may establish new clans in the other hemisphere.

That the immediate motives of their desertion must be imputed to their landlords, may be reasonably concluded, because some Lairds of more prudence and less rapacity have kept their vassals undiminished. From Raasay only one man had been seduced, and at Col there was no wish to go away.

The traveller who comes hither from more opulent countries, to speculate upon the remains of pastoral life, will not much wonder that a common Highlander has no strong adherence to his native soil; for of animal enjoyments, or of physical good, he leaves nothing that he may not find again wheresoever he may be thrown.

The habitations of men in the Hebrides may be distinguished into huts and houses. By a *house*, I mean a building with one storey over another; by a *hut*, a dwelling with only one floor. The Laird, who formerly lived in a castle, now lives in a house; sometimes sufficiently neat, but seldom very spacious or splendid. The Tacksmen and the Ministers have commonly houses. Wherever there is a house, the stranger finds a welcome, and to the other evils of exterminating Tacksmen may be added the unavoidable cessation of hospitality, or the devolution of too heavy a burden on the Ministers.

Of the houses little can be said. They are small, and by the necessity of accumulating stores, where there are so few opportunities of purchase, the rooms are very heterogeneously filled. With want of cleanliness it were ingratitude to reproach them. The servants having been bred upon the naked earth, think every floor clean, and the quick succession of guests, perhaps not always over-elegant, does not allow much time for adjusting their apartments.

Huts are of many gradations; from murky dens, to commodious dwellings.

The wall of a common hut is always built without mortar, by a skilful adaptation of loose stones. Sometimes perhaps a double wall of stones is raised, and the intermediate space filled with earth. The air is thus completely excluded. Some walls are, I think, formed of turfs, held together by a wattle, or texture of twigs. Of the meanest huts, the first room is lighted by the entrance, and the second by the smoke-hole. The fire is usually made in the middle. But there are huts, or dwellings, of only one storey, inhabited by gentlemen, which have walls cemented with mortar, glass windows, and boarded floors. Of these all have chimneys, and some chimneys have grates.

The house and the furniture are not always nicely suited. We were driven once, by missing a passage, to the hut of a gentleman, where, after a very liberal supper, when I was conducted to my chamber, I found an elegant bed of Indian cotton, spread with fine sheets. The accommodation was flattering; I undressed myself, and felt my feet in the mire. The bed stood upon the bare earth, which a long course of rain had softened to a puddle.

In pastoral countries the condition of the lowest rank of people is sufficiently wretched. Among manufacturers, men that have no property may have art and industry, which make them necessary, and therefore valuable. But where flocks and corn are the only wealth, there are always more hands than work, and of that work there is little in which skill and dexterity can be much distinguished. He therefore who is born poor never can be rich. The son merely occupies the place of the father, and life knows nothing of progression or advancement.

The petty tenants, and labouring peasants, live in miserable cabins, which afford them little more than shelter from the storms. The boor of Norway[30] is said to make all his own utensils. In the Hebrides, whatever might be their ingenuity, the want of wood leaves them no materials. They are probably content with such accommodations as stones of different forms and sizes can afford them.

Their food is not better than their lodging. They seldom taste the flesh of land animals; for here are no markets. What each man eats is from his own stock. The great effect of money is to break property into small parts. In towns, he that has a shilling may have a piece of meat; but where there is no commerce, no man can eat mutton but by killing a sheep.

Fish in fair weather they need not want; but, I believe, man never lives long on fish, but by constraint, he will rather feed upon roots and berries.

The only fuel of the Islands is peat. Their wood is all consumed, and coal they have not yet found. Peat is dug out of the marshes, from the depth of one foot to that of six. That is accounted the best which is nearest the surface. It appears to be a mass of black earth held together by vegetable fibres. I know not whether the earth be bituminous, or whether the fibres be not the only combustible part; which by heating the interposed earth red hot, make a burning mass. The heat is not very strong nor lasting. The ashes are yellowish, and in a large quantity. When they dig peat, they cut it into square pieces, and pile it up to dry beside the house. In some places it has an offensive smell. It is like wood charked for the smith. The common method of making peat fires, is by heaping it on the hearth; but it burns well in grates, and in the best houses is so used.

The common opinion is, that peat grows again where it has been cut which, as it seems to be chiefly a vegetable substance, is not unlikely to be true, whether known or not to those who relate it.

There are water mills in Sky and Raasay; but where they are too far distant, the housewives grind their oats with a quern, or handmill, which consists of two stones, about a foot and a half in diameter; the lower is a little convex, to which the concavity of the upper must be fitted. In the middle of the upper stone is a round hole, and on one side is a long handle. The grinder sheds the corn gradually into the hole with one hand, and works the handle round with the other. The corn slides down the convexity of the lower stone, and by the motion of the upper is ground in its passage. These stones are found in Lochabar.

The Islands afford few pleasures, except to the hardy sportsman, who can tread the moor and climb the mountain. The distance of one family from another, in a country where travelling has so much difficulty, makes frequent intercourse impracticable. Visits last several days, and are commonly paid by water; yet I never saw a boat furnished with benches, or made commodious by any addition to the first fabric. Conveniences are not missed where they never were enjoyed.

The solace which the bagpipe can give, they have long enjoyed; but among other changes, which the last Revolution introduced, the use of the bagpipe begins to be forgotten. Some of the chief families still entertain a piper, whose office was anciently hereditary. Macrimmon was piper to Macleod, and Rankin to Maclean of Col.

The tunes of the bagpipe are traditional. There has been in Sky, beyond all time of memory, a college of pipers, under the direction of Macrimmon, which is not quite extinct. There was another in Mull, superintended by Rankin, which expired about sixteen years ago. To these colleges, while the pipe retained its honour, the students of music repaired for education. I have had my dinner exhilarated by the bagpipe, at Armidale, at Dunvegan, and in Col.

The general conversation of the Islanders has nothing particular. I did not meet with the inquisitiveness of which I have read, and suspect the judgement to have been rashly made. A stranger of curiosity comes into a place where a stranger is seldom seen: he importunes the people with questions, of which they cannot guess the motive, and gazes with surprise on things which they, having had them always before their eyes, do not suspect of any thing wonderful. He appears to them like some being of another world, and then thinks it peculiar that they take their turn to inquire whence he comes, and whither he is going.

The Islands were long unfurnished with instruction for youth, and none but the sons of gentlemen could have any literature. There are now parochial schools, to which the lord of every manor pays a certain stipend. Here the children are taught to read; but by the rule of their institution, they teach only English, so that the natives read a language which they may never use or understand. If a parish, which often happens, contains several islands, the school being but in one, cannot assist the rest. This is the state of Col, which, however, is more enlightened than some other places; for the deficiency is supplied by a young gentleman, who, for his own improvement, travels every year on foot over the Highlands to the session at Aberdeen; and at his return, during the vacation, teaches to read and write in his native island.

In Sky there are two grammar schools, where boarders are taken to be regularly educated. The price of board is from three pounds, to four pounds ten shillings a year, and that of instruction is half a crown a quarter. But the scholars are birds of passage, who live at school only in the summer; for in winter provisions cannot be made for any considerable number in one place. This periodical dispersion impresses strongly the scarcity of these countries.

Having heard of no boarding-school for ladies nearer than Inverness, I suppose their education is generally domestic. The elder daughters of the higher families are sent into the world, and may contribute by their acquisitions to the improvement of the rest.

Women must here study to be either pleasing or useful. Their deficiences are seldom supplied by very liberal fortunes. A hundred pounds is a portion beyond the hope of any but the Laird's daughter. They do not indeed often give money with their daughters; the question is, How many cows a young lady will bring her husband. A rich maiden has from ten to forty; but two cows are a decent fortune for one who pretends to no distinction.

The religion of the Islands is that of the Kirk of Scotland. The gentlemen with whom I conversed are all inclined to the English liturgy; but they are obliged to maintain the established Minister, and the country is too poor to afford payment to another, who must live wholly on the contribution of his audience.

They therefore all attend the worship of the Kirk, as often as a visit from their Minister, or the practicability of travelling gives them opportunity; nor have they any reason to complain of insufficient pastors; for I saw not one in the Islands, whom I had reason to think either deficient in learning, or irregular in life; but found several with whom I could not converse without wishing, as my respect increased, that they had not been Presbyterians.

The ancient rigour of puritanism is now very much relaxed, though all are not yet equally enlightened. I sometimes met with prejudices sufficiently malignant, but they were prejudices of ignorance. The Ministers in the Islands had attained such knowledge as may justly be admired in men, who have no motive to study, but generous curiosity, or, what is still better, desire of usefulness; with such politeness as so narrow a circle of converse could not have supplied, but to minds naturally disposed to elegance.

Reason and truth will prevail at last. The most learned of the Scottish Doctors would now gladly admit a form of prayer, if the people would endure it. The zeal or rage of congregations has its different degrees. In some parishes the Lord's Prayer is suffered: in others it is still rejected as a form; and he that should make it part of his supplication would be suspected of heretical pravity.[31]

The principle upon which extemporary prayer was originally introduced, is no longer admitted. The Minister formerly, in the effusion of his prayer, expected immediate, and perhaps perceptible inspiration, and therefore thought it his duty not to think before what he should say. It is now universally confessed, that men pray as they speak on other occasions, according to the general measure of their abilities and attainments. Whatever each may think of a form prescribed by another, he cannot but believe that he can himself compose by study and meditation a better prayer than will rise in his mind at a sudden call; and if he has any hope of supernatural help, why may he not as well receive it when he writes as when he speaks.

In the variety of mental powers, some must perform extemporary prayer with much imperfection; and in the eagerness and rashness of contradictory opinions, if public liturgy be left to the private judgement of every Minister, the congregation may often be offended or misled.

There is in Scotland, as among ourselves, a restless suspicion of popish machinations, and a clamour of numerous converts to the Romish religion. The report is, I believe, in both parts of the Island equally false. The Romish religion is professed only in Egg and Canna, two small islands, into which the Reformation never made its way. If any missionaries are busy in the Highlands, their zeal entitles them to respect, even from those who cannot think favourably of their doctrine.

The political tenets of the Islanders I was not curious to investigate, and they were not eager to obtrude. Their conversation is decent and inoffensive. They disdain to drink for their principles, and there is no disaffection at their tables. I never heard a health offered by a Highlander that might not have circulated with propriety within the precincts of the King's palace.

Legal government has yet something of novelty to which they cannot perfectly conform. The ancient spirit, that appealed only to the sword, is yet among them. The tenant of Scalpa, an island belonging to Macdonald, took no care to bring his rent; when the landlord talked of exacting payment, he declared his resolution to keep his ground, and drive all intruders from the island, and continued to feed his cattle as on his own land, till it became necessary for the Sheriff to dislodge him by violence.

The various kinds of superstition which prevailed here, as in all other regions of ignorance, are by the diligence of the Ministers almost extirpated.

Of Browny, mentioned by Martin, nothing has been heard for many years. Browny was a sturdy Fairy; who, if he was fed, and kindly treated, would, as they said, do a great deal of work. They now pay him no wages, and are content to labour for themselves.

In Troda, within these three-and-thirty years, milk was put every Saturday for Greogach, or the *Old Man with the Long Beard*. Whether Greogach was courted as kind, or dreaded as terrible, whether they meant, by giving him the milk, to obtain good, or avert evil, I was not informed. The Minister is now living by whom the practice was abolished.

They have still among them a great number of charms for the cure of different diseases; they are all invocations, perhaps transmitted to them from the times of popery, which increasing knowledge will bring into disuse.

They have opinions, which cannot be ranked with superstition, because they regard only natural effects. They expect better crops of grain, by sowing their seed in the moon's increase. The moon has great influence in vulgar philosophy. In my memory it was a precept annually given in one of the English Almanacks, *to kill hogs when the moon was increasing, and the bacon would prove the better in boiling*.

We should have had little claim to the praise of curiosity, if we had not endeavoured with particular attention to examine the question of the *Second Sight*. Of an opinion received for centuries by a whole nation, and supposed to be confirmed through its whole descent, by a series of successive facts, it is desirable that the truth should be established, or the fallacy detected.

The *Second Sight* is an impression made either by the mind upon the eye, or by the eye upon the mind, by which things distant or future are perceived and seen as if they were present. A man on a journey far from home falls from his horse, another, who is perhaps at work about the house, sees him bleeding on the ground, commonly with a landscape of the place where the accident befalls him. Another seer, driving home his cattle, or wandering in idleness, or musing in the sunshine, is suddenly surprised by the appearance of a bridal ceremony, or funeral procession, and counts the mourners or attendants, of whom, if he knows them, he relates the names, if he knows them not, he can describe the dresses. Things distant are seen at the instant when they happen. Of things future I know not that there is any rule, for determining the time between the sight and the event.

This receptive faculty, for power it cannot be called, is neither voluntary nor constant. The appearances have no dependence upon choice: they cannot be summoned, detained, or recalled. The impression is sudden, and the effect often painful.

By the term *Second Sight*, seems to be meant a mode of seeing, superadded to that which Nature generally bestows. In the Erse it is called *Taisch;* which signifies likewise a spectre, or a vision. I know not, nor is it likely that the Highlanders ever examined, whether by *Taisch*, used for *Second Sight*, they mean the power of seeing, or the thing seen.

I do not find it to be true, as it is reported, that to the *Second Sight* nothing is presented but phantoms of evil. Good seems to have the same proportion in those visionary scenes, as it obtains in real life: almost all remarkable events have evil for their basis; and are either miseries incurred, or miseries escaped. Our sense is so much stronger of what we suffer, than of what we enjoy, that the ideas of pain predominate in almost every mind. What is recollection but a revival of vexations, or history but a record of wars, treasons, and calamities? Death, which is considered as the greatest evil, happens to all. The greatest good, be it what it will, is the lot but of a part.

That they should often see death is to be expected; because death is an event frequent and important. But they see likewise more pleasing incidents. A gentleman told me, that when he had once gone far from his own island, one of his labouring servants predicted his return, and described the livery of his attendant, which he had never worn at home; and which had been, without any previous design, occasionally given him.

Our desire of information was keen, and our inquiry frequent. Mr

Boswell's frankness and gaiety made every body communicative; and we heard many tales of these airy shows, with more or less evidence and distinctness.

It is the common talk of the Lowland Scots, that the notion of the *Second Sight* is wearing away with other superstitions; and that its reality is no longer supposed, but by the grossest people. How far its prevalence ever extended, or what ground it has lost, I know not. The Islanders of all degrees, whether of rank or understanding, universally admit it, except the Ministers, who universally deny it, and are suspected to deny it, in consequence of a system, against conviction. One of them honestly told me, that he came to Sky with a resolution not to believe it.

Strong reasons for incredulity will readily occur. This faculty of seeing things out of sight is local, and commonly useless. It is a breach of the common order of things, without any visible reason or perceptible benefit. It is ascribed only to a people very little enlightened; and among them, for the most part, to the mean and the ignorant.

To the confidence of these objections it may be replied, that by presuming to determine what is fit, and what is beneficial, they presuppose more knowledge of the universal system than man has attained; and therefore depend upon principles too complicated and extensive for our comprehension; and that there can be no security in the consequence, when the premises are not understood; that the *Second Sight* is only wonderful because it is rare, for, considered in itself, it involves no more difficulty than dreams, or perhaps than the regular exercise of the cogitative faculty; that a general opinion of communicative impulses, or visionary representations, has prevailed in all ages and all nations; that particular instances have been given, with such evidence, as neither Bacon nor Bayle has been able to resist; that sudden impressions, which the event has verified, have been felt by more than own or publish them; that the *Second Sight* of the Hebrides implies only the local frequency of a power, which is nowhere totally unknown; and that where we are unable to decide by antecedent reason, we must be content to yield to the force of testimony.

By pretension to *Second Sight*, no profit was ever sought or gained. It is an involuntary affection, in which neither hope nor fear are known to have any part. Those who profess to feel it, do not boast of it as a privilege, nor are considered by others as advantageously distinguished. They have no temptation to feign; and their hearers have no motive to encourage the imposture.

To talk with any of these seers is not easy. There is one living in Sky, with whom we would have gladly conversed; but he was very gross and ignorant, and knew no English. The proportion in these countries of the poor to the rich is such, that if we suppose the quality to be accidental, it can very rarely happen to a man of education; and yet on such men it has sometimes fallen. There is now a Second Sighted gentleman in the Highlands, who complains of the terrors to which he is exposed.

The foresight of the seers is not always prescience: they are impressed with images, of which the event only shows them the meaning. They tell what they have seen to others, who are at that time not more knowing than themselves, but may become at last very adequate witnesses, by comparing the narrative with its verification.

To collect sufficient testimonies for the satisfaction of the public, or of ourselves, would have required more time than we could bestow. There is, against it, the seeming analogy of things confusedly seen, and little understood; and for it, the indistinct cry of national persuasion, which may be perhaps resolved at last into prejudice and tradition. I never could advance my curiosity to conviction; but came away at last only willing to believe.

As there subsists no longer in the Islands much of that peculiar and discriminative form of life, of which the idea had delighted our imagination, we were willing to listen to such accounts of past times as would be given us. But we soon found what memorials were to be expected from an illiterate people, whose whole time is a series of distress; where every morning is labouring with expedients for the evening; and where all mental pains or pleasure arose from the dread of winter, the expectation of spring, the caprices of their Chiefs, and the motions of the neighbouring clans; where there was neither shame from ignorance, nor pride in knowledge; neither curiosity to inquire, nor vanity to communicate.

The Chiefs indeed were exempt from urgent penury, and daily difficulties; and in their houses were preserved what accounts remained of past ages. But the Chiefs were sometimes ignorant and careless, and sometimes kept busy by turbulence and contention; and one generation of ignorance effaces the whole series of unwritten history. Books are faithful repositories, which may be a while neglected or forgotten; but when they are opened again, will again impart their instruction: memory, once interrupted, is not to be recalled. Written learning is a fixed luminary, which, after the cloud that had hidden it has passed away, is again bright in its proper station. Tradition is but a meteor, which, if once it falls, cannot be rekindled.

It seems to be universally supposed, that much of the local history was preserved by the Bards, of whom one is said to have been retained by every great family. After these Bards were some of my first inquiries; and I received such answers as, for a while, made me please myself with my increase of knowledge; for I had not then learned how to estimate the narration of a Highlander.

They said that a great family had a Bard and a Senachi, who were the poet and historian of the house; and an old gentleman told me that he remembered one of each. Here was a dawn of intelligence. Of men that had lived within memory, some certain knowledge might be attained. Though the office had ceased, its effects might continue; the poems might be found, though there was no poet.

Another conversation indeed informed me, that the same man was both Bard and Senachi. This variation discouraged me; but as the practice might be different in different times, or at the same time in different families, there was yet no reason for supposing that I must necessarily sit down in total ignorance.

Soon after I was told by a gentleman, who is generally acknowledged the greatest master of Hebridian antiquities, that there had indeed once been both Bards and Senachies; and that Senachi signified *the man of talk*, or of conversation; but that neither Bard nor Senachi had existed for some centuries. I have no reason to suppose it exactly known at what time the custom ceased, nor did it probably cease in all houses at once. But whenever the practice of recitation was disused, the works, whether poetical or historical, perished with the authors; for in those times nothing had been written in the Erse language.

Whether the *Man of talk* was a historian, whose office was to tell truth, or a story-teller, like those which were in the last century, and perhaps are now among the Irish, whose trade was only to amuse, it now would be vain to inquire.

Most of the domestic offices were, I believe, hereditary; and probably the laureat of a clan was always the son of the last laureat. The history of the race could no otherwise be communicated, or retained; but what genius could be expected in a poet by inheritance?

The nation was wholly illiterate. Neither Bards nor Senachies could write or read; but if they were ignorant, there was no danger of detection; they were believed by those whose vanity they flattered.

The recital of genealogies, which has been considered as very efficacious to the preservation of a true series of ancestry, was anciently made, when the heir of the family came to manly age. This practice has never subsisted within time of memory, nor was much credit due to such rehearsers, who might obtrude fictitious pedigrees, either to please their masters, or to hide the deficiency of their own memories.

Where the Chiefs of the Highlands have found the histories of their descent is difficult to tell; for no Erse genealogy was ever written. In general this only is evident, that the principal house of a clan must be very ancient, and that those must have lived long in a place, of whom it is not known when they came thither.

Thus hopeless are all attempts to find any traces of Highland learning. Nor are their primitive customs and ancient manner of life otherwise than very faintly and uncertainly remembered by the present race.

The peculiarities which strike the native of a commercial country, proceeded in a great measure from the want of money. To the servants and dependents that were not domestics, and if an estimate be made from the capacity of any of their old houses which I have seen, their domestics could have been but few, were appropriated certain portions of land for their support. Macdonald has a piece of ground yet, called the Bards', or Senachies' field. When a beef was killed for the house, particular parts were claimed as fees by the several officers, or workmen. What was the right of each I have not learned. The head belonged to the smith, and the udder of a cow to the piper: the weaver had likewise his particular part; and so many pieces followed these prescriptive claims, that the Laird's was at last but little.

The payment of rent in kind has been so long disused in England, that it is totally forgotten. It was practised very lately in the Hebrides, and probably still continues; not only in St Kilda, where money is not yet known, but in others of the smaller and remoter islands. It were perhaps to be desired, that no change in this particular should have been made. When the Laird could only eat the produce of his lands, he was under the necessity of residing upon them; and when the tenant could not convert his stock into more portable riches, he could never be tempted away from his farm, from the only place where he could be wealthy. Money confounds subordination, by overpowering the distinctions of rank and birth, and weakens authority by supplying power of resistance, or expedients for escape. The feudal system is formed for a nation employed in agriculture, and has never long kept its hold where gold and silver have become common.

Their arms were anciently the Glaymore,[32] or great two-handed sword, and afterwards the two-edged sword and target, or buckler, which was sustained on the left arm. In the midst of the target, which was made of wood, covered with leather, and studded with nails, a slender lance, about two feet long, was sometimes fixed; it was heavy and cumbrous, and accordingly has for some time past been gradually laid aside. Very few targets were at Culloden. The dirk, or broad dagger, I am afraid, was of more use in private quarrels than in battles. The Lochaber-axe is only a slight alteration of the old English bill.

After all that has been said of the force and terror of the Highland sword, I could not find that the art of defence was any part of common education. The gentlemen were perhaps sometimes skilful gladiators, but the common men had no other powers than those of violence and courage. Yet it is well known, that the onset of the

Highlanders was very formidable. As an army cannot consist of philosophers, a panic is easily excited by any unwonted mode of annoyance. New dangers are naturally magnified; and men accustomed only to exchange bullets at a distance, and rather to hear their enemies than see them, are discouraged and amazed when they find themselves encountered hand to hand, and catch the gleam of steel flashing in their faces.

The Highland weapons gave opportunity for many exertions of personal courage, and sometimes for single combats in the field; like those which occur so frequently in fabulous wars. At Falkirk, a gentleman now living, was, I suppose after the retreat of the King's troops, engaged at a distance from the rest with an Irish dragoon. They were both skilful swordsmen, and the contest was not easily decided: the dragoon at last had the advantage, and the Highlander called for quarter; but quarter was refused, and the fight continued till he was reduced to defend himself upon his knee. At that instant one of the Macleods came to his rescue; who, as it is said, offered quarter to the dragoon, but he thought himself obliged to reject what he had before refused, and, as battle gives little time to deliberate, was immediately killed.

Funerals were formerly solemnized by calling multitudes together, and entertaining them at great expense. This emulation of useless cost has been for some time discouraged, and at last in the Isle of Sky is almost suppressed.

Of the Erse language, as I understand nothing, I cannot say more than I have been told. It is the rude speech of a barbarous people, who had few thoughts to express, and were content, as they conceived grossly, to be grossly understood. After what has been lately talked of Highland Bards, and Highland genius, many will startle when they are told, that the Erse never was a written language; that there is not in the world an Erse manuscript a hundred years old; and that the sounds of the Highlanders were never expressed by letters, till some little books of piety were translated, and a metrical version of the Psalms was made by the Synod of Argyle. Whoever therefore now writes in this language, spells according to his own perception of the sound, and his own idea of the power of the letters. The Welsh and the Irish are cultivated tongues. The Welsh, two hundred years ago, insulted their English neighbours for the instability of their orthography; while the Erse merely floated in the breath of the people, and could therefore receive little improvement.

When a language begins to teem with books, it is tending to refinement; as those who undertake to teach others must have undergone some labour in improving themselves, they set a proportionate value on their own thoughts, and wish to enforce them by efficacious expressions; speech becomes embodied and permanent; different modes and phrases are compared, and the best obtains an establishment. By degrees one age improves upon another. Exactness is first obtained, and afterwards elegance. But diction, merely vocal, is always in its childhood. As no man leaves his eloquence behind him, the new generations have all to learn. There may possibly be books without a polished language, but there can be no polished language without books.

That the Bards could not read more than the rest of their countrymen, it is reasonable to suppose; because, if they had read, they could probably have written; and how high their compositions may reasonably be rated, an inquirer may best judge by considering what stores of imagery, what principles of ratiocination, what comprehension of knowledge, and what delicacy of elocution he has known any man attain who cannot read. The state of the Bards was yet more hopeless. He that cannot read, may now converse with those that can; but the Bard was a barbarian among barbarians, who, knowing nothing himself, lived with others that knew no more.

There has lately been in the Islands one of these illiterate poets, who hearing the Bible read at church, is said to have turned the sacred history into verse. I heard part of a dialogue, composed by him, translated by a young lady in Mull, and thought it had more meaning than I expected from a man totally uneducated; but he had some opportunities of knowledge; he lived among a learned people. After all that has been done for the instruction of the Highlanders, the antipathy between their language and literature still continues; and no man that has learned only Erse is, at this time, able to read.

The Erse has many dialects, and the words used in some islands are not always known in others. In literate nations, though the pronunciation, and sometimes the words of common speech may differ, as now in England, compared with the south of Scotland, yet there is a written diction, which pervades all dialects, and is understood in every province. But where the whole language is colloquial, he that has only one part, never gets the rest, as he cannot get it but by change of residence.

In an unwritten speech, nothing that is not very short is transmitted from one generation to another. Few have opportunities of hearing a long composition often enough to learn it, or have inclination to repeat it so often as is necessary to retain it: and what is once forgotten is lost for ever. I believe there cannot be recovered, in the whole Erse language, five hundred lines of which there is any evidence to prove them a hundred years old. Yet I hear that the father of Ossian[33] boasts of two chests more of ancient poetry, which he suppresses, because they are too good for the English.

He that goes into the Highlands with a mind naturally acquiescent, and a credulity eager for wonders, may come back with an opinion very different from mine; for the inhabitants knowing the ignorance of all strangers in their language and antiquities, perhaps are not very scrupulous adherents to truth; yet I do not say that they deliberately speak studied falsehood, or have a settled purpose to deceive. They have inquired and considered little, and do not always feel their own ignorance. They are not much accustomed to be interrogated by others; and seem never to have thought upon interrogating themselves; so that if they do not know what they tell to be true, they likewise do not distinctly perceive it to be false.

Mr Boswell was very diligent in his inquiries; and the result of his investigations was, that the answer to the second question was commonly such as nullified the answer to the first.

We were a while told, that they had an old translation of the scriptures; and told it till it would appear obstinacy to inquire again. Yet by continued accumulation of questions we found, that the translation meant, if any meaning there were, was nothing else than the Irish Bible.

We heard of manuscripts that were, or that had been in the hands of somebody's father, or grandfather; but at last we had no reason to believe they were other than Irish. Martin mentions Irish, but never any Erse manuscripts, to be found in the Islands in his time.

I suppose my opinion of the poems of Ossian is already discovered. I believe they never existed in any other form than that which we have seen. The editor, or author, never could show the original; nor can it be shown by any other; to revenge reasonable incredulity, by refusing evidence, is a degree of insolence, with which the world is not yet acquainted; and stubborn audacity is the last refuge of guilt. It would be easy to show it if he had it; but whence could it be had? It is too long to be remembered, and the language formerly had nothing written. He has doubtless inserted names that circulate in popular stories, and may have translated some wandering ballads, if any can be found; and the names, and some of the images being recollected, make an inaccurate auditor imagine, by the help of Caledonian bigotry, that he has formerly heard the whole.

I asked a very learned Minister in Sky, who had used all arts to make me believe the genuineness of the book, whether at last he believed it himself? but he would not answer. He wished me to be deceived, for the honour of his country; but would not directly and formally deceive me. Yet has this man's testimony been publicly produced, as of one that held Fingal to be the work of Ossian.

It is said, that some men of integrity profess to have heard parts of it, but they all heard them when they were boys; and it was never said that any of them could recite six lines. They remember names, and perhaps some proverbial sentiments; and, having no distinct ideas, coin a resemblance without an original. The persuasion of the Scots, however, is far from universal; and in a question so capable of proof, why should doubt be suffered to continue? The editor has been heard to say, that part of the poem was received by him, in the Saxon character. He has then found, by some peculiar fortune, an unwritten language, written in a character which the natives probably never beheld.

I have yet supposed no imposture but in the publisher, yet I am far from certainty, that some translations have not been lately made, that may now be obtruded as parts of the original work. Credulity on one part is a strong temptation to deceit on the other, especially to deceit of which no personal injury is the consequence, and which flatters the author with his own ingenuity. The Scots have something to plead for their easy reception of an improbable fiction: they are seduced by their fondness for their supposed ancestors. A Scotchman must be a very sturdy moralist, who does not love Scotland better than truth: he will always love it better than inquiry; and if falsehood flatters his vanity, will not be very diligent to detect it. Neither ought the English to be much influenced by Scotch authority; for of the past and present state of the whole Erse nation, the Lowlanders are at least as ignorant as ourselves. To be ignorant is painful; but it is dangerous to quiet our uneasiness by the delusive opiate of hasty persuasion.

But this is the age in which those who could not read, have been supposed to write; in which the giants of antiquated romance have been exhibited as realities. If we know little of the ancient Highlanders, let us not fill the vacuity with Ossian. If we have not searched the Magellanic regions, let us however forbear to people them with Patagons.

Having waited some days at Armidel, we were flattered at last with a wind that promised to convey us to Mull. We went on board a boat that was taking in kelp, and left the Isle of Sky behind us. We were doomed to experience, like others, the danger of trusting to the wind, which blew against us, in a short time, with such violence, that we, being no seasoned sailors, were willing to call it a tempest. I was sea-sick and lay down. Mr Boswell kept the deck.[34] The master knew not well whither to go; and our difficulties might perhaps have filled a very pathetic page, had not Mr Maclean of Col, who, with every other qualification which insular life requires, is a very active and skilful mariner, piloted us safe into his own harbour.

Col

In the morning we found ourselves under the Isle of Col, where we landed; and passed the first day and night with Captain Maclean, a gentleman who has lived some time in the East Indies; but having dethroned no Nabob,[35] is not too rich to settle in his own country.

Next day the wind was fair, and we might have had an easy passage to Mull; but having, contrarily to our own intention, landed upon a new island, we would not leave it wholly unexamined. We therefore suffered the vessel to depart without us, and trusted the skies for another wind.

Mr Maclean of Col, having a very numerous family, has, for some time past, resided at Aberdeen, that he may superintend their education, and leaves the young gentleman, our friend, to govern his dominions, with the full power of a Highland Chief. By the absence of the Laird's family, our entertainment was made more difficult, because the house was in a great degree disfurnished; but young Col's kindness and activity supplied all defects, and procured us more than sufficient accommodation.

Here I first mounted a little Highland steed; and if there had been many spectators, should have been somewhat ashamed of my figure in the march. The horses of the Islands, as of other barren countries, are very low: they are indeed musculous and strong, beyond what their size gives reason for expecting; but a bulky man upon one of their backs makes a very disproportionate appearance.

From the habitation of Captain Maclean, we went to Grissipol, but called by the way on Mr Hector Maclean, the Minister of Col, whom we found in a hut, that is, a house of only one floor, but with windows and chimney, and not inelegantly furnished. Mr Maclean has the reputation of great learning: he is seventy-seven years old, but not infirm, with a look of venerable dignity, excelling what I remember in any other man.

His conversation was not unsuitable to his appearance. I lost some of his goodwill, by treating a heretical writer with more regard than, in his opinion, a heretic could deserve. I honoured his orthodoxy, and did not much censure his asperity. A man who has settled his opinions, does not love to have the tranquillity of his conviction disturbed; and at seventy-seven it is time to be in earnest.

Mention was made of the Erse translation of the New Testament, which has been lately published, and of which the learned Mr Macqueen of Sky spoke with commendation; but Mr Maclean said he did not use it, because he could make the text more intelligible to his auditors by an extemporary version. From this I inferred, that the language of the translation was not the language of the Isle of Col.

He has no public edifice for the exercise of his ministry; and can officiate to no greater number, than a room can contain; and the room of a hut is not very large. This is all the opportunity of worship that is now granted to the inhabitants of the island, some of whom must travel thither perhaps ten miles. Two chapels were erected by their ancestors, of which I saw the skeletons, which now stand faithful witnesses of the triumph of Reformation.

The want of churches is not the only impediment to piety: there is likewise a want of Ministers. A parish often contains more islands than one; and each island can have the Minister only in its own turn. At Raasay they had, I think, a right to service only every third Sunday. All the provision made by the present ecclesiastical constitution, for the inhabitants of about a hundred square miles, is a prayer and sermon in a little room, once in three weeks: and even this parsimonious distribution is at the mercy of the weather; and in those islands where the Minister does not reside, it is impossible to tell how many weeks or months may pass without any public exercise of religion . . .

Mull

As we were to catch the first favourable breath, we spent the night not very elegantly, nor pleasantly in the vessel, and were landed next day at Tobor Morar,[36] a port in Mull, which appears to an unexperienced eye formed for the security of ships; for its mouth is closed by a small island, which admits them through narrow channels into a basin sufficiently capacious. They are indeed safe from the sea, but there is a hollow between the mountains, through which the wind issues from the land with very mischievous violence.

There was no danger while we were there, and we found several other vessels at anchor; so that the port had a very commercial appearance.

The young Laird of Col, who had determined not to let us lose his company, while there was any difficulty remaining, came over with us. His influence soon appeared; for he procured us horses, and conducted us to the house of Dr Maclean, where we found very kind entertainment, and very pleasing conversation. Miss Maclean, who was born, and had been bred at Glasgow, having removed with her father to Mull, added to other qualifications, a great knowledge of the Erse language, which she had not learned in her childhood, but gained by study, and was the only interpreter of Erse poetry that I could ever find.

The Isle of Mull is perhaps in extent the third of the Hebrides. It is not broken by waters, not shot into promontories, but is a solid and compact mass, of breadth nearly equal to its length. Of the dimensions of the larger islands, there is no knowledge approaching to exactness. I am willing to estimate it as containing about three hundred square miles.[37]

Mull had suffered like Sky by the black winter of seventy-one, in which, contrary to all experience, a continued frost detained the snow eight weeks upon the ground. Against a calamity never known, no provision had been made, and the people could only pine in helpless misery. One tenant was mentioned, whose cattle perished to the value of three hundred pounds; a loss which probably more than the life of man is necessary to repair. In countries like these, the descriptions of famine become intelligible. Where by vigorous and artful cultivation of a soil naturally fertile, there is commonly a superfluous growth both of grain and grass; where the fields are crowded with cattle; and where every hand is able to attract wealth from a distance, by making something that promotes ease, or gratifies vanity, a dear year produces only a comparative want, which is rather seen than felt, and which terminates commonly in no worse effect, than that of condemning the lower orders of the community to sacrifice a little luxury to convenience, or at most a little convenience to necessity.

But where the climate is unkind, and the ground penurious, so that the most fruitful years will produce only enough to maintain themselves; where life unimproved, and unadorned, fades into something little more than naked existence, and every one is busy for himself, without any arts by which the pleasure of others may be increased; if to the daily burden of distress any additional weight be added, nothing remains but to despair and die. In Mull the disappointment of a harvest, or a murrain among the cattle, cuts off the regular provision; and they who have no manufactures can purchase no part of the superfluities of other countries. The consequence of a bad season is here not scarcity, but emptiness; and they whose plenty was barely a supply of natural and present need, when that slender stock fails, must perish with hunger.

All travel has its advantages. If the passenger visits better countries, he may learn to improve his own, and if fortune carries him to worse, he may learn to enjoy it.

Mr Boswell's curiosity strongly impelled him to survey Iona, or Icolmkil, which was to the early ages the great school of Theology, and is supposed to have been the place of sepulture for the ancient kings. I, though less eager, did not oppose him.

That we might perform this expedition, it was necessary to traverse a great part of Mull. We passed a day at Dr Maclean's, and could have been well contented to stay longer. But Col provided us horses, and we pursued our journey. This was a day of inconvenience, for the country is very rough, and my horse was but little. We travelled many hours through a tract, black and barren, in which, however, there were the reliques of humanity; for we found a ruined chapel in our way.

It is natural, in traversing this gloom of desolation, to inquire, whether something may not be done to give nature a more cheerful face, and whether those hills and moors that afford health cannot with a little care and labour bear something better? The first thought that occurs is to cover them with trees, for that in many of these naked regions trees will grow, is evident, because stumps and roots are yet remaining; and the speculatist hastily proceeds to censure that negligence and laziness that has omitted for so long a time so easy an improvement.

To drop seeds into the ground, and attend their growth, requires little labour and no skill. He who remembers that all the woods, by which the wants of man have been supplied from the Deluge till now, were self-sown, will not easily be persuaded to think all the art and preparation necessary, which the Georgic writers[38] prescribe to planters. Trees certainly have covered the earth with very little culture. They wave their tops among the rocks of Norway, and might thrive as well in the Highlands and Hebrides.

But there is a frightful interval between the seed and timber. He that calculates the growth of trees, has the unwelcome remembrance of the shortness of life driven hard upon him. He knows that he is doing what will never benefit himself; and when he rejoices to see the stem rise, is disposed to repine that another shall cut it down.

Plantation is naturally the employment of a mind unburdened with care, and vacant to futurity, saturated with present good, and at leisure to derive gratification from the prospect of posterity. He that pines with hunger, is in little care how others shall be fed. The poor man is seldom studious to make his grandson rich. It may be soon discovered, why in a place, which hardly supplies the cravings of necessity, there has been little attention to the delights of fancy, and why distant convenience is unregarded, where the thoughts are turned with incessant solicitude upon every possibility of immediate advantage.

Neither is it quite so easy to raise large woods, as may be conceived. Trees intended to produce timber must be sown where they are to grow; and ground sown with trees must be kept useless for a long time, inclosed at an expense from which many will be discouraged by the remoteness of the profit, and watched with that attention, which, in places where it is most needed, will neither be given nor bought. That it cannot be ploughed is evident; and if cattle be suffered to graze upon it, they will devour the plants as fast as they rise. Even in coarser countries, where herds and flocks are not fed, not only the deer and the wild goats will browse upon them, but the hare and rabbit will nibble them. It is therefore reasonable to believe, what I do not remember any naturalist to have remarked, that there was a time when the world was very thinly inhabited by beasts, as well as men, and that the woods had leisure to rise high before animals had bred numbers sufficient to intercept them.

Sir James Macdonald, in part of the wastes of his territory, set or sowed trees, to the number, as I have been told, of several millions, expecting, doubtless, that they would grow up into future navies and cities; but for want of inclosure, and of that care which is always necessary, and will hardly ever be taken, all his cost and labour have been lost, and the ground is likely to continue an useless heath.

Having not any experience of a journey in Mull, we had no doubt of reaching the sea by daylight, and therefore had not left Dr Maclean's very early. We travelled diligently enough, but found the country, for road there was none, very difficult to pass. We were always struggling with some obstruction or other, and our vexation was not balanced by any gratification of the eye or mind. We were now long enough acquainted with hills and heath to have lost the emotion that they once raised, whether pleasing or painful, and had our mind employed only on our own fatigue. We were however sure, under Col's protection, of escaping all real evils. There was no house in Mull to which he could not introduce us. He had intended to lodge us, for that night, with a gentleman that lived upon the coast, but discovered on the way, that he then lay in bed without hope of life.

We resolved not to embarrass a family, in a time of so much sorrow, if any other expedient could be found; and as the Island of Ulva was over-against us, it was determined that we should pass the strait and have recourse to the Laird, who, like the other gentlemen of the Islands, was known to Col. We expected to find a ferry-boat, but when at last we came to the water, the boat was gone.

We were now again at a stop. It was the sixteenth of October, a time when it is not convenient to sleep in the Hebrides without a cover, and there was no house within our reach, but that which we had already declined.

Ulva

While we stood deliberating, we were happily espied from an Irish ship, that lay at anchor in the strait. The master saw that we wanted a passage, and with great civility sent us his boat, which quickly conveyed us to Ulva, where we were very liberally entertained by Mr Macquarry.

To Ulva we came in the dark, and left it before noon the next day. A very exact description therefore will not be expected. We were told, that it is an island of no great extent, rough and barren, inhabited by the Macquarrys; a clan not powerful nor numerous, but of antiquity, which most other families are content to reverence. The name is supposed to be a depravation of some other; for the Erse language does not afford it any etymology. Macquarry is proprietor both of Ulva and some adjacent islands, among which is Staffa, so lately raised to renown by Mr Banks.

When the Islanders were reproached with their ignorance, or insensibility of the wonders of Staffa, they had not much to reply. They had indeed considered it little, because they had always seen it; and none but philosophers, nor they always, are struck with wonder, otherwise than by novelty. How would it surprise an unenlightened ploughman, to hear a company of sober men, inquiring by what power the hand tosses a stone, or why the stone, when it is tossed, falls to the ground!

Of the ancestors of Macquarry, who thus lies hid in his unfrequented island, I have found memorials in all places where they could be expected.

Inquiring after the relic of former manners, I found that in Ulva, and I think, no where else, is continued the payment of the *Mercheta mulierum*;[39] a fine in old times due to the Laird at the marriage of a virgin. The original of this claim, as of our tenure of *Borough English*, is variously delivered. It is pleasant to find ancient customs in old families. This payment, like others, was, for want of money, made anciently in the produce of the land. Macquarry was used to demand a sheep, for which he now takes a crown, by that inattention to the uncertain proportion between the value and the denomination of money, which has brought much disorder into Europe. A sheep has always the same power of supplying human wants, but a crown will bring at one time more, at another less.

Ulva was not neglected by the piety of ancient times: it has still to show what was once a church.

Inch Kenneth

In the morning we went again into the boat, and were landed on Inch Kenneth, an island about a mile long, and perhaps half a mile broad, remarkable for pleasantness and fertility. It is verdant and grassy, and fit both for pasture and tillage; but it has no trees. Its only inhabitants were Sir Allan Maclean, and two young ladies, his daughters, with their servants.

Romance does not often exhibit a scene that strikes the imagination more than this little desert in these depths of Western obscurity, occupied not by a gross herdsman, or amphibious fisherman, but by a gentleman and two ladies, of high birth, polished manners, and elegant conversation, who, in a habitation raised not very far above the ground, but furnished with unexpected neatness and convenience, practised all the kindness of hospitality, and refinement of courtesy.

Sir Allan is the Chieftain of the great clan of Maclean, which is said to claim the second place among the Highland families, yielding only to Macdonald. Though by the misconduct of his ancestors, most of the extensive territory, which would have descended to him, has been alienated, he still retains much of the dignity and authority of his birth. When soldiers were lately wanting for the American war, application was made to Sir Allan, and he nominated a hundred men for the service, who obeyed the summons, and bore arms under his command.

He had then, for some time, resided with the young ladies in Inch Kenneth, where he lives not only with plenty, but with elegance, having conveyed to his cottage a collection of books, and what else is necessary to make his hours pleasant.

When we landed, we were met by Sir Allan and the ladies, accompanied by Miss Macquarry, who had passed some time with them, and now returned to Ulva with her father.

We all walked together to the mansion, where we found one cottage for Sir Allan, and I think two more for the domestics and the offices. We entered, and wanted little that palaces afford. Our room was neatly floored, and well lighted; and our dinner, which was dressed in one of the other huts, was plentiful and delicate.

In the afternoon Sir Allan reminded us, that the day was Sunday, which he never suffered to pass without some religious distinction, and invited us to partake in his acts of domestic worship; which I hope neither Mr Boswell nor myself will be suspected of a disposition to refuse. The elder of the ladies read the English service.

Inch Kenneth was once a seminary of ecclesiastics, subordinate, I suppose, to Icolmkill. Sir Allan had a mind to trace the foundation of the college, but neither I nor Mr Boswell, who *bends* a keener *eye on vacancy*, were able to perceive them.

Our attention, however, was sufficiently engaged by a venerable chapel, which stands yet entire, except that the roof is gone. It is about sixty feet in length, and thirty in breadth. On one side of the altar is a bas relief of the blessed Virgin, and by it lies a little bell; which, though cracked, and without a clapper, has remained there for ages, guarded only by the venerableness of the place. The ground round the chapel is covered with grave-stones of Chiefs and ladies; and still continues to be a place of sepulture.

Inch Kenneth is a proper prelude to Icolmkill. It was not without some mournful emotion that we contemplated the ruins of religious structures, and the monuments of the dead.

On the next day we took a more distinct view of the place, and went with the boat to see oysters in the bed, out of which the boatmen forced up as many as were wanted. Even Inch Kenneth has a subordinate island, named Sandiland, I suppose, in contempt, where we landed, and found a rock, with a surface of perhaps four acres, of which one is naked stone, another spread with sand and shells, some of which I picked up for their glossy beauty, and two covered with a little earth and grass, on which Sir Allan has a few sheep. I doubt not but when there was a college at Inch Kenneth, there was a hermitage upon Sandiland.

Having wandered over those extensive plains, we committed ourselves again to the winds and waters; and after a voyage of about ten minutes, in which we met with nothing very observable, were again safe upon dry ground.

We told Sir Allan our desire of visiting Icolmkill, and entreated him to give us his protection, and his company. He thought proper to hesitate a little, but the ladies hinted, that as they knew he would not finally refuse, he would do better if he preserved the grace of ready compliance. He took their advice, and promised to carry us on the morrow in his boat.

We passed the remaining part of the day in such amusements as were in our power. Sir Allan related the American campaign, and at evening one of the ladies played on her harpsichord, while Col and Mr Boswell danced a Scottish reel with the other.

We could have been easily persuaded to a longer stay upon Inch Kenneth, but life will not be all passed in delight. The session at Edinburgh was approaching, from which Mr Boswell could not be absent.

In the morning our boat was ready: it was high and strong. Sir Allan victualled it for the day, and provided able rowers. We now parted from the young Laird of Col, who had treated us with so much kindness, and concluded his favours by consigning us to Sir Allan. Here we had the last embrace of this amiable man, who, while these pages were preparing to attest his virtues, perished in the passage between Ulva and Inch Kenneth.

Sir Allan, to whom the whole region was well known, told us of a very remarkable cave, to which he would show us the way. We had been disappointed already by one cave, and were not much elevated by the expectation of another.

It was yet better to see it, and we stopped at some rocks on the coast of Mull. The mouth is fortified by vast fragments of stone, over which we made our way, neither very nimbly, nor very securely. The place, however, well repaid our trouble. The bottom, as far as the flood rushes in, was encumbered with large pebbles, but as we advanced was spread over with smooth sand. The breadth is about forty-five feet: the roof rises in an arch, almost regular, to a height which we could not measure; but I think it about thirty feet.

This part of our curiosity was nearly frustrated; for though we went to see a cave, and knew that caves are dark, we forgot to carry tapers, and did not discover our omission till we were wakened by our wants. Sir Allan then sent one of the boatmen into the country, who soon returned with one little candle. We were thus enabled to go forward, but could not venture far. Having passed inward from the sea to a great depth, we found on the right hand a narrow passage, perhaps not more than six feet wide, obstructed by great stones, over which we climbed and came into a second cave, in breadth twenty-five feet. The air in this apartment was very warm, but not oppressive, nor loaded with vapours. Our light showed no tokens of a feculent[40] or corrupted atmosphere. Here was a square stone, called, as we are told, *Fingal's Table*.

If we had been provided with torches, we should have proceeded in our search, though we had already gone as far as any former adventurer, except some who are reported never to have returned; and, measuring our way back, we found it more than a hundred and sixty yards, the eleventh part of a mile.

Our measures were not critically exact, having been made with a walking pole, such as it is convenient to carry in these rocky countries, of which I guessed the length by standing against it. In this there could be no great error, nor do I much doubt but the Highlander, whom we employed, reported the number right. More nicety however is better, and no man should travel unprovided with instruments for taking heights and distances.

There is yet another cause of error not always easily surmounted, though more dangerous to the veracity of itinerary narratives, than imperfect mensuration. An observer deeply impressed by any remarkable spectacle, does not suppose, that the traces will soon vanish from his mind, and having commonly no great convenience for writing, defers the description to a time of more leisure, and better accommodation.

He who has not made the experiment, or who is not accustomed to require rigorous accuracy from himself, will scarcely believe how much a few hours take from certainty of knowledge, and distinctness of imagery; how the succession of objects will be broken, how separate parts will be confused, and how many particular features and discriminations will be compressed and conglobated into one gross and general idea.

To this dilatory notation must be imputed the false relations of travellers, where there is no imaginable motive to deceive. They trusted to memory, what cannot be trusted safely but to the eye, and told by guess what a few hours before they had known with certainty. Thus it was that Wheeler and Spon[41] described with irreconcilable contrariety things which they surveyed together, and which both undoubtedly designed to show as they saw them.

When we had satisfied our curiosity in the cave, so far as our penury of light permitted us, we clambered again to our boats, and proceeded along the coast of Mull to a headland, called Atun, remarkable for the columnar form of the rocks, which rise in a series of pilasters, with a degree of regularity, which Sir Allan thinks not less worthy of curiosity than the shore of Staffa.

Not long after we came to another range of black rocks, which had the appearance of broken pilasters, set one behind another to a great depth. This place was chosen by Sir Allan for our dinner. We were easily accommodated with seats, for the stones were of all heights, and refreshed ourselves and our boatmen, who could have no other rest till we were at Icolmkill.

The evening was now approaching, and we were yet at a considerable distance from the end of our expedition. We could therefore stop no more to make remarks in the way, but set forward with some degree of eagerness. The day soon failed us, and the moon presented a very solemn and pleasing scene. The sky was clear, so that the eye commanded a wide circle: the sea was neither still not turbulent: the wind neither silent nor loud. We were never far from one coast or another, on which, if the weather had become violent, we could have found shelter, and therefore contemplated at ease the region through which we glided in the tranquillity of the night, and saw now a rock and now an island grow gradually conspicuous and gradually obscure. I committed the fault which I have just been censuring, in neglecting, as we passed, to note the series of this placid navigation.

We were very near an island, called *Nun's Island*, perhaps from an ancient convent. Here is said to have been dug the stone that was used in the buildings of Icolmkill. Whether it is now inhabited we could not stay to inquire.

At last we came to Icolmkill, but found no convenience for landing. Our boat could not be forced very near the dry ground, and our Highlanders carried us over the water.

We were now treading that illustrious island,[42] which was once the luminary of the Caledonian regions, whence savage clans and roving barbarians derived the benefits of knowledge, and the blessings of religion. To abstract the mind from all local emotion would be impossible, if it were endeavoured, and would be foolish, if it were possible. Whatever withdraws us from the power of our senses; whatever makes the past, the distant, or the future predominate over the present, advances us in the dignity of thinking beings. Far from me and from my friends, be such frigid philosophy as may conduct us indifferent and unmoved over any ground which has been dignified by wisdom, bravery, or virtue. That man is little to be envied, whose patriotism would not gain force upon the plain of Marathon, or whose piety would not grow warmer among the ruins of Iona!

We came too late to visit monuments: some care was necessary for ourselves. Whatever was in the island, Sir Allan could command, for the inhabitants were Macleans; but having little they could not give us much. He went to the headman of the island, whom Fame, but Fame delights in amplifying, represents as worth no less than fifty pounds. He was perhaps proud enough of his guests, but ill prepared for our entertainment; however, he soon produced more provision than men not luxurious require. Our lodging was next to be provided.

We found a barn well stocked with hay, and made our beds as soft as we could.

In the morning we rose and surveyed the place. The churches of the two convents are both standing, though unroofed. They were built of unhewn stone, but solid, and not inelegant. I brought away rude measures of the buildings, such as I cannot much trust myself, inaccurately taken, and obscurely noted. Mr Pennant's delineations, which are doubtless exact, have made my skilful description less necessary.

The episcopal church consists of two parts, separated by the belfry, and built at different times. The original church had, like others, the altar at one end, and tower at the other; but as it grew too small, another building of equal dimension was added, and the tower then was necessarily in the middle.

That these edifices are of different ages seems evident. The arch of the first church is Roman, being part of a circle; that of the additional building is pointed, and therefore Gothic, or Saracenical; the tower is firm, and wants only to be floored and covered.

Of the chambers or cells belonging to the monks, there are some walls remaining but nothing approaching to a complete apartment.

The bottom of the church is so incumbered with mud and rubbish, that we could make no discoveries of curious inscriptions, and what there are have been already published. The place is said to be known where the black stones lie concealed, on which the old Highland Chiefs, when they made contracts and alliances, used to take the oath, which was considered as more sacred than any other obligation, and which could not be violated without the blackest infamy. In those days of violence and rapine, it was of great importance to impress upon savage minds the sanctity of an oath, by some particular and extraordinary circumstances. They would not have recourse to the black stones, upon small or common occasions, and when they had established their faith by this tremendous sanction, inconstancy and treachery were no longer feared.

The chapel of the nunnery is now used by the inhabitants as a kind of general cow-house, and the bottom is consequently too miry for examination. Some of the stones which covered the later abbesses have inscriptions, which might yet be read, if the chapel were cleansed. The roof of this, as of all the other buildings, is totally destroyed, not only because timber quickly decays when it is neglected, but because in an island utterly destitute of wood, it was wanted for use, and was consequently the first plunder of needy rapacity.

The chancel of the nuns' chapel is covered with an arch of stone, to which time has done no injury; and a small apartment communicating with the choir, on the north side, like the chapter-house in cathedrals, roofed with stone in the same manner, is likewise entire.

In one of the churches was a marble altar, which the superstition of the inhabitants has destroyed. Their opinion was, that a fragment of this stone was a defence against shipwrecks, fire, and miscarriages. In one corner of the church the basin for holy water is yet unbroken.

The cemetery of the nunnery was, till very lately, regarded with such reverence, that only women were buried in it. These relics of veneration always produce some mournful pleasure. I could have forgiven a great injury more easily than the violation of this imaginary sanctity.

South of the chapel stand the walls of a large room, which was probably the hall, or refectory of the nunnery. This apartment is capable of repair. Of the rest of the convent there are only fragments.

Besides the two principal churches, there are, I think, five chapels yet standing, and three more remembered. There are also crosses, of which two bear the names of St John and St Matthew.

A large space of ground about these consecrated edifices is covered with gravestones, few of which have any inscription. He that surveys it, attended by an insular antiquary, may be told where the Kings of many nations are buried, and if he loves to soothe his imagination with the thoughts that naturally rise in places where the great and the powerful lie mingled with the dust, let him listen in submissive silence; for if he asks any questions, his delight is at an end.

Iona has long enjoyed, without any very credible attestation, the honour of being reputed the cemetery of the Scottish Kings. It is not unlikely that, when the opinion of local sanctity was prevalent, the

Chieftains of the Isles, and perhaps some of the Norwegian or Irish princes were reposited in this venerable enclosure. But by whom the subterraneous vaults are peopled is now utterly unknown. The graves are very numerous, and some of them undoubtedly contain the remains of men, who did not expect to be so soon forgotten.

Not far from this awful ground, may be traced the garden of the monastery: the fishponds are yet discernible, and the aqueduct, which supplied them, is still in use.

There remains a broken building, which is called the Bishop's house, I know not by what authority. It was once the residence of some man above the common rank, for it has two stories and a chimney. We were shown a chimney at the other end, which was only a niche, without perforation, but so much does antiquarian credulity, or patriotic vanity prevail, that it was not much more safe to trust the eye of our instructor than the memory.

There is in the island one house more, and only one, that has a chimney: we entered it, and found it neither wanting repair nor inhabitants; but to the farmers, who now possess it, the chimney is of no great value; for their fire was made on the floor, in the middle of the room, and notwithstanding the dignity of their mansion, they rejoiced, like their neighbours, in the comforts of smoke.

It is observed, that ecclesiastical colleges are always in the most pleasant and fruitful places. While the world allowed the monks their choice, it is surely no dishonour that they chose well. This island is remarkably fruitful. The village near the churches is said to contain seventy families, which, at five in a family, is more than a hundred inhabitants to a mile. There are perhaps other villages; yet both corn and cattle are annually exported.

But the fruitfulness of Iona is now its whole prosperity. The inhabitants are remarkably gross, and remarkably neglected: I know not if they are visited by any Minister. The island, which was once the metropolis of learning and piety, has now no school for education, nor temple for worship, only two inhabitants that can speak English, and not one that can write or read.

The people are of the clan of Maclean; and though Sir Allan had not been in the place for many years, he was received with all the reverence due to their Chieftain. One of them being sharply reprehended by him, for not sending him some rum, declared after his departure, in Mr Boswell's presence, that he had no design of disappointing him, 'for,' said he, 'I would cut my bones for him; and if he had sent his dog for it, he should have had it.'

When we were to depart, our boat was left by the ebb at a great distance from the water, but no sooner did we wish it afloat, than the islanders gathered round it, and, by the union of many hands, pushed it down the beach; every man who could contribute his help seemed to think himself happy in the opportunity of being, for a moment, useful to his Chief.

We now left those illustrious ruins, by which Mr Boswell was much affected, nor would I willingly be thought to have looked upon them without some emotion. Perhaps, in the revolutions of the world, Iona may be sometime again the instructress of the Western Regions.

It was no long voyage to Mull, where, under Sir Allan's protection, we landed in the evening, and were entertained for the night by Mr Maclean, a Minister that lives upon the coast, whose elegance of conversation, and strength of judgement, would make him conspicuous in places of greater celebrity. Next day we dined with Dr Maclean, another physician, and then travelled on to the house of a very powerful Laird, Maclean of Lochbuy; for in this country every man's name is Maclean.

Where races are thus numerous and thus combined, none but the Chief of a clan is addressed by his name. The Laird of Dunvegan is called Macleod, but other gentlemen of the same family are denominated by the places where they reside, as Raasay, or Talisker. The distinction of the meaner people is made by their Christian names. In consequence of this practice, the late Laird of Macfarlane, an eminent genealogist, considered himself as disrespectfully treated, if the common addition was applied to him. Mr Macfarlane, said he, may with equal propriety be said to many; but I, and I only, am Macfarlane.

Our afternoon journey was through a country of such gloomy desolation, that Mr Boswell thought no part of the Highlands equally terrific, yet we came without any difficulty, at evening, to Lochbuy, where we found a true Highland Laird, rough and haughty, and tenacious of his dignity; who, hearing my name, inquired whether I was of the Johnstons of Glencoe, or of Ardnamurchan.

Lochbuy has, like the other insular Chieftains, quitted the castle that sheltered his ancestors, and lives near it, in a mansion not very spacious or splendid. I have seen no houses in the Islands much to be envied for convenience or magnificence, yet they bear testimony to the progress of arts and civility, as they show that rapine and surprise are no longer dreaded, and are much more commodious than the ancient fortresses.

The castles of the Hebrides, many of which are standing, and many ruined, were always built upon points of land, on the margin of the sea. For the choice of this situation there must have been some general reason, which the change of manners has left in obscurity. They were of no use in the days of piracy, as defences of the coast; for it was equally accessible in other places. Had they been sea-marks or lighthouses, they would have been of more use to the invader than the natives, who could want no such directions on their own waters: for a watch-tower, a cottage on a hill would have been better, as it would have commanded a wider view.

If they be considered merely as places of retreat, the situation seems not well chosen; for the Laird of an island is safest from foreign enemies in the centre: on the coast he might be more suddenly surprised than in the inland parts; and the invaders, if their enterprise miscarried, might more easily retreat. Some convenience, however, whatever it was, their position on the shore afforded; for uniformity of practice seldom continues long without good reason.

A castle in the Islands is only a single tower of three or four stories, of which the walls are sometimes eight or nine feet thick, with narrow windows, and close winding stairs of stone. The top rises in a cone, or pyramid of stone, encompassed by battlements. The intermediate floors are sometimes frames of timber, as in common houses, and sometimes arches of stone, or alternately stone and timber; so that there was very little danger from fire. In the centre of every floor, from top to bottom, is the chief room, of no great extent, round which there are narrow cavities, or recesses, formed by small vacuities, or by a double wall. I know not whether there be ever more than one fireplace. They had not capacity to contain many people, or much provision; but their enemies could seldom stay to blockade them; for if they failed in the first attack, their next care was to escape.

The walls were always too strong to be shaken by such desultory hostilities; the windows were too narrow to be entered, and the battlements too high to be scaled. The only danger was at the gates, over which the wall was built with a square cavity, not unlike a chimney, continued to the top. Through this hollow the defendants let fall stones upon those who attempted to break the gate, and poured down water, perhaps scalding water, if the attack was made with fire. The castle of Lochbuy was secured by double doors, of which the outer was an iron grate.

In every castle is a well and a dungeon. The use of the well is evident. The dungeon is a deep subterraneous cavity, walled on the sides, and arched on the top, into which the descent is through a narrow door, by a ladder or a rope, so that it seems impossible to escape, when the rope or ladder is drawn up. The dungeon was, I suppose, in war, a prison for such captives as were treated with severity, and, in peace, for such delinquents as had committed crimes within the Laird's jurisdiction; for the mansions of many Lairds were, till the late privation of their privileges, the halls of justice to their own tenants.

As these fortifications were the productions of mere necessity, they are built only for safety, with little regard to convenience, and with none to elegance or pleasure. It was sufficient for a Laird of the Hebrides, if he had a strong house, in which he could hide his wife and children from the next clan. That they are not large nor splendid is no wonder. It is not easy to find how they were raised, such as they are, by men who had no money, in countries where the labourers and artificers could scarcely be fed. The buildings in different parts of the Islands show their degrees of wealth and power. I believe that for all the castles which I have seen beyond the Tweed, the ruins yet remaining of some one of these which the English built in Wales, would supply materials.

These castles afford another evidence that the fictions of romantic chivalry had for their basis the real manners of the feudal times, when every Lord of a seignory lived in his hold lawless and unaccountable, with all the licentiousness and insolence of uncontested superiority and unprincipled power. The traveller, whoever he might be, coming to the fortified habitation of a Chieftain, would, probably, have been interrogated from the battlements, admitted with caution at the gate, introduced to a petty Monarch, fierce with habitual hostility, and vigilant with ignorant suspicion; who, according to his general temper, or accidental humour, would have seated a stranger as his guest at the table, or as a spy confined him in the dungeon.

Lochbuy means the *Yellow Lake*, which is the name given to an inlet of the sea, upon which the castle of Mr Maclean stands. The reason of the appellation we did not learn.

We were now to leave the Hebrides, where we had spent some weeks with sufficient amusement, and where we had amplified our thoughts with new scenes of nature, and new modes of life. More time would have given us a more distinct view, but it was necessary that Mr Boswell should return before the courts of justice were opened; and it was not proper to live too long upon hospitality, however liberally imparted.

Of these Islands it must be confessed, that they have not many allurements, but to the mere lover of naked nature. The inhabitants are thin, provisions are scarce, and desolation and penury give little pleasure.

The people collectively considered are not few, though their numbers are small in proportion to the space which they occupy. Mull is said to contain six thousand, and Sky fifteen thousand.[43] Of the computation respecting Mull, I can give no account; but when I doubted the truth of the numbers attributed to Sky, one of the Ministers exhibited such facts as conquered my incredulity.

Of the proportion, which the product of any region bears to the people, an estimate is commonly made according to the pecuniary price of the necessaries of life; a principle of judgement which is never certain, because it supposes what is far from truth, that the value of money is always the same, and so measures an unknown quantity by an uncertain standard. It is competent enough when the markets of the same country, at different times, and those times not too distant, are to be compared; but of very little use for the purpose of making one nation acquainted with the state of another. Provisions, though plentiful, are sold in places of great pecuniary opulence for nominal prices, to which, however scarce, where gold and silver are yet scarcer they can never be raised.

In the Western Islands there is so little internal commerce, that hardly anything has a known or settled rate. The price of things brought in, or carried out, is to be considered as that of a foreign market; and even this there is some difficulty in discovering, because their denominations of quantity are different from ours; and when there is ignorance on both sides, no appeal can be made to a common measure.

This, however, is not the only impediment. The Scots, with a vigilance of jealousy[44] which never goes to sleep, always suspect that an Englishman despises them for their poverty, and to convince him that they are not less rich than their neighbours, are sure to tell him a price higher than the true. When Lesley, two hundred years ago, related so punctiliously, that a hundred hen eggs, new laid, were sold in the Islands for a penny, he supposed that no inference could possibly follow, but that eggs were in great abundance. Posterity has since grown wiser; and having learned, that nominal and real value may differ, they now tell no such stories, lest the foreigner should happen to collect, not that eggs are many, but that pence are few.

Money and wealth have by the use of commercial language been so long confounded, that they are commonly supposed to be the same; and this prejudice has spread so widely in Scotland, that I know not whether I found man or woman, whom I interrogated concerning payments of money, that could surmount the illiberal desire of deceiving me, by representing every thing as dearer than it is.

From Lochbuy we rode a very few miles to the side of Mull, which faces Scotland, where, having taken leave of our kind protector, Sir Allan, we embarked in a boat, in which the seat provided for our accommodation was a heap of rough brushwood; and on the twenty-second of October reposed at a tolerable inn on the mainland.

On the next day we began our journey southwards. The weather was tempestuous. For half the day the ground was rough, and our horses were still small. Had they required much restraint, we might have been reduced to difficulties; for I think we had amongst us but one bridle. We fed the poor animals liberally, and they performed their journey well. In the latter part of the day, we came to a firm and smooth road, made by the soldiers, on which we travelled with great security, busied with contemplating the scene about us. The night came on while we had yet a great part of the way to go, though not so dark, but that we could discern the cataracts which poured down the hills, on one side, and fell into one general channel that ran with great violence on the other. The wind was loud, the rain was heavy, and the whistling of the blast, the fall of the shower, the rush of the cataracts, and the roar of the torrent, made a nobler chorus of the rough music of nature than it had ever been my chance to hear before. The streams, which ran across the way from the hills to the main current, were so frequent, that after a while I began to count them; and, in ten miles, reckoned fifty-five, probably missing some, and having let some pass before they forced themselves upon my notice. At last we came to Inverary, where we found an inn, not only commodious, but magnificent.

The difficulties of peregrination were now at an end.

THE LIFE OF COWLEY

'ON METAPHYSICAL POETRY'

COWLEY, like other poets who have written with narrow views and, instead of tracing intellectual pleasure to its natural sources in the mind of man, paid their court to temporary prejudices, has been at one time too much praised and too much neglected at another.

Wit, like all other things subject by their nature to the choice of man, has its changes and fashions, and at different times takes different forms. About the beginning of the seventeenth century appeared a race of writers that may be termed the metaphysical poets, of whom in a criticism on the works of Cowley it is not improper to give some account.

The metaphysical poets were men of learning, and to show their learning was their whole endeavour; but, unluckily resolving to show it in rhyme, instead of writing poetry they only wrote verses, and very often such verses as stood the trial of the finger better than of the ear; for the modulation was so imperfect that they were only found to be verses by counting the syllables.

If the father of criticism[1] has rightly denominated poetry τέχνη μιμητική, *an imitative art*, these writers will without great wrong lose their right to the name of poets, for they cannot be said to have imitated anything: they neither copied nature nor life; neither painted the forms of matter nor represented the operations of intellect.

Those however who deny them to be poets allow them to be wits. Dryden confesses of himself and his contemporaries that they fall below Donne in wit, but maintains that they surpass him in poetry.

If Wit be well described by Pope as being 'that which has been often thought, but was never before so well expressed', they certainly never attained nor ever sought it, for they endeavoured to be singular in their thoughts, and were careless of their diction. But Pope's account of wit is undoubtedly erroneous; he depresses it below its natural dignity, and reduces it from strength of thought to happiness of language.

If by a more noble and more adequate conception that be considered as Wit which is at once natural and new, that which though not obvious upon its first production, acknowledged to be just; if it be that, which he that never found it, wonders how he missed; to wit of this kind the metaphysical poets have seldom risen. Their thoughts are often new, but seldom natural; they are not obvious, but neither are they just; and the reader, far from wondering that he missed them, wonders more frequently by what perverseness of industry they were ever found.

But Wit, abstracted from its effects upon the hearer, may be more rigorously and philosophically considered as a kind of *discordia concors*; a combination of dissimilar images, or discovery of occult resemblances in things apparently unlike. Of wit, thus defined, they have more than enough. The most heterogeneous ideas are yoked by violence together; nature and art are ransacked for illustrations, comparisons, and allusions; their learning instructs, and their subtlety surprises; but the reader commonly thinks his improvement dearly bought, and, though he sometimes admires, is seldom pleased.

From this account of their compositions it will be readily inferred that they were not successful in representing or moving the affections. As they were wholly employed on something unexpected and surprising they had no regard to that uniformity of sentiment, which enables us to conceive and to excite the pains and the pleasure of other minds: they never inquired what on any occasion they should have said or done, but wrote rather as beholders than partakers of human nature; as beings looking upon good and evil, impassive and at leisure; as Epicurean deities making remarks on the actions of men and the vicissitudes of life, without interest and without emotion. Their courtship was void of fondness and their lamentation of sorrow.

Their wish was only to say what they hoped had been never said before.

Nor was the sublime more within their reach than the pathetic; for they never attempted that comprehension and expanse of thought which at once fills the whole mind, and of which the first effect is sudden astonishment, and the second rational admiration. Sublimity is produced by aggregation, and littleness by dispersion. Great thoughts are always general,[2] and consist in positions not limited by exceptions, and in descriptions not descending to minuteness. It is with great propriety that subtlety, which in its original import means exility of particles,[3] is taken in its metaphorical meaning for nicety of distinction. Those writers who lay on the watch for novelty could have little hope of greatness; for great things cannot have escaped former observation. Their attempts were always analytic: they broke every image into fragments, and could no more represent by their slender conceits and laboured particularities the prospects of nature or the scenes of life, than he who dissects a sunbeam with a prism can exhibit the wide effulgence of a summer noon.

What they wanted however of the sublime they endeavoured to supply by hyperbole; their amplification had no limits: they left not only reason but fancy behind them, and produced combinations of confused magnificence that not only could not be credited, but could not be imagined.

Yet labour directed by great abilities is never wholly lost: if they frequently threw away their wit upon false conceits, they likewise sometimes struck out unexpected truth: if their conceits were far-fetched, they were often worth the carriage. To write on their plan it was at least necessary to read and think. No man could be born a metaphysical poet, nor assume the dignity of a writer by descriptions copied from descriptions, by imitations borrowed from imitations, by traditional imagery and hereditary similes, by readiness of rhyme and volubility of syllables.

In perusing the works of this race of authors the mind is exercised either by recollection or inquiry; either something already learned is to be retrieved, or something new is to be examined. If their greatness seldom elevates, their acuteness often surprises; if the imagination is not always gratified, at least the powers of reflection and comparison are employed; and in the mass of materials, which ingenious absurdity has thrown together, genuine wit and useful knowledge may be sometimes found, buried perhaps in grossness of expression, but useful to those who know their value, and such as, when they are expanded to perspicuity and polished to elegance, may give lustre to works which have more propriety though less copiousness of sentiment.

This kind of writing, which was, I believe, borrowed from Marino and his followers, had been recommended by the example of Donne, a man of very extensive and various knowledge, and by Jonson, whose manner resembled that of Donne more in the ruggedness of his lines than in the cast of his sentiments.

When their reputation was high they had undoubtedly more imitators than time has left behind. Their immediate successors, of whom any remembrance can be said to remain, were Suckling, Waller, Denham, Cowley, Cleveland, and Milton. Denham and Waller sought another way to fame, by improving the harmony of our numbers. Milton tried the metaphysic style only in his lines upon Hobson the Carrier.[4] Cowley adopted it, and excelled his predecessors; having as much sentiment and more music. Suckling neither improved versification nor abounded in conceits. The fashionable style remained chiefly with Cowley: Suckling could not reach it, and Milton disdained it.

FROM

THE LIFE OF WALLER

'ON DEVOTIONAL POETRY'

It has been the frequent lamentation of good men that verse has been too little applied to the purposes of worship, and many attempts have been made to animate devotion by pious poetry; that they have very seldom attained their end is sufficiently known, and it may not be improper to inquire why they have miscarried.

Let no pious ear be offended if I advance, in opposition to many authorities, that poetical devotion cannot often please. The doctrines of religion may indeed be defended in a didactic poem, and he who has the happy power of arguing in verse will not lose it because his subject is sacred. A poet may describe the beauty and the grandeur of Nature, the flowers of the Spring, and the harvests of Autumn, the vicissitudes of the Tide, and the revolutions of the Sky, and praise the Maker for his works in lines which no reader shall lay aside. The subject of the disputation is not piety, but the motives to piety; that of the description is not God, but the works of God.

Contemplative piety, or the intercourse between God and the human soul, cannot be poetical. Man admitted to implore the mercy of his Creator and plead the merits of his Redeemer is already in a higher state than poetry can confer.

The essence of poetry is invention; such invention as, by producing something unexpected, surprises and delights. The topics of devotion are few, and being few are universally known; but, few as they are, they can be made no more; they can receive no grace from novelty of sentiment, and very little from novelty of expression.

Poetry pleases by exhibiting an idea more grateful to the mind than things themselves afford. This effect proceeds from the display of those parts of nature which attract, and the concealment of those which repel, the imagination: but religion must be shown as it is; suppression and addition equally corrupt it, and such as it is, it is known already.

From poetry the reader justly expects, and from good poetry always obtains, the enlargement of his comprehension and elevation of his fancy; but this is rarely to be hoped by Christians from metrical devotion. Whatever is great, desirable, or tremendous, is comprised in the name of the Supreme Being. Omnipotence cannot be exalted; Infinity cannot be amplified; Perfection cannot be improved.

The employments of pious meditation are Faith, Thanksgiving, Repentance, and Supplication. Faith, invariably uniform, cannot be invested by fancy with decorations. Thanksgiving, the most joyful of all holy effusions, yet addressed to a Being without passions, is confined to a few modes, and is to be felt rather than expressed. Repentance, trembling in the presence of the judge, is not at leisure for cadences and epithets. Supplication of man to man may diffuse itself through many topics of persuasion, but supplication to God can only cry for mercy.

Of sentiments purely religious, it will be found that the most simple expression is the most sublime. Poetry loses its lustre and its power, because it is applied to the decoration of something more excellent than itself. All that pious verse can do is to help the memory and delight the ear, and for these purposes it may be very useful; but it applies nothing to the mind. The ideas of Christian Theology are too simple for eloquence, too sacred for fiction, and too majestic for ornament; to recommend them by tropes and figures is to magnify by a concave mirror the sidereal hemisphere.

FROM

THE LIFE OF MILTON

'ON MILTON'S POETRY'

In the examination of Milton's poetical works I shall pay so much regard to time as to begin with his juvenile productions. For his earlier pieces he seems to have had a degree of fondness not very laudable: what he has once written he resolves to preserve, and gives to the public an unfinished poem, which he broke off because he was 'nothing satisfied with what he had done', supposing his readers less nice than himself. These preludes to his future labours are in Italian, Latin, and English. Of the Italian I cannot pretend to speak as a critic, but I have heard them commended by a man well qualified to decide their merit. The Latin pieces are lusciously elegant; but the delight which they afford is rather by the exquisite imitation of the ancient writers, by the purity of the diction, and the harmony of the numbers, than by any power of invention or vigour of sentiment. They are not all of equal value; the elegies excel the odes, and some of the exercises on Gunpowder Treason might have been spared.

The English poems, though they make no promises of *Paradise Lost*, have their evidence of genius, that they have a cast original and unborrowed. But their peculiarity is not excellence: if they differ from verses of others, they differ for the worse; for they are too often distinguished by repulsive harshness; the combinations of words are new, but they are not pleasing; the rhymes and epithets seem to be laboriously sought and violently applied.

That in the early parts of his life he wrote with much care appears from his manuscripts, happily preserved at Cambridge, in which many of his smaller works are found as they were first written, with the subsequent corrections. Such relics show how excellence is acquired: what we hope ever to do with ease we may learn first to do with diligence.

Those who admire the beauties of this great poet sometimes force their own judgement into false approbation of his little pieces, and prevail upon themselves to think that admirable which is only singular. All that short compositions can commonly attain is neatness and elegance. Milton never learned the art of doing little things with grace; he overlooked the milder excellence of suavity and softness: he was a 'Lion'[1] that had no skill 'in dandling the Kid'.

One of the poems on which much praise has been bestowed is *Lycidas*; of which the diction is harsh, the rhymes uncertain, and the numbers unpleasing. What beauty there is we must therefore seek in the sentiments and images. It is not to be considered as the effusion of real passion; for passion runs not after remote allusions and obscure opinions. Passion plucks no berries from the myrtle and ivy, nor calls upon Arethuse and Mincius, nor tells of 'rough satyrs and fauns with cloven heel'. Where there is leisure for fiction there is little grief.

In this poem there is no nature, for there is no truth; there is no art, for there is nothing new. Its form is that of a pastoral, easy, vulgar, and therefore disgusting:[2] whatever images it can supply are long ago exhausted; and its inherent improbability always forces dissatisfaction on the mind. When Cowley tells of Hervey[3] that they studied together, it is easy to suppose how much he must miss the companion of his labours and the partner of his discoveries; but what image of tenderness can be excited by these lines!

> We drove a field, and both together heard
> What time the grey fly winds her sultry horn,
> Battening our flocks with the fresh dews of night.

We know that they never drove a field, and that they had no flocks to batten; and though it be allowed that the representation may be allegorical, the true meaning is so uncertain and remote that it is never sought because it cannot be known when it is found.

Among the flocks and copses and flowers appear the heathen deities, Jove and Phœbus, Neptune and Æolus, with a long train of mythological imagery, such as a College easily supplies. Nothing can less display knowledge or less exercise invention than to tell how a shepherd has lost his companion and must now feed his flocks alone, without any judge of his skill in piping; and how one god asks another god what is become of Lycidas, and how neither god can tell. He who thus grieves will excite no sympathy; he who thus praises will confer no honour.

This poem has yet a grosser fault. With these trifling fictions are mingled the most awful and sacred truths, such as ought never to be polluted with such irreverent combinations. The shepherd likewise is now a feeder of sheep, and afterwards an ecclesiastical pastor, a superintendent of a Christian flock. Such equivocations are always unskilful; but here they are indecent, and at least approach to impiety, of which, however, I believe the writer not to have been conscious.

Such is the power of reputation justly acquired that its blaze drives away the eye from nice examination. Surely no man could have fancied that he read *Lycidas* with pleasure had he not known its author.

Of the two pieces, *L'Allegro* and *Il Penseroso*, I believe opinion is uniform; every man that reads them, reads them with pleasure. The author's design is not, what Theobald has remarked, merely to show how objects derived their colours from the mind, by representing the operation of the same things upon the gay and the melancholy temper, or upon the same man as he is differently disposed; but rather how, among the successive variety of appearances, every disposition of mind takes hold on those by which it may be gratified.

The *cheerful* man hears the lark in the morning; the *pensive* man hears the nightingale in the evening. The *cheerful* man sees the cock strut, and hears the horn and hounds echo in the wood; then walks 'not unseen' to observe the glory of the rising sun or listen to the singing milk-maid, and view the labours of the ploughman and the mower; then casts his eyes about him over scenes of smiling plenty, and looks up to the distant tower, the residence of some fair inhabitant: thus he pursues rural gaiety through a day of labour or of play, and delights himself at night with the fanciful narratives of superstitious ignorance.

The *pensive* man at one time walks 'unseen' to muse at midnight, and at another hears the sullen curfew. If the weather drives him home he sits in a room lighted only by 'glowing embers'; or by a lonely lamp outwatches the North Star to discover the habitation of separate souls, and varies the shades of meditation by contemplating the magnificent or pathetic scenes of tragic and epic poetry. When the morning comes, a morning gloomy with rain and wind, he walks into the dark trackless woods, falls asleep by some murmuring water, and with melancholy enthusiasm expects some dream of prognostication or some music played by aerial performers.

Both Mirth and Melancholy are solitary, silent inhabitants of the breast that neither receive nor transmit communication; no mention is therefore made of a philosophical friend or a pleasant companion. The seriousness does not arise from any participation of calamity, nor the gaiety from the pleasures of the bottle.

The man of *cheerfulness* having exhausted the country tries what 'towered cities' will afford, and mingles with scenes of splendour, gay assemblies, and nuptial festivities; but he mingles a mere spectator as, when the learned comedies of Jonson or the wild dramas of Shakespeare are exhibited, he attends the theatre.

The *pensive* man never loses himself in crowds, but walks the cloister or frequents the cathedral. Milton probably had not yet forsaken the Church.

Both his characters delight in music; but he seems to think that cheerful notes would have obtained from Pluto a complete dismission of Eurydice, of whom solemn sounds only procured a conditional release.

For the old age of Cheerfulness he makes no provision; but Melancholy he conducts with great dignity to the close of life. His Cheerfulness is without levity, and his Pensiveness without asperity.

Through these two poems the images are properly selected and nicely distinguished, but the colours of the diction seem not sufficiently apart. No mirth can, indeed, be found in his melancholy; but I am afraid that I always meet some melancholy in his mirth. They are two noble efforts of imagination.

The greatest of his juvenile performances is the *Mask of Comus*, in which may very plainly be discovered the dawn or twilight of *Paradise Lost*. Milton appears to have formed very early that system of diction and mode of verse[4] which his maturer judgement approved, and from which he never endeavoured nor desired to deviate.

Nor does *Comus* afford only a specimen of his language: it exhibits likewise his power of description and his vigour of sentiment, employed in the praise and defence of virtue. A work more truly poetical is rarely found; allusions, images, and descriptive epithets embellish almost every period with lavish decoration. As a series of lines, therefore, it may be considered as worthy of all the admiration with which the votaries have received it.

As a drama it is deficient. The action is not probable. A Masque, in those parts where supernatural intervention is admitted, must indeed be given up to all the freaks of imagination; but so far as the action is merely human it ought to be reasonable, which can hardly be said of the conduct of the two brothers, who, when their sister sinks with fatigue in a pathless wilderness, wander both away in search of berries too far to find their way back, and leave a helpless Lady to all the sadness and danger of solitude. This however is a defect over-balanced by its convenience.

What deserves more reprehension is that the prologue spoken in the wild wood by the attendant Spirit is addressed to the audience; a mode of communication so contrary to the nature of dramatic representation that no precedents can support it.

The discourse of the Spirit is too long, an objection that may be made to almost all the following speeches; they have not the spriteliness of a dialogue animated by reciprocal contention, but seem rather declamations deliberately composed and formally repeated on a moral question. The auditor therefore listens as to a lecture, without passion, without anxiety.

The song of Comus has airiness and jollity; but, what may recommend Milton's morals as well as his poetry, the invitations to pleasure are so general that they excite no distinct images of corrupt enjoyment, and take no dangerous hold on the fancy.

The following soliloquies of Comus and the Lady are elegant, but tedious. The song must owe much to the voice, if it ever can delight. At last the Brothers enter, with too much tranquillity; and when they have feared lest their sister should be in danger, and hoped that she is not in danger, the Elder makes a speech in praise of chastity, and the Younger finds how fine it is to be a philosopher.

Then descends the Spirit in form of a shepherd; and the Brother, instead of being in haste to ask his help, praises his singing, and inquires his business in that place. It is remarkable that at this interview the Brother is taken with a short fit of rhyming. The Spirit relates that the Lady is in the power of Comus, the Brother moralizes again, and the Spirit makes a long narration, of no use because it is false, and therefore unsuitable to a good Being.

In all these parts the language is poetical and the sentiments are generous, but there is something wanting to allure attention.

The dispute between the Lady and Comus is the most animated and affecting scene of the drama, and wants nothing but a brisker reciprocation of objections and replies, to invite attention and detain it.

The songs are vigorous and full of imagery; but they are harsh in their diction, and not very musical in their numbers.

Throughout the whole the figures are too bold and the language too luxuriant for dialogue: it is a drama in the epic style, inelegantly splendid, and tediously instructive.

The *Sonnets* were written in different parts of Milton's life upon different occasions. They deserve not any particular criticism; for of the best it can only be said that they are not bad, and perhaps only the eighth and the twenty-first[5] are truly entitled to this slender commendation. The fabric of a sonnet, however adapted to the Italian language, has never succeeded in ours, which, having a greater variety of termination, requires the rhymes to be often changed.

Those little pieces may be dispatched without much anxiety; a greater work calls for greater care. I am now to examine *Paradise Lost*, a poem which, considered with respect to design, may claim the first place, and with respect to performance the second, among the productions of the human mind.

By the general consent of critics the first praise of genius is due to the writer of an epic poem, as it requires an assemblage of all the powers which are singly sufficient for other compositions. Poetry is the art of uniting pleasure with truth,[6] by calling imagination to the help of reason. Epic poetry undertakes to teach the most important truths by the most pleasing precepts, and therefore relates some great event in the most affecting manner. History must supply the writer with the rudiments of narration, which he must improve and exalt by a nobler art, must animate by dramatic energy, and diversify by retrospection and anticipation; morality must teach him the exact bounds and different shades of vice and virtue; from policy and the practice of life he has to learn the discriminations of character and the tendency of the passions, either single or combined; and physiology[7] must supply him with illustrations and images. To put these materials to poetical use is required an imagination capable of painting nature and realizing fiction. Nor is he yet a poet till he has attained the whole extension of his language, distinguished all the delicacies of phrase, and all the colours of words, and learned to adjust their different sounds to all the varieties of metrical modulation.

Bossu[8] is of opinion that the poet's first work is to find a *moral*, which his fable is afterwards to illustrate and establish. This seems to have been the process only of Milton: the moral of other poems is incidental and consequent; in Milton's only it is essential and intrinsic. His purpose was the most useful and the most arduous: 'to vindicate the ways of God to man'; to show the reasonableness of religion, and the necessity of obedience to the Divine Law.

To convey this moral there must be a *fable*, a narration artfully constructed so as to excite curiosity and surprise expectation. In this part of his work Milton must be confessed to have equalled every other poet. He has involved in his account of the Fall of Man the events which preceded, and those that were to follow it: he has interwoven the whole system of theology with such propriety that every part appears to be necessary, and scarcely any recital is wished shorter for the sake of quickening the progress of the main action.

The subject of an epic poem is naturally an event of great importance. That of Milton is not the destruction of a city, the conduct of a colony, or the foundation of an empire.[9] His subject is the fate of worlds, the revolutions of heaven and of earth; rebellion against the Supreme King raised by the highest order of created beings; the overthrow of their host and the punishment of their crime; the creation of a new race of reasonable creatures; their original happiness and innocence, their forfeiture of immortality, and their restoration to hope and peace.

Great events can be hastened or retarded only by persons of elevated dignity. Before the greatness displayed in Milton's poem all other greatness shrinks away. The weakest of his agents are the highest and noblest of human beings, the original parents of mankind; with whose actions the elements consented; on whose rectitude or deviation of will depended the state of terrestrial nature and the condition of all the future inhabitants of the globe.

Of the other agents in the poem the chief are such as it is irreverence to name on slight occasions. The rest were lower powers;

> of which the least could wield
> Those elements, and arm him with the force
> Of all their regions;[10]

powers which only the control of Omnipotence restrains from laying creation waste, and filling the vast expanse of space with ruin and confusion. To display the motives and actions of beings thus superior, so far as human reason can examine them or human imagination represent them, is the task which this mighty poet has undertaken and performed.

In the examination of epic poems much speculation is commonly employed upon the *characters*. The characters in the *Paradise Lost* which admit of examination are those of angels and of man; of angels good and evil, of man in his innocent and sinful state.

Among the angels the virtue of Raphael is mild and placid, of easy condescension and free communication; that of Michael is regal and lofty, and, as may seem, attentive to the dignity of his own nature. Abdiel and Gabriel appear occasionally, and act as every incident requires; the solitary fidelity of Abdiel is very amiably[11] painted.

Of the evil angels the characters are more diversified. To Satan, as Addison observes, such sentiments are given as suit 'the most exalted and most depraved being'. Milton has been censured by Clarke for the impiety which sometimes breaks from Satan's mouth. For there are thoughts, as he justly remarks, which no observation of character can justify, because no good man would willingly permit them to pass, however transiently, through his own mind. To make Satan speak as a rebel, without any such expressions as might taint the reader's imagination, was indeed one of the great difficulties in Milton's undertaking, and I cannot but think that he has extricated himself with great happiness. There is in Satan's speeches little that can give pain to a pious ear. The language of rebellion cannot be the same with that of obedience. The malignity of Satan foams in haughtiness and obstinacy; but his expressions are commonly general, and no otherwise offensive than as they are wicked.

The other chiefs of the celestial rebellion are very judiciously discriminated in the first and second books; and the ferocious character of Moloch appears, both in the battle and the council, with exact consistency.

To Adam and to Eve are given during their innocence such sentiments as innocence can generate and utter. Their love is pure benevolence and mutual veneration; their repasts are without luxury and their diligence without toil. Their addresses to their Maker have little more than the voice of admiration and gratitude. Fruition[12] left them nothing to ask, and Innocence left them nothing to fear.

But with guilt enter distrust and discord, mutual accusation, and stubborn self-defence; they regard each other with alienated minds, and dread their Creator as the avenger of their transgression. At last they seek shelter in his mercy, soften to repentance, and melt in supplication. Both before and after the Fall the superiority of Adam is diligently sustained.

Of the *probable* and the *marvellous*, two parts of a vulgar epic poem which immerge the critic in deep consideration, the *Paradise Lost* requires little to be said. It contains the history of a miracle, of Creation and Redemption; it displays the power and the mercy of the Supreme Being: the probable therefore is marvellous, and the marvellous is probable. The substance of the narrative is truth; and as truth allows no choice, it is, like necessity, superior to rule. To the accidental or adventitious parts, as to every thing human, some slight exceptions may be made. But the main fabric is immovably supported.

It is justly remarked by Addison that this poem has, by the nature of its subject, the advantage above all others, that it is universally and perpetually interesting. All mankind will, through all ages, bear the same relation to Adam and to Eve, and must partake of that good and evil which extend to themselves.

Of the *machinery*, so called from Θεὸς ἀπὸ μηχανῆς,[13] by which is meant the occasional interposition of supernatural power, another fertile topic of critical remarks, here is no room to speak, because every thing is done under the immediate and visible direction of Heaven; but the rule is so far observed that no part of the action could have been accomplished by any other means.

Of *episodes*[14] I think there are only two, contained in Raphael's relation of the war in heaven and Michael's prophetic account of the changes to happen in this world. Both are closely connected with the great action; one was necessary to Adam as a warning, the other as a consolation.

To the completeness or *integrity* of the design nothing can be objected; it has distinctly and clearly what Aristotle requires, a beginning, a middle, and an end. There is perhaps no poem of the same length from which so little can be taken without apparent mutilation. Here are no funeral games,[15] nor is there any long description of a shield. The short digressions at the beginning of the third, seventh, and ninth books might doubtless be spared; but superfluities so beautiful who would take away? or who does not wish that the author of the *Iliad* had gratified succeeding ages with a little knowledge of himself? Perhaps no passages are more frequently or more attentively read than those extrinsic paragraphs; and, since the end of poetry is pleasure, that cannot be unpoetical with which all are pleased.

The questions, whether the action of the poem be strictly *one*, whether the poem can be properly termed *heroic*, and who is the hero, are raised by such readers as draw their principles of judgement rather from books than from reason. Milton, though he entitled *Paradise Lost* only a 'poem,' yet calls it himself 'heroic song.' Dryden, petulantly and indecently,[16] denies the heroism of Adam because he was overcome; but there is no reason why the hero should not be unfortunate except established practice, since success and virtue do not go necessarily together. Cato is the hero of Lucan,[17] but Lucan's authority will not be suffered by Quintilian to decide. However, if success be necessary, Adam's deceiver was at last crushed; Adam was restored to his Maker's favour, and therefore may securely resume his human rank.

After the scheme and fabric of the poem must be considered its component parts, the sentiments, and the diction.

The *sentiments*, as expressive of manners or appropriated to characters, are for the greater part unexceptionably just.

Splendid passages containing lessons of morality or precepts of prudence occur seldom. Such is the original formation of this poem that as it admits no human manners till the Fall, it can give little assistance to human conduct. Its end is to raise the thoughts above sublunary cares or pleasures. Yet the praise of that fortitude, with which Abdiel maintained his singularity of virtue against the scorn of multitudes, may be accommodated to all times; and Raphael's reproof of Adam's curiosity after the planetary motions, with the answer returned by Adam, may be confidently opposed to any rule of life which any poet has delivered.

The thoughts which are occasionally called forth in the progress are such as could only be produced by an imagination in the highest degree fervid and active, to which materials were supplied by incessant study and unlimited curiosity. The heat of Milton's mind might be said to sublimate his learning, to throw off into his work the spirit of science,[18] unmingled with its grosser parts.

He had considered creation in its whole extent, and his descriptions are therefore learned. He had accustomed his imagination to unrestrained indulgence, and his conceptions therefore were extensive. The characteristic quality of his poem is sublimity. He sometimes descends to the elegant, but his element is the great. He can occasionally invest himself with grace; but his natural port is gigantic loftiness. He can please when pleasure is required; but it is his peculiar power to astonish.

He seems to have been well acquainted with his own genius, and to know what it was that Nature had bestowed upon him more bountifully than upon others; the power of displaying the vast, illuminating the splendid, enforcing the awful, darkening the gloomy, and aggravating the dreadful: he therefore chose a subject on which too much could not be said, on which he might tire his fancy without the censure of extravagance.

The appearances of nature and the occurrence of life did not satiate his appetite of greatness. To paint things as they are requires a minute attention, and employs the memory rather than the fancy. Milton's delight was to sport in the wide regions of possibility; reality was a scene too narrow for his mind. He sent his faculties out upon discovery, into worlds where only imagination can travel, and delighted to form new modes of existence, and furnish sentiment and action to superior beings, to trace the counsels of hell, or accompany the choirs of heaven.

But he could not be always in other worlds: he must sometimes revisit earth, and tell of things visible and known. When he cannot raise wonder by the sublimity of his mind he gives delight by its fertility.

Whatever be his subject he never fails to fill the imagination. But his images and descriptions of the scenes or operations of Nature do not seem to be always copied from original form, nor to have the freshness, raciness, and energy of immediate observation. He saw Nature, as Dryden expresses it, 'through the spectacles of books'; and on most occasions calls learning to his assistance. The garden of Eden brings to his mind the vale of Enna, where Proserpine was gathering flowers. Satan makes his way through fighting elements, like Argo between the Cyanean rocks, or Ulysses between the two Sicilian whirlpools, when he shunned Charybdis 'on the larboard'. The mythological allusions have been justly censured, as not being always used with notice of their vanity;[19] but they contribute variety to the narration and produce an alternate exercise of the memory and the fancy.

His similes are less numerous and more various than those of his predecessors. But he does not confine himself within the limits of rigorous comparison: his great excellence is amplitude, and he expands the adventitious image beyond the dimensions which the occasion required. Thus, comparing the shield of Satan to the orb of the Moon, he crowds the imagination with the discovery of the telescope and all the wonders which the telescope discovers.

Of his moral sentiments it is hardly praise to affirm that they excel those of all other poets; for this superiority he was indebted to his acquaintance with the sacred writings. The ancient epic poets, wanting the light of Revelation, were very unskilful teachers of virtue: their principal characters may be great, but they are not amiable. The reader may rise from their works with a greater degree of active or passive fortitude, and sometimes of prudence; but he will be able to carry away few precepts of justice, and none of mercy.

From the Italian writers it appears that the advantages of even Christian knowledge may be possessed in vain. Ariosto's pravity[20] is generally known; and, though the *Deliverance of Jerusalem*[21] may be considered as a sacred subject, the poet has been very sparing of moral instruction.

In Milton every line breathes sanctity of thought and purity of manners, except when the train of the narration requires the introduction of the rebellious spirits; and even they are compelled to acknowledge their subjection to God in such a manner as excites reverence and confirms piety.

Of human beings there are but two; but those two are the parents of mankind, venerable before their fall for dignity and innocence, and amiable after it for repentance and submission. In their first state their affection is tender without weakness, and their pity sublime without presumption. When they have sinned they show how discord begins in mutual frailty, and how it ought to cease in mutual forbearance; how confidence of the divine favour is forfeited by sin, and how hope of pardon may be obtained by penitence and prayer. A state of innocence we can only conceive, if indeed in our present misery it be possible to conceive it; but the sentiments and worship proper to a fallen and offending being we have all to learn, as we have all to practise.

The poet whatever be done is always great. Our progenitors in their first state conversed with angels; even when folly and sin had degraded them they had not in their humiliation 'the port of mean suitors'; and they rise again to reverential regard when we find that their prayers were heard.

As human passions did not enter the world before the Fall, there is in the *Paradise Lost* little opportunity for the pathetic; but what little there is has not been lost. That passion which is peculiar to rational nature, the anguish arising from the consciousness of transgression and the horrors attending the sense of the Divine Displeasure, are very justly described and forcibly impressed. But the passions are moved only on one occasion; sublimity is the general and prevailing quality in this poem – sublimity variously modified, sometimes descriptive, sometimes argumentative.

The defects and faults of *Paradise Lost*,[22] for faults and defects every work of man must have, it is the business of impartial criticism to discover. As in displaying the excellence of Milton I have not made long quotations, because of selecting beauties there had been no end, I shall in the same general manner mention that which seems to deserve censure; for what Englishman can take delight in transcribing passages, which, if they lessen the reputation of Milton, diminish in some degree the honour of our country?

The generality of my scheme does not admit the frequent notice of verbal inaccuracies which Bentley,[23] perhaps better skilled in grammar than in poetry, has often found, though he sometimes made them, and which he imputed to the obtrusions of a reviser whom the author's blindness obliged him to employ. A supposition rash and groundless, if he thought it true; and vile and pernicious, if, as is said, he in private allowed it to be false.

The plan of *Paradise Lost* has this inconvenience, that it comprises neither human actions nor human manners. The man and woman who act and suffer are in a state which no other man or woman can ever know. The reader finds no transaction in which he can be engaged, beholds no condition in which he can by any effort of imagination place himself; he has, therefore, little natural curiosity or sympathy.

We all, indeed, feel the effects of Adam's disobedience; we all sin like Adam, and like him must all bewail our offences; we have restless and insidious enemies in the fallen angels, and in the blessed spirits we have guardians and friends; in the Redemption of mankind we hope to be included: in the description of heaven and hell we are surely interested, as we are all to reside hereafter either in the regions of horror or of bliss.

But these truths are too important to be new: they have been taught to our infancy; they have mingled with our solitary thoughts and familiar conversation, and are habitually interwoven with the whole texture of life. Being therefore not new they raise no unaccustomed emotion in the mind: what we knew before we cannot learn; what is not unexpected, cannot surprise.

Of the ideas suggested by these awful scenes, from some we recede with reverence, except when stated hours require their association; and from others we shrink with horror, or admit them only as salutary inflictions, as counterpoises to our interests and passions. Such images rather obstruct the career of fancy than incite it.

Pleasure and terror are indeed the genuine sources of poetry; but poetical pleasure must be such as human imagination can at least conceive, and poetical terror such as human strength and fortitude may combat. The good and evil of Eternity are too ponderous for the wings of wit; the mind sinks under them in passive helplessness, content with calm belief and humble adoration.

Known truths however may take a different appearance, and be conveyed to the mind by a new train of intermediate images. This Milton has undertaken, and performed with pregnancy and vigour of mind peculiar to himself. Whoever considers the few radical positions which the Scriptures afforded him will wonder by what energetic operations he expanded them to such extent and ramified them to so much variety, restrained as he was by religious reverence from licentiousness of fiction.

Here is a full display of the united force of study and genius; of a great accumulation of materials, with judgement to digest and fancy to combine them: Milton was able to select from nature or from story, from ancient fable or from modern science, whatever could illustrate or adorn his thoughts. An accumulation of knowledge impregnated his mind, fermented by study and exalted by imagination.

It has been therefore said without an indecent hyperbole by one of his encomiasts, that in reading *Paradise Lost* we read a book of universal knowledge.

But original deficience cannot be supplied.[24] The want of human interest is always felt. *Paradise Lost* is one of the books which the reader admires and lays down, and forgets to take up again. None ever wished it longer than it is. Its perusal is a duty rather than a pleasure. We read Milton for instruction, retire harassed and over-burdened, and look elsewhere for recreation; we desert our master, and seek for companions.

Another inconvenience of Milton's design is that it requires the description of what cannot be described, the agency of spirits. He saw that immateriality supplied no images, and that he could not show angels acting but by instruments of action; he therefore invested them with form and matter. This being necessary was therefore defensible; and he should have secured the consistency of his system by keeping immateriality out of sight, and enticing his reader to drop it from his thoughts. But he has unhappily perplexed his poetry with his philosophy. His infernal and celestial powers are sometimes pure spirit and sometimes animated body. When Satan walks with his lance upon the 'burning marle' he has a body; when in his passage between hell and the new world he is in danger of sinking in the vacuity and is supported by a gust of rising vapours he has a body; when he animates the toad he seems to be mere spirit that can penetrate matter at pleasure; when he 'starts up in his own shape', he has at least a determined form; and when he is brought before Gabriel he has 'a spear and a shield', which he had the power of hiding in the toad, though the arms of the contending angels are evidently material.

The vulgar inhabitants of Pandæmonium, being 'incorporeal spirits', are 'at large though without number' in a limited space, yet in the battle when they were overwhelmed by mountains their armour hurt them, 'crushed in upon their substance, now grown gross by sinning'. This likewise happened to the uncorrupted angels, who were overthrown 'the sooner for their arms, for unarmed they might easily as spirits have evaded by contraction or remove'. Even as spirits they are hardly spiritual, for 'contraction' and 'remove' are images of matter; but if they could have escaped without their armour, they might have escaped from it and left only the empty cover to be battered. Uriel, when he rides on a sunbeam, is material; Satan is material when he is afraid of the prowess of Adam.

The confusion of spirit and matter[25] which pervades the whole narration of the war of heaven fills it with incongruity; and the book in which it is related is, I believe, the favourite of children, and gradually neglected as knowledge is increased.

After the operation of immaterial agents which cannot be explained may be considered that of allegorical persons, which have no real existence. To exalt causes into agents, to invest abstract ideas with form, and animate them with activity has always been the right of poetry. But such airy beings are for the most part suffered only to do their natural office, and retire. Thus Fame tells a tale and Victory hovers over a general or perches on a standard; but Fame and Victory can do no more. To give them any real employment or ascribe to them any material agency is to make them allegorical no longer, but to shock the mind by ascribing effects to non-entity. In the *Prometheus* of Æschylus we see Violence and Strength, and in the *Alcestis* of Euripides we see Death, brought upon the stage, all as active persons of the drama; but no precedents can justify absurdity.

Milton's allegory of Sin and Death is undoubtedly faulty. Sin is indeed the mother of Death, and may be allowed to be the portress of hell; but when they stop the journey of Satan, a journey described as real, and when Death offers him battle, the allegory is broken. That Sin and Death should have shown the way to hell might have been allowed; but they cannot facilitate the passage by building a bridge, because the difficulty of Satan's passage is described as real and sensible, and the bridge ought to be only figurative. The hell assigned to the rebellious spirits is described as not less local than the residence of man. It is placed in some distant part of space, separated from the regions of harmony and order by a chaotic waste and an unoccupied vacuity; but Sin and Death worked up a 'mole of aggregated soil', cemented with asphaltus; a work too bulky for ideal architects.

This unskilful allegory appears to me one of the greatest faults of the poem; and to this there was no temptation, but the author's opinion of its beauty.

To the conduct of the narrative some objections may be made. Satan is with great expectation brought before Gabriel in Paradise, and is suffered to go away unmolested. The creation of man is represented as the consequence of the vacuity left in heaven by the expulsion of the rebels; yet Satan mentions it as a report 'rife in heaven' before his departure.

To find sentiments for the state of innocence was very difficult; and something of anticipation perhaps is now and then discovered. Adam's discourse of dreams seems not to be the speculation of a new-created being. I know not whether his answer to the angel's reproof for curiosity does not want something of propriety;[26] it is the speech of a man acquainted with many other men. Some philosophical notions, especially when the philosophy is false, might have been better omitted. The angel in a comparison speaks of 'timorous deer', before deer were yet timorous, and before Adam could understand the comparison.

Dryden remarks that Milton has some flats among his elevations. This is only to say that all the parts are not equal. In every work one part must be for the sake of others; a palace must have passages, a poem must have transitions. It is no more to be required that wit should always be blazing than that the sun should always stand at noon. In a great work there is a vicissitude of luminous and opaque parts, as there is in the world a succession of day and night. Milton, when he has expatiated in the sky, may be allowed sometimes to revisit earth; for what other author ever soared so high or sustained his flight so long?

Milton, being well versed in the Italian poets, appears to have borrowed often from them; and, as every man catches something from his companions, his desire of imitating Ariosto's levity has disgraced his work with the 'Paradise of Fools'; a fiction not in itself ill-imagined, but too ludicrous for its place.

His play on words, in which he delights too often; his equivocations, which Bentley endeavours to defend by the example of the ancients; his unnecessary and ungraceful use of terms of art[27], it is not necessary to mention, because they are easily remarked and generally censured, and at last bear so little proportion to the whole that they scarcely deserve the attention of a critic.

Such are the faults of that wonderful performance *Paradise Lost;* which he who can put in balance with its beauties must be considered not as nice but as dull, as less to be censured for want of candour than pitied for want of sensibility.

Of *Paradise Regained* the general judgement seems now to be right, that it is in many parts elegant, and everywhere instructive. It was not to be supposed that the writer of *Paradise Lost* could ever write without great effusions of fancy and exalted precepts of wisdom. The basis of *Paradise Regained* is narrow; a dialogue without action can never please like an union of the narrative and dramatic powers. Had this poem been written, not by Milton but by some imitator, it would have claimed and received universal praise.

If *Paradise Regained* has been too much depreciated, *Samson Agonistes* has in requital been too much admired. It could only be by long prejudice and the bigotry of learning that Milton could prefer the ancient tragedies with their encumbrance of a chorus to the exhibitions of the French and English stages; and it is only by a blind confidence in the reputation of Milton that a drama can be praised in which the intermediate parts have neither cause nor consequence, neither hasten nor retard the catastrophe.

In this tragedy are however many particular beauties, many just sentiments and striking lines; but it wants that power of attracting attention which a well-connected plan produces.

Milton would not have excelled in dramatic writing; he knew human nature only in the gross, and had never studied the shades of character, nor the combinations of concurring or the perplexity of contending passions. He had read much and knew what books could teach; but had mingled little in the world, and was deficient in the knowledge which experience must confer.

Through all his greater works there prevails an uniform peculiarity of *Diction*,[28] a mode and cast of expression which bears little resemblance to that of any former writer, and which is so far removed from common use that an unlearned reader when he first opens his book finds himself surprised by a new language.

This novelty has been, by those who can find nothing wrong in Milton, imputed to his laborious endeavours after words suitable to the grandeur of his ideas. 'Our language,' says Addison, 'sunk under him.' But the truth is, that both in prose and verse, he had formed his style by a perverse and pedantic principle. He was desirous to use English words with a foreign idiom. This in all his prose is discovered and condemned, for there judgement operates freely, neither softened by the beauty nor awed by the dignity of his thoughts; but such is the power of his poetry that his call is obeyed without resistance, the reader feels himself in captivity to a higher and a nobler mind, and criticism sinks in admiration.

Milton's style was not modified by his subject: what is shown with greater extent in *Paradise Lost* may be found in *Comus*. One source of his peculiarity was his familiarity with the Tuscan poets: the disposition of his words is, I think, frequently Italian; perhaps sometimes combined with other tongues. Of him, at last, may be said what Jonson says of Spenser, that 'he wrote no language', but has formed what Butler calls 'a Babylonish Dialect', in itself harsh and barbarous, but made by exalted genius and extensive learning the vehicle of so much instruction and so much pleasure that, like other lovers, we find grace in its deformity.

Whatever be the faults of his diction he cannot want the praise of copiousness and variety; he was master of his language in its full extent, and has selected the melodious words with such diligence that from his book alone the Art of English Poetry might be learned.

After his diction something must be said of his versification. 'The measure,' he says, 'is the English heroic verse without rhyme.' Of this mode he had many examples among the Italians, and some in his own country. The Earl of Surrey is said to have translated one of Virgil's books without rhyme[29], and besides our tragedies a few short poems had appeared in blank verse; particularly one tending to reconcile the nation to Raleigh's wild attempt upon Guiana, and probably written by Raleigh himself. These petty performances cannot be supposed to have much influenced Milton, who more probably took his hint from Trisino's *Italia Liberata*; and, finding blank verse easier than rhyme, was desirous of persuading himself that it is better.

'Rhyme,' he says, and says truly, 'is no necessary adjunct of true poetry.' But perhaps of poetry as a mental operation metre or music is no necessary adjunct; it is however by the music of metre that poetry has been discriminated in all languages, and in languages melodiously constructed with a due proportion of long and short syllables metre is sufficient. But one language cannot communicate its rules to another; where metre is scanty and imperfect some help is necessary. The music of the English heroic line strikes the ear so faintly that it is easily lost, unless all the syllables of every line coopcrate together; this cooperation can be only obtained by the preservation of every verse unmingled with another as a distinct system of sounds, and this distinctness is obtained and preserved by the artifice of rhyme. The variety of pauses, so much boasted by the lovers of blank verse, changes the measures of an English poet to the periods of a declaimer; and there are only a few skilful and happy readers of Milton who enable their audience to perceive where the lines end or begin. 'Blank verse,' said an ingenious critic,[30] 'seems to be verse only to the eye.'

Poetry may subsist without rhyme, but English poetry will not often please; nor can rhyme ever be safely spared but where the subject is able to support itself. Blank verse makes some approach to that which is called the 'lapidary style';[31] has neither the easiness of prose nor the melody of numbers, and therefore tires by long continuance. Of the Italian writers without rhyme, whom Milton alleges as precedents, not one is popular; what reason could urge in its defence has been confuted by the ear.

But whatever be the advantage of rhyme I cannot prevail on myself to wish that Milton had been a rhymer, for I cannot wish his work to be other than it is; yet like other heroes he is to be admired rather than imitated. He that thinks himself capable of astonishing may write blank verse, but those that hope only to please must condescend to rhyme.

The highest praise of genius is original invention. Milton cannot be said to have contrived the structure of an epic poem, and therefore owes reverence to that vigour and amplitude of mind to which all generations must be indebted for the art of poetical narration, for the texture of the fable, the variation of incidents, the interposition of dialogue, and all the stratagems that surprise and enchain attention. But of all the borrowers from Homer, Milton is perhaps the least indebted. He was naturally a thinker for himself, confident of his own abilities and disdainful of help or hindrance; he did not refuse admission to the thoughts or images of his predecessors, but he did not seek them. From his contemporaries he neither courted nor received support; there is in his writings nothing by which the pride of other authors might be gratified or favour gained, no exchange of praise nor solicitation of support. His great works were performed under discountenance and in blindness, but difficulties vanished at his touch; he was born for whatever is arduous; and his work is not the greatest of heroic poems, only because it is not the first.

FROM

THE LIFE OF ADDISON

'ADDISON AS CRITIC AND ESSAYIST'

Addison is now to be considered as a critic; a name which the present generation is scarcely willing to allow him. His criticism is condemned as tentative or experimental rather than scientific, and he is considered as deciding by taste rather than by principles.

It is not uncommon for those who have grown wise by the labour of others to add a little of their own, and overlook their masters. Addison is now despised by some who perhaps would never have seen his defects, but by the lights which he afforded them. That he always wrote as he would think it necessary to write now cannot be affirmed; his instructions were such as the character of his readers made proper. That general knowledge which now circulates in common talk was in his time rarely to be found. Men not professing learning were not ashamed of ignorance; and in the female world any acquaintance with books was distinguished only to be censured. His purpose was to infuse literary curiosity by gentle and unsuspecting conveyance into the gay, the idle, and the wealthy; he therefore presented knowledge in the most alluring form, not lofty and austere, but accessible and familiar. When he showed them their defects, he showed them likewise that they might be easily supplied. His attempt succeeded; inquiry was awakened, and comprehension expanded. An emulation of intellectual elegance was excited, and from his time to our own life has been gradually exalted, and conversation purified and enlarged.

Dryden had not many years before scattered criticism over his *Prefaces* with very little parsimony; but, though he sometimes condescended to be somewhat familiar, his manner was in general too scholastic for those who had yet their rudiments to learn, and found it not easy to understand their master. His observations were framed rather for those that were learning to write, than for those that read only to talk.

An instructor like Addison was now wanting, whose remarks being superficial,[1] might be easily understood, and being just might prepare the mind for more attainments. Had he presented *Paradise Lost*[2] to the public with all the pomp of system and severity of science, the criticism would perhaps have been admired, and the poem still have been neglected; but by the blandishments of gentleness and facility he has made Milton an universal favourite, with whom readers of every class think it necessary to be pleased.

He descended now and then to lower disquisitions; and by a serious display of the beauties of *Chevy Chase*[3] exposed himself to the ridicule of 'Wagstaff', who bestowed a like pompous character on *Tom Thumb*; and to the contempt of Dennis, who, considering the fundamental position of his criticism, that *Chevy Chase* pleases, and ought to please, because it is natural, observes 'that there is a way of deviating from nature, by bombast or tumour, which soars above nature, and enlarges images beyond their real bulk; by affectation, which forsakes nature in quest of something unsuitable; and by imbecility, which degrades nature by faintness and diminution, by obscuring its appearances and weakening its effects.' In *Chevy Chase* there is not much of either bombast or affectation; but there is chill and lifeless imbecility.[4] The story cannot possibly be told in a manner that shall make less impression on the mind.

Before the profound observers of the present race repose too securely on the consciousness of their superiority to Addison let them consider his *Remarks on Ovid*, in which may be found specimens of criticism sufficiently subtle and refined; let them peruse likewise his *Essays on Wit* and on *The Pleasures of Imagination*, in which he founds art on the base of nature, and draws the principles of invention from dispositions inherent in the mind of man with skill and elegance, such as his contemners will not easily attain.

As a describer of life and manners he must be allowed to stand perhaps the first of the first rank. His humour, which, as Steele observes, is peculiar to himself, is so happily diffused as to give the grace of novelty to domestic scenes and daily occurrences. He never 'outsteps the modesty of nature',[5] nor raises merriment or wonder by the violation of truth. His figures neither divert by distortion, nor amaze by aggravation. He copies life with so much fidelity that he can be hardly said to invent; yet his exhibitions have an air so much original that it is difficult to suppose them not merely the product of imagination.

As a teacher of wisdom he may be confidently followed. His religion has nothing in it enthusiastic[6] or superstitious: he appears neither weakly credulous nor wantonly sceptical; his morality is neither dangerously lax, nor impracticably rigid. All the enchantment of fancy and all the cogency of argument are employed to recommend to the reader his real interest, the care of pleasing the Author of his being. Truth is shown sometimes as the phantom of a vision, sometimes appears half-veiled in an allegory, sometimes attracts regard in the robes of fancy, and sometimes steps forth in the confidence of reason. She wears a thousand dresses, and in all is pleasing.

'Mille habet ornatus, mille decenter habet.'

His prose is the model of the middle style; on grave subjects not formal, on light occasions not grovelling; pure without scrupulosity, and exact without apparent elaboration; always equable, and always easy, without glowing words or pointed sentences. Addison never deviates from his track to snatch a grace; he seeks no ambitious ornaments, and tries no hazardous innovations. His page is always luminous, but never blazes in unexpected splendour.

It was apparently his principal endeavour to avoid all harshness and severity of diction; he is therefore sometimes verbose in his transitions and connexions, and sometimes descends too much to the language of conversation: yet if his language had been less idiomatical it might have lost somewhat of its genuine Anglicism. What he attempted, he performed; he is never feeble, and he did not wish to be energetic; he is never rapid, and he never stagnates. His sentences have neither studied amplitude, nor affected brevity; his periods, though not diligently rounded, are voluble[7] and easy. Whoever wishes to attain an English style, familiar but not coarse, and elegant but not ostentatious, must give his days and nights to the volumes of Addison.

FROM

THE LIFE OF CONGREVE

'CONGREVE AS COMIC DRAMATIST'

Congreve has merit of the highest kind: he is an original writer, who borrowed neither the models of his plot nor the manner of his dialogue. Of his plays I cannot speak distinctly, for since I inspected them many years have passed; but what remains upon my memory is that his characters are commonly fictitious and artificial, with very little of nature, and not much of life. He formed a peculiar idea of comic excellence, which he supposed to consist in gay remarks and unexpected answers; but that which he endeavoured, he seldom failed of performing. His scenes exhibit not much of humour, imagery, or passion; his personages are a kind of intellectual gladiators; every sentence is to ward or strike; the contest of smartness is never intermitted; his wit is a meteor playing to and fro with alternate coruscations. His comedies have therefore, in some degree, the operation of tragedies: they surprise rather than divert, and raise admiration oftener than merriment. But they are the works of a mind replete with images, and quick in combination.

FROM

THE LIFE OF PRIOR

'ON TEDIOUSNESS'

Tediousness is the most fatal of all faults; negligences or errors are single and local, but tediousness pervades the whole: other faults are censured and forgotten, but the power of tediousness propagates itself. He that is weary the first hour is more weary the second; as bodies forced into motion, contrary to their tendency, pass more and more slowly through ever successive intervals of space.

Unhappily this pernicious failure is that which an author is least able to discover. We are seldom tiresome to ourselves; and the act of composition fills and delights the mind with change of language and succession of images: every couplet when produced is new, and novelty is the great source of pleasure. Perhaps no man ever thought a line superfluous when he first wrote it, or contracted his work till his ebullitions of invention had subsided. And even if he should control his desire of immediate renown, and keep his work nine years unpublished,[1] he will be still the author, and still in danger of deceiving himself; and if he consults his friends, he will probably find men who have more kindness than judgement, or more fear to offend than desire to instruct.

FROM

THE LIFE OF POPE

'POPE'S CHARACTER AND HIS POETRY'

The person of Pope is well known not to have been formed by the nicest model. He has, in his account of the 'Little Club', compared himself to a spider, and by another is described as protuberant behin 1 and before. He is said to have been beautiful in his infancy; but he was of a constitution originally feeble and weak, and as bodies of a tender frame are easily distorted his deformity was probably in part the effect of his application. His stature was so low that, to bring him to a level with common tables, it was necessary to raise his seat. But his face was not displeasing, and his eyes were animated and vivid.

By natural deformity or accidental distortion his vital functions were so much disordered that his life was a 'long disease'.[1] His most frequent assailant was the headache, which he used to relieve by inhaling the steam of coffee, which he very frequently required.

Most of what can be told concerning his petty peculiarities was communicated by a female domestic of the Earl of Oxford, who knew him perhaps after the middle of life. He was then so weak as to stand in perpetual need of female attendance; extremely sensible of cold, so that he wore a kind of fur doublet under a shirt of very coarse warm linen with fine sleeves. When he rose he was invested in boddice[2] made of stiff canvas, being scarce able to hold himself erect till they were laced, and he then put on a flannel waistcoat. One side was contracted. His legs were so slender that he enlarged their bulk with three pair of stockings, which were drawn on and off by the maid; for he was not able to dress or undress himself, and neither went to bed nor rose without help. His weakness made it very difficult for him to be clean.

His hair had fallen almost all away, and he used to dine sometimes with Lord Oxford, privately, in a velvet cap. His dress of ceremony was black, with a tie-wig[3] and a little sword.

The indulgence and accommodation which his sickness required had taught him all the unpleasing and unsocial qualities of a valetudinary man. He expected that every thing should give way to his ease or humour, as a child whose parents will not hear her cry has an unresisted dominion in the nursery.

> *C'est que l'enfant toujours est homme,*
> *C'est que l'homme est toujours enfant.*

When he wanted to sleep he 'nodded in company'[4]; and once

slumbered at his own table while the Prince of Wales was talking of poetry.

The reputation which his friendship gave procured him many invitations; but he was a very troublesome inmate. He brought no servant, and had so many wants that a numerous attendance was scarcely able to supply them. Wherever he was he left no room for another, because he exacted the attention and employed the activity of the whole family. His errands were so frequent and frivolous that the footmen in time avoided and neglected him, and the Earl of Oxford discharged some of the servants for their resolute refusal of his messages. The maids, when they had neglected their business, alleged that they had been employed by Mr Pope. One of his constant demands was of coffee in the night, and to the woman that waited on him in his chamber he was very burdensome; but he was careful to recompense her want of sleep, and Lord Oxford's servant declared that in a house where her business was to answer his call she would not ask for wages.

He had another fault, easily incident to those who suffering much pain think themselves entitled to whatever pleasures they can snatch. He was too indulgent to his appetite: he loved meat highly seasoned and of strong taste, and, at the intervals of the table, amused himself with biscuits and dry conserves. If he sat down to a variety of dishes he would oppress his stomach with repletion, and though he seemed angry when a dram was offered him, did not forbear to drink it. His friends, who knew the avenues to his heart, pampered him with presents of luxury, which he did not suffer to stand neglected. The death of great men is not always proportioned to the lustre of their lives. Hannibal, says Juvenal,[5] did not perish by a javelin or a sword; the slaughters of Cannæ were revenged by a ring. The death of Pope was imputed by some of his friends to a silver saucepan, in which it was his delight to heat potted lampreys.

That he loved too well to eat is certain; but that his sensuality shortened his life will not be hastily concluded when it is remembered that a conformation so irregular lasted six and fifty years, notwithstanding such pertinacious diligence of study and meditation.

In all his intercourse with mankind he had great delight in artifice, and endeavoured to attain all his purposes by indirect and unsuspected methods. 'He hardly drank tea without a stratagem'.[6] If at the house of his friends he wanted any accommodation he was not willing to ask for it in plain terms, but would mention it remotely as something convenient; though, when it was procured, he soon made it appear for whose sake it had been recommended. Thus he teased Lord Orrery till he obtained a screen. He practised his arts on such small occasions that Lady Bolingbroke used to say, in a French phrase, that 'he played the politician about cabbages and turnips.' His unjustifiable impression of *The Patriot King*, as it can be imputed to no particular motive, must have proceeded from his general habit of secrecy and cunning; he caught an opportunity of a sly trick, and pleased himself with the thought of outwitting Bolingbroke.

In familiar or convivial conversation it does not appear that he excelled. He may be said to have resembled Dryden, as being not one that was distinguished by vivacity in company. It is remarkable that, so near his time, so much should be known of what he has written, and so little of what he has said: traditional memory retains no sallies of raillery nor sentences of observation; nothing either pointed or solid, either wise or merry. One apophthegm only stands upon record. When an objection raised against his inscription for Shakespeare was defended by the authority of Patrick, he replied, – '*horresco referens*'[7] – that 'he would allow the publisher of a Dictionary to know the meaning of a single word, but not of two words put together.'

He was fretful and easily displeased, and allowed himself to be capriciously resentful. He would sometimes leave Lord Oxford silently, no one could tell why, and was to be courted back by more letters and messages than the footmen were willing to carry. The table was indeed infested by Lady Mary Wortley,[8] who was the friend of Lady Oxford, and who, knowing his peevishness, could by no entreaties be restrained from contradicting him, till their disputes were sharpened to such asperity that one or the other quitted the house.

He sometimes condescended to be jocular with servants or inferiors; but by no merriment, either of others or his own, was he ever seen excited to laughter.

Of his domestic character frugality was a part eminently remarkable. Having determined not to be dependent he determined not to be in want, and therefore wisely and magnanimously rejected all temptations to expense unsuitable to his fortune. This general care must be universally approved; but it sometimes appeared in petty artifices of parsimony, such as the practice of writing his compositions on the back of letters, as may be seen in the remaining copy of the *Iliad*, by which perhaps in five years five shillings were saved; or in a niggardly reception of his friends and scantiness of entertainment, as when he had two guests in his house he would set at supper a single pint upon the table, and having himself taken two small glasses would retire and say, 'Gentlemen, I leave you to your wine.' Yet he tells his friends that 'he has a heart for all, a house for all, and, whatever they may think, a fortune for all.'[9]

He sometimes, however, made a splendid dinner, and is said to have wanted no part of the skill or elegance which such performances require. That this magnificence should be often displayed, that obstinate prudence with which he conducted his affairs would not permit; for his revenue, certain and casual, amounted only to about eight hundred pounds a year, of which, however, he declares himself able to assign one hundred to charity.

Of this fortune, which as it arose from public approbation was very honourably obtained, his imagination seems to have been too full: it would be hard to find a man, so well entitled to notice by his wit, that ever delighted so much in talking of his money. In his Letters and in his Poems, his garden and his grotto, his quincunx[10] and his vines, or some hints of his opulence, are always to be found. The great topic of his ridicule is poverty[11]: the crimes with which he reproaches his antagonists are their debts, their habitation in the Mint, and their want of a dinner. He seems to be of an opinion, not very uncommon in the world, that to want money is to want every thing.

Next to the pleasure of contemplating his possessions seems to be that of enumerating the men of high rank with whom he was acquainted, and whose notice he loudly proclaims not to have been obtained by any practices of meanness or servility; a boast which was never denied to be true, and to which very few poets have ever aspired. Pope never set genius to sale: he never flattered those whom he did not love, or praised those whom he did not esteem. Savage, however, remarked that he began a little to relax his dignity when he wrote a distich for 'his Highness's dog'[12].

His admiration of the great seems to have increased in the advance of life. He passed over peers and statesmen to inscribe his *Iliad* to Congreve, with a magnanimity of which the praise had been complete, had his friend's virtue been equal to his wit. Why he was chosen for so great an honour it is not now possible to know; there is no trace in literary history of any particular intimacy between them. The name of Congreve appears in the letters among those of his other friends, but without any observable distinction or consequence.

To his latter works, however, he took care to annex names dignified with titles, but was not very happy in his choice; for, except Lord Bathurst, none of his noble friends were such as that a good man would wish to have his intimacy with them known to posterity: he can derive little honour[13] from the notice of Cobham, Burlington, or Bolingbroke.

Of his social qualities, if an estimate be made from his letters,[14] an opinion too favourable cannot easily be formed; they exhibit a perpetual and unclouded effulgence of general benevolence and particular fondness. There is nothing but liberality, gratitude, constancy, and tenderness. It has been so long said as to be commonly believed that the true characters of men may be found in their letters, and that he who writes to his friend lays his heart open before him. But the truth is that such were simple friendships of the *Golden Age*, and are now the friendships only of children. Very few can boast of hearts which they dare lay open to themselves, and of which, by whatever accident exposed, they do not shun a distinct and continued view; and certainly what we hide from ourselves we do not show to our friends. There is, indeed, no transaction which offers stronger temptations to fallacy and sophistication than epistolary intercourse. In the eagerness of conversation the first emotions of the mind often burst out before they are considered; in the tumult of business interest and passion have their genuine effect; but a friendly letter is a calm and deliberate performance in the cool of leisure, in the stillness of solitude, and surely no man sits down to depreciate by design his own character.

Friendship has no tendency to secure veracity, for by whom can a man so much wish to be thought better than he is as by him whose kindness he desires to gain or keep? Even in writing to the world there is less constraint: the author is not confronted with his reader, and takes his chance of approbation among the different dispositions of mankind; but a letter is addressed to a single mind of which the prejudices and partialities are known, and must therefore please, if not by favouring them, by forbearing to oppose them.

To charge those favourable representations, which men give of their own minds, with the guilt of hypocritical falsehood, would show more severity than knowledge. The writer commonly believes himself. Almost every man's thoughts, while they are general, are right; and most hearts are pure while temptation is away. It is easy to awaken generous sentiments in privacy; to despise death when there is no danger; to glow with benevolence when there is nothing to be given. While such ideas are formed they are felt, and self-love does not suspect the gleam of virtue to be the meteor of fancy.

If the letters of Pope are considered merely as compositions they seem to be premeditated and artificial. It is one thing to write because there is something which the mind wishes to discharge and another to solicit the imagination because ceremony or vanity requires something to be written. Pope confesses his early letters to be vitiated with 'affectation and ambition': to know whether he disentangled himself from these perverters of epistolary integrity his book and his life must be set in comparison.

One of his favourite topics is contempt of his own poetry. For this, if it had been real, he would deserve no commendation, and in this he certainly was not sincere; for his high value of himself was sufficiently observed, and of what could he be proud but of his poetry? He writes, he says, when 'he has just nothing else to do': yet Swift complains that he was never at leisure for conversation because he 'had always some poetical scheme in his head'. It was punctually required that his writing-box should be set upon his bed before he rose; and Lord Oxford's domestic related that, in the dreadful winter of Forty, she was called from her bed by him four times in one night to supply him with paper, lest he should lose a thought.

He pretends insensibility to censure and criticism, though it was observed by all who knew him that every pamphlet disturbed his quiet, and his extreme irritability laid him open to perpetual vexation; but he wished to despise his critics, and therefore hoped that he did despise them.

As he happened to live in two reigns when the Court paid little attention to poetry he nursed in his mind a foolish disesteem of Kings, and proclaims that 'he never sees Courts'. Yet a little regard shown him by the Prince of Wales melted his obduracy, and he had not much to say when he was asked by his Royal Highness 'how he could love a Prince while he disliked Kings'.

He very frequently professes contempt of the world, and represents himself as looking on mankind, sometimes with gay indifference, as on emmets[15] of a hillock below his serious attention, and sometimes with gloomy indignation, as on monsters more worthy of hatred than of pity. These were dispositions apparently counterfeited.[16] How could he despise those whom he lived by pleasing, and on whose approbation his esteem of himself was superstructed?[17] Why should he hate those to whose favour he owed his honour and his ease? Of things that terminate in human life the world is the proper judge: to despise its sentence, if it were possible, is not just; and if it were just is not possible. Pope was far enough from this unreasonable temper; he was sufficiently 'a fool to Fame',[18] and his fault was that he pretended to neglect it. His levity and his sullenness were only in his letters; he passed through common life, sometimes vexed and sometimes pleased, with the natural emotions of common men.

His scorn of the great is repeated too often to be real: no man thinks much of that which he despises; and as falsehood is always in danger of inconsistency he makes it his boast at another time that he lives among them.

It is evident that his importance swells often in his mind. He is afraid of writing lest the clerks of the Post-office should know his secrets; he has many enemies; he considers himself as surrounded by universal jealousy; 'after many deaths, and many dispersions, two or three of us,' says he, 'may still be brought together, not to plot, but to divert ourselves, and the world too, if it pleases'; and they can live together, and 'show what friends wits may be, in spite of all the fools in the world'. All this while it was likely that the clerks did not know his hand: he certainly had no more enemies than a public character like his inevitably excites, and with what degree of friendship the wits might live very few were so much fools as ever to inquire.

Some part of this pretended discontent he learned from Swift, and expresses it, I think, most frequently in his correspondence with him. Swift's resentment was unreasonable, but it was sincere; Pope's was the mere mimicry of his friend, a fictitious part which he began to play before it became him. When he was only twenty-five years old he related that 'a glut of study and retirement had thrown him on the world', and that there was danger lest 'a glut of the world should throw him back upon study and retirement'. To this Swift answered with great propriety that Pope had not yet either acted or suffered enough in the world to have become weary of it. And, indeed, it must be some very powerful reason that can drive back to solitude him who has once enjoyed the pleasures of society.

In the letters both of Swift and Pope there appears such narrowness of mind as makes them insensible of any excellence that has not some affinity with their own, and confines their esteem and approbation to so small a number, that whoever should form his opinion of the age from their representation would suppose them to have lived amidst ignorance and barbarity, unable to find among their contemporaries either virtue or intelligence, and persecuted by those that could not understand them.

When Pope murmurs at the world, when he professes contempt of fame, when he speaks of riches and poverty, of success and disappointment, with negligent indifference, he certainly does not express his habitual and settled sentiments, but either wilfully disguises his own character, or, what is more likely, invests himself with temporary qualities, and sallies out in the colours of the present moment. His hopes and fears, his joys and sorrows acted strongly upon his mind, and if he differed from others it was not by carelessness. He was irritable and resentful:[19] his malignity to Philips, whom he had first made ridiculous, and then hated for being angry, continued too long. Of his vain desire to make Bentley contemptible, I never heard any adequate reason. He was sometimes wanton in his attacks, and before Chandos, Lady Wortley, and Hill, was mean in his retreat.

The virtues which seem to have had most of his affection were liberality and fidelity of friendship, in which it does not appear that he was other than he describes himself. His fortune did not suffer his charity to be splendid and conspicuous, but he assisted Dodsley with a hundred pounds that he might open a shop; and of the subscription of forty pounds a year that he raised for Savage twenty were paid by himself. He was accused of loving money, but his love was eagerness to gain, not solicitude to keep it.

In the duties of friendship he was zealous and constant: his early maturity of mind commonly united him with men older than himself, and therefore, without attaining any considerable length of life, he saw many companions of his youth sink into the grave; but it does not appear that he lost a single friend by coldness or by injury: those who loved him once continued their kindness. His ungrateful mention of Allen[20] in his will was the effect of his adherence to one whom he had known much longer, and whom he naturally loved with greater fondness. His violation of the trust reposed in him by Bolingbroke could have no motive inconsistent with the warmest affection; he either thought the action so near to indifferent that he forgot it, or so laudable that he expected his friend to approve it.

It was reported, with such confidence as almost to enforce belief, that in the papers entrusted to his executors was found a defamatory

Life of Swift, which he had prepared as an instrument of vengeance to be used, if any provocation should be ever given. About this I inquired of the Earl of Marchmont, who assured me that no such piece was among his remains.

The religion in which he lived and died was that of the Church of Rome, to which in his correspondence with Racine[21] he professes himself a sincere adherent. That he was not scrupulously pious in some part of his life is known by many idle and indecent applications of sentences taken from the Scriptures; a mode of merriment which a good man dreads for its profaneness, and a witty man disdains for its easiness and vulgarity. But to whatever levities he has been betrayed, it does not appear that his principles were ever corrupted, or that he ever lost his belief of Revelation. The positions which he transmitted from Bolingbroke he seems not to have understood, and was pleased with an interpretation that made them orthodox.

A man of such exalted superiority and so little moderation would naturally have all his delinquencies observed and aggravated: those who could not deny that he was excellent would rejoice to find he was not perfect.

Perhaps it may be imputed to the unwillingness with which the same man is allowed to possess many advantages that his learning has been depreciated. He certainly was in his early life a man of great literary curiosity, and when he wrote his *Essay on Criticism* had for his age a very wide acquaintance with books. When he entered into the living world it seems to have happened to him as to many others that he was less attentive to dead masters: he studied in the academy of Paracelsus, and made the universe his favourite volume. He gathered his notions fresh from reality, not from the copies of authors, but the originals of Nature. Yet there is no reason to believe that literature ever lost his esteem; he always professed to love reading, and Dobson, who spent some time at his house translating his *Essay on Man*, when I asked him what learning he found him to possess, answered, 'More than I expected.' His frequent references to history, his allusions to various kinds of knowledge, and his images selected from art and nature, with his observations on the operations of the mind and the modes of life, show an intelligence perpetually on the wing, excursive, vigorous, and diligent, eager to pursue knowledge, and attentive to retain it.

From this curiosity arose the desire of travelling, to which he alludes in his verses to Jervas, and which, though he never found an opportunity to gratify it, did not leave him till his life declined.

Of his intellectual character the constituent and fundamental principle was Good Sense,[22] a prompt and intuitive perception of consonance and propriety. He saw immediately, of his own conceptions, what was to be chosen, and what to be rejected; and, in the works of others, what was to be shunned, and what to be copied.

But good sense alone is a sedate and quiescent quality, which manages its possessions well, but does not increase them; it collects few materials for its own operations, and preserves safety, but never gains supremacy. Pope had likewise genius; a mind active, ambitious, and adventurous, always investigating, always aspiring; in its widest searches still longing to go forward, in its highest flights still wishing to be higher; always imagining something greater than it knows, always endeavouring more than it can do.

To assist these powers he is said to have had great strength and exactness of memory. That which he had heard or read was not easily lost; and he had before him not only what his own meditation suggested, but what he had found in other writers that might be accommodated to his present purpose.

These benefits of nature he improved by incessant and unwearied diligence; he had recourse to every source of intelligence, and lost no opportunity of information; he consulted the living as well as the dead; he read his compositions to his friends, and was never content with mediocrity when excellence could be attained. He considered poetry as the business of his life, and, however he might seem to lament his occupation, he followed it with constancy: to make verses was his first labour, and to mend them was his last.

From his attention to poetry he was never diverted. If conversation offered anything that could be improved he committed it to paper; if a thought, or perhaps an expression more happy than was common, rose to his mind, he was careful to write it; an independent distich was preserved for an opportunity of insertion, and some little fragments have been found containing lines, or parts of lines, to be wrought upon at some other time.

He was one of those few whose labour is their pleasure; he was never elevated to negligence, nor wearied to impatience; he never passed a fault unamended by indifference, nor quitted it by despair. He laboured his works first to gain reputation, and afterwards to keep it.

Of composition there are different methods. Some employ at once memory and invention, and, with little intermediate use of the pen, form and polish large masses by continued meditation, and write their productions only when, in their own opinion, they have completed them. It is related of Virgil that his custom was to pour out a great number of verses in the morning, and pass the day in retrenching exuberances and correcting inaccuracies. The method of Pope, as may be collected from his translation, was to write his first thoughts in his first words, and gradually to amplify, decorate, rectify, and refine them.

With such faculties and such dispositions he excelled every other writer in *poetical prudence*; he wrote in such a manner as might expose him to few hazards. He used almost always the same fabric of verse; and, indeed, by those few essays which he made of any other, he did not enlarge his reputation. Of this uniformity the certain consequence was readiness and dexterity. By perpetual practice language had in his mind a systematical arrangement; having always the same use for words, he had words so selected and combined as to be ready at his call. This increase of facility he confessed himself to have perceived in the progress of his translation.

But what was yet of more importance, his effusions were always voluntary, and his subjects chosen by himself. His independence secured him from drudging at a task, and labouring upon a barren topic: he never exchanged praise for money, nor opened a shop of condolence or congratulation. His poems, therefore, were scarce ever temporary. He suffered coronations and royal marriages to pass without a song, and derived no opportunities from recent events, nor any popularity from the accidental disposition of his readers. He was never reduced to the necessity of soliciting the sun to shine upon a birthday,[23] of calling the Graces and Virtues to a wedding, or of saying what multitudes have said before him. When he could produce nothing new, he was at liberty to be silent.

His publications were for the same reason never hasty. He is said to have sent nothing to the press till it had lain two years under his inspection: it is at least certain that he ventured nothing without nice examination. He suffered the tumult of imagination to subside, and the novelties of invention to grow familiar. He knew that the mind is always enamoured of its own productions, and did not trust his first fondness. He consulted his friends, and listened with great willingness to criticism; and, what was of more importance, he consulted himself, and let nothing pass against his own judgement.

He professed to have learned his poetry from Dryden, whom, whenever an opportunity was presented, he praised through his whole life with unvaried liberality; and perhaps his character may receive some illustration if he be compared with his master.

Integrity of understanding and nicety of discernment were not allotted in a less proportion to Dryden than to Pope. The rectitude of Dryden's mind was sufficiently shown by the dismission of his poetical prejudices,[24] and the rejection of unnatural thoughts and rugged numbers. But Dryden never desired to apply all the judgement that he had. He wrote, and professed to write, merely for the people; and when he pleased others, he contented himself. He spent no time in struggles to rouse latent powers; he never attempted to make that better which was already good, nor often to mend what he must have known to be faulty. He wrote, as he tells us, with very little consideration; when occasion or necessity called upon him, he poured out what the present moment happened to supply, and, when once it had passed the press, ejected it from his mind; for when he had no pecuniary interest, he had no further solicitude.

Pope was not content to satisfy; he desired to excel, and therefore always endeavoured to do his best: he did not court the candour, but dared the judgement of his reader, and, expecting no indulgence from others, he showed none to himself. He examined lines and words with minute and punctilious observation, and retouched every part with indefatigable diligence, till he had left nothing to be forgiven.

For this reason he kept his pieces very long in his hands, while he considered and reconsidered them. The only poems which can be supposed to have been written with such regard to the times as might hasten their publication, were the two satires of *Thirty-eight*[25]; of which Dodsley told me that they were brought to him by the author, that they might be fairly copied. 'Almost every line,' he said, 'was then written twice over; I gave him a clean transcript, which he sent some time afterwards to me for the press, with almost every line written twice over a second time.'

His declaration that his care for his works ceased at their publication was not strictly true. His parental attention never abandoned them; what he found amiss in the first edition, he silently corrected in those that followed. He appears to have revised the *Iliad*, and freed it from some of its imperfections; and the *Essay on Criticism* received many improvements after its first appearance. It will seldom be found that he altered without adding clearness, elegance, or vigour. Pope had perhaps the judgement of Dryden; but Dryden certainly wanted the diligence of Pope.

In acquired knowledge the superiority must be allowed to Dryden, whose education was more scholastic[26] and who before he became an author had been allowed more time for study, with better means of information. His mind has a larger range, and he collects his images and illustrations from a more extensive circumference of science. Dryden knew more of man in his general nature, and Pope in his local manners. The notions of Dryden were formed by comprehensive speculation, and those of Pope by minute attention. There is more dignity in the knowledge of Dryden, and more certainty in that of Pope.

Poetry was not the sole praise of either, for both excelled likewise in prose; but Pope did not borrow his prose from his predecessor. The style of Dryden is capricious and varied, that of Pope is cautious and uniform; Dryden obeys the motions of his own mind, Pope constrains his mind to his own rules of composition. Dryden is sometimes vehement and rapid; Pope is always smooth, uniform, and gentle. Dryden's page is a natural field, rising into inequalities, and diversified by the varied exuberance of abundant vegetation; Pope's is a velvet lawn, shaven by the scythe, and levelled by the roller.

Of genius, that power which constitutes a poet; that quality without which judgement is cold and knowledge is inert; that energy which collects, combines, amplifies, and animates – the superiority must, with some hesitation, be allowed to Dryden. It is not to be inferred that of this poetical vigour Pope had only a little, because Dryden had more, for every other writer since Milton must give place to Pope; and even of Dryden it must be said that if he has brighter paragraphs, he has not better poems. Dryden's performances were always hasty, either excited by some external occasion, or extorted by domestic necessity; he composed without consideration, and published without correction. What his mind could supply at call, or gather in one excursion, was all that he sought, and all that he gave. The dilatory caution of Pope enabled him to condense his sentiments, to multiply his images, and to accumulate all that study might produce, or chance might supply. If the flights of Dryden therefore are higher, Pope continues longer on the wing. If of Dryden's fire the blaze is brighter, of Pope's the heat is more regular and constant. Dryden often surpasses expectation, and Pope never falls below it. Dryden is read with frequent astonishment, and Pope with perpetual delight.

This parallel will, I hope, when it is well considered, be found just; and if the reader should suspect me, as I suspect myself, of some partial fondness[27] for the memory of Dryden, let him not too hastily condemn me; for meditation and inquiry may, perhaps, show him the reasonableness of my determination.

The works of Pope are now to be distinctly examined, not so much with attention to slight faults or petty beauties, as to the general character and effect of each performance.

It seems natural for a young poet to initiate himself by pastorals, which, not professing to imitate real life, require no experience, and, exhibiting only the simple operation of unmingled passions, admit no subtle reasoning or deep inquiry. Pope's *Pastorals* are not however composed but with close thought; they have reference to the times of the day, the seasons of the year, and the periods of human life. The last, that which turns the attention upon age and death, was the author's favourite. To tell of disappointment and misery, to thicken the darkness of futurity, and perplex the labyrinth of uncertainty, has been always a delicious employment of the poets. His preference was probably just. I wish, however, that his fondness had not overlooked a line in which the 'Zephyrs' are made 'to lament in silence'.

To charge these *Pastorals* with want of invention is to require what never was intended. The imitations are so ambitiously frequent that the writer evidently means rather to show his literature than his wit. It is surely sufficient for an author of sixteen not only to be able to copy the poems of antiquity with judicious selection, but to have obtained sufficient power of language and skill in metre to exhibit a series of versification, which had in English poetry no precedent, nor has since had an imitation.

The design of *Windsor Forest* is evidently derived from *Cooper's Hill*,[28] with some attention to Waller's poem on *The Park*; but Pope cannot be denied to excel his masters in variety and elegance, and the art of interchanging description, narrative and morality. The objection made by Dennis is the want of plan, of a regular subordination of parts terminating in the principal and original design. There is this want in most descriptive poems, because as the scenes, which they must exhibit successively, are all subsisting at the same time, the order in which they are shown must by necessity be arbitrary, and more is not to be expected from the last part than from the first. The attention, therefore, which cannot be detained by suspense, must be excited by diversity, such as his poem offers to its reader.

But the desire of diversity may be too much indulged: the parts of *Windsor Forest* which deserve least praise are those which were added to enliven the stillness of the scene, the appearance of Father Thames and the transformation of Lodona.[29] Addison had in his *Campaign* derided the 'Rivers' that 'rise from their oozy beds' to tell stories of heroes, and it is therefore strange that Pope should adopt a fiction not only unnatural but lately censured. The story of Lodona is told with sweetness; but a new metamorphosis is a ready and puerile expedient: nothing is easier than to tell how a flower was once a blooming virgin, or a rock an obdurate tyrant.

The Temple of Fame has, as Steele warmly declared, 'a thousand beauties'. Every part is splendid; there is great luxuriance of ornaments; the original vision of Chaucer was never denied to be much improved; the allegory is very skilfully continued, the imagery is properly selected and learnedly displayed: yet, with all this comprehension of excellence, as its scene is laid in remote ages, and its sentiments, if the concluding paragraph be excepted, have little relation to general manners or common life, it never obtained much notice, but is turned silently over, and seldom quoted or mentioned with either praise or blame.

That *The Messiah* excels the *Pollio* is no great praise, if it be considered from what original the improvements are derived.

The *Verses on the unfortunate Lady* have drawn much attention by the illaudable singularity of treating suicide with respect, and they must be allowed to be written in some parts with vigorous animation, and in others with gentle tenderness; nor has Pope produced any poem in which the sense predominates more over the diction. But the tale is not skilfully told: it is not easy to discover the character of either the lady or her guardian. History relates that she was about to disparage herself by a marriage with an inferior; Pope praises her for the dignity of ambition, and yet condemns the uncle to detestation for his pride: the ambitious love of a niece may be opposed by the interest, malice, or envy of an uncle, but never by his pride. On such an occasion a poet may be allowed to be obscure, but inconsistency never can be right.

The *Ode for St Cecilia's Day* was undertaken at the desire of Steele: in this the author is generally confessed to have miscarried, yet he has miscarried only as compared with Dryden; for he has far outgone other competitors. Dryden's plan is better chosen; history will always take stronger hold of the attention than fable: the passions excited by Dryden are the pleasures and pains of real life, the scene of Pope is laid in imaginary existence. Pope is read with calm acquiescence, Dryden with turbulent delight; Pope hangs upon the ear, and Dryden finds the passes of the mind.

Both the odes want the essential constituent of metrical compositions, the stated recurrence of settled numbers. It may be alleged that Pindar is said by Horace to have written '*numeris lege solutis*',[30] but as no such lax performances have been transmitted to us, the meaning of that expression cannot be fixed; and perhaps the like return might properly be made to a modern Pindarist, as Mr Cobb received from Bentley, who, when he found his criticisms upon a Greek exercise, which Cobb had presented, refuted one after another by Pindar's authority, cried out at last, 'Pindar was a bold fellow, but thou art an impudent one.'

If Pope's Ode be particularly inspected it will be found that the first stanza consists of sounds well chosen indeed, but only sounds.

The second consists of hyperbolical common-places, easily to be found, and perhaps without much difficulty to be as well expressed.

In the third, however, there are numbers, images, harmony, and vigour, not unworthy the antagonist of Dryden. Had all been like this – but every part cannot be the best.

The next stanzas place and detain us in the dark and dismal regions of mythology, where neither hope nor fear, neither joy nor sorrow can be found: the poet however faithfully attends us; we have all that can be performed by elegance of diction or sweetness of versification; but what can form avail without better matter?

The last stanza recurs again to common-places. The conclusion is too evidently modelled by that of Dryden; and it may be remarked that both end with the same fault, the comparison of each is literal on one side, and metaphorical on the other.

Poets do not always express their own thoughts; Pope, with all this labour in the praise of music, was ignorant of its principles, and insensible of its effects.

One of his greatest though of his earliest works is the *Essay on Criticism*, which if he had written nothing else would have placed him among the first critics and the first poets, as it exhibits every mode of excellence that can embellish or dignify didactic composition, selection of matter, novelty of arrangement, justness of precept, splendour of illustration and propriety of digression. I know not whether it be pleasing to consider that he produced this piece at twenty, and never afterwards excelled it: he that delights himself with observing that such powers may be so soon attained, cannot but grieve to think that life was ever after at a stand.

To mention the particular beauties of the *Essay* would be unprofitably tedious; but I cannot forbear to observe that the comparison of a student's progress in the sciences with the journey of a traveller in the Alps is perhaps the best that English poetry can show.[31] A simile, to be perfect, must both illustrate and ennoble the subject; must show it to the understanding in a clearer view, and display it to the fancy with greater dignity: but either of these qualities may be sufficient to recommend it. In didactic poetry, of which the great purpose is instruction, a simile may be praised which illustrates, though it does not ennoble; in heroics, that may be admitted which ennobles, though it does not illustrate. That it may be complete it is required to exhibit, independently of its references, a pleasing image; for a simile is said to be a short episode. To this antiquity was so attentive that circumstances were sometimes added, which, having no parallels, served only to fill the imagination, and produced what Perrault ludicrously called 'comparisons with a long tail'. In their similes the greatest writers have sometimes failed: the ship-race, compared with the chariot-race, is neither illustrated nor aggrandised; land and water make all the difference: when Apollo running after Daphne is likened to a greyhound chasing a hare, there is nothing gained; the ideas of pursuit and flight are too plain to be made plainer, and a god and the daughter of a god are not represented much to their advantage by a hare and dog. The simile of the Alps has no useless parts, yet affords a striking picture by itself: it makes the foregoing position better understood, and enables it to take faster hold on the attention; it assists the apprehension, and elevates the fancy.

Let me likewise dwell a little on the celebrated paragraph, in which it is directed that 'the sound should seem an echo to the sense'[32]; a precept which Pope is allowed to have observed beyond any other English poet.

This notion of representative metre, and the desire of discovering frequent adaptations of the sound to the sense, have produced, in my opinion, many wild conceits and imaginary beauties. All that can furnish this representation are the sounds of the words considered singly, and the time in which they are pronounced. Every language has some words framed to exhibit the noises which they express, as *thump*, *rattle*, *growl*, *hiss*. These, however, are but few, and the poet cannot make them more, nor can they be of any use but when sound is to be mentioned. The time of pronunciation was in the dactylic measures of the learned languages capable of considerable variety; but that variety could be accommodated only to motion or duration, and different degrees of motion were perhaps expressed by verses rapid or slow, without much attention of the writer, when the image had full possession of his fancy: but our language having little flexibility our verses can differ very little in their cadence. The fancied resemblances, I fear, arise sometimes merely from the ambiguity of words; there is supposed to be some relation between a *soft* line and a *soft* couch, or between *hard* syllables and *hard* fortune.

Motion, however, may be in some sort exemplified; and yet it may be suspected that even in such resemblances the mind often governs the ear, and the sounds are estimated by their meaning. One of the most successful attempts has been to describe the labour of Sisyphus:

> With many a weary step, and many a groan,
> Up a [the] high hill he heaves a huge round stone;
> The huge round stone, resulting with a bound,
> Thunders impetuous down, and smoaks along the ground.

Who does not perceive the stone to move slowly upward, and roll violently back? But set the same numbers to another sense:

> While many a merry tale, and many a song,
> Cheer'd the rough road, we wish'd the rough road long.
> The rough road then, returning in a round,
> Mock'd our impatient steps, for all was fairy ground.

We have now surely lost much of the delay, and much of the rapidity.

But to show how little the greatest master of numbers can fix the principles of representative harmony, it will be sufficient to remark that the poet, who tells us that

> When Ajax strives some rock's vast weight to throw,
> The line too labours and the words move slow:
> Not so when swift Camilla scours the plain,
> Flies o'er th' unbending corn, and skims along the main;

when he had enjoyed for about thirty years the praise of Camilla's lightness of foot, tried another experiment upon *sound* and *time*, and produced this memorable triplet:

> Waller was smooth; but Dryden taught to join⎫
> The varying verse, the full resounding line, ⎬
> The long majestic march, and energy divine. ⎭

Here are the swiftness of the rapid race and the march of slow-paced majesty exhibited by the same poet in the same sequence of syllables, except that the exact prosodist will find the line of *swiftness* by one time longer than that of *tardiness*.

Beauties of this kind are commonly fancied; and when real are technical and nugatory, not to be rejected and not to be solicitied.

To the praises which have been accumulated on *The Rape of the Lock* by readers of every class, from the critic to the waiting-maid, it is difficult to make any addition. Of that which is universally allowed to be the most attractive of all ludicrous compositions, let it rather be now inquired from what sources the power of pleasing is derived.

Dr Warburton, who excelled in critical perspicacity, has remarked that the preternatural agents are very happily adapted to the purposes of the poem. The heathen deities can no longer gain attention: we should have turned away from a contest between Venus and Diana. The employment of allegorical persons always excites conviction of its own absurdity: they may produce effects, but cannot conduct actions; when the phantom is put in motion, it dissolves; thus Discord may raise a mutiny, but Discord cannot conduct a march, nor besiege a town. Pope brought into view a new race of beings, with powers and passions proportionate to their operation. The sylphs and gnomes act at the toilet and the tea-table what more terrific and more powerful phantoms perform on the stormy ocean or the field of battle; they give their proper help, and do their proper mischief.

Pope is said by an objector[33] not to have been the inventor of this petty nation; a charge which might with more justice have been brought against the author of the *Iliad*, who doubtless adopted the religious system of his country; for what is there but the names of his agents which Pope has not invented? Has he not assigned them characters and operations never heard of before? Has he not, at least, given them their first poetical existence? If this is not sufficient to denominate his work original, nothing original ever can be written.

In this work are exhibited in a very high degree the two most engaging powers of an author: new things are made familiar, and familiar things are made new. A race of aerial people never heard of before is presented to us in a manner so clear and easy, that the reader seeks for no further information, but immediately mingles with his new acquaintance, adopts their interests and attends their pursuits, loves a sylph and detests a gnome.

That familiar things are made new every paragraph will prove. The subject of the poem is an event below the common incidents of common life; nothing real is introduced that is not seen so often as to be no longer regarded, yet the whole detail of a female-day is here brought before us invested with so much art of decoration that, though nothing is disguised, everything is striking, and we feel all the appetite of curiosity for that from which we have a thousand times turned fastidiously away.

The purpose of the Poet is, as he tells us, to laugh at 'the little unguarded follies of the female sex'. It is therefore without justice that Dennis charges *The Rape of the Lock* with the want of a moral, and for that reason sets it below *The Lutrin*,[34] which exposes the pride and discord of the clergy. Perhaps neither Pope nor Boileau has made the world much better than he found it; but if they had both succeeded, it were easy to tell who would have deserved most from public gratitude. The freaks, and humours, and spleen, and vanity of women, as they embroil families in discord and fill houses with disquiet, do more to obstruct the happiness of life in a year than the ambition of the clergy in many centuries. It has been well observed[35] that the misery of man proceeds not from any single crush of overwhelming evil, but from small vexations continually repeated.

It is remarked by Dennis likewise that the machinery is superfluous; that by all the bustle of preternatural operation the main event is neither hastened nor retarded. To this charge an efficacious answer is not easily made. The sylphs cannot be said to help or to oppose, and it must be allowed to imply some want of art that their power has not been sufficiently intermingled with the action. Other parts may likewise be charged with want of connection; the game at *ombre* might be spared, but if the lady had lost her hair while she was intent upon her cards, it might have been inferred that those who are too fond of play will be in danger of neglecting more important interests. Those perhaps are faults; but what are such faults to so much excellence!

The *Epistle of Eloise to Abelard* is one of the most happy productions of human wit: the subject is so judiciously chosen that it would be difficult, in turning over the annals of the world, to find another which so many circumstances concur to recommend. We regularly interest ourselves most in the fortune of those who most deserve our notice. Abelard and Eloise were conspicuous in their days for eminence of merit. The heart naturally loves truth. The adventures and misfortunes of this illustrious pair are known from undisputed history. Their fate does not leave the mind in hopeless dejection; for they both found quiet and consolation in retirement and piety. So new and so affecting is their story that it supersedes invention, and imagination ranges at full liberty without straggling into scenes of fable.

The story thus skilfully adopted has been diligently improved. Pope has left nothing behind him which seems more the effect of studious perseverance and laborious revisal. Here is particularly observable the *curiosa felicitas*[36], a fruitful soil, and careful cultivation. Here is no crudeness of sense, nor asperity of language.

The sources from which sentiments which have so much vigour and efficacy have been drawn are shown to be the mystic writers by the learned author[37] of the *Essay on the Life and Writings of Pope*; a book which teaches how the brow of criticism may be smoothed, and how she may be enabled, with all her severity, to attract and to delight.

The train of my disquisition has now conducted me to that poetical wonder, the translation of the *Iliad*; a performance which no age or nation can pretend to equal. To the Greeks translation was almost unknown; it was totally unknown to the inhabitants of Greece. They had no recourse to the Barbarians for poetical beauties, but sought for every thing in Homer, where, indeed, there is but little they might not find.

The Italians have been very diligent translators; but I can hear of no version, unless perhaps Anguillara's *Ovid* may be excepted, which is read with eagerness. The *Iliad* of Salvini every reader may discover to be punctiliously exact; but it seems to be the work of a linguist skilfully pedantic, and his countrymen, the proper judges of its power to please, reject it with disgust.

Their predecessors the Romans have left some specimens of translation behind them, and that employment must have had some credit in which Tully and Germanicus engaged; but unless we suppose, what is perhaps true, that the plays of Terence were versions of Menander, nothing translated seems ever to have risen to high reputation. The French, in the meridian hour of their learning, were very laudably industrious to enrich their own language with the wisdom of the ancients; but found themselves reduced, by whatever necessity, to turn the Greek and Roman poetry into prose. Whoever could read an author could translate him. From such rivals little can be feared.

The chief help of Pope in this arduous undertaking was drawn from the versions of Dryden. Virgil had borrowed much of his imagery from Homer, and part of the debt was now paid by his translator. Pope searched the pages of Dryden for happy combinations of heroic diction, but it will not be denied that he added much to what he found. He cultivated our language with so much diligence and art that he has left in his *Homer* a treasure of poetical elegances to posterity. His version may be said to have tuned the English tongue,[38] for since its appearance no writer, however deficient in other powers, has wanted melody. Such a series of lines so elaborately corrected and so sweetly modulated took possession of the public ear; the vulgar was enamoured of the poem, and the learned wondered at the translation.

But in the most general applause discordant voices will always be heard. It has been objected by some, who wish to be numbered among the sons of learning,[39] that Pope's version of Homer is not Homerical; that it exhibits no resemblance of the original and characteristic manner of the Father of Poetry, as it wants his awful simplicity, his artless grandeur, his unaffected majesty. This cannot be totally denied, but it must be remembered that *necessitas quod cogit defendit*, that may be lawfully done which cannot be forborne. Time and place will always enforce regard. In estimating this translation consideration must be had of the nature of our language, the form of our metre, and, above all, of the change which two thousand years have made in the modes of life and the habits of thought. Virgil wrote in a language of the same general fabric with that of Homer, in verses of the same measure, and in an age nearer to Homer's time by eighteen hundred years; yet he found even then the state of the world so much altered, and the demand for elegance so much increased, that mere nature would be endured no longer; and perhaps, in the multitude of borrowed passages, very few can be shown which he has not embellished.

There is a time when nations emerging from barbarity, and falling into regular subordination, gain leisure to grow wise, and feel the shame of ignorance and the craving pain of unsatisfied curiosity. To this hunger of the mind plain sense is grateful; that which fills the void removes uneasiness, and to be free from pain for a while is pleasure; but repletion generates fastidiousness, a saturated intellect soon becomes luxurious, and knowledge finds no willing reception till it is recommended by artificial diction. Thus it will be found in the progress of learning that in all nations the first writers are simple, and that every age improves in elegance. One refinement always makes way for another, and what was expedient to Virgil was necessary to Pope.

I suppose many readers of the English *Iliad*, when they have been touched with some unexpected beauty of the lighter kind, have tried to enjoy it in the original, where, alas! it was not to be found. Homer doubtless owes to his translator many Ovidian graces not exactly suitable to his character; but to have added can be no great crime if nothing be taken away. Elegance is surely to be desired if it be not gained at the expense of dignity. A hero would wish to be loved as well as to be reverenced.

To a thousand cavils one answer is sufficient; the purpose of a writer is to be read, and the criticism which would destroy the power of pleasing must be blown aside. Pope wrote for his own age and his own nation: he knew that it was necessary to colour the images and point the sentiments of his author; he therefore made him graceful, but lost him some of his sublimity.

The copious notes with which the version is accompanied and by which it is recommended to many readers, though they were undoubtedly written to swell the volumes, ought not to pass without praise: commentaries which attract the reader by the pleasure of perusal have not often appeared; the notes of others are read to clear difficulties, those of Pope to vary entertainment.

It has, however, been objected with sufficient reason that there is in the commentary too much of unseasonable levity and affected gaiety; that too many appeals are made to the ladies, and the ease which is so carefully preserved is sometimes the ease of a trifler. Every art has its terms and every kind of instruction its proper style; the gravity of common critics may be tedious, but is less despicable than childish merriment.

Of the *Odyssey* nothing remains to be observed; the same general praise may be given to both translations, and a particular examination of either would require a large volume. The notes were written by Broome, who endeavoured not unsuccessfully to imitate his master.

Of *The Dunciad* the hint is confessedly taken from Dryden's *Mac Flecknoe*, but the plan is so enlarged and diversified as justly to claim the praise of an original, and affords perhaps the best specimen that has yet appeared of personal satire ludicrously pompous.

That the design was moral, whatever the author might tell either his readers or himself, I am not convinced. The first motive was the desire of revenging the contempt with which Theobald[40] had treated his *Shakespeare*, and regaining the honour which he had lost, by crushing his opponent. Theobald was not of bulk enough to fill a poem, and therefore it was necessary to find other enemies with other names, at whose expense he might divert the public.

In this design there was petulance and malignity enough; but I cannot think it very criminal. An author places himself uncalled before the tribunal of criticism, and solicits fame at the hazard of disgrace. Dullness or deformity are not culpable in themselves, but may be very justly reproached when they pretend to the honour of wit or the influence of beauty. If bad writers were to pass without reprehension what should restrain them? '*impune diem consumpserit ingens Telephus*'[41]; and upon bad writers only will censure have much effect. The satire which brought Theobald and Moore into contempt, dropped impotent from Bentley, like the javelin of Priam.

All truth is valuable, and satirical criticism may be considered as useful when it rectifies error and improves judgement: he that refines the public taste is a public benefactor.

The beauties of this poem are well known; its chief fault is the grossness of its images. Pope and Swift had an unnatural delight in ideas physically impure, such as every other tongue utters with unwillingness, and of which every ear shrinks from the mention.

But even this fault, offensive as it is, may be forgiven for the excellence of other passages; such as the formation and dissolution of Moore, the account of the Traveller, the misfortune of the Florist, and the crowded thoughts and stately numbers which dignify the concluding paragraph.[42]

The alterations which have been made in *The Dunciad,* not always for the better, require that it should be published, as in the last collection, with all its variations.

The *Essay on Man* was a work of great labour and long consideration, but certainly not the happiest of Pope's performances. The subject is perhaps not very proper for poetry, and the poet was not sufficiently master of his subject; metaphysical morality was to him a new study, he was proud of his acquisitions, and, supposing himself master of great secrets, was in haste to teach what he had not learned. Thus he tells us, in the first Epistle, that from the nature of the Supreme Being may be deduced an order of beings such as mankind, because Infinite Excellence can do only what is best. He finds out that these beings must be 'somewhere', and that 'all the question is whether man be in a wrong place'. Surely if, according to the poet's Leibnitzian reasoning, we may infer that man ought to be only because he is, we may allow that his place is the right place, because he has it. Supreme Wisdom is not less infallible in disposing than in creating. But what is meant by 'somewhere' and 'place' and 'wrong place' it had been vain to ask Pope, who probably had never asked himself.

Having exalted himself into the chair of wisdom he tells us much that every man knows, and much that he does not know himself; that we see but little, and that the order of the universe is beyond our comprehension, an opinion not very uncommon; and that there is a chain of subordinate beings 'from infinite to nothing', of which himself and his readers are equally ignorant. But he gives us one comfort which, without his help, he supposes unattainable, in the position 'that though we are fools, yet God is wise'.

This *Essay* affords an egregious instance of the predominance of genius, the dazzling splendour of imagery, and the seductive powers of eloquence. Never were penury of knowledge and vulgarity of sentiment so happily disguised.[43] The reader feels his mind full, though he learns nothing; and when he meets it in its new array no longer knows the talk of his mother and his nurse. When these wonder-working sounds sink into sense and the doctrine of the *Essay*, disrobed of its ornaments, is left to the powers of its naked excellence, what shall we discover? That we are, in comparison with our Creator, very weak and ignorant; that we do not uphold the chain of existence; and that we could not make one another with more skill than we are made. We may learn yet more: that the arts of human life were copied from the instinctive operations of other animals; that if the world be made for man, it may be said that man was made for geese. To these profound principles of natural knowledge are added some moral instructions equally new: that self-interest well understood will produce social concord; that men are mutual gainers by mutual benefits; that evil is sometimes balanced by good; that human advantages are unstable and fallacious, of uncertain duration and doubtful effect; that our true honour is not to have a great part, but to act it well; that virtue only is our own; and that happiness is always in our power.

Surely a man of no very comprehensive search may venture to say that he has heard all this before, but it was never till now recommended by such a blaze of embellishment or such sweetness of melody. The vigorous contraction of some thoughts, the luxuriant amplification of others, the incidental illustrations, and sometimes the dignity, sometimes the softness of the verses, enchain philosophy, suspend criticism, and oppress judgement by overpowering pleasure.

This is true of many paragraphs; yet if I had undertaken to exemplify Pope's felicity of composition before a rigid critic I should not select the *Essay on Man*, for it contains more lines unsuccessfully laboured, more harshness of diction, more thoughts imperfectly expressed, more levity without elegance, and more heaviness without strength, than will easily be found in all his other works.

The *Characters of Men and Women*[44] are the product of diligent speculation upon human life; much labour has been bestowed upon them, and Pope very seldom laboured in vain. That his excellence may be properly estimated I recommend a comparison of his *Charac-*

ters of Women with Boileau's *Satire*; it will then be seen with how much more perspicacity female nature is investigated and female excellence selected; and he surely is no mean writer to whom Boileau shall be found inferior. The *Characters of Men*, however, are written with more, if not with deeper, thought, and exhibit many passages exquisitely beautiful. 'The Gem and the Flower'[45] will not easily be equalled. In the women's part are some defects: the character of Atossa[46] is not so neatly finished as that of Clodio, and some of the female characters may be found perhaps more frequently among men; what is said of Philomede[47] was true of Prior.

In the *Epistles to Lord Bathurst* and *Lord Burlington* Dr Warburton has endeavoured to find a train of thought which was never in the writer's head, and, to support his hypothesis, has printed that first which was published last. In one, the most valuable passage is perhaps the eulogy on Good Sense[48], and in the other the End of the Duke of Buckingham.

The *Epistle to Arbuthnot*, now arbitrarily called the *Prologue to the Satires*, is a performance consisting, as it seems, of many fragments wrought into one design, which by this union of scattered beauties contains more striking paragraphs than could probably have been brought together into an occasional work. As there is no stronger motive to exertion than self-defence, no part has more elegance, spirit, or dignity than the poet's vindication of his own character. The meanest passage is the satire upon Sporus[49].

Of the two poems which derived their names from the year, and which are called the *Epilogue to the Satires*, it was very justly remarked by Savage that the second was in the whole more strongly conceived and more equally supported, but that it had no single passages equal to the contention in the first for the dignity of Vice and the celebration of the triumph of Corruption.

The *Imitations of Horace* seem to have been written as relaxations of his genius. This employment became his favourite by its facility; the plan was ready to his hand, and nothing was required but to accommodate as he could the sentiments of an old author to recent facts or familiar images; but what is easy is seldom excellent: such imitations cannot give pleasure to common readers. The man of learning may be sometimes surprised and delighted by an unexpected parallel; but the comparison requires knowledge of the original, which will likewise often detect strained applications. Between Roman images and English manners there will be an irreconcilable dissimilitude, and the work will generally be uncouth and party-coloured; neither original nor translated, neither ancient nor modern.

Pope had, in proportions very nicely adjusted to each other, all the qualities that constitute genius. He had Invention, by which new trains of events are formed and new scenes of imagery displayed, as in *The Rape of the Lock*, and by which extrinsic and adventitious embellishments and illustrations are connected with a known subject, as in the *Essay on Criticism*; he had Imagination, which strongly impresses on the writer's mind and enables him to convey to the reader the various forms of nature, incidents of life, and energies of passion, as in his *Eloisa*, *Windsor Forest*, and the *Ethic Epistles*; he had Judgement, which selects from life or nature what the present purpose requires, and, by separating the essence of things from its concomitants, often makes the representation more powerful than the reality; and he had colours of language always before him ready to decorate his matter with every grace of elegant expression, as when he accommodates his diction to the wonderful multiplicity of Homer's sentiments and descriptions.

Poetical expression includes sound as well as meaning. 'Music,' says Dryden, 'is inarticulate poetry'; among the excellences of Pope, therefore, must be mentioned the melody of his metre. By perusing the works of Dryden he discovered the most perfect fabric of English verse[50], and habituated himself to that only which he found the best; in consequence of which restraint his poetry has been censured as too uniformly musical, and as glutting the ear with unvaried sweetness. I suspect this objection to be the cant of those who judge by principles rather than perception; and who would even themselves have less pleasure in his works if he had tried to relieve attention by studied discords, or affected to break his lines and vary his pauses.

But though he was thus careful of his versification he did not oppress his powers with superfluous rigour. He seems to have thought with Boileau that the practice of writing might be refined till the difficulty should overbalance the advantage. The construction of his language is not always strictly grammatical; with those rhymes which prescription[51] had conjoined he contented himself, without regard to Swift's remonstrances, though there was no striking consonance; nor was he very careful to vary his terminations or to refuse admission at a small distance to the same rhymes.

To Swift's edict for the exclusion of alexandrines and triplets he paid little regard; he admitted them, but, in the opinion of Fenton, too rarely: he uses them more liberally in his translation than his poems.

He has a few double rhymes[52], and always, I think, unsuccessfully, except once in *The Rape of the Lock*.

Expletives[53] he very early ejected from his verses; but he now and then admits an epithet rather commodious than important. Each of the six first lines of the *Iliad* might lose two syllables with very little diminution of the meaning; and sometimes, after all his art and labour, one verse seems to be made for the sake of another. In his latter productions the diction is sometimes vitiated by French idioms[54], with which Bolingbroke had perhaps infected him.

I have been told that the couplet by which he declared his own ear to be most gratified was this:

> Lo, where Maeotis sleeps, and hardly flows
> The freezing Tanais thro' a waste of snows.[55]

But the reason of this preference I cannot discover.

It is remarked by Watts that there is scarcely a happy combination of words or a phrase poetically elegant in the English language which Pope has not inserted into his version of Homer. How he obtained possession of so many beauties of speech it were desirable to know. That he gleaned from authors, obscure as well as eminent, what he thought brilliant or useful, and preserved it all in a regular collection, is not unlikely. When, in his last years, Hall's *Satires* were shown him he wished that he had seen them sooner.

New sentiments and new images others may produce, but to attempt any further improvement of versification will be dangerous. Art and diligence have now done their best, and what shall be added will be the effort of tedious toil and needless curiosity.

After all this it is surely superfluous to answer the question that has once been asked, Whether Pope was a poet?[56] otherwise than by asking in return, If Pope be not a poet, where is poetry to be found? To circumscribe poetry by a definition will only show the narrowness of the definer, though a definition which shall exclude Pope will not easily be made. Let us look round upon the present time, and back upon the past; let us inquire to whom the voice of mankind has decreed the wreath of poetry; let their productions be examined and their claims stated, and the pretensions of Pope will be no more disputed. Had he given the world only his version the name of poet must have been allowed him; if the writer of the *Iliad* were to class his successors he would assign a very high place to his translator, without requiring any other evidence of genius.

FROM

THE LIFE OF EDMUND SMITH

'ON GILBERT WALMSLEY'

Of Gilbert Walmsley, thus presented to my mind, let me indulge myself in the remembrance. I knew him very early; he was one of the first friends that literature procured me, and I hope that at least my gratitude made me worthy of his notice.

He was of an advanced age, and I was only not a boy; yet he never received my notions with contempt. He was a Whig, with all the virulence and malevolence of his party; yet difference of opinion did not keep us apart. I honoured him, and he endured me.

He had mingled with the gay world without exemption from its vices or its follies, but had never neglected the cultivation of his mind;

his belief of Revelation was unshaken; his learning preserved his principles: he grew first regular, and then pious.

His studies had been so various that I am not able to name a man of equal knowledge. His acquaintance with books was great; and what he did not immediately know he could at least tell where to find. Such was his amplitude of learning and such his copiousness of communication that it may be doubted whether a day now passes in which I have not some advantage from his friendship.

At this man's table I enjoyed many cheerful and instructive hours, with companions such as are not often found: with one who has lengthened and one who has gladdened life; with Dr James,[1] whose skill in physic will be long remembered; and with David Garrick,[2] whom I hoped to have gratified with this character of our common friend: but what are the hopes of man! I am disappointed by that stroke of death, which has eclipsed the gaiety of nations and impoverished the public stock of harmless pleasure.

FROM

THE LIFE OF SHENSTONE

'LANDSCAPE-GARDENING AT THE LEASOWES'

Now was excited his delight in rural pleasures,[1] and his ambition of rural elegance; he began from this time to point his prospects, to diversify his surface, to entangle his walks, and to wind his waters, which he did with such judgement and such fancy as made his little domain the envy of the great and the admiration of the skilful: a place to be visited by travellers, and copied by designers. Whether to plant a walk in undulating curves, and to place a bench at every turn where there is an object to catch the view; to make water run where it will be heard, and to stagnate where it will be seen; to leave intervals where the eye will be pleased, and to thicken the plantation where there is something to be hidden, demands any great powers of mind, I will not inquire: perhaps a sullen and surly speculator may think such performances rather the sport than the business of human reason. But it must be at least confessed that to embellish the form of nature is an innocent amusement, and some praise must be allowed by the most supercilious observer to him who does best what such multitudes are contending to do well.

This praise was the praise of Shenstone; but, like all other modes of felicity, it was not enjoyed without its abatements. Lyttelton[2] was his neighbour and his rival, whose empire, spacious and opulent, looked with disdain on the '*petty State*' that '*appeared behind it*'. For a while the inhabitants of Hagley affected to tell their acquaintance of the little fellow that was trying to make himself admired; but when by degrees the Leasowes forced themselves into notice, they took care to defeat the curiosity which they could not suppress, by conducting[3] their visitants perversely to inconvenient points of view, and introducing them at the wrong end of a walk to detect a deception; injuries of which Shenstone would heavily complain. Where there is emulation there will be vanity, and where there is vanity there will be folly.

The pleasure of Shenstone was all in his eye; he valued what he valued merely for its looks: nothing raised his indignation more than to ask if there were any fishes in his water.

His house was mean, and he did not improve it: his care was of his grounds. When he came home from his walks he might find his floors flooded by a shower through the broken roof; but could spare no money for its reparation.

In time his expenses brought clamours about him, that overpowered the lamb's bleat and the linnet's song; and his groves were haunted by beings very different from fauns and fairies.[4] He spent his estate in adorning it, and his death was probably hastened by his anxieties. He was a lamp that spent its oil in blazing. It is said that if he had lived a little longer he would have been assisted by a pension: such bounty could not have been ever more properly bestowed; but that it was ever asked is not certain: it is too certain that it never was enjoyed.

THE LIFE OF GRAY

Thomas Gray, the son of Mr Philip Gray, a scrivener of London, was born in Cornhill, 26 November, 1716. His grammatical education he received at Eton under the care of Mr Antrobus, his mother's brother, then assistant to Dr George, and when he left school, in 1734, entered a pensioner at Peterhouse in Cambridge.

The transition from the school to the college is, to most young scholars, the time from which they date their years of manhood, liberty, and happiness; but Gray seems to have been very little delighted with academical gratifications: he liked at Cambridge neither the mode of life nor the fashion of study, and lived sullenly on to the time when his attendance on lectures was no longer required. As he intended to profess the Common Law he took no degree.

When he had been at Cambridge about five years, Mr Horace Walpole, whose friendship he had gained at Eton, invited him to travel with him as his companion. They wandered through France into Italy, and Gray's letters contain a very pleasing account of many parts of their journey. But unequal friendships are easily dissolved: at Florence they quarrelled and parted, and Mr Walpole is now content to have it told that it was by his fault. If we look, however, without prejudice on the world we shall find that men, whose consciousness of their own merit sets them above the compliances of servility, are apt enough in their association with superiors to watch their own dignity with troublesome and punctilious jealousy, and in the fervour of independence to exact that attention which they refuse to pay. Part they did, whatever was the quarrel, and the rest of their travels was doubtless more unpleasant to them both. Gray continued his journey in a manner suitable to his own little fortune, with only an occasional servant.

He returned to England in September, 1741, and in about two months afterwards buried his father, who had, by an injudicious waste of money upon a new house, so much lessened his fortune that Gray thought himself too poor to study the law. He therefore retired to Cambridge, where he soon after became Bachelor of Civil Law, and where, without liking the place or its inhabitants, or professing to like them, he passed, except a short residence at London, the rest of his life.

About this time he was deprived of Mr West,[1] the son of a chancellor of Ireland, a friend on whom he appears to have set a high value, and who deserved his esteem by the powers which he shows in his letters, and in the *Ode to May*, which Mr Mason has preserved, as well as by the sincerity with which, when Gray sent him part of *Agrippina*, a tragedy that he had just begun, he gave an opinion which probably intercepted the progress of the work, and which the judgement of every reader will confirm. It was certainly no loss to the English stage that *Agrippina* was never finished.

In this year (1742) Gray seems first to have applied himself seriously to poetry, for in this year were produced the *Ode to Spring*, his *Prospect of Eton*, and his *Ode to Adversity*. He began likewise a Latin Poem, *De Principiis Cogitandi*.

It may be collected from the narrative of Mr Mason, that his first ambition was to have excelled in Latin poetry: perhaps it were reasonable to wish that he had prosecuted his design; for though there is at present some embarrassment in his phrase, and some harshness in his lyric numbers, his copiousness of language is such as very few possess, and his lines, even when imperfect, discover a writer whom practice would quickly have made skilful.

He now lived on at Peterhouse, very little solicitous what others did or thought, and cultivated his mind and enlarged his views without any other purpose than of improving and amusing himself; when Mr Mason, being elected fellow of Pembroke-hall, brought him a companion who was afterwards to be his editor, and whose fondness and fidelity has kindled in him a zeal of admiration, which cannot be reasonably expected from the neutrality of a stranger and the coldness of a critic.

In this retirement he wrote (1747) an ode on *The Death of Mr Walpole's Cat*, and the year afterwards attempted a poem of more importance, on *Government and Education*, of which the fragments which remain have many excellent lines.

His next production (1750) was his far-famed *Elegy in the Church-yard*, which, finding its way into a magazine, first, I believe, made him known to the public.

An invitation from Lady Cobham about this time gave occasion to an odd composition called *A Long Story*, which adds little to Gray's character.

Several of his pieces were published (1753), with designs, by Mr Bentley, and, that they might in some form or other make a book, only one side of each leaf was printed. I believe the poems and the plates recommended each other so well, that the whole impression was soon bought. This year he lost his mother.

Some time afterwards (1756) some young men of the college, whose chambers were near his, diverted themselves with disturbing him by frequent and troublesome noises, and, as is said, by pranks yet more offensive and contemptuous. This insolence, having endured it a while, he represented to the governors of the society, among whom perhaps he had no friends, and, finding his complaint little regarded, removed himself to Pembroke-hall.

In 1757 he published *The Progress of Poetry* and *The Bard*, two compositions at which the readers of poetry were at first content to gaze in mute amazement. Some that tried them confessed their inability to understand them,[2] though Warburton said that they were understood as well as the works of Milton and Shakespeare, which it is the fashion to admire. Garrick wrote a few lines in their praise. Some hardy champions undertook to rescue them from neglect, and in a short time many were content to be shown beauties which they could not see.

Gray's reputation was now so high that, after the death of Cibber, he had the honour of refusing the laurel,[3] which was then bestowed on Mr Whitehead.

His curiosity not long after drew him away from Cambridge to a lodging near the Museum, where he resided near three years, reading and transcribing; and, so far as can be discovered, very little affected by two odes on *Oblivion* and *Obscurity*, in which his lyric performances were ridiculed with much contempt and much ingenuity.

When the Professor of Modern History at Cambridge died he was, as he says, 'cockered and spirited up', till he asked it of Lord Bute, who sent him a civil refusal; and the place was given to Mr Brocket, the tutor of Sir James Lowther.

His constitution was weak, and believing that his health was promoted by exercise and change of place he undertook (1765) a journey into Scotland, of which his account, so far as it extends, is very curious and elegant; for as his comprehension was ample his curiosity extended to all the works of art, all the appearances of nature, and all the monuments of past events. He naturally contracted a friendship with Dr Beattie, whom he found a poet, a philosopher, and a good man. The Mareschal College at Aberdeen offered him the degree of Doctor of Laws, which, having omitted to take it at Cambridge, he thought it decent to refuse.

What he had formerly solicited in vain was at last given him without solicitation. The Professorship of History became again vacant, and he received (1768) an offer of it from the Duke of Grafton. He accepted, and retained it to his death; always designing lectures, but never reading them; uneasy at his neglect of duty,[4] and appeasing his uneasiness with designs of reformation, and with a resolution which he believed himself to have made of resigning the office, if he found himself unable to discharge it.

Ill health made another journey necessary, and he visited (1769) Westmorland and Cumberland. He that reads his epistolary narration wishes that to travel, and to tell his travels, had been more of his employment; but it is by studying at home that we must obtain the ability of travelling with intelligence and improvement.

His travels and his studies were now near their end. The gout, of which he had sustained many weak attacks, fell upon his stomach, and, yielding to no medicines, produced strong convulsions, which (30 July, 1771) terminated in death.

His character I am willing to adopt, as Mr Mason has done, from a letter written to my friend Mr Boswell, by the Rev. Mr Temple, rector of St Gluvias in Cornwall; and am as willing as his warmest well-wisher to believe it true.

Perhaps he was the most learned man in Europe. He was equally acquainted with the elegant and profound parts of science, and that not superficially but thoroughly. He knew every branch of history, both natural and civil; had read all the original historians of England, France, and Italy; and was a great antiquarian. Criticism, metaphysics, morals, politics made a principal part of his study; voyages and travels of all sorts were his favourite amusements; and he had a fine taste in painting, prints, architecture, and gardening. With such a fund of knowledge, his conversaticn must have been equally instructing and entertaining; but he was also a good man, a man of virtue and humanity. There is no character without some speck, some imperfection; and I think the greatest defect in his was an affectation in delicacy, or rather effeminacy, and a visible fastidiousness, or contempt and disdain of his inferiors in science. He also had, in some degree, that weakness which disgusted Voltaire so much in Mr Congreve: though he seemed to value others chiefly according to the progress they had made in knowledge, yet he could not bear to be considered himself merely as a man of letters; and though without birth, or fortune, or station, his desire was to be looked upon as a private independent gentleman, who read for his amusement. Perhaps it may be said, What signifies so much knowledge, when it produced so little? Is it worth taking so much pains to leave no memorial but a few poems? But let it be considered that Mr Gray was, to others, at least innocently employed; to himself, certainly beneficially. His time passed agreeably; he was every day making some new acquisition in science; his mind was enlarged, his heart softened, his virtue strengthened; the world and mankind were shown to him without a mask; and he was taught to consider every thing as trifling, and unworthy of the attention of a wise man, except the pursuit of knowledge and practice of virtue, in that state wherein God hath placed us.

To this character Mr Mason has added a more particular account of Gray's skill in zoology. He has remarked that Gray's effeminacy was affected most 'before those whom he did not wish to please'; and that he is unjustly charged with making knowledge his sole reason of preference, as he paid his esteem to none whom he did not likewise believe to be good.

What has occurred to me, from the slight inspection of his letters in which my undertaking has engaged me, is that his mind had a large grasp; that his curiosity was unlimited, and his judgement cultivated; that he was a man likely to love much where he loved at all, but that he was fastidious and hard to please. His contempt, however, is often employed, where I hope it will be approved, upon scepticism and infidelity. His short account of Shaftesbury I will insert.

You say you cannot conceive how lord Shaftesbury came to be a philosopher in vogue; I will tell you: first he was a lord; secondly, he was as vain as any of his readers; thirdly, men are very prone to believe what they do not understand; fourthly, they will believe anything at all, provided they are under no obligation to believe it; fifthly, they love to take a new road, even when that road leads nowhere; sixthly, he was reckoned a fine writer, and seems [seemed] always to mean more than he said. Would you have any more reasons? An interval of above forty years has pretty well destroyed the charm. A dead lord ranks [but] with commoners: vanity is no longer interested in the matter; for a new road is [has] become an old one.

Mr Mason has added from his own knowledge that though Gray was poor, he was not eager for money, and that out of the little that he had, he was very willing to help the necessitous.

As a writer he had this peculiarity, that he did not write his pieces first rudely, and then correct them, but laboured every line as it arose in the train of composition, and he had a notion not very peculiar, that he could not write but at certain times, or at happy moments; a fantastic foppery, to which my kindness for a man of learning and of virtue wishes him to have been superior.

Gray's poetry is now to be considered, and I hope not to be looked on as an enemy to his name if I confess that I contemplate it with less pleasure than his life.

His *Ode on Spring* has something poetical, both in the language and the thought; but the language is too luxuriant, and the thoughts have nothing new. There has of late arisen a practice of giving to adjectives, derived from substantives, the termination of participles, such as the *cultured* plain, the *daisied* bank; but I was sorry to see, in the lines of a scholar like Gray, 'the *honied* Spring'. The morality is natural, but too stale; the conclusion is pretty.

The poem on the Cat was doubtless by its author considered as a trifle, but it is not a happy trifle. In the first stanza 'the azure flowers that blow' show resolutely a rhyme is sometimes made when it cannot easily be found. Selima, the Cat, is called a nymph, with some violence both to language and sense; but there is good use made of it when it is done; for of the two lines,

> What female heart can gold despise?
> What cat's averse to fish?

the first relates merely to the nymph, and the second only to the cat. The sixth stanza contains a melancholy truth, that 'a favourite has no friend', but the last ends in a pointed sentence of no relation to the purpose; if what glistered had been 'gold', the cat would not have gone into the water; and, if she had, would not less have been drowned.

The *Prospect of Eton College* suggests nothing to Gray which every beholder does not equally think and feel. His supplication to Father Thames, to tell him who drives the hoop or tosses the ball, is useless and puerile. Father Thames has no better means of knowing than himself. His epithet 'buxom health' is not elegant; he seems not to understand the word.[5] Gray thought his language more poetical as it was more remote from common use: finding in Dryden 'honey redolent of Spring', an expression that reaches the utmost limits of our language, Gray drove it a little more beyond common apprehension, by making 'gales' to be 'redolent of joy and youth'.

Of the *Ode on Adversity* the hint was at first taken from *O Diva, gratum quae regis Antium*;[6] but Gray has excelled his original by the variety of his sentiments and by their moral application. Of this piece, at once poetical and rational, I will not by slight objections violate the dignity.

My process has now brought me to the 'Wonderful Wonder of Wonders', the two Sister Odes; by which, though either vulgar ignorance or common sense at first universally rejected them, many have been since persuaded to think themselves delighted. I am one of those that are willing to be pleased, and therefore would gladly find the meaning of the first stanza of *The Progress of Poetry*.

Gray seems in his rapture to confound the images of 'spreading sound' and 'running water'. A 'stream of music' may be allowed; but where does Music, however 'smooth and strong', after having visited the 'verdant vales', 'roll down the steep amain', so as that 'rocks and nodding groves rebellow to the roar'? If this be said of Music, it is nonsense; if it be said of Water, it is nothing to the purpose.

The second stanza, exhibiting Mars's car and Jove's eagle, is unworthy of further notice. Criticism disdains to chase a schoolboy to his common-places.

To the third it may likewise be objected that it is drawn from mythology, though such as may be more easily assimilated to real life. 'Idalia's velvet-green' has something of cant.[7] An epithet or metaphor drawn from Nature ennobles Art; an epithet or metaphor drawn from Art degrades Nature. Gray is too fond of words arbitrarily compounded. 'Many-twinkling' was formerly censured as not analogical; we may say *many-spotted*, but scarcely *many-spotting*. This stanza, however, has something pleasing.

Of the second ternary of stanzas the first endeavours to tell something, and would have told it had it not been crossed by Hyperion; the second describes well enough the universal prevalence of poetry, but I am afraid that the conclusion will not rise from the premises. The caverns of the North and the plains of Chili are not the residences of 'Glory' and 'generous Shame'. But that Poetry and Virtue go always together is an opinion so pleasing that I can forgive him who resolves to think it true.

The third stanza sounds big with Delphi, and Egean, and Ilissus, and Meander, and 'hallowed fountain' and 'solemn sound'; but in all Gray's odes there is a kind of cumbrous splendour which we wish away. His position is at last false: in the time of Dante and Petrarch, from whom he derives our first school of poetry, Italy was overrun by 'tyrant power' and 'coward vice'; nor was our state much better when we first borrowed the Italian arts.

Of the third ternary the first gives a mythological birth of Shakespeare. What is said of that mighty genius is true; but it is not said happily: the real effects of this poetical power are put out of sight by the pomp of machinery.[8] Where truth is sufficient to fill the mind, fiction is worse than useless; the counterfeit debases the genuine.

His account of Milton's blindness, if we suppose it caused by study in the formation of his poem, a supposition surely allowable, is poetically true, and happily imagined. But the 'car' of Dryden, with his 'two coursers', has nothing in it peculiar; it is a car in which any other rider may be placed.

The Bard appears at the first view to be, as Algarotti and others have remarked, an imitation of the prophecy of Nereus.[9] Algarotti thinks it superior to its original, and, if preference depends only on the imagery and animation of the two poems, his judgement is right. There is in *The Bard* more force, more thought, and more variety. But to copy is less than to invent, and the copy has been unhappily produced at a wrong time. The fiction of Horace was to the Romans credible; but its revival disgusts us with apparent and unconquerable falsehood. 'Incredulus odi.'[10]

To select a singular event, and swell it to a giant's bulk by fabulous appendages of spectres and predictions, has little difficulty, for he that forsakes the probable may always find the marvellous. And it has little use: we are affected only as we believe; we are improved only as we find something to be imitated or declined. I do not see that *The Bard* promotes any truth, moral or political.

His stanzas are too long, especially his epodes; the ode is finished before the ear has learned its measures, and consequently before it can receive pleasure from their consonance and recurrence.

Of the first stanza the abrupt beginning has been celebrated; but technical beauties can give praise only to the inventor. It is in the power of any man to rush abruptly upon his subject, that has read the ballad of *Johnny Armstrong*,

'Is there ever a man in all Scotland—'

The initial resemblances, or alliterations, 'ruin,' 'ruthless,' 'helm nor hauberk,' are below the grandeur of a poem that endeavours at sublimity.

In the second stanza the Bard is well described; but in the third we have the puerilities of obsolete mythology. When we are told that Cadwallo 'hush'd the stormy main', and that Modred 'made huge Plinlimmon bow his cloud-top'd head', attention recoils from the repetition of a tale that, even when it was first heard, was heard with scorn.

The 'weaving' of the 'winding sheet' he borrowed, as he owns, from the northern bards; but their texture, however, was very properly the work of female powers, as the art of spinning the thread of life in another mythology. Theft is always dangerous; Gray has made weavers of his slaughtered bards by a fiction outrageous and incongruous. They are then called upon to 'Weave the warp, and weave the woof', perhaps with no great propriety; for it is by crossing the woof with the warp that men weave the web or piece; and the first line was dearly bought by the admission of its wretched correspondent, 'Give ample room and verge enough'. He has, however, no other line as bad.

The third stanza of the second ternary is commended, I think, beyond its merit. The personification is indistinct. Thirst and Hunger are not alike, and their features, to make the imagery perfect, should have been discriminated. We are told, in the same stanza, how 'towers' are 'fed'. But I will no longer look for particular faults; yet let it be observed that the ode might have been concluded with an action of better example:[11] but suicide is always to be had without expense of thought.

These odes are marked by glittering accumulations of ungraceful ornaments: they strike, rather than please; the images are magnified by affectation; the language is laboured into harshness. The mind of the writer seems to work with unnatural violence. 'Double, double, toil and trouble.' He has a kind of strutting dignity, and is tall by walking on tiptoe. His art and his struggle are too visible, and there is too little appearance of ease and nature.

To say that he has no beauties would be unjust: a man like him, of great learning and great industry, could not but produce something valuable. When he pleases least, it can only be said that a good design was ill directed.

His translations of Northern and Welsh poetry deserve praise: the imagery is preserved, perhaps often improved; but the language is unlike the language of other poets.

In the character of his *Elegy* I rejoice to concur with the common reader; for by the common sense of readers uncorrupted with literary prejudices, after all the refinements of subtlety and the dogmatism of learning, must be finally decided all claim to poetical honours. The *Church-yard* abounds with images which find a mirror in every mind, and with sentiments to which every bosom returns an echo. The four stanzas beginning 'Yet even these bones' are to me original: I have never seen the notions in any other place; yet he that reads them here persuades himself that he has always felt them. Had Gray written often thus it had been vain to blame, and useless to praise him.

TO WILLIAM DRUMMOND

Sir

I did not expect to hear that it could be, in an assembly convened for the propagation of Christian knowledge, a question whether any nation uninstructed in religion should receive instruction; or whether that instruction should be imparted to them by a translation of the holy books into their own language. If obedience to the will of GOD be necessary to happiness, and knowledge of his will be necessary to obedience, I know not how he that with-holds this knowledge, or delays it, can be said to love his neighbour as himself. He that voluntarily continues ignorance, is guilty of all the crimes which ignorance produces; as to him that should extinguish the tapers of a light-house, might justly be imputed the calamities of shipwrecks. Christianity is the highest perfection of humanity; and as no man is good but as he wishes the good of others, no man can be good in the highest degree who wishes not to others the largest measures of the greatest good. To omit for a year, or for a day, the most efficacious method of advancing Christianity, in compliance with any purposes that terminate on this side of the grave, is a crime of which I know not that the world has yet had an example, except in the practice of the planters of America, a race of mortals whom, I suppose, no other man wishes to resemble.

The Papists have, indeed, denied to the laity the use of the Bible; but this prohibition, in few places now very rigorously enforced, is defended by arguments, which have for their foundation the care of souls. To obscure, upon motives merely political, the light of revelation, is a practice reserved for the reformed; and, surely, the blackest midnight of popery is meridian sunshine to such a reformation. I am not very willing that any language should be totally extinguished. The similitude and derivation of languages afford the

*See Editor's Notes.

most indubitable proof of the traduction of nations, and the genealogy of mankind. They add often physical certainty to historical evidence; and often supply the only evidence of ancient migrations, and of the revolutions of ages which left no written monuments behind them.

Every man's opinions, at least his desires, are a little influenced by his favourite studies. My zeal for languages may seem, perhaps, rather over-heated, even to those by whom I desire to be well-esteemed. To those who have nothing in their thoughts but trade or policy, present power, or present money, I should not think it necessary to defend my opinions; but with men of letters I would not unwillingly compound, by wishing the continuance of every language, however narrow in its extent, or however incommodious for common purposes, till it is reposited in some version of a known book, that it may be always hereafter examined and compared with other languages, and then permitting its disuse. For this purpose, the translation of the bible is most to be desired. It is not certain that the same method will not preserve the Highland language, for the purposes of learning, and abolish it from daily use. When the Highlanders read the Bible, they will naturally wish to have its obscurities cleared, and to know the history, collateral or appendant. Knowledge always desires increase: it is like fire, which must first be kindled by some external agent, but which will afterwards propagate itself. When they once desire to learn, they will naturally have recourse to the nearest language by which that desire can be gratified; and one will tell another that if he would attain knowledge, he must learn English.

This speculation may, perhaps, be thought more subtle than the grossness of real life will easily admit. Let it, however, be remembered that the efficacy of ignorance has been long tried, and has not produced the consequence expected. Let knowledge, therefore, take its turn; and let the patrons of privation stand awhile aside, and admit the operation of positive principles.

You will be pleased, Sir, to assure the worthy man who is employed in the new translation, that he has my wishes for his success; and if here or at Oxford I can be of any use, that I shall think it more than honour to promote his undertaking.

> I am sorry that I delayed so long to write.
>
> I am, Sir, your most humble servant,

Johnson's-court, Fleet-street,   Sam: Johnson

  13 August, 1766.

To Mrs Aston

17 November, 1767.

Madam

If you impute it to disrespect or inattention, that I took no leave when I left Lichfield, you will do me great injustice. I know you too well not to value your friendship.

When I came to Oxford, I inquired after the product of our walnut-tree, but it had, like other trees this year, but very few nuts, and for those few I came too late. The tree, as I told you, Madam, we cannot find to be more than thirty years old, and, upon measuring it, I found it, at about one foot from the ground, seven feet in circumference, and at the height of about seven feet, the circumference is five feet and a half; it would have been, I believe, still bigger, but that it has been lopped. The nuts are small, such as they call single nuts; whether this nut is of quicker growth than better I have not yet inquired; such as they are, I hope to send them next year.

You know, dear Madam, the liberty I took of hinting that I did not think your present mode of life very pregnant with happiness. Reflection has not yet changed my opinion. Solitude excludes pleasure, and does not always secure peace. Some communication of sentiments is commonly necessary to give vent to the imagination, and discharge the mind of its own flatulencies. Some lady surely might be found, in whose conversation you might delight, and in whose fidelity you might repose. *The World*, says Locke, *has people of all sorts.* You will forgive me this obtrusion of my opinion; I am sure I wish you well.

Poor Kitty has done what we have all to do, and Lucy has the world to begin anew: I hope she will find some way to more content than I left her possessing.

Be pleased to make my compliments to Mrs Hinckley and Miss Turton.

> I am, Madam,
> > Your most obliged and most humble servant,
> > > SAM: JOHNSON.

TO MRS THRALE

> Lichfield, 11 July, 1770.

Madam

Since my last letter nothing extraordinary has happened. Rheumatism, which has been very troublesome, is grown better. I have not yet seen Dr Taylor, and July runs fast away. I shall not have much time for him, if he delays much longer to come or send. Mr Grene, the apothecary, has found a book, which tells who paid levies in our parish, and how much they paid, above an hundred years ago. Do you not think we study this book hard? Nothing is like going to the bottom of things. Many families that paid the parish rates are now extinct, like the race of Hercules. *Pulvis et umbra sumus.*[1] What is nearest us touches us most. The passions rise higher at domestic than at imperial tragedies. I am not wholly unaffected by the revolutions of Sadler-street; nor can forbear to mourn a little when old names vanish away, and new come into their place.

Do not imagine, Madam, that I wrote this letter for the sake of these philosophical meditations; for when I began it, I had neither Mr Grene, nor his book, in my thoughts; but was resolved to write, and did not know what I had to send, but my respects to Mrs Salusbury, and Mr Thrale, and Harry, and the Misses.

> I am, dearest Madam,
> > Yours, &c.,
> > > SAM: JOHNSON.

To Dr Taylor

Dear Sir

I am sorry to find both from your own letter and from Mr Langley that your health is in a state so different from what might be wished. The Langleys impute a great part of your complaints to a mind unsettled and discontented. I know that you have disorders, though I hope not very formidable, independent of the mind, and that your complaints do not arise from the mere habit of complaining. Yet there is no distemper, not in the highest degree acute, on which the mind has not some influence, and which is not better resisted by a cheerful than a gloomy temper. I would have you read when you can force your attention, but that perhaps will be not so often as is necessary to increase the general cheerfulness of Life. If you could get a little apparatus for chemistry or experimental philosophy it would offer you some diversion, or if you made some little purchase at a small distance, or took some petty farm into your own hands, it would break your thoughts when they become tyrannous and troublesome, and supply you at once with exercise and amusement.

You tell me nothing of Kedlestone, which you went down with a design of visiting, nor of Dr Butler, who seems to be a very rational man, and who told you with great honesty that your cure must in the greatest measure depend upon yourself.

Your uneasiness at the misfortunes of your relations, I comprehend perhaps too well. It was an irresistible obtrusion of a disagreeable image, which you always wished away but could not dismiss, an incessant persecution of a troublesome thought neither to be pacified nor ejected. Such has of late been the state of my own mind. I had formerly great command of my attention, and what I did not like could forbear to think on. But of this power, which is of the highest importance to the tranquillity of life, I have been so much exhausted, that I do not go into a company towards night, in which I foresee anything disagreeable, nor inquire after any thing to which I am not indifferent, lest something, which I know to be nothing, should fasten upon my imagination, and hinder me from sleep. Thus it is that the progress of life brings often with it diseases, not of the body only, but of the mind. We must endeavour to cure both the one and the other. In our bodies we must ourselves do a great part, and for the mind it is very seldom that any help can be had, but what prayer and reason shall supply.

I have got my work so far forward that I flatter myself with concluding it this month, and then shall do nothing so willingly as come down to Ashbourne. We will try to make October a pleasant month.

> I am, Sir,
> Yours affectionately,

31 August 1772.   SAM: JOHNSON.

I wish we could borrow of Dr Bentley the *Preces in usum Sarum.*

TO MRS THRALE

[Ashbourne, July 1775.]

Now, thinks my dearest Mistress to herself, sure I am at last gone too far to be pestered every post with a letter: he knows that people go into the country to be at quiet; he knows too that when I have once told the story of Ralph, the place where I am affords me nothing that I shall delight to tell, or he will wish to be told; he knows how troublesome it is to write letters about nothing; and he knows that he does not love trouble himself, and therefore ought not to force it upon others.

But, dearest Lady, you may see once more how little knowledge influences practice, notwithstanding all this knowledge, you see, here is a letter.

Everybody says the prospect of harvest is uncommonly delightful; but this has been so long the Summer talk, and has been so often contradicted by Autumn, that I do not suffer it to lay much hold on my mind. Our gay prospects have now for many years together ended in melancholy retrospects. Yet I am of opinion that there is much corn upon the ground. Every dear year encourages the farmer to sow more and more, and favourable seasons will be sent at last. Let us hope that they will be sent now.

The Doctor and Frank are gone to see the hay. It was cut on Saturday, and yesterday was well wetted; but to day has its fill of sunshine. I hope the hay at Streatham was plentiful, and had good weather.

Our lawn is as you left it, only the pool is so full of mud that the water-fowl have left it. Here are many calves, who, I suppose, all expect to be great bulls and cows.

Yesterday I saw Mrs Diot at church, and shall drink tea with her some afternoon.

I cannot get free from this vexatious flatulence, and therefore have troublesome nights, but otherwise I am not very ill. Now and then a fit, and not violent. I am not afraid of the waterfall. I now and then take physic; and suspect that you were not quite right in omitting to let blood before I came away. But I do not intend to do it here.

You will now find the advantage of having made one at the regatta. You will carry with you the importance of a public personage, and enjoy a superiority which, having been only local and accidental, will not be regarded with malignity. You have a subject by which you can gratify general curiosity, and amuse your company without bewildering them. You can keep the vocal machine in motion, without those seeming paradoxes that are sure to disgust; without that temerity of censure which is sure to provoke enemies; and that exuberance of flattery which experience has found to make no friends. It is the good of public life that it supplies agreeable topics and general conversation. Therefore wherever you are, and whatever you see, talk not of the Punic war; nor of the depravity of human nature; nor of the slender motives of human actions; nor of the difficulty of finding employment or pleasure; but talk, and talk, and talk of the regatta, and keep the rest for, dearest Madam,

Your, &c.,
SAM: JOHNSON.

Samuel Johnson

To Mrs Thrale

[Ashbourne], 6 September 1777.

Dearest Lady

It is true that I have loitered, and what is worse, loitered with very little pleasure. The time has run away, as most time runs, without account, without use, and without memorial. But to say this of a few weeks, though not pleasing, might be borne, but what ought to be the regret of him who, in a few days, will have so nearly the same to say of sixty-eight years? But complaint is vain.

If you have nothing to say from the neighbourhood of the metropolis, what can occur to me in little cities and petty towns; in places which we have both seen, and of which no description is wanted? I have left part of the company with which you dined here, to come and write this letter; in which I have nothing to tell, but that my nights are very tedious. I cannot persuade myself to forbear trying something.

As you have now little to do, I suppose you are pretty diligent at the Thraliana, and a very curious collection posterity will find it. Do not remit the practice of writing down occurrences as they arise, of whatever kind, and be very punctual in annexing the dates. Chronology you know is the eye of history; and every man's life is of importance to himself. Do not omit painful casualties, or unpleasing passages, they make the variegation of existence; and there are many transactions, of which I will not promise with Æneas, *et haec olim meminisse juvabit.*[1] Yet that remembrance which is not pleasant may be useful. There is however an intemperate attention to slight circumstances which is to be avoided, lest a great part of life be spent in writing the history of the rest. Every day perhaps has something to be noted, but in a settled and uniform course few days can have much.

Why do I write all this, which I had not thought of when I begun? The Thraliana drove it all into my head. It deserves however an hour's reflection, to consider how, with the least loss of time, the loss of what we wish to retain may be prevented.

488

Do not neglect to write to me, for when a post comes empty, I am really disappointed.

Boswell, I believe, will meet me here.

I am, dearest Lady,

Your, &c.,

SAM: JOHNSON.

TO MRS THRALE

London, 10 July 1780.

Dear Madam

If Mr Thrale eats but half his usual quantity, he can hardly eat too much. It were better however to have some rule, and some security. Last week I saw flesh but twice, and I think fish once, the rest was pease.

You are afraid, you say, lest I extenuate myself too fast, and are an enemy to violence: but did you never hear nor read, dear Madam, that every man has his *genius*, and that the great rule by which all excellence is attained, and all success procured, is, to follow *genius*; and have you not observed in all our conversations that my *genius* is always in extremes; that I am very noisy, or very silent; very gloomy, or very merry; very sour, or very kind? And would you have me cross my *genius*, when it leads me sometimes to voracity and sometimes to abstinence? You know that the oracle said follow your *genius*. When we get together again (but when alas will that be?) you can manage me, and spare me the solicitude of managing myself.

Poor Miss Owen called on me on Saturday, with that fond and tender application which is natural to misery, when it looks to everybody for that help which nobody can give. I was melted; and soothed and counselled her as well as I could, and am to visit her tomorrow.

She gave a very honourable account of my dear Queeney; and says of my master,[1] that she thinks his manner and temper more altered than his looks, but of this alteration she could give no particular account; and all that she could say ended in this, that he is now sleepy in the morning. I do not wonder at the scantiness of her narration, she is too busy within to turn her eyes abroad.

I am glad that Pepys is come, but hope that resolute temperance will make him unnecessary. I doubt he can do no good to poor Mr Scrase.

I stay at home to work, and yet do not work diligently; nor can tell when I shall have done, nor perhaps does anybody but myself wish me to have done; for what can they hope I shall do better? yet I wish the work was over, and I was at liberty. And what would I do if I was at liberty? Would I go to see Mrs Aston and Mrs Porter, and see the old places, and sigh to find that my old friends are gone? Would I recall plans of life which I never brought into practice, and hopes of excellence which I once presumed, and never have attained? Would I compare what I now am with what I once expected to have been? Is it reasonable to wish for suggestions of shame, and opportunities of sorrow?

If you please, Madam, we will have an end of this, and contrive some other wishes. I wish I had you in an evening, and I wish I had you in a morning; and I wish I could have a little talk, and see a little frolic. For all this I must stay,[2] but life will not stay.

I will end my letter and go to Blackmore's Life, when I have told you that

I am, &c.,
SAM: JOHNSON.

To Robert Chambers

19 April 1783.

Dear Sir

Of the books which I now send you I sent you the first edition, but it fell by the chance of war into the hands of the French. I sent likewise to Mr Hastings. Be pleased to have these parcels properly delivered.

Removed as we are with so much land and sea between us, we ought to compensate the difficulty of correspondence by the length of our letters, yet searching my memory, I do not find much to communicate. Of all public transactions you have more exact accounts than I can give; you know our foreign miscarriages and our intestine discontents, and do not want to be told that we have now neither power nor peace, neither influence in other nations nor quiet amongst ourselves. The state of the public, and the operations of government have little influence upon the private happiness of private men, nor can I pretend that much of the national calamities is felt by me; yet I cannot but suffer some pain when I compare the state of this kingdom, with that in which we triumphed twenty years ago. I have at least endeavoured to preserve order and support Monarchy.

Having been thus allured to the mention of myself, I shall give you a little of my story. That dreadful illness which seized me at New Inn Hall, left consequences which have I think always hung upon me. I have never since cared much to walk. My mental abilities I do not perceive that it impaired. One great abatement of all miseries was the attention of Mr Thrale, which from our first acquaintance was never intermitted. I passed far the greater part of many years in his house where I had all the pleasure of riches without the solicitude. He took me into France one year, and into Wales another, and if he had lived would have shown me Italy and perhaps many other countries, but he died in the spring of eighty-one, and left me to write his epitaph.

But for much of this time my constitutional maladies pursued me. My thoughts were disturbed, my nights were insufferably restless, and by spasms in the breast I was condemned to the torture of sleepiness without the power to sleep. These spasms after enduring them more than twenty years I eased by three powerful remedies, abstinence, opium and mercury, but after a short time they were succeeded by a strange oppression of another kind which when I lay down disturbed me with a sensation like flatulence or intumescence which I cannot describe. To this supervened a difficulty of respiration, such as sometimes makes it painful to cross a street or climb to my chamber; which I have eased by venisection till the Physician forbids me to bleed, as my legs have begun to swell.

Almost all the last year past in a succession of diseases ἐκ κακῶν κακά[1] and this year till within these few days has heaped misery upon me. I have just now a lucid interval.

With these afflictions, I have the common accidents of life to suffer. He that lives long must outlive many, and I am now sometimes to seek for friends of easy conversation and familiar confidence. Mrs Williams is much worn; Mr Levet died suddenly in my house about a year ago. Doctor Lawrence is totally disabled by a palsy, and can neither speak nor write. He is removed to Canterbury. Beauclerc died about two years ago and in his last sickness desired to be buried by the side of his Mother. Langton has eight children by Lady Rothes. He lives very little in London, and is by no means at ease. Goldsmith died partly of a fever and partly of anxiety, being immoderately and disgracefully in debt. Dier lost his fortune by dealing in the East India stock, and, I fear, languished into the grave. Boswell's father is lately dead, but has left the estate incumbered; Boswell has, I think, five children. He is now paying us his annual visit, he is all that he was, and more. Doctor Scot prospers exceedingly in the commons, but I seldom see him; he is married and has a daughter.

Jones, now Sir William, will give you the present state of the club, which is now very miscellaneous, and very heterogeneous; it is therefore without confidence, and without pleasure. I go to it only as to a kind of public dinner. Reynolds continues to rise in reputation and in riches, but his health has been shaken. Dr Percy is now Bishop of Dromore, but has I believe lost his only son. Such are the deductions from human happiness.

I have now reached an age which is to expect many diminutions of the good, whatever it be, that life affords; I have lost many friends, I am now either afflicted or threatened by many diseases, but perhaps not with more than are commonly incident to increase of years, and I am afraid that I bear the weight of time with unseemly, if not with sinful impatience. I hope that God will enable me to correct this as well as my other faults, before he calls me to appear before him.

In return for this history of myself I shall expect some account of you, who by your situation have much more to tell. I hope to hear that the Ladies and the Children are all well, and that your constitution accommodates itself easily to the climate. If you have health, you may study, and if you can study, you will surely not miss the opportunity which place and power give you, beyond what any Englishman qualified by previous knowledge, ever enjoyed before, of inquiring into Asiatic Literature. Buy manuscripts, consult the scholars of the country, learn the languages, at least select one, and master it. To the Malabaric Books Europe is, I think, yet a stranger. But my advice comes late; what you purpose to do, you have already begun, but in all your good purposes persevere. Life is short, and you do not intend to pass all your life in India.

How long you will stay, I cannot conjecture. The effects of English Judicature are not believed here to have added anything to the happiness of the new dominions. Of you, Sir, I rejoice to say that I have heard no evil. There was a trifling charge produced in parliament, but it seems to be forgotten, nor did it appear to imply anything very blamable. This purity of character you will, I hope, continue to retain. One of my last wishes for you, at a gay table was ἀρετήν τε καὶ ὄλβόν.[2] Let me now add in a more serious hour, and in more powerful words, *Keep innocency, and take heed to the thing that is right, for that shall bring a Man peace at the last.*[3]

I shall think myself favoured by any help that you shall give to Mr Joseph Fowke, or Mr Lawrence. Fowke was always friendly to me, and Lawrence is the son of a man, whom I have long placed in the first rank of my friends. Do not let my recommendation be without effect.

Let me now mention an occasion on which you may perhaps do great good without evil to yourself. Langton is much embarrassed by a mortgage made, I think, by his grandfather, and perhaps aggravated by his father. The creditor calls for his money, and it is in the present general distress very difficult to make a *versura*.[4] If you could let him have six thousand pounds upon the security of the same land, you would save him from the necessity of selling part of his estate under the great disadvantage produced by the present high price of money. This proposal needs give you no pain, for Langton knows nothing of it, and may perhaps have settled his affairs before the answer can be received. As the security is good, you should not take more than four per cent.

Nothing now, I think, remains but that I assure you, as I do, of my kindness and good wishes, and express my hopes that you do not forget

Your old Friend and humble servant,
SAM: JOHNSON.

Bolt Court, Fleet Street, 19 April 1783.

Mr Langton, who is just come in, sends his best respects but he knows still nothing.

TO MRS THRALE

Bolt Court, Fleet Street,
19 June 1783.

Dear Madam

I am sitting down in no cheerful solitude to write a narrative which would once have affected you with tenderness and sorrow, but which you will perhaps pass over now with the careless glance of frigid indifference. For this diminution of regard however, I know not whether I ought to blame you, who may have reasons which I cannot know, and I do not blame myself, who have for a great part of human life done you what good I could, and have never done you evil.

I had been disordered in the usual way, and had been relieved by the usual methods, by opium and cathartics, but had rather lessened my dose of opium.

On Monday the 16th I sat for my picture, and walked a considerable way with little inconvenience. In the afternoon and evening I felt myself light and easy, and began to plan schemes of life. Thus I went to bed, and in a short time waked and sat up, as has been long my custom, when I felt a confusion and indistinctness in my head, which lasted I suppose about half a minute; I was alarmed, and prayed God, that however he might afflict my body, he would spare my understanding. This prayer, that I might try the integrity of my faculties, I made in Latin verse.[1] The lines were not very good, but I knew them not to be very good: I made them easily, and concluded myself to be unimpaired in my faculties.

Soon after I perceived that I had suffered a paralytic stroke, and that my speech was taken from me. I had no pain, and so little dejection in this dreadful state, that I wondered at my own apathy, and considered that perhaps death itself when it should come would excite less horror than seems now to attend it.

In order to rouse the vocal organs I took two drams. Wine has been celebrated for the production of eloquence. I put myself into violent motion, and I think repeated it; but all was vain. I then went to bed, and, strange as it may seem, I think, slept. When I saw light, it was time to contrive what I should do. Though God stopped my speech he left me my hand, I enjoyed a mercy which was not granted to my dear friend Lawrence, who now perhaps overlooks me as I am writing, and rejoices that I have what he wanted. My first note was necessarily to my servant, who came in talking, and could not immediately comprehend why he should read what I put into his hands.

I then wrote a card to Mr Allen, that I might have a discreet friend at hand to act as occasion should require. In penning this note I had some difficulty, my hand, I knew not how nor why, made wrong letters. I then wrote to Dr Taylor to come to me, and bring Dr Heberden, and I sent to Dr Brocklesby, who is my neighbour. My physicians are very friendly and very disinterested, and give me great hopes, but you may imagine my situation. I have so far recovered my vocal powers, as to repeat the Lord's Prayer with no very imperfect articulation. My memory, I hope, yet remains as it was; but such an attack produces solicitude for the safety of every faculty.

How this will be received by you I know not. I hope you will sympathize with me; but perhaps

My mistress gracious, mild and good,
Cries! Is he dumb? 'Tis time he shou'd.[2]

But can this be possible? I hope it cannot. I hope that what, when I could speak, I spoke of you, and to you, will be in a sober and serious hour remembered by you; and surely it cannot be remembered but with some degree of kindness. I have loved you with virtuous affection; I have honoured you with sincere esteem. Let not all our endearments be forgotten, but let me have in this great distress your pity and your prayers. You see I yet turn to you with my complaints as a settled and unalienable friend; do not, do not drive me from you, for I have not deserved either neglect or hatred.

To the girls, who do not write often, for Susy has written only once, and Miss Thrale owes me a letter, I earnestly recommend, as their guardian and friend, that they remember their Creator in the days of their youth.

I suppose you may wish to know how my disease is treated by the physicians. They put a blister upon my back, and two from my ear to my throat, one on a side. The blister on the back has done little, and those on the throat have not risen. I bullied and bounced (it sticks to our last sand)[3] and compelled the apothecary to make his salve according to the Edinburgh Dispensatory, that it might adhere better. I have two on now of my own prescription. They likewise give me salt of hartshorn,[4] which I take with no great confidence, but am satisfied that what can be done is done for me.

O God! give me comfort and confidence in Thee: forgive my sins; and if it be Thy good pleasure, relieve my diseases for Jesus Christ's sake. Amen.

I am almost ashamed of this querulous letter, but now it is written, let it go.

I am, &c.,
SAM: JOHNSON.

To Mrs Thrale

London, 10 March 1784.

Madam,

You know I never thought confidence with respect to futurity any part of the character of a brave, a wise, or a good man. Bravery has no place where it can avail nothing; wisdom impresses strongly the consciousness of those faults, of which it is itself perhaps an aggravation; and goodness, always wishing to be better, and imputing every deficience to criminal negligence, and every fault to voluntary corruption, never dares to suppose the condition of forgiveness fulfilled, nor what is wanting in the crime supplied by penitence.

This is the state of the best, but what must be the condition of him whose heart will not suffer him to rank himself among the best, or among the good? Such must be his dread of the approaching trial, as will leave him little attention to the opinion of those whom he is leaving for ever; and the serenity that is not felt, it can be no virtue to feign.

The sarcocele ran off long ago, at an orifice made for mere experiment.

The water passed naturally, by God's mercy, in a manner of which Dr Heberden has seen but few examples. The chirurgeon has been employed to heal some excoriations; and four out of five are no longer under his cure. The physician laid on a blister, and I ordered, by their consent, a salve; but neither succeeded, and neither was very easily healed.

I have been confined from the fourteenth of December, and I know not when I shall get out; but I have this day dressed me, as I was dressed in health.

Your kind expressions gave me great pleasure; do not reject me from your thoughts. Shall we ever exchange confidence by the fireside again?

I hope dear Sophy is better; and intend quickly to pay my debt to Susy.

I am, Madam,

Your, &c.,

Sam: Johnson.

To Mrs Thrale

Madam

If I interpret your letter right, you are ignominiously married; if it is yet undone, let us once more talk together. If you have abandoned your children and your religion, God forgive your wickedness: if you have forfeited your fame and your country, may your folly do no further mischief. If the last act is yet to do, I who have loved you, esteemed you, reverenced you, and served you, I who long thought you the first of humankind, entreat that, before your fate is irrevocable, I may once more see you. I was, I once was,

Madam, most truly yours,

2 July 1784.   SAM: JOHNSON.

I will come down, if you permit it.

To Mrs Thrale

London, 8 July 1784.

Dear Madam

What you have done, however I may lament it, I have no pretence to resent, as it has not been injurious to me: I therefore breathe out one sigh more of tenderness, perhaps useless, but at least sincere.

I wish that God may grant you every blessing, that you may be happy in this world for its short continuance, and eternally happy in a better state; and whatever I can contribute to your happiness I am very ready to repay, for that kindness which soothed twenty years of a life radically wretched.

Do not think slightly of the advice which I now presume to offer. Prevail upon Mr Piozzi to settle in England: you may live here with more dignity than in Italy, and with more security: your rank will be higher, and your fortune more under your own eye. I desire not to detail all my reasons, but every argument of prudence and interest is for England, and only some phantoms of imagination seduce you to Italy.

I am afraid however that my counsel is vain, yet I have eased my heart by giving it.

When Queen Mary[1] took the resolution of sheltering herself in England, the Archbishop of St Andrew's, attempting to dissuade her, attended on her journey; and when they came to the irremeable[2] stream that separated the two kingdoms, walked by her side into the water, in the middle of which he seized her bridle, and with earnestness proportioned to her danger and his own affection pressed her to return. The Queen went forward. – If the parallel reaches thus far, may it go no further. – The tears stand in my eyes.

I am going into Derbyshire, and hope to be followed by your good wishes, for I am, with great affection,

Your, &c.,

Sam: Johnson.

Any letters that come for me hither will be sent me.

PROLOGUE TO
THE GOOD NATUR'D MAN

Prest by the load of life, the weary mind
Surveys the general toil of human kind;
With cool submission joins the labouring train,
And social sorrow loses half its pain:
5   Our anxious Bard, without complaint, may share
This bustling season's epidemic care;
Like Caesar's pilot,[1] dignified by fate,
Tost in one common storm with all the great;
Distrest alike, the statesman and the wit,
10   When one a borough courts, and one the pit.
The busy candidates for power and fame,
Have hopes, and fears, and wishes, just the same;
Disabled both to combat, or to fly,
Must hear all taunts, and hear without reply.
15   Uncheck'd on both, loud rabbles[2] vent their rage,
As mongrels bay the lion in a cage.
Th' offended burgess hoards his angry tale,[3]
For that blest year when all that vote may rail;
Their schemes of spite the poet's foes dismiss,
20   Till that glad night when all that hate may hiss.
This day the powder'd curls and golden coat,
Says swelling Crispin, begg'd a cobbler's vote.[4]
This night our wit, the pert apprentice cries,
Lies at my feet, I hiss him, and he dies.
25   The great, 'tis true, can charm th' electing tribe;
The bard may supplicate, but cannot bribe.
Yet judg'd by those, whose voices ne'er were sold,
He feels no want of ill-persuading[5] gold;
But confident of praise, if praise be due,
30   Trusts without fear, to merit, and to you.

THREE PARODIES OF PERCY'S
*HERMIT OF WARKWORTH**

I

The tender infant, meek and mild,
   Fell down upon the stone;
The nurse took up the squealing child,
   But still the child squeal'd on.

II

I put my hat upon my head
   And walk'd into the Strand,
And there I met another man
   Whose hat was in his hand.

III

I therefore pray thee, Renny dear,
   That thou wilt give to me,
With cream and sugar soften'd well,
   Another dish of tea.

Nor fear that I, my gentle maid,   5
   Shall long detain the cup,
When once unto the bottom I
   Have drunk the liquor up.

Yet hear, alas! this mournful truth,
   Nor hear it with a frown; —   10
Thou canst not make the tea so fast
   As I can gulp it down.

* See Editor's Notes.

A SHORT SONG OF CONGRATULATION*

LONG-EXPECTED one and twenty
Ling'ring year at last is flown,
Pomp and Pleasure, Pride and Plenty,
Great Sir John, are all your own.

5   Loosen'd from the minor's tether,
Free to mortgage or to sell,
Wild as wind, and light as feather
Bid the slaves of thrift farewell.

Call the Betties, Kates, and Jennies,
10   Ev'ry name that laughs at care,
Lavish of your Grandsire's guineas,
Show the spirit of an heir.

All that prey on vice and folly
Joy to see their quarry fly,
15   Here the gamester light and jolly,
There the lender grave and sly.

Wealth, Sir John, was made to wander,
Let it wander as it will;
See the jockey, see the pander,
20   Bid them come, and take their fill.

When the bonny blade carouses,
Pockets full, and spirits high,
What are acres? What are houses?
Only dirt, or wet or dry.

25   If the guardian or the mother
Tell the woes of wilful waste,
Scorn their counsel and their pother,
You can hang or drown at last.

* See Editor's Notes.

ON THE DEATH OF DR ROBERT LEVET

CONDEMN'D to hope's delusive mine,[1]
  As on we toil from day to day,
By sudden blast,[2] or slow decline,
  Our social comforts drop away.

Well tried through many a varying year,   5
  See LEVET to the grave descend;
Officious,[3] innocent, sincere,
  Of ev'ry friendless name the friend.

Yet still he fills affection's eye,
  Obscurely wise, and coarsely kind;   10
Nor, letter'd arrogance, deny
  Thy praise to merit unrefin'd.

When fainting nature call'd for aid,
  And hov'ring death prepar'd the blow,
His vig'rous remedy display'd   15
  The power of art without the show.

In misery's darkest caverns known,
  His useful care was ever nigh,
Where hopeless anguish pour'd his groan,
  And lonely want retir'd to die.   20

No summons mock'd by chill delay,
  No petty gain[4] disdain'd by pride,
The modest wants of ev'ry day
  The toil of ev'ry day supplied.

His virtues walk'd their narrow round,   25
  Nor made a pause, nor left a void;
And sure th' Eternal Master found
  The single talent well employ'd.

The busy day, the peaceful night,
  Unfelt, uncounted, glided by;   30
His frame was firm, his powers were bright,
  Tho' now his eightieth year was nigh.[5]

Then with no throbbing fiery pain,
    No cold gradations of decay,
35 Death broke at once the vital chain,
    And free'd his soul the nearest[6] way.

20 APRIL 1764 GOOD FRIDAY. I have made no reformation, I have lived totally useless, more sensual in thought and more addicted to wine and meat; grant me, O God, to amend my life for the sake of Jesus Christ. Amen.

I hope,

To put my rooms in order.[1]*

I fasted all day

21 APRIL 1764 – 3 – M. My indolence, since my last reception of the Sacrament, has sunk into grosser sluggishness, and my dissipation spread into wilder negligence. My thoughts have been clouded with sensuality, and, except that from the beginning of this year I have in some measure forborn excess of strong drink, my appetites have predominated over my reason. A kind of strange oblivion has overspread me, so that I know not what has become of the last year, and perceive that incidents and intelligence pass over me without leaving any impression.

This is not the life to which Heaven is promised. I purpose to approach the altar again tomorrow. Grant, O Lord, that I may receive the sacrament with such resolutions of a better life as may by thy Grace be effectual, for the sake of Jesus Christ. Amen.

21 APRIL. I read the whole Gospel of St John. Then sat up till the 22nd.

My Purpose is from this time

1 To reject or expel sensual images, and idle thoughts.

To provide some useful amusement for leisure time.

2 To avoid idleness.

To rise early.

To study a proper portion of every day.

3 To worship God diligently.

*Disorder I have found one great cause of idleness.

4 To read the Scriptures.

To let no week pass without reading some part.

To write down my observations.

I will renew my resolutions made at Tetty's death.

I perceive an insensibility and heaviness upon me. I am less than commonly oppressed with the sense of sin, and less affected with the shame of idleness. Yet I will not despair. I will pray to God for resolution, and will endeavour to strengthen my faith in Christ by commemorating his death.

I prayed for Tett.

EASTER DAY

22 APRIL. Having before I went to bed composed the foregoing meditation and the following prayer, I tried to compose myself but slept unquietly. I rose, took tea, and prayed for resolution and perseverance. Thought on Tetty, dear poor Tetty, with my eyes full.

I went to Church, came in at the first of the Psalms, and endeavoured to attend the service which I went through without perturbation. After sermon I recommended Tetty in a prayer by herself, and my Father, Mother, Brother, and Bathurst in another. I did it only once, so as it might be lawful for me.

I then prayed for resolution and perseverance to amend my life. I received soon, the communicants were many. At the altar it occurred to me that I ought to form some resolutions. I resolved in the presence of God, but without a vow,[1] to repel sinful thoughts, to study eight hours daily, and, I think, to go to church every Sunday and read the Scriptures. I gave a shilling, and seeing a poor girl at the Sacrament in a bedgown, gave her privately a crown, though I saw Hart's hymns[2] in her hand. I prayed earnestly for amendment, and repeated my prayer at home. Dined with Miss W. Went to prayers at church. Went to Davies's, spent the evening not pleasantly. Avoided wine and tempered a very few glasses with sherbet. Came home, and prayed.

I saw at the Sacrament a man meanly dressed whom I have always seen there at Easter.

EASTER DAY

22 APRIL 1764. AT 3. M. Almighty and most merciful Father, who hast created and preserved me, have pity on my weakness and corruption. Let me not be created to misery, nor preserved only to multiply sin. Deliver me from habitual wickedness, and idleness, enable me to purify my thoughts, to use the faculties which thou hast given me with honest diligence, and to regulate my life by thy holy word.

Grant me, O Lord, good purposes and steady resolution, that I may repent my sins, and amend my life. Deliver me from the distresses of vain terror and enable me by thy Grace to will and to do what may please thee, that when I shall be called away from this present state I may obtain everlasting happiness through Jesus Christ our Lord. Amen.

Against loose thoughts and idleness.

SUNDAY 8 OCTOBER 1767. Yesterday, Oct. 17 at about ten in the morning I took my leave for ever of my dear old Friend Catherine Chambers, who came to live with my Mother about 1724, and has been but little parted from us since. She buried my Father, my Brother, and my Mother. She is now fifty-eight years old.

I desired all to withdraw, then told her that we were to part for ever, that as Christians we should part with prayer, and that I would, if she was willing, say a short prayer beside her. She expressed great desire to hear me, and held up her poor hands, as she lay in bed, with great fervour, while I prayed, kneeling by her, nearly in the following words.

Almighty and most merciful Father, whose loving kindness is over all thy works, behold, visit, and relieve this thy Servant who is grieved with sickness. Grant that the sense of her weakness may add strength to her faith, and seriousness to her repentance. And grant that by the help of thy Holy Spirit after the pains and labours of this short life, we may all obtain everlasting happiness through Jesus Christ, our Lord, for whose sake hear our Prayers. Amen.

Our Father.

I then kissed her. She told me that to part was the greatest pain that she had ever felt, and that she hoped we should meet again in a better place. I expressed with swelled eyes and great emotion of tenderness the same hopes. We kissed and parted, I humbly hope, to meet again, and to part no more.

18 SEPTEMBER 1768 AT NIGHT. Townmalling in Kent.

I have now begun the sixtieth year of my life. How the last year has passed I am unwilling to terrify myself with thinking. This day has been past in great perturbation. I was distracted at Church in an uncommon degree, and my distress has had very little intermission. I have found myself somewhat relieved by reading, which I therefore intend to practise when I am able. This day it came into my mind to write the history of my melancholy. On this I purpose to deliberate. I know not whether it may not too much disturb me.

I this day read a great part of Pascal's Life.

1 JUNE 1770. Every man naturally persuades himself that he can keep his resolutions, nor is he convinced of his imbecility but by length of time, and frequency of experiment. This opinion of our own constancy is so prevalent, that we always despise him who suffers his general and settled purpose to be overpowered by an occasional desire. They therefore whom frequent failures have made desperate cease to form resolutions, and they who are become cunning do not tell them. Those who do not make them, are very few, but of their effect little is perceived, for scarcely any man persists in a course of life planned by choice, but as he is restrained from deviation by some external power. He who may live as he will, seldom lives long in the observation of his own rules. I never yet saw a regular family unless it were that of Mrs Harriots, nor a

regular man except Mr Campbell[1] whose exactness I know only by his own report, and Psalmanazar[2] whose life was, I think, uniform.

25 JULY 1774. We saw Hawkestone, the seat of Sir Rowland Hill, and were conducted by Miss Hill over a large tract of rocks and woods, a region abounding with striking scenes and terrific grandeur. We were always on the brink of a precipice, or at the foot of a lofty rock, but the steeps were seldom naked; in many places oaks of uncommon magnitude shot up from the crannies of stone, and where there were not tall trees, there were underwoods and bushes. Round the rocks is a narrow path, cut upon the stone which is very frequently hewn into steps, but art has proceeded no further than to make the succession of wonders safely accessible. The whole circuit is somewhat laborious, it is terminated by a grotto cut in the rock to a great extent with many windings and supported by pillars, not hewn into regularity, but such as imitate the sports of nature, by asperities and protuberances. The place is without any dampness, and would afford a habitation not uncomfortable. There were from space to space seats in the rock. Though it wants water it excels Dovedale, by the extent of its prospects, the awfulness of its shades, the horrors of its precipices, the verdure of its hollows and the loftiness of its rocks. The ideas which it forces upon the mind, are the sublime, the dreadful, and the vast. Above, is inaccessible altitude, below, is horrible profundity. But it excels the garden of Ilam only in extent. Ilam has grandeur tempered with softness. The walker congratulates his own arrival at the place, and is grieved to think that he must ever leave it. As he looks up to the rocks his thoughts are elevated; as he turns his eyes on the valley, he is composed and soothed. He that mounts the precipices at Hawkestone, wonders how he came hither, and doubts how he shall return. His walk is an adventure and his departure an escape. He has not the tranquillity, but the horror of solitude, a kind of turbulent pleasure between fright and admiration. Ilam is the fit abode of pastoral virtue, and might properly diffuse its shades over nymphs and swains. Hawkestone can have no fitter inhabitants than 'Giants of mighty bone, and bold emprise', men of lawless courage

and heroic violence. Hawkestone should be described by Milton and Ilam by Parnel.

Miss Hill showed the whole succession of wonders with great civility.

The house was magnificent compared with the rank of the owner.

SATURDAY 21 OCTOBER 1775. In the night I got ground.[1] We came home to Paris. – I think we did not see the chapel. Tree broken by the wind.

The French chairs made all of boards painted.

Soldiers at the court of Justice. Soldiers not amenable to the magistrates. Dijon. Woman.

Fagot in the palace, everything slovenly, except in chief rooms. Trees in the roads some tall, none old, many very young and small.

Women's saddles seem ill made. Queen's bridle woven with silver. Tags to strike the horse.

SUNDAY OCTOBER 22. To Versailles, a mean town. Carriages of business passing. Mean shops against the wall. Our way lay through Sevre, where the China manufacture. Wooden bridge at Sevre in the way to Versailles. The Palace of great extent. The front long. I saw it not perfectly. The Menagerie. Cygnets dark, their black feet, on the ground, tame. Halcyons, or gulls. Stag and hind – young. Aviary very large, the net wire. Black stag of China, small. Rhinoceros. The horn broken, and pared away which I suppose will grow. The basis I think four inches across. The skin folds like loose cloth doubled, over his body, and cross his hips, a vast animal though young, as big perhaps as four oxen. The young elephant with his tusks just appearing. The brown bear put out his paws. All very tame. The lion. The tigers I did not well view. The camel or dromedary with two bunches, called the Highgeen taller than any horse. Two camels with one bunch. Among the birds was a pelican who being let out went to a fountain, and swam about to catch fish. His feet were webbed. He dipped his head, and turned his long bill sidewise. He caught two or three fish but did not eat them.

MONDAY 23 OCTOBER. Last night I wrote to Levet.

We went to see the looking glasses wrought. They come from Normandy in cast plates perhaps the third of an inch thick. At Paris they are ground upon a marble table by rubbing one plate on another with grit between them. The various sands, of which there are said to be five, I could not learn. The handle by which the upper glass is moved has the form of a wheel which may be moved in all directions. The plates are sent up with their surfaces ground but not polished and so continue till they are bespoken, lest time should spoil the surface, as we were told. Those that are to be polished are laid on a table covered with several thick cloths, hard strained that the resistance may be equal, they are then rubbed with a hand rubber held down hard by a contrivance which I did not well understand. The powder which is used last seemed to me to be iron dissolved in aqua fortis. They called it, as Baretti said, Mar de l'eau forte, which he thought was dregs. They mentioned vitriol and saltpetre. The cannon ball swam in the quicksilver. To silver them, a leaf of beaten tin is laid, and rubbed with quicksilver to which it unites. Then more quicksilver is poured upon it which by its mutual attraction rises very high. Then a paper is laid at the nearest end of the plate, over which the glass is slided till it lies upon the plate, having driven much of the quicksilver before it. It is then, I think, pressed upon cloths, and then set sloping to drop the superfluous mercury, the slope is daily heightened towards a perpendicular.

EASTER DAY

7 APRIL 1776. The time is again at which, since the death of my poor dear Tetty, on whom God have mercy, I have annually commemorated the mystery of Redemption, and annually purposed to amend my life. My reigning sin, to which perhaps many others are appendent, is waste of time, and general sluggishness, to which I was always inclined and in part of my life have been almost compelled by morbid melancholy and disturbance of mind. Melancholy has had in me its paroxysms and remissions, but I have not improved the intervals, nor sufficiently resisted my natural inclination, or sickly habits. I will resolve henceforth to rise at eight in the morning, so far as resolution is proper, and will pray that God will strengthen me. I have begun this morning.

Though for the past week I have had an anxious design of communicating today, I performed no particular act of devotion, till on Friday I went to Church. My design was to pass part of the day in exercises of piety but Mr Boswell interrupted me; of him however I could have rid myself, but poor Thrale, orbus et exspes,[1] came for comfort and sat till seven when we all went to Church.

In the morning I had at Church some radiations of comfort.

I fasted though less rigorously than at other times. I by negligence poured milk into the tea, and in the afternoon drank one dish of coffee with Thrale yet at night after a fit of drowsiness I felt myself very much disordered by emptiness, and called for tea with peevish and impatient eagerness. My distress was very great.

Yesterday I do not recollect that to go to Church came into my thoughts, but I sat in my chamber, preparing for preparation, interrupted I know not how. I was near two hours at dinner.

I go now with hope

To rise in the morning at eight.

To use my remaining time with diligence.

To study more accurately the Christian Religion.

Almighty and most merciful Father, who hast preserved me by thy tender forbearance, once more to commemorate thy Love in the Redemption of the world, grant that I may so live the residue of my days, as to obtain thy mercy when thou shalt call me from the present state. Illuminate my thoughts with knowledge, and inflame my heart with holy desires. Grant me to resolve well, and keep my resolutions. Take not from me thy Holy Spirit, but in life and in death have mercy on me for Jesus Christ's sake. Amen.

acts of forgiveness.

P.M. In the pew I read my prayer and commended my friends, and those that θ^2 this year. At the altar I was generally attentive, some thoughts of vanity[3] came into my mind while others were communicating, but I found when I considered them, that they did not tend to irreverence of God. At the altar I renewed my resolutions. When I received, some tender images struck me. I was so mollified by the concluding address to our Saviour that I could not utter it. The communicants were mostly women. At intervals I read collects, and recollected, as I could, my prayer. Since my return I have said it.

21 MAY. Those resolutions I have not practised nor recollected. O God, grant me to begin now for Jesus Christ's sake. Amen.

AGAINST INQUISITIVE AND PERPLEXING THOUGHTS

12 AUGUST 1784. O Lord, my Maker and Protector, who hast graciously sent me into this world, to work out my salvation, enable me to drive from me all such unquiet and perplexing thoughts as may mislead or hinder me in the practice of those duties which thou hast required. When I behold the works of thy hands and consider the course of thy providence, give me grace always to remember that thy thoughts are not my thoughts, nor thy ways my ways. And while it shall please thee to continue me in this world where much is to be done and little to be known, teach me by thy Holy Spirit to withdraw my mind from unprofitable and dangerous inquiries, from difficulties vainly curious, and doubts impossible to be solved. Let me rejoice in the light which thou hast imparted, let me serve thee with active zeal, and humble confidence, and wait with patient expectation for the time in which the soul which Thou receivest, shall be satisfied with knowledge. Grant this, O Lord, for Jesus Christ's sake. Amen.

PRECES

31 OCTOBER 1784.

Against the incursion of wicked thoughts.
Repentance and Pardon.
In disease.

On the loss of friends by death; by his own fault; or friend's.
On unexpected notice of the death of other.

Prayer generally recommendatory.
To understand their prayers.
Under dread of death.

Prayer commonly considered as a stated and temporary duty –
performed and forgotten – without any effect on the following day.
Prayer a vow.

SCEPTICISM CAUSED BY

1 Indifference about opinions.
2 Supposition that things disputed are disputable.
3 Denial of unsuitable evidence.
4 False judgement of evidence.
5 Complaint of the obscurity of Scripture.
6 Contempt of Fathers and of authority.
7 Absurd method of learning objection first.
8 Study not for truth but vanity.
9 Sensuality and a vicious life.
10 False honour, false shame.
11 Omission of prayer and religious exercises.

Against Despair

NOTES

Part I

TRANSLATION OF HORACE, ODES BOOK II, 14 (p. 41)

This fine translation of *Eheu fugaces, Posthume, Posthume* is worth inclusion both for its own merits and because it was made when Johnson was a schoolboy of fifteen.

The translation is by no means a literal 'crib'. It shows great confidence in its willingness to cut down on the mythological elaborations and detailed allusiveness which make close translations of Horace such heavy going. In the fifth stanza, for instance, Horace has Sisyphus as well as the daughters of Danaus, and in the last he specifies the kind of wine – 'Caecuban'.

1. *Sirius:* the dog-star, the star of the midsummer heats, when plague was most likely.

2. *Danaus' bloody brood:* the fifty daughters of Danaus, all of whom, save one (Hypermnestra), murdered their husbands on the wedding-night, because their father had been informed that one of his sons-in-law would murder *him*. The surviving one, needless to say, did just that.

LONDON (pp. 42–9)

There has been much discussion whether the Thales of this poem is to be identified with Richard Savage. Hawkins, Johnson's first biographer, said he was; Boswell denied it. The point is not of crucial importance, since the man who quits the city is there already in Juvenal's poem. If by Thales Johnson did intend Savage, he was paying him an undeserved compliment; for it was not as a gesture of proud moral disgust that Savage left London, but as a desperate expedient (arranged by his well-wishers) to save him from himself.

1. *That gave Eliza birth:* 'Queen Elizabeth was born at Greenwich' (Johnson's note).

2. *Excise:* Walpole's Excise Act, first attempted (but abandoned) in 1733, aroused more savage and unscrupulous opposition than any other of his actions. Johnson's definition of 'Excise' in his dictionary is well-known: 'A hateful tax levied upon commodities, and adjudged not by

the common judges of property, but wretches hired by those to whom excise is paid.'

3. *Warbling eunuchs:* the *castrati* singers of Italian opera, then very popular in London.

4. *Licensed stage:* this alludes to the recent Act (1737) requiring all stage-plays to be licensed by the Lord Chamberlain – from which absurdity we have just ceased to suffer.

5. *The Gazetteer:* 'the paper which at that time contained apologies for the Court' (Johnson's note – made necessary because the paper in question, created as an organ of Walpole's administration, later became independent).

6. *H—y:* Lord John Hervey, Pope's Sporus, one of Walpole's principal supporters at court.

7. *Illustrious Edward:* King Edward III, who defeated the French at Crecy. 'Henry' of i. 120 is of course Henry V of Agincourt. Johnson is here expressing the jingoist spirit which Walpole's pacific foreign policy was frustrating. In later years, Johnson was somewhat ashamed that he had yielded to it.

8. *Of France the mimic* etc: The French here replace the Greeks of Juvenal's poem – somewhat awkwardly, since imperial Rome *was* full of Greeks plying a variety of occupations, but Johnson's London was certainly not overrun by French.

9. *Gropes:* has the obsolete meaning of 'grasps'.

10. *Hated poverty* etc: The lines on poverty have a power and concentration not found in the rest of the poem; the reason, of course, is their bitterly personal application to Johnson himself at the time.

11. *Unclaim'd by Spain:* 'The Spaniards at this time were said to make claim to some of our American provinces' (Johnson's note).

12. *Should heaven's . . . wealth confound* etc: 'This was by Hitch a Bookseller justly remarked to be no picture of modern manners, though it might be true at Rome' (Johnson's note). 'Hitch a Bookseller' was right.

13. *Tyburn:* the place where public executions were held until 1783; they were then moved to Newgate, and the long procession of death through the city, which haunted the age's imagination from the *Beggar's Opera* on, was discontinued. See the Introduction for Johnson's changing opinions on this subject.

14. *Ways and Means:* 'a cant term in the House of Commons for methods of raising money' (Johnson's note).

15. *To rig . . . the k—g:* This line refers to George II's frequent visits (at the public expense) to his native Hanover, which the Opposition were fond of sniping at.

16. *Deep'd the Sword:* a disputed reading; it is certainly a very unusual use of the verb, but is probably correct. The meaning is 'lowered'. The alternative reading 'dropp'd' gives the wrong meaning, 'let fall'. Johnson means that Justice, in 'Alfred's golden reign', did not have to *use* her sword – but she still kept it in her hand.

17. *Kent:* Why 'Kent'? No special reason, it seems, except the rhyme; and perhaps the fact that Johnson is faithfully giving an equivalent to Juvenal's 'Aquino'. Aquinus was near Rome, as Kent is to London.

LIFE OF SAVAGE (pp. 50–133)

1. *Discovered a resolution of disowning:* i.e., revealed it.

2. *The Author to be Let:* a brief prose squib against Grub Street hacks and hirelings; it is also, incidentally, a defence of Pope's attacks on such writers in the *Dunciad*.

3. *The Wanderer:* 'a moral and descriptive poem in five cantos'. Johnson's criticism of it (which is rather lenient) may be found on p. 78.

4. *Fallacious and evasive answers:* i.e., deceiving answers.

5. *The Bangorian controversy:* this politico-ecclesiastical wrangle began in 1717 with a sermon by Benjamin Hoadly, Bishop of Bangor, who argued for reducing the temporal authority of the Church of England.

6. *Caressed:* this meaning of 'caressed' – treated with kindness – is a standard eighteenth-century usage.

7. *Bailiffs . . . with an execution:* i.e., officers of the law with a writ to seize property against a debt.

8. *Less often in his profession than in others:* Johnson had a lifelong prejudice against actors, of which Boswell's *Life* gives many examples, most of them directed against Garrick. E.g. on 19 October 1769:

I complained that he had not mentioned Garrick in his 'Preface to Shakespeare', and asked him if he did not admire him. Johnson: 'Yes, as a "poor player, who frets and struts his hour upon the stage"; – as a shadow'. Boswell: 'But has he not brought Shakespeare into notice?' Johnson: 'Sir, to allow that, would be to lampoon the age.'

In this prejudice, as in so many things, Johnson was swimming against the current of his age. The modern adulation of the 'players' was just beginning, and Garrick was the pioneer. See p. 559 below.

9. *Mrs Oldfield:* Anne Oldfield (1683–1730), probably the most famous actress of the early eighteenth century. She achieved the distinction of burial in Westminster Abbey, which provoked Voltaire (by contrast) into a denunciation of the Paris ecclesiastics' refusal of a church burial to the French actress Adrienne Lecouvreur, who died in the same year as Anne Oldfield:

> Le sublime Dryden et le sage Addison
> Et la charmante Oldfield et l'immortel Newton
> Ont part au temple de mémoire,
> Et Lecouvreur à Londre aurait eu des tombeaux
> Parmi les beaux esprits, les rois et les héros.

Johnson's slightly snide remarks about Mrs Oldfield's 'general character' and 'faults' refer to her well-known liaisons – with Marlborough's brother among others. Colley Cibber denied Johnson's story that she had given Savage a pension, and maintained that she strongly disapproved of him.

10. *Sir Thomas Overbury:* the central figure and victim of a scandalous affair in 1613. Because, apparently, he opposed the marriage of Robert Carr, one of James I's favourites, with the Countess of Essex (a divorcée), he was sent to the Tower, and there, allegedly, poisoned by persons in the pay of Lady Essex. The agents were all duly hanged; the principals, Carr and his wife, were let off, though found guilty.

11. *Mr Hill:* Aaron Hill, a minor poet.

12. *Button's coffeehouse:* one of the best-known meeting-places of literary men.

13. *Discharge another lodging:* i.e., pay off what he owed there.

14. *Mr Page:* Mr Justice Page was perhaps the most notorious 'hanging judge' of his time. Pope scarifies him in the *Imitations of Horace*, book II, satire 1:

> Slander or poison dread from Delia's rage,
> Hard words and hanging if your judge be Page.

15. *Candidly:* as very commonly in eighteenth-century usage, this means 'fairly'.

16. *Had the front:* i.e., the impudence.

17. *The true author:* in fact Pope. Johnson may not have known this when he wrote the *Life of Savage;* he certainly knew it later, for he mentions it in the *Life of Pope*.

18. . . . *Sold the copy for ten guineas:* Johnson got the same for *London*, and only five more for *The Vanity of Human Wishes* – so we may feel that Savage was not too scandalously underpaid.

19. *A superstitious regard to the correction of his sheets*, etc: Johnson's amusement at Savage's textual fussiness is no doubt derived from remembering his own cheerful carelessness. He is also, of course, sardonically commenting on the contrast between Savage's meticulousness in this respect and heedlessness in everything else.

20. *one particular person:* Sir Robert Walpole.

21. *When he was afterwards ridiculed . . .:* in *An Author to be Let*, Savage, following Pope's example, makes fun of the poverty of the poetasters he is lampooning – and also defends Pope for having done the same in the *Dunciad*. The bitter irony of Johnson's justified reproach of Savage here (and, by implication, of Pope also) is sharpened by the fact that Johnson too, when he wrote this, was 'a distressed poet'.

22. *The vivacious sallies of thought:* these include the only line Savage wrote which has become at all famous:

> He [the Bastard] lives to build, not boast, a gen'rous race;
> No tenth transmitter of a foolish face.

The doctrine is that of Edmund in *King Lear:*

> . . . Who, in the lusty stealth of Nature, take
> More composition and fierce quality
> Than doth within a dull, stale, tired bed
> Go to the creating a whole tribe of fops
> Got 'tween asleep and wake.

23. *But he was at other times more favourable to mankind:* the moral wisdom of this and the next two paragraphs is very Johnsonian. He is willing to allow to unhappy humanity a degree of self-deception and wish-fulfilment; but he knows their dangers if indulged in too far. Compare Imlac's account of the genesis of insanity in *Rasselas* (chapter 44):

There is no man whose imagination does not sometimes predominate over his reason, who can regulate his attention wholly by his will, and whose ideas come and go at his command. . . . All power of fancy over reason is a degree of insanity; but while this power is such as we can control and suppress, it is not visible to others, nor considered as any deprivation of the mental faculties: it is not pronounced madness, but when it becomes ungovernable and apparently influences speech or action.

24. *Not so much a good man, as the friend of goodness:* Johnson, in his profound humility, would probably have applied this description to himself. He was always bitterly conscious of the weakness of man's will and the gulf between belief and practice.

25. *Upon the death of Eusden:* he died in 1730.

26. *The dispute between the Bishop of London and the Chancellor:* this was over the appointment of one Dr Rundle to be Bishop of Gloucester. He was made, instead, Bishop of Derry in Ireland.

27. *The Progress of a Divine:* a thoroughly unpleasant poem, in which a strong taste for sadistic sexual fantasy is presented under the guise of moral indignation.

28. *Particular:* i.e., peculiar.

29. *The ministry of the last years of Queen Anne:* the Tory ministry of Oxford and Bolingbroke, of which Swift was an ardent supporter and almost a member.

30. *The prince was now extremely popular:* this was Frederick, Prince of Wales. In the usual style of his family, he hated his father with a cordiality which was thoroughly returned, and set up what was in effect a rival court in opposition to the real one. Many of the 'wits', including Pope, were adherents of the Prince, in varying degrees and for various reasons, either because he subsidized them or because they really thought he would put an end to the corrupt regime of Walpole. But the Prince died before his father, and received as his epitaph the anonymous lines:

> Here lies Fred,
> Who was alive and is dead ...

31. *The enormous wickedness of making war upon barbarous nations ...:* this praise is one of the earliest passages to reveal Johnson's life-long detestation of imperial conquests. Compare *Idler* 81 (p. 229).

32. *Upon a bulk:* Johnson's Dictionary defines 'bulk' as 'a part of a building jutting out'. The bulks seem to have been the traditional sleeping-places of the penniless writer. Compare Pope's brutal couplet in the *Dunciad:*

> Thus the soft gifts of sleep conclude the day,
> And stretch'd on bulks, as usual, poets lay.
>
> (II. 419)

33. *He wrote to him, not in a style of supplication or respect:* one of Savage's letters to Lord Tyrconnel began in this style – 'Right Honourable BRUTE, and BOOBY ...'

It is fairly obvious, if one reads between the lines of Johnson's account, that Savage was almost paranoiac: permanently and incurably immature.

34. *The petulance of his wit:* 'sharpness' would be the modern equivalent.

35. *Duck:* Stephen Duck, who enjoyed a brief period of fame as 'the thresher-poet'. He was, it seems, a genuinely self-taught peasant. Queen Caroline made him her librarian, and in due course (like Crabbe) he became a clergyman. But his success did not make him happy; he drowned himself in the Thames.

36. *One of them wrote a letter to him:* this was Pope.

37. *Scenes of flowery felicity:* Johnson's witty mocking of Savage's daydreams of rustic happiness reminds one of his contempt for pastoral as a literary genre. In life and literature alike, his criterion is truth to reality.

38. *The liberties of the Fleet:* an area round the Fleet prison in the City, in which debtors were free from arrest.

39. *A letter was written for him ...:* again, the writer was Pope.

40. *Parted from the author of this narrative:* this is the only hint in the biography of the intimate friendship between Savage and Johnson.

41. *An embargo laid upon the shipping:* because a war with Spain ('the war of Jenkins' ear') had just begun.

42. *Mr Nash at Bath:* this is 'Beau Nash', the 'legislator' of Bath and founder of its eighteenth-century heyday.

43. *Since Monday last was se'nnight:* i.e., a week ago last Monday.

44. *Any of his subscribers except one:* i.e., Pope.

45. *He received from one of his friends:* Pope again. Pope, who had treated Savage with great generosity and a forbearance which was remarkable considering his own acute sensitiveness, had at last been goaded by Savage's insane and insolent bombast into informing him that 'our correspondence is now likely to be closed. Your language is really too high ...'

46. *His mind was in an uncommon degree active . . .*: Birkbeck Hill remarks justly that 'in this paragraph and the two following much of Johnson's own character is described'.

Was Johnson aware of this? Are the power and poignancy of the *Life of Savage* partly due to the fact that Johnson was indirectly describing himself? And was Savage really the writer of genius, the tragic, almost Promethean figure that Johnson makes of him?

We can never know. But it seems certain that when he wrote his story of Savage, Johnson was condensing all the essentials of his own early experience. He himself was a reluctant autobiographer, especially of the disagreeable parts of his life; he had found in Savage, perhaps, the 'objective correlative' which enabled him to write what he would otherwise have suppressed. (In the last weeks of his life, according to Boswell, he 'burnt large masses [of his private papers], with little regard, as I apprehend, to discrimination'.) That the composition of the *Life of Savage* was for Johnson a passionate, cathartic experience may be guessed from Boswell's account. 'The rapidity with which this work was composed is a wonderful circumstance. Johnson has been heard to say, 'I wrote 48 of the printed octavo pages of the *Life of Savage* at a sitting; but then I sat up all night.' (*Life*, 1744.)

LETTERS TO EDWARD CAVE (pp. 134–5)

These two letters to the editor of *The Gentleman's Magazine* (see Introduction) are included as showing how Johnson began, a miscellaneous writer ready to try his hand at anything.

In the second letter, the poem he sends to Cave as if it were by some other poverty-stricken scribbler was in fact his own *London*. Dodsley published it, and paid ten guineas for it.

Part II

THE VANITY OF HUMAN WISHES (pp. 139–48)

1. *Let observation . . . China to Peru*: On these two lines Wordsworth made the well-known criticism, that they said no more than 'Let observation with extensive observation observe mankind extensively.'

But Coleridge was being obtuse; he failed to see how Johnson's deliberate tautology renders the effect of a slow, steady, repeated scrutiny.

2. *Afflictive:* i.e., 'causing affliction'.

3. *Precipitates on death:* the preposition goes together with the verb – 'hurries on death'.

4. *For gold his sword . . . the treasures rise:* These lines form part of the widespread protest through the mid-eighteenth century against the increasing power of commerce and wealth. Compare *Idler* 73 (p. 227).

5. *The wealthy traitor:* in the first edition, this read 'the bonny traitor' – the Scots word being a clear allusion to the Jacobite leaders of the Forty-five who had died on the scaffold only two or three years before *The Vanity of Human Wishes* was published. It may be thought that the epithet reflects the younger Johnson's sympathy with and admiration for the victims.

6. *Hover round:* the first edition has 'clang around' – changed, presumably, because Johnson – a very accurate writer, except when dealing with horses' pasterns – remembered that vultures do not 'clang' like geese or seagulls.

7. *Unnumbered suppliants . . . th' indignant wall:* These lines are a much more *literal* description of the signs of an eighteenth-century statesman's decline and fall than we may appreciate. The 'clients' besieging the great man's town mansion; the hired journalists; the poets or dramatists dedicating their works with fulsome flattery; the portrait in oils, less valuable (when the great man is great no more) than its elaborate gilt frame: all these were accurate barometers of political fortunes.

8. *Palladium:* The original 'Palladium' was the statue of Pallas Athene on which the fortune of Troy depended. Here it means something like 'the most precious and worshipped object'.

9. *Wolsey:* The superb passage on Cardinal Wolsey is derived quite closely from Shakespeare's *Henry VIII*, especially Act III, scene 2. Johnson's 'at length his sov'reign frowns' is a reminiscence of Shakespeare's stage-direction: 'Exit King, frowning upon Cardinal Wolsey.'

10. *The wisest justice:* the first edition has 'the richest landlord'. The new reading (if one takes 'wisest' as having a tinge of irony) seems to envisage a harmless, Justice Shallow-like figure instead of the mighty dictator of the nation. 'Trent' is a sly joke; it refers to Johnson's hometown of Lichfield, like Marvell's mention of his native Humber in the *Coy Mistress*.

11. *Great Villiers:* the first Duke of Buckingham, who was assassinated by an army captain with a grievance (he hadn't been promoted, like Iago).

12. *Harley:* the Earl of Oxford, Queen Anne's Tory minister and Swift's idol.

13. *Wentworth:* the Earl of Strafford, Charles I's minister, impeached by Parliament and executed in 1641; *Hyde* is the Earl of Clarendon, who was exiled in 1667.

14. *When first the college rolls . . . name* etc.: Mrs Thrale relates that when Johnson one day read aloud the great lines describing the ills of the scholar's life, he 'burst into a passion of tears'.

15. *And Bacon's Mansion . . . head:* 'There is a tradition, that the study of friar Bacon, built on an arch over the bridge, will fall, when a man greater than Bacon shall pass under it' (Johnson's note).

16. *Toil, envy . . . jail:* This line includes Johnson's most famous textual alteration. The first edition reads 'garret' for 'patron'. The change was occasioned by his bitter experience of Lord Chesterfield's 'patronage' of the *Dictionary*. See the letter to Chesterfield, p. 252.

17. *The tardy busts:* 'Tardy busts' of poets, in Westminster Abbey, included those of Milton, erected in 1731, 63 years after his death; of Samuel Butler, 1721, 41 years after; and of Shakespeare, 1741, 125 years after. But Samuel Johnson was to get *his* monument (in St Paul's) less than 12 years after his death.

18. *Lydiat:* Thomas Lydiat, a sixteenth-century Oxford scholar, cited by Johnson, apparently, because he was always poor. He was an obscure figure even when Johnson mentioned him, and many readers were puzzled. He doesn't seem an adequate counter-balance to Galileo.

19. *And fatal learning . . . block:* Macaulay remarked, with justice, that it wasn't 'fatal learning', but fatal meddling with politics, that led Archbishop Laud (in 1645) 'to the block'.

20. *The rapid Greek:* Alexander the Great.

21. *Swedish Charles:* Charles XII of Sweden. A few years before *The Vanity of Human Wishes* was written, Johnson was thinking of writing a drama about him.

22. *Pultowa's day:* At the battle of Pultowa Peter the Great's Russian army completely defeated Charles XII and his followers.

23. *His fall . . . adorn a tale:* T. S. Eliot has a good comment on these lines. 'These lines, especially the first two, with their just inevitable

sequence of *barren*, *petty*, and *dubious*, still seem to me among the finest that have ever been written in that particular idiom.' ('Poetry in the Eighteenth Century', in *Pelican Guide to English Literature*, vol. 4, pp. 271-7.)

On the whole passage about Charles, Eliot remarks in the same essay: 'If these lines are not poetry, I do not know what it is.'

The ironic point of line 222 is that Johnson himself, in this very poem, is using 'the name, at which the world grew pale' for just these purposes.

24. *The encumber'd oar . . . floating host:* Johnson himself, it seems, regarded this couplet as his best effort in verse. It is hard to agree with him.

25. *The bold Bavarian:* Charles Albert, Elector of Bavaria, who made a bid for the imperial throne in the 1740s. This led to the 'war of the Austrian Succession'.

26. *Fair Austria:* Maria Theresa.

27. *Luxury:* In eighteenth-century usage 'luxury' had a meaning close to 'extravagance' or 'wasteful display of excessive wealth'. It was a favourite word of those many writers who were uneasy about the increasing wealth and commercialization of the country. See Boswell for 13 April 1773, when Johnson denies that 'luxury' is harmful, and also *Idler* 73 (p. 227).

28. *Positively:* 'emphatically'.

29. *Till they make his will:* There is a witty and savage pun in 'will', which means both 'will-power' (contrasted with 'passions') and 'last will and testament'.

30. *Lydia's monarch:* Croesus, the fabulously wealthy king in Herodotus.

31. *Vane:* Anne Vane, mistress of Frederick Prince of Wales, son to George II.

32. *Sedley:* Catherine Sedley, one of the mistresses of the Duke of York who became King James II. It is not clear why she should have 'curs'd her form' (i.e., beauty). She did quite well by it: His Majesty made her Countess of Dorchester. Anna Seward reports that when she cross-examined Johnson on 'Sedley', he told her that he had completely forgotten why she was in the poem.

33. *Ye nymphs . . . radiant eyes* etc.: This passage describes what one might call the 'official' sexual morality of the age, whereby one 'fall from virtue' ruined a woman for life. It was a morality which Johnson

inflexibly supported: compare his remark to Boswell about a much-wronged woman who had at last cuckolded her husband and whom Boswell had tried to defend – 'Sir, the woman's a whore, and there's an end on 't.' (7 May 1773.) This was also the sexual morality of the society which Jane Austen lived in and wrote about; the process described in these lines is followed, in essentials, by Maria Bertram in *Mansfield Park*, and her end also – dismissed to a 'remote' establishment with Mrs Norris and never again 'countenanced' by her father – is the 'hissing infamy' of line 342.

34. *Where then shall Hope . . . find* etc.: Johnson's ending departs from its Roman model far more widely than do the other parts of his poem. He adds his own Christian faith, austere, hard-won and hard-held, but deeply sincere, to Juvenal's 'existentialist' stoicism. The deity who presides over the last lines of Juvenal's satire is Fortune – not 'celestial wisdom' – and even she, Juvenal says, is made a goddess only by man's folly.

35. *Must helpless man . . . of his fate:* This wonderful couplet (which I, for one, would set far above Johnson's own favourite about the defeat of the Persian fleet) has an interesting linguistic detail. Johnson, as his dictionary proves, thought that 'darkling' was a present participle from a lost verb *darkle*, and uses it thus in line 346, meaning 'becoming darker and darker'. It is really an adverb, meaning 'in darkness': as the Fool says in *King Lear* (I, 4) – 'out went the candle, and we were left darkling.'

36. *Safe in his pow'r . . . a specious prayer:* The image of these lines is by no means easy to see. Is it the idea that someone (like the King in *Hamlet*) who puts up an insincere prayer, is trying to trap God into believing him? If so, it seems a very 'metaphysical' conceit. But Johnson has many such; his wit has often a distinctly seventeenth-century cast.

THE RAMBLER (pp. 149–85)

No. 4. This is probably the first attempt to give what was then the new literary form, the novel, a serious critical attention. Johnson's lead was little followed; some 160 years later, Henry James was still claiming, with justice, that such attention was precisely what the novel hardly ever received.

Johnson lays stress on three points in particular: that what distinguished the novel from earlier forms of fiction was its closeness to contemporary reality; that it was read, largely, by an unsophisticated public – 'the young, the ignorant, and the idle'; and that therefore its moral effect, for good or evil, would be particularly strong and widespread.

When this essay was written, Fielding's *Tom Jones* (1749) and Richardson's *Clarissa* (1748) had just appeared. Hence, perhaps, Johnson's references to the danger of presenting vice associated with gaiety and courage in such a way as to 'reconcile it to the mind'. He is thinking of Lovelace and Tom Jones.

No. 18. The 'characters' through which this sardonic survey of marriage is presented are done somewhat in the manner of Pope: e.g., the *Moral Essay* 'On the Characters of Women'.

What Johnson really thought of marriage is no doubt summed up in the famous saying in *Rasselas:* 'Marriage has many pains; but celibacy has no pleasures.'

No. 21. This disillusioned account of the life of a professional author is obviously written from first-hand knowledge. Johnson, on the whole, approved of the commercialization of literature; but he knew its evils and heartbreaks as well as anyone.

No. 50. This essay is one of generalized moral reflection, one of the kind which won for the *Rambler* its fame as a storehouse of moral wisdom – and also its obloquy as a repository of tedious commonplaces. But if one looks at it closely, one sees that its thought is the opposite of 'commonplace'; Johnson is concerned to demolish the truisms that humanity is always degenerating and that every younger generation is insolent and irreverent towards its elders. He had in fact a distinct tenderness for the young, which grew as he himself grew older; he remarked to Boswell in 1763 (21 July): 'Sir, I love the acquaintance of young people; because, in the first place, I don't like to think myself growing old . . . and then, Sir, young men have more virtue than old men; they have more generous sentiments in every respect. I love the young dogs of this age: they have more wit and humour and knowledge of life than we had . . .'

The essay is interesting also as marking a kind of watershed in Johnson's life. He was in his early forties when he wrote it, on the way from 'young Sam Johnson', rebel and friend of Savage, to the moral sage and scholar; and this is reflected in the nice balance which the essay holds between the claims of young and old, and the way in which the writer's own age and generation are left undefined.

1. *Or, why does he imagine . . . the general condition of man?*: Compare *The Vanity of Human Wishes*:

> Yet hope not life from grief or danger free,
> Nor think the doom of man revers'd for thee.
>
> (155)

2. *There are many who live merely to hinder happiness*: another parallel with *The Vanity of Human Wishes* – the passage (255 etc.) which describes the miseries and cruelties of old age.

No. 60. Boswell tells us that Johnson was always of the opinion expressed here, that biography is the most interesting and valuable form of literature. It is a preference in consonance with the general principle of all his criticism, most obvious in his criticism of Shakespeare – to bring everything to the test of real life.

Boswell, not surprisingly, cited Johnson's defence of including in biographies 'the minute details of daily life' against those many critics of his own life of Johnson who disapproved of his exhibiting the great man's failings and oddities.

1. '*Parva . . . quotidie*': 'things which would be trivial if they didn't happen daily.'

No. 144. This essay shows the 'Rochefoucauldian' side of Johnson's mind – his disillusioned contemplation of the selfishness and unmotivated malevolence of which humanity is capable. The last paragraph is notable, with its sudden outburst of bitter anger. It reminds one of the line in *London*: 'SLOW RISES WORTH, BY POVERTY OPPRESS'D.'

No. 155. The last paragraph of this essay, when Johnson instances indolence as one of the vices most difficult to cure, is one of those passages of unconfessed autobiography which are frequent in his essays. For indolence, in his own opinion, was his besetting sin; and the method which he here recommends to his readers, of 'reviewing' one's life 'at certain stated days', was the method he employed (to little purpose) for himself.

1. *Nearly examined*: 'closely examined'.

2. *Adscititious excellence*: Johnson's dictionary defines *adscititious* as 'that which is taken in to complete something else, though originally extrinsic; supplemental; additional'.

Notes

No. 185. Like *Idler* 32, this is really a sermon: see the solemn eloquence of the last paragraph. It has that uncompromising directness which Johnson shows when his deepest convictions are engaged. 'Nothing can be great which is not right.'

The Adventurer (pp. 186–204)

No. 67. This almost poetic panegyric on the vastness and multiplicity of London may be compared with Wordsworth's description of it in the 7th book of the *Prelude*, and with that by Henry James (which also is almost poetic) in his *Notebooks:*

It is difficult to speak adequately or justly of London. It is not a pleasant place; it is not agreeable, or cheerful, or easy, or exempt from reproach. It is only magnificent. You can draw up a tremendous list of reasons why it should be insupportable. The fogs, the smoke, the dirt, the darkness, the wet, the distances, the ugliness, the brutal size of the place, the horrible numerosity of society, the manner in which this senseless bigness is fatal to amenity, to convenience, to conversation, to good manners – all this and much more you may expatiate upon. You may call it dreary, heavy, stupid, dull, inhuman, vulgar at heart and tiresome in form. I have felt these things at times so strongly that I have said – 'Ah London, you too then are impossible?' But these are occasional moods; and for one who takes it as I take it, London is on the whole the most possible form of life. I take it as an artist and as a bachelor; as one who has the passion of observation and whose business is the study of human life. It is the biggest aggregate of human life – the most complete compendium of the world. The human race is better represented there than anywhere else, and if you learn to know your London you learn a great many things.

> *The Notebooks of Henry James*, ed. Matthiessen and Murdock
> (Oxford, 1947): pp. 27–8.

No. 99. 'Projector' in this essay means what we would call 'pioneer', 'inventor' or 'scientist'. The Latin tag describing Catiline means: 'He always desired what was excessive, unbelievable, and too lofty.'

Johnson's attitude to science is more encouraging than otherwise, and three of the 'projects' which he cites as mocked at have been achieved: 'a flight through the air in a winged chariot', the movement of a mighty engine by the steam of water', and the making of a Thames-Severn canal.

No. 107. Johnson, as this essay shows, felt deeply the complexities and unaccountability of human nature, and for the understanding of that, he felt, exact science was no useful guide. The phrase in the last paragraph – 'life is not the object of science' – reminds one of a saying in the *Life* of Milton: 'We are perpetually moralists, but we are geometricians only by chance.'

No. 137. The Adventurer was coming to an end; Johnson is reviewing his work in it, and considering, with his usual sense of moral responsibility, what good or evil it may have done. The essay keeps a steady balance between egotism and frivolousness. He doesn't flatter himself that his writings have had an enormous effect; but he knows that all writings have some effect, evil or good.

THE IDLER (pp. 205–34)

No. 17. This essay demonstrates Johnson's passionate opposition to vivisection and his ironic scepticism about the 'minute' sciences, in which he shares some common ground with Swift (*Gulliver*, Book III) and Pope (*Dunciad* IV). But his scepticism was not total and obscurantist; he was himself a great dabbler in chemistry, and another essay (*Adventurer* 99, p. 191) shows he was far too intelligent to be crudely 'anti-science'.

The Latin motto means: 'Arise, at last, an executioner' – said by Maecenas to Augustus.

No. 18. A very Johnsonian comment on human nature, sad, disillusioned, but not bitter, and always aware of 'the importance of little things' (see letters to Mrs Thrale, pp. 484 and 487). 'Drugget' is a character in *Idler No. 16*, a London shopkeeper who retires to the country.

No. 22. Johnson himself, it seems, had doubts about this splendidly ferocious attack on war; he kept it out of the first collected edition of the *Idlers*. It is a fine example (as the Yale editors point out) of the 'Swiftian' side of Johnson's mind.

No. 30. This essay is not really an attack on journalism, but on the degradation of it from telling the truth to looking for a 'good story'. Those who imagine that it is only the twentieth century which has discovered the first casualty of war to be truth may read the last three paragraphs.

No. 31. Mrs Thrale informs us that 'Sober' was 'intended as [Johnson's] own portrait'. It is in fact a rather ruthless self-analysis: laziness, continual self-reproach for it, terror of solitude, and clutching at all expedients to avoid it, were elements in Johnson's character of which he was well aware.

No. 32. The eloquence of this essay – the tone is almost solemn enough to be a sermon, and in fact many of Johnson's essays *were* used as sermons – has an almost seventeenth-century resonance: e.g. the sentence beginning 'The most diligent enquirer . . .' and the beautiful and elegiac ending.

No. 38. This attack on imprisonment for debt and on the evils of contemporary prisons shows (like *Idler* 17, with its denunciation of vivisection) that Johnson was deeply involved in the great humanitarian spirit of the eighteenth century. One is sometimes inclined to associate that spirit only with the men of 'sensibility' and the political radicals, such as Blake: but no one could have felt it more strongly than Johnson.

No. 60. The critical opinions which Dick Minim retails are carefully chosen from among the most threadbare literary platitudes of the day. Some of them – e.g. the notion of the 'sound' being an echo to the 'sense' – are also platitudes which Johnson denounced elsewhere.

No. 73. This is one of Johnson's contributions to the age's debate on 'Luxury', by which was meant the great increase of commerce and consequently of wealth in eighteenth-century England. Goldsmith's *Deserted Village* is one offshoot of it; so, in certain of its aspects, is Johnson's own *Journey to the Western Islands*.

Most of those who attacked 'luxury' took the simple position that increase of wealth was bad in itself; it led to corruption, decadence, and finally moral and social ruin. Rome had 'fallen' because of luxury; England would go the same way. Such was the commonplace. Johnson was too intelligent ever to take that position; he knew poverty well enough to know that wealth in itself was a blessing rather than a curse. (See his argument with Goldsmith in Boswell for 13 April 1773.) And he denied that the acquisition of wealth was always morally harmful – as he observed to George Strahan: 'There are few ways in which a man can be more innocently employed than in getting money.' (Boswell 17 March 1775). What worried him was not the mere increase of wealth, but the resultant shift in moral and social standards. The possession of wealth, it seemed to him, was becoming more and more the criterion for respect; it was displacing the old standards – rank, land, status in the

Church or the other learned professions. Rich men no longer felt in a sense ashamed of being rich, as the old morality had taught them to feel; society no longer felt that a poor parson or gentleman was a more *respectable* figure than a rich merchant.

Had society ever really felt this? One may certainly suspect Johnson here of some sentimental idealizing of the past, which accounts in part for his very indulgent picture of the old clan society in the Highlands. It contrasts oddly with his hard-headed grasp on the realities of wealth and poverty – and with his deep respect for that typical rich merchant, Mr Henry Thrale the brewer of Southwark. But the truth is that Johnson's attitude in this, as in so many things, was deeply 'ambivalent'.

1. *counterfeit mediocrity:* i.e., pretend to have only a moderate fortune.

2. *To be rich is to have more than is desired . . . avarice is always poor:* This line of thought seems to derive from a medieval-Renaissance Latin saying (I have not been able to find its source), which goes: *Quis est dives? Qui nil cupit. Quis est pauper? Avarus.* (Who is the rich man? He who desires nothing. Who is the poor man? The miser.)

No. 81. This essay was written just after the English conquest of Quebec (September 1759). It expresses one of Johnson's strongest political convictions – his detestation of the wrongs done by white settlers to the American Indians and to Negro slaves. It was this – much more than any reactionary 'Toryism' – which was the real cause of his opposition to the American Revolution: as he said in *Taxation no Tyranny*, 'How comes it that we hear the loudest yelps for liberty from the drivers of Negroes?' Johnson's was a mind of astonishing insight; he had seen, in 1776, the terrible anomaly which still, in the 1960s, tortures and corrupts American society.

All three of Johnson's series of essays were written during the course of the Seven Years' War against France. This triumphantly successful war produced in most of the British a frenzy of jingoist enthusiasm, of which Garrick's *Heart of Oak* (1759) is typical:

> Come, cheer up, my lads! 'tis to Glory we steer,
> To add something more to this wonderful year.
> To Honour we call you, not press you like slaves,
> For who are so free as we sons of the waves . . .

But this essay, together with *Idler* Nos. 22 and 30, shows how little Johnson shared in the general bellicosity.

No. 89. The last two paragraphs of this 'sermon', with their image of the 'rivulet of life', may be compared with the conclusion of *The Vanity of Human Wishes*. The moral is the same: endure this life, which is incurably miserable, in the hope of a better one.

Preface to the Dictionary (pp. 235–43)

1. *I trusted more to memory . . . .:* Johnson was always doing this; hence his quotations (e.g. in the *Lives of the Poets*) are perpetually inaccurate.

2. *. . . . The obscure recesses of northern learning:* by this he no doubt meant Anglo-Saxon, Old-Norse, and in general the Teutonic languages. This reference is interesting, as showing his awareness of his own classically trained mind's comparative ignorance in these regions. But later, when he came to consider as a literary critic the Celtic or Norse ventures of such as Macpherson, Collins and Gray, he found for them nothing but contempt.

3. *. . . . Whether appellative or technical:* i.e., general or technical.

4. *The academicians della Crusca:* the Accademia della Crusca was founded in 1582, with the same object as the later-formed Académie Française, that of reforming and standardizing the language. It produced its Italian dictionary in 1612.

Many patriots commented with pride on the fact that Johnson, single-handed (more or less), had accomplished what the Italians and French required whole Academies to complete.

5. *Fugitive cant:* i.e., short-lived slang.

6. *Cursory words:* i.e., lasting only for a short time.

7. *The French language has visibly changed:* the point of this reference to the two translations of Paolo Sarpi's *History of the Council of Trent* (see Johnson's first letter to Edward Cave, p. 134) is that only some fifty years separated them.

The Italian writers mentioned all wrote before the lexicographical efforts of the Accademia della Crusca.

8. *Commerce, however necessary . . . :* an example of Johnson's uneasiness about the growing industrialization of the country.

9. *As by the cultivation . . . original sense:* W. K. Wimsatt's analysis of Johnson's prose style shows that he himself practised what he here describes with apparent disapproval. His own style is full of such 'metaphors' derived from science.

10. .... *To babble a dialect of France:* it is difficult to understand the reasons for this wildly exaggerated fear. Largely, no doubt, it was simply a facet of Johnson's general disapproval of the French; there seems to have been little truly linguistic justification for it. The Dictionary itself contains some examples of what Johnson is fulminating against: *e.g.* his comments on *trait, traverse,* and *rapport* (p. 245).

11. .... *Without any patronage of the great:* a reference to the encounter with Chesterfield. Johnson's letter to him is on p. 252.

12. .... *In this gloom of solitude:* He is presumably referring to the death of his wife, three years before.

LETTERS 1754–58 (pp. 251–5)

To Thomas Warton, 21 December 1754

1. *The book:* i.e. Johnson's Dictionary.

2. *Poor Collins:* the poet William Collins, for whose insanity Johnson felt a deep sympathy sharpened by his own perpetual terror of madness.

3. *The loss of mine:* Mrs Johnson had died more than two years before this letter was written. The Greek quotation, which is from a lost play, the *Bellerophon,* by Euripides, means: 'Alas! but why *alas*? I have suffered only what all mortals suffer.'

To the Earl of Chesterfield, 7 February 1755

The genesis of this, Johnson's most famous letter, is best given in his own words, as spoken to Boswell:

Sir, after making great professions, he had for many years taken no notice of me; but when my *Dictionary* was coming out, he fell a-scribbling in the *World* about it. Upon which I wrote him a letter expressed in civil terms, but such as might show him that I did not mind what he said or wrote, and that I had done with him. (*Life*, 1754.)

It was as a result of this encounter with Chesterfield that Johnson changed 'garret' to 'patron' in the list of the 'ills' which 'the scholar's life assail' in *The Vanity of Human Wishes.* But the literary-historical cliché that the episode 'dealt the death-blow to patronage' is rather meaningless. The forces of commercialization were dealing it much more effectively, and the Chesterfield-Johnson clash was more between two utterly antipathetic personalities than between two social or economic tendencies.

1. *A native of the rocks:* The reference to Virgil is to the eighth Eclogue (line 43) – as translated by Dryden: 'I know thee, Love: in deserts thou wert bred.'

2. *Solitary:* another allusion to the death of his wife.

3. *Cynical:* The word seems to be used in the original Greek meaning, 'dog-like', i.e. curmudgeonly, with reference to the deliberately uncouth behaviour of the Stoic philosophers like Diogenes.

To Samuel Richardson, 16 March 1756

This letter (to Richardson the novelist) is one of many which might be cited to illustrate the financial straits in which Johnson frequently found himself, even after *The Vanity of Human Wishes*, the *Rambler*, and the *Dictionary* had made him famous, until he was granted his pension in 1762. Strahan and Millar were publishers, members of the consortium which had published the *Dictionary*.

To Warton, 15 April 1756

1. *An octavo book:* Warton's essay on Pope's poetry – a work of some literary-historical interest, since it exhibits for the first time the Romantic doubt whether Pope was a 'true poet'. The 'kind of royalty' which Johnson facetiously bestows on Warton refers to his having been appointed Second Master of Winchester.

2. *Collins:* Collins had become incurably insane, and was to die three years later. Johnson's reflections on the terror of madness should be compared with the passage from *Rasselas* (chapter 43):

'Ladies', said Imlac, 'to mock the heaviest of human afflictions is neither charitable nor wise. Few can attain this man's knowledge, and few practise his virtues; but all may suffer his calamity. Of the uncertainties of our present state, the most dreadful and alarming is the uncertain continuance of reason.'

To Bennet Langton, 21 September 1758

This is a letter of consolation on the death in action of Langton's uncle, a general in the Guards. The moral principle, 'let us endeavour to see things as they are', is the basis of all Johnson's philosophy. It is also

Samuel Johnson

the basis of his literary criticism – which links it with Matthew Arnold's dictum: 'to see the object as in itself it really is'.

PRAYERS 1752 AND 1759 (pp. 256–7)

Prayers on his wife's death, 1752

Mrs Johnson died on 17 March 1752. Johnson put these prayers on his wife's coffin, but kept a copy for himself. Eight years later, he was making an entry in his journal: 'To consult the resolves on Tetty's coffin.' The prayer for 26 April 1752 shows Johnson's readiness to give at least partial credence to the existence of spirits of the dead and their employment by God to minister to the living. Both beliefs were contrary to the general current of his age against 'superstition', and in fact he was mocked by the satirist Charles Churchill for his alleged belief in the 'ghost of Cock Lane'.

Easter Prayer, 1759
Prayer on Scruples, 1759?

These two prayers begin what are to be the recurring themes of Johnson's prayers and journals: the struggles against sensuality, especially in thought and imagination, against sloth, and against 'vain scruples', i.e. religious doubts. On two occasions in every year – at Easter and on his birthday – he was accustomed to review his life with particular scrupulousness.

What Johnson suffered from was a profound but general sense of guilt and sin: because this *was* general, no particular reformation (even if he managed to accomplish any) could alleviate it. It is obvious that in spite of his perpetual self-reproofs for indolence, Johnson accomplished a great deal; there is no evidence that he was more than the *homme moyen sensuel*; he forced himself to become a great deal soberer than the average in that hard-drinking age; and his religious faith was much more passionate than most men's. But all this was quite useless against that devouring guilt, that terror of being one of those whom God had chosen to 'punish everlastingly', which shadowed his whole life. In this respect, as in others, Johnson seems much closer to the temper of the seventeenth-century Puritans than to that of his contemporaries; there is no more moving or understanding description of this side of him than

Notes

Bunyan's characterization of Mr Fearing in the second part of *Pilgrim's Progress*:

The Celestial City, he said he should die if he came not to it; and yet was dejected at every difficulty, and stumbled at every straw that anybody cast in his way. . . . He had, I think, a Slough of Despond in his mind; a slough that he carried everywhere with him, or else he could never have been as he was. . . . Difficulties, lions, or Vanity Fair, he feared not at all. It was only sin, death, and hell that was to him a terror, because he had some doubts about his interest in that celestial country.

Part III

Preface to Shakespeare (pp. 261–88)

1. *Established fame and prescriptive veneration:* i.e., veneration as for an established tradition.

2. *At least above all modern writers:* i.e., other than the writers of ancient Greece and Rome. This exception is doubtless made with Homer in mind.

3. *The progress of his fable:* in the sense of Latin *fabula*, 'plot' or 'story'.

4. *Dennis and Rymer think his Romans not sufficiently Roman . . .:* these two critics, and Voltaire, were probably picked out by Johnson as the best-known representatives of the neo-classicist attack on Shakespeare, which was based on his disobedience of the 'Rules'. It is noteworthy that Johnson does not answer by another literary argument, but by a direct appeal to real life.

5. *The players, who in their edition . . .:* i.e., the First Folio of 1623, edited by Shakespeare's fellow-actors, John Heminge and Henry Condell.

6. *The rules of the ancients were yet known to few:* this is very doubtful. All educated Elizabethans would have known of them: Sidney and Ben Jonson certainly did. If Shakespeare disregarded the 'Rules', he did not do so unknowingly.

7. *The Gothic mythology of fairies:* i.e., medieval.

8. *A quibble is to Shakespeare . . .:* i.e., a pun or word-play of any kind. Johnson, like eighteenth-century taste in general, could not imagine the use of the pun in a serious context, such as Donne's 'when thou hast done [finished], thou hast not done [Donne]'.

9. *A mind wandering in ecstasy:* i.e., in madness.

10. *Calenture:* fever.

11. *The truth is that the spectators are always in their senses . . .':* Johnson's triumph over the 'Unities' is so complete, and expressed with such vigour and wit, that he may be forgiven for overstating his case. In this passage he surely exaggerates the audience's degree of detachment and self-awareness; he doesn't allow enough for the temporary absorption and self-forgetfulness which true drama demands and obtains.

12. 'Non usque adeo permiscuit imis . . .': these lines (from Lucan's *Pharsalia*, III. 138) may be paraphrased: 'The passing of time has not as yet made such confusion between the lowest and the highest, that the "Rules" wouldn't prefer to be broken by a great writer than obeyed by a small one.' Addison had said much the same in *Spectator* No. 592: 'Our inimitable Shakespeare is a stumbling-block to the whole tribe of these rigid critics. Who would not rather read one of his plays, where there is not a single rule of the stage observed, than any production of a modern critic, where there is not one of them violated?'

13. *Every man's performances, to be rightly estimated . . . :* the account of Elizabethan culture which follows suffers from the general eighteenth-century conviction that the Elizabethans, though giants of course, were crude and barbarous giants, compared with their 'polite' descendants. It is undeniable that the weakest aspect of Johnson's Shakespearean scholarship was his understanding of the 'background'.

14. *The philology of Italy:* Johnson uses the word with a wider sense than its modern meaning; 'literature and linguistic scholarship' is what he means.

15. *'The Death of Arthur':* i.e., Sir Thomas Malory's *Morte Darthur*. *Palmerin* and *Guy of Warwick* were well-known medieval romances, both of which were printed in the sixteenth century.

16. *'Small Latin, and less Greek'* (Johnson misquotes): Ben Jonson's famous phrase comes from his verses 'To the Memory of My Beloved, Mr William Shakespeare' in the Folio. Johnson does not mention that his namesake was judging from his own standard, the standard of a very (and very self-consciously) educated man. By the standard of the average product of twentieth-century education, Shakespeare's Latin, if not his Greek, would seem far from 'small'.

17. *'I cried to sleep again':* another of Johnson's numerous misquota-

tions from memory. The correct reading (*Tempest*, III. iii) is 'I cried to dream again.'

18. *As dew-drops from a lion's mane'*: *Troilus and Cressida*, III. iii.

19. *Gorboduc* is a Senecan drama in blank verse, written by Sackville and Norton in 1561. By *Hieronimo* Johnson means Thomas Kyd's *Spanish Tragedy*, of which Hieronimo is the hero.

20. *Little 'declined into the vale of years'*: the phrase is from *Othello*, III. iii. If Shakespeare 'retired to ease and plenty' in about 1612, he did so at the age of 48.

NOTES ON SHAKESPEARE (pp. 289–305)

Measure for Measure, III. i. Johnson's beautiful comment on 'Thou hast nor youth nor age . . .' shows two qualities of his criticism: his real ability to respond to great tragic poetry – cf. Eliot's use of the passage as epigraph to *Gerontion* – and the way in which he related the poetry to his own experience of life.

As You Like It. Johnson's complaint that Shakespeare should have written a scene showing the interview between 'the usurper and the hermit' is an example of one of his general complaints against Shakespeare – that he was not always careful enough to point the moral.

Henry IV, *1 and 2*, *and Henry V*. It is probable that Johnson enjoyed the English history plays more than any others of Shakespeare's. He was always slightly uneasy before high tragedy, of which the tendency to bombastic heroics annoyed and disconcerted him; the histories, with their closer relation to reality, suited him better. No later critic has equalled his analyses of Prince Hal and Falstaff.

His delightful tribute to the disappearance of Falstaff's camp-followers in *Henry V* illustrates one of his best-known heterodox opinions – his conviction that Shakespeare was by nature more a comic than a tragic genius. This judgement may seem odd at first sight; but it deserves to be thought about. It is worth considering in its light the characterization of Cleopatra, the scene of Gloucester's 'suicide' in *Lear*, and a great deal of *Hamlet*.

King Lear. Johnson's criticism of the 'Dover cliff' speech (IV. vi) is based on the principle that poetry is an art of generalization rather than of particularity. The principle is expressed in a well-known passage of *Rasselas* (chapter 10):

'The business of the poet', said Imlac, 'is to examine, not the individual, but the species; to remark general properties and large appearances. He does not number the streaks of the tulip . . .'

By this principle, Johnson judges that Shakespeare's lines fail to convey the essential feeling of terror when looking down from a great height, because they are too occupied with the details of one particular precipice.

Macbeth. Behind all these comments on the poetic diction of *Macbeth* lies a clear coherent doctrine of the language appropriate to poetry. The doctrine is expressed in the Preface: 'There is a conversation above grossness and below refinement, where propriety resides'; and again in the *Life* of Dryden: 'It is a general rule in poetry, that all appropriate terms of art should be sunk in general expressions, because poetry is to speak a universal language.'

Coriolanus. 'Amusing' in the 'General Observation' on this play means 'interesting'.

Antony and Cleopatra. In the note on Cleopatra's 'never palates more the dung', Johnson is rejecting Theobald's and Warburton's emendation *dug*, which was inspired by a feeling that the metaphor should be rationalized by a word connecting logically with 'nurse'. Johnson had a better understanding of the Shakespearean use of language: see Introduction, p. 31.

Hamlet. The 'General Observation' gets the essential quality of the play with the word 'variety'. The remark that Hamlet's madness 'causes much mirth' is an indication of how the part was still being played in the eighteenth century – in a style probably much nearer to the original intention than the neurotic pathos with which it is usually done today.

Two of Johnson's other comments, that there seems no 'adequate cause' for Hamlet's 'feigned madness' and that Hamlet is 'rather an instrument than an agent', anticipate a great deal of nineteenth and twentieth-century criticism.

Othello. It seems likely that of all Shakespeare's tragedies Johnson found *Othello* the most congenial. He liked its 'classical' qualities – the absence of sub-plot or comic effects, the rigid concentration on the central issue, and the clear-cut outlines of the characterization. In his analysis of the characters he is troubled by no 'romantic' feelings about the inadequacy of Iago's stated motives and no twentieth-century doubts about Othello's 'magnanimity'. He is ready to accept the characters as being what the text says they are. I could wish that the Shakespearean criticism of our own time were occasionally modest enough to follow him.

JOURNEY TO THE WESTERN ISLANDS (pp. 306–402)

The real 'meat' of the *Journey* is that part in which the travellers are going through the true West Highlands: Gaelic-speaking, almost roadless and wheel-less. My selection is therefore taken entirely out of that part, which starts from Inverness and ends at Inverary.

1. *A profundity scarcely credible:* in fact, the maximum depth of Loch Ness is 754 feet, or 125 fathoms: so Johnson's scepticism was hardly justified. It is also a fact that it very rarely freezes.

2. *An old woman:* Boswell's account of the old woman in her hut tells us that 'she was afraid we wanted to go to bed with her. This *coquetry*, or whatever it may be called, of so wretched a being, was truly ludicrous. Dr Johnson and I afterwards were merry upon it' (*Journal*, 30 August).

3. *Wade:* General Wade was the English commander-in-chief whose road-building activities (designed to facilitate the military reduction of the clans) gave the Highlands the first system of roads they had ever known. As the old jingle put it:

> Had you known these roads before they were made,
> You'd have lifted your hands and blessed General Wade.

4. *Prideaux's Connection:* a work of theology, properly entitled *The Old and New Testament Connected*, by Humphrey Prideaux. Johnson regarded it with much respect.

5. *I presented her with a book:* Boswell tells us what the book was. 'This book has given rise to much inquiry, which has ended in ludicrous surprise.' The book was *Cocker's Arithmetic* (*Journal*, 31 August).

6. *The next sea:* i.e., 'nearest.'

7. *I sat down on a bank:* this paragraph was picked out for special praise by many contemporary reviewers of the *Journey*.

8. *Deserts:* i.e., wildernesses of any kind.

9. *A very savage wildness:* Johnson remarks on the 'savage wildness' of the people here. Boswell had in fact said: 'It was much the same as being with a tribe of Indians.' To which Johnson replied: 'Yes, Sir; but not so terrifying' (*Journal*, 1 September).

10. *We came to our inn weary and peevish:* Johnson's narrative suppresses the fact that he and Boswell had had a tremendous scene, in which Johnson had been 'in a passion' with his companion, and had berated him with 'a tremendous shout' and 'extraordinary warmth', with the result that poor Boswell 'slept ill' on the following night and arose next morning 'very uneasy' (*Journal*, 1 and 2 September).

11. *Moorgame:* presumably grouse.

12. *Apicius:* an ancient Roman writer on gastronomy.

13. *Empyreumatic:* defined by Johnson himself in the Dictionary as 'having the smell or taste of burnt substances'.

14. *The art of making poison pleasant:* Johnson was drinking no alcohol at this period of his life – having discovered previously that if he drank at all, he was sure to drink too much.

15. *Refuse them a version of the holy scriptures:* Johnson's letter of protest against the attempt to suppress the Gaelic Bible is given on p. 481.

16. *Martin:* Martin Martin, whose *Description of the Western Isles of Scotland* (1719) went with Johnson and Boswell on their journey and had been an original cause of Johnson's interest in the Hebrides.

17. *Phoeacia:* the land of perfect happiness which Odysseus encounters in Book V of the *Odyssey*. The reference clinches, with beautiful appropriateness, the air of antique and heroic idyll which Johnson found on Raasay.

18. *Flora Macdonald:* she had earned Johnson's stately tribute by the heroism she had displayed in aiding the escape of Prince Charles (disguised as her maid) after the defeat of Culloden.

19. *Standing traditions:* i.e., still kept up.

20. *Tasted lotus:* like the comparison of Raasay to Phoeacia, this is an elegant classical compliment. The lotus was the magic herb which (in Book IX of the Odyssey) was offered by the lotus-eaters to some of Odysseus's companions, from whom it took away all desire to return home.

21. *The Czar of Muscovy:* Peter the Great, who had won himself much publicity by working in Deptford dockyard when touring the West in order to improve Russian technology.

22. *Than those of the Highlands:* Johnson seems to use the last word, here, in the sense of 'mainland'.

23. *A crooked spade:* The instrument here described is the *cas crom*. It

has still been in use in the twentieth century – perhaps is still used even
in the 1960s. Johnson's description is minute and accurate. He was
fascinated by all *processes*, all forms of human work and ingenuity.
Compare his account of the mirror-factory at Versailles, p. 511.

24. *Perflation:* i.e., 'the act of blowing through, ventilation' (O.E.D.).

25. *Malignant:* as here used, means simply 'infertile'.

26. *Meal:* the quantity of milk yielded at one milking.

27. *Chirurgery:* i.e., surgery.

28. *Trembling on the brink of his own climacteric:* there is a hidden piece
of autobiography here. The 'climacteric' age was 63 (7 times 9), and
Johnson had completed his own climacteric year during the Hebridean
journey. He refers to it in one of his letters from Scotland to Mrs Thrale:

Boswell, with some of his troublesome kindness, has informed this family and
reminded me that the 18th of September is my birthday. The return of my
birthday, if I remember it, fills me with thoughts which it seems to be the general care of humanity to escape. I can now look back upon three-score and four
years in which little has been done, and little has been enjoyed; a life diversified
by misery, spent part in the sluggishness of penury, and part under the violence
of pain, in gloomy discontent or importunate distress. But perhaps I am better
than I should have been if I had been less afflicted. With this I will try to be
content (21 September 1773).

29. *American conversation:* i.e., association with Americans (assumed to
be seditious rogues). This was written three years before the Declaration
of Independence.

30. *The boor of Norway:* i.e., peasant.

31. *Pravity:* i.e., depravity.

32. *Glaymore:* Claymore is the usual modern form. It is Gaelic for
'big sword'.

33. *Father of Ossian:* this, of course, is Johnson's phrase for James
Macpherson. 'Father' implies that in Johnson's opinion Macpherson
was the creator of *Ossian*.

34. *Mr Boswell kept the deck:* these five words conceal one of the most
amusing incidents of the journey. While Johnson lay 'quiet and unconcerned' below, Boswell, in a state of great perturbation on deck, had
been told by 'young Col' to hold on to a certain rope – which, as he
later realized, was perfectly useless: but it kept him from worrying
about the 'danger we were in' (*Journal*, 3 October). The danger was very
real: not many months later Col himself was drowned in the same seas.

35. *Having dethroned no Nabob:* a reference to the extortions of the East India Company, which were to lead up to the great trial of Warren Hastings. Johnson, as always, takes the side of the oppressed and exploited, whether they were Indian 'nabobs' (princes) or Negro slaves in America.

36. *Tobar Morar:* Tobermory.

37. *About three hundred square miles:* Johnson's estimate of the area of Mull is reasonably accurate; it is in fact 351.2 square miles.

38. *Georgic writers:* i.e., writers on agriculture.

39. *Mercheta mulierum:* this is the probably fabulous *droit de seigneur*, or 'right of the first night'.

40. *Feculent:* i.e., foul, fetid.

41. *Wheeler and Spon:* these two men travelled together in Italy and Greece in 1675–6, and each published a narrative of the journey.

42. *We are now treading that illustrious island . . .:* this paragraph also was much admired by contemporaries. Boswell quotes it in his *Journal* (19 October) and adds the note:

Had our Tour produced nothing else but this sublime passage, the world must have acknowledged that it was not made in vain. The present respectable President of the Royal Society was so much struck on reading it, that he clapped his hands together, and remained for some time in an attitude of silent admiration.

43. *Mull is said to contain . . . and Skye fifteen thousand:* The present population of Mull is 2903, and of Skye 9908. The population of the rest of Britain has of course increased enormously since the eighteenth century.

44. *The Scots, with a vigilance of jealousy . . . .:* this jealousy (i.e., suspiciousness) was thoroughly justified, for the eighteenth-century English were perpetually sneering at the comparative poverty of the Scots. Johnson did it himself very often: e.g., his conversation with Wilkes, reported by Boswell in the *Life* for 15 May 1776.

LIVES OF THE POETS (pp. 403–80)

COWLEY ('*On Metaphysical Poetry*')

This famous piece of criticism is the first to look on the followers of Donne as a 'school' and to give them the label of 'metaphysical' which they have had ever since. This, in itself, has been rather unfortunate, resulting in their total or partial isolation from the main stream of English poetry until the twentieth century; but Johnson's account of their characteristics, however unappreciative, is a brilliant piece of critical description.

1. *The father of criticism:* Aristotle.

2. *Great thoughts are always general:* one of the basic principles of Johnson's criticism. Compare note to his comments on the 'Dover cliff' speech in *Lear* (p. 294). The answer was provided by William Blake, in one of his annotations to Joshua Reynolds's *Discourses:* 'To generalize is to be an Idiot!'

3. *Exility of particles:* i.e., minuteness.

4. *Only in his lines upon Hobson the Carrier:* there are 'metaphysical' conceits to be found in the *Nativity Ode* also, e.g.:

> So when the sun in bed
> Curtained with cloudy red,
> Pillows his chin upon an orient wave ...

WALLER ('*On Devotional Poetry*')

Mrs Thrale tells a story which throws a revealing light on Johnson's argument against devotional poetry:

Dr Johnson ... could never pass the stanza (in the *Dies Irae*) ending thus, *Tantus labor non sit cassus*, without bursting into a flood of tears; which sensibility I used to quote against him when he would inveigh against devotional poetry.

It may be suspected that Johnson's real, unavowed and perhaps unknown, reason was the precise opposite of the reason he declared. He disliked devotional poetry because he feared it; he feared it because it stirred up some of his most agonizing emotions.

Birkbeck Hill, after quoting the above passage from Mrs Thrale, comments: 'In the Latin hymns is to be found the best answer to Johnson's criticism.' One might add also the devotional poetry of the English seventeenth century – the poetry of Herbert, Vaughan and Traherne.

MILTON

1. *He was a 'Lion':* Johnson is alluding to these lines in *Paradise Lost*.

> Sporting the lion ramp'd, and in his paw
> Dandled the kid. (IV. 243)

2. *Easy, vulgar, and therefore disgusting:* the two last of this splendid trio of epithets do not have quite their modern meanings. 'Vulgar' means commonplace; 'disgusting' means distasteful. It is worth noting – because the point is often misunderstood – that Johnson is not saying *Lycidas* itself is 'easy, vulgar and therefore disgusting'; he is saying this of the pastoral form, which he always disliked and despised.

3. *When Cowley tells of Hervey**. . .: Johnson refers to Cowley's elegy in memory of William Hervey, and especially to these lines:

> We spent them [our hours] not in toys, or lusts, or wine;
>> But search of deep philosophy,
>>> Wit, eloquence, and poetry,
> Arts which I lov'd, for they, my friend, were thine.
> Ye fields of Cambridge, our dear Cambridge, say,
> Have ye not seen us walking every day?

It is quite true that Cowley feels and expresses a far stronger personal grief for Hervey than Milton for Edward King. But the true subject of *Lycidas* is not Edward King; it is John Milton.

4. *That system of diction and mode of verse:* Johnson's opinion that in *Comus* can be found the 'system of diction and mode of verse' of *Paradise Lost* seems perverse. To most ears, the verse of *Comus* is very different from that of *Paradise Lost*.

5. *Only the eighth and the twenty-first* . . . : these are the sonnets 'When the assault was intended to the city' and that addressed to Cyriack Skinner. Both are comparatively light in tone, without the preaching or propagandist element present in some of the others: hence perhaps Johnson's approval of them, very modified though it be.

6. *Poetry is the art of uniting pleasure with truth* . . .: Johnson is echoing the Horatian tag, *miscere utile dulci*. He had said the same in the Preface to his Shakespeare: 'The end of all writing is to instruct; the end of poetry is to instruct by pleasing.'

7. *Physiology:* i.e., in Johnson's own dictionary definition, 'the doctrine of the constitution of the works of nature'.

8. *Bossu:* Le Bossu, a French critic in the age of Louis XIV, who was one of the most influential of the neo-classical critics, expressed this opinion in his *Traité du Poème Epique*.

9. *Not the destruction of a city* . . . *or the foundation of an empire:* Johnson is thinking of the stories of the *Iliad* and *Aeneid*.

10. *Of which the least could wield . . . their regions:* Paradise Lost, VI, 22 – slightly misquoted, 'which' instead of 'whom' and 'those' for 'these'.

11. *Amiably:* i.e., attractively.

12. *Fruition:* i.e., enjoyment. The contemporary use of this word with the meaning *maturity* is as wrong as the use of 'disinterested' meaning *uninterested*. The word has no connexion with *fruit*; it comes from Latin *fruor,* 'enjoy'.

13. θεὸς ἀπὸ μηχανῆς: i.e., the god from the machine, the supernatural intervention which resolves the tangle at the end of the Greek tragedy.

14. *Episodes:* as used in the technical language of neo-classical criticism, the word means, more or less, parts of the whole work which seem comparatively detachable, self-sufficient.

15. *Here are no funeral games . . . :* funeral games occur in both *Iliad* (book 23) and *Aeneid* (book 5); the description of Achilles' shield is in *Iliad* 18. 'The short digressions' in *Paradise Lost* are those in which Milton gives some personal or autobiographic matter: on his blindness at the beginning of book 3, on his loneliness after the Restoration at the beginning of book 7, and on his opinions about epic poetry at the beginning of book 9. As Johnson implies, they may be critically indefensible, but they are remarkably interesting.

16. *Petulantly and indecently:* two of Johnson's favourite critical terms, neither of which has quite its modern meaning. 'Cantankerously and inappropriately' is something near it.

17. *Cato is the hero of Lucan:* i.e., Cato 'Uticensis', hero of Lucan's *Pharsalia.* Cato, defeated in his last-ditch defence of the Roman Republic, committed suicide – but, in Lucan's own words, *victrix causa diis placuit sed victa Catoni:* which might be 'imitated', rather than translated, as 'God was on the side of the big battalions, but the moral victory was Cato's.'

18. *The spirit of science:* the word still held for Johnson its earlier, unspecialized meaning, derived from Latin *scientia* – 'learning'.

19. *. . . Not always used with notice of their vanity:* i.e., their falsity. Johnson is making the same complaint as he made against *Lycidas,* that the false mythology of the heathens should not be mingled with the truthful narratives of the Bible.

20. *Ariosto's pravity:* i.e., wickedness.

21. *The Deliverance of Jerusalem:* i.e., Tasso's *Gierusalemne Liberata.*

22. *The defects and faults of Paradise Lost:* it is at this point that Johnson begins his stately critical somersault.

23. *Bentley:* Richard Bentley's notorious edition of *Paradise Lost* proposed an immense number of emendations, made necessary, in his opinion, by minute errors of logic or language. E.g., Bentley objected to the last lines of the poem –

> Then hand in hand with wand'ring steps and slow,
> Through Eden took their solitary way

– on the ground that Adam and Eve, being two, were not 'solitary'.

24. *But original deficience . . . supplied* etc.: it may be suspected that in this paragraph Johnson is giving his genuine personal response to the poem.

25. *The confusion of spirit and matter:* this was, there is no doubt, one of Milton's major difficulties. He himself, presumably, believed in angels and demons not as corporeal creatures, but as spirits; but the fact that he had elected to write a poem purporting to be a narrative, a 'story', compelled him to pretend that they were material. As Johnson observes, his pretence is inconsistent.

26. *Propriety:* i.e., appropriateness (to Adam as the first and still the only man).

27. *Terms of art:* i.e., technical expressions. E.g., earlier Johnson had objected to Milton's use of *larboard.* This was a basic tenet of neo-classical criticism; Johnson makes the same objection to Dryden's use, in *Annus Mirabilis,* of technical ship-building terms such as 'oakum' and 'caulking-iron'. He there lays down the basic principle: 'It is a general rule of poetry that all appropriated (i.e., specialized) terms of art should be sunk in general expressions, because poetry is to speak an universal language.' (*Life of Dryden*).

28. *Peculiarity of Diction:* Johnson's comments on the diction of *Paradise Lost,* and especially his remark that Milton 'was desirous to use English words with a foreign idiom', anticipate the famous observation of Keats:

The Paradise Lost, though so fine in itself, is a corruption of our language . . . a northern dialect accommodating itself to the Greek and Latin inversions and intonations. (Letter to George Keats, September 1819)

29. *The Earl of Surrey is said to have translated . . . rhyme:* in fact,

Surrey (about 1540) translated *two* books of the *Aeneid*, books 2 and 4, into what is usually taken to be the first example of English blank verse.

Johnson's vagueness and inaccuracy about Surrey illustrates how scanty, in the eighteenth century, even among the learned, was knowledge of early English literature. Vernacular scholarship was regarded, on the whole, with much disdain: cf. Pope's contempt for Theobald, who was a far better English scholar than himself. The only *real* scholarship was in Latin and Greek.

30. *An ingenious critic:* this critic appears to be Johnson himself. His dislike of blank verse is often quoted as a proof of the deficiencies of his ear in the criticism of poetry. This is probably true, up to a point: but it may be said in his defence that he had doubtless been prejudiced against blank verse in general, and Miltonic blank verse in particular, by the immense and tedious tracts of the stuff turned out in the eighteenth century.

31. *'The lapidary style':* i.e., the style appropriate to inscriptions on monuments. This comment indicates that to Johnson's ear blank verse must have sounded something like 'free verse'.

Addison

Johnson's analysis of Addison as critic and prose-writer is an example of his criticism at its finest: judicious without being pompous, balanced but decisive. He is here evaluating a writer who, he feels, has been unduly depreciated, and one who was admittedly a 'popularizer' and not a talent of the highest order. He resists the temptations inherent in such an undertaking: he neither reacts to the opposite extreme and overpraises, nor does he make his description of Addison's techniques of popularization sound condescending. He believes (with justice) that Addison made a significant contribution to the improving of English culture. For that he pays him due honour; but he knows that he was not a supreme genius.

1. *Superficial:* the word, as used here, has no pejorative sense.

2. *Paradise Lost:* Addison wrote a *Spectator* on *Paradise Lost* every Saturday through eighteen weeks, beginning with No. 267 on 5 January 1712. Johnson's statement that they 'made Milton an universal favourite' seems exaggerated. *Paradise Lost* did not immediately become popular.

3. *Chevy Chase:* in *Spectators* 70 and 74.

4. *Imbecility:* the meaning then was nearer to 'weakness' or 'silliness' than the stronger modern meaning.

5. *'Outsteps the modesty of nature':* from Hamlet's instructions to the players (III. ii). Johnson, as he often does, misquotes slightly ('outsteps' for 'o'ersteps').

6. *Enthusiastic:* used in the old sense (beginning to grow obsolete by this time) of 'fanatical'. Johnson's dictionary definitions of 'enthusiasm' show the changing significance of the word:

(1) A vain belief of private revelation; a vain confidence of divine favour or communication.

(2) Heat of imagination; violence of passion; confidence of opinion.

(3) Elevation of fancy; exaltation of ideas.

7. *Voluble:* i.e., smooth-flowing.

CONGREVE

This paragraph is Johnson's summing-up of Congreve as comic dramatist. To my mind, it is a brilliant distillation of his essential quality. Especially provocative is Johnson's remark that Congreve's comedies have in them a quality strangely like tragedy, because 'they surprise rather than divert'. They do have this effect: an elegiac undertone, a flirting with poetry, which no other Restoration comedies possess.

PRIOR

These two paragraphs from the *Life of Prior* were occasioned by Prior's long serious poem *Solomon*, 'the work', as Johnson put it, 'to which he entrusted the protection of his name, and which he expected succeeding ages to regard with veneration.' By the time Johnson came to write the *Lives of the Poets, Solomon* was already dead and forgotten.

One of Johnson's supreme merits as critic (and one in which modern criticism is singularly deficient) is that he *never forgets the reader*. His criticism never gives the impression that it is a kind of private dialogue between critic and author – or, sometimes, between critic and himself, with author merely as pretext. And another of Johnson's critical merits which these paragraphs reveal is a wholesome lack of solemnity about *being an author*. No writer had a higher concept of the duties of literature than he had; but none was less arrogant about the literary character.

1. *Nine years unpublished:* the reference is to Horace's advice (*Ars Poetica*, 388) to keep your work in a drawer for nine years before you

let it out (*nonum prematur in annum*). Prior claimed to have done this with his *Solomon*.

POPE

1. *A 'long disease'*: the phrase comes from Pope's *Epistle to Dr Arbuthnot* – 'this long disease, my life'.

2. *Boddice*: the word was really a plural, meaning 'bodies'. What Johnson is describing seems to have been a sort of corset.

3. *Tie-wig*: 'a wig having the hair gathered together behind and tied with a knot of ribbon' (O.E.D.).

4. *'Nodded in company'*: also from the *Epistle to Arbuthnot* – 'I nod in company, I wake at night, Fools rush into my head, and so I write.'

5. *Hannibal, says Juvenal*: in his tenth satire, Juvenal relates the story that Hannibal died of a poisoned ring – the equivalent of the obscure death of Charles XII in Johnson's imitation.

6. *'He hardly drank tea . . . stratagem'*: Johnson adapts a line from Young's *Satires* (VI. 188) – 'nor take her tea without a stratagem'.

7. *Horresco referens*: 'I shudder when I refer to it' (Aeneid II. 204). This is of course a sly allusion to Johnson's own 'dictionary-making'. 'Publisher' here must mean 'compiler' or 'producer'.

8. *Lady Mary Wortley*: Lady Mary Wortley Montagu became the object of Pope's bitter hatred because, according to her own tale, she had laughed in his face when he made some passionate declarations of love to her. Her story may not be true; but it is certain that Pope had at least carried on an epistolary flirtation with her.

9. *'A heart for all . . . a fortune for all'*: Pope actually wrote this to Swift, inviting him in 1737 to come with his household from Dublin and stay with him at Twickenham.

10. *Quincunx*: a favourite arrangement of trees, shrubs, etc., in the old-style formal garden. It is 'an arrangement of five things with one at each corner and one in the middle of a square'. Sir Thomas Browne wrote a treatise on 'The Garden of Cyrus, or, The Quincunciall, Lozenge, or Net-work Plantations of the Ancients, Artificially, Naturally, Mystically Considered'.

11. *The great topic of his ridicule is poverty*: Pope was often attacked – and not without justice – for sneering at the poverty of writers less successful than himself. His defence was that they deserved their poverty;

they should have known better, with their miserable talents, than to endeavour at writing.

12. '*His highness's dog*': i.e., the Prince of Wales's dog. Pope's distich is:

> I am his Highness' dog at Kew;
> Pray tell me, Sir, whose dog are you?

13. *He can derive little honour ... Bolingbroke:* Johnson detested Bolingbroke for his deistic opinions; but it is not clear why he disapproved so strongly of Cobham and Burlington. The former was a distinguished soldier, and the latter one of the most effective amateurs and patrons of architecture that the country has ever known. He was the principal agent in popularizing the Palladian manner in England.

14. *Of his social qualities ... letters:* Johnson is entirely justified in regarding with extreme scepticism Pope's claim that his letters revealed his 'true character'. The fact is that he regarded his 'private' correspondence as part of his 'creative work', and when he printed it himself, he indulged in a great deal of shameless cutting, doctoring, and downright forgery.

15. *Emmets:* ants.

16. *Dispositions apparently counterfeited:* i.e., obviously. Johnson's devastating account of Pope's innumerable deceptions and contradictions is entirely accurate, but perhaps too unsympathetic. In many instances, Pope was striving for an ideal which he was incapable of reaching; but his striving was not always hypocritical.

17. *Superstructed:* 'built upon something else, constructed upon a foundation' (O.E.D.)

18. '*A fool to Fame*': another quotation from the *Epistle to Arbuthnot* – 'As yet a child, nor yet a fool to fame, I lisped in numbers, for the numbers came.'

19. *He was irritable and resentful:* there is no need to give the details of the various quarrels which Johnson here alludes to. Ambrose Philips, a minor poet, had been Pope's butt for his 'namby-pamby' pastorals. Richard Bentley, the great Hellenist, was detested by all the Swift–Pope–Arbuthnot circle largely because of his formidable professional accuracy, which they (who stood for the 'amateur', humanist ideal) called pedantry – as it sometimes really was. Bentley is the main victim of the fourth book of the *Dunciad*. The Duke of Chandos was allegedly – but Pope denied it – the original of the tasteless plutocrat 'Timon' in

the fourth of the *Moral Essays*. For 'Lady Wortley' see note 8 above. Hill was Aaron Hill, another minor poet, whom Pope had attacked, under his initials, in a *Dunciad* note. When Hill complained, Pope tried to wriggle out of it.

20. *His ungrateful mention of Allen:* Martha Blount, Pope's closest female friend – perhaps his mistress – had quarrelled with the Allens, who had been very generous to Pope. Pope left Ralph Allen £150, with the remark that that was more or less what Allen had given him. Allen gave the bequest to charity, commenting that Pope was always 'a bad accountant' and that £1500 would have been nearer to the true figure.

21. *Racine:* Louis Racine, son of the poet. He had attacked Pope for the alleged irreligion of the *Essay on Man*. Pope replied, protesting that he was really a devout and submissive Catholic. 'The positions which he transmitted from Bolingbroke' refer to the deistical ideas of the *Essay on Man*.

22. *Good Sense:* this was of course one of the basic standards of the Augustans, and Johnson's definition of it here is the best ever made by any of them. By 'consonance' Johnson means 'absence of incongruities'. Note that he recognizes the limitations of Good Sense and its essentially negative character – 'a sedate and quiescent quality'.

23. *Soliciting the sun to shine upon a birth-day:* Johnson refers to the fact that eighteenth-century Poets Laureate were supposed to produce Birthday Odes for members of the royal family.

24. *The dismission of his poetical prejudices:* refers to the 'metaphysical' conceits to be found in Dryden's early verse, and his subsequent abandonment of them.

Johnson's description of Dryden's way of writing is very similar to his own. His remark that when Dryden 'had no pecuniary interest', his solicitude for his work ceased, reminds one of his famous saying: 'No man but a blockhead ever wrote, except for money.' (Boswell, 5 April 1776).

25. . . . *The two satires of Thirty-eight:* i.e., the two Dialogues which make up the *Epilogue to the Satires*, first published in 1738 and originally entitled *1738*.

26. . . . *Whose education was more scholastic:* Dryden had been to public school and university; Pope, partly because of his health, partly because of his Roman Catholicism, had been educated largely by tutors.

27. *some partial fondness:* Johnson's suspicion that he is too partial to Dryden will probably be shared by most modern readers. He seems to have been deceived by the appearance of vigour always present in Dryden's verse, which does not always mean that the real thing is there too; and conversely, by the appearance of urbanity and polish always present in Pope's verse, which does not necessarily mean a lack of true vigour behind it.

28. *Cooper's Hill:* a poem by Sir John Denham, which contains these once much-quoted lines on the Thames:

> O could I flow like thee, and make thy stream
> My great example, as it is my theme!
> Though deep, yet clear; though gentle, yet not dull;
> Strong without rage; without o'erflowing, full.

These lines, no doubt, Pope greatly admired; but that did not prevent him from parodying them in the *Dunciad:*

> Flow, Welsted, flow! like thine inspirer, Beer,
> Though stale, not ripe; though thin, yet never clear.
>
> (III. 169)

29. *Lodona:* in *Windsor Forest* is the nymph who is pursued by Pan with lecherous intent and saved by being metamorphosed into the River Loddon. Johnson is quite right to say that this episode (lines 171–218) is very inferior to the rest of *Windsor Forest;* but he was prejudiced, in general, against what he called in his critique of Gray 'the puerilities of obsolete mythology'.

30. *'Numeris lege solutis':* Horace, Odes IV. 2 – 'verses freed from law', i.e., from metrical rules.

31. *Perhaps the best that English poetry can show:* Johnson refers to lines 219–32, beginning

> Fir'd at first sight with what the Muse imparts,
> In fearless youth we tempt the heights of Arts ...

and ending

> Th' increasing prospect tires our wand'ring eyes,
> Hills peep o'er hills, and Alps on Alps arise.

Johnson's admiration for this simile – which modern taste is unlikely to value so highly – is probably due to its studiously 'Homeric' character.

It is elaborate, but clear; every part in the comparison corresponds with precision to a part in the thing compared. And also, it is 'sublime'.

32. '*The sound should seem an echo to the sense*': Pope actually wrote 'must seem' (line 365).

Johnson's scepticism on this, like his dislike of blank verse, is sometimes cited as proof of the deficiency of his ear: but though he may be a trifle too intransigent, he is surely right in essence when he remarks that 'in such resemblances the mind often governs the ear' – and not vice versa. I. A. Richards's devastating experiment in *Practical Criticism* may be cited in support:

It should be possible to take some recognised masterpiece of poetic rhythm and compose, with nonsense syllables, a double or dummy which at least comes recognisably near to possessing the same virtue.

> J. Droostan-Sussting Benn
> Mill-down Leduren N.
>   Telamba-taras oderwainto weiring
> Hwersey zet bidreen
> Ownd istellester sween
>   Lithabian tweet ablissood owdswown stiering
> Apleven aswetsen sestinal
> Yintomen I adaits afurf gallas Ball.

If the reader has any difficulty in scanning these verses, reference to Milton, On the Morning of Christ's Nativity, XV, will prove of assistance ... (Chap. IV).

33. *Pope is said by an objector:* the objector was Joseph Warton, who pointed out in his *Essay on the Genius of Pope* that the sylphs were borrowed from a French romance, *Le Comte de Gabalis*. But, as Birkbeck Hill says, Pope had acknowledged this in his own preface to *The Rape of the Lock*.

34. *The Lutrin: Le Lutrin* is Boileau's most famous satire.

35. *It has been well observed:* by Johnson himself. Birkbeck Hill quotes the couplet which Johnson inserted into Goldsmith's *Traveller:*

> How small of all that human hearts endure
> That part which laws or kings can cause or cure

– and the conviction that the greater part of human misery had private and domestic causes rather than public ones was one of Johnson's consistent beliefs, expressed in many places.

36. '*Curiosa felicitas*': Petronius on Horace. The phrase is virtually

untranslatable. 'Brilliant phrasing which appears to have been arrived at by chance, but is really the result of hard work and thought' is a clumsy but accurate paraphrase. It was one of the ideals of Augustan art; Pope expressed it in the *Essay on Criticism:*

> True ease in writing comes from art, not chance,
> As those move easiest who have learned to dance.
>
> (362)

37. *The learned author:* Joseph Warton, in the *Essay on the Genius of Pope.*

38. *To have tuned the English tongue:* Johnson is quite right to see Pope's Homer as one of the great sources – perhaps *the* great source – of the rhythm and diction of much eighteenth-century verse. Some forty years later, Wordsworth – from a hostile viewpoint – made exactly the same comment when he observed that it would be many years before the 'poison' of that translation had worked itself out of English poetry.

39. *Some, who wish to be numbered among the sons of learning:* Johnson is no doubt alluding in particular to Richard Bentley and his famous remark: 'A very pretty poem, Mr Pope; but we must not call it Homer'. On which Matthew Arnold was to comment that the translation was thereby 'judged'.

Johnson is clearly a little uneasy in his defence of Pope's Homer. He is aware that its general spirit is scarcely Homer's – that Pope tones down the ferocity and barbarism, the bloodshed and delight in bloodshed, the occasional raucous and cruel humour, the frequently comic and un-dignified behaviour of gods and goddesses. He is not quite prepared to say in effect: 'This is to be enjoyed as a great contemporary poem, and never mind about Homer' – but he comes very near to it when he observes that 'Pope wrote for his own age and his own nation.'

40. *Theobald:* i.e., Lewis Theobald, who in his *Shakespeare Restored* had exposed the many deficiencies and errors in Pope's edition of Shakespeare.

41. *Impune diem ... Telephus:* from Juvenal's first satire (line 4). 'Should such an interminable play be allowed to waste a whole day – and the author get away with it?'

42. *The concluding paragraph:* i.e., the great vision of 'universal dark-ness' which begins 'In vain, in vain – the all-composing hour ...' (IV. 627).

43. *Never were penury of knowledge ... happily disguised:* Johnson's

scathing contempt for the 'philosophy' of the *Essay on Man* is somewhat exaggerated. He was prejudiced because he believed it to have been entirely, and uncomprehendingly, stolen from Bolingbroke, whom he regarded as a vile 'infidel'.

44. *Characters of Men and Women:* i.e., the *Moral Essays*, as Pope eventually decided to call them. Johnson's title is perhaps better: what one remembers best in these poems are certainly the 'characters'.

45. '*The Gem and the Flower*': Johnson refers to a passage in the first *Moral Essay*, in which Pope is arguing that characters in 'high life' afford better material for understanding human traits than obscure persons:

> Though the same sun with all-diffusive rays
> Blush in the rose, and in the diamond blaze,
> We prize the stronger effort of his power,
> And justly set the gem above the flower.

(145)

46. *Atossa:* a 'character' in *Moral Essay* II, based on the Duchess of Marlborough; 'Clodio' in *Moral Essay* I was the Duke of Wharton.

47. *Philomede:* she is in *Moral Essay* II, and is said (l. 83) to have 'lectured all mankind On the soft passion and the taste refined' – but then to have 'made her hearty meal upon a dunce'. As for Prior, Johnson's own *Life* of him remarks:

Tradition represents him as willing to descend from the dignity of the poet and the statesman to the low delights of mean company. His Chloe probably was sometimes ideal; but the woman with whom he cohabited was a despicable drab of the lowest species.

48. *The eulogy on Good Sense:* in *Moral Essay* IV. The passage on the death of Buckingham is in *Moral Essay* III. The second – the wonderful lines beginning 'In the worst inn's worst room' (l. 299) – is certainly one of Pope's greatest achievements.

49. *The satire upon Sporus:* the virulent attack on Lord Hervey beginning 'Let Sporus tremble' (l. 305). Johnson finds this 'mean' for the same reason, perhaps, as makes him uneasy about the *Dunciad:* for Pope hints pretty plainly at Hervey's alleged homosexuality and at the contrast between his powdered, painted, exquisite surface and the stinking corruption beneath. If one takes the passage on 'Sporus' only as a personal invective, Johnson's comment is just. But take it as an exposure (perhaps unintended) of what often *did* lie behind the eighteenth

century's 'elegance', and it will seem a brilliant and profound piece of analysis.

50. *The most perfect fabric of English verse:* i.e., the heroic couplet. Johnson often uses 'fabric' in the sense of 'metre'.

51. *Prescription:* i.e., tradition.

52. *Double rhymes:* i.e., rhymes in two syllables. The one Johnson refers to in the *Rape of the Lock* is 'dissever' and 'sever' (III. 153). Johnson's comment means, of course, that very few of Pope's lines have eleven syllables or 'feminine endings.'

53. *Expletives:* i.e., words like 'does' and 'do', used to supply an extra syllable. Pope makes fun of them in the *Essay on Criticism:* 'and expletives their feeble aid *do join.*'

54. *Sometimes vitiated by French idioms:* Johnson's prejudice against what he regarded as harmful and unnecessary borrowings from the French is revealed in more than one place of the Dictionary; but it is not clear which expressions of Pope's he is referring to here.

55. '*Lo, where Maeotis sleeps . . . snows*': Johnson's inability to discover 'the reason of this preference' may have been caused by his indifference to that poetic quality which Marlowe and Milton had in common with Pope – a delight in exotic and sonorous names for their own sakes as well as for their associational powers. The beauty of Pope's couplet clearly resides in 'Maeotis' and 'Tanais'; it is therefore of the same kind as the beauty of Marlowe's

> To ride in triumph through Persepolis

and Milton's

> Where the great vision of the guarded mount
> Looks toward Namancos and Bayona's hold.

56. *Whether Pope was a poet:* Johnson is probably referring in particular to Joseph Warton's essay mentioned above. Birkbeck Hill is surely wrong in suggesting that Johnson did not 'perceive' the reaction against Pope's poetry. He perceived it very clearly, and this peroration is his reply. It is notable that he ends with a cunning reference to Homer – the suggestion being that Pope was a worthy member of the great line of European poets which Homer began – and with the defiant word 'genius'; just the quality which the new romantic taste, though ready to concede to Pope 'wit' and 'cleverness', was beginning to deny him.

SMITH '*On Gilbert Walmsley*'

Gilbert Walmsley was Registrar of the Ecclesiastical Court at Lichfield. Johnson slides him into his *Life* of the very minor poet Edmund Smith on the pretext that Walmsley had known Smith and supplied Johnson with some information about him. Walmsley's wife was a sister of 'Molly' Aston (see Introduction, p. 9). Boswell observes that in this passage Johnson draws Walmsley's character 'in the glowing colours of gratitude', with the implication, it seems, that there is a modicum of exaggeration. Perhaps there is: but it is a superb piece of writing, and nothing could be more skilful than the way in which the eulogy of Walmsley seems to lead with complete naturalness into the praises of James and Garrick.

1. *Dr James:* James (who had died three years before this passage was written) invented a once-famous patent medicine called 'Dr James's Powder', much used for the treatment of fevers. Its chief constituents were phosphate of lime and oxide of antimony. A hearty dose of it was alleged to have killed Oliver Goldsmith.

2. *David Garrick:* Garrick had died early in 1779, when *The Lives of the Poets* was going through the press. Johnson's famous tribute may be compared with the letter he wrote to Garrick's widow:

Dr Johnson sends most respectful condolence to Mrs Garrick, and wishes that any endeavour of his could enable her to support a loss which the world cannot repair.

Johnson's attitude to Garrick was splendidly 'ambivalent' throughout the course of their long friendship. He felt toward 'Davy' a combination of the feelings of master toward pupil (Garrick had in fact been one of his pupils when he kept a school at Lichfield), of a provincial who had made good in the big city toward a fellow-provincial who had made even better, of contempt for a 'player' combined with respect for one who had made 'playing' respectable, of envy for a man who had become much richer than himself mixed with respect for one who used his wealth with discretion – all in all, a teasing blend of affection, admiration and contempt. It was all summed up in what Garrick himself remarked to Boswell – that Johnson 'would let nobody attack Garrick but himself' (15 May 1776).

SHENSTONE

1. *His delight in rural pleasures:* Shenstone's landscape-gardening at the

Leasowes was famous; the tone of Johnson's witty description sufficiently indicates that *he* thought of those who took such activities
seriously.

2. *Lyttelton:* George, Lord Lyttelton, a well-known politician and
minor versifier. He had a considerable following, especially among the
bluestockings, to whom this passage, and the *Life* of Lyttelton itself, gave
great offence. Johnson's judgement on him as a poet is in fact generous rather than unkind: 'Lord Lyttelton's poems are the works of a
man of literature and judgement, devoting part of his time to versification. They have nothing to be despised, and little to be admired.'

3. *Conducting . . . to inconvenient points of view:* this reminds one of
Peacock's criticism in *Headlong Hall:*

'Allow me', said Mr Gall. 'I distinguish the picturesque and the beautiful, and
I add to them in the laying out of grounds, a third and distinct character, which
I call unexpectedness.'

'Pray, sir', said Mr Milestone, 'by what name do you distinguish this
character, when a person walks round the grounds for the second time?'

The kind of landscaping of which the Leasowes was an outstanding
example did depend very largely on 'deceptions': e.g., the fake bridge
at Ken House which makes what is really a small lake look like a stretch
of river – from the right viewpoint.

4. *In time his expenses . . . fauns and fairies:* Shenstone's friends indig-
nantly denied Johnson's comic account of his financial embarrassments.

GRAY

1. *Mr West:* Richard West, Gray's schoolfellow at Eton, to whose
memory he wrote the sonnet 'In vain to me the smiling mornings
shine', which Wordsworth criticized but Hopkins admired ('an
exquisite piece of art, whatever Wordsworth may say').

2. *Inability to understand them:* the universal criticism of these two odes
when they first appeared was about their 'obscurity'. Gray himself
remarked of them: 'I hear we are not at all popular; the great objection
is obscurity.' Walpole (like Roger Fry with Eliot's *Waste Land*) persuaded Gray to supply notes, but not as many as he wished.

3. *Refusing the laurel:* i.e., declining to be made Poet Laureate.

4. *Uneasy at his neglect of duty:* Birkbeck Hill remarks that Johnson is
here describing a state of mind – a paralysis of the will to act in spite of

a perfectly clear knowledge of what ought to be done – which he knew 'only too well' in himself.

5. *He seems not to understand the word:* it is not clear why Johnson objects to Gray's 'buxom health'. His own dictionary defines 'buxom' as follows:

(1) obedient, obsequious; (2) gay, lively, brisk; (3) wanton, jolly.

– and Gray is presumably using the word in the last two senses.

6. '*O Diva, gratum . . . Antium*': first line of Horace's Odes, book I, 35. 'O goddess, who rulest over pleasant Antium' – the goddess is Fortune.

7. *Something of cant:* one of Johnson's favourite words. As used here it has presumably the fourth meaning in Johnson's own dictionary definition: 'barbarous jargon'.

8. *That Poetry and Virtue go always together . . . to think it true:* this as Johnson says, is nonsense. But it was an opinion constantly expressed by the 'pre-romantic' poets of the mid-eighteenth century, who usually added to it (as Gray does) the proposition that primitive or 'savage' life goes with them both. E.g., the lines in Collins's *Ode on the Popular Superstitions of the Highlands of Scotland*, which urge the poet to find his subject-matter and inspiration in the remotest of the Hebrides.

9. *The pomp of machinery:* Johnson uses the word in the old literary-critical sense of 'mythological allusions'. Gray himself, in one of his letters, made the damaging revelation that one of his readers (though she was 'a lady of quality') was unaware that Shakespeare and Milton were the real subjects of stanzas III. i and III. ii of the ode.

10. *The prophecy of Nereus:* Horace, Odes I, 15. Nereus prophesies the war and destruction of Troy which will follow on Paris's abduction of Helen. The ode was taken to be meant as a warning to Mark Antony of what would follow if he did not break with Cleopatra.

11. *Incredulus odi:* from Horace, *Ars Poetica*, 188. 'I hate what I can't believe in.'

12. *An action of better example: The Bard* ends with the bard's committing suicide. Johnson's objection, that suicide is a sin, seems rather pedantic, since the bard was a pagan, who might be supposed to have known no better.

Samuel Johnson

To William Drummond, 13 August 1766

This letter was addressed to an Edinburgh bookseller (publisher), but was obviously intended to be made public. The occasion for it is given by Boswell:

It seems some of the members of the Society in Scotland for Propagating Christian Knowledge had opposed the scheme of translating the Holy Scriptures into the Erse or Gaelic language, from political considerations of the disadvantage of keeping up the distinction between the Highlanders and the other inhabitants of North Britain.

Johnson's letter, according to Boswell, was effective – 'the opponents of this pious scheme being made ashamed of their conduct, the benevolent undertaking was allowed to go on.'

The letter shows Johnson's sympathetic interest in the Highlands and their inhabitants, seven years before he visited them. The caustic reference to 'the planters of America' indicates a kind of subconscious parallel in Johnson's mind between the brutal crushing of the Highlanders by the English after the '45 and the cruelties perpetrated on Indians and Negroes by the American (and West Indian) colonists. Compare *Idler* 81 (p. 229).

To Mrs Aston, 17 November 1767

The advice which Johnson gives to Mrs Aston is based, as he says, on his own opinion and experience. He was always terrified of solitude.

To Mrs Thrale, 11 July 1770

What Johnson here says semi-facetiously – 'the passions rise higher at domestic than at imperial tragedies' – he enounces as a serious critical principle in his comment on Shakespeare's *Timon*: 'The play of *Timon* is a domestic tragedy and therefore strongly fastens on the attention of the reader.' In Johnson's critical mind there was a strong resistance against the Sublime and the Grand Style; it is a major reason for his coolness towards Milton and Gray.

1. *Pulvis et umbra sumus:* 'we are dust and shade,' Horace, Odes IV, 7.

To Dr Taylor, 31 August 1772

This letter is an example of a tendency very often seen in Johnson (as in lesser men), that of giving to others the advice he was always giving to himself. What he urges on Taylor – stop being melancholy, don't be introspective, you can cure your own glooms if you try and no one else can, keep yourself incessantly but innocently busy – is what he kept urging both on Boswell and on himself, with no success in either case.

Johnson himself was a great experimenter in chemistry; Mr Thrale fitted up a small laboratory for him at Streatham. (Cf. 'Sober' in *Idler*, No. 31, p. 216). 'Experimental philosophy' is what we call physics and chemistry.

To Mrs Thrale, July 1775

Johnson's remarks to Mrs Thrale about 'the advantage of having made one at the regatta' are not entirely facetious. Like Jane Austen, Johnson was deeply convinced of the importance of 'little things,' of which by far the greater part of life is composed. As he put it in a later letter to Mrs Thrale (13 August 1777), 'the variations of life consist of little things'.

To Mrs Thrale, 6 September 1777

Johnson was to reach his 68th birthday twelve days after this letter was written. As his prayers and meditations reveal, he was accustomed to take stock of himself as his birthdays came round, and his stock-takings became increasingly unhappy the older he grew. 'But complaint was vain.'

1. *Et haec olim meminisse juvabit:* 'even these things, one day, will be pleasant to remember.'

To Mrs Thrale, 10 July 1780

It seems not uncommon for Johnson to tell the real truth about himself in a tone of self-guarding facetiousness. What he says here about his genius being 'always in extremes' is in fact perfectly true, and one of the clues to understanding his mind. The facade of 'classical restraint' is completely misleading.

The work whose progress he reports on with such despondency is *The Lives of the Poets*.

1. *My master:* Mr Thrale, who was already ill and died in the following April.

2. *For all this I must stay:* i.e., wait.

To Robert Chambers, 19 April 1783

Chambers, a former member of the 'Club', had become a Judge in Bengal, and this is a kind of news-letter which gives a vivid impression of the sadness of Johnson's last years and the fortitude with which he faced it. The conviction of national decline which he expresses in the second paragraph was very widespread at the time; Walpole and Cowper, among others, express the same sentiments. Johnson always maintained, as he does here, that he was not seriously upset by public affairs: compare his remark to Boswell, during this same year, when the latter asked if he was not 'vexed' by the goings-on of the Opposition – 'I would have knocked the factious dogs on the head, to be sure; but I was not *vexed*.' (15 May 1783). How much truth there was in this indifference is hard to ascertain. I suspect that he was more deeply concerned than he liked to admit.

The theme of 'he that lives long must outlive many' is found also in the poem in memory of Levet (p. 503).

1. *ἐκ κακῶν κακά:* evil upon evil.

2. *ἀρετήν τε και ὀλβὸν:* virtue and wealth.

3. *Keep innocency . . . peace at the last:* Psalm 38.

4. *Versura:* a legal expression meaning 'transfer' (of a mortgage).

To Mrs Thrale, 19 June 1783

This account of the stroke which Johnson suffered on 16 June is one of the most moving of all his letters; but what makes it so is not the story of his bodily suffering but the desperate anxiety it shows lest he has lost Mrs Thrale's affection. The Italian musician Piozzi, whom she was to marry in July 1784, had already appeared on the scene, and Johnson knew that she was beginning to find himself tedious and demanding.

1. *In Latin verse:* The Latin verses which Johnson composed to test if his mind was unimpaired are extant; the lines whose meaning he paraphrases for Mrs Thrale are these:

> Summe Pater, quodcumque tuum de corpore numen
> Hoc statuat, precibus Christus adesse velit;
> Ingenio parcas, nec sit mihi culpa rogasse,
> Qua solum potero parte placere tibi.

2. *My mistress gracious . . .' Tis time he shou'd:* a parody of lines from Swift's *Verses on the Death of Dr Swift:*

> The Queen, so gracious, mild and good,
> Cries: 'Is he gone? 'Tis time he 'should.'

3. *It sticks to our last sand:* 'we retain our natural characteristics to our last moments.' The phrase comes from Epistle I of Pope's *Moral Essays* (line 225).

4. *Salt of hartshorn:* sal volatile.

To Mrs Thrale, 10 March 1784

The terror of death and damnation was always with Johnson; it was an element in his religion which many people deplored as 'gloomy' or 'fanatical'. His first biographer, Sir John Hawkins, described his religion as having 'a tincture of enthusiasm [i.e., fanaticism], arising, as is con-jectured, from the fervour of his imagination . . .' Boswell is rather embarrassed by it; after relating how Johnson shocked the bland Oxford dons by expressing ('passionately and loudly') his fear lest he should be 'sent to Hell, Sir, and punished everlastingly', he explains: 'If what has now been stated should be urged by the enemies of Christianity, as if its influence on the mind were not benignant, let it be remembered, that Johnson's temperament was melancholy . . .' (13 June 1784). In a way, of course, Boswell is right. The 'gloom' of Johnson's religion was largely an aspect of his constitutional melancholia. I must all the same admit (though I am not one of 'the enemies of Christianity') that it is hard to see how Johnson's piety did much to make his life more bear-able, and only too easy to find occasions when it seems to have made it worse. See note on his prayers for Easter, 1759, p. 536.

To Mrs Thrale, 2 July 1784 and 8 July 1784

Mrs Thrale (widowed three years earlier) married Gabriele Piozzi on 24 July 1784; both these letters were therefore written just before the marriage, though it is clear that Johnson believed it had taken place before the letter of 8 July. Mrs Thrale replied with dignity, forbearance and truthfulness to the first letter:

Sir, I have this morning received from you so rough a letter in reply to one which was both tenderly and respectfully written, that I am forced to desire the conclusion of a correspondence which I can bear to continue no longer.

The birth of my second husband is not meaner than that of my first; his sentiments are not meaner; his profession is not meaner, and his superiority in what
he professes acknowledged by all mankind. . . . The religion to which he has
been always a zealous adherent will, I hope, teach him to forgive insults he has
not deserved; mine will, I hope, enable me to bear them at once with dignity
and patience . . . God bless you.

1. *Queen Mary:* Mary Queen of Scots; the 'parallel', in Johnson's
view, is that when she went into England, she was going to her death.

2. *irremeable:* 'admitting of no return.' The word comes from Virgil's
'*irremeabilis unda*' in *Aeneid* VI, 425, through Dryden's translation:

> The keeper charm'd, the chief without delay
> Pass'd on and took the irremeable way.

In Virgil also the crossing of the stream led Aeneas to the abode of the
dead. Did Johnson deliberately seek to evoke in Mrs Thrale's mind
these associations with death? Was he trying to tell her that if she married Piozzi she would be 'dead' to him? Or was it that his own mind,
close as he was now to his end, was filled with the thoughts of death?

Whatever he may have meant, it is a fact that five months after
writing these heart-broken letters, he was dead. Mrs Thrale, having crossed her 'irremeable stream,' went on living on the farther side of it for
another thirty-seven years of busy sociability. She had earned them.

PROLOGUE TO THE GOOD NATURED MAN (p. 500)

This prologue was written for the first production of Goldsmith's play
in January 1768. Its sardonic and melancholy tone is quite inappropriate
to Goldsmith's cheerful farce.

The parallel between an author seeking the audience's applause and a
politician seeking the people's votes, which is the central idea of the
prologue, was topical because a general election was imminent. Parliament was actually dissolved six weeks later.

1. *Caesar's pilot:* In Plutarch's life of Julius Caesar, it is related that
Caesar went to sea 'in a little pinnace of twelve oars only'. A storm came
up and the master of the vessel wished to put back to land.

But Caesar then taking him by the hand said unto him: 'Good fellow, be of
good cheer and forwards hardily; fear not, for thou hast Caesar and his fortune
with thee.' (North's translation).

2. *Loud rabbles:* hardly complimentary either to audience or voters; one wonders how Goldsmith's audience liked being thus addressed.

3. *Hoards his angry tale:* i.e., keeps quiet about his grievances till election-time gives him his chance.

4. *This day . . . a cobbler's vote:* The 'powder'd curls and golden coat' belong to the wealthy and aristocratic candidate for parliament. Crispin was the patron saint of shoemakers; so 'swelling Crispin' means 'the boastful shoemaker'.

5. *Ill-persuading:* i.e., persuading to ill.

THREE PARODIES OF PERCY'S *Hermit of Warkworth* (p. 501)

Dr Thomas Percy, editor of the *Reliques of Ancient English Poetry*, 1765, one of the most influential collections of verse ever published, was not only the leading pioneer in the 'pre-romantic' revival of the old ballads; he also wrote some imitation-ballads himself. Of these the *Hermit of Warkworth* was probably the best known. Johnson regarded the ballads, ancient and imitation alike, with much disdain. In Boswell's words: 'The conversation having turned on modern imitations of ancient ballads, and some one having praised their simplicity, he treated them with that ridicule which he always displayed, when that subject was mentioned' (3 April 1773).

These three parodies were all improvised on various social occasions. The third, and perhaps the second, were composed at the tea-table of Miss Reynolds, Sir Joshua's sister; she is the 'Renny' of the first line of the third.

As Wordsworth pointed out in his preface to the second edition of *Lyrical Ballads*, the point of Johnson's ridicule lies more in the absurdity and triviality of the content than in the simplicity of the language.

A SHORT SONG OF CONGRATULATION (p. 502)

This poem celebrates the coming of age, in 1780, of Sir John Lade, Baronet. He was the son of Mr Thrale's sister: hence Johnson's interest in him. The young gentleman, it appears, took the advice which the poem ironically offers him; he dissipated his inheritance, which was vast, with much celerity. Mrs Piozzi (Thrale) records that he once asked Johnson if he would advise him to marry, and received the splendid answer: 'I would advise no man to marry, Sir, who is not likely to propagate understanding.' He disregarded *this* advice, and married a 'notorious woman'; but Johnson's fear was not fulfilled, for Sir John died childless.

Johnson sent the poem to Mrs Thrale with a letter in which he says: 'I have enclosed a short song of congratulation, which you must not show to anybody. It is odd that it should come into my head. I hope you will read it with candour; it is, I believe, one of the author's first essays in that way of writing, and a beginner is always to be treated with tenderness.'

'Candour' in eighteenth-century usage means 'fairness', and by 'that way of writing' Johnson must mean satire. It is true that this poem is almost the only overtly satirical piece of writing by him, but he had a strong satirical streak, suppressed, perhaps, because he feared that cultivation of it would increase those tendencies to bitterness and anger the power of which he well knew in himself.

On the Death of Dr Robert Levet (p. 503)

The best account of the subject and genesis of this wonderful poem is given by Mrs Thrale:

Dr Johnson has been writing Verses on his old Inmate Mr Levett he tells me: that poor Creature was 84 or 85 years old this Winter, when after an uninterrupted Series of Health he died suddenly by a Spasm or Rupture of some of the Vessels of the Heart. He lived with Johnson as a sort of *necessary Man*, or Surgeon to the wretched Household he held in Bolt Court . . . Levett used to bleed one, and blister another, and be very useful, tho' I believe disagreeable to all: he died while his Patron was with me in Harley Street – and very sorry he was – in his way of being sorry – and he wrote these Verses.

(Thraliana, Oxford 1942: I, 531–2)

Walter Scott was a great admirer of the lines on Levet; he alludes to them at least three times in his correspondence. In a letter of consolation to his friend Morritt (3 October 1810) he calls the poem 'beautiful and feeling', and adds that although he, Scott, is 'a tolerably ardent Scotchman', these lines 'atone for a thousand of Johnson's prejudices.' There is an admirable remark on the poem by Mr Christopher Hollis. He calls it (I quote from memory) 'one of the very few really sincere tributes paid by one whom the world calls successful to one whom the world calls a failure.' For my own part, I can only say that I find it the most personally and directly moving elegy in the language.

1. *Hope's delusive mine:* The image is of slaves toiling in a mine. The mine is 'delusive' because they always hope, but in vain, to be set free.

2. *Blast:* The Oxford edition reads 'blasts', but there is good authority for 'blast', which I prefer for reasons of euphony.

3. *Officious:* here with the old meaning, derived from Latin *officium*, of 'dutiful.'

4. *Petty gain:* Boswell (*Life*, 1752) thus describes the 'petty gains' of Levet's medical practice: '. . . his fees being sometimes very small sums, sometimes whatever provisions his patients could afford him.' Levet was not a 'qualified' doctor, but it is wrong to call him a 'quack,' as he often is called. 'Qualifications' in the eighteenth century were distinctly elastic, and Levet seems to have been a great deal more conscientious and self-sacrificing than many of the highly qualified, then and now.

5. *His eightieth year was nigh:* Johnson was more accurate than Mrs Thrale on Levet's age; he was 76 when he died.

6. *Nearest:* in modern usage this would be 'quickest'.

PRAYERS AND JOURNALS 1764–84 (pp. 505–14)

Good Friday, 1764

1. *To put my rooms in order:* There are many descriptions of the chaotic conditions in which Johnson usually lived. His resolutions to 'put them in order' were always in vain. There was probably in him, as in Walter Scott, some profound terror of tidying up his chaotic papers, etc. which may have been a psychological symbol of stirring up ideas and memories he wished to keep buried. In Scott's *Journal* there is an agonizing description of his ordeal when he sorted through his accumulated papers.

Easter Day, 1764

1. *Without a vow:* Johnson felt very strongly the unwisdom of making vows, and often cautioned Boswell against them because he knew

only too well the virtual certainty he would break them and the added burden of guilt which this would entail. He has a clearly personal note to *Love's Labour's Lost* (I, i) on this theme:

Biron amidst his extravagancies, speaks with great justice against the folly of vows. They are made without sufficient regard to the variations of life, and are therefore broken by some unforeseen necessity. They proceed commonly from a presumptuous confidence, and a false estimate of human power.

2. *Hart's hymns:* these were apparently full of a somewhat 'revivalist' emotionalism; hence Johnson's implied disapproval of them.

18 September 1768

Johnson's fear that 'to write the history' of his melancholy (which he never did) would 'too much disturb' him is again reminiscent of Scott. Compare Scott's *Journal* for 23 May 1830 (after he had discontinued it for nearly a year): 'I thought it made me abominably selfish, and that by recording my gloomy fits I encouraged their recurrence.'

1 June 1770

This passage is in fact a brilliant piece of self-analysis, though expressed as if it were impersonal observation.

1. *Mr Campbell:* Elsewhere Johnson makes a characteristic remark on Mr Campbell to Boswell:

I am afraid he has not been in the inside of a church for many years; but he never passes a church without pulling off his hat. This shows that he has good principles. (1 July 1763).

2. *Psalmanazar:* George Psalmanazar, a celebrated fraud and impostor, who later reformed and won Johnson's deep admiration for his piety.

25 July 1774

This is an extract from the journal which Johnson kept when touring with the Thrales in Wales and neighbouring counties. Hawkstone Park is in Shropshire. The passage may suffice to show the falsity of the popular notion that Johnson was 'blind' to 'wild Nature' and incapable of 'romantic' feelings about it. One could not easily imagine a better definition of the quintessential romantic *frisson* than Johnson's 'a kind of turbulent pleasure between fright and admiration'.

21–23 October 1775

In 1775 Johnson, with the Thrales and Baretti, went on a tour to France. These are extracts from the journal he kept. Their somewhat sour and critical note may reflect his habitual prejudice against the French. Compare his note to *Henry V* (Act III, iv):

It may be noted that there is in this scene not only the French language but the French spirit. Alice compliments the princess upon her knowledge of four words and tells her that she pronounces like the English themselves. The princess suspects no deficiency in her instructress, nor the instructress in herself. Throughout the whole scene there may be found French servility and French vanity.

But Johnson's notes on the menagerie and the manufactory of mirrors at Versailles shows that even if he disapproved, he was keenly interested. The meticulous description of the mirror-making process illustrates his invariable absorption in any form of industry or craft: e.g. in Thrale's brewery at Southwark.

1. *I got ground:* 'My health improved.'

Easter Day, 1776

1. *Poor Thrale, orbus et exspes:* 'bereaved and without hope'. This refers to the recent death of Thrale's only surviving son Harry, of whom Johnson said: 'I would have gone to the extremity of the earth to have preserved this boy.' (Boswell, 25 March 1776).

2. *θ:* The Greek letter theta is used by Johnson as a symbol for 'died' ($\theta\nu\acute{\eta}\tau o\varsigma$).

3. *Thoughts of vanity:* 'worldly, trivial thoughts'.

12 August 1784

This prayer 'against inquisitive and perplexing thoughts' is perhaps the most eloquent of all Johnson's prayers and one of the finest things he wrote. It shows how, even near the end of his life, he was still tormented with doubt.

31 October 1784

'Preces' means 'prayers'; the list which follows is of possible subjects for prayers, presumably to be written by himself.

Johnson died on 13 December, just six weeks after this entry was written. The last words 'Against Despair' are in a sense a concentration of his entire religious life.

MORE ABOUT PENGUINS, PELICANS
AND PUFFINS

For further information about books available from Penguins please write to Dept EP, Penguin Books Ltd, Harmondsworth, Middlesex UB7 0DA.

In the U.S.A.: For a complete list of books available from Penguins in the United States write to Dept DG, Penguin Books, 299 Murray Hill Parkway, East Rutherford, New Jersey 07073.

In Canada: For a complete list of books available from Penguins in Canada write to Penguin Books Canada Limited, 2801 John Street, Markham, Ontario L3R 1B4.

In Australia: For a complete list of books available from Penguins in Australia write to the Marketing Department, Penguin Books Australia Ltd, P.O. Box 257, Ringwood, Victoria 3134.

In New Zealand: For a complete list of books available from Penguins in New Zealand write to the Marketing Department, Penguin Books (N.Z.) Ltd, Private Bag, Takapuna, Auckland 9.

In India: For a complete list of books available from Penguins in India write to Penguin Overseas Ltd, 706 Eros Apartments, 56 Nehru Place, New Delhi 110019.

ENGLISH AND AMERICAN
LITERATURE IN PENGUINS

☐ *Emma* Jane Austen   £1.25

'I am going to take a heroine whom no one but myself will much like,' declared Jane Austen of Emma, her most spirited and controversial heroine in a comedy of self-deceit and self-discovery.

☐ *Tender is the Night* F. Scott Fitzgerald   £2.95

Fitzgerald worked on seventeen different versions of this novel, and its obsessions – idealism, beauty, dissipation, alcohol and insanity – were those that consumed his own marriage and his life.

☐ *The Life of Johnson* James Boswell   £2.95

Full of gusto, imagination, conversation and wit, Boswell's immortal portrait of Johnson is as near a novel as a true biography can be, and still regarded by many as the finest 'life' ever written. This shortened version is based on the 1799 edition.

☐ *A House and its Head* Ivy Compton-Burnett   £4.95

In a novel 'as trim and tidy as a hand-grenade' (as Pamela Hansford Johnson put it), Ivy Compton-Burnett penetrates the facade of a conventional, upper-class Victorian family to uncover a chasm of violent emotions – jealousy, pain, frustration and sexual passion.

☐ *The Trumpet Major* Thomas Hardy   £1.50

Although a vein of unhappy unrequited love runs through this novel, Hardy also draws on his warmest sense of humour to portray Wessex village life at the time of the Napoleonic wars.

☐ *The Complete Poems of Hugh MacDiarmid*

☐ Volume One   £8.95
☐ Volume Two   £8.95

The definitive edition of work by the greatest Scottish poet since Robert Burns, edited by his son Michael Grieve, and W. R. Aitken.

ENGLISH AND AMERICAN
LITERATURE IN PENGUINS

☐ *Main Street* **Sinclair Lewis**   £4.95

The novel that added an immortal chapter to the literature of America's Mid-West, *Main Street* contains the comic essence of Main Streets everywhere.

☐ *The Compleat Angler* **Izaak Walton**   £2.50

A celebration of the countryside, and the superiority of those in 1653, as now, who love *quietnesse, vertue* and, above all, *Angling*. 'No fish, however coarse, could wish for a doughtier champion than Izaak Walton' – Lord Home

☐ *The Portrait of a Lady* **Henry James**   £2.50

'One of the two most brilliant novels in the language', according to F. R. Leavis, James's masterpiece tells the story of a young American heiress, prey to fortune-hunters but not without a will of her own.

☐ *Hangover Square* **Patrick Hamilton**   £3.95

Part love story, part thriller, and set in the publands of London's Earls Court, this novel caught the conversational tone of a whole generation in the uneasy months before the Second World War.

☐ *The Rainbow* **D. H. Lawrence**   £2.50

Written between *Sons and Lovers* and *Women in Love*, *The Rainbow* covers three generations of Brangwens, a yeoman family living on the borders of Nottinghamshire.

☐ *Vindication of the Rights of Woman*
   Mary Wollstonecraft   £2.95

Although Walpole once called her 'a hyena in petticoats', Mary Wollstonecraft's vision was such that modern feminists continue to go back and debate the arguments so powerfully set down here.

ENGLISH AND AMERICAN LITERATURE IN PENGUINS

☐ *Nostromo* **Joseph Conrad** £1.95

In his most ambitious and successful novel Conrad created an entire imaginary republic in South America. As he said, 'you shall find there according to your deserts: encouragement, consolation, fear, charm – all you demand – and, perhaps, also that glimpse of truth for which you forgot to ask.'

☐ *A Passage to India* **E. M. Forster** £2.50

Centred on the unsolved mystery at the Marabar Caves, Forster's masterpiece conveys, as no other novel has done, the troubled spirit of India during the Raj.

These books should be available at all good bookshops or newsagents, but if you live in the UK or the Republic of Ireland and have difficulty in getting to a bookshop, they can be ordered by post. Please indicate the titles required and fill in the form below.

NAME _____ BLOCK CAPITALS

ADDRESS _____

_____

_____

Enclose a cheque or postal order payable to The Penguin Bookshop to cover the total price of books ordered, plus 50p for postage. Readers in the Republic of Ireland should send £1R equivalent to the sterling prices, plus 67p for postage. Send to: The Penguin Bookshop, 54/56 Bridlesmith Gate, Nottingham, NG1 2GP.

You can also order by phoning (0602) 599295, and quoting your Barclaycard or Access number.

Every effort is made to ensure the accuracy of the price and availability of books at the time of going to press, but it is sometimes necessary to increase prices and in these circumstances retail prices may be shown on the covers of books which may differ from the prices shown in this list or elsewhere. This list is not an offer to supply any book.

This order service is only available to residents in the UK and the Republic of Ireland.

● ● ●